BY DEMI WINTERS

THE ASHEN SERIES

The Road of Bones

Kingdom of Claw

KINGDOM OF CLAW

KINGDOM OF CLAW

THE ASHEN SERIES

BOOK TWO

DEMI WINTERS

DELACORTE PRESS | NEW YORK

Copyright © 2024 by Demi Winters

Penguin Random House values and supports copyright. Copyright fuels creativity, encourages diverse voices, promotes free speech, and creates a vibrant culture. Thank you for buying an authorized edition of this book and for complying with copyright laws by not reproducing, scanning, or distributing any part of it in any form without permission. You are supporting writers and allowing Penguin Random House to continue to publish books for every reader. Please note that no part of this book may be used or reproduced in any manner for the purpose of training artificial intelligence technologies or systems.

All rights reserved.

Published in the United States by Delacorte Press, an imprint of Random House, a division of Penguin Random House LLC, New York.

DELACORTE PRESS is a registered trademark and the DP colophon is a trademark of Penguin Random House LLC.

Originally self-published in the United States by the author in 2024.

Hardback ISBN 978-0-593-97563-3
Ebook ISBN 978-1-73899-605-6
International edition ISBN 978-0-593-98322-5

Printed in the United States of America on acid-free paper

randomhousebooks.com

1st Printing

First Delacorte Edition

Design by Betty Lew

Map design by Megan Wyreweden

FOR THOSE WHOSE SAFE SPACE
HAS BECOME THEIR PRISON. YOU ARE BRAVE.
YOU ARE STRONG. YOU ARE WARRIORS.

AUTHOR'S NOTE

Kingdom of Claw takes place in a dark fantasy world and is intended for mature readers. Some scenes may make certain readers uncomfortable including, but not limited to, depictions of addiction, agoraphobia, PTSD, bloodletting, human and animal sacrifice, and explicit sex scenes. A full list of content warnings is available at:

demiwinters.com/trigger-warnings/

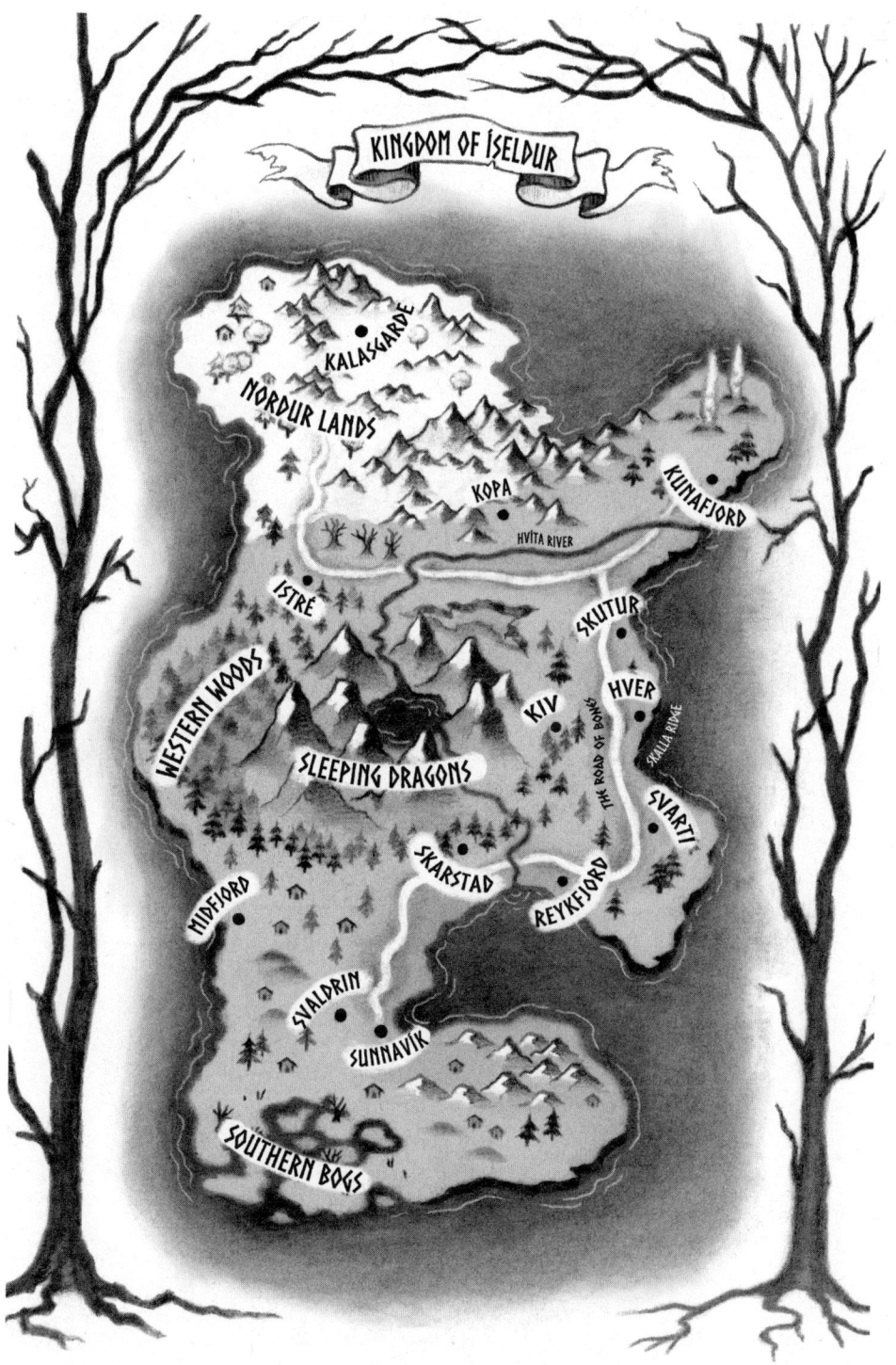

THE ROAD OF BONES RECAP

Silla Nordvig was on the run after the queen's warriors killed her father while trying to capture her. Her father's last words sent her to seek a shield-home in the city of Kopa, which required her to travel the Road of Bones. After only narrowly surviving the first leg of the journey, Silla climbed into a supply wagon, without realizing it belonged to the Bloodaxe Crew, who were on their way to complete a dangerous job in the town of Istré (just west of Kopa).

Upon discovery, Silla brokered a deal with their leader, Reynir "Axe Eyes" Bjarg, to help him obtain information from the Crew's former leader, Kraki, in exchange for a ride partway. But in the process, Silla learned that Rey had been using a false last name, and she used his real last name (Galtung) to blackmail him into giving her a ride all the way to Kopa. Despite their antagonistic relationship, Rey revealed to Silla that the skjöld leaves she was taking for headaches were dangerous. When she decided to quit taking them, Rey supported her and kept her addiction secret.

Much to Silla's surprise, the leaves had been causing her to hallucinate the little blond girl only she could see, and suppressing a big secret—she was one of the Galdra, a class of magic-wielders hunted and executed by Íseldur's king. During a confrontation with the queen's assassin, Skraeda, Silla also learned that she was Eisa Volsik, a princess thought to have been executed seventeen years prior, and that the girl she hallucinated was her older sister, Saga.

Meanwhile, Silla had begun a secret relationship with Jonas "the Wolf" Svik. When Skraeda tried to capture Silla, Jonas discovered that Silla had been hiding the truth of her past from him. He was hurt, but he agreed to help her. Then when the queen's warriors again came for Silla, and Jonas's younger brother was killed, everything changed. Jonas felt betrayed by her and used the skjöld leaves to drug her and hand her in to the Klaernar in Kopa.

When brought to Kommandor Valf of the Klaernar, Silla fought for her life, smashing his skull in with a statue and climbing out the window. She ran to the man who'd told her father of shield-homes, only to find him dead and Skraeda waiting for her. Silla and Skraeda fought, Silla at last killing the assassin. When Silla left the home, the Klaernar were waiting for her, and they chased her into the forest bordering Kopa.

Meanwhile, it was revealed that Rey was the smoke-wielding Galdra who'd been killing people along the Road of Bones. Upon entering a hidden passageway to Kopa to help Silla, he was forced to use his magic on a group of Klaernar. Unfortunately one escaped before he could kill them. Rey found Silla fleeing the others and pulled her into the bushes, shielding her from discovery.

Silla and Rey escaped Kopa together, Rey with the goal of reuniting with the Bloodaxe Crew in Istré, and Silla with a rough plan of going north to a place called Kalasgarde. At the end of *The Road of Bones,* Silla had not revealed her identity to Rey, much as Rey had not revealed his to Silla.

Meanwhile, in Askaborg Castle, Saga was summoned to a meeting with Queen Signe, where it was revealed Saga had spent a month without leaving her chambers. The queen informed Saga she was to rejoin them for meals and take her place at her betrothed's side. As she returned to her chambers, Saga began to panic, and she fled into a secret passage before anyone could see her. While hiding, she overheard Signe and Maester Alfson's conversation in the room beyond, learning that her sister, Eisa, was alive.

KINGDOM
OF
CLAW

PROLOGUE

Seventeen years ago
City of Sunnavík, Kingdom of Íseldur

It was a good thing queasiness had been trained from Ivar Ironheart as a child, because victory smelled an awful lot like blood and shit. The scent drifted on the wind as Ivar paced a path into the black sand beach. Behind him, Askaborg, his new castle, loomed over a fresh boatload of Norvalander thralls laboring to clear the corpses from Sunnavík's streets. Before him, a woman was secured to the ruined pier as the tide flowed into the bay.

Frustration gathered in Ivar's gut. He'd vanquished King Kjartan and had taken Íseldur's throne for himself. He should be able to relax at last. But instead, *this*.

Ivar let himself remember the look in the Volsik king's eyes as he'd told him he'd be blood-eagled while his people looked on. But even the memory of peeling the king's flesh from his back, of cracking his ribs open and pulling the lungs from his body, did little to temper Ivar's current irritation.

"Tell me!" he bellowed at the infernal, stubborn woman. "What is in this weaving, Galdra?"

But she only pressed her lips together. Strands of brown hair were plastered to her face, the tide swirling around her shoulders. How much longer did the woman have? Fifteen minutes? Ivar paced another lap into the sand.

Now that Íseldur was claimed, Ursir demanded Ivar set his focus on his next campaign—to raise strong sons. One to follow his Sea

King ancestors and claim the next isle in Ursir's name. The other to inherit Íseldur's throne. But before he could consider any of that, Ivar had to ensure his Norvalander wife could bear him sons. Little Yrsa was a few years old, and while his iron heart warmed a few degrees in her presence, she was still only a *daughter.*

It was *sons* Ivar needed: strong, capable warriors to carry out Ursir's Edict. Without sons, he was shackled. He'd done his husbandly duty; he'd even set aside his whores for two months now. Yet month after month passed with Signe's bloods coming on cue. The maesters and midwives could find no physical deformities, but Ivar was growing impatient. If his wife was defective, he must know so he could find an alternative, and quickly.

Which was how Ivar had found himself standing in the doorway of a ramshackle home belonging to a Galdra woman. He was familiar enough with the magic-wielding warriors of Íseldur—the impossibly strong Blade Breakers and impossibly quick Harefeet. And of course the infernal Shadow Hounds, who'd slipped past Ivar's lines and caused chaos in their war camps.

But he was told this woman was a different type of Galdra, with gifts of the mind. A Weaver, they called her. The rest, Ivar did not understand. *Threads of the past, present, and future,* she'd told him. A prick of his blood, and the Weaver could find his threads in the webwork of the world. Would weave them into a tapestry.

All Ivar drew from this talk was that the woman could glimpse his future. If he could only reassure himself he would father sons, Ivar could set his frustrations aside and begin his reign in earnest.

But it had all gone awry. The woman had taken his blood—had gone into a strange trance and worked at her loom. And after she had spent hours weaving a tapestry filled with bright colors, a black thread had appeared. The Weaver had recoiled—had turned to the king with a bloodless pallor.

"My apologies, Your Majesty. I cannot complete the tapestry today," she'd said. "Might you return on the morrow?"

"You will finish the tapestry," Ivar had growled, nodding at his chief hirdman. Magnus Hansson had stepped forward, drawing his blade and holding it to the woman's throat. She'd swallowed then turned back to her weaving. And with that, she'd continued.

Hours later, when the Weaver had stepped away from her loom, Ivar had approached the tapestry.

At the top, he saw his past—the forests and fjords of Norvaland, a bear and a woman in white. It transitioned to his battle for Íseldur—battleaxes and berserker warriors, a crown made of claws. But at the bottom of the tapestry, where Ivar might have expected to see the blues of the ocean, or perhaps a Sea King's prowed ship, was an angry mix of black and crimson. He stared at the piles of corpses—at the V-shaped pillars dripping blood. And at the top of the pile, a king.

There was no mistaking the king's identity. Not with the long blond hair and the twin braids in his beard. The Weaver had seen his death.

Which is how Ivar now found himself pacing the beach, ravens screaming over the churning dark sea. Ivar could read a person well enough to know this Weaver had a greater understanding of the threads than she'd revealed. But the foolish woman refused to divulge any details.

He glared at the woman. Her lips were nearly blue, water lapping just below her chin, hands secured above her head. It would take but a single word for Ivar's men to shoot through her binds, freeing her from her watery grave. But hours had now passed as the tide flowed into the bay, and this Weaver had not revealed a thing.

Why? Why would she choose death over the truth?

"Whatever knowledge she holds, she values it more than her own life," he mused. Realization crystallized, and he whirled to Magnus. "This secret endangers someone she loves."

Magnus tugged at the thick warrior's braid cresting along his skull. "A child?" His keen eyes narrowed. "Shall I root out her kin?"

Wordlessly, Ivar nodded, then watched his hirdman's broad back as he ambled into the streets of Sunnavík.

"He will bring me your child," Ivar called to the woman, hoping

Magnus had guessed right. "And then he will cut off parts until you share what you've seen in your threads."

The corners of her mouth tightened ever so slightly, and Ivar knew he had her. "We shall start with the fingers. Slow, steady cuts. I'll have my healers called to bandage the wounds. We wouldn't want the child to bleed out too quickly." The woman's eyes flew open, and she didn't even bother to hide her terror.

Foolish woman. Ivar shook his head.

"The screams shall be the worst part for you. They will carry clear across the water. They will fill the streets of Sunnavík, and all will understand what it means to cross their king."

The woman's mouth opened, then closed. She now had to tilt her head upward to draw breath. The tide's pace had increased, and it wouldn't be long until she was submerged completely.

"Do you know of Magnus Heart Eater? His skill with the knife is unmatched. He's known for opening your chest while you still breathe. Pulling out the heart and eating it fresh."

"Please," she begged. "Please, take my life, but not that, please, anything but that."

"The decision is in your hands, woman," growled Ivar. "Tell me what you read, and I will spare your child." He paused in thought. "I will order my men to shoot you down from that post, so you'll be free to return to your kin."

"Galdur!"

Ivar's mouth snapped shut as he stared at the woman. Galdur—that strange Íseldurian magic.

"Explain," he barked.

"You will—" She coughed out a mouthful of salt water. "You will meet your end by galdur's hand!" she called out before a wave crashed into her, submerging her completely for a heartbeat.

Ivar's brows plummeted, his iron stomach giving a single queasy lurch. *Meet his end by galdur's hand.*

"What else?" he demanded.

"That is all," called the woman. "There is nothing else. Free me!" she pleaded, not a moment before another wave struck her, salt water rushing into her lungs. More coughing. More spluttering. She fought against her binds with a ragged cry. "Free me!"

Ivar turned his back to her.

By the time Magnus returned, an unconscious child slung over his shoulder, the pillar was submerged, and a plan had solidified in the king of Íseldur's mind.

"Kill the child," said Ivar coldly, striding toward Askaborg, "and gather the Galdra. Things will be changing in this kingdom."

PART I

DUSK

DUHSK

1. The state or period of partial darkness between day and night; the dark part of twilight.

2. Partial darkness; shade; gloom.

CHAPTER 1

Two days west of Kopa

Silla Nordvig had once vowed no force in this world could draw her to the true north of Íseldur, but clearly she'd underestimated the gods' twisted sense of humor. Because here she was, on a horse with Axe Eyes, heading for that very place.

The canyon's black walls climbed up on either side of them as Horse walked beside a flat-bedded river. Nature had made a valid attempt to reclaim the space, moss and greenery carpeting the riverbanks and exposed ledges. But black volcanic stone dominated, the sheer canyon walls stark and raw in their beauty.

They'd ridden through the canyon for two full days now. The sun rose and set, the world moving on as though it hadn't been smashed to pieces. But with each passing day, Silla's spirits sank lower. It was starting to settle in—there would be no Kopa.

Instead, there was Kalasgarde.

Silla exhaled. Rey claimed to know people in Kalasgarde who could help her hide from the queen and Klaernar. He thought it would be safe for her. But Silla knew better than to hope; her foolish heart had been bruised too many times. The truth was, there was no place safe for her. Not now that she knew her true name.

Eisa Volsik.

Heir of King Ivar's sworn enemy. Hunted by Queen Signe for her mysterious, wicked plans. Political pawn to those in power. Easy reward for those who were not. The name brought nothing but misery. Chest tightening, Silla clamped her hands around the saddle horn until her knuckles grew white.

Not her. Not her. Not her.

Silla drew in a long breath. Exhaled it slowly.

Kopa had been Matthias's decision, and Kalasgarde was Rey's. As the days wore on, the idea of choosing for herself grew in Silla's mind. Perhaps there were better options for her than the northern wilds of this kingdom. A southbound ship leaving Íseldur had a pleasing feel to it. She could go to the Southern Continent or Karthia, perhaps. Anywhere she could fade into obscurity.

For the time being, Silla had resigned herself to Rey's plan. Istré for now. It was easier not to decide for herself. A relief, if she was being honest. But between the black walls of the canyon, Silla had nothing but time to think. To remember their names.

Ilías Svik. Matthias Nordvig. Skeggagrim.

Good men, all dead because of her. Perhaps living was her punishment. To wake each morning with the anguish of their blood on her hands, with the ache of Jonas's betrayal etched into her soul, knowing that Metta was in the Klaernar's prison, suffering at the hands of her captors.

Certainly, Silla bore the bruises of Kopa—a beating so thorough that her eye had swelled up and her ribs ached with each slight movement. Even so, she couldn't help but think she deserved far worse.

They rounded a bend, the canyon widening. The lower levels of the wall had eroded away in one spot, leaving a thin black spire topped with a wider rock.

"They call it Hábrók's Hammer," said Rey from behind her. "We will camp here tonight. There is an overhang there to shelter under. Plenty of grass for Horse . . ." Her mind drifted to the rumble of his voice along her back. It was impossible to keep their distance while on horseback, and in her exhaustion, she'd given up trying. Though she'd never admit it to anyone but herself, his presence behind her—a solid wall of warrior—was reassuring.

"Silla?"

She shook her head, trying to disperse the haze clouding her mind. Rey had dismounted and was staring at the small crescent-shaped scar at the corner of her eye.

Stop staring at it! she wanted to scream. This scar was her damnation. It had allowed those men near Skarstad to identify her; it had gotten her father killed. Silla turned her head, dismounting from Horse.

Over the past days spent traveling together, she and Rey had settled into a routine of sorts. Mindlessly, Silla removed Horse's saddle and brushed her down, while Rey pulled supplies from the saddlesack and set up camp. By the time Horse's coat gleamed and she'd wandered to a lush patch of grass, Rey had a fire roaring. As it happened, he was remarkably adept at kindling a fire, even from the wettest wood.

She sank onto the grass. Pulled at an errant thread dangling from her cuff. It was Rey's tunic, as were the breeches belted around her waist. His clothing swam on her, but it didn't matter. She'd burned the red dress Valf had put her in. If only she could burn the memories of his hand, clutching her neck while the other went to his belt.

Scream, dear. I do so enjoy it.

Rey's voice diverted her thoughts. "Tomorrow we'll travel past a village. I'll stop and have a falcon sent north to the warriors who will fetch you." He paused, eyeing her. "And we shall reach Istré after dark."

Silla's temples throbbed at the mere thought of Istré. Days now, it had been the two of them plodding through this canyon. Here, she'd settled into a numb existence. Not quite safe, yet not quite in danger: It was an in-between. But the words *village* and *people* had her survival instincts on edge, making her pulse beat erratically.

A weighted silence hung in the air, and Silla knew Rey was choosing his words. "You must eat more tonight, Silla." He pulled a few strips of dried elk from his bag and offered them to her.

Silla stared at his outstretched hand. The thought of food made her stomach roil, and the thought of Kalasgarde was like an anchor tied to her, pulling her down, down, down. She felt lost and so very tired. Not just her body, but her bones.

Her soul.

But she took the dried elk all the same. Forced herself to bite into it. What she wouldn't give for her skjöld leaves, to fly away from everything for a moment or two. Would there be an apothecary in Istré? Silla had lost all her belongings, sólas included. Rey, though . . . he kept coins in a pouch on his battle belt, others in the false bottom of Horse's saddlesack. She could pilfer a few. Sneak off to the apothecary in Istré.

She was filled with self-loathing at the vile thought. Rey had saved her life in Kopa. She could not *steal* from him. But the longings were fiercer than she'd felt in days . . . weeks.

Without the leaves how could she distract herself from the gloom of her thoughts? Before, she'd had Jonas to help her escape. But like the leaves, he'd brought nothing but misery. All of the bandages for Silla's grief were now gone, and gods, but it hurt.

Rey had busied himself sharpening one of his many daggers, but she felt the touch of his gaze on her skin. Silla glanced his way. With the fire's flames reflected in his eyes, with that sharp jaw and the sprawl of his legs, the man looked like a malevolent god honing his blade. Utterly unbothered by anything. Impenetrable to human emotion. Brutally handsome.

Her eyes trailed across his broad frame and landed on his hip.

"May I?" she asked, nodding at the flask.

Rey hesitated before pushing to his full height and stepping around the fire. Crouching down to her level, he pressed the flask firmly into her palm. "Go easy," he said, a groove deepening between his brows.

She wanted to reach out. Smooth the line away. Instead, she lifted the flask to her lips and took a large swallow. It burned a path down her throat, making her wince. Still, Rey stared at her scar so intently that she squirmed.

"Why do you stare at it?" she asked, blinking against the burn of the fire whiskey. "My scar?"

Rey seemed to shake free from his reverie. Running a hand down his face, for a moment he looked a little unsettled. "It reminds me," he said, "of a life long ago."

Silla puzzled over his words for a moment before helping herself to another gulp of brennsa. "Tell me," she said.

Rey settled back across the fire, passing his dagger across a whetstone. "I prefer not to think of it."

"Bad memories?" she asked, though of course he did not answer.

Tendrils of warmth unfurled in her belly, sending tiny vibrations all through her. Silla took yet another large mouthful of the fire whiskey, closing her eyes as it took effect. It was like a full-body exhalation, her tangled worries loosening, the burn of guilt soothed.

She lifted the flask for another drink.

"Silla." Rey's voice floated across the fire, carrying irritation and warning all at once. Silla, of course, ignored him. He wanted her to be responsible and sensible when all she wanted was to forget.

Pushing onto her feet, she arched her back in a stretch. She felt better already. Almost happy. "In a life long ago, I had chickens," she said. The brennsa flowed through her with a silent rhythm that made her want to move. "And a swing. And I played a game. Do you want to play it, Axe Eyes?"

He scowled at her. The light from the fire caught his black curls, the warm brown of his curving cheekbone. Rey's normally fastidiously trimmed beard hadn't been touched in some time, and Silla considered that the past few days must have held their challenges for him as well. A better woman would offer to trim it for him—would try to lighten his burden.

A better woman was not her.

After taking another large gulp of fire whiskey, Silla coughed. It burned her throat, her lungs, her stomach, but she was learning to appreciate this kind of discomfort—it was one she could control. One she was choosing.

"Come now, Axe Eyes. Have fun with me." Her hand reached out, and she longed for him to grab it. To let down those stern barriers he kept in place. After a moment, it became clear he had no intention of joining her. "Fine," Silla muttered. "I'll play by myself."

Spreading her arms wide, she looked up. Darkness had fallen, stars spattering the sliver of sky above. Curious plants unfurled moonlight-seeking tentacles from coves in the canyon's walls, their luminescence making it feel as though she were inside her own constellation. Warmth and euphoria glimmered through her body, and for the first time in days, everything felt so . . . easy. Staring at the stars, Silla began to turn. Her smile spread wide, her body growing light as a feather.

"Round 'n' round 'n' round we go." Laughter spilled from her lips, and for the barest moment, Silla was free. She was a bird soaring through the skies, ready to fly away from it all. Faster she spun, until the stars and strange, glowing plants blurred together, and the ground grew unsteady.

Without warning, the flask was pulled from her grip, an arm wrenching her to an abrupt stop. Her vision continued to spin, and it was a moment before she could make out Rey's furious expression. "What did you say?" he demanded.

The walls of the canyon with its living stars swayed, her mind growing slippery. This was what she'd needed. To drown in nothingness. For the currents of the drink to pull her into their flow. "A game," she whispered, leaning into his arm. "From a life long ago."

Rey was strangely quiet, and Silla forced herself to look at him. Again, he stared at her scar, his pulse throbbing furiously.

"What is it?" she asked.

"Sometimes I think"—he shook his head—"you remind me of someone."

A curious feeling filled Silla, as though she was trying to recall something important. But it was gone in an instant, and Silla found herself being eased onto a bedroll, tucked into an alcove in the canyon's wall.

She lay back on the bed, trying to steady her whirling vision. "Who?" she asked.

Rey crouched before her, but it was difficult to make out his shadowed expression. "A girl who liked to play spinning games," he said distantly. "But she's long dead."

"Too much spinning," groaned Silla, putting a hand to her forehead.

"I told you to go easy."

A large, warm hand skimmed around her back, bringing her into a sitting position. Head swimming, Silla blinked. A waterskin was pressed to her lips, and cool water slid down her throat. But it only seemed to agitate the fire in her stomach.

"I cannot feel anymore," she whispered. "I wish only to forget."

Rey let out a long sigh, lowering onto the bedroll beside hers. She wanted to curl into his warmth, to surrender and trust in his strength. "Forget for a moment," said Rey wearily. "I'll be here."

Silla wanted to weep at his words. How long had it been since she'd been able to truly let go? Her eyes slid shut, and she fell deep into slumber.

Silla woke to bright morning light and a throbbing skull. For one dizzying moment, she could not place her surroundings—the curving black stone overhead, the trickle of running water from somewhere nearby. The canyon, she remembered. She was tucked into the canyon's alcove.

Sitting up, she found Rey, kneeling by the stream. He'd stripped down to a thin undertunic and his sleeves were rolled up to reveal thick, muscled forearms covered in tattooed coils. Transfixed, she watched him scrub his hands and forearms clean before scooping water over his hair and neck.

A life long ago—the words echoed in her mind, memories of the night before coming back in a nauseating rush. The way he'd stared at her scar. The girl she reminded him of, long dead.

Pain pulsed in her skull as she tried to wrestle meaning into these details. Hot, restless panic exasperated her hangover. Everything hurt, her mind swam, and all she could think of was how the one person who'd discovered her true name had taken less than a day to betray her.

Now she tried to reassure herself—Rey didn't know who she was; it was only a queasy feeling brought on by the brennsa. But what if he did? Or what if he figured it out? Silla's fingers found the patch of short, spiky hair left by Kommandor Valf's blade.

Can't, she thought, the decision growing more solid with each heartbeat. *Can't go back.*

In that moment, Silla made herself a vow. She would never allow another to know her true name. She would hold it so tightly she strangled it from this world.

And no matter what it took, she would never end up in the Klaernar's cells again.

CHAPTER 2

Rey's long exhale misted the air, his body swaying with Horse as she trudged through the canyon. The bright morning sunlight slanted between the black walls, warming his face. Soon they'd reach the canyon's end, climb back into the forest, and be another step closer to Istré.

Though his memory was fuzzy, Rey recalled a few villages along their route and had decided to stop at the first one. He must send a falcon to Vig and Runný in Kalasgarde, and Silla needed better attire than his oversized tunic and breeches.

Casting his gaze on Silla's messy curls, Rey battled the urge to twist a tendril around his finger and pull it taut. His teeth clenched together.

She was too damned quiet.

Hábrók's hairy arse. Rey could not believe it irritated him, but there was something *unnatural* about her silence. She should be pointing at the rock formations or humming incessantly. He'd never admit it aloud, but he'd grown to like the sound of her chatter. It uplifted him. Kept him from the dark places he so often retreated to.

And he couldn't help but think of the night before. *Round 'n' round 'n' round we go,* she'd said. When she'd started twirling, when she'd spoken those words, it was as though Rey'd been sent back to another time. Back to those gardens.

A lifetime ago. Not to mention, the girl was long dead.

But Silla had curled into him. Had trusted in him enough to forget for a while. Why did this woman's trust feel like a thing to be cherished? Like a sapling he yearned to shelter so it might grow stronger...

Rey gave himself a shake. Those were dangerous thoughts—ones he needed to rid himself of.

The canyon grew more and more shallow until at last they climbed back into the forest. The familiar scent of pine needles and loam filled his senses as they followed a narrow goat track through the woods. Wet foliage brushed against them, the path thankfully soon widening.

Why is the queen hunting her?

The question shouldered into Rey's thoughts as it had a hundred times in the past few days. In the aftermath of Kopa, he'd asked Silla why the queen hunted her. But that look in her eyes—haunted and terrified—he'd never wanted to see it again. And so he'd urged her to tell him when she was ready. Rey knew well enough that some secrets were essential to keep a person safe. He wanted to respect her need for secrets. But the gods damned *queen* hunted her. The Klaernar were involved. Warbands and assassins had been sent after her. This was no small secret, and knowing some details could be a matter of life or death.

Again and again he ran over each strange detail he'd collected about the curly-haired woman who'd climbed into his supply wagon in Reykfjord. Like Rey, she was Galdra. There was the spinning game and the scar, just where *hers* had been. She'd led a sheltered life, as though she'd been hidden away from prying eyes.

It takes a small man to be ruled by fear, and a large one to show mercy. And anyone can see you are no small man.

The words she'd spoken to him on the Road of Bones flitted through Rey's skull. At the time, he'd brushed them off as a curious coincidence, but now he wondered if it could be more than that. What if their fathers had known each other? It would fit with the girl's identity...

No. Rey ground his teeth. The girl was dead. There had been a body. Everyone in this kingdom knew the gruesome details.

Unless she hadn't died that day. What if she'd escaped the castle, hidden away for all these years before being discovered near Skarstad? He thought of her father—a supposed farmhand—killing six of the queen's warriors before succumbing to his wounds. Considering each strange detail alone, it seemed an unlikely answer. But when they were all added up, no other explanation fit.

It was her.

Rey's temples squeezed. It couldn't be. It was impossible.

But the facts were piling up too high, and with each pound of his heart, the impossible grew ever more plausible. By some miracle, she hadn't died that day. She was alive and had been sitting right in his wagon all these weeks. A feeling of wonder filled him, and Rey opened his mouth to say something. But he slammed it shut as a woven fence came into view, followed soon by a longhouse, smoke twisting up from it.

Rey drew Horse to a stop near a patch of grass. "We'll stop here for a few minutes," he told Silla, dismounting. He couldn't keep his eyes from roaming her face, searching for similarities to the girl. But Rey's jaw clenched as his gaze found the bruise on her cheek instead. "I think it best you stay out of sight. Draw your hood up and linger behind the fence. I'll be gone only a few minutes to send word north."

Rey had thought this place a village, but soon discovered it was merely a cluster of steadings. Thankfully, the old mothers were happy to allow Rey use of their falcon for the generous coin he offered. They also readily parted with boots and garments in Silla's size. Rey found his gratitude waning as the old mothers pressed their unwed granddaughters forward, imploring him to stay the night. After sending the message to Kalasgarde, it had taken all his patience not to snap at the boldest of the granddaughters, who'd taken his arm and tried to steer him to the yard for a stroll.

"Married," he'd barked, watching the women scowl at his ringless finger. "My wife is just there!" Exiting the home, Rey had tucked the garments under his arm and broken into a run. He was desperate to talk to Silla. To tell her what he knew . . . but his feet came to a sudden halt.

Silla was gone. As was his gods damned horse.

Anger quickly replaced his excitement. She'd fled into monster-filled woods while warriors combed the countryside for her.

"I know you're more clever than this, Sunshine!" he bellowed through cupped hands. From the corner of his eye, he saw the women of the steadings gather in the doorway. "You don't know how to ride, not to mention you're on *my* gods damned horse!" He put two fingers into his mouth and let out a shrill whistle.

Hoofbeats and Silla's frustrated cry soon met his ears. A moment later, Horse emerged from the woods.

"Other way!" begged Silla, pulling on the reins. "Horse, *please*!"

But Horse merely tossed her head, whinnying in greeting to Rey. He snatched the reins, then stroked Horse's velvety nose as he glared at Silla. "No amount of treats will buy her loyalty."

Silla's gaze met his, flustered and guilty.

"Why are you running?" he asked in a low voice. Casting a cautious look at the women gathered in the longhouse's doorway, he swung up on the saddle behind her and shoved the garments into the saddlesack. Rey urged Horse forward, and they rode in silence along the track until he judged they were far enough away not to be overheard.

"What has happened?" he demanded, lifting an arm to shield her from a low-hanging bough. "You no longer trust me?" Rey went over everything he'd said in the last day.

She'd tried to *run*, would have put herself in danger's way, and, as a strange dry laugh choked out of her, the flames of Rey's anger were fanned.

"Do you think this is funny?" he demanded. "Do you think it a game?"

"Not in the slightest," she said with a sniffle.

Gods, but Rey hated her tears. His hands fisted tightly around the reins.

"You knew I'd come after you, as I did in Kopa," he said with quiet violence as Horse stepped over a fallen tree.

Her shoulders sagged. "I just wanted chickens."

"You cannot run into danger! This is bigger than your wants."

Her entire body stiffened. "What do you mean 'bigger than your wants'?"

Rey had planned to be gentle with the subject—perhaps coax answers from her gradually—but her attempt to flee had rattled him. She'd tried to put herself in *harm's way*, and he felt himself coming unhinged.

"I know who you are," he heard himself say.

She went stone-still.

"I know why the queen is hunting you."

She tensed as though bracing for the words to come.

"Your scar. I was with you when you got it, Eisa."

Rey's words sliced into Silla's skin. Her breath seized in her lungs as she realized she'd been right to trust her instincts—Rey knew who she was. And now she'd missed her opportunity to flee.

Your scar. I was with you when you got it, Eisa.

Her body trembled. He knew who she was, and Silla knew what came next. Jonas hadn't even taken a day to turn on her. How long would it take Rey to do the same?

Now panic climbed through her limbs. *Run,* her instincts told her once more. But some sliver of logic reminded her Rey would only chase her down.

"You were trying to flee," he growled.

"Please," begged Silla, gazing longingly into the forest. "Let me slip into the wilds . . . let me vanish. I'll take a ship south somewhere, and when I have the coin, I'll ensure you get your reward . . . I swear it to you."

Rey stiffened behind her. "You're *Eisa-gods-damned-Volsik,* and you want to abandon Íseldur?"

The air between them vibrated with his fury, leaving Silla disoriented. Shouldn't he be happy? He'd just stumbled upon the kingdom's biggest bounty. Why was he so angry?

"You're a *Volsik!*" continued Rey. "Don't you understand what that means?"

Manacles, she thought. Another cell. Her choices taken from her.

"Please," begged Silla. "You said you would not turn me in. You are nothing if not a man of honor."

"This is bigger than my honor," he grumbled. "And if you are incapable of making smart choices, I will have you bound to the saddle and carried to Kalasgarde by force."

"*Kalasgarde?*" Surprise furrowed through her. "You don't want a reward?"

Rey did not reply.

"Kalasgarde," Silla repeated. She shook with relief. Not a cell. She wasn't going back to a cell. Silla drew in a long breath. Let it flow slowly out of her. The trembling eased a touch, but the rest of his words finally sank into her. "You'll *force* me to go to Kalasgarde?"

He was tense as a bowstring behind her. "I've done many unsavory things for this kingdom, and I shall do many more."

"I can't be Eisa," she whimpered. It wasn't a cell in Kopa, wasn't Kommandor Valf, but he wasn't listening to her, wouldn't let her explain . . . "I *cannot be her;* don't you understand?"

"Don't *you* understand?" he flung back. "People *died* to protect your family. Ivar came for all Volsik supporters and killed them in the most vile ways."

The burn of guilt was spreading through her. "Please," Silla begged. "I must leave this isle. It is the only way to stop the bloodshed that follows me."

"Or," said Rey, "you could stand for your people. Do you not know what your existence would mean to so many? How much hope you could bring?"

"How?" cried Silla. "Don't you understand I can barely be Silla? How can I possibly be *her*?"

"I understand nothing but your cowardice."

It was just as she'd feared: The name would bind her, turn her into a thing to be used. Already her choices were being stripped from her, and her sense of self was vanishing into thin air. "You're just like Jonas, taking away my choice." She felt him flinch but continued. "But you said *Kalasgarde,* not Sunnavík, which means you don't want the reward. So why, Rey? What are you playing at? Why are you doing this?"

She could sense him choosing his words. Forcing them past his teeth. "Because all the good people have died, yet still I breathe. I must honor them and their deaths. Make them mean *something*."

"That's what Jonas said." Her voice trembled. "He handed me to the Klaernar so Ilías's death would *mean* something."

Rey stilled, hardly daring to breathe. "It is not the same."

"Truly?" Anger rose in her, and she was relieved to feel anything beyond fear. "Or is that simply an excuse made by violent men to allow them to sleep at night?"

"Do not pretend you know a thing about me."

"How can anyone know a thing about you, *Reynir Galtung*?" Silla spat. "You, who demand all my truths yet provide none of your own? You're more guarded than Askaborg."

The air was thick with tension. "You won't be troubled by my presence much longer," said Rey. His voice was cold, void of any emotion. "We will arrive in Istré tonight. You will stay in hiding. The warriors I've sent for are honorable. They'll put you in touch with people—good, trustworthy ones who know best how to handle you."

Handle me. Silla gritted her teeth. Anger festered in her stomach and burned through her limbs. She opened her mouth to protest but slammed it shut as Rey said, "There are wild things in these woods. Best we keep silent."

Silla blinked back her tears. Tried to gather her resolve. But all she could think of was Kalasgarde.

It was nothing but another cold cell.

CHAPTER 3

Askaborg Castle, Sunnavík

Saga Volsik wore black to the Bear God's service—the first she'd attended in over a month. It was practical, really. Though perhaps she should not worry; by now the washing thralls had grown quite adept at removing bloodstains from the clothing of the royals.

Her lady's maid had woven one side of her hair into intricate Urkan braids, and Saga had completed the look with her favorite winterwing brooch. If she was to bleed for the Bear God, then she'd damned well do it wearing what she pleased.

And now she sat beside Princess Yrsa in Ursir's House as the king's favored nobles trailed in for the weekly Letting. The room was well lit, despite the lack of windows. Braziers lining the central dais both brightened and heated the room, while gold-foiled pillars reflected and amplified the light.

Outwardly, Saga projected an air of boredom. But inside, she was a mess. For a month, she'd managed to avoid this—the crowd, the spectacle, the helplessness of her situation. Saga felt like a leashed animal, trotted out for their viewing pleasure.

Look how well she sits. Look how well she bleeds. Such a good little pet.

Her fingers twitched in search of her charcoal and drawing board, desperate to quell her growing nerves. Days had now passed since Saga had overheard Maester Alfson and Signe's conversation, discovering that Eisa—the little sister she'd thought dead for the last seventeen years—was alive. Not only had her foster mother known and not told Saga, but the queen had been hunting Eisa for *months*. It had been a staggering revelation, one that was still difficult to believe.

But as the days passed, with Saga waiting for a chance to do something—to do *anything*—to help Eisa, her nerves had only worsened. She could hardly sleep. Went through her days with a fog in her mind. Hours she'd spent in the hidden corridor behind Alfson's study, waiting to overhear another conversation, but she had nothing to show for her efforts.

Overwhelm consumed her some days, her mind like a cup overfilled, spilling over the sides until all she could do was to fetch her charcoals and parchment and draw, draw, draw. It was the only thing capable of restoring balance to her mind—by taking her out of her head entirely.

But drawing was not an option now. Her eyes swept the room for at least the tenth time, marking each doorway in Ursir's House. The main exit. The High Gothi's doorway. The trapdoor under the rug at the back of the dais—unless they'd boarded it up.

She repeated these exits to herself over and over, reminding herself that she was safe. Not trapped. Yet she couldn't shake the primal need to flee to the safety of her chambers.

Pulse pounding, Saga glanced to her right, where Princess Yrsa sat. Her emerald-green gown contrasted with her Norvalander white-gold hair and pale skin. Yrsa's spine was straight, her lips curved into a demure smile, and her brown eyes shone, as though there was nowhere else she'd rather be. Saga opened her mouth to say something to her foster sister—to quell the strange tension hanging between them these days—but the words were nowhere to be found. Instead, her gaze returned to the bloodstained altar stone at the front of the room.

It was said that the Bear God gained strength from blood. This was what moved Urkan warriors to such violence in battle. The more blood they loosed, the more glory they were granted. But other less glorious methods—sacrifice of oneself or one's belongings—could also gain Ursir's blessing. Farmers often slaughtered the best of their animals during Ursir's Spring Awakening to ensure a fertile growing season, while some Urkan warrior chiefs sacrificed the strongest of their human thralls before battle. But for the average citizen, the easiest way to gain Ursir's favor was to take part in a Letting.

Gods, but she couldn't do this. She needed to get to safety—back to her chambers. Pushing up from her chair, Saga prepared to flee the room. But as Queen Signe entered, accompanied by six bondswomen, any chance of leaving was extinguished. Numbly, Saga sank into her chair, resigning herself to her fate. She'd have to face this—would have to roll up her sleeve.

"Ursir shall be glad to see you, Lady Saga," came a woman's grating voice. Saga quickly identified the source as Lady Geira. As the High Gothi's pious new wife, she was one of Signe's most trusted confidants, and the pity in her eyes made Saga crave violence. Instead, she nodded curtly.

"'Tis a beautiful thing to recognize your own faults and move to correct them," said Geira, toying with a set of keys strung from her neck. The bondswomen surrounding her clucked their agreement.

"Darling Saga," came the queen's clear voice. The women parted, and she stepped through, a crown of iron claws atop her white-blond hair. Saga stood, dropping her brow in deference to the queen. Signe took Saga's gloved hand, stroking it gently. "I sought the High Gothi's wise counsel on your behalf."

Saga's heart pounded.

"He believes an extra Letting should help in healing your . . . *nerves*." Signe's bondswomen nodded and murmured in collective agreement, Lady Geira the loudest among the bunch.

Of course the answer was blood. Low spirits? Give blood. Bashed your toe? Give blood. Fighting the plague? Most definitely, give blood.

Saga nodded blankly. The queen moved to her daughter, collecting Yrsa's face in her hands. "Green suits you, my sweet girl." Signe placed a loving kiss on each of Yrsa's cheeks.

"Thank you, Mother."

Signe settled into a chair beside her daughter, bondswomen in the row behind.

Saga swallowed back the burn of jealousy. She should be grateful that the queen had taken an interest in her health. Her foster mother was befuddling. Harsh and unyielding, and yet every so often, she sprinkled in small acts of caring. And Saga, like a starved dog, ate each small scrap up.

A hush fell over the room as Thorir the Giant entered, heralding the king's arrival. With his bushy red beard and imposing height, the warrior was impossible to miss in any room. But in the flickering light of Ursir's House, he seemed somehow more enormous than usual.

Following Thorir came King Ivar Ironheart. Though Ivar was several inches shorter than Thorir, his commanding presence was felt across the room. The king had shoulder-length blond hair streaked with gray, his beard styled in dual Urkan braids. And though Ivar's eyes were cold and hard, they gleamed with satisfaction as they landed on Saga.

She shifted, looking away. There had always been a discomforting feeling in the king's gaze. Rather than lustful, it felt . . . covetous. As though he looked upon a jewel he'd gained for his treasure hoard.

Prince Bjorn, Saga's betrothed, came next. At age thirteen—nine years her junior—Bjorn had already gained his father's height but was lanky and awkward as he loped after Ivar. Clad in a red tunic matching his father's, and with his blond hair worn similarly, he was certain to be the king's spitting image when he came of age. Saga did not begrudge Bjorn for her situation—he had no more choice in their betrothal than she. But she had watched warily as Ivar drew Bjorn further into his affairs—had noticed the hardening of his face and the cooling of his eyes. Saga spent a great deal of energy trying not to think of what kind of man her future husband would become.

But she'd survived this long by molding herself to their expectations, so Saga forced a smile at her husband-to-be.

The rest of the king's retinue filed in after the prince, burly men with dour expressions, finding their seats in the warriors' section. The last warrior of the bunch ambled into the room with a familiar gait, and as light revealed his face, Saga's stomach lurched violently. Thin, cruel eyes were set in a windblown, ruddy complexion with a long, graying beard. She forced her gaze back to the altar stone, trying to quell the violent thrashing of her heart.

Magnus Hansson had returned from Reykfjord.

Saga dared not look, but she tracked the Heart Eater from the corner of her vision as he sat to King Ivar's right, the pair bowing their heads in quiet conference.

She repeated the exits in her mind. The main exit. The High Gothi's doorway. The trapdoor under the rug.

Thankfully, the High Gothi entered before she lost her wits entirely and fled. He was clad in flowing brown robes, and light caught the gold-embossed bear tooth strung around his neck. Several acolytes flanked him, one carrying a gilded cage, another tugging a leashed goat. Conversation quieted as they climbed the steps of the dais. The goat screamed loudly and dug its hooves in.

Thorir stood, hefting the goat with ease and setting it on the stone slab atop the dais before returning to his seat. The acolytes rushed to take Thorir's place, pinning the goat down as the High Gothi faced the crowd and pulled a ceremonial dagger from the folds of his cloak.

"We honor you, Ursir, God of Gods, with the blood of our finest beasts."

It was quick, bloody business. The Gothi murmured soft words while cutting the goat's neck and collecting the blood in a golden bowl, then pouring the contents over the altar stone. They then repeated the process with a dove pulled from the cage.

The High Gothi launched into a sermon, but the words were lost to Saga. Instead, she stared at that altar stone—at the runes carved into its bloodstained surface. It told the story of Ursir—of how He'd defeated the Moonhound to claim the Great Forest and the wolf beast's wife as His own. She couldn't help but think of all the others raided and defeated by the Urkans, of all the daughters taken. It was all an endless cycle of violence, driven by the need for the Bear God's blessing. The need for blood. The need to take.

At last, the High Gothi's voice trailed off and the warriors' section stood to begin the Letting. But the Speaker of the God raised a hand, quelling the hushed conversations around the room. Apprehension knotted in Saga's stomach.

"Before we begin, I'm told one of Ursir's daughters has come to us in poor health. Lady Saga, please join me on the dais so I might look upon your face."

Saga's body prickled as all eyes in the room turned toward her. Their gazes were like acid spilling over her, burning her skin, dissolving her bones. Saga swallowed and pushed to her feet. Took a step forward. She couldn't feel her feet, couldn't think. But she was doing it. Stepping up the dais stairs. Sitting in the chair. Looking at the faces of those who either pitied her or wished her dead.

The High Gothi was before her, dark eyes surveying her face. His stubby fingers prodded at her cheeks, turning her face this way and that. Squeezing her jaw, he pulled her mouth open and peered at her tongue.

"It is as I thought," he proclaimed to the crowd. "Impurities have gathered in her body, feeding on her health." The rasp of whispers gathered in the room. "I prescribe a heavy Letting to clean the blood and grant Ursir's blessing."

Saga wanted to rip herself out of the chair and run from the room. But their eyes were upon her, and the High Gothi was rolling up her sleeve and scowling.

"Ah," he said, loud enough for the entire room to hear. "Her vein has healed!" He yanked Saga's arm up, exposing her inner elbow to the crowd with unnecessary enthusiasm. A collective gasp filled the room as they peered at the freshly healed scars. "Proof of her half-hearted faith! Look what is wrought from frugality—ill health. What you give to Ursir, He will repay tenfold!"

The blood rushed in Saga's ears.

"I see now. This is far worse than I'd thought," said the High Gothi. "I fear I must change my prescription. A Grand Offering is in order."

Saga tried with all her might not to think of what that meant. It did not matter how she felt about the matter. She must be good, pliable Saga who did what she was told. But inside, she kicked and screamed. Much like the animals, her blood would be *taken,* not given.

As an acolyte approached, Saga retreated into the folds of her mind.

She was not here.

No. Saga was running through the gardens, her younger sister squealing behind her. Birds chittered from the hedges, the scent of fresh foliage thick in the air. Eisa was turning 'round and 'round and 'round and falling over . . .

"There," said the Gothi, as pain sliced into the crook of her arm.

She closed her eyes, and then she was lying on her stomach in the library, surrounded by tall shelves stretching toward the rafters. A fire crackled low in the fireplace, a cat lounging in Queen Svalla's lap.

"Another cup," murmured the Gothi.

Her eyelids fluttered, a glint of gold catching her eye—the gilded bowl, filling with a slow drizzle of her life force.

"Another cup."

Wrath and judgment scraped across her skin. They watched her, waiting for her to shatter. Didn't they know she was already broken? They'd taken her family, her castle, her kingdom, and now they'd taken her blood. What was there left to take? Surely they'd find it and take that, too.

Eisa. An ember buried deep within flared. Eisa needed her. But as the fourth—fifth?—cup of blood drained from Saga, her fight bled with it.

"She is pale," murmured the acolyte.

"Another cup," barked the High Gothi.

. . . It is what she has earned, flowed someone's thoughts.

. . . She must pay in blood like her family, added another.

. . . She deserves every bit of punishment she's earned . . .

The words throbbed in her skull, alerting Saga that her mental barriers had fallen and the thoughts of the crowd flowed freely to her. She could handle one, perhaps two people at a time with her Sense, but any more than that grew overwhelming.

More thoughts assaulted her. Saga knew she had to pull her barrier back into place—needed to keep her Sense at bay. Grabbing at the frayed edges, she wove together a shoddy barricade. It would have to do; she could manage nothing else.

The room swelled and rippled as her head lolled to the side. "That will do."

Her elbow was bandaged while the Gothi spoke to the crowd.

But Saga was spinning, turning, whirling, crashing. They watched her, all of them, as she stood. Stumbled.

Red flashed in her vision—the beard of Thorir the Giant as he scooped her up and carried her down the dais. The crowd was murmuring; braziers crackling; her heart thump, thump, thumping, too hard, too fast. And then Saga was placed back in her chair.

"You did well," whispered Yrsa.

Saga blinked, biting back on the urge to laugh. Did well. Bled well. Submitted like a good little captive.

But as her vision swirled, she saw herself and Yrsa as girls—playing in the gardens and riding ponies through the royal forest. For a time, they'd almost been like sisters. But now there was only distance.

... My Little Bear has grown so tall ...

A chill ran down Saga's spine. Signe ... she called Bjorn her Little Bear. Her mental barricades were still not intact, and it seemed Signe's thoughts were drifting through a gap.

... and soon he shall be wed. I do hope we can restore Saga to health in time. I cannot help but wonder if Ivar chose the wrong sister. Blond hair is certainly not a measure of one's strength ...

Saga's hands clasped tightly, her Sense widening, reaching toward Signe ...

... and Eisa has certainly proven herself resilient. But we shall see how she fares against the Wolf Feeders. It shall be my first task today—to see to the letter ...

Saga inhaled sharply, her barriers shredding through abruptly, inundating her senses with all the thoughts in the room at once. It was loud, a cacophony of noise that made it nearly impossible to snatch the fraying edges and weave barricades back into place.

Somehow, she managed.

Her gaze fell to her hands, Signe's thoughts pinging through her mind. The Wolf Feeders. A letter. *Today.*

The Letting began, warriors and worshippers queuing through the room. Saga stayed in her seat, mind gradually clearing. The ember in her chest flared hotter, hope spreading through her. After days of waiting, the opportunity had arrived.

She needed to stop Signe; she needed to intercept that letter.

And as the bloodletting continued, a dazed smile spread across her face.

CHAPTER 4

Immediately after leaving Ursir's House, Saga made her way toward the falconry tower. Askaborg consisted of a central keep and four branching wings, a maze of tunnels sprawling beneath. When King Ivar seized control, all loyal Volsik supporters were executed, including the help. Little did he know, knowledge of Askaborg's tunnels had perished with them. And while the Urkans had found some of them, the vast majority were known to Saga alone.

But as she groped along the cold stone walls leading through the western wing, Saga couldn't recall a single tunnel. Stars danced in her vision, her head throbbing viciously in the wake of her Letting. It was slow going through the corridor, but she made steady progress. Thankfully, there was little risk of encountering anyone. Deep in Askaborg's western wing, this corridor was solely used to deliver correspondence to and from the falconry tower.

Despite her dreamlike state, Saga traced her path to the tower in her mind. Through the corridor. To the dead end. And then she could pass through the old defensive walls without setting foot outdoors.

Saga's heart pounded with twice its normal vigor as it tried to fuel her body with what little blood it had left. The walls seemed to bend, and the floor was unsteady beneath her feet. Yet, despite the dizziness, she would not be stopped.

This was her chance.

She paused, bracing herself against the cold stone wall, grasping for a plan. Would Signe send a thrall or one of her bondswomen to the tower? And if Saga could intercept this person, could somehow obtain the letter before they posted it, then . . . what?

Then she'd read it. Burn it. But no. She'd surely be reported to Signe and quickly punished. Saga bit her lip, trying to think. But her heart was hammering, and she needed to lie down for a moment, or perhaps a day.

One step in front of the other. She would figure it out when she got there. Minutes bled together until, at last, she rounded a corner. Her feet stilled.

Ancient stone pillars bracketed the long, straight corridor. But the formerly solid wall of the dead end was now a mass of crumbling stone. Her heart pounded. The defensive walls had been her plan, but now they were entirely inaccessible.

Her gaze fell on the doors. Set perpendicular to the hall and located several paces before the crumbling stonework, the double doors led to Askaborg's inner courtyard. And that, Saga realized with growing panic, was where she needed to go.

A noise sounded from beyond the doors, and Saga rushed toward the rubble, concealing herself behind an arched pillar.

The door groaned open, someone stepping through. A woman's soft hum filled the air. Saga hazarded a glance around the pillar, taking in the woman's muted-gray dress and long auburn braids. Slowly Saga lowered her barriers, letting her Sense stretch out.

. . . That new quill was quite splendid. I shall send a note of appreciation . . .

As the woman walked, the faint jangle of iron met Saga's ears, and she knew the woman's identity at once.

It was Lady Geira and those keys she kept tethered around her neck.

Saga's heart crashed against her chest. How long had she taken to get here? Long enough, it seemed, for Signe's letter to be penned and delivered to the falconry tower. Which meant Saga had scant time to intercept it. She counted the fading footfalls as Geira retreated down the corridor.

The moment it felt safe, she dashed to the doors. Stared at the iron latch.

The defensive walls were no longer an option. In order to reach the letter, Saga would have to cross the castle's inner courtyard.

She'd need to step outdoors.

Nausea roiled in her stomach, her heart trying to beat free from her chest. Saga braced against the wall, repeating Eisa's name in her mind as her gloved hand found the iron latch. Lifted it. Pushed the door open.

She looked across the grassy courtyard to the tower. Her heart was in her throat now, hammering faster than she had thought possible. Twenty steps. She could do it. She *had* to do it. But what if . . . what if she became cornered? What if she was seen?

Go! she urged herself. Surely it wouldn't take long to select the right falcon—to affix a scroll to its leg? But a raven screamed from above. There had been ravens that day five years ago. She'd smelled the iron forge, the smoke of the fire. Had heard the sizzle of flesh and bloodcurdling screams.

The hand around her ribs squeezed tighter, tighter.

You should have been strung on a pillar next to them.

Her heart bucked wildly, the tower before Saga warping. Hand bracing on the oak door, she flinched as a breeze rushed at her. She *would* do this. But as she stared through the doorway, she saw it—a lone bird taking flight from the top with a scroll attached to its foot.

A cry ripped free from deep in her chest, and Saga stumbled away from the door. She could have made it, *would* have made it, had she not succumbed to her nerves. And now she was too late.

"Eisa," she whispered, eyes burning, as panic crashed over her. No tears. She would not cry.

Motion in her periphery caught Saga's attention—a woman peering down at her through the tower's window. Staggering backward, Saga tried to drive the raven's cries from her skull. *Punished!* they screamed. *Punished!*

Saga's vision went white, and she collapsed to the floor. She tried to breathe, but it felt as though her chest was caving in on her. How could she have thought she could simply cross the courtyard when she hadn't stepped outdoors in five long years?

You deserve to be punished.

Gasping desperately, Saga saw death on the horizon. Would she drown on dry land, or would her heart give out first? The wild pounding was not sustainable . . .

Tap.

She blinked at the gentle pat on her shoulder.

Tap. Tap.

She focused.

Tap. Tap. Tap.

"Breathe," came a deep voice, the commanding tone reassuring. The taps continued, firm and even, and she tried to ground herself with the sensation.

Closing her eyes, Saga followed the instructions and tried desperately to breathe. Her chest seemed to move up and down, but panic held a firm grip, and the room spun around her.

"Easy. Do not fight it. Go with it."

The fingers tapped her shoulder with a slow, calming rhythm. Saga focused on the touch until all else faded away. There was only gentle pressure and the expansion of her rib cage—the courtyard, the ravens, her failure all ceased to exist. Air gradually returned to her body, the terror in her chest loosening.

As the wild pounding of her heart dulled, the hand lifted from her shoulder. Everything in her body seemed to have a pulse, and her chest seized with spasms of pain. Her eyes fluttered open, but the walls were still spinning. Where was she? How had she gotten here? And who was the stranger staring down at her? Saga's eyes slammed shut.

"You fell," said the man in heavily accented Íseldurian. "There is blood." He paused. "You are all right, miss?"

"You're not here," Saga replied, squeezing her eyes tighter.

"Perhaps I am not understanding your language," said the stranger with a nervous laugh. Of course the man was nervous—he thought her madder than a bag of marmots. "Tell to me where you are hurt? Where is blood coming from?"

Saga prodded her mental barriers, shocked to find them already lowered. Her Sense was exposed, and yet she could hear no trace of this stranger's thoughts. Reluctantly, Saga pried one eye open. Looked up at the stranger. Her vision danced with lights, and she could not make out the man's face, but she could immediately tell he had a warrior's build.

Her heart resumed its thunderous beat, her mind screaming at her to flee. *Danger! Escape!* "I-I . . ." She glanced around in search of an exit, eyes falling on the opened door to the courtyard. "Door," Saga blurted. "Please, can you close it? I'm . . . cold."

The man moved away, and Saga pushed to her feet. Bracing an arm against the wall, she patted her hair—good gods, it was utter mayhem, pulled from her braid and strewn all about. She used it like a shield, pulling it around her face and peering at the man through her tresses.

He'd turned back to her, and she got her first glimpse of him. His skin was lightly tanned, his hair dark and wavy. But her eyes fell at once to his jaw—bare and angular, with a shallow cleft in the middle of his chin. To see a grown man's naked chin felt oddly obscene. It was not smooth, like Bjorn's boyishly unbearded chin. No, this was rough, textured with the coarse grain of regrowth. It was, decidedly, a *man's* chin.

Saga frowned. In Íseldur, beards were revered—a sign of male potency.

"You're not Íseldurian," she murmured.

"*Ochevidno,*"* the man said with clear impatience. "Tell to me where you are hurt."

Saga, you loaf-eater, stop ogling his chin. She blinked, gaze darting to his eyes. Worse. They were green as emeralds, framed with dark lashes and thick brows, pulled into a look of concern.

She forced her gaze to the roof above him. Roof. Beams. Cobwebs. All good, normal things.

"You are hurt?" demanded the stranger, his voice growing more impatient.

"No," replied Saga, trying to shove some sense back into her skull. The man before her was decidedly *large*. Her eyes darted from

---

*Obviously.

the enormous hand braced against the wall back to his bare chin. Not Íseldurian, which meant . . .

"Are you from the Zagadkian party?"

"*Zdravstvuyte,*"* he said, his penetrating green gaze prickling her skin.

"Oh, gods," Saga muttered, rubbing a hand over her face. *Make a good impression,* Signe had said. *We must foster a good relationship with the Zagadkians.* She dropped her hands. Tried for a smile.

"Why you are smelling of blood?" asked the man, his huge hand sliding over her shoulder, shaking her gently. Saga blinked at the man. *Smelling?* "You are bleeding. Where you are hurt?"

Saga looked down. Blood had trickled down her arm and was dripping onto the stone floor. Rolling up her sleeve, she found the bandage dangling loose. "I gave blood," she said, trying to retie it one-handed. "For the Bear God."

The man's expression grew stony. "Let me," he said, producing a fresh pocket linen. One hand slid around the back of her arm, cradling it gingerly, while the other pulled the strip of linen into place. He tied it deftly. "And that?" he asked, gesturing to the door.

"Blood loss," Saga mumbled, hiding her flush behind her hair. Gods, but this was humiliating. "I-I thank you for your help."

"Was not so much . . ." He put a hand to his forehead, mimicking fainting. "Was seeming more"—the man searched for the word, coming up short—"different. *Bezumiye.*†" His brows drew together, making his green eyes somehow more piercing.

Saga rubbed her gloved hands together, unwilling to share any more than she must.

"Come, miss . . ." He looked at her inquiringly.

Saga opened her mouth in reply. But then the realization struck her. He didn't know who she was. Telling this man her name would place Saga at the falconry tower. And if that was made known to the queen, it could make her suspicious of Saga.

---

*Greetings.
†Madness.

"Árlaug," Saga answered, thinking of her lady's maid. "I thank you, my lord, for your help."

The man smiled, and Saga's head spun at the glorious sight. Soft curving lips. Shallow lines flanking them. Gods, the blood loss was truly getting to her.

"I am Rurik," he said quickly, holding out a giant hand. "Kassandr Rurik."

The name flowed from him, somehow soft and sharp all at once. Hesitantly, Saga slid her gloved hand into his, blinking as she felt the friction straight down to her toes. "Let me to"—he seemed to struggle with the words—"help you to your rooms."

"I thank you for your assistance, Lord Rurik, but I'm afraid I must..."

The man uttered something in Zagadkian, slipping a steadying arm around her waist. "No, Árlaug," he replied, his words as immovable as stone. "I will not allow it. You are alone and needing someone to catch you."

Saga's insides squirmed in discomfort. She needed to find the exits, but her only option besides the outdoors was to return the way she'd come. Weak from blood loss and from the crisis she'd suffered, Saga could scarcely stand, let alone reach her chambers in the northern wing. She tilted her head so that her hair tumbled over her shoulder, a barrier of sorts between the two.

"Kitchens," she blurted, thinking of the passage in the back of the pantry. "That is, I work in the kitchens and would appreciate your assistance returning there."

"I think you must rest, Árlaug," he protested, leading her down the corridor. "You are not in condition for working."

"I thank you for your concern, Lord Rurik," she murmured, leaning against his sturdy form more than she ought to. "Cook will prepare a replenishing broth, and I'll be back to rights."

"Very well," grumbled the man, clearly unconvinced. He began leading her down the hall. "While we are walking, tell to me about this place."

"What do you wish to know?" asked Saga cautiously.

They passed an alcove, a polished granite bust glaring at them from atop a pedestal. Saga knew that in the alcove's corner lay a hidden passage running beneath the castle, and she fought the urge to flee into the tunnel's dark solitude.

"Who is this unsmiling man?" asked Rurik.

"That is King Harald the Hard, King Ivar's father. He is ruler of—"

"Norvaland," answered Rurik. "He is often visiting?"

Saga cleared her throat. She supposed a kitchen thrall would know such a thing. "He last visited when Prince Hávar was born." She paused. "Two years past."

"They are treating you well here?" he asked, studying her.

Saga felt faint under his perusal. "Y-yes, my lord."

"But this"—he gestured to her arm—"they are often taking blood from you? From all workers?"

"Yes." There was no point in lying, she supposed.

"And their . . . ward," said Rurik. "Do you often see her?"

"Lady Saga?" asked Saga, clutching his arm tighter as the hallway spun before her.

"Yes."

"She is . . . present." Saga watched him through her hair, wondering why the man sought information about her. "I'm told she'll soon be wed to Prince Bjorn."

Rurik muttered something under his breath. "How old is this boy?"

"Thirteen," replied Saga.

"And Printsessa Yrsa?"

"She'll soon be eighteen, my lord." They walked through the winding corridors, Rurik peppering her with questions about the various tapestries they passed. Much to Saga's chagrin, the man was quite talkative and, it appeared, rather curious. By the time they arrived at the kitchens, Saga was exhausted from keeping up her guise as Árlaug.

"Thank you for your assistance, Lord Rurik," said Saga, hastening into the kitchens before he could reply.

She leaned against the wall in the pantry for several minutes before she was ready to venture into the passageway. Not long after that, she was collapsing on her bed, utterly exhausted.

With an oatcake stolen from the kitchens in her belly, she felt her energy crawling back. An afternoon of rest and she should be back to rights. But as sleep closed in on her, the thing she'd walled away surged forth at last.

By now, the falcon was well on its way north. The Wolf Feeders would come for Eisa, and Saga had missed her chance to warn her. Had missed her chance to *do something*.

Twenty steps, perhaps less. Saga wanted to scream. Wanted to punch a wall. Wanted to pull her hair out. Long had she honored her need to feel safe by staying within Askaborg's walls. Five years it had been since she'd set foot outdoors. Her affliction was merely a part of herself—a thing she worked around. But today, here, *now*, she saw it for what it was.

Hers was a cage with no bars.

Because of it, the Wolf Feeders were coming for Eisa. And there was nothing Saga could do.

CHAPTER 5

Somewhere east of Istré

Silla and Rey trudged along the trail, growing ever closer to Istré. As the day progressed, the volcanic rocks mottling the forest slowly vanished, a familiar patchwork of northern lichens joining the moss.

Rey shifted in the saddle, trying to distance himself from Silla's mass of curly hair. For the dozenth time that hour, he tried and failed to find the right words. They hadn't spoken since her attempt to flee, and with each passing hour, his guilt gnawed more viciously.

You're just like Jonas, taking away my choice.

He gritted his teeth against the burn of guilt as her words invaded his mind once more. Again, he'd spoken too harshly to her. He raked a hand down his face, wondering how he'd grown so unhinged. It wasn't the recognition of her identity but her attempt to flee that had knocked him off balance. Rey had yelled at her. Malla's tits. He'd called her a coward.

Her lack of self-preservation had been kindling to Rey's anger, but her pleas to leave Íseldur were the winds fanning it higher. Eisa Volsik was alive but wanted nothing to do with this kingdom. The realization more than disappointed Rey. It *enraged* him.

It was a slap in the face to those who'd fought—to those who'd *died*—for her family. Silla had inadvertently picked at an old wound of his; it felt as raw and exposed as it had seventeen years ago. Dead, all of them. It was only him now, left to sift through the rubble. To find meaning in it all.

To seek vengeance.

And the woman lacked the common sense to keep herself alive. If Rey had to force her into the northern reaches of Íseldur for her own good, then so be it.

On they rode, but the closer Istré loomed, the higher Rey's unease grew. Was it merely the prospect of reaching his destination after a full month's travel from Reykfjord? The anticipation of tackling this challenging job without two of his Bloodaxe brothers?

Or was it something more?

Days now, Rey had been pushing memories of Kopa from his mind. Now he could think of nothing else but the escaped Klaernar he'd failed to kill at Kopa's hidden entrance. It was a loose end Rey would normally have tied up. But there hadn't been time.

And now it was too late.

As they neared Istré, Rey found himself glancing over his shoulder. The sun had set, though the cloud-cloaked skies meant an absence of moonlight and the slumber of luminescent forest plants. Ravens called out, and a wolf howled from the woods nearby.

"Grimwolves?" asked Silla, tensing.

"Could be," said Rey, eyes searching either side of the road. "As we're on horseback, they should not attack."

Had it truly been a grimwolf? Rey rolled his shoulders, the strange sense of foreboding crawling through his body. Was it the eyes of wild things that had him reaching for his dagger?

Or was it merely their nearness to Istré, with its deadly mist and mysterious creatures the Bloodaxe Crew had been sent to deal with? Yes. That must be the reason for this strange apprehension.

They rode for several minutes until, at last, they rounded a bend in the road and the torchlit walls of Istré came into view. Silla shivered, drawing her new cloak tight around her.

Rey remained silent as they approached the closed gates, torches lighting sheep skulls and weathered shields mounted on the timber walls.

Istré.

His heart pounded. The trip north had been rife with troubles, and the job with the mist would be a challenge to tackle, but he'd made it, and in that moment, it was all that mattered.

Before he could stop her, Silla slid from Horse, rushing to the closed gates of Istré. "Oh, gods," she muttered, pulling at something.

"What is it?" he asked, casting a look at the top of Istré's walls. Where were the guards at this hour?

Her body had gone preternaturally still as she stared at something in her hands. "How? What?" Slowly, Silla turned, holding a birchbark etching.

The breath left his lungs in a sharp exhale. Rey's body grew weightless, his mind spinning, as he stared at the image painted on the bark. As the threads of his fate unraveled before his very eyes.

Rey's own face stared back at him.

Silla's was beneath it. And below that were the words serving as the final stones on his burial mound.

REWARD:
Slátrari—ten thousand sólas.
Companion—twenty thousand sólas.
Must be brought in alive.

CHAPTER 6

"Slátrari," Silla read, looking at him in confusion.

Rey could not reply; he was too busy trying to wake from this nightmare. But each time he blinked, he was met with the damning image of his face paired with that name. *Slátrari*.

"The noticeboard calls you the Slátrari. They've made a terrible mistake . . ." Silla's voice trailed off as she caught something in his expression. She took a cautious step backward, her hand reaching to where that damnable vial used to hang.

"No," she murmured, taking another step back.

But his mind could not function. He could only stare at the birchbark etching and wonder how this troublesome woman could have climbed into his wagon and ruined his life so thoroughly.

"—the burnt corpses at the door to Kopa—"

His face was now linked to the name *Slátrari*, illuminating nearly a decade of work in the shadows to the entire kingdom. How long would this take to reach Sunnavík—for Magnus to realize that the leader of his favorite warband had been using him to collect information for the Uppreisna? How long would it take for the entire gods damned kingdom to be searching for him?

"—oh gods, *oh gods—*"

Rey's vision tunneled as he fought the urge to scream—to drive his fist through Istré's cursed gates.

"—you're him. *You're* the murderer—" Silla's back hit the wall, her eyes wide with panic.

Rey knew that look well—the look of prey about to bolt. Gods, but she would do it again, wouldn't she? Infuriated, he leaped from

Horse, striding toward her while drawing his galdur to the surface of his palms.

"You," was all he could manage. He was beyond words, beyond anything except the wrath burning through him. With an exhale, ribbons of ash peeled up from his palms.

"No!" she shrieked, stumbling on a loose stone and landing on her backside. Her eyes were wide, the pulse in her throat hammering. She scrambled to her feet. Turned.

And then Silla fled. *Again.*

"Too late," Rey growled, his smoke swarming after her, sliding up her spine and hooking around her shoulders to halt her.

"Don't kill me!" she begged, struggling against the hold of his smoke. Rey was practiced enough to maintain a light touch and not burn her.

His boots crunched on the rocky road as he stepped toward her. She writhed like a wild animal, trying to wrestle free. "In case it wasn't clear, *Eisa*," he said roughly, "if you run, I will come after you. If you cannot make smart choices, I will make them for you. And, *Sunshine*"—he tugged on his smoke, twisting her around to face him—"running into those woods is *not* a smart decision." With that, he strode back toward Horse, dragging Silla like a leashed animal behind him.

"Why?" she spluttered. "Why would you kill those people? What will you do with me?"

He opened his mouth to reply but stopped short as something whizzed past his ear, embedding into the timber gates with a *thwack*. Rey's warrior instincts kicked back in. Grabbing Silla around the waist, he threw her into the saddle and launched himself up after her. With a pull on the reins, he whirled Horse to flee.

Ten warriors blocked the roadway, arrows nocked in longbows.

Silla wailed, thrashing against him.

"Hush," he growled in her ear, tightening his smoke's grip.

Thankfully, with the glint of arrows trained on them, she stilled. Yanking on the reins, he turned Horse to retreat, only to face eight more archers, aiming straight at them. Panic flared inside him as

Rey assessed the situation. Eighteen warriors he could handle, but if he maintained his smoke's grip on her, he risked losing control and burning her...

"Do you want to live?" he whispered roughly. "If you do, your only chance is with me. Do you understand?" Slowly, she nodded. "Good. I will release you, but you must be still and silent. If we wish to escape, we must work together." He eased his smoke away from her and was relieved she did not bolt like a frightened rabbit. Perhaps she'd finally realized the murderer she knew was a far better option than the warbands and monsters.

Rey assessed the archers before him—helmless and clad in boiled-leather armor. He recognized the wolf sigil etched on their breasts.

"Wolf Feeders," he muttered.

Fool. He should have seen this coming. Should have known what came of loose ends. The lone Klaernar who'd escaped in Kopa . . . Rey should have chased him down. Now it was too late. He scanned the surrounding woods.

"You're outnumbered, warrior," said one archer. "Best to give yourself over."

Without another thought, Rey drew more galdur forth, the warm familiarity of it calming his heartbeat. They knew his identity; he might as well give them a show. Rey hoped the reputation of the Slátrari had preceded him—fear was an equal weapon to any blade.

Silla whimpered as smoke hissed from his skin.

He assessed the situation while drawing from the pool of galdur nestled next to his pounding heart. Numbers. Weapons. Weaknesses. Escape. Not all battles must be won. It was counter to Rey's nature to flee, but he had Eisa-gods-damned-Volsik with him. Had walked her straight into a trap.

Escape. If they could outrun these warriors . . . but they were two on one horse with eighteen arrows drawn on them, and the gods knew how many more on horseback in the shadows.

"I-I can startle them," whispered Silla, much to his surprise. "M-my light."

Rey glanced down, noting how she hugged her forearms against herself, muting the light that poured from her wrists—her fear must have primed her.

"You speak the truth," called Rey to the Wolf Feeders. "We are indeed outnumbered. But I have a proposition for you." He lowered his voice, whispering to Silla, "When they decline, unsheathe your light upon them."

"Go on," said one of the central archers, his arrow nocked.

"If you let us go, I will double the reward."

A coarse laugh bounced off Istré's gates. "You carry sixty thousand sólas on you, warrior?"

"I can get it within a fortnight. And it comes with a bonus: You won't be roasted like a boar on a spit."

"Bold words for a man surrounded," said the warrior. "But we're oathsworn to the queen. It is not personal, warrior. 'Tis merely business."

With that, Silla wrenched her arms free, pure white light cutting through the darkness and straight into the eyes of the Wolf Feeders. The archers cried out in surprise and sent arrows spearing through the air without precision. Rey, meanwhile, expressed more smoke as quickly as he could, shaping dark, twisting tendrils that struck out with serpentine speed.

Bowstrings twanged behind him, and Rey lurched to the side in the saddle, his thighs pulling Silla with him. Arrows sang through the air, bare inches from his ear. One struck the scales of his armor at the wrong angle, deflecting harmlessly. His luck ran out after that. An arrow slashed through the seams in his lébrynja armor, sinking into the flesh of his shoulder.

Bellowing, Rey channeled his pain and fury into his galdur. A grim smile tilted the corners of his lips as his smoke tunneled down the throats of the archers before him. The hiss of searing flesh met his ears as he poured wrath and heat into it, sparing not an ounce of mercy.

It's not personal, he thought grimly as their flesh blistered and burst, as they crumbled to the ground and tried to crawl away.

Silla made a sound of distress but somehow maintained enough clarity of mind to grab the reins. Horse tore down the road while Rey held his smoke in place. The screams of dying warriors chased them, gradually dissolving into silence.

But Rey knew the Wolf Feeders' reputation well enough to know he'd seen a mere sliver of their plan. He glanced over his shoulder, his chest clenching down: Riders, twelve, perhaps fifteen, darting from the woods. He expected they had even more. Pulling his shield from the saddle hook, Rey swung it overhead just as arrows rained down upon them.

Quickly, Rey sifted through his options. His galdur required too much focus to manage while riding; best to save his reserves for later. A fresh idea took shape in his mind.

"Climb up," barked Rey, hooking his shield back in place. "Pull the arrow from my shoulder."

"Climb . . . up?" she spluttered.

"Stand in the saddle. I'll hold you in place. Pull out the arrow, then climb behind me."

Awkwardly, she stood, clutching his shoulders as he gripped her hips. Jostling with the movement of Horse, she looked over his shoulder, gingerly touching the shaft of the arrow.

"This is no time to be gentle!" he bellowed. "Pull it out n—" Rey unleashed a string of feral curses as she yanked the arrow free and flung it aside. Sucking a sharp breath in through his nose, he breathed through the pain. "Climb behind me and get ready to catch the arrows."

"Catch . . . the arrows?"

"Now!" he growled.

Thankfully, something shook loose within her, and Silla edged around him, one foot on his thigh, the other on the saddle behind.

"This is madness," she muttered. At that exact moment, Horse jostled to the left. Silla shrieked as her foot slipped from the saddle and she tumbled off Horse. Dropping the reins, Rey's arm struck out, wrapping around her waist. He yelled in agony—the pain from the wound in his shoulder was knife-sharp.

Silla's feet dangled freely from the side of Horse, the ground a blur beneath her. Rey's eyes met hers as a bead of sweat rolled down his temple.

"Don't drop me!"

"Would make my life easier," he muttered. Muscles screaming in protest, he hauled her upward inch by painstaking inch.

An arrow hissed by his head, thudding into the earth; the thunder of hooves behind them grew louder by the moment. At last, Silla could grasp onto the saddle, kicking Rey as she clambered gracelessly up behind him and arranged herself with her back to his.

"Rey!" she cried out. "They're gaining on us!"

"And so the fun begins." Reaching down, he unhooked the shield and passed it to her.

"If you're trying to put me at ease, you're failing."

"I was certain it was a lost cause when you watched those men burn."

The unmistakable twang of loosed arrows met his ears, and Rey said a silent prayer to the gods she could keep him from becoming arrow fodder.

With a squeal, she shifted behind him, and he heard a series of *thwacks* as arrows struck the shield. He exhaled—they'd survived the first wave.

"Hang on tight!" He directed Horse off the road and into the woods. "Light!"

Thankfully, she understood his clipped commands and raised her free arm above his shoulder, twisting to illuminate his path. Rey smiled grimly—they were badly outnumbered, and he would take whatever advantage he could get. Horse darted between pine trunks, leaping over fallen logs and dried creek beds.

"Duck!" he barked, lying back and flattening her on Horse's rump. They rode beneath a fallen tree, bark whizzing inches above his nose. Moments later, several Wolf Feeders cried out, horses screaming as their riders were knocked off.

"Light!" he called out, straightening in the saddle. And so they continued—Silla lighting their way, Horse expertly weaving between trunks and beneath logs, as they weeded out the Wolf Feeders one at a time. After several more long minutes in the woods, he directed them back out onto the open road. They'd lost all but two of the Wolf Feeders on their tail in the forest's darkness, but Rey was not so naïve as to think there wouldn't be others waiting in the wings.

"More!" Silla cried, confirming his suspicions.

"How many?"

She paused, counting. "Twelve!"

With a vicious curse, he urged Horse on. Silla shrieked behind him, hefting the shield up as another volley of arrows fell upon them.

"One of them is breaking off!"

Rey gritted his teeth, passing the reins to one hand and unsheathing his hevrít with the other. Two on one horse, they had no chance to outrun the Wolf Feeders. But if they each had their own mount, they could even the odds . . .

Ears primed, he listened as the hoofbeats grew louder, louder, until the rider was beside them. And then Rey made his move. With a swift swing of his leg, and a push off Horse, he launched himself onto the Wolf Feeder, burying his dagger in the warrior's neck.

The man let out a cry of surprise as Rey shoved him loose. As the warrior crashed to the ground, Rey grabbed the reins, smiling once more at the yells from behind him.

"You arse!" came a cry, followed by a shriek—Silla, seated backward on Horse, was clutching the saddle blanket in pure terror as they careened down the road.

Glancing over his shoulder, Rey assessed their pursuers. About a dozen riders with quivers full of arrows, and it seemed Silla had lost their only shield. As another arrow whizzed past his ear, Rey traced the landscape in his mind. An idea quickly took shape.

Kicking his mount and whistling for Horse to follow with a screeching Silla, Rey drove them down the road with even greater speed. Without Silla's light, it was difficult to make out the terrain, but his instincts sensed when the bridge came into range, and he readied himself.

Drawing from his source, Rey also pulled from the additional reserves tattooed on his chest until an exhilarating river of power rushed through his veins. With an exhale, he expressed, pulling thick ropes of smoke and weaving them together until a storm of ash and shadows churned wildly above him. Heat lashed down on him, embers crackling angrily, and when he felt the bottom of his source, Rey drove the smoldering tempest toward the bridge.

Ignite. Another arrow sang through the air, inches from his head. The soft crackle of embers met his ears, hooves pounding on timber as he galloped across the bridge, straight through the churning mass of smoke.

Leaping off his mount, Rey waited until Horse and Silla had crossed the bridge, then forced all of his power onto the wooden structure. He could feel the dry bottom of his source and knew that if this did not work, they'd be in grave trouble. But as he felt his magic catch—as he felt it begin to consume—a maniacal laugh escaped him.

The Wolf Feeders gathered on the opposite side of the bridge. In the firelight, it was difficult to see, but Rey remembered this gorge well and knew how perilously deep it went.

One of the Wolf Feeders was brave enough to attempt a crossing. Rey's heart pounded with the force of hammer strikes as the warrior's horse took one step, two. The horse reared as they neared the flames, throwing his rider. Screams bounced from the walls of the gorge as he plummeted down, down, down, and landed with a sickening crunch.

The bridge was now a blazing bonfire, illuminating the Wolf Feeders' angry faces on the opposite side of the canyon. Glowering, they whirled their horses, riding off into the night.

And at last, Rey allowed himself to exhale. It would take them hours to bypass this canyon, which meant he and Silla would have plenty of time to vanish into the wilds.

Something struck him in the back. Turning, Rey took her in. Lit by the swirling light of her forearms, Silla's eyes burned with rage.

"You wretch!" She slapped his chest. "You murderer!" She pushed him. "All those people on the Road of Bones—you murdered them all!"

Silla reared back as though to punch him, but Rey's hands lashed out, wrapping around her wrists. With a yank, he pinned them in place at her sides, causing her to stumble forward, her chest colliding with his. Her breath hitched, but she quickly recovered, trying to shake loose from his ironclad grip.

She struggled against him, her rage palpable. "You killed them!"

"I saved us."

It was difficult to think with bare inches separating them. With the light from her forearms, he could count each curving eyelash, trace the lines of her brows, the constellation of freckles across her nose.

"You burned them!" she shouted. "You brought them agony until their last breath—"

Rey tried to focus on her words. "You're Eisa-gods-damned-Volsik," he gritted out. "What would you have me do?"

"But all those people along the Road of Bones! How many were there?"

"It does not matter."

"*How?*" she demanded. "How can it not matter? All I can think of when I look at you is the flesh melting off their faces—"

"You shouldn't have watched."

Silla stilled against him, and he sensed she was trying to gather herself. "Explain," she pushed. "Explain it to me."

Rey looked away, releasing her. His stomach burned. How could she understand when she wanted nothing but to flee this kingdom?

She made a sound of irritation. "How can you preach honor while murdering good men?"

He scowled. "There was nothing *good* about the men I've killed. Death, in fact, was too easy for them."

She pressed her lips together, then continued. "And who decides this? What gives you the right to dispense justice as you see fit?"

"*I* do not decide it." He sent her a look as hard as granite. "That is done by men far wiser than me. I am simply the blade."

It was clear a thousand new questions had sprung into her mind, but Rey was done answering them. The reality of his situation was sinking in. The birchbark etching flashed in his mind, and a wave of raw fury consumed him.

"Fuck!" he bellowed. He picked up a branch and swung at a tree edging the road. Over and over, he swung the branch until it had shattered and nothing remained. Leaning forward, he rested his forehead against the tree's trunk.

Rey's likeness was now linked to the name Slátrari. Life as he knew it had just ended. Istré was no longer safe for him. The entire Kingdom of Íseldur was no longer safe for him.

A hard lump formed in his throat. There was only one place for him to go. One place where he'd be safe.

Turning, Rey glowered at the curly-haired woman staring at him with pure loathing.

"Well, *Sunshine,* it looks as though you'll have company in Kalasgarde."

CHAPTER 7

Kopa

Jonas Svik needed to punch someone. Or perhaps bed someone. But most preferably, both.

He needed *something* to remind him he was alive. Despite the raucous crowd in the mead hall, he'd never felt so alone.

Ilías had always loved the oddities of Íseldur's north, and this place would have been no exception. Besides the obvious—the hall was crafted from volcanic stone, the hearths of polished obsidian—he'd appreciate the eccentric details the most. There were the garlands of bones dangling from the rafters, and light flared from a cage of flíta in the room's corner. But the thing setting this mead hall firmly in Kopa was the pure abundance of dragons—carved into the pillars, painted on decorative shields, embroidered on the barmaids' dresses.

With a sigh, Jonas took a long draught from his horn of ale. He'd come here to forget, but it seemed there was no amount of ale that could wipe his brother from his mind. Everywhere he looked were memories of Ilías—a flash of golden hair, the rumble of falling dice, a certain pitch of laughter. Should he turn, certainly his brother would be there.

"I got you!" Ilías would joke. "My most elaborate jest to date!"

Then Jonas would drag him into a headlock and trounce him as only an older brother could. Laughing, they'd settle on the bench, drinking and speaking of the farmstead, until they floated along on a warm wave of contentment.

Lies. His fingers found the talisman strung around his neck and smoothed over the interlocking triangles. His brother was gone; the sooner Jonas accepted it, the better off he'd be. But Jonas didn't want to accept that his younger brother's light had been snuffed from this world.

For a time, he'd thought he'd be able to move on from the tragedy. That if Ilías's death had *meant* something, he could go forth with his life. And when Silla's true identity had been revealed, it felt like he could see the threads of his fate clearly for once. Jonas needed only to turn Eisa in to the Klaernar, collect his reward, and retake what had been stolen from them all those years ago. He could reclaim his family's lands.

Ilías's death had made sense to him at last, and with that had come a measure of peace.

Yet here he now sat, plans in ruin, and even more bereft than in the days following Ilías's death.

Jonas had lost his brother—his shadow, his better half. He'd lost the Bloodaxe Crew—better than most of the true kin he'd known in his life. And he'd lost her—the one he'd thought could change him. Could make him a good man.

And for what? *Eisa* had escaped, and now the Klaernar refused to pay his reward. Jonas failed to see how that was his fault—he'd delivered her right to them. *They* were the fools who'd allowed her to escape. Whispers had reached him—she'd killed their gods damned kommandor. A small corner of his heart had smiled at that, but he quickly stomped it down.

She deserved to be in a cell—deserved whatever brand of cruelty the Klaernar dished out. But like the serpent she was, she'd slithered free.

And Jonas was left with nothing. Utterly . . . nothing.

He should feel something. Sad or angry or . . . *anything.* Instead, there was this blasted numbness, as though he were trapped between life and death. After draining his horn of ale, he slammed it into the stand and gestured to the barmaid. As she swished over to him, he caught the hopeful glimmer in her eye.

"Hello, Jonas," she purred, replacing the empty horn with a fresh one. "Thirsty tonight, are we?" She trailed her fingers along his shoulder. "Do you *hunger* for anything?"

He sighed. In a moment of weakness... desperate to feel something... he'd taken the barmaid to bed. The woman had been eager to please him, and yet it hadn't been enough. She'd mewled like a cat in heat, her every move so... wrong. Jonas had been forced to flip her on her stomach so he could imagine it was *her* he fucked.

And even then, there was no pleasure to be found. It was an empty, joyless thing. He'd been relieved just to kick the woman out.

Another thing *she* had ruined for him.

"Just the ale," he growled, shaking the barmaid's hand free. Scowling, she retreated.

Jonas drank deeply, eyes surveying the crowd in search of a worthy foe. Who would challenge him enough to wake his battle lust? Who would slake his need to feel alive?

A burst of laughter a short distance down the long table caught Jonas's attention. A group of warriors, four strong, heads bent in a less-than-quiet conversation. Drunk, clearly, but they had the look of battle-hardy men.

"Heard it was a draugur, rose from the dead."

"Draugur don't roast a man like a spring rabbit," barked a second man, slamming his ale down. "Galdra, it was—one of those Ashbringers. Burned more'n twenty Klaernar without breakin' a sweat. Look, 'ere's the etching." The man rummaged around in his sack, then pulled an item out and flattened it on the table. "Says 'ere, REWARD: SLÁTRARI—TEN THOUSAND SÓLAS. COMPANION—TWENTY THOUSAND SÓLAS. MUST BE BROUGHT IN ALIVE. Pretty thing, she is."

"She's one of 'em!" chimed in a third man. "One of 'em Galdra. Heard he freed 'er from the Klaernar. Helped her escape the city."

Jonas knew in an instant who they spoke of. Anger roared to life deep in his chest. So she'd had help to escape the Klaernar, then? Curiosity prickled through him, and he found himself rising. Found his feet moving toward the group of warriors.

They scowled at him as he approached, snatching the birch bark away from his eyes. "What you want, warrior?" asked a bald man with a scar running from forehead to chin.

"Might I have a look at that?" asked Jonas, nodding at the drawing.

"You want them sólas for yerself, huh?" asked the man's companion—red-bearded, with thick biceps. "What if we don' feel like sharing?"

Jonas fished in his pocket, then tossed a handful of sólas onto the table. "For your next round."

The bald man hesitated, then gave his companion a curt nod. Scowling, the warrior passed the birch bark to Jonas.

He stared at it. Blinked to clear his vision. But there was no mistaking who stared back at him from the etching.

Jonas's vision tunneled as he stared into the eyes of Reynir Bjarg.

Below, the name SLÁTRARI.

First came denial. It was impossible. Not his good, honorable headman. Rey, who had always demanded honesty from his Crew. Five years Jonas had known the man. There was no way his Bloodaxe brother was Galdra, let alone the gods damned Slátrari.

But below Rey's likeness was *her*. Curly hair. Large, dark eyes. That tiny scar on her cheek. The spawn of Myrkur, who chewed people up and used their bones to pick her teeth clean.

Doubt crept in. Jonas allowed himself to consider the possibility. Allowed himself to remember the accounts of the Slátrari chasing them all the way north. All those evening walks Rey liked to take. And then there was the morning the Bloodaxe Crew had chosen to fight for Silla on the Road of Bones. When Silla's lies had been exposed to the Crew, and Rey—who held honesty above all else—had deflected their questions. Had protected her.

Wouldn't that confounding incident make sense if Rey, too, was Galdra?

Jonas's grip on the etching tightened, the voices in the mead hall growing muffled. More secrets. More lies. Did no one in this kingdom value honesty?

I was dishonest for my own safety, Silla had told him. But what about Ilías? Who had cared for *his* safety? Not Silla, when she'd withheld the truth about who hunted her. Not Rey, when he'd led them into that battle, unprepared.

Nausea burned in his gut, but his anger was hotter, hungrier—it consumed him.

"All right, pretty boy?" asked the red-bearded warrior. "You know the pair?"

"No," replied Jonas numbly. He was beginning to realize he'd never known either of them at all.

Long had Jonas yearned to feel something, but the fresh knife in his back was too painful to bear. It hurt to breathe. Hurt to think.

He couldn't feel this. Needed to forget.

Jonas drew his fist back.

Smashed it into the red-bearded warrior's face.

The mead hall erupted.

And as the battle thrill coursed through him, at last, Jonas felt something tolerable.

CHAPTER 8

Sunnavík

Saga's back ached. As she sat in the hidden passageway, her ears were primed for conversation beyond the cold stone wall, as they had been for hours. To pass the time, she'd brought her drawing board, and her charcoal raced across the parchment.

The man's nose was straight, his eyes piercing, but the scar on his cheek and the golden hair knotted at his crown made it clear he was a warrior. Her gaze settled on the pendant hanging from his neck, etched with three interlocking triangles. Saga frowned. There was something unsettling about the man, despite his handsomeness, despite the hint of a smile. She felt as though she knew him, and yet she could not place him.

The light guttered, and she glanced at the torch. It had burned nearly through, and she was down to her last one. That gave Saga . . . thirty minutes more before she'd be engulfed in complete darkness.

With a sigh, Saga set her drawing board aside and touched the torches together. The pitch-soaked cloth caught at once, and light spilled into the corridor anew. She leaned against the wall, head thunking back. How long had she been here?

It didn't matter. She would stay here as long as it took to discover Eisa's fate. Had the Wolf Feeders captured her? Was she shackled in a boat bound for Sunnavík? The hours passed with no answers, and the gnawing in her gut only worsened.

Using her Sense to listen in on Signe's thoughts during meals had proven disastrous. She could manage, at most, two threads of thought at a time. So the great hall, filled with dozens of people, had quickly overwhelmed her. Instead, Saga had returned to the passageway in which she'd originally overheard Queen Signe and Maester Alfson converse. She'd lost count of how many days she'd spent in this secret corridor, ear pressed to the wall. Though she'd also freed her Sense, the thick stone impeded her gift for reasons she did not understand.

Saga had quickly realized it was Maester Alfson's study beyond the stone wall, and it was him she most often heard. So far, she'd discovered nothing but the maester's irritation at poor test results of some sort and his fondness for pickled herring.

There'd been no word from the north—no mention of the Wolf Feeders. Days passed with nothing to show for Saga's efforts save for yet another dress coated in dust. What had happened to Eisa? Why hadn't Saga heard any news?

Staring at the shadows dancing along the roof, Saga tried not to let her worry get the best of her. But it was looking like yet another fruitless day.

It was impossible to keep the images from invading her mind's eye. Her little sister, running through the wilds of the north, hunted by the Wolf Feeders. Little Eisa, caged like an animal—forced to come south against her will.

Anger festered in her veins. Saga could not allow this to happen. She was the older sister. She *had* to protect Eisa. But the longer she sat here, the worse these nightmare visions got. She needed to clear her mind before she went mad. With a long exhale, Saga pushed to her feet and began beating the dust from her skirts.

"Alfson!"

Saga froze, a prickle of recognition rushing down her spine. That was Signe's voice. Heart pounding, Saga pressed her ear to the wall.

The muffled sound of a slamming door. "Your Highness." It was Alfson.

"What have you to say of this?" barked the queen.

Silence stretched out, and Saga forced herself to breathe. Alfson mumbled in a low voice, and she pressed her ear tighter to the wall. "Arrow struck one target . . . bridge burned . . . targets escaped while we bypassed the gorge . . ."

Saga's heart quickened. This *had* to be Eisa. Had she escaped the Wolf Feeders and slipped into the wilds? Elation filled her at the prospect, making Saga so buoyant she might float to the roof.

"Well?" demanded Signe, and Saga forced in a calming breath.

Alfson cleared his throat. "I assure you, Your Highness, they came highly recommended."

"Not recommended enough!" Glass shattered beyond the wall.

Signe's anger was like a quiet storm, always held between carefully placed words. Knowing that Eisa had caused the queen's loss of control brought a malevolent smile to Saga's lips.

"'Tis a positive sign that one of them was wounded," said Alfson.

"*Wounded,* not captured. Not on a ship bound south!"

"They are the best trackers in the kingdom, Your Highness. We must be patient."

"You well know I have plenty of patience, Alfson. It is *incompetence* I cannot tolerate!"

Alfson's low reply was difficult to hear, and Saga's ears strained. "The girl is cunning," he said. "And her companion . . . he's Galdra. Used to concealing himself. Unafraid to spill blood, and it seems he's quite adept at it."

Saga's heart was dancing in her chest. Eisa had a companion—someone to help her, perhaps to keep her safe. It eased the worry in her gut.

"What do you suggest?" demanded the queen.

"We must get into their minds—think like them. Were you in their place, what would you do?"

Silence for a moment, then, "I'd hide until the search died down."

"The north is vast," said Alfson. "Hundreds of villages."

"It is an impossible task!" exclaimed the queen.

"Not *impossible*," replied Alfson. "A challenge, to be sure, but not impossible. Let us consider the pair. Based on what we know, does Eisa have knowledge of the north?"

"No," mused the queen. "But this Slátrari . . . what of him?"

"Precisely, Your Highness," said Alfson. "Her companion is the key to finding Eisa."

"His likeness has been spread throughout the north," said Signe. "*Someone* knows this man."

"It will take some time for the etchings to reach each remote village in Nordur," said Alfson. "In the meantime, I suggest we change our tactics. Seek information rather than capture. We will learn how this man thinks. Which connections he has."

"Let them grow comfortable," said the queen. "Lay out the noose. And when they least expect it, pull it taut around their necks."

"According to this message, the Wolf Feeders are trekking through the eastern wilds of Nordur and will send an update when they reach Völfell," said Alfson.

"How long will that be?"

"Difficult to say," said Alfson. "Perhaps a week? This will give us some time to gather information about the man. Here is what I propose, my queen: Have the Black Cloak spread word in the northern cities that we now merely seek information. And when someone comes forth, have Geira pen a letter with this information and send it to the Wolf Feeders to narrow their search."

Saga reeled. *Geira*. Her mind returned to the queen's bondswoman, returning from the falconry tower. It seemed Lady Geira was involved in more than delivery of correspondence. With a shake of her head, Saga tried to refocus.

The queen's sigh could be heard through the thick stone wall. "Very well," she said. "But what is to say the Wolf Feeders won't fail once more?"

"They've been shamed," said Alfson. "I'm certain it has only spurred their resolve. They'll hunt the pair down with even more vigor."

"Very well," said Signe after a long pause. "But if the Wolf Feeders fail once more, I want their heads on pikes."

"Yes, Your Highness."

Fading footsteps. A door closing. The conversation, it seemed, was done. Saga's head swirled with what she'd just heard. Eisa had escaped. She had a companion. But she was far from safe.

"I won't let them find you," whispered Saga. She sank to the floor, staring at the wall as she considered her options. By the time she stood and beat the dust from her skirts, Saga had the bones of a plan. And unfortunately, it involved befriending Lady Geira.

But Saga vowed she would do what it took. The next time Signe sent word to the north, she would be ready.

CHAPTER 9

As Saga climbed out through the hidden panel in the library's oldest hearth, her blood flowed with vigor. Thankfully, this fireplace was infrequently used and located well out of sight in the back corner of the room. But as Saga stepped out, it was impossible to keep old ash from fluttering up and joining the dust on her skirts.

"Plague and boils," she muttered, beating her skirts. But despite the ash on her slippers, Saga felt as though she could fly. Finally, she had news. Finally, she had hope. She need only return to her chambers and map out her plan.

As she neared the end of the aisle, a voice fractured the hush of the library. Saga hesitated. It wasn't that she was *ever* in the mood to engage in small talk, but today, her need to avoid it was high. She peered between the shelves, identifying the source of the noise—one of King Ivar's advisers, trailed by a group of ten or so men. Based on the tailoring of their jackets and the rolling lilt of their voices, they seemed to be Zagadkian.

"The library was built in the six hundredth and fifty-fifth year of the Volsik Dynasty, under the rule of King Adils," droned Ivar's adviser, allowing the Zagadkian translator to speak. After a long moment, he continued. "His great-grandson, King Sigurd, expanded upon it in the six hundred and thirtieth year."

"Seven hundred and thirtieth," muttered Saga under her breath. Mortification crept through her as she recognized Kassandr Rurik in the bunch.

A week ago, when she'd first dined with the Zagadkians, Saga had waited for Rurik to recognize her. Seated at the farthest end of the high table, she'd worn a vibrant gown of Zagadkian silk. Her hair was immaculately styled, eyes lined with kohl, and when they were introduced, there had not been so much as a flicker of recognition in Kassandr Rurik's eye. If Saga had it her way, he'd never realize the disheveled woman he'd met near the falconry tower was really Lady Saga.

She'd quickly realized the man had the kind of charisma she preferred to keep far away from. The serving thralls and jarls' wives alike turned to watch him enter the great hall at mealtimes, whispers and giggles following in his wake. And the irritating man seemed to feed on the attention of others—always laughing, always speaking in his loud, carrying voice, his spoon waving in the air as he conversed with King Ivar. What in the gods' burning bollocks could Ivar have possibly said that was so amusing? Nothing, that was what.

Mind back in the present, Saga retreated a step. She'd just hasten down the aisle and skirt the library's outer edge.

"Lady Saga," came a deep voice in heavily accented Íseldurian. Her feet faltered. "May you repeat this?"

Saga held her breath, pressing her back into the wooden shelves. She should have known she wouldn't escape unnoticed. But how had she been heard?

A figure appeared between the rows of books. Though light filtering from the windows cast the man's form in silhouette, Saga had no problem identifying him as Kassandr Rurik. For one thing, he was tall among Urkan and Zagadkian warriors alike. And for another, he walked with a graceful sort of arrogance, near silent despite all the blades strapped against the strange, armored surcoat he wore.

The last time she'd tried, Saga had been unable to hear this man's thoughts. Now she eased her barriers down, longing to know what exactly he wanted. But as she allowed her Sense to stretch out, she was met with silence. Her brows lifted in surprise.

"Perhaps I should be calling you Árlaug?" Rurik said in a lowered voice, leaning against a shelf.

The world seemed to drop out from beneath her. "I beg your pardon?" she managed, gripping the shelves to steady herself.

Rurik rolled his eyes. "You can stop this"—he gestured at her—"game."

Saga's mind whirled in search of a reply. "How did you know?" she asked.

Rurik prowled closer, and Saga's heart pounded faster with each step. "Bird," he said, his large hand reaching out, flicking a dangling winterwing earring. Saga forced herself not to recoil.

"Bird," she repeated. It felt as though a bird were trapped in her rib cage, thrashing about.

"You are wearing the birds, as did Árlaug."

She was an utter sculpin. Of course she'd worn that blasted winterwing pin the day she'd called herself Árlaug.

"Why did you give yourself new name?" he asked, thankfully in a low voice.

Saga swallowed. "I did not wish for you to know it was me," she confessed.

Rurik's brows drew together. "Why?"

Saga searched for the right words but came up blank.

"First, you give to me wrong name. Now you try to run away. It appears you wish not to see me."

"I was *not* running," she lied.

"Shall I call for my Druzhina, Lady Saga? Ask them what they think of this?"

"No," she blurted. She grabbed the man's sleeve. Pulled him deeper down the aisle before she could think better.

"I apologize for my deceit," she whispered. "I meant you no dishonor, Lord Rurik."

He watched her, his mouth twisted up to one side, and she could tell he needed more convincing. Though she despised herself a little, Saga decided the damsel in distress might be warranted. She made her eyes wide. Looked up at him through her lashes. "Please, my lord, I beg for your discretion in this matter."

But Rurik didn't leap to play her rescuer. Instead, a sly smile crossed his lips. "Ah. A secret? And what you will give to me for holding your secret, Lady Saga?"

She gaped up at the man.

"Perhaps," continued Rurik, "you will give us a tour of Askaborg." At her scowl, his eyes flashed with glee. "After all, is best to learn from the one who lived here longest."

Saga closed her eyes, swallowing. She had no choice; she'd have to do this. There was the fact that Signe had made it clear they needed the Zagadkian grain. But this man could now place her at the falconry tower, and Saga did not want this information to reach Signe's ears.

"I'd be pleased to show you around," she forced out.

"Again," he said, smiling victoriously. "Will be second time now, will it not?"

Good gods, the man was delighting in her misery. "I suppose it is."

Rurik's eyes scoured her from her ash-covered slippers to the top of her head. Reaching forward, he plucked something from her hair.

Saga's face heated as she looked up at him.

"You have cobweb in hair," he said genially. He leaned closer, whispering in her ear, "Is from reading of books, I suppose."

The heat in her face rushed through her body in an angry torrent. Damn this man. Entirely too perceptive. There was no choice but to get it over with. Pushing past Rurik, she made her way to the rest of the group.

"Pleasing news," Kassandr told Ivar's adviser. "Lady Saga will give to us the tour." He repeated this to the group in a rapid flurry of Zagadkian.

"B-but," sputtered the adviser, his face reddening.

"We are thanking you," said Lord Rurik. "But you are"—he appeared to search for the right word—"dismissed."

"Lord Rurik, surely Lady Saga is too busy. I have orders from His Majesty to—"

"I am not liking to repeat myself, Oslo." Lord Rurik waved his hand in a dismissive gesture that made Saga's teeth grind.

"Oslak," muttered the adviser as he reluctantly shuffled toward the exit.

"Rude," she muttered under her breath.

Rurik's assessing look told her it had not been low enough. "Come," he said, "I will introduce to you Druzhina."

Numbly, Saga turned to the Zagadkian retinue. Her heart pounded like a cornered rabbit's. *The passageway in the hearth,* she recited, trying to calm herself. *The library's main doors. The thralls' door. The western door.*

A tall man with warm-brown skin and a nose that appeared to have been broken more than once barked out rapid-fire Zagadkian, Rurik replying in an argumentative tone. Saga watched as Rurik gestured to her, then to the library's door. After scrubbing a hand through his close-cropped hair, the other man turned to Saga with a broad smile.

"Lady Saga," he said jovially. "Is good to be meeting you. I am Yuri Rovgolod. Lord like Kassandr, but better looks and manners."

Rurik barked something in Zagadkian.

Rovgolod's smile only deepened. He offered his hand. "You can call me Rov."

"Saga," she said, sliding her hand into his, bracing herself as he shook it with shocking enthusiasm.

"Rest of Druzhina is not speaking the language," continued Rov. "I am translating for them."

"Druzhina?" Saga asked.

"Is name for retinue."

Saga turned to the rest of the Druzhina, her legs numb. She tried for a smile, but it felt flimsy at best. "Welcome to Íseldur," she said, feeling like a fool. Gods, they were doomed if acquiring Zagadkian grain depended on Saga's social skills. Names flew her way as Rov introduced her to the rest of the Druzhina.

"We were to visit collection of tapestries and—" Rurik turned to Rov and spoke in a rapid burst of Zagadkian.

"Obsidian busts," chirped Rov.

"Yes," said Rurik. "This is right."

Saga examined the group of warriors. "Surely you'd rather shoot something in the royal forest or try to outdrink Thorir the Giant."

"Lady Saga, once more it seems you try to rid yourself of me," said Rurik, watching her closely. Too closely.

"Is not first time someone tries such a thing," Rov said wryly. "Man is like barnacle. Difficult to get rid of."

Saga smothered a smile. "Very well, I shall show you the tapestries, if you're certain you wish to see them."

"Yes," asserted Rurik.

"This way," Saga said, reluctantly leading them to the library's exit.

She would show them the artwork, then return to her chambers to consider her plans. Taking a stabilizing breath, she led them toward the rainbow corridor. They walked in awkward silence, Rurik beside her, Rov behind.

"How fare your meetings?" she asked, aiming for the breezy conversation Yrsa made look effortless. But her voice came out too harsh, too brisk.

"Some badly, some good," said Rurik. Behind them, Rov made a sound of irritation.

Saga blinked at his candor. "What does that mean?"

"Is . . . games of reason." Lord Rurik ran a hand through his hair, and Saga's gaze lingered on his dark waves. "Negotiation on treaties is more stroking of the tender egos than doing something useful."

Saga glanced at Rurik. His strides were fluid yet edged with silent power. "Your Íseldurian is quite good."

"So it must be," said Rov. "Kassandr prepared for full moon cycle before we sailed. Barely letting his poor teacher come out from his rooms," Rov added conspiratorially. "I . . . I am poor teacher."

The corners of Saga's lips tugged up.

Rubbing her gloved hands, Saga led the Zagadkians into the hallway. The walls and pillars in the corridor were hewn from a pale volcanic stone, the perfect canvas for the rainbows projected through prismatic glass. "This is the rainbow corridor," she said, a small smile on her lips. It was impossible not to smile with millions of rainbows dancing along the corridor's white pillars.

She turned to find Kassandr Rurik watching her once more, the prisms casting rainbows on his sun-kissed skin. Her smile faltered. "The arches are made from fortified rhyolite, I believe, and the windows are made of special prismatic glass, creating the ... uh ... rainbows." She tried to recall which king had commissioned this corridor, but with Rurik's eyes on her, she could scarcely remember her own name.

Rov and the rest of the Druzhina wandered along the corridor, but Rurik hung back.

"How it was made, this glass?" he asked, rapping a knuckle along the intricately assembled panes.

"Galdra," Saga said in a hushed voice, glancing over her shoulder. "There are many Galdra-made structures left in the palace. Despite efforts to remove them," she added in a flat tone.

"Galdra. Is your ... magic people?" asked Rurik, running a large hand along the glass.

"They were," she said, desperate to change the subject. "Where is your high prince?" Immediately, Saga cringed.

But Rurik was unfazed. "He is not liking boats," he replied, his face an inch from the glass as he inspected it.

She choked on a laugh, taken aback once more by his candor. King Ivar would have a man's tongue for sharing a weakness like that. "Truly?" she managed.

"It makes him sick."

"And his famous heir?" Sunnvald Almighty, Saga was on a roll.

"Is not permitted. You wish to meet him?" Rurik turned from the windows, assessing her with unabashed curiosity.

"No," she blurted. "I mean, yes, of course. It would be good to foster ... relationships, but ..." She was unsure how, exactly, to climb out from the hole she'd just dug herself.

"But ..." urged Rurik.

"Perhaps it's best he stayed behind."

Rurik turned to her, the rainbows cast upon his face doing nothing to soften the intensity in his eyes. "Tell to me what you have heard."

Saga swallowed. This was precisely why she was the wrong

woman to tour the Zagadkians—it had taken bare minutes for her to stick her foot in her mouth. And yet . . . her mouth was still moving.

"Only that he has a beastly temper and a penchant for tearing out throats." Saga cringed, gloved palms rubbing nervously together.

"Is true," said Rurik, watching her intently. "In Zagadka, our customs are different. A ruler must show strength. Must show the kingdom what happens to deceivers."

Deceivers. Saga swallowed. *She'd* deceived Rurik only days ago.

Rurik chuckled softly, as though reading her thoughts. "Do not worry. High prince has forbidden his heir to come. Is not good man for . . . diplomacy."

He turned away, and Saga exhaled. *Get through this,* she told herself. One tour and she could put a safe distance between herself and Lord Rurik.

Saga led the Zagadkians through the corridor, down a flight of stairs, and into the eastern wing of the palace. At last, they entered the gallery. Hewn from the same granite as the rest of Askaborg Castle, the gallery had high ceilings and plenty of natural light flowing in from tall, glass-paned windows. The walls were crowded with fading tapestries, sculptures, weathered shields, and chipped weapons.

"Well," Saga sighed. "Tapestries. Obsidian busts."

The Druzhina scattered throughout the room, examining the artwork on display. Rurik studied a wooden carving depicting Ursir in his Sacred Forest. "Is all Urkan here?"

"Mostly. There may be a few Íseldurian relics lingering about, but most of them were considered blasphemous and destroyed."

Saga's gaze bounced around the room. She hadn't been here in years—possibly a decade. To think of what once had been here, what had been destroyed . . . Saga's feet itched to leave, but she held herself in place. *Focus. Appease the man's ego. Smooth any feathers you've ruffled.* She must finish the tour and leave on good terms.

"Is pity," said Rurik, wandering down the gallery.

One of the Druzhina pushed his shoulder against a door midway along the wall, causing Rov to unleash a flurry of Zagadkian. Sheepishly, the man withdrew and continued perusing the art.

"'Tis merely a storage room, if I recall," Saga told Rov.

"Tell to me about this, my lady," said Rurik. He now stood before a large tapestry of black and fiery oranges.

"Please, my lord, just Saga."

"Very well. Tell to me, *Just Saga.*" Gods, but she hated how much she enjoyed the man's accent. She wanted to ask him to say *bogblossom* or *flying fairy caps* and close her eyes to let the sound roll over her skin. But instead, she said, "This one is Íseldurian. It is a rendition of the Sleeping Dragons."

"Why volcanoes are called this?"

"It's a name derived from an old tale."

"Tell me," he urged.

Saga glanced around the room. Satisfied that Signe could not have any mice listening in, she continued. "It involves our old gods. Legend tells that long ago, the Íseldurian god of chaos tried to destroy the world." Saga's vision grew unfocused as she tried to remember the tale.

"The great dragon Kraugeir woke, and with him the volcanoes, spewing ash and fire and opening the gateway to Myrkur's underworld. With great effort, Sunnvald was able to defeat Myrkur and banish Him back below."

"The fire and death? We have this thing, too."

Saga stared at the tapestry, frowning. Eisa was in the north. Would she have passed the Sleeping Dragons? Where had she gone? What if the Wolf Feeders found her before Saga could put her plan into motion?

"Where did you go, Saga?"

She blinked, turning to Lord Rurik. This man was dangerous—he saw too much. Already, he knew far too many of her secrets. And in a world where safety meant staying hidden, she could not allow him to see any more of her. Saga's protective thorns slid into place. "Have I satisfied your requirements yet, my lord?"

He watched her carefully, but she kept her expression stony.

"If you wish to see more, you might ask Princess Yrsa. She's spent many years learning her history and probably knows it better than I do."

"I did not want Printsessa Yrsa to show me," he said slowly.

She eyed him warily. "Why not?"

"I wanted to know little pet of Ivar."

Flames of anger licked up her spine. "I'm no one's pet."

Rurik's lips twitched. "What is it you say . . . hostage? How you prefer to call this?"

Saga's heart beat loudly, pushing fire through her veins. "Is that what they tell you in Zagadka? That I'm a hostage?"

"Do you truly wish to know?"

Her hands balled into fists. "Yes."

Rurik's face grew serious, and he was silent for a moment before replying. "Survivor, they call you. Yes, most think you hostage."

"I don't want your pity." She could hear it in his voice, and it made her want to scream.

Rurik held his palms up defensively, but it only made her blood boil.

Saga took a menacing step closer. "Do I *look* like a hostage? I am free to do what I want. They treat me well."

The man had the audacity to chuckle—*chuckle*! Saga's muscles trembled. She tried to let it go, to no avail. "What, exactly, is so amusing to you?"

His smirk made her want to take the priceless tapestry off the wall and bash it over his head. "You sound of perfect trained pet. They must give you excellent treats."

"You are *insufferable*!"

He looked utterly delighted. "Here you are." Rurik's gaze swept her face. "I am pleased to see the *true* Lady Saga. Like tapestry, in you there is the fire."

"You've a knack for bringing it out," she seethed, searching for her self-control. But it seemed that with a few choice words, the man had unraveled all her restraint.

"I have *many* talents, Saga," Rurik drawled, his emerald-green eyes alight. "Why do you hide yourself?"

"Because I don't have a death wish!"

"Better I will die standing than live in collar."

Saga reared back as if slapped. And in a single sentence, Rurik had doused the flames of her anger. Now she was naught but ash, certain to blow away in a gust of wind.

Because he was right. Saga was a pet. A leashed thing trotted out for others to admire. Soon she'd wed Bjorn. Would become one of them. Would bear Urkan children, would be part of their legacy. Bloodshed and war and taking, taking, taking...

"Saga," began Rurik. His jaw flexed, his confident demeanor faltering.

"I'm done," she said, hugging herself.

Silence for a long moment, then, "I thank you for showing the gallery to us. And I can assure you, I will hold your secret."

"Good day, Lord Rurik," said Saga. Turning, she made her way toward the doorway.

"Kassandr," he called out. "Call me Kass."

Saga huffed. As far as she was concerned, if she never laid eyes on that man again, it would be too soon.

CHAPTER 10

North of Istré

Silla glared at the curious assortment of lichen covering the trees and surrounding forest, ignoring the harsh stare of the man sitting across from her. A crisp, late-summer morning, it was the day after the Wolf Feeders' attack. They'd fled down the road for several hours afterward before trudging deep into the woods and making camp for the night.

And now, Silla and Rey were up with the sun, readying for another long day of travel. As Rey wrapped clean linen around his arrow wound, Silla pulled her new cloak tighter around her shoulders and bit into her smoked elk.

Rallying cry, Silla, she thought. *You didn't die yesterday. You're not alone right now. Even if your companion has a penchant for burning people alive . . .*

She huffed, chewing harder. It was impossible to shake the image from her vision—Rey, melting the Wolf Feeders' flesh from their faces with a mere flick of his wrist. He'd killed them in the most vile of ways . . . had *been* killing people as the Slátrari for the gods knew how long.

I am simply the blade, he'd explained, but it did little to quell her nausea. Instead, it brought to mind the queen's warriors who'd killed her adoptive father and Ilías Svik. It made her think of Skraeda, stalking her along the Road of Bones at the queen's behest. Were they not *simply blades* as well?

It all made her want to flee once more. But in the aftermath of the Wolf Feeders' attack, Silla was more clearheaded. Her choices were grim: escape and take her chances with the monsters and warbands, or stay with the murderous man before her.

It wasn't really a choice.

Despite Rey's violence, it was clear he intended to keep her . . . uncooked. For now at the very least.

"Aren't you going to ask me?" grumbled Rey, drawing Silla from her thoughts. "Don't you wish to know how we know each other, *Eisa?*" He jabbed a stick into the campfire, sending embers floating skyward.

Every muscle in her body tensed. "Don't call me that."

His brows drew together, gaze lifting to meet hers. "Why not?"

Silla massaged her temples. "I cannot think of it all, not now."

"You'll have to face it eventually," he bit out.

"I know I'm a coward. You do not need to remind me of it."

Rey opened his mouth, but snapped it shut.

"Fine," sighed Silla, staring into the fire. "Tell me how you know her."

He eyed her for a long moment before he began. "My father was a member of King Kjartan's retinue, and we visited Askaborg often. When I was eight years old, we came to Sunnavík. And while our parents visited, the children went into the gardens to play. Kristjan and Saga were close in age, and they ran off together, leaving me with the baby sister."

Met with her silence, Rey continued. "The nursemaid was with us for some time, but there was an emergency she had to rush off to attend. And that left me, an eight-year-old boy who wished only to play swords or climb trees, to watch a two-year-old princess who wanted to play a spinning game."

Round 'n' round 'n' round we go echoed in Silla's mind. Was this game a remnant of Eisa's childhood? Suddenly, she felt as dizzy as she had that night in the canyon.

Rey pressed his lips together as though he did not wish to continue. "Eisa climbed on Sunnvald's fountain to walk round 'n' round it, then fell and hit her eye on the ledge," he said in a rush. Absently, Silla's fingertips skimmed along the small scar. "And I received a stern verbal lashing from my father for failing to protect the princess from harm."

"That's it?" she asked, disappointed. "I thought it would be something more fanciful—clawed by a grimwolf or wrestled a bear. A fountain. I was told it was a table." Numbness was creeping in from all corners. "It seems my whole life was a lie."

Rey's eyes narrowed as he examined her. "When did you realize you were *her*?"

"Skutur. Skraeda . . . she pulled on a memory and . . ."

Confusion, then disbelief, crossed Rey's face. "You've only just discovered," he mumbled, more to himself. Silla watched him fight inwardly with something. "I thought . . ." He exhaled, his gaze lifting to hers. "I thought you knew all along."

Silla shook her head, trying to push back the pain. A new thought entered her mind, and she could not push it aside. "If you knew my birth father, did you—"

Several moments passed before he prompted her. "Did I what?"

"Did you know my adoptive father? Tómas, he was called." It stung to ask this question. To admit she knew so little of the man who'd raised her.

"Tómas was King Kjartan's bodyguard," replied Rey, studying her. "My father knew him well."

Somehow, Silla had thought answers might assuage her grief and anger. Instead, they only exasperated them further. "I suppose that explains how he killed six mercenaries near Skarstad," she said bitterly. "And my foster mother, Ina? Unless that was a false name as well."

Rey's brows drew together. "Eisa's nursemaid. Her name was Ina."

"Nursemaid," she muttered. "And bodyguard." Pieces were sliding into place—Tómas and the nursemaid, stealing Eisa away from the palace, unable to get to Saga in time. An ache began to grow in her chest.

Silla drew a long breath and pushed to her feet. Lichen crunched underfoot as she wandered into the bushes under the guise of relieving herself. But once behind a copse of trees, she braced against a scaled trunk, gasping for breath. The lies were endless, each new one more painful than the last. Why hadn't Matthias—*Tómas,* she corrected bitterly—told her? Why hadn't he *trusted* her?

Her entire body ached, tears burning in her eyes. But she could not afford to fall apart now. She needed to wrangle the grief flowing through her and shove it in a cage.

And when she strode back into camp, her expression was as hard and unyielding as Rey's *axe eyes.*

Rey watched her emerge from the bushes, bleary-eyed and tense as a bowstring. The swelling around her eye had faded, but purple bruises lingered, reminding him of all she'd suffered in Kopa. He should be kinder. Gentler. But neither of these words described him in the least.

Grabbing his stick, Rey jabbed a burning log.

She'd only *just* learned her true name, and the discovery left Rey reeling. How could Tómas have withheld this from her? Fed her those poisonous leaves and treated her like a child? Anger burned in Rey's gut at the very thought.

He searched for something to say that would put her at ease. It would be many days until they reached Kalasgarde and the safety of a shield-home . . . gods, *Kalasgarde.* Bile pushed up his throat at the very thought.

From the corner of his eye, he tracked Silla. She peered at the horse he'd stolen from the Wolf Feeders, now tethered to a tree. The mare was a deep chestnut brown, and already it was clear that she had a temperamental disposition. Rey watched with apprehension as Silla approached and the horse's tail swished.

"Good morning, beauties," said Silla with forced brightness. "What brilliant and valiant warriors you were yesterday." Horse snorted, stepping forward and nuzzling against her palm. "In case your rider forgets to tell you this, I insist that you do not forget it."

The new horse snorted, ears flicking back in irritation. Rey pushed to his feet, moving forward on instinct. "A lot has changed for you in a short time, hasn't it?" Silla said softly to the new horse, reaching out to stroke her cheek. Rey lunged a moment before the horse did, arm snaking around Silla's waist and hauling her back. The horse's teeth snapped together where Silla's hand had been moments before.

As her back came flush to his chest, a jolt ran through him. Instinctively, Rey's arms tightened around her, and she relaxed against him. But after a heartbeat, she came to her senses. Whirling, she wiped a furious tear from her cheek.

"She's a warrior's steed," Rey grumbled, stepping back. The feel of her lingered, and he ran a flustered hand over his face. "You must earn her trust." He gazed at the new horse. "But her ears are not pinned, and she hasn't reared or kicked out, so she should be safe for you to ride."

"Ride?" Silla asked, aghast. "She tried to bite me!"

"It was merely a warning nip," he said gruffly. "I advise you not to pat her." Rey tried to soften his voice. "I know you do not trust me, but I hope you know I wouldn't compromise your safety."

Those dark eyes met his for one moment, and once again, Rey could feel the ghost of her leaning into his touch. Grinding his teeth, he turned to gather his belongings.

Thank the gods above, the horse tolerated Silla in the saddle, though a lead tied to his own mount was an unfortunate necessity. At last, Rey had Horse back to himself. At last, he could *think*. But with each step closer to Kalasgarde, the burn in his stomach intensified. Kalasgarde, the last place in all of Íseldur he wished to go. Rey had worked so hard to leave Reynir Galtung behind him—to create a new version of himself as Rey Bjarg.

Yet, it seemed fate had other plans. In the better part of a decade that Rey had worked for the Uppreisna, he'd never needed a shield-home. And now he'd be stuck in hiding. With *her*.

And yet he knew with utter certainty he would do it all over again. Even before he'd discovered she was Eisa-gods-damned-Volsik, Rey had known Silla was worthy of protection. He'd thought her one of the last good things in this cursed kingdom.

Still, he brooded over the implosion of his life and turned his attention to salvaging the Istré job in his absence. First, Rey would contact Eyvind, a childhood friend who owed him favors. Eyvind was a talented warrior who had a genial way about him—he could win over even the most ornery of men. The Bloodaxe Crew would not like a stranger stepping into Rey's shoes, but given the difficult circumstances, they had little choice.

Next, the Uppreisna would need to be informed of Eisa. Yet on this matter, Rey hesitated. *I cannot be her,* Silla had told him, a look of panic in her eye. He frowned. Perhaps that needn't happen right away.

He glanced behind him. Took in the droop of her shoulders. And decided Eisa Volsik could wait.

In his anger, Rey had pushed too hard, but now the truth was plain to see. Right now, Silla Nordvig had her own battles to fight.

CHAPTER 11

For six long days, Silla and Rey rode north. The terrain shifted from the flat acres near the Western Woods to rolling foothills, the winds from cold gusts to ice-tinged gales. Silla pulled on all the clothing she owned and accepted Rey's wolfskin gloves with grim resignation. Despite the cold, the countryside was rather lovely. The pinewoods covered wild and rugged mountains, the road branching frequently and growing ever narrower. Alongside the road, clusters of blue lilies bloomed between lichen-crusted boulders, and when a family of frost foxes darted across their path one day, Silla's breath caught in her throat.

She decided frost foxes were a good omen. A reminder of adaptability. Like the foxes, whose fur shifted to blend in with their surroundings, Silla, too, could reshape herself.

On the long, silent days, Silla had nothing but time to think. Over and over, her mind's eye showed Rey killing a horde of warriors with barely a thought. It had been horrific, so gruesome, and yet . . . he'd wielded such *power*. It was the first time Silla had considered that her galdur could be more than a death sentence. Shifting the reins to one hand, she pulled up the sleeve of her tunic and examined the smooth, pale underside of her forearm.

Could she wield power like that?

Ashbringer, Skraeda had called her, as well as Blade Breaker. Silla did not know these terms. But now that she'd had a glimpse of what Rey could do, an idea began to take root in her mind. At first, she nearly dismissed it. But with each passing day, it grew and expanded until it had taken over completely. It seemed so clear now.

Come and find me, the little blond girl had said. Saga was trapped in Askaborg with those who'd killed their parents.

And if Silla could wield power like Rey's, perhaps she could free her sister.

With each mile they traveled, her purpose became clearer.

She would master her galdur and free her sister.

Each time Silla found sadness creeping in from the edges; each time she dreamed of her father dying on that road; each time their names echoed in her mind—*Ilías Svik, Matthias Nordvig, Skeggagrim*—Silla reminded herself of Saga.

Saga needed her.

On the sixth day, they met Vig and Runný, the warrior siblings Rey had sent to fetch Silla from Istré. To say it shocked the pair to discover that Rey was now also in need of a shield-house was an understatement. Once their surprise had faded, they'd handed Silla a pair of wool-lined boots that had made her groan with delight as she'd pulled them on. But with the howling winds and frigid temperatures, they'd had to set quickly off down the road.

Now they clustered around a campfire, and Silla stared into the flames, glad for the warmth. She'd layered not one but two blankets beneath her cloak, hugging them tighter as a frigid gust made the flames stutter. From beneath her hood, Silla examined their new companions.

Runný looked to have seen perhaps twenty winters. She had pale skin and dark, angular eyes, and her hair was styled into a dozen black braids adorned with glinting silver rings. Her brother Vig was as broad as Rey, with black hair twisted into a thick braid. Most curiously, Vig's tunic ended at his elbows, revealing thick, and decidedly *bare* forearms. As she looked closer, Silla realized the man had forgone a cloak in favor of a simple wolf pelt.

Vig's eyes met Silla's from across the fire. "Aren't you *freezing?*" she blurted.

The man's stern face cracked into a smile, and laughter boomed from him. "This is summer weather, Silla." He shook his head. "Southerners."

Runný cast a sidelong look at Silla. "Do not worry," she said. "Your blood will grow used to the north."

"'Tis true!" said Vig, folding his arms over his chest. Firelight danced in his eyes. "And once you grow used to it, you'll want to seek out more. Perhaps when you've adjusted, I can take you to the glacial lakes for a true Nordurian ice bath."

That sounded horrid, but Silla kept her mouth shut.

Vig bellowed a laugh, reading her expression. "It is invigorating. Reminds you that you're alive. Even my mother swears by it."

"Do not listen to him, Silla," said Runný wryly. "He wishes only to see what is under your cloak."

Vig shrugged. "I think you are jealous I asked her first, Runný."

Silla felt her face flush, despite the frigid temperatures.

"Leave her be," Rey bit out. Silla's eyes darted to his in surprise. "She has been through much and should not be expected to weather yet another of your sibling rivalries."

Vig chuckled. "It has not yet been a day and already you're ordering us about. You've not changed, Galtung."

Silla's brows drew together. *Galtung,* not *Bjarg,* which meant Vig and Runný knew Rey's true name. Her eyes darted between Vig and Rey, trying to understand their history.

"After you've faced the strife we have, Vig, you can give orders," snapped Rey.

"Don't expect you can act like the king of Kalasgarde, Galtung. Some may kiss the ground you walk on, but others . . . we take our roots more seriously. We remember the scrawny northern boy you were."

"Vig," muttered Runný as Rey released an irritated breath.

But Silla was stuck on what Vig had revealed. "You're *from* Kalasgarde?" Suddenly, Rey's knowledge of the shield-house made sense. And his sullen resignation at having to accompany her made it clear there was something in Kalasgarde he did not wish to face. A fresh wave of irritation rushed through Silla. The man told her nothing!

Silla turned her gaze to Runný. "Are you both Galdra?"

"Subtle as thunder, aren't you?" chuckled Runný.

Silla's cheeks heated, but Vig merely shrugged. "I like it. No games or wasted words. Direct and to the point. We are Galdra, all of us in our family. I am a Blade Breaker; my sister is a Shadow Hound; our youngest brother, Snorri, is showing Ashbringer intuition—"

"How old is he now?" Rey cut in.

"Nearly twelve," grumbled Vig. "The twins are sixteen. Which you'd know if you cared to open your correspondence—"

Runný cut her brother off. "Has Rey shown you his tricks, Silla?"

"Not by choice," grumbled Rey.

Silla's head was spinning. "What do all these names mean? Blade Breaker? Shadow Hound? I gather Ashbringers make . . . fire . . ."

Runný made an irritated sound. "Galtung has told you nothing, has he?"

"*Nothing.*"

Runný sighed. "How very *predictable* of you, Galtung. A man of deeds, not words. *Never* words." She gestured to Vig. "A Blade Breaker is one of the Warrior Galdra. They are capable of bursts of great strength. And a Shadow Hound . . . we play tricks with the light that help us blend with the shadows, bend light, and reshape it to our will. Of course, it depends on the individual, as all are different in subtle ways."

Silla was silent, digesting these words. Blade Breaker. She thought of that buzzing sensation—of Rey and Skraeda, each sailing through the air after she'd pushed them. But her arms had glowed with that strange white light. So surely that meant she was an Ashbringer?

"Warrior Galdra," Silla repeated. "Is there another type?"

"There are the Mind Galdra as well," said Vig. "While the Warrior Galdra have gifts of the body, the Mind Galdra have gifts of thought and memory. Solacers, Readers, Weavers."

Silla's head swam with this information, and she wanted to wrap her hands around Reynir Galtung's neck and squeeze for not explaining any of it to her.

"And you, Silla?" asked Vig with a gleaming smile. "You are Galdra?"

"I . . . suppose I am," she admitted. It was strange to say this so openly. "I am adjusting to the thought, as I've only recently discovered it."

"*Recently* discovered?" asked Runný, incredulous. "What, have you been living in a mountain cave?"

"Something like that," said Silla. "My father gave me skjöld leaves under the guise that they treated headaches."

The tightness in her chest spread through her body, and she took a deep breath. Gods, but she couldn't think of her father now. Silla soldiered forward. "Once I became aware of the dangers of the leaves, I stopped taking them and began to glow, and now it seems I might be an Ashbringer."

Silence stretched in the wake of her rushed confession, but Silla felt Runný's gaze on her. "You're not Cohesed then? Your heart and your mind remain unlinked?"

Silla nodded.

"It is unheard of to have such a late learner," said Runný. "It could be quite a challenge."

Silla tried not to let her heart sink at that. "I like a challenge," she said defiantly. "When there is something I want, I am quite persistent."

Rey let out a long sigh. "Unfortunately," he said, "I can affirm that."

"So you'll bring her to Harpa, then?" asked Runný.

At Rey's subtle nod, Silla's brows shot down. "Harpa?"

"An instructor," said Rey wearily. "She'll anchor you through your Rite and teach you."

A curious look passed between the siblings, but before Silla could ask more, Vig had focused his gaze onto Rey. "And you, Galtung?" he asked. "What happened to Istré?"

Rey only stared into the flames.

"If you need the shield-house, too, that must mean the mighty Axe Eyes has been exposed." When Rey did not reply, Vig continued his goading. "What happened? Did the Klaernar come for you? Try to cleanse your soul on one of those pillars?"

Rey's glower deepened, and so Vig went on. "Your letter asked us to fetch Silla from Istré, and yet here you are, quite a bit north from there. So that must mean—"

"It means it's a long story not meant for your ears," snapped Rey, pointedly ignoring Silla's gaze.

"Because you're so *important*, aren't you?" spat Vig. "With your secretive endeavors."

"Stop!" exclaimed Silla. Both Rey and Vig looked her way, startled. "It's my fault he's been exposed."

Rey's stare was like a hot poker sizzling into her skin. Thankfully, Vig seemed stunned into silence.

Gathering her courage, Silla continued. "Can you not make peace?"

"I'm afraid that ship has long sailed," said Vig. "I will suffer your presence in Kalasgarde, Galtung. I will honor my word and keep a watchful eye on the shield-home, but I do so for Silla, not for you."

With a long sigh, Rey rose to his feet. "I would expect no less from you. I fear I am tired and shall retire for the night." And with that, he disappeared into the tent, leaving Silla alone with Vig and Runný.

"Irritating kunta," muttered Vig, taking a long drink from his flask.

"What happened between you?" Silla asked. "I sense things were once different. Were you friends?"

Vig added another log to the fire, nudging it into position with a stick. "Aye, we were friends. Inseparable from a young age. But he decided himself better than us in Kalasgarde. Left without a second thought."

Silla pursed her lips in quiet contemplation. All she'd known in her life was leaving, and she did not understand this sentiment. "And that is . . . bad? To leave Kalasgarde?"

"'Tis when you forget your roots, forget where you came from. We were like kin, and yet he . . . bah!" Vig waved a hand in the air. "I do not wish to speak of it."

She could feel his gaze settle on her.

"What is he to you?" he asked. "Are you two—"

"No. The man tried to kill me . . . twice!" She laughed, the sound a little off kilter. "But he's also saved my life. He has a . . . curious sense of honor." She thought of how Rey had helped her quit the skjöld leaves—of the hours he'd spent teaching her to defend herself. She thought of how he'd reacted to her galdur with such wonder, the way he'd dragged his fingers along her inner wrist.

You truly are filled with sunshine, aren't you?

Silla shivered, staring into the fire. "All things considered, he's helped me quite a lot. Even if his methods leave something to be desired." Silla thought of the vampire deer attacking her, of the faces of the Wolf Feeders as they burned. A scowl settled in place. "I suppose I don't know what he is to me. Friend, perhaps?"

Vig studied her from across the fire, and Silla felt as though she'd said too much.

"Best you heed my warning," he muttered. "Galtung considers *friends* in the loosest form of the word. In truth, he cares only for his cause."

"Cause?" asked Silla. "What is this *cause*?"

"Uppreisna," said Runný. "'Tis the old word for *'uprising.'* Those who stand against King Ivar. A network of rebels across the kingdom, working in concert to undermine the Usurper."

Silla chewed her lip, watching her across the fire. "And what is the goal of this . . . Uppreisna?"

"To put the rightful heir back on the throne," Runný replied. "The Uppreisna believe the Volsiks are protectors of Íseldur, that one of that bloodline must always be seated on the throne. Without a Volsik, the realm is unbalanced, and chaos will only grow."

Silla felt suddenly hot, her clothing too tight. "Oh," she managed. "And the Uppreisna send Rey—"

"Rushing about the kingdom, doing *great deeds*?" said Vig bitterly. "Yes. 'Course, I'm not privy to the details. But he's been on their leash for years."

Silla chewed on her lip. *I am simply the blade,* Rey had said. So this . . . this must explain the murders. The victims had been targeted by the Uppreisna, and Rey . . . Rey would now take the fall for this. He'd be branded as a murderer, doomed to a lifetime in the shadows. The very thought made Silla's stomach twist.

"And you?" she asked Vig and Runný. "Are you part of the Uppreisna?"

Runný opened her mouth, but Vig spoke first. "We do what we can from the north. The Galdra have been pushed to the farthest corners of this realm, and here my family has found a sense of peace. But we help where we can, when there are Galdra in need. And we keep ourselves informed on the goings-on of the south."

Silla's head was spinning with all this information.

"And you, Silla of the South? You seek a shield-house in which to hide for some time. And you wish to learn how to use your fire. Is there anything else we must know?"

I'm Eisa Volsik, she thought, but the tightness in her body squeezed until every muscle was taut. How could she be Eisa when she could hardly manage Silla?

"I like chickens," Silla offered, fatigue setting in once more.

"Very well," said Vig jovially. "We have those in Kalasgarde."

"Excellent," she said.

CHAPTER 12

They rode for another four long days. Silla spent it largely in silence, bracing herself against the cold. The wind somehow grew more frigid, the mountain snow creeping lower. They climbed over mountain passes and followed snaking paths into valleys where vibrant blue lakes glittered like jewels. They passed few animals but saw evidence of them everywhere—a paw print so large it could only belong to a grimwolf, tree bark scratched by grizzly claws. And while they met few travelers in the pass, each one had Silla pulling her hood as low as she could.

On the second day, the back of Silla's neck prickled, telling her something was watching them. Wordlessly, Rey dropped back, and Silla's stomach was knotted tight until he rejoined them the better part of an hour later. Horse's white coat was flecked with black blood, but Rey's face was impassive. After that, the feeling of being watched had vanished.

On the third morning, they climbed through a long, snaking mountain pass wedged between towering rocky ridges, a river rushing alongside the trail.

"This pass is called Svangormr," Vig explained, his voice low. "It means 'hungry serpent' in the old language. In the winter, you must speak no louder than a whisper. Many a loudmouthed warrior has found himself buried beneath an avalanche through these parts."

"And yet you still live," Rey muttered under his breath, which, as expected, began a fresh wave of bickering.

Late the next day, they arrived in Kalasgarde. The town was both larger and far more beautiful than Silla had expected. Surrounded by a stone stockade wall, the hundred or so buildings fit perfectly in the valley's basin, mountains climbing all around it like the walls of a fortress. Silla's eye was drawn to the tallest, a blue glint shining from atop it.

"Those are the glacial terraces," murmured Runný, following her gaze.

Silla stared in wonder. Layers upon layers of blue ice terraces dripped down from the mountain like something out of a fairy story.

"That is Jökull," said Runný, pointing at the glacial terraces. "Its smaller neighbor is Snowspear. While Jökull houses Sunnvald's many shields, Snowspear holds His armory of spears—a waterfall with great heights of frozen icicles."

As they rode through the gates of Kalasgarde, a confusing range of emotions chased through her. Relief that their journey would soon end. Apprehension at being in a strange place, surrounded by people she did not know. Eagerness to meet this Harpa and learn how to master her galdur.

Silla studied Kalasgarde from beneath her hood. The homes were timber-sided and turf-roofed. But beyond that, there were a few peculiarities. For one thing, there were markings on many of the doors—symbols that felt familiar and foreign all at once. And for another, each home held iron plates secured next to its door with remnants of left-behind offerings. Silla understood at once. These plates served as altars. But to whom?

Runný seemed to notice her interest. "The ice spirits have been restless as of late," she murmured.

"What do they favor?"

"Butter and fresh sheep's milk are their favorite. But when those are scarce, they're content with bread and mead."

Silla's brows dipped. "In the south, offerings are done in secrecy. Do you not fear the Klaernar?"

Runný scoffed. "The Klaernar don't bother us much up here. They come twice a year, if that, and our allies south of here warn of their approach. I think you will find Kalasgarde quite different from the Íseldur you know."

"And the markings on the doors?"

"Protection runes," said Vig, apprehensively. "There have been some . . . troubling happenings about these parts."

The hairs on the backs of Silla's arms lifted. She opened her mouth to ask what sort of happenings when a boy called out.

"Vig!" he exclaimed, rushing over. Silla pulled her hood lower on her face. Rey had informed her that while in Kalasgarde, they'd stay at the shield-home, avoiding the town as much as they could. He'd said while he trusted the local Uppreisna members, he did not know how the rest of the townspeople would react when those birch etchings eventually made their way north.

But as the boy approached, it was difficult for Silla to imagine him as a threat. He looked to have seen near twelve winters, large brown eyes set in a pale face, cheeks rosy from the northern wind.

"Well met, young Váli," said Vig, jovially. "Suppose you're wondering about Snorri?"

The boy nodded. A basket hung from his elbow, a fur-trimmed cloak secured around his shoulders with a leaf-shaped pin. "He said he'd join me hunting snowcap mushrooms."

Vig cleared his throat. "Snorri'll be elbow-deep in horse shite about now. While I was away, he's had to shoulder my chores."

"Very well," sighed Váli, turning away.

"Don't be going out alone, Váli," cautioned Vig. "Snorri'll be free in a few days' time. I'll go with the pair of you."

Váli hesitated a moment, then nodded. As the boy walked off, Vig glanced at Rey, then quickly away. "As I said, strange happenings about Kalasgarde. Best our young don't go out alone."

The words sent an ominous prickle down Silla's spine, and yet she could sense Vig was not ready to say more.

At last, they reached the edge of town, riding through another gate onto a path that climbed up the mountain they called Snowspear. But before they gained much elevation, they veered from the road and into an empty clearing.

"Here we are," proclaimed Vig with a broad smile.

"What—" Silla started, but it felt as though something pressed against her skin. And then, as though she were looking through the glassy surface of a lake, a small home swirled into view.

"What was that?" she asked, blinking.

"My sister has her uses," said Vig happily. "She has bent the light to disguise the area. The barriers stretch to the edges of this clearing, so you can venture outdoors without being seen."

"Impressive," murmured Rey, his gaze drifting to Runný. She shrugged, but the tilt at the corner of her mouth suggested she was pleased. "When did you learn to affix your galdur?"

"Last year. Though it works only for stationary things."

Silla examined the shield-home. It was made of weathered timber beams and topped with a turf roof; the windows were covered with animal hides. Beyond the home was a pair of outbuildings—a privy and a small stable perfect for the animals. And beyond that, a stream cut through the clearing, vanishing into the forest.

As Silla examined the woods, a bright glint of blue caught her eye. Was it an ice spirit? She blinked, then stared hard. But her eyes found only lichen-covered trees and scraggly bushes.

She pressed the heels of her palms into her eyes. Clearly, she'd been riding too long.

They dismounted and secured the horses. Vig fished through his saddlesack for an iron key, which he used to unlock the shield-home's door, and Silla followed the warriors inside. It was small and dark, with a single rectangular hearth in the center of the room, a cauldron hanging from a chain above it. On one side of the room sat a table and benches; cabinets and shelves were on the other. A curtain separated a sleeping space at the back of the room from the rest, and that was the entirety of the home.

"We, erm, were not expecting two of you," said Vig. "I'll send Snorri over with some more furs and hay for the horses." He paused for a moment. "Mother has gathered provisions at the farm, so you needn't go into town. We know you plan to keep your presence hidden. But Mother'll certainly come by to see you, Galtung."

And with that, Vig and Runný departed. The door clicked shut, and Silla found herself watching Rey uneasily. Given the events of the past few weeks, she didn't know how to act around him. It was difficult to accept that Rey was the killer haunting the Road of Bones. But his words had echoed in her mind.

I am simply the blade.

She didn't like it one bit, but knowing there was a reason behind the murders—that they weren't random—put her mind partly at ease.

In the confines of the small shield-home, he seemed somehow larger. But the set of his shoulders and deep scowl on his face told her he'd rather be anywhere in the entire kingdom than here.

"It's not much," he muttered, glancing her way. In that small gesture, he seemed so unlike himself—almost self-conscious. And Silla found herself wanting to put him at ease.

"It reminds me of . . ." the homes she and her father used to live in, she wanted to say, but found she could not. Her hand moved to the place on her chest where the vial used to hang, and she quickly pulled it away. "It will be more than enough."

Wordlessly, Rey vanished outdoors, returning a moment later with an armful of firewood. After arranging it in the hearth, he used his galdur to spark the fire.

"To think all this time you've hidden such a useful skill."

His gaze was flat. "The bed is yours. I'll sleep on a bench."

"Rey," she started, but he turned on his heel and strode out the door.

"I'll be back late," he called over his shoulder as he mounted Horse. And with that, Rey departed, leaving Silla alone in the shield-house.

Sitting on the bench, Silla warmed her hands over the hearthfire. She breathed in. Exhaled slowly. A shield-home. She'd made it.

After running for so long, at last she could stop and rest her feet. Wasn't this what she'd craved for so many years? Silla waited for the hollowness in her chest to be filled with something—*anything*. But the jubilation she'd anticipated for so long did not come.

Instead, there was only more emptiness.

B ad beginnings bring terrible endings.

It was all Rey could think of as he stared into the glassy waters of Kalasgarde Lake, mountainous peaks reflected within. He and Silla'd had a bad start. Rey should have been able to see the threads of fate clearly back then—should have known to cut them swiftly.

Now Ilías was cold in the ground, and the Bloodaxe Crew were in tatters. And *this*.

Rey was back in Kalasgarde. As the cold sank into his bones, so, too, did this realization. He'd fought valiantly—had run so very long.

But fate had brought him back all the same.

Ashes, but he hated it here. Each miserable mountain peak; each bend in the gods damned road; every oddly familiar face they'd passed in the town—memories, all of them, painful as sharpened flint driven into his skin.

They knew him here as Rey Galtung. Once, he'd *been* one of them. A spoke in their wheel, an essential part of this community. Now he was a deserter. An outsider.

Rey had worked long to become Axe Eyes—had worked hard to bury *Galtung* alongside Kristjan and his parents. He'd become *Bjarg*—the word in the old language for "rock." Rey had made himself immovable, impenetrable. But he should have known that even rocks can crack with enough force.

He was back. In. Kalasgarde.

As the temperature dropped, his misery only climbed higher. This was *not* his plan. The plan had been Istré, and then it would have been Kopa for further instructions. Not this. *Not* Kalasgarde.

Everything had been smashed so thoroughly, he struggled to find fragments to piece back together. Rey had spent years working himself into a position with access to Magnus Hansson; he had fed countless bits of information to the Uppreisna and countless lies to the Heart Eater. And now . . . now not only was that ruined, but it was possible the entire kingdom would soon know his secret.

What now?

What now?

As the auroras woke, the skies were painted in brushstrokes of greens reflected in the lake below. Bitterly, Rey stood and turned away.

The muffled flap of wings made his feet pause. *Don't look*. But he was powerless against the pull. His gaze lifted, and there it was—bottomless black eyes; ghostly white face; tawny feathers tipped in black.

The barn owl.

As he stared at the creature, Rey felt the wound opening, sinew and muscle tearing, bones wrenched apart. It was agony all over again, the pain so sharp it could have been the day he'd buried Kristjan. "Fuck," he muttered.

The owl hooted softly, and with that, the spell broke. He couldn't do this. Couldn't be here.

Rey forced his gaze away. Stumbled down the hill. Why had he come here, of all places? Everywhere he looked was like pushing on a bruise, but this . . . this was a raw and open wound, the pain so brutal it hurt to breathe.

Time to go home.

Home? The shield-home was no home. It was as good as a cell.

And so he returned to his prison.

The cabin was dark and quiet as he approached, but from the light of the sister moons, Rey saw the symbol scrawled on the door. She'd drawn the protection rune in ash. The sight made him clench his teeth against the sting of self-loathing. He shouldn't have left her here all alone in this new place.

Do better, he thought, tripping through the doorway into darkness. The hearth had burned to coals, and the curtain had been slung shut. Remorse tasted bitter in the back of his throat as Rey stared at that curtain, wondering if she had enough furs.

Curiously, there was no sign of provisions. It seemed Vig's mother, Gyda, had not come after all. Had Silla found food and water in the saddlesacks? Had she been frightened when Rey had not returned?

As Rey settled onto the hard bench, pulling a fur over his body, he vowed that tomorrow, he would do better.

CHAPTER 13

Sunnavík

Saga forced her eager feet to slow as she dashed through the hearth hall. It was a pleasant late-summer day, and bright light streamed through the windows, casting deep shadows behind the columns.

Saga's gloved hand slipped into her pocket, wrapping around the small tin. She could hardly believe what she was about to do. In the aftermath of learning Signe and Alfson's new plans, Saga had been busy. Gently, she'd pried into Lady Geira's role in the queen's entourage and had confirmed that the woman acted as Signe's scribe.

The revelation had been a pleasing one. Surely, Lady Geira's chambers would be far less guarded than the queen's. Perhaps this was why the queen trusted Geira to pen her scheming letters—fewer prying eyes.

It had taken her a day to come up with a plan. Two days she'd spent poring through botany tomes and digging up luna bulbs from the solarium in the dead of night. It had required some careful timing to avoid patrolling guards, and twice Saga had thought herself caught for certain. Yet she'd crept in and out of the solarium undetected before spending hours grinding the damned bulbs and picking out each fibrous bit. It had taken another day for the paste to fully dry into a transparent powder.

Altogether, it meant Saga had three days left to get the queen's wax sealer and a sample of Lady Geira's handwriting. Those two items meant she'd be ready to forge the queen's instructions for the

Wolf Feeders—ready to buy Eisa some time. But if today's ploy didn't work, Saga wasn't sure what she'd do.

She'd questioned the plan a thousand times. Between the hours spent grinding the luna root paste, she'd diligently met with the queen and her bondswomen—had tried using her Sense to uncover any updates on Eisa. But Signe was so rarely alone, and it had proven impossible to listen in on her thoughts with so many others present.

Saga had made certain to seat herself beside Lady Geira, to show interest in the woman. Thus far, she knew Geira to be the most pious of the bunch—knew she enjoyed singing and had a collection of figurines carved from bear bones. As a lover of art, Saga had expressed her interest in viewing the collection. And to her great delight, Geira had taken the bait.

Saga entered a high-ceilinged landing, large arched passages branching off in opposite directions. To the left lay Askaborg's eastern wing, housing Geira and her husband, the High Gothi, while the passage on the right led to the garrison hall.

Saga moved to the eastern wing, but paused as the clash of steel assaulted her senses. Unbidden, her feet moved to the double doors leading to the sparring grounds. She peered through the window, finding a crowd of black-clad Klaernar.

After a moment, the crowd parted, and she saw him. The light caught a sheen of sweat on Kassandr Rurik's brow, his dark waves damp. Clad in that same armored jacket, he held a blade in each hand, but no shield. His green eyes were homed in with feral intensity as his Klaernar opponent rushed at him, and he blocked a sword strike with his twin blades.

The men circled each other, Rurik lithe and smooth while his opponent seemed encumbered in heavy chain mail. As the Klaernar swung his blade with power, Rurik ducked easily, his smile deepening. Perplexed, Saga watched them circle anew. Rurik was patient, his gaze never wavering from his opponent. The Klaernar, on the other hand, grew increasingly angry, the grip on his sword tightening with each step.

Rurik was baiting him.

Sure enough, the Klaernar warrior burst recklessly at the Zagadkian lord in a move even Saga recognized as sloppy. And then Rurik made his move. With confusing grace and speed for a man of his size, he ducked beneath the sword, driving the hilt of his blade against the man's knee, his shoulder into the man's side. The Klaernar quickly toppled to the ground, and Rurik straightened, blades poised at his opponent's throat.

Saga rolled her eyes. Why did it not surprise her that the man taunted his adversaries?

"Yield!" the Klaernar called, raising a chorus of groans from the crowd. Rurik's face split into a grin as he offered his opponent a hand up. Even from here, she could see the mischievous glint in those eyes as he surveyed the crowd.

"Who is next?" he asked in accented Íseldurian.

Saga took that as her cue to leave, hastening into the eastern wing and far, far away from him.

"I am pious," Saga recited to herself as she walked. "I am repentant. I crave Ursir's blessing." The wound at her inner elbow throbbed in disagreement, and Saga's lips tugged down.

A raven-haired serving thrall with shadows beneath her eyes led Saga into the drawing room.

In contrast with the opulence of Queen Signe's chambers, Lady Geira appeared to have far simpler tastes. The room centered on a modest hearth cut into the wall, a pair of carved chairs positioned before it. The dark stone flooring was softened with a crimson rug, and the only hint of splendor was the golden braziers burning in each corner of the room.

"Lady Saga is here, my lady," said the thrall with a curtsy.

Geira stood, greeting Saga with her stern, no-nonsense expression. Her gown was a pale green with golden stitching, and her auburn hair hung in a tight braid. "Refreshments, Valka," barked Lady Geira.

The thrall scurried away, leaving Saga alone with the High Gothi's wife.

"Thank you for having me," Saga said awkwardly. It was impossible to keep her eyes from darting around the room. Wax sealer. Handwriting sample. Where would Geira keep them?

"Sit, Lady Saga," said Geira, gesturing to the chairs near the fire. "Valka will bring the figurines out in but a moment."

Saga eased into a chair. Reluctantly, she allowed her mental barriers to slip down, bracing herself for whatever abhorrent thoughts her Sense might pull from Lady Geira.

. . . Valka was up well into the night, came Geira's thoughts. *They'd best be polished to a shine . . .*

That explained the dark circles beneath the poor thrall's eyes. Saga felt a twinge of pity that the girl had been drawn into her scheme.

"I'm eager to see them," Saga said, far too brightly. *Stop smiling like a wolverine,* she told herself. "They are all bone-carved, you say?"

Geira nodded, prattling on about the collection. Saga nodded along, surveying the room from the corner of her eye. She guessed this space was for receiving guests, not for everyday living, and doubted correspondence would be located here.

The serving thrall reappeared, pouring mead into a pair of silver goblets and setting them on a table between them.

. . . Valka had best not have confused the plain mead with juniper again, thought Geira.

"Fetch the figurines, Valka," ordered Lady Geira aloud.

Please, thought Saga, biting her tongue.

"I can see your coloring has not changed," said Geira, turning her blunt gaze on Saga. "Have you felt more vigor since your Grand Offering?"

Saga managed a crisp "Somewhat." When she held the wax sealer in hand, she had a feeling she'd be positively vibrant.

Geira pursed her lips. "You must not be worshipping with a whole heart. Ursir can sense when a Letting is done without devotion and may withhold His blessing."

It took every ounce of Saga's strength to hold her tongue.

. . . Everyone knows ill health is the body purging itself of malevolence,

thought Lady Geira, sipping her mead. *The girl must have much malignance to rid* . . .

Thankfully, the serving thrall returned, setting a tray of ivory figurines down on the table.

Bones with a side of mead was not what Saga would call the most appetizing of pairings, but she feigned a look of awe. Setting down her goblet, she picked up the largest figurine of the bunch. Ursir's likeness snarled at her from within the polished bone.

"How splendid."

"This one hails all the way from Norvaland," said Geira, a rare smile curving her lips. "Carved from the bones of a Spring Awakening sacrifice."

"What . . . kind?" Saga asked, trying not to think of the poor victim of the bloodiest Ursinian holiday.

"Cave bear, I'm told. A rare breed."

. . . and a bringer of ample blessings, thought Geira.

Saga set the figurine back, one gloved hand sliding into her pocket and loosening the tin's lid. With her other hand, Saga selected a smaller figurine with a yellowish glint. "And this one?"

"A gift from the wife of a Gothi in Urka," answered Geira with pride. "We've exchanged many letters over the years, and she sent this to me as a token of friendship. The yellow tint comes with age, but I find it rather fetching. It gives the appearance that Ursir is bathed in golden light."

Saga nodded, fingers dipping into the translucent powder. "This one *is* ancient," she said, pulling her hand out of her pocket to hold the figurine up to the light. "Do you see this groove here?" Saga's powder-coated gloves slid along the bear's snout. "It once would have been etched in black. Charcoal, I suspect, or perhaps a botanical dye. And here"—Saga's fingers skimmed along the bear's back—"I see the faintest remnants of knotwork."

"Truly?" asked Geira, reaching eagerly for the figurine. Saga bit down on a smile as Geira's bare fingers contacted the polished bone, and the woman held it up to the firelight, trying to see knotwork that was not, nor had ever been, there.

Saga slipped the lid of the tin back in place, wiping her powder-coated gloves off on the inside of her pocket. She reminded herself she'd have to burn this dress before the day was through.

The next several minutes moved with a glacial pace. Saga's gaze tracked each movement of Geira's fingers—scratching her nose, pushing a strand of hair behind her ear. But when Geira's hand went to that necklace of keys, absently running along the tether—up, down, up, down—Saga held her breath.

The seconds ticked by slower than Saga thought possible. And as Geira picked up the tenth—eleventh?—carving, worry set in. What if she'd dug up the wrong plant? What if she'd read the recipe incorrectly? What if she'd wasted four days and it was all for naught? The thought of leaving this room empty-handed was enough to make her want to cry.

But as Geira reached for her goblet, Saga saw it—a faint pink flush spreading from the woman's ink-stained fingertips. A minute later, it had spread across the backs of Geira's hands and bloomed on her nose. The woman scratched absently at first, then with more vigor. And after a second minute had passed, raised welts had formed.

"Oh!" exclaimed Geira, swiping a thumb across the back of her hand. "By Ursir's Paw, what is this?"

Malevolence is being purged from your body, Saga thought, a little too eagerly. "My goodness, Lady Geira!" exclaimed Saga, leaping to her feet. "Shall I fetch Valka?"

Geira tugged at the collar of her dress, wincing when it contacted her necklaces. "Oh, but it stings!" exclaimed Geira, pulling more vigorously.

Blisters began to form, ranging in size from pinpricks to the dimensions of Saga's smallest fingernail, all filled with clear liquid.

"What is this curse?" exclaimed Saga, perhaps a little too enthusiastically. "What is this foulness?"

Geira's face twisted into a look of pure horror.

... Ursir, oh my beloved Ursir, what have I done to displease You? came the woman's thoughts. Her whole body jerked and spasmed as though she were trying to escape her own skin.

"It bites!" cried Geira, yanking at her neckline.

"Let me assist you with the lacings," suggested Saga, her gaze trained on the pair of necklaces.

"Get it off!" shrieked Geira. "Oh, Ursir, save me!"

Ursir isn't here right now, thought Saga wickedly. Darting to Lady Geira's back, Saga's fingers pulled at the lacings. "One moment, Lady Geira, and you shall have relief. My, but what could have caused this?" Geira was writhing, howling in pain. "It has the look of a pox."

. . . Surely not! Geira thought desperately. *Oh, Ursir, what have I done? How have I wronged You?*

Loosening Geira's binds at last, Saga pulled the back of the gown open, but the marks had formed anywhere the woman's necklaces touched. "By the Holy Claw," Saga murmured. "Lady Geira, let us take your necklaces off. Those blisters look fit to burst!"

"Off!" wailed Geira, tugging at the tethers. Saga grasped them, slipping them over Geira's head and tucking them deftly into her own pocket.

Valka entered the room, carrying a plate of fresh flatbreads.

"Where have you been?" bellowed Geira, causing Valka to stumble back.

"My lady!" exclaimed Valka. "What has befallen you?"

But Geira was beyond words, flailing about wildly. The table toppled to the side, mead and bone-carved figurines falling in disarray.

"It is morbid matter pushing itself out of your body!" cried Valka, only adding to Geira's distress. "The Bear God punishes you!"

. . . But I have been devoted, Geira thought. A blister burst, liquid seeping across her skin and causing the woman to howl.

"Bath!" ordered Saga, in her most stern voice. "The lady must bathe in warmed milk. Add honey and lavender to soothe the skin." With a clap of her hands, Valka was scuttling off in search of supplies.

"Hush now, Lady Geira," soothed Saga, linking their arms together. With her long-sleeved gown and gloved hands, Saga had little exposed skin at risk, but she was careful to avoid Geira's fingers all the same. "Come now. Let us bring you to your chambers, where you might rest."

"C-corridor," gasped Geira, sagging against Saga.

Saga eased her down the corridor, cooing in sympathy as she glanced through each door they passed—a second sitting room, a bedchamber, a study. Writing desk. Cabinets. Stool and trunk. It was gone in a flash, but Saga exhaled sharply. That had to be it.

"Down here!" called Valka, scurrying after them.

"Milk bath," repeated Saga. She didn't want the woman permanently disfigured.

"I've sent word for it to be heated, my lady," said Valka. "We can make a cold compress for now."

Together they eased Geira onto her bed, the woman clawing at her dress, begging Valka to remove it.

"I can take it from here, my lady," said Valka, ushering Saga to the door.

"Please send word to update me on her health," said Saga, trying for her best look of concern.

With Valka's quick nod, the door closed, and Saga was alone in Geira's quarters, the keys heavy in her pocket.

She wasted no time in rushing to the study, excitement coursing through her veins. Saga forced herself to slow down and assess the room—tall glass-paned windows, heavy curtains thrown wide; cabinets lining one wall; a solid desk in the middle. On the desk was a slanted writing surface, upon which parchment was secured, ink pots and quills neatly arranged on one side; at the desk's foot sat a trunk.

Rushing to the windows, Saga pulled the tether from her pocket, wiping the keys and her gloves on the curtain to remove any traces of the luna root powder. Heart pounding, Saga knew she hadn't time to waste.

Saga examined the writing desk first. The parchment secured to the slanted writing surface was blank, but based on the pile of ash adjacent to it, Saga guessed correspondence had recently been burned. She turned to the cabinet, sliding key after key into the hole, until she heard the telltale click. She pulled the cabinet doors wide. Her heart lurched at what she saw—*hundreds* of scrolls tucked into storage nooks.

"Bog badgers," she hissed, pulling a scroll out. There was no outer parchment, no evidence of a royal seal, but Saga unrolled it just in case.

The Bear is the embodiment of the Father, the Husband, the Son, He who shall be worshipped and obeyed . . .

That was enough to tell Saga this was the High Gothi's writings. Fighting against the instinct to set fire to the thing, she re-rolled it and slid it back into the cabinet. Her gaze slashed back and forth across the rows of scrolls. There was nothing to be done but to examine them.

Scroll after scroll she pulled out, her heart sinking lower with each passing minute and no sign of a royal seal. After sliding the last scroll back into place, Saga checked the trunk. Nothing but books. Frantically, Saga ran through her memory. Did she have it wrong? Or did Lady Geira use another room for scribing the queen's letters?

"Where is she?" came a loud male voice from beyond the door.

Saga froze, the fine hairs on the back of her neck standing on end. Unfortunately, she knew that voice all too well—it belonged to the High Gothi.

"What has befallen her?" he demanded, and Saga exhaled. He was speaking of Lady Geira, not her, thank the gods above. The High Gothi's heavy footfalls thudded beyond the door. But then they paused. "Why is this door shut?"

Panic seized Saga, but thankfully, it channeled her into action. She dove behind the heavy curtains and pressed her back to the wall. Blood rushed in her ears as she held her breath.

The door groaned open. Footsteps entered the room. She heard the rustle of the High Gothi's robes—each breath he drew in.

Sweat dotted her brow, but she did not dare wipe it away. Surely the man could hear the breakneck pace of her heartbeat. Surely he'd sweep the curtains back to reveal her hiding place.

Chest tightening, Saga began reciting the exits.

The door through which she'd entered.

The window.

That was it. The realization was not calming in the least. She tried to slow her breathing but could not seem to get anything but quick sips of air. Gods, she needed to flee, needed to get back to the safety of her chambers . . .

Valka's distant call had the High Gothi's footfalls reluctantly turning. And then they retreated, leaving Saga alone once again in the study.

Her heartbeat was deafening in her skull. That was far too close. Saga could *not* be discovered here. Tears burning up her throat, she was forced to decide—stay and risk discovery, or leave and regroup for another day. Three days, she still had three days, but if she were discovered in this room, the ruse would be up—Saga would be punished and unable to help Eisa. With a shaky exhale, she eased her way out from behind the curtains and moved toward the door.

Her slipper caught on the rug and Saga stumbled. Righting herself, she turned. The rug had folded back on itself, revealing a floor plank a hair's breadth higher than those surrounding it. Saga crouched. Prodded the board's edges. The corner pressed down with a gentle click. And then the entire board lifted, revealing a hidden alcove.

Time seemed to slow as Saga reached into the compartment, then pulled out a scroll and stack of parchment. She turned the scroll over, frustrated at the lack of seal. But as her eyes fell upon the name, Saga wanted to scream with joy. It was addressed to Signe. She unrolled it and read.

> *We've unraveled the mystery behind our poor results. It appears our samples were contaminated. An individual has confessed to letting a red-haired woman into the room three months past. We believe it was Skraeda Clever Tongue who persuaded him, and that she made off with our most vigorous stock. As she would not have been properly washed, contamination ensued. It has taken us two months to understand our troubles.*
>
> *It would be wise to send the Black Cloak after Clever Tongue and to speed our timeline. Svaldrin may be compromised.*
>
> *—Maester Lekka*

She turned to the stack of parchment. Unlike the small, cramped writing she'd seen on the High Gothi's scrolls, this penmanship had a curving flourish to it. This had to be Lady Geira's writing. Glancing at the open doorway, Saga swallowed. And then she read.

AN URSINE AWAKENING, PART 3

I walk into the forest, barefoot and clad in naught but a wolfskin, as Ursir requested. My heart pounds and I am frightened, but I know what I must do. I am a sacrifice. Chosen by Him. And now I walk willingly . . .

Saga's nose wrinkled, and she turned the parchment over. Gods, it continued for quite a few pages.

. . . I yield to Him, and He lays me on the soft moss, unsheathing His husky staff. Ursir cleaves into me, and I'm naught but sensation. A creature of pain and pleasure. His appetite is fervid, His motions quick, and the Bear God tilts His head and roars to the skies . . .

Saga didn't know whether she wanted to laugh or cry. This was devotion on an entirely different level. Reluctantly, she tucked Geira's story into her bodice—a handwriting sample was a handwriting sample. Even if Geira noticed a single page missing, Saga doubted she'd risk the humiliation of retrieving it. But the letter to Signe—were that to go missing, Geira would surely need to inform the queen.

After a moment's hesitation, Saga slid Lekka's letter back into the alcove, her last desperate hope fading as she felt around for the sealer stamp. It was not there.

After pressing the board back in place and smoothing the rug over it, Saga dashed out of the study and down the corridor.

The High Gothi's voice carried from the bedchambers. "I shall fetch the cup, wife. An extra Letting shall purge the malevolence from your blood."

If Saga were a better person, perhaps she'd feel a twinge of sympathy for Lady Geira. Instead, she felt only a perverse sense of justice. Reaching the drawing room, she pulled Lady Geira's necklaces from her pockets and tossed them into the chaos.

And then Saga slipped from Geira's quarters and dashed down the hall.

The parchment lay heavily against her chest, but as Saga rushed through the eastern wing of Askaborg, she couldn't help but feel a twinge of worry.

The wax sealer stamp hadn't been there. And now, only three days remained before word would be sent north.

CHAPTER 14

Kalasgarde

Silla and Rey followed a winding trail between shivering pine trees up Snowspear. Despite the afternoon sun, the air was decidedly cool. Silla sat atop Brown Horse, as she'd taken to calling her mount, a lead connected to Rey's Horse necessary to urge her stubborn beast forward.

As they rode, Silla couldn't shake her excitement.

"I'm taking you to a Galdra instructor," Rey had informed her earlier.

Silla smiled to herself. She was eager to start her new life as a Galdra—to learn what flowed through her veins and take the first step toward rescuing Saga. How she'd accomplish this, Silla was not quite certain, but she was determined to claw together a plan.

As they rode up Snowspear to meet this instructor, snow dusted the surrounding ground. *Snow,* though midsummer had been a mere month ago.

"Early," Rey muttered as though reading her thoughts.

Early, as in another long winter. Silla tried to count how many it had been—three now, each one coming sooner. It would be another season of stunted crops.

Around them, it was quiet and still. But inside, Silla was filled with maddening energy—the impatient need to get on with things.

"Tell me again," she begged Rey.

"Her name is Harpa," he answered. "She'll anchor you through the Cohesion Rite and teach you how to express and weave your galdur."

Silla let out a long breath, watching it cloud the crisp northern air. "The Cohesion Rite will link my heart and my mind?"

"Yes."

"And then I will be able to control the light?"

"In time."

The man's voice was gruff with irritation, and Silla felt the urge to tease him. "And perhaps I'll be able to knock you on your arse once more," she continued.

"You can try," Rey grunted.

"It shall earn me a place in a warband," she continued. "Hammer Hand seems unfitting for such a skill." Silla frowned. "Perhaps Silla the Strong. Or Silla the *Slayer*."

"Silla the Stone Whisperer," muttered Rey.

"It was *one* time," retorted Silla, recalling Rey's appalled look after she'd apologized to a stone she'd tripped over. "Tell me more. What is the Rite? How long will it take? And how do you know Harpa?"

"She'll *love* you."

"Do you ever offer information willingly?" Silla demanded sharply. Brown Horse snorted, tossing her head in agitation. "Sorry, my darling," Silla cooed, stroking her shining black mane. But the horse ducked away, and Silla drew her hand back, swallowing her disappointment.

"We're here," grumbled Rey. "Soon, all of your questions will be answered."

Rey steered them off the trail, twisting between trees until a wide, empty clearing stretched before them. It was a confusing befuddlement of seasons all in one place. Sunbaked grasses and wildflowers peeked from beneath the dusting of snow while rowan trees bordering the property held showy displays of reds and yellows.

"This is it."

"Where?" asked Silla, eyes darting around.

"It seems Runný has affixed her wards here as well," said Rey.

Indeed, as they moved across the clearing's halfway point, the familiar cold press of Runný's galdur touched Silla's skin. The empty clearing shifted, and a weathered home with a few scattered outbuildings came into view.

"Burning stars," she breathed. Each time she witnessed this strange magic, Silla remembered there was an entire world awaiting her that she knew nothing about.

Rey's shoulders rose and fell with a heavy breath as he steered them toward the cabin.

"Something troubles you, Rey. Are you nervous?"

"No."

"Right," she said tartly. "A waste of your time—I recall it. But the set of your shoulders says otherwise."

Rey dismounted without reply, then led the horses to a weathered stable. Silla stared at the hollow segments of wood affixed to the sides of the stables, blinking when half a dozen birds poked their heads out.

"Hello?" she whispered to them.

"This is new," Rey muttered, staring at the birds.

She followed him to the cabin, noting several altars welded to the worn timber beams, crumbs of offerings left behind. As they strode to the door, Silla examined the wind chimes flanking it. Dozens of polished bones and bits of smooth wood were threaded together into a ladder-like structure, thunking as the breeze caught them.

"For luck and protection," Rey said, following her gaze. He looked at the door with a long exhale. Silla shifted impatiently as she waited for Rey to knock. But he only stood there, picking at a decaying piece of wood on the doorframe.

"Oh, for the love of the gods," Silla exclaimed, pushing past him and knocking on the door.

It was several moments before it scraped open and an older woman peered out. The first thing Silla noticed was the woman's striking hair—tight coils spilling around her face and over her shoulders, midnight black save for twin swaths of white framing her face. The second thing she noticed was Harpa's eyes—the amber vivid against coppery-brown skin. It was impossible to guess how many winters the woman had seen—it could be forty or just as easily eighty. The only hints of aging were the fine lines bracketing her mouth and eyes.

Silla's gaze trailed lower. Harpa wore a heavy wool overdress fastened with twin brooches, the garment cinched around her waist with a belt of stunning tablet weave.

The woman's eyes widened for the briefest of moments then quickly narrowed.

"Harpa—" began Rey.

"No," she snapped, shoving the door shut.

Silla swallowed her shock as Rey jammed his foot between door and frame. "Wait," he said. "Harpa, I ask only for a minute—"

"I've retired." She kicked at his foot but was no match for Rey's towering form.

"You know I would not come to you without good cause," said Rey through gritted teeth. "Harpa, I implore you to listen—"

"No, Reynir. Leave me in peace. Rykka!"

"Wait," said Rey, but it was too late. The acrid scent of burnt leather met her nostrils. With a foul curse, Rey rushed from the door back into the yard, snow hissing as he extinguished the tip of his boot into it.

Predictably, the door slammed shut. Silla watched incredulously as Rey strode back to the door and pounded so hard the wood bent beneath his fist.

"Harpa! Open the gods damned door!"

Birds squawked behind them, and Silla shook her head. "I should have guessed there was bad blood between you and this woman."

"She is only stubborn," he barked, continuing to pound against the door. "Harpa! I swear to you, this is important. Let us in." Rey cursed again. "She has Ashbringer *and* Breaker intuition!" he bellowed through the door. "Her light is cold to the touch. White as moonlight!"

After several minutes of this, Rey quieted, crossing his arms over his chest and leaning against the wall. "We have nothing but time, Harpa. You know well enough I will not relent. You can settle in for a day of loud unrest or let me speak my piece." He scowled at the snow, voice lowering. "You owe me this much, Harpa."

Silla watched him carefully. For the briefest of moments, Rey's mask slipped away, and he looked despondent . . . a little lost. Something inside Silla woke up and growled. She despised this look; she wanted to batter it away and bring back the surly man she knew.

A murmur of voices carried from within the home. After several long moments, the door ground open, and Harpa stood with her arms crossed in the doorway.

"Five minutes," she said, retreating inside with the door left wide.

Silla followed Rey as he stalked inside. She examined the space. Like their shield-home, it was small and basic. Above the central hearth bubbled a cauldron, and bundles of dried foliage were strung along the walls. To the left of the entry stood a heavy table. Behind it, shelves were littered with clay cups and glass jars filled with dried mushrooms, nuts and seeds, preserves, and more.

At the back of the cabin, Silla spotted an enormous warp-weighted loom, taller than herself and at least as broad as her arms stretched wide. Threads of red and gold glinted from a partially completed weaving, stones knotted to the ends of the warp threads holding them taut.

Harpa and Rey stared at each other for an awkward moment. "In my day, we had more respect for our elders," Harpa finally grumbled.

"Harpa, this is Silla," said Rey, his voice surprisingly level. "She needs an anchor."

"She's too old, Reynir. You know this." Harpa's gaze was far too hard and thorough for Silla's liking. "Who is she?"

She, as if Silla did not stand right before her with two perfectly functioning ears. "Well met, Harpa," said Silla as brightly as she could manage. She extended her arm to shake the old woman's hand, but Harpa grabbed her by the wrist and yanked her forward with frightful force. Holding her forearm aloft, she drew something from her pocket.

Pain speared from her finger, and Silla tried to yank her hand back, but Harpa held it in place. A crimson bead welled from her fingertip, and Harpa smeared it between her own. There seemed a pulse in the air, a subtle shift of the room, and Harpa's eyes turned milky white. Silla gasped.

Rey placed a large, warm hand on Silla's shoulder. "Do not worry."

"Difficulty," muttered Harpa, staring vacantly at Silla. "Troubles. Snarls in the yarn. Tangles." The deep brown of her irises bled back through Harpa's eyes, and she scowled at Rey. "You've delivered danger to my doorstep, Reynir."

Rey glowered back in equal strength.

"Who is she?" came a voice from the back of the cabin. Silla looked around but could see no other being in the home.

Harpa's gaze narrowed. "A Volsik."

"How?" Silla exclaimed, clutching Rey's arm for support.

"Your aura screams it at me. A room, a little blond girl, and Kjartan's bodyguard—"

"What . . . how . . ."

"I am a Weaver," replied Harpa. "I can see the threads of your past, present, and future. Yours are very tangled—very confusing." She turned to Rey. "How have you found yourself in the company of a Volsik, Reynir?"

"Volsik?" rasped the voice from the corner. "Harpa, that name brings trouble. Cast her out."

"Rykka," warned Rey, gazing at something in the room's back corner. Turning to Harpa, he answered in clipped words. "She climbed into my wagon."

Harpa's hand went to her chin as she puzzled over this answer. "The weavings did not show this," she muttered. "Threads hidden from my eye—gaps in the web. How has she hidden?" Her amber eyes settled back on Silla. "You are not Saga. So you must be Eisa."

She flinched. "I'm Silla."

"Danger!" rasped the voice from the corner. "Trouble is what she is!"

"What?" asked Silla, turning around. "Where is that voice coming from?" Staring at the loom, she spotted a twist of smoke rising from it. Alarm pricked her skin, but the smoke churned into the shape of a tiny, winged woman. As Silla watched, the creature's shape grew less translucent, until she was dark as a thundercloud. And apparently as angry as one, too.

Silla gasped. "Wha-what's that?"

"What's that?" repeated the creature in an appalled voice. "I'm not a *what*. I'm a *who*."

"That's Rykka," said Harpa, waving a hand. "She is a smoke spirit."

Silla clasped her hands together, her mouth falling open. "Ashes, but you are darling!"

"Not in the slightest," grumbled Rey, looking at the burnt toe of his boot.

Rykka erupted into flames that quickly burned out. "I'm no darling. I'll burn you alive!"

Silla pressed her lips together, nodding her head enthusiastically. "Oh, yes. I'm certain you would."

"Rey," purred Rykka. "I hope you'll forgive me. I'm so very glad to see your face once more." Her tiny charcoal lips pouted, and Silla's heart squeezed.

Rey rubbed the back of his neck in exasperation.

"Are you friends with the ice spirits?" asked Silla.

Rykka flared, embers popping within her. "I do not associate with ice spirits! Frigid little hissers, they are."

"I hope to see one," continued Silla. "I thought I caught a glimpse when we first arrived."

"Do not trust the frost vixens," said Rykka. "They are spiteful creatures. Dangerous to mortals. Get too near and they'll bite that pretty nose of yours."

Silla frowned, prodding her nose. She'd need to ask this Gyda woman for butter and fresh goat's milk to offer the ice spirits. If the woman actually showed up tonight—

"Well," said Rey, dragging her back to the conversation. "Now you've heard all I have to say. And what is your answer, Harpa?"

The older woman stared at Rey for the better part of a minute. Silla counted her breaths, trying to calm her racing heart. She'd never considered the possibility that the Galdra instructor would not wish to teach her, but now dread crept through her. If Harpa would not teach her, what did this mean for her plans to rescue Saga?

"She's too old," Harpa said at last. "Her mind is too firm."

"She's determined," countered Rey.

She's right here, Silla wanted to say, but she wisely kept her mouth clamped shut.

"*I'm* too old," muttered Harpa.

"Eisa *Volsik,* Harpa."

Another long silence stretched through the cabin. Embers hissed in the hearth, joined by the soft lull of the boiling cauldron.

"I cannot," Harpa said at last.

Silla's chest clenched tight, objections gathering on her tongue . . .

"Disappointing," muttered Rey, grabbing Silla's hand and pulling her to the door. "I should have known better than to hope."

"I'm retired," protested Harpa as Rey tugged Silla outdoors. "I have my weavings to tend to."

"Yes, your precious weavings," spat Rey. "How could I forget?"

Silla trailed him to the horses, panic and frustration battling within her. Was he truly just going to leave? As Rey gripped Brown Horse's reins to keep her still, Silla climbed sullenly into the saddle. She waited for him to say something, to fight harder with Harpa, but he only climbed onto Horse.

Silla cast a look over her shoulder. Harpa watched from the doorway, arms crossed over her chest. There was uncertainty in her posture, a question in her eyes. But as Rey nudged Horse forward and Harpa said nothing, despair flooded Silla. What would they do now?

"Can *you* perform the Cohesion Rite?" Silla asked Rey, a panicked edge to her voice. "Can *you* teach me how to wield power like yours—"

"Wait," mumbled Rey, so low she barely heard him.

"For what?" demanded Silla. Tears of frustration gathered in her eyes. Kalasgarde was supposed to be a fresh start, and already things were falling apart . . .

"Trust me," he said.

Trust is earned, she wanted to retort. But at that moment, Harpa's voice reached her ears.

"Wait!" exclaimed the older woman. "Stop, Reynir!"

Rey exhaled, halting Horse. Harpa's grumblings could be heard as she trudged across the snowy yard, tugging a shawl around her shoulders. At last, the old woman reached them, and Silla felt herself being examined once more.

"You look like him," Harpa said. "Your father." After a moment, she added, "King Kjartan."

Silla tried desperately to keep her face neutral. All her life, *Matthias* had been her father, but now it was a confusing, tangled mess. Another man had been there first—another man who'd entrusted her life to his bodyguard. As with Matthias, one of her birth father's last acts had been to protect her.

Grief pushed open its cage, sliding over the threshold. But Silla slammed the door shut, confining the darkness for now.

"You have your father's eyes but your mother's hair," continued Harpa. Something passed behind her amber eyes. It could have been a thousand things, but for the briefest of moments, Silla thought it looked a bit like remorse.

"You knew my parents?"

"I taught them both."

A thousand questions sprang to mind, but Silla forced herself to remain quiet. Harpa turned to Rey, her breath misting the air.

"I will do it," said Harpa, "for Kjartan and Svalla. For Íseldur." The old woman took a deep breath. Seemed to struggle with the next words. "And I will do it for you, Reynir."

CHAPTER 15

Rey rode down the mountain with a lighter heart. It was a monumental obstacle overcome. He wouldn't tell Silla how much he'd dreaded this day. How hard it had been to look into those amber eyes that looked so much like Kristjan's . . .

But it was done.

"I wish we could have done the Rite today," muttered Silla from behind him.

"Harpa will not be rushed," he warned her. "She does things at her own pace."

Silla huffed. "I must learn it quickly."

Rey's brows drew together. "Why?"

"You'll only laugh."

"I swear to you, I won't."

She was silent a long moment before answering. "My sister. She's all alone, living with murderers. I must learn my galdur so I can free her."

Inwardly, Rey groaned. Dozens of attempts had been made, countless lives lost trying to rescue Saga. But Silla had weathered so much in the past weeks, and Rey couldn't bring himself to snuff out her hope.

"Hakon," he said instead. "Jarl Hakon in Kopa is who you'd need to speak to."

"Jarl Hakon," she repeated.

"After the search for us has quieted, I will take you to him. Hakon has ways . . . he can help us slip into the city undetected."

"Yes," she said brightly, to herself more than Rey. "Yes." She began to hum, and the corners of Rey's lips tugged up. But Silla stopped abruptly. "Reynir. Harpa called you Reynir."

Rey scowled, knowing what would come next. Gods, but he never should have told her.

"You said Kraki and your grandmother were the only ones to call you that. Harpa is your *grandmother?*" Silla cackled gleefully behind him. "Oh, I understand you much better now."

Rey groaned inwardly—he could practically hear the questions brewing.

"Did Harpa raise you?"

Instinct had Rey pulling his walls higher. No one got in, not anymore. But he knew this woman was relentless, and he'd be stuck in the shield-home with her for the gods knew how long. Perhaps, in this case, the better defense was to answer and move on. He took a stabilizing breath. "Harpa raised my brother and me when we fled north."

"Fled north?"

Rey ignored the ache in his chest, digging deeper for the cold, impenetrable place inside him. "My parents sent us north the moment Ivar came ashore in Íseldur," he said. "As some of the staunchest Volsik supporters, they knew if things went awry . . ."

Rey's throat constricted. *Continue,* he urged himself. *Say it once and you need never speak of it again.*

"They were not wrong," he continued at last. "When Ivar took the throne, he came for them. Came for *all* Volsik supporters." He took a deep breath. "Ivar killed my parents. He sliced the backs of their ankles, then forced them into Askaborg's pits with his pet bears. They could not run. A crowd of Urkans and Ivar's supporters cheered as they were devoured."

A sound of distress came from Silla, and Rey wondered if he'd said too much. But this wasn't about her, or even about him. This was about those who could no longer speak. Those who deserved justice.

"He saved his vilest methods for Volsik supporters," said Rey. "He made a sport of it. And yet my uncles had more honor than to flee."

"You were a child," interjected Silla. "There is no dishonor in fleeing—"

"My cousins were scarcely old enough to bear arms, but they did. They died with honor, as did any with a drop of Galtung blood in their veins. It was only the two of us left, with Harpa to care for us."

The silence was as awful as the words he'd just spoken. "I'm sorry," she said at last.

"Don't be," he snapped, then forced his voice to soften. "Now you know why I do what I do. Why I cannot be complacent."

"Yes," she said softly. "I do."

Rey couldn't help but wonder—did she still think him the same as Jonas? A violent man filled with excuses?

They rode in silence down the mountain, fatigue settling into Rey. He couldn't recall the last time he'd spoken of his parents. But they'd been gone for seventeen years. The wounds had long ago scabbed over—had healed into toughened, scarred flesh. His brother, on the other hand . . . this wound was raw and untended, had festered in the years since he'd acquired it.

He did what he always did. Rey shoved his mind away from Kristjan.

Silla's stomach was growling by the time they rode through Runný's wards, but as voices carried from within the shield-home, her whole body tensed.

"It's Gyda," said Rey. "Vig's mother. I recognize her voice." After dismounting, he held Brown Horse still while Silla clambered out of the saddle.

Reluctantly, she trailed him into the bright chaos of the shield-home, blinking in shock. The scent of cooked food made her stomach twist with hunger. Six bodies were packed into the small space. Vig leaned on the table while a pair of identically awkward boys rolled on the floor, a blur of elbows and flying fists; Runný was seated on a bench, weaving a younger boy's hair into a black braid along the top of his skull. An older woman was stirring the cauldron and barking over her shoulder at the wrestling boys.

"Rey!" exclaimed the boys, their quarrel forgotten as they rushed at him. He absorbed their impact with a soft grunt, looking down at them in surprise.

"Which of you is Haki and which is Haddi?" he asked. "Gods above, you've grown."

"Aside, boys!" boomed the woman. "Rey Galtung. Come here, lad."

With a heavy breath, Rey shook free from the twins and stepped toward the woman, whom Silla presumed to be Gyda. Clad in a heavy woolen overdress fastened with brooches, she was both tall and sturdy. Without hesitation, she pulled Rey into a smothering hug. Silla watched in amusement. This was a whole new side to Axe Eyes.

Silla studied the woman's hair. Black with gray streaks, it was woven into dozens of small braids and embellished with beads and silver cuffs.

"This is Silla," said Rey the moment Gyda released him.

Silla forced a smile, lifting a nervous hand. But Gyda stormed toward her, wrapping her up in the same motherly embrace she'd forced upon Rey. Gods, but it felt good to be hugged. Silla sagged against her, not wanting to let go.

"Any friend of the Galtungs is a friend of ours," said Gyda, pulling back. Hands firm on Silla, Gyda held her at shoulder's reach to examine her face. Thankfully, the swelling was gone, but the remnants of Kopa's bruises still lingered. "Bless you, poor girl. I hear the Klaernar have given you a hard time."

Silla's hand rose to the short patch of hair, prickly to the touch. "Yes."

"Vig says you didn't even know you were Galdra!" said the boy sitting before Runny. "Is that true?"

"I'm afraid so," said Silla, forcing another smile at the boy, whom she guessed to be Snorri. He wore a woolen cloak with bare arms beneath it. "Ah, you must be Vig's brother."

He nodded proudly.

"Snorri, help me convince Silla to take a Nordurian ice bath." Vig laughed from the table.

A cautious smile spread across Snorri's face. "Oh, you *must*. It is only cold for the first few seconds. Then you cannot feel a thing." He frowned. "Until you get out and near the fire and then it *burns*. But . . . in a good way."

Silla collapsed on the bench beside Runný. "Is that so?"

"Hush, Snorri." Gyda chuckled. "Silla has only just arrived. Give her a minute to settle in before you have her jumping through holes in the ice." The older woman turned around in the cabin. "Meant to come by last night with the furs and provisions, but we had some troubling news." Gyda wandered to the cupboards and selected a clay jar that had certainly not been there this morning. "One of Snorri's friends went missing."

A prickling sensation crawled down Silla's spine.

"Aye," muttered Vig, running a hand over his weary face. "It seems young Váli did not heed my warnings. He ventured out to pick snowcaps alone and failed to return."

Snorri's eyes glistened, and the boy turned his head away.

Runný slid an arm around her younger brother's shoulder. "Surely he's taken shelter somewhere. We'll find him, Snorri."

"The whole of Kalasgarde has been up the mountain searching for him," continued Gyda, adding a pinch of something to the cauldron. "Went back up this morning to search in the light, but we've found no trace thus far."

"You should have told me," said Rey, settling down at the table. "I'd have joined the search."

Gyda's face melted into a knowing smile. "Of course you would have, Rey." Her dark eyes slid from Rey to Silla, then back again. "But you've just traveled so far, and we thought you might not wish yourselves known in these parts."

Rey nodded slowly. "It is best to keep our presence quiet. But I know how to stay hidden and lend a helping hand."

Gyda sighed, cupping Rey's cheek in a surprisingly affectionate gesture. "Have you been eating enough? Sleeping well?" She glanced around the cabin. "Suppose there is only one bed in this place. I should have fetched a spare pallet for you." Gyda paused. "I am sorry you've been forced into hiding, lad. But I am not sorry it brought you back to us."

But Rey shook Gyda's hand from his cheek, grumbling something about firewood before retreating outdoors. Gyda only smiled, fetching a battered kettle and handing it to Snorri, who bounded out the door.

"That man has not changed one bit. Still so solemn outwardly, but his heart . . ." She sighed as Snorri returned and handed her the filled kettle, which she hung over the flames. Gyda turned to Silla. "And you, dúlla? What is your story?"

Story. Silla supposed she should have one of those. Her skin felt itchy, her stomach knotted tight. The old Silla would have woven herself in with these people, would have absorbed all the fun and affection they so obviously shared. But she'd seen too much, had weathered too much heartache. The new Silla understood that getting too close to these people would only endanger their lives.

"I'm afraid there isn't much to say," she muttered, hating herself. "I hope you'll forgive me, but I must lie down. The day has quite exhausted me."

"Ashes, how could I forget?" said Gyda, adding róa bark to the kettle. The rich, spiced scent filled the air. "You've just met Harpa. That can be a harrowing experience indeed. Of course, dúlla, rest. We shan't be here for long, and there will be plenty of leavings for you when you wake."

Silla looked away, blinking furiously. "My thanks, Gyda," she said, retreating behind the curtain.

Though she tried, sleep did not find her. Instead, Silla listened to the clamor beyond the curtain, breathing in the scents of spiced róa and hearty stew, wishing she were out there with them. Wishing she wasn't a danger to their lives.

Beyond the curtain, the cabin brimmed with voices. She heard Vig settle into a game of dice with the twins, heard Snorri rousing himself from his sorrow to pepper Rey with questions: "What's it like to kill an illmarr?"; "Do you truly prefer a longsword to a greataxe?"; "Did you want to punch the Heart Eater when you met him?"

Silla listened keenly, touched by the way Rey indulged the boy's questions. He would have been an excellent older brother, she realized with sorrow.

As Rey offered to train Snorri in swordplay, Vig huffed. "No true northerner would choose a longsword over a greataxe for battle."

"Hush, bjáni," chided Gyda.

It was not long after that Gyda and her brood began pulling on clothing for the return trip to their farmstead. Gyda informed Rey their cabin was now stocked with provisions—apples, carrots, hard cheese, róa bark, a loaf of bread, and limited supply of grains. Leavings from the evening meal were tucked away in a cold storage space beneath the floorboards. Fresh firewood was stacked on the front porch and hay in the stables. They'd left clothes for the pair in the cabinet—linen and wool tunics, breeches and leg wrappings, and a thick fur-lined cloak for Silla.

"For her southern blood," Vig proclaimed loudly, as though he knew she listened in.

As the door to the shield-home ground open, Rey cleared his throat. "If ever you have need of men to go searching, I want you to fetch me."

"I will," said Gyda in a smiling voice.

As the door clicked shut, Silla exhaled. She allowed a few minutes to pass before wrapping a fur around her shoulders and treading beyond the curtain.

"What was that about?" asked Rey. Her feet faltered as she saw he was fastening the buckles of his armored jacket.

"I was not much in the mood for visitors," she lied. "What are you—" Her heart pounded as understanding settled in her. "You're going to search for him. That boy."

Rey simply grunted, unable to meet her eye. Silla's fur tumbled to the ground. "I shall go, too."

His gaze slid to hers, *axe eyes* cutting into her skin. "You will do no such thing."

"I want to help!"

"No," he answered coldly. "It's too dangerous for you."

"So," she spat, "*you* may leave the cabin, but *I* may not. Am I understanding this correctly?"

Much to her chagrin, tears pricked her eyes. Alone, he was leaving her alone, venturing out into the unknown to find the missing boy. What if he didn't return? What if someone found her here, alone? The night before had been torturous, lying awake in the empty shield-home, wondering if he'd abandoned her for good.

Turning his back to her, Rey pulled on his wolfskin gloves. "*I* can handle myself. *You* cannot."

Her hands trembled, yet somehow, her voice was steady. "It is darkening. What chance have you when dozens of others have failed—"

"I must try," he snapped, then sighed. He tugged the fur-trimmed cloak around his shoulders and secured it with a bronzed pin. Rey took a deep breath. "I will be late. No one but Vig's family knows you are here, and it will take some time for the birch etchings to spread this far. With the wards, you'll be safe."

Silla fell numbly onto the bench. "And you?" she asked. "Who will watch over you, Rey? Who will keep you safe?"

She felt his surprise from across the room. Felt him search for words.

"I look out for myself," he said at last. And then the door rasped shut and Silla was left alone in the cabin for the second night in a row.

It was somewhere close to morning when Rey finally returned to the cabin. His limbs ached from climbing steep slopes, the cold sunk deep into his bones. Hours he'd searched in the dark.

Rey had sought all the hiding places from his youth—the cave notched into the rock on the far side of Kalasgarde Lake and the valley where he and Kristjan had spent hours sledding. But there had been no trace of the boy. No tracks. No shreds of fabric. No broken branches or crushed foliage. As the hour neared morning and Rey's eyelids became heavy as boulders, he'd been forced to relent.

Again he returned to the shield-home with guilt in his heart. He'd left Silla alone for the second night in a row. Was she warm enough? Had she fallen into a quick slumber? Loosing a wide yawn, Rey pushed the shield-home's door open.

He was unprepared for the dark figure leaping from the shadows. As they collided with his shoulder and sent him stumbling sideways, Rey's warrior instincts kicked in. He righted himself just in time to block a blow, snatching his opponent's wrist and driving them against the wall. Forearm pressed into his attacker's neck, Rey held them in place.

"Silla," he murmured, releasing his arm from her throat. "What—are you—"

Chest heaving, she looked up at him with wide, dark eyes. Eternal fucking fires, the woman was terrified. "Rey," she said tremulously. "It's you."

"What has happened?" Rey demanded, searching her face for evidence of harm. "Are you hurt?"

"I thought"—she started shakily—"I thought you were an intruder."

"It's me," said Rey softly. Gods, he was such an arse. He should not have left her alone, not after all she'd weathered. "You're safe here."

"Oh," she said, her voice thin and fragile. "Did you find him?"

Rey shook his head, sorrow filling his chest. He'd known it was unlikely he'd find the boy, yet he'd had to do something. But as Silla sniffled, he gathered her to his chest, desperate to comfort her. Red spots blurred Rey's vision. *He'd* done this. Had made her cry. And he felt like the biggest arse in the realm.

Slowly, he led her through the dark cabin, settling her onto the bench. The fire had burned down to the coals, but Rey refused to let go of her to revive it. As she sobbed against him, her fingertips stroked along that patch of spiky hair, and he began to understand.

Kopa had left bruises on Silla's skin and unseen scars on her soul. Jonas. The Klaernar. Each warrior the queen had sent after her. In that moment, Rey wanted to hunt them all down and pull them apart piece by piece.

"You're safe," he repeated, cursing himself for such insufficient words. Slowly, Rey pulled Silla into the crook where his arm met shoulder. Holding his breath, Rey waited for her to push away. But she only sank into him, soft and so warm. His heart thrummed at her nearness, the walls around it crumbling to ash.

"A-am I?" she choked out. "It seems only a matter of time before I'm running, yet again. Before someone else tries to harm me . . ."

"No one knows—"

"Yet," she said in a watery voice. "I know you trust Vig and Runný, but I do not know them. And besides, Jonas showed how quickly a person can turn."

The thrum of his heart turned thunderous with rage. "He did a vile, despicable thing. He betrayed the Bloodaxe Crew, but you . . . he betrayed you in the worst way."

Silla said nothing, and so Rey continued. "You can trust me." He cursed under his breath. Her body trembled as if she were in the after-throes of a battle. "I'm sorry for leaving you alone."

She lowered her head to his chest in a move of such familiarity, Rey thought his heart might break free from his ribs. The sapling of trust was growing once more, and this time, he would not trample it. He would nurture this precious thing until it grew strong. Arm sliding down her spine, he hauled her closer.

"Do not be sorry," she said into his chest. "Of course you went looking for Váli. I couldn't stop thinking of him. He is so young." She paused. "I shouldn't act like such a child. I didn't know it, but it seems I don't like to be alone."

Rey smoothed her hair with caution and tenderness, waiting for her to flinch away. Instead, she closed her eyes. Exhaling, he stroked the curls that had taunted him for so long. "You . . . didn't know it?"

"I've never felt alone."

Rey's brows drew together. "Never?"

"All my life it has been my father and me. After he died, I *was* alone in the Twisted Pinewoods, but I . . ." She drew a deep breath. "You'll think I'm mad."

"Unlikely." His fingertips traced the contours of a curl.

She hesitated. "I saw phantom visions. A little blond girl I've only recently realized was Saga as I remembered her. She . . ." Silla shuddered. "She was my constant companion."

His stomach felt as heavy as a stone. "The skjöld leaves," he murmured. Kristjan had seen visions as well—had spent hours talking to their long-dead parents.

Silla nodded. "She came and went, and yet, she was the most constant thing in my life. And so, you see, I've never truly been alone."

"I've always been alone," Rey found himself saying.

Silla drew back. A flush crossed her cheeks, as though she was suddenly aware of how near they'd grown. She scooted a few inches away, and while Rey knew he should feel relief, he felt the loss of her touch like an ache.

"I'm sorry," she said, a tendril falling over her forehead. "For attacking you. And for weeping on you."

"You have nothing to apologize for," said Rey, willing himself not to reach for the coil of hair. To tug it straight, then let it bounce back up.

As she looked at him, her brows drew together. "Have you truly always been alone?"

"Not with the Bloodaxe Crew. But in between jobs, especially after my brother . . ." He found himself unable to complete the sentence. It was too raw, too vulnerable. To explain Kristjan's death was not a thing he could survive twice. It was easier to be a lone wolf. To keep everyone out.

"I don't *like* being alone," Silla admitted. She pushed the tendril up, but it fell back across her forehead.

"You'll get used to it," Rey said, staring at the curl.

Silla let out a long breath. "My behavior is appalling. I do not even recognize myself."

He shook his head. "I should not have left you alone."

They stared at each other, a new uncertainty hanging in the air. Rey didn't like it one bit. He wanted to gather her back to him. To hold her until all her fears melted away.

Silla stood, smothering a yawn. "Now that I know you are safe, perhaps sleep will find me." She hesitated. "Good night, Rey."

"Good night, Silla."

As she retreated behind the curtain, Rey stared into the hearthfire's orange coals. Seeing the woman who'd fearlessly faced down the Bloodaxe Crew so utterly undone had shaken something loose inside him. Rey tried to imagine all she must be going through now—alone, confused, and haunted. Lone wolf he might be, but now Silla needed a pack.

With a long sigh, Rey tossed another log on the fire.

CHAPTER 16

Sunnavik

Saga's heart hammered as her eyes swept the colorful jars lining the shelves in Maester Alfson's study. For the dozenth time she questioned this plan.

A day had passed since she'd dosed Lady Geira with luna root powder and gained a sample of her handwriting. Saga had pondered the discovery of Geira's curious hobby. On the one hand, Geira was unlikely to report her salacious story missing. And on the other, there was a chance to use it as leverage. It was rather improper for the High Gothi's wife to write erotic stories about the Bear God. Could Saga use this damning evidence to get Geira's compliance in handing over the queen's correspondence?

But it appeared Geira was still bedbound, and Alfson had stated the letter would be sent in two days' time. Saga was growing increasingly worried about acquiring the wax sealer. She needed that stamp. With it, she'd be able to buy *weeks* for Eisa while the Wolf Feeders scoured the wilds in the wrong direction.

Which brought Saga to Maester Alfson's study with the request for a tonic to "ease her nerves." The tin of luna root lay heavy in her pocket, yet Saga did not want to use it on Alfson. Should the maester come down with the same affliction as Geira immediately after meeting with Saga, it would be rather obvious who was the culprit. She'd brought it only as a last, desperate resort.

But when the maester's young adherent had let her into the

empty study minutes earlier, Saga was shocked to be left alone while Alfson finished up whatever maesterly things he did all day. Naturally, Saga had jumped at the opportunity to search the place.

She tried to ignore the eyes following her as she threw cabinet doors open, scouring the shelves for anything that might help her cause. It was bad enough that the maester had a dozen dead animals mounted on his walls. But these animals . . . their eyes were not as they'd been at birth. They'd been swapped—a wolf's yellow eyes with something far larger, the fox fitted with some other creature's unearthly blues. The rabbit's eyes looked reptilian—brilliant green, the pupils a vertical slit. There were countless more, but she'd tried to banish them from her mind.

She moved to the maester's worktable, eye twitching at the cluttered space. Snatching a piece of parchment, Saga read the cramped writing.

- Salvia—*bled out (12)*
- Burning nettle—*weakened heart (11)*
- Alpine catspaw—*reduce dosage. Day 5 infection (13)*

Saga stared at the parchment, unsure of what to make of it. After a moment, she cast it aside and dropped to her knees. Beneath the table was a cabinet, double doors locked shut. As her hand wrapped around the iron padlock, a prickling sensation crawled up her arm and down her spine. Saga was filled with the sudden urgent need to discover what lay behind these locked doors. She jiggled the iron padlock, tugged on the handles, trying in vain to pry open the door. Why had she never learned how to pick a lock? She *had* to get into this cabinet . . .

"What are you doing?" she whispered, shaking herself. As she pulled her hands back from the cabinet, the strange urgency dissipated. Saga pushed to her feet, glancing at the door. Her Sense was unleashed, but it had trouble penetrating through walls, and she sent a prayer to her patron goddess Marra that Alfson would not make a stealthy approach.

Her gaze landed on the desk drawer, and she rushed to it. But her heart sank as she saw another padlock secured in place. With a sigh, Saga gave it a tug.

The padlock fell open.

Saga stared at it in disbelief for several heartbeats. Surely, it couldn't be. But there it hung. She sprang into action, sliding the padlock out and pulling open the drawer. Her mouth fell open. Nestled among feathered quills and sticks of wax was a sealer stamp. She picked it up, examined the sigil. A Norvalander wasp.

Time seemed to slow, her mind entirely blank.

This was the queen's sigil. *Alfson* had the queen's wax sealer stamp.

Saga's knees threatened to buckle at this discovery. And all she could think was how *fortunate* she was to have discovered not only the unlocked drawer, but also the precise thing she'd sought all week. She scowled. This must be a trick. It had been too easy. Too lucky for a woman like her. All the same, she slipped the sealer into her bodice.

Saga had just replaced the padlock when a throat cleared beyond the door. She threw herself into the chair across from the desk, just as the iron hinges creaked and Maester Alfson shuffled in. Short and balding, the maester was clad in evergreen robes. Her heart galloped, and Saga gripped the chair's arms.

The wax sealer was in her bodice. The *wax sealer*! She wanted to rush back to her room with the stamp, wanted to jump for joy on her bed and scream into her pillow. But she forced herself to be cautious. Above all else, she must not rouse suspicion.

. . . dosage numbers for Maester Lekka, came Maester Alfson's thoughts, reminding Saga that her barriers were lowered. She recognized the name as the one from Geira's hidden scroll.

"Saga," said Maester Alfson, settling into the chair behind the desk. "I'm told your nerves have worsened."

. . . a shame it is not Saga who carries a strong warrior's gift, thought the maester. *But I tested her thrice in her adolescence and never did the catalyst have any effect . . .*

"Yes," she said, trying to comprehend what this meant. Alfson had... tested her? Realizing she was staring, Saga overcompensated by nodding eagerly—too eagerly. *Act normal, featherhead.*

Alfson peered at her from across the desk. It was impossible to miss the red scar slashing from forehead to cheek, the pale, lumpy mass where an eye should be. Saga focused on his intact eye—dark and assessing, as though he could read her deepest secrets.

... such lovely eyes ...

Saga's gloved hands clasped tightly together.

"Nerves," said the maester. "Yes. I can make you a tonic to help with that."

"My thanks." Saga was scarcely aware of what she was saying as threads of the maester's thoughts diffused into her mind.

... How irritating for Geira to be abed, leaving the scribing to me, he thought. *Surely we can bring another scribe under wing. It is well beneath my skills ...*

Saga blinked at the maester, trying her best to look natural. For the first time in years—possibly in her life—Saga felt giddy. Like she could jump up from her chair and dance like a fool. She had the wax sealer. She *had* it!

"A particular tonic comes to mind. One used to treat battle shock," the maester was saying. "It soothes the mind and body alike."

"It sounds promising," murmured Saga.

... Svaldrin compromised, filtered Alfson's thoughts. *Yet Rökksgarde is not ready. Do we risk housing them here for the time being? ...*

"Passionflower, valerian root, and essence of losna," the maester said, rising from his chair. Alfson made his way to the wall of shelves, scanning its length with a raised finger. After collecting various items, he moved to his worktable.

... one drop losna, he thought. *Steady hands, two drops would knock down a horse ...*

Saga blinked.

... at least there's good tidings from the north, thought Alfson.

Pulse jumping, Saga held herself preternaturally still.

... a Svangormr Pass sighting. 'Tis not a precise location, but it narrows the search considerably ...

"Now, dear," the maester said, turning with a clay cup in hand. "This will make you braver. Try this today, and we shall meet again. On, now, drink it up, then try to get some sun on your face."

Saga accepted the cup. "My thanks."

... Yes, yes, on with it, thought Alfson, retrieving a key and sliding it into the padlock on his desk drawer. *Must pen this letter to the Wolf Feeders first thing. Bother managing this search from the south, we ought to send the Black Cloak ...*

That last thought held Saga immobile. He would send word to the Wolf Feeders *today,* not in two days. She felt as though her mind was no longer connected to her body but floating somewhere above it.

Watching with wide eyes, Saga brought the cup to her mouth and tipped the liquid down her throat. Alfson had pulled the padlock aside. Was staring into the drawer.

... I distinctly told Gorm to fetch the wax sealer from Lady Geira, he thought, moving the quills and ink pots around. *This is Gorm's second blunder today alone. One more and he'll be out of chances ...*

With a long, slow exhale, Saga placed the empty cup on Alfson's desk.

Already, she could feel the tonic at work. Much like an egg cracked over her head, it dripped down her neck and shoulders, loosening the knots of tension wherever it touched. Oh ... it was *wonderful.*

"We may have to adjust the dose," said Maester Alfson, eyeing her. "But 'tis a good start. Now go."

Saga nodded, standing. She hoped Alfson attributed her quivering body to the effects of the tonic but did not wait for him to comment.

Turning on her heel, Saga fled from the room.

CHAPTER 17

Svangormr Pass, thought Saga, hand skimming along the stone walls. *Eisa was seen in Svangormr Pass...*

She pushed deeper down the corridor, passing tapestries, busts, and that awful taxidermied bear. Saga scowled at the poor thing. It belonged in the wilds with the birds and wolves and wildflowers, not stuffed with wool and posed in this dark, musty corridor. Saga looked down, realizing her feet had paused.

Eisa, she reminded herself, forcing them forward. Gods, but her thoughts were like water, slipping through her mind before she could grasp them. And she was light as a cloud, floating down the hallway. She felt *good.* Gods, she felt *happy.* What a strange, foreign sensation it was, like the first few seconds after sliding into a hot bath. Saga pressed a hand to her lips, surprised to find them spread wide in a smile.

She looked down. Her feet had stopped again. Turning around, she examined her surroundings—a high-ceilinged landing with two arched doorways leading off. She knew this place, and the clash of swords from beyond the doorway only confirmed it. Saga stepped to the window and peered into the sparring grounds. Was *he* there among them, taunting the Klaernar and playing for the crowd?

"Lady Saga," came a voice from behind her, making her jump in fright.

Saga whirled to face the man in question. How did he know she'd been thinking of him? "You," she blurted. "Did you read my thoughts?"

Arms crossed over his chest, Rurik leaned casually against a shadowed arch, watching her with those eyes. Green like ferns . . . or poison ivy. But the longer she looked, the more Saga thought they were more like the green eyes of a mountain cat—the kind you wouldn't dare turn your back to.

Thankfully, Rurik ignored her question. "Many days now I've wanted to speak with you."

Saga stared at the cleft in his chin. It appeared he'd shaved just this morning, the hints of a beard battling back. "What are you doing here?" she said dazedly.

His brows drew together. "I think better question is why *you* are at sparring grounds, Lady Saga?"

"I don't know," she answered honestly. She'd been on her way to complete a task, yet she'd forgotten entirely what it had been. It nagged at her, this important thing just out of her grasp.

"Something is"—he paused, mountain cat eyes assessing—"not regular with you. Are you well?"

"*Very* well," Saga replied, turning to look through the window. "The best I've ever been!" She could feel him puzzling over her, and so she continued. "I took a tonic." Saga leaned in, whispering loudly. "For my nerves."

"What is this . . . tonic?"

"Tohn-eek," Saga repeated, smiling so wide her cheeks hurt. "Say it again!"

"Now I know you are not . . . regular," Rurik said, eyeing her. "What is this? You are drinking something? You are *drunk*?"

A cough from down the hall had her grasping his forearm in surprise. Saga stared down, adding her other hand and trying to encircle it. It was so thick her thumbs could not touch. "What do you have in here? Iron plates?"

"Is my arm," he said, amused.

"It's hard as steel," she said, kneading it like a cat.

"What it was in this . . . tonic?"

"Valderion root and passionflower and essence of fosna. Lesna. Something -*na*." She waved her hand dismissively. "I feel *quite* relaxed."

"It seems that way," he said.

"Only," she continued, "I have the most peculiar sensation." Saga paused, reaching for the niggling thought, dangling just out of her reach. "I believe I was meant to do something, yet I cannot recall. Do *you* know what it was, Rurik?"

"Kass," he corrected. "And no. I'm afraid I do not know it. But I wished to apologize to you."

"Apologize?" Saga laughed. The very idea was humorous.

"Yes," he said slowly. "For what I said in gallery. I have . . . disobedient tongue. Often it speaks without permission. I should not have said that to you."

But Saga was lost deep in thought, trying to recall what, precisely, she was meant to be doing.

Rurik cleared his throat. "I see today you wear birds on your gloves—"

"Bird!" Saga exclaimed, clapping a hand to her mouth. "The falcons!" It rushed back to her in an instant—the messages, the wax sealer nestled inside her bodice. And without excusing herself, she turned to flee. But she made it only a few steps before stumbling to the side. Rurik was there, his arm sliding around her, holding her steady.

"Easy, Lady Saga," he said softly. "You must lie down. Let me help you to your chambers."

But Saga clutched his arm tightly. "Falconry tower," she asserted, trying to wrangle her flailing thoughts. Now that she had the memory, she could not let it slip free. "I must get to the falconry tower."

"You barely can be walking," he protested.

"You *owe* me, Rurik," she hissed, distantly aware it was far too bold.

He frowned. "And I will take you to your *chambers,* Lady Saga."

"Falconry tower," Saga repeated. "Take me there, and I'll . . . I'll accept your apology."

Rurik's face drew into a scowl as he pondered her proposition. "Very well," he relented at long last, directing her toward the exit. "I will do you this favor, and then we might be friends. Come, lean on my shoulder, yes, there."

She put her head on his shoulder, a scent hitting her nose—fresh and herbal, like sage or perhaps juniper. "You smell good."

He chuckled softly. "I see this tonic is making you feel very free. Your feet must be answering. Now tell them to step. Good, yes."

She felt him moving forward, pulling her with him, and her feet moved quickly to keep up. They entered a windowless corridor lit by wall-mounted torches, firelight dancing along the ancient stone walls. The dark corridors only made Saga's eyelids grow heavier. She blinked a few times, trying to keep them open, but they just wanted to close.

Rurik snorted. "Usually I treat a lady to supper before she falls asleep on shoulder."

Eisa, Saga reminded herself, desperate to stay awake. *Eisa is in danger!* She'd waited many days for this opportunity and could not ruin it. Saga leaned against Rurik's sturdy form, her arm sliding around his back. She tried not to think of the muscles bunching and releasing just beneath her fingers.

The sound of approaching voices had Saga's feet slowing. "We cannot be seen," she mumbled. "'Twould be . . . improper." As she whirled them around to get her bearings, her gaze collided with Harald the Hard's. His cold eyes stared at her from the threads of a tapestry, longsword held aloft as he prepared to plunge it into the king of Norvaland's chest. And with that, Saga knew how to avoid detection. "This way."

Rurik let out a deep sigh. "Will you tell to me where you are taking us?"

But Saga was busy counting out the stones. When she reached twelve, she stared at the wall in search of the right stone—one that was incrementally smaller than the rest. Spotting it, she pushed with the heel of her hand.

Nothing happened.

The voices were louder now—a pair of women, and gods, the voices belonged to members of the queen's retinue. She could not let it reach the queen's ears that she was alone in Rurik's company. Gritting her teeth, Saga put her whole body's weight against it, pushing with all her might.

Beside her, Rurik cleared his throat. "I think I should be taking you to your—"

His voice broke off at the sound of stone scraping against stone. Saga felt the latch click before a doorway swung inward.

"A tunnel," Rurik said, a look of keen interest spreading across his face.

"Torch," was Saga's only reply. Rurik snatched one off the wall, and she yanked him through the doorway. With a quick shove, Rurik had the door shut, entombing them between the ancient stone walls.

"Now we shan't be seen," Saga murmured, leaning her swaying body against the wall. "This path leads beneath the castle keep and up to the western wing."

Rurik muttered something in Zagadkian, surveying the crumbling stone walls. The tonic's grip seemed to grow ever tighter with each passing heartbeat, pulling Saga down toward sleep. Thankfully, Rurik slipped a stabilizing arm around her waist, drawing her into the corridor.

As they made their way down a set of spiral stairs, the press of his fingers filled her mind with curious thoughts—like burying her face in his chest and drawing deep pulls of his scent, or plunging her fingers into his hair to discover if it was as silky as it looked.

The air chilled and grew heavier with each passing step, yet Saga found it more a comfort than anything. In these tunnels, she was safe. Her secret, protective space.

Not secret, a part of her chastised. Saga blinked in the dim torchlight, the realization beginning to dawn. She'd shared this tunnel with *him,* which meant one less place of safety for her.

Eisa, she countered. Nothing mattered except intercepting that letter.

"Tell to me a story while we walk," said Rurik, thankfully diverting Saga from her inner turmoil. "To keep you from sleep."

Looking up, she blinked. Those mountain cat eyes were assessing her, learning how she moved, how fast she might run. A shiver rolled down her spine.

"Tell to me why always you are wearing bird," Rurik tried.

Saga glanced down at her gloves, examining the delicately embroidered birds along the cuffs. "My mother," she murmured.

"Why?"

"She had a flock of winterwing birds."

Rurik held the torch aloft, helping Saga down the last of the steps. They were now in the bowels of Askaborg, deeper than the crypt and dungeons. The air was so cool that their breaths clouded.

Saga found herself continuing, "They were housed in a gilded cage large enough to fit even you, Rurik. But they made my mother sad. She thought they deserved better than a cage, and so we decided to set them free. We opened the cage door together."

Saga frowned. She hated this part.

"What happened?" urged Rurik.

"They . . ." The words resisted her, but she pushed them out. "The birds wouldn't leave. They were too frightened to leave their cage."

Rurik was silent behind her, and Saga tried to remember the end of the story—the good part. "We left breadcrumbs for them. Slowly, the birds grew braver." Saga swallowed as the memory flashed before her eyes. She and her mother, hiding in the bushes of the solarium, waiting for the birds to realize they were free.

"Did they leave?" asked Rurik.

Saga nodded. "It took some time, but eventually they did. I shall never forget the sight of those birds, wings stretched wide. Free at last."

"I am thinking," said Rurik, "perhaps you and birds have much in common." Silence for a beat, and then, "I know it was not blood loss that had you falling, Lady Saga. How long is it since you've stepped outdoors?"

Saga wrung her gloved hands. She'd said too much—had exposed things that were best left hidden away. Thankfully, right now, the tonic had her floating like a cloud. "You're too pershep . . . perceptive," Saga said with a yawn. The tonic was pulling at her, dragging her down into its murky depths.

At long last, they reached the spiral staircase leading up to the western wing of Askaborg. After several minutes of climbing, they reached the hidden exit. Saga leaned against the stone wall as Rurik searched for the hidden latch of the door. "Do you recall the bust of

Harald the Hard? *Unsmiling man* as you called him?" Rurik nodded. "The doorway lets out there. A short walk to the falconry tower," she mumbled, forcing her drooping eyelids to lift.

Rurik turned, holding the torchlight between them, and as Saga studied the hard and soft contrasts on the man's face, she decided she wanted to draw him.

"What is your business?" he asked, nodding to the sealed doorway. "What have you planned?"

Saga shoved her hand artlessly down her bodice, retrieving the wax sealer and holding it up like a prize. "I shall interkept . . . intercept the letter." Her body swayed, and Rurik placed a steadying hand on her hip. *Yes,* her body seemed to say, leaning into his touch.

He was speaking Zagadkian, those sharp and soft sounds blending together. Her eyes fell shut, and she felt the words rolling over her skin like the gentlest caress. "No, Lady Saga," urged Rurik, giving her a shake. "You are not in health for intercepting letters."

Rurik took the wax sealer from her grasp, examining it while Saga used every ounce of her energy to stay upright. "Is queen's sigil."

Saga's knees buckled, and Rurik eased her to the ground. "Just need to find Alfson's adherent," Saga mumbled. "Perhaps his thrall. Get the letter. Change some things. And she'll be safe."

"What you are doing, Lady Saga?" asked Rurik. "Taking queen's letters? Is dangerous."

Even through the haze of sleep, Saga knew she shouldn't have told him. But she refused to give up, and with her muddled mind, she was in no state to accomplish this task herself. "You," she said, reaching for Rurik's arm, missing it by miles. "I need your help."

"I have given you my help." She could hear the wariness in his voice.

"You must get the letters," Saga soldiered on.

"I cannot," he said. Perhaps it was the narrow space or the torchlight that made Rurik seem impossibly tall. But in his expression—in those stunning green hunter's eyes—Saga also saw remorse.

Rurik crouched, lowering his voice. "You must understand—I am sorry for your situation. It makes me sick, Saga, what these Urkans have done. But I cannot wrap myself in your troubles. Would cause great problems for my country."

Problems.

The word echoed in her skull, the tonic's grip ever tightening. Distantly, Saga felt smoldering anger. She knew it had been too good . . . too perfect. The wax sealer and then the information—it had fallen into her lap too easily. The gods toyed with her, reveling in her misery.

"I'll give you anything you want," she whispered. And in that moment, it was true. Her life was already forfeit. But Eisa . . . Eisa was out there, with a chance to live free.

"I do not want—"

"Anything," she pleaded. Rurik had never leered at her in the way that made her feel soiled, but she sent a silent prayer he wouldn't ask for . . . that. And when she forced herself to meet his gaze, it was clear it was the farthest thing from his mind. He looked as though he waged an inner war. He was silent for so long, she was certain he'd refuse. But when Rurik opened his mouth, the most unexpected word fell out.

"Tunnels."

"Tunnels," she repeated.

"There are other tunnels in Askaborg?"

"*Many*," replied Saga. Gods, but she couldn't hold on much longer. She'd just close her eyes for a moment. Just for a heartbeat. But as she blinked at Rurik, she realized the confident, arrogant Zagadkian looked slightly undone. Raking a hand through his hair, he muttered something incomprehensible under his breath.

"And you need me to—"

"Intercept letters," said Saga. She dug deep for her energy. Nodded at the wax sealer. "Tell them the queen sent you with the wax sealer to vouch for her word. The letters' details were incorrect. And then after I've changed them, you will bring them back for sending."

Rurik's eyes narrowed.

"I'll be quick," said Saga. "Just a few details to change."

Rurik scowled at her. "What have you gotten into, Saga?"

"Please," she begged. "Lives are at stake. Please, Kass."

Distantly, she could tell his name on her lips had impacted him in some way. Rurik scrubbed a hand down his face. "All of tunnels," was his hard reply. "I will do this for you, Saga, one time. But you . . . you will draw for me a map with all tunnels of Askaborg Castle on it."

Saga was nodding. It didn't matter what he asked of her, she'd do it. *Eisa*. She shoved back at sleep. Eisa was all that mattered.

"We shake to seal deal," said Rurik, sliding his palm into her gloved hand. It was warm and firm, shaking hers with enviable strength.

"Wait here," he said brusquely. "I will be back." The wax sealer slid into his pocket. The door swung open then closed.

Saga was alone in the passageway with nothing but a torch for light. She curled onto her side. Stopped fighting the tonic's pull.

And within a few measured heartbeats, Saga was sound asleep.

CHAPTER 18

Kalasgarde

As she and Rey entered Harpa's home, Silla's stomach swarmed with butterflies. Her gaze jumped from a pallet laid out in the farthest back corner to Rykka, twisting and whirling about in the hearthfire's flames, but as it landed on Harpa eyeing her intently, her restlessness grew.

She was eager to get on with this. Ready to go through her Cohesion Rite and join the ranks of the Galdra. But what if Harpa had changed her mind?

Harpa's focus turned to her grandson. "I am old and set in my ways," she said, breaking the silence. "You know that about me, Reynir."

Rey merely grunted.

"But I have thought long and hard about it. It seems threads long thought severed have merely been frayed." Harpa paused, thumb rubbing along the lovely tablet weave belt she wore today. "I am honor-bound to play my part."

Silla's brows drew together.

Harpa appeared to chew on words she did not wish to voice. "I've realized this is bigger than you or me, Reynir," she said after a long moment. "It is my duty to see this through."

Rey nodded. "After this, I will ask nothing else of you."

Harpa and Rey stared at each other, as though they held a silent conversation to which Silla was not privy. "Very well," said Harpa.

She turned her stern gaze to Silla. "If I agree to do this, you must listen to what I say. You must not question my methods."

Silla nodded eagerly.

"You're old," said Harpa, making Silla's smile fall.

"I'm twenty—"

"It is difficult to teach galdur past a certain age. Your mind has firmed. It will fight against what needs to be done."

"I think you'll find I'm quite determined."

Harpa ignored her, turning to Rey. "Explain everything."

Rey sighed, running a hand over his textured curls. Silla turned away, embarrassed she'd attacked him like a madwoman the night before. But Rey . . . he'd shown her softness. Had pulled her close and let her cry into his chest.

"King Kjartan's bodyguard took her from Askaborg," Rey was saying. "He kept her safely hidden in Sudur lands for seventeen years, had her taking skjöld to suppress her priming. She seems to have Ashbringer intuition—a cold white light. And perhaps Breaker strength."

"What?" Harpa had her back to them, rummaging through the jar-laden shelves.

"Strength," repeated Rey. "She pushed me clear across a field."

Harpa whirled on Silla, eyes narrowed. "You're not a twin."

Silla lifted a shoulder in a casual shrug.

"How can this be?" asked Harpa. "Perhaps you *had* a twin, but the other never quickened in the womb?" She went back to picking jars from the shelves. "What do you know of the Galdra, Eisa?"

"Please, call me Silla." She swallowed hard. "I know there are Warrior Galdra and Mind Galdra."

"Yes," said Harpa. "And you are a Warrior Galdra."

Her heart warmed to hear this. She needed to become a warrior—needed to be as powerful as Rey . . .

"Warrior Galdra," continued Harpa, "include the Blade Breakers, capable of great strength. The Shadow Hounds, who bend light to their will. The Harefeet, who generate great bursts of speed. Ashbringers, with fire at their fingertips. And the Smiths, who can sever and forge the bonds of this world."

"Wait," said Silla. "I've not heard of the Smiths. What do you mean by bonds?"

"Bonds are the weavings of this universe," said Harpa. "They are everywhere—in everything, so small that you cannot see them. They shape the stones and each blade of grass. The Smiths can change these bonds; can cut them or forge them anew; can create new things from what nature has provided."

"My armor," said Rey, smoothing a hand along the intricate leather-like scales. "It was made by a Smith we call the Tailor. He specializes in creating new textiles: armor as durable as chain mail but a fraction of the weight, or blankets holding as much heat as ten furs."

Silla held herself absolutely still, taking in each word.

"The buildings in Kopa and some in Sunnavík," Rey continued, "were made by the Stone Masons. They specialize in cleaving the bonds within stone."

A memory rattled in Silla's mind. "Hekla's prosthesis."

Rey nodded. "A collaboration between a Metal Smith and the Tailor. Together, they've made many limbs and helpful devices for Galdra warriors."

Her brows furrowed. "But it is so useful," she mused. "How could the king not wish to use such skills to his advantage?"

"Pah!" Harpa threw her hand in the air, back hunched over her worktable. "He fears the Galdra, that man. He tries to outrun his fate, but he should know better. Not even a king can escape such a thing."

Silla looked at Rey, hoping for clarification. "There are stories," he said slowly, glancing at his grandmother. "That Ivar once sought a Weaver to read his future. She was never seen again. It was then Ivar's vendetta against the Galdra began. They were rounded up in large groups and executed. But many escaped, fleeing to the far corners of the kingdom."

"What did the Weaver tell him?" asked Silla.

"That he will fall by galdur's hand," said Harpa.

"Speculation," muttered Rey.

Harpa straightened, handing a clay cup to Rey. "Add water to this, Reynir."

"What will happen today?" asked Silla, unable to hold her questions at bay. "How long will it take? Will I be as powerful as Rey?"

"You talk a lot," said Rykka, twisting up from the hearthfire's flames. "I will call you Trilla. Like the squirrel in the yard, always chattering for food."

"Rykka," warned Rey, pressing the cup of steaming liquid into Silla's hands. "Be kind."

"I'm always kind, Reynir," she purred. "Squirrels are the most darling of rodents."

"Off with you, Rykka," barked Harpa. "We need peace." She turned to Silla. "You will drink this, and then we will start your Cohesion Rite."

"Now?" asked Silla, bouncing onto the tips of her toes. All morning, thoughts of this moment had consumed her, but now that it was here, apprehension knotted her gut.

"Yes, *now*. Today, I will guide you through the Rite, and then you must rest. Tomorrow we will work on expression and weaving your galdur into physical shape." Harpa's gaze dipped to the cup. "Drink."

Gazing at the cup, Silla had a moment of trepidation. She'd learned the dangers of accepting food and drink from others the hard way. "What's in it?"

"An herb that will help draw your powers from the heart of your magic. It makes it easy for your mind to find this part of yourself and link them together."

Rey watched her carefully. "It will prime you. Draw the light to your arms and nothing more."

Prime me. Her heart palpitated as Silla stared at the steaming mug. "The catalyst?"

Rey's jaw tightened. "How do you know that?"

Silla's hand lifted to that short patch of hair. "Valf. Kommandor Valf had it baked into my f-food." Tapestries flashed in her mind—gleaming locks of brown woven with blond; hands wrapping around her throat; *scream, dear. I do so enjoy it.*

The cup fell from her hand, clattering on the floor and making Silla jump. She looked down, surprised to see liquid splashed across her boots.

"Harpa," said Rey. "We need a moment."

Arm sliding around her shoulders, Rey held on to Silla firmly as he guided her through the door and into the yard. An icy gust scraped her cheeks, the cold rousing her from the shock.

"You did not tell me," said Rey, his voice low. Large hands slid over her shoulders, turning her to face him while holding her steady. "You did not tell me he gave you the catalyst."

"Why did you think I was glowing like the auroras?"

"I thought it was battle thrill or fear. Both can help to prime you."

Silla's gaze grew unfocused as she stared into the woods.

Rey cursed viciously. "The death you granted that man was far too swift." She met his eyes, golden embers sparking in an ocean of deep brown. "I'd have been far less merciful."

Silla opened her mouth, but nothing came out.

"You're safe."

Safe, Silla reminded herself. *Not trapped. Your choice.*

"We can try another day."

But Saga needed her, and there wasn't time to waste. She pulled back, looking him in the eye. "No. Tell me what will happen."

Rey observed her. "After you drink the catalyst, you will clear your mind of thoughts and retreat inward to a place of deep consciousness. I cannot say what you will see for certain. Some see flashes of memories, glimpses of the past. Others are visited by the spirit of an ancestor. Most see a light. Follow the light, and you will find your heart—the source of your power. Place your hands upon it, and heart and mind will become Cohesed."

Silla bit her lip. "And if I don't?"

"If you don't, your galdur will continue to prime with no way to express it."

"What does that mean?"

"When you are filled with tension," said Rey, "or fear or anger or other powerful emotions, your galdur is pushed to the surface. You are *primed*. But your mind cannot control it. You cannot *express* it or weave it into form. Does that make sense?"

She nodded.

"When you're Cohesed, you'll be able to control your priming and send the galdur back to your source when you do not wish to light up like a torch."

She bit down on a smile. "That would be helpful." Silla took a steadying breath, staring up at him. There was only forward. Only this. "I . . . don't want to lose control."

He took a slow breath. "Harpa has done this hundreds of times, and if you wish, I can leave—"

"I want you to stay."

"Very well." His gaze locked onto hers and held steady. "I'll stay."

Goosebumps prickled her skin as the moment stretched on. Silla cleared her throat. Turned to the cabin.

"I'm ready."

They reentered the cabin. Harpa had readied a fresh cup of hot water steeped with the catalyst, and Silla drank it as quickly as she could without scalding her tongue. She followed Harpa to a reed pallet, dozens of candles arranged around it.

"Lie here," said Harpa, gesturing to the pallet. As Silla stretched out, Harpa began. "We light candles for the Father of Light, as He is the source of our galdur."

Silla's eyes met Rey's, candle flames shimmering in his gaze.

"Close your eyes," ordered Harpa. Silla did as she was told, her heart rate speeding up. "We call upon the Bright One. We ask You, Sunnvald, to grant Your power and blessings to Eisa. Fill her with Your divine grace so she might bind her mind to her heart."

Silla already felt the catalyst at work. It began as a trickle of power, growing wilder by the minute, until a glacial river coursed through her veins. That tension . . . that excruciating tension that begged . . . pleaded with her for release.

Soon. Soon they would be one.

Bracing against the strange pressure, Silla could feel it gathering in her forearms. She cracked an eyelid open, catching Harpa's face bathed in that pure white light.

"Close your eyes," snapped Harpa. "Empty your mind."

Adjusting herself on the hard pallet, Silla took a deep breath and tried to clear her mind. Her nose itched. A lump dug into her spine. Her tongue slid along the roof of her mouth, back and forth, back and forth.

Harpa exhaled sharply, her impatience stirring the air. Silla could feel the tickle of their gazes like ants marching across her skin. Maddeningly, it seemed the harder she tried to clear her mind, the more her thoughts wandered.

"Count your breaths," said Harpa. "Deeply in, deeply out."

Silla took a great, deep breath. Let it out slowly. Tried to clear her mind, allowing her body to relax.

Ice-blue eyes flashed in her mind's eye. Rusted red blood matting his hair, oozing from his wounds. Then brown eyes, wide with fear. Hair mussed like a cave bear. Then Skeggagrim, a man she'd never known, neck slashed wide, eyes open and lifeless.

Your fault. Your fault. Your fault!

Silla's eyes flew open, her breaths growing shallow. "I cannot quiet my mind."

Harpa sighed, then bent toward Rey and whispered in his ear. He vanished from beside her, then returned a moment later with a jar. Unlatching it, Harpa plucked out a slender, gnarled mushroom and handed it to Silla.

"Chew this. It will ease your nerves and clear your mind for you."

Bitterness pricked at the back of her tongue as she chewed and swallowed. But as she closed her eyes, that ice-blue gaze, the guilt and shame, melted like snow under a spring sun. At last, her mind was blissfully empty.

And then, Silla drifted downward until blackness pulled her under.

CHAPTER 19

Silla landed on hands and knees, chin snapping forward with the force of her fall. Stunned, she held herself still for several heartbeats, picking out the details she could. Below, a gray stone floor stretched in either direction—a corridor, it seemed.

It was remarkably silent.

After pushing herself up, Silla wiped her palms on her knees and tried to get her bearings. But before she could decide what to do, the faint sound of footfalls met her ears. Her stomach fluttered in trepidation as the steps grew nearer. There was nowhere to hide—nothing but barren corridor in either direction. Should she run?

But the knowing feeling held her rooted in place. A man soon rounded the corner, and she pulled in a deep breath and held it. A crown sat atop the man's head, simple gold, free of ornamentation. His silver curls caught the light, blue eyes set into a face deeply lined with age. Silla felt she should know him, was certain he was a king, yet not King Ivar.

Sadness clung to this king; she saw it in the hunch of his shoulders—in his heavy-footed walk. The blackness in the corner of Silla's mind rattled its cage, and she knew: Grief held this man in its tight embrace.

Who was this king, and what had happened to him?

Curiously, the man did not seem to see her—he walked straight past without so much as a glance. Silla lurched after him.

"Excuse me?" she tried.

Still no reaction. Rushing forward, Silla placed a hand on his shoulder, gasping as it passed right through the king's back.

Some see flashes of memories, glimpses of the past. Others are visited by the spirit of an ancestor. Most see a light. Rey's words hung in her mind. *Light,* she thought. *Perhaps this king will lead me to the light.*

Dazed, Silla trailed the man. They walked together until they reached an enormous tapestry of black and fiery oranges hung on the wall. After glancing over his shoulder, the king pulled it aside, the heel of his hand pushing hard into a stone. The whole section of wall swung inward.

"A doorway," Silla gasped, following the king through it.

Darkness swallowed them as the door swung back into place, but it was not long before the old king cupped a thin, orange flame in his palm. *Ashbringer.* A smile curved Silla's lips. This king was Galdra! Which meant . . . he must be an ancestor of hers.

Silla watched the old king carefully. His flame cast light upon the stone wall, and he edged along it in search of something. At last, he put his flameless palm on a stone, pushing until it clicked softly. Silla gasped as the flooring sank in a spiral pattern, revealing a twisting, shadowy stairwell.

Silla and the king descended. The stairwell went far deeper than Silla had guessed; the air grew heavy and dank, with a strange, ancient feel to it. At last they reached the bottom, a small room opening before them.

An oily chill slid through Silla's veins. The ancient presence was stronger here, dark intoxication unfurling within the heart of her being. Hand rising to her chest, Silla searched in vain for the comforting feel of the vial.

She surveyed the small room, examining the candles nestled into stone-carved alcoves and the hidebound book sitting on a pedestal.

A strange sensation stirred in her blood—recognition, but not, like a dream she could not quite recall. This presence welcomed her like a friend long forgotten, invisible tendrils sliding through her in a dark, seductive caress.

The king lit the candles until the room danced with light, then stood before the book, flipping through the pages. Silla gasped as the king pulled out a white-hilted dagger and sliced deep into his palm. After dipping his fingers in the blood, the king drew a series of symbols on the wall.

"Dark One, I call to you," he said in a low voice. Silla held her breath as they waited in silence. Nothing happened.

"Dark One, I *implore* you." The man's voice cracked, his desperation tangible.

The candles flickered, the temperature plunging in an instant. Silla's breath clouded the air. The presence grew stronger, more commanding, and a sudden wave of need snaked through Silla's blood.

One leaf to numb yourself. A second to push the guilt away. Three to stop feeling altogether . . .

Silla clutched at her chest, seeking that vial. She hungered for those leaves like she hadn't in weeks, was driven to her knees with a sound of agony. Need. She *needed* them. Was incomplete without them, would *die* if she could not get them . . .

Another flicker of candlelight, and the longings vanished in an instant.

Breaths heaving from her, Silla clambered to her feet, trying to calm her racing heart. Movement in her periphery diverted her attention—a shadow creeping up the wall. Slowly, it grew, loose lines fusing into the form of a man, a crown of tall, thin spikes protruding from his skull.

"You have chosen," said an unearthly voice. Deep and disembodied, it seemed to come from nowhere and everywhere all at once. Goosebumps raced up Silla's arms.

The king turned to the shadow, conflict carved into his face. "Is there not another?"

"No," said the voice with quiet malevolence. "I will say it once more, King. My answer has never wavered, nor will it today."

The king closed his eyes, shadows pooling in the hollows of his cheeks.

"Think of your beloved back in your arms," said the voice. "You were robbed of time with her, Hrolf. You can undo this grave wrong."

"But . . . my bloodline."

"Your son is not so old. He might yet sire more children."

A woman's voice filled the air. "Hrolf, my dearest. It is agony for me without you. Each moment is a pain only curable by your love. Make the right choice, darling, so we can be together once more."

The king's eyes shone with unshed tears, his hand going to his heart. "Brida?" he whispered.

"Make the right choice, my love," cried the woman, "I implore you."

The king closed his eyes, hugging himself. Like this, he did not seem a king at all—only a broken man consumed by grief. But as he opened his eyes, hardness replaced the pain and anguish. The king straightened his spine. "I will do it."

The shadow crackled with glee. "A life for a life," it said.

The king nodded solemnly.

"Use the knife," said the disembodied voice. "Take it. Deliver the girl's life to me, and you will hold your beloved Brida once more."

A slow shudder rolled through Silla as the king's intent became clear. It was wrong, a terrible deed, and yet . . . she understood. His grief had broken him—had twisted his thoughts, so that wrongs seemed right. Darkness was his path to the light.

Your fault, chanted the deep dark voice, penetrating her skull and burrowing deep into her mind. *Your fault they are all dead.*

Matthias's face flashed in her mind's eye. Then Ilías and Skeggagrim. A man with an iron brand looming over her. She deserved to be punished. Should have been strung up on a pillar with her family. The raw, black grief she'd caged away seeped through the bars, oozing through her like poison until she was choking on it, drowning in anguish . . .

Something hooked behind her navel and tugged. And then, once more, she was falling through blackness.

Silla landed. Blinked into the darkness. That smothering presence was gone, her grief caged away in the back corner of her mind. A light was growing, somewhere distant in this empty place.

"Where did you go?" snapped Harpa, amber eyes gleaming as she strode toward Silla. Harpa. Silla wanted to hug the woman.

"A room," she managed. "There was a book . . ."

"Never mind that now," said Harpa briskly. "You are where you must be. Follow the lights and trust the knowing feeling inside you. It will guide you into your power."

Silla followed her gaze to the flickering lights. After pushing to her feet, she moved toward them. As she approached, it became apparent that they were not, in fact, lights. They were flíta—thousands of the butterfly-like creatures, flapping gauzy, luminescent wings. She walked among them in wonder. Some of the flíta's wings caught fire before burning up in tiny infernos and yielding to darkness. And somewhere in those ashes, a caterpillar would emerge.

Death and rebirth. A new phase of their lives beginning.

Much like her own. When Silla woke, her life as an ordinary woman would be over. She'd be Galdra. An Ashbringer. And she'd be one step closer to freeing Saga.

As she walked among the flíta, a larger light caught Silla's attention, off in the distance. Unlike the flame-yellow glow of the flíta, this larger orb was pure white. As she neared, its form became clear—a churning, throbbing orb.

Trust the knowing feeling inside you, Harpa had said, and Silla found she did indeed know exactly what to do. The light pulled at her, not with the book's dark seduction but rather a bright, steady flow—like a slow-moving current drawing her forward. And whereas the book had felt like a ruinous craving, this light felt *right*—as though she were uniting with another fragment of her very being.

The orb's light warmed her face, exultation filling her. At last, she would embrace this fundamental part of herself. Soon, she would do what she'd been born to do.

Reaching out, Silla clasped the orb.

Energy surged into her body, and for one infinitesimal moment, Silla understood the weavings of the world. She saw the connections Harpa had spoken of—the complex webwork of bonds holding this world together, organizing it into structures and beings and air and water. She saw threads of emotion and thought and memory, the weavings of the past and the future to come. The balance of it all was exquisite—warp and weft; darkness and light; chaos and order—so beautiful Silla could weep.

But then it was gone. The wave crested. This knowledge and awareness grew liquid, slipping through her fingers and beyond her grasp.

The white radiance sank into her, settling in place just behind her rib cage. It was a gently lapping pool of galdur, and with it came the awareness that it felt so much like her because it *was* her—it had always been there. But now that her heart and mind were linked, Silla could sense her galdur.

Silla felt a smile curving her lips as her eyes opened and she stared at the rafters of Harpa's cabin.

CHAPTER 20

Sunnavík

Saga woke with a full-body jolt. Disoriented, she stared up at crimson pleats spilling and wrapping all around her like a silken cocoon. Immediately, her muscles eased in recognition—it was her bed's canopy.

Her fingers pressed into her throbbing temples. She'd slept like the dead. Groggily, Saga sat up, pulling aside the curtains surrounding her bed. Pushing to the edge of the mattress, she peered into her chambers. The window curtains were thrown wide. It seemed to be the last light of the day, which meant Saga had missed the evening meal. She'd had a nap and . . .

"No," she moaned, as the memories surged forth. The tonic, the wax sealer. Kassandr Rurik.

I need your help.

"A dream," she muttered, pressing the heels of her palms into her eyes. Surely it had been a dream. Because even in her worst nightmares, she didn't reveal such information to a man like Rurik. But her eyes found a scrap of parchment atop her dressing table, and Saga knew . . . somehow, she *knew* it had been no dream. Head protesting, she rushed across the room and read the parchment.

Asla Tower, tomorrow, 20th chime.

She turned it over, but there was nothing more. Rurik, it seemed, was a man of few words. Saga presumed the purpose of the note was to pass him the forged letter so he could fulfill his end of the bargain. Plus, the man would want his promised map.

Saga gritted her teeth, staring at the note. The last thing she remembered was giving in to sleep's pull in that dark passageway. Had Rurik *carried* her to her chambers? The thought of being unconscious—so *vulnerable*—around a man she scarcely knew made her squirm. Gods, how embarrassing, but also how utterly risky. Saga was betrothed to Ivar Ironheart's son. What if Rurik had been seen?

Saga cast a cursory glance around the room in search of the scroll. Her eyes dropped to the dressing table drawer's handle. She yanked it open. And there they were—the sealer lying next to a single scroll, the queen's wasp sigil stamped in wax. Hands shaking, Saga picked up the scroll. Tore the seal. Read the letter within.

The girl and her companion were spotted in Svangormr Pass, confirming she's entered the central corridor of Nordur lands. They must be apprehended at all costs. I don't need to remind you what is at stake should the Wolf Feeders fail once more.

Yours,
S.

Alfson's cramped letters blurred together, then came apart as Saga's heartbeat thundered. This was it—the letter she'd sought. He'd done it. Rurik had intercepted the scroll, and now Saga held the power to help Eisa in her hand.

Gratitude swelled in her chest, making Saga feel light as air. And now she would merely change a word or two, sending the Wolf Feeders in entirely the wrong direction. By the time the error was discovered, it would be simple enough to seem innocent, yet would buy more time for Eisa.

Saga's body tingled with excitement, but nausea quickly sliced through it. She'd obtained the letter, but at what cost? Rurik now knew Saga interfered with the queen's letters—that she had Signe's wax sealer stamp. Her head dropped into her hands at the realization; she'd just handed him the power to destroy her.

But Rurik's words rang in her ears.

You will draw for me a map with all tunnels of Askaborg.

Saga's brows furrowed. She'd exposed too much of herself to Rurik, but he, too, had revealed something to her. What need had the man for a map? As she pondered in silence, several details slid into place: Rurik, discovering her near the falconry tower that first day—a remote location the man had no business being—and now, his interest in the tunnels.

"He searches for something," she murmured, pushing a blond lock back from her face. What did Rurik seek? Did his Druzhina search for it as well? Were they truly here for diplomatic reasons, or was it merely a ruse? But another realization settled, easing the burn of discomfort in her stomach. "Rurik cannot expose me without risking the revelation of his own secret." It was a thin, fragile thing, this hope, but Saga clung to it with everything she had.

"Focus," she told herself, rising to unsteady feet. Right now, there was only the scroll. Only Eisa. Saga poured water from a pitcher into a washbasin and splashed her cheeks. And as her mind steadied, she listed each step.

Forge the instructions. Reseal the scrolls. Meet Rurik in Asla Tower.

And with that, Saga got to work.

Saga's heart pounded like a war hammer as she climbed the spiral staircase to Asla Tower. Tucked into one sleeve was the forged scroll, freshly resealed. She'd struggled for hours to match Maester Alfson's scratchy handwriting and finally achieved something close to it. With these new directions, the Wolf Feeders would traipse along the western coast of Nordur, far from Svangormr Pass and, Saga hoped, Eisa.

In her other sleeve, Rurik's map was folded. Saga had slaved over that map, had included Askaborg's main passages—including those known by the Urkans—and just enough obscure ones to satisfy his curiosity. But others, Saga had kept to herself. She'd not been of sound mind when she'd agreed to share this with him. Were she to reveal all of Askaborg's secrets, it would not only jeopardize her safety but also give Rurik everything he needed.

And she planned to leave him wanting just a little more.

Saga went over the offer she'd propose to Rurik—a partnership of sorts. He'd intercept future letters for her, and she'd reward him with new passageways. How Rurik would react to this, Saga was unsure. But the man deserved it for striking that deal while her mind was addled from the tonic.

Asla Tower had long been abandoned yet was accessible through corridors within the old defensive walls of the castle's northern wing. Not only that, but it was only a few minutes' walk from Saga's own bedchambers. Had Rurik selected the tower for this reason? It was disturbing to realize this man had learned so much of the castle in so little time.

Saga pushed through the door and into an empty tower room. The rounded space had five glass-paned windows, each with a breathtaking view of the castle grounds and Sunnavík's districts beyond. Saga drew nearer to the easternmost window, gazing out at the sister moons reflected in the bay's waters. Tonight, the largest moon was at her fullest.

A full Malla is a good omen for those in need of courage, came a curious thought. Before Saga could question where she'd heard such a thing, a scuff sounded from behind her.

"I've got your—" Saga began, cutting off as shock jolted through her. It was not Rurik's large frame filling the doorway, but a woman Saga did not recognize. Her stomach turned over, heartbeat kicking up.

Clad in a thrall's blue apron dress, the woman bobbed an awkward curtsy. "Good evening, Your Majesty."

"Who—what—"

"I'm Ana, Your Majesty," said the woman, stepping into the room.

Saga's heart leaped into her throat. This was not Rurik at all. "*Your Majesty* is reserved for royalty," said Saga, more harshly than she'd intended.

"Aye," replied Ana, unperturbed. "It is."

Discomfort wrapped itself around Saga's ribs, and she cast a look over Ana's shoulder. "I thought you were . . ." She pressed her lips together.

"Lord Rurik?" the girl guessed. She shook her head. "I must tell you, the man is most brash. Had he encountered anyone else in the falconry tower, word would already have reached the king."

Saga felt the blood leave her face. "You were in the falconry tower. You gave him the . . ." Again, she found herself not wanting to reveal too much.

"Scroll," finished Ana. "He came into the falconry tower just as I was securing the scroll. I'll admit, the man is *quite* persuasive." Ana raised her brows in mock amusement, but Saga only scowled. She should have known the man would be a shameless seducer.

"I was about ready to give him the keys to the building," continued Ana. "Thankfully, some shred of my wits remained intact. And his unexpected presence had me thinking—had me remembering a woman trying to cross the castle's inner bailey not long ago."

Saga's body flushed with shame, a memory surging forth—a face peering down at her from the falconry tower's window while she fell to pieces. "You saw . . ."

"Do not be embarrassed," Ana said with a wave of her hand. "Please, Your Highness, that is the last thing I wish to do."

"And what is it you wish to do?" Saga snapped. She took a slow breath, trying to summon her patience. But she'd rather discuss Ursir's wisdom than her affliction with a stranger.

"I passed the scroll and note to Lord Rurik because I wanted to tell you . . ." Ana rolled her lips together, then spoke. "Should you find yourself in need of intercepting another letter, perhaps I could be of assistance."

Surprise prickled down Saga's spine. "Assistance," she repeated, dumbstruck.

"Yes," said Ana, carefully. The two women looked at each other assessingly. It was a dangerous line being toed, and both of them knew it.

Saga stared at the woman before her, uncertain what to think. Slowly, she eased her mental barriers down, letting her Sense stretch out.

... How can I convince her? wafted Ana's thoughts. *I must share something to gain her trust ...*

"Assistance could be . . . agreeable," said Saga slowly. "You would help me with this?"

... Yes! burst Ana's thoughts. *Tell her, but do not be too eager. You'll frighten her off ...*

"Yes," Ana replied aloud. "Though I fear I must ask something of you as well. An exchange of sorts. I think we could be of great help to each other."

"Help . . ."

Ana's hands balled into fists, but she shook them out. "I work with a group seeking information housed within Askaborg's walls. And you, Your Majesty, have access to areas off limits to a palace thrall."

Saga's brows drew together. "Information?"

... Oh, they'll have my head for involving her in this, thought Ana, observing Saga quietly, *but it is the only way ...*

"Yes," Ana said aloud. "Would this arrangement agree with you?"

"You want me to find this information," mused Saga. "And in exchange, you'll intercept Queen Signe's letters?"

... Should I tell her reading the queen's letters helps us as well? thought Ana. *Never mind that she has access to the palace, and that wax sealer stamp ...*

Ana nodded. "They have stationed me in the falconry tower to investigate the queen. But with such limited access, I'm only able to record addresses from the queen's correspondence."

"Addresses?"

Ana nodded again. "Mere scraps of what we seek."

Saga considered Ana silently. "How do I know I can trust you?"

... Tell her, thought Ana. *Share something to help her trust you ...*

"Galdra!" Ana said aloud.

Saga blinked.

. . . Oh, gods, thought Ana. *Should I have said that? What if she hands me over? No, calm yourself. She wouldn't. She's a Volsik . . .*

Ana cleared her throat. "That is to say, I'm Galdra," she said aloud. "I only tell you this so you might trust me. Should I not come through on my side of the bargain, you can have me put to the pillar."

. . . Why did you suggest that? Ana thought, panicked.

"I would not do *that*," Saga rushed to say. But the information combined with what her Sense had heard eased Saga's protective thorns ever so slightly. "There are Galdra left in this kingdom?"

"Of course!" said Ana, then shook her head. "I'm sorry . . . it makes sense that you wouldn't know."

Saga watched Ana carefully, her curiosity getting the best of her. When Saga's Sense had awakened at age sixteen, she'd known at once she was Galdra. She recalled that when her parents had still ruled, there had been a Galdra ritual. But in this castle, under Ivar Ironheart's rule, Saga had not gone through it. Instead, she'd learned how to build mental barriers and hide her Sense away.

But she'd never met anyone else like her, and a thousand questions jostled in her mind. "What can you do?"

. . . That's good, thought Ana. *She's asking questions . . .*

"I am what they called a Harefoot," said Ana. "It means I can move with great bursts of speed. But I dare not use such a skill in this place."

Saga chewed the inside of her cheek. *I can hear thoughts,* was on the tip of her tongue. *Do you know others like me?* Yet her protective instincts held her back. She could not say this. Not yet. "I would never tell," she promised instead. "No matter what, your secret is safe with me, Ana."

. . . I knew it, thought Ana, her eyes beginning to shine. *She's just as Mother described the Volsiks. Good and honorable . . .*

"Thank you, Your Majesty," said Ana aloud.

Feeling slightly nauseous at Ana's use of that title, Saga looked away. Working the scroll out from her sleeve, she considered it. She'd toiled and struggled to obtain this scroll, to buy Eisa a few short weeks. But soon, there would be other plans, other letters, and Saga would need help to intercept them. "I need to know more," Saga said. "What information do you seek?"

"A name," replied Ana, cautiously.

"A name," repeated Saga.

... They'll be so cross with me for involving Lady Saga in this, thought Ana, *but it is the only way ...*

Ana blew out a long breath. "We believe the queen is directing the Klaernar for her own twisted deeds."

"The Klaernar?"

"Yes," said Ana. "We have knowledge to suggest someone is pulling the strings for her. A liaison of sorts. And we seek this name."

Saga stared at her, thoughts zipping madly through her mind. "What are the Klaernar doing on the queen's behalf?"

... Murder and treason are the best of the bunch, came the woman's exasperated thoughts.

Ana winced. "I'm afraid I cannot reveal the details. Suffice it to say, the people I work for have a vested interest in discovering who this person is."

Saga turned and stared out the window, Ana's thoughts dulling as her own mind whirred. The Klaernar. Treason. This was bigger than mere mail tampering. But then she recalled that first conversation she'd heard between Alfson and the queen.

What kind of incompetent imbecile was your friend, Maester? Kommandor of the Eystri branch of the Klaernar. How could an untrained girl best him?

The Klaernar were involved in the queen's hunt for Eisa. And with that realization, her decision was made.

"I'll do it," said Saga, handing the scroll to Ana. "This must be sent with haste."

Ana took the scroll, turning to examine all sides of it. "Clever, Your Majesty," murmured Ana. "Outer parchment replaced, wax seal an exact replica, and your penmanship looks like a precise match. I shall send them at once." Ana paused. "We must burn the original letters. But the sealer stamp—do you have a hiding place for it?"

"A loose stone in the wall," replied Saga.

Ana nodded. "We need you to search for the name of this liaison between the queen and the Klaernar."

"I shall find this information," vowed Saga, steel in her voice.

"I wish I could speak to you all day, Your Majesty," continued Ana. "You must know it is a great honor just to meet you. My parents... my family..." Her eyes shone.

... Oh hush, Ana's thoughts chided. *Stop being so sentimental...*

"Your parents were good and fair rulers, worthy of our devotion and sacrifice," said Ana aloud. "Long have the Volsiks been protectors of the realm. The throne belongs to you."

Ana's words made Saga squirm. Years she'd spent burying such sentiments. Years she'd spent molding herself to fit *their* ideals.

"You must know," said Ana, "there have been many plans to free you from this prison over the years. They've all gone astray for one reason or another."

Saga's throat stung, and she swallowed back her emotion.

... They treat her like a child, when clearly she has grit, thought Ana. *Why they've never included her in their plans, I'll never understand...*

"I think," said Ana, her dark eyes sweeping Saga's face, "after you deliver us the name, I'll demand my foreman put out a call for a new plan to free you."

... and this time, I'll demand they include Saga in their plans, thought Ana.

Saga was speechless, her mind awhirl. The thought of leaving Askaborg should fill her with exhilaration. But she hadn't set foot outdoors for five long years. How could she leave the castle? The familiar hand of panic wrapped around her ribs and began to squeeze, tighter, tighter...

"Remember this," continued Ana, oblivious to her plight. "A white linen flying from the falconry tower means I've intercepted the queen's mail. We shall meet that night in this very tower. I'll bring the wax and spare parchment; you bring the sealer and any information you've gathered. A black linen means trouble. Do not linger near the falconry tower and deny any knowledge of me."

Saga nodded, drawing in a deep breath.

"You can descend first," said Ana. "I will wait ten minutes and follow. And I'll ensure this letter is posted immediately." Ana performed a rough curtsy. "This will be a wonderful partnership, Your Majesty!"

Saga managed a shaky smile and left. She'd come to the tower hoping for an alliance with Rurik, but she'd left it with so much more. Now she had the chance to *do* something that mattered. Because if the information Ana sought could expose Signe's schemes—if she could bring evidence to Ivar that his wife undermined his rule—Saga could do far better than misdirecting a warband.

She could stop Signe once and for all.

CHAPTER 21

Kalasgarde

Rey stared bleary-eyed into his bowl of porridge. Already, his back complained from sleeping on the hard bench, but now Vig was here, talking far too loudly.

"I heard Silla's voice coming from the stables," said Vig from across the table as Rey shoveled porridge into his mouth. "Is she . . . speaking to your horse?"

"Probably."

"It sounded quite grave. A true heart-to-heart."

Rey let out a long breath. "Why are you here, Vig?"

"Falcon arrived with a letter for you," said Vig, pulling a scroll from the folds of his cloak and handing it to Rey. "Important business from Kopa, I presume."

Rey's eyes fell upon the dragon sigil stamped into the wax—Jarl Hakon's mark. Rey's pulse drummed as he tore the seal and read the letter.

Soot Fingers,

Ten men, be there in six days. Try not to die.

Yours,
Fire Breath

Rey felt a rare smile tugging at his lips. Eyvind hadn't changed a lick. Shaking his head, he turned the scroll over, frowning. No word of Metta, the girl Silla had begged him to save from the Klaernar's custody in Kopa. He hoped it had merely slipped Eyvind's mind and didn't bode poorly for the woman. Rey rolled the letter back up and tucked it into his cloak.

Vig watched him hawkishly. "What're you playing at, Galtung?"

"Cleaning up an unfinished mess." Rey filled his mouth with more porridge. He was not in the mood to deal with Vig's shite.

"How unlike you to finish things."

Rey swallowed and closed his eyes. *Marra, grant me the patience to deal with this eelhead.* With a long exhale, he fixed his best *axe eyes* on Vig. "I'm planning for the job I can no longer complete in Istré, so people do not continue to be murdered."

It was more than he should say—more than he *meant* to say—but Vig's blink of surprise was worth it. Did he truly think Rey rushed about this kingdom *playing* warrior as they'd done as children?

"What is killing the people of Istré?" asked Vig.

"I do not know," Rey answered honestly, which was what troubled him the most. He could send men to be sure, but without being there himself to sift through the evidence, and with the delay in correspondence, his unease grew stronger. The last thing he wanted was to send his broken and battered Bloodaxe Crew into danger unprepared—again.

"Troubling times indeed," muttered Vig.

"What do you mean by that?"

Vig watched Rey, and for once, the contempt was missing from his face. "It might be nothing, but . . ."

"But?"

"Váli's disappearance has me thinking."

"A rare thing," muttered Rey, but he frowned in unease. Still Váli had not been found. Rey had retraced his search for the boy in his mind's eye—planned to ask Runný to stay with Silla so he could search for him in daylight.

Vig shot him a sharp glare. "A few weeks past, we had a flock of sheep go missing." As he stroked his dark beard, Vig's expression matched the worry gathering in Rey's gut. "We found only scattered tufts of wool in the pasture."

"Claw marks? Mist?" demanded Rey, before he could think better of it. Magnus had said the troubles in Istré had begun with missing livestock...

"No and no," replied Vig, and Rey let out a long breath. Thank the gods above. "But it had a strange... smell."

"Smell," repeated Rey. "What kind of smell?"

"Rot," Vig said. "The smell of moldered things. Yet there were no corpses."

Rey's curiosity was piqued. *Take me to the field,* he wanted to demand.

But logic quickly forced the thought back. He had Silla to worry about. Arrangements for Istré. The Uppreisna to contact. And he still had to consider how he'd put his life back together. "It is likely a pack of grimwolves," he said instead, focusing back on his porridge.

"Good," said Vig, exhaling in clear relief. "Good. I am glad an expert can put my fears to rest." Rey eyed his former friend with a faint note of respect. Regardless of his personal quarrels, Vig would do what it took to ensure the safety of those around him.

"Good," said Rey. And with that, Vig departed.

Silla's breath clouded the northern air as she stared up at the enormous mountains. Turning in a full circle, she took them in—jagged snowcapped peaks spearing clear blue skies. The raw beauty of Nordur was astounding, its wildness making her feel like a small thing at nature's mercy.

Shaking herself, Silla prodded inwardly, as she'd done a dozen or more times already this morning. There it was—the heart of her magic shimmering brightly within. It was real. She hadn't dreamed it.

A smile spread across her lips, and it deepened as Rey's voice reached her from within the shield-home. Warmth spread across her cheeks as she recalled the rest of that day. After her Cohesion

Rite, they'd ridden back to the shield-home. Rey had groomed the horses while Silla collapsed on the bench, utterly exhausted.

Rey had soon joined her, sprawled on the bench with an arm slung over the back of it. "How do you feel?" he'd asked gruffly. Perhaps she'd been delirious with fatigue, but she'd decided she rather adored that stern, sharp voice of his.

"Like . . . I'm more myself than ever before," Silla had said, eyeing the space between his arm and his chest. It was a little Silla-sized pocket—one she now knew she fit rather well. Gods, she needed a pet.

Rey had nodded. "You've found a part of yourself you never knew you were missing."

"Exactly." Impulsively, she'd scooted along the bench, closer to Rey.

"You've expended a great deal of energy," he said, eyeing her, "but a night's sleep shall restore you."

Silla's thigh had brushed against his, sending a jolt of heat through her.

"What are you doing?" he'd asked, in that harsh Axe Eyes voice.

"I'm . . . cold." She'd stared at the cozy-looking crook, hoping he'd understand.

"Fine," he'd relented, rolling his eyes.

Silla had eagerly leaned against him, tucking her feet up on the bench. "You're like my own personal hearthfire," she murmured, curling against him and trying to ignore the expanse of firm muscle. Warmth. She was merely seeking warmth.

Rey tensed beneath her, as though he was deeply uncomfortable. Uncertainty had filled her at that, and Silla had lifted her head, locking eyes with him. She'd felt foolish in that moment, wondering what she'd been thinking. This was Axe Eyes, not a puppy for her to cuddle.

She made to push away from him, but Rey's arm slid off the back of the bench, scooping her even closer. Silla's heart had pounded a little faster at that. In truth, she'd felt dizzy. She'd gone through her Rite and claimed her magic. And now she was one step closer to rescuing Saga.

"I won't tell anyone," she'd murmured after a long while. At that point, she'd scarcely been able to speak through her fatigue. "I won't tell a soul that the fearsome Axe Eyes has a soft side."

And as blackness had pulled her into sleep, she could have sworn she'd heard him say, "Only for you, Sunshine."

Turning away from the shield-home, Silla gave herself a mental shake. In her grief, she'd turned to Jonas for comfort. She could not fall into such habits with Rey. Not when they had to share such close quarters and he was her only link to the Galdra.

With a deep breath, Silla continued across the yard. But as she moved, she caught a blur of bright blue zipping back and forth in the woods. Her breath hitched. This time, she was certain—it was an ice spirit.

"I left you some butter last night," Silla whisper-called into the bushes. "Was it to your liking?" But the spirit didn't stir. Her feet itched to chase after it, but she knew it would be pointless. Spirits who did not wish to be seen were quite adept at remaining hidden. With a sigh, she turned to the stables.

That was when she saw it: a symbol drawn in shimmering frost on the stable's post. With a single vertical line and two diagonal arms pointing downward, Silla recognized it at once as the protection rune, though upside down. As the symbol melted in the morning light, Silla whirled in search of the ice spirit.

Had the spirit drawn the symbol? What did this mean?

But the ice spirit was nowhere to be seen, and so she continued on to the stables. As she stepped under the roof, the scent of hay and horse met her.

"Good morning, lovelies," she said softly, approaching the two horses. Horse drew nearer, nuzzling her palm, while Brown Horse looked away. Irritation flared inside Silla, chased quickly by determination. She was going to get this horse to love her if it was the last thing she did.

At the very least, the obstinate creature hadn't nipped at her in some time. And after feeding half of an oatcake to Horse, Silla gathered her bravery. Flattening her palm, she held the other half out for

Brown Horse to take. She watched for the telltale signs of the horse's agitation—flattened ears and swishing tail.

Brown Horse's nostrils flared as she scented the treat. "You might be used to brash, rude warriors," said Silla softly, "but in time, you'll adjust to me." Brown Horse's large, dark eyes settled on the treat, and for the barest of moments, Silla thought she might finally break through.

But this horse, it seemed, was as stubborn as a mule. Brown Horse turned, showing Silla her backside. And then, the rude creature lifted her tail and shat on the floor.

Silla crossed her arms over her chest. "Unfortunately for you," she said through gritted teeth, "I've abundant experience in dealing with ill-tempered brutes."

After grabbing a shovel propped near the stable's entrance, she scooped up Brown Horse's offering and flung it into the woods. "In case you were wondering," she told her mount's rear end, "I shall be back tomorrow. And the day after that. And one day, you insolent creature, you'll love me."

As she stormed from the stables, Silla pulled up short. Vig's horse was gone, and Rey was alone, working through one of his defensive routines with a longsword. He'd trimmed the sides of his skull and neatened his beard, his clean-cut look only enhancing the intensity in his eyes.

"May I join you?" she asked. "After Kopa, I . . ." Silla drew a deep breath. "It's clear I must continue my defensive lessons."

Rey stopped and examined her. "Grab the practice swords. Let's see if you can knock me on my arse."

And suddenly, Silla's irritation at Brown Horse was channeled into something new. Wordlessly, she fetched the wooden swords and came to stand before Rey, handing one to him. "What now?" she asked, watching him keenly.

The sun caught the golden flecks in Rey's eyes. "First, your stance," he said, examining her posture. Silla forced her gaze ahead, ignoring the pounding of her heart. "Widen your feet," said Rey, rounding behind her. "Loosen your hips."

Silla gasped as his large warm large hands landed on her hips, tingles rushing down her spine. Rey adjusted her to the left. "Good," he grunted. "Now your sword." His arm brushed along hers, a warm palm sliding over her sword hand. His hand closed over hers, adjusting her grip. "Hold it higher. There."

Silla's eyes fluttered shut as she tried to focus on his direction. But all she could think of was the feel of him at her back and the fact that she'd fallen asleep against him last night. That she'd woken in her bed with the furs tucked neatly around her.

"Your other hand will be busy with a shield," Rey was saying. His left hand slid under her elbow, nudging it upward.

As he eased away from her, Silla's body throbbed in protest. Rey stepped back in front of her, his lips twitching. "Now I'll show you the routine, and you'll repeat it."

After demonstrating, Rey gestured for Silla to try it. As he watched her, arms folded over his chest and an unimpressed expression on his face, Silla was reminded of all those lessons on the Road of Bones. "What do you think Hekla is doing right now?" she asked, an ache growing in her chest.

Rey's scowl deepened. "Causing trouble in Istré's mead halls."

"I hope so." Silla's lips twisted up. "I miss her. And Sigrún. And Gunnar and . . ." *Ilías,* she could not say. *Jonas. The way things were for so many weeks.* She was hit with an intense yearning for the past. For the ability to go back in time and take Ilías's place.

Guilt's familiar scald spread through her body. Scowling, Silla gripped her sword and forced herself into the routine. Her moves were awkward, her swing hesitant. With an irritated huff, Silla returned to the starting stance.

"Gods above," muttered Rey, running a hand down his face. "Did you make that up? That had no resemblance to what I showed you."

"Kindness, Reynir," chided Silla.

"I'll attempt kindness if you attempt intelligence. I've seen better from drunken children."

"Who is letting children get drunk?" she asked, aghast.

But a smile crept across her face, and she readied herself for another try. And so it went for the better part of an hour—Rey running Silla through the routine, correcting her posture and grip as needed. Slowly, Silla sank into it, losing herself in the movement of her body. This, she decided, was precisely what she'd needed. A new purpose. A way to relax.

And with that, a new morning routine was born.

CHAPTER 22

After an hour of sparring, Silla saddled the horses while Rey dipped into the stream behind the home. Then she followed him up Snowspear to Harpa's cabin. With no sign of Váli, Silla couldn't help but look over her shoulder as they rode. Was something dangerous lurking in the wilds of Kalasgarde? Or had Váli merely gotten lost?

Now she stood in Harpa's yard, amid the confusing disarray of summer and autumn and winter, trying to keep such thoughts out of her mind. It was a gray midmorning, and yesterday's dusting of snow had grown incrementally deeper. In the distance, Harpa's wind chimes clunked together while Brown Horse chewed grass at an ungodly volume.

Today, Harpa looked like a queen, lounging on a bench surrounded by her subjects. If birds could be subjects, that was. They squawked and chattered around her, swarming over bits of bread she tossed to the ground.

A loud thud drew her attention to Harpa's home. Rey was in there, doing the gods knew what.

"Now that you're Cohesed," began Harpa, "you should be able to sense the heart of your galdur—your source. Can you feel it?"

Silla nodded. She did not need to search for the warm shimmering pool of magic sitting behind her breastbone; though it had not even been a full day since her Rite, already it felt like an essential part of her being.

"Your source is individual," continued Harpa. "It generates the magic, yes, but also gives it a shape and signature. My source gives my galdur the shape of a Weaver's; Rey's gives him his Ashbringer skill. But even among classes of Galdra, there is diversity. Rey's Ashbringer skill, for example, presents as smoke, while other Ashbringers produce flames."

Silla nodded along.

"Each being in this kingdom carrying Sunnvald's gift has a different source."

Silla's brows drew together. "Sunnvald's gift?"

Harpa's amber eyes grew steely. "Tell me Tómas was not so cod-brained as to forget the old ways."

"He taught me of the old gods," Silla said defensively. "We left offerings for the gods and the spirits—"

"And did he teach you of Sunnvald's blessings?" Harpa cut in. "The origin of the Ashen?"

Silla shook her head slowly.

"The Ashen," began Harpa, "are all things in this kingdom blessed by Sunnvald." The older woman scowled at whatever Silla's expression revealed. "You doubt this? They are as real as you and me. The proof is in your very body. Can you not feel it?"

Silla pressed her lips together, trying to tamp down her irritation. "I thought you were going to teach me how to express my galdur."

"Impatience is your enemy in this." Harpa's head cocked to the side. "It is a thing that must be taken one step at a time. First, you must understand the nature of your galdur. The origin of the Ashen and the gift you carry inside you."

Silla remained silent. She would let Harpa speak her piece. Then Harpa would teach her how to use her galdur. And then, on with retrieving Saga.

"It is a tale of darkness and light—of the balance between chaos and order," said Harpa. "The thread begins with Sunnvald—the Father of Light—and His wife, Stjarna—the Mother Star. You know, of course, of their moon goddess daughters, Malla and Marra. All beings of light, of order and protection of Íseldur. But Sunnvald had also a brother—Myrkur, god of chaos and darkness.

"Unlike the Father of Light, Myrkur thirsts for disorder and unrest, and He loves most of all to play tricks on His brother. One day, Myrkur stole Stjarna, Malla, and Marra, pulling them into the night and binding them with unbreakable magic. And so it became that the stars and moons were separated from Sunnvald, shining only in the darkness of night.

"When Sunnvald discovered His beloved kin had been stolen, He grew so angry that He shook the skies, causing stars to crash to the land. As the stars fell, they burned into motes of ash, magic sprouting wherever they fell. Where they landed on plants, they became the hjarta trees, moonflowers, and snowcap mushrooms. Where they landed on rocks and soil, halda deposits were formed. Where they landed on animals, they became the frost foxes, the flíta, the skarplings, and so on."

Harpa paused for a moment. "And where the stardust fell on the people, they were gifted with galdur. This is why the Galdra are sometimes called the Ashen. Each of these beings, plant or animal, has a heart of galdur distinct to only them, their own flavor of magic. And that is how these weavings began."

Silla nodded absently.

"And the Volsiks," continued Harpa, rubbing her chin. "That, I'm afraid, is a tale frayed through, too many details lost over the centuries. But it is said that the Volsiks contain an additional blessing from Sunnvald. The Volsik gift is not understood, but it is thought to be a formidable weapon to be used against Myrkur."

"A weapon?"

Harpa nodded. "This means, child, that Sunnvald selected among all humankind *your* bloodline to keep order in the kingdom. A Volsik must always sit on the throne, lest the kingdom fall into turmoil."

Silla's throat tightened, her skin itching. Too much; it was too much. She just wanted to learn her galdur and get on with rescuing Saga . . .

"Long has there been a single Volsik in this kingdom, imprisoned though she is. But now"—Harpa allowed herself a small smile—"now there is another."

With those words, Silla felt a kingdom full of expectations

heaped onto her, and she looked away. Even so, Harpa's gaze lingered, studying her far more closely than Silla would have liked.

"I wonder sometimes," said Harpa, almost to herself, "if I had trained them better—if I had done something differently—perhaps things might have turned out differently."

Silla's gaze snapped back to Harpa. "Were you sent north as well?" she could not help herself from asking. Why had Harpa not died with the rest of her kin? Why had she gone north?

Harpa ignored her question. "I fear I have wandered too far off today's path. It is time you try priming yourself, Volsik."

"Silla," she snapped.

Harpa scowled. "You must accept it sooner or later."

"You sound like your grandson."

The faintest of smiles touched Harpa's lips. "Close your eyes and reach for your source. Get used to the shape and feel of it, then pull the galdur from it into your blood."

Obediently, Silla closed her eyes and found her source in an instant. She reached for the luminescence and drew it into her veins, that familiar cold tension swirling through her. Opening her eyes, she found the white light glowing from her arms.

"Good," said Harpa. "Now you will express. Clear your mind, then relax into your galdur. Trust the knowing feeling inside you, and let it do what it will."

Squaring her feet, Silla took a deep breath, then exhaled as though that would release her galdur—ridiculous, of course. After several long moments of absolutely nothing, she shook herself out, then tried visualizing white light bursting from her palms—imagined that irritating tension releasing—still, not a cursed thing.

A distant bang from the cabin reminded Silla that Rey was here. What was he doing in there while she and Harpa were out in the cold?

"Center yourself."

Silla breathed in deeply. *Expression,* she told herself. *Fire. Poof. White light.*

But her father's face flashed in her mind's eye.

Your fault. It's all your fault.

"Ay! Girl! Back on track!" Silla jumped at the sound of Harpa's clapping hands, birds chittering wildly in response.

"How do I express?" asked Silla. "I cannot seem to *make* it."

"Your impatience," said Harpa, watching her quietly, "clouds your path. Until you master it, you will never succeed."

Truly, that was so helpful. She shook out her body. Tried counting by twos, then backward from one hundred. Tried focusing on an imaginary dot on the back of her eyelids. Tried focusing on long, deep breaths.

Yet nothing could drive the thoughts from her mind—impatience at how long this was taking, irritation that she was faring so poorly. Her thoughts bounced to her father, and then she was stuck in the trap, the endless blame and self-loathing and why couldn't she do this one thing and make something good come from it all?

"Clear your mind," barked Harpa.

"I *cannot*!" Silla's eyes snapped open, irritation and impatience prickling her skin. She didn't have time to waste. Right now, Saga was in that castle, surrounded by murderers . . . by the same vile humans who had slaughtered her parents and a child they'd thought was Eisa.

Harpa watched her in that studious way of hers, and Silla turned away, trying to gather herself.

"You are not ready," said Harpa in a flat voice. "You must take a step back before you can move forward. You must learn how to surrender."

"Surrender?" Silla blinked back tears.

"Let us first take some róa and warm ourselves."

Silla trudged after her to the cabin.

Rey's back ached as he bent low, scrubbing another layer of grime from Harpa's walls. The pain seemed to grow each morning he woke on that damned bench, despite his attempts to ignore it. He was used to making do with what he had—had spent years sleeping on the rock-riddled ground and dusty floors. But somehow that bench had knotted his spine. Hábrók's arse. He was an old man at twenty-six winters.

"Hello, Reynir," cooed Rykka, a cloud of black smoke churning into the form of a miniature woman. Charcoal hair spilled around her face. Her wings were as delicately veined as a dragonfly's.

"Rykka," he grunted, scouring at a stubborn spot.

"Harpa is so fortunate to have you as a grandson," said Rykka, strolling along the patch he'd just cleaned, ash sprinkling in her wake.

"I'm certain she'd disagree with you on that." He scowled.

"Oh, no," smiled Rykka, running a tiny hand through her smoky tresses. "She's missed you, as have I. Will you stay for long?"

Rey shook his head. "Not if I can help it."

The smoke spirit pouted. "A shame."

"Rykka," grumbled Rey. "You're dropping ash on my clean walls."

With a laugh, the spirit zipped away, entwining herself with the hearthfire's smoke and leaving Rey in peace.

He swiped the ash away, wondering how long it had been since Harpa cleaned the place. From the looks of things, not since he'd last been here.

Five years.

Five years since he'd placed the last stone on Kristjan's burial mound and turned his back on this place forever. Or so he'd thought.

The speed at which his life had flipped over disoriented Rey. He was back in the place he'd vowed never to return. Hiding like a craven while his Bloodaxe Crew faced deadly foes in Istré and his brothers and sisters in the Uppreisna fought Ivar Ironheart's regime. He felt powerless.

There is nothing to be done about it, he tried to tell himself. If the Klaernar had his likeness, Kalasgarde was the safest place for him in all the kingdom. And she . . . she was Eisa Volsik. The moment he'd realized, some part of him had known: If this wasn't the hand of the gods at play, Rey did not know what was. How else could she have climbed into *his* of all the wagons? How else, after seventeen years, could they have been brought back together?

She was bigger than Istré, bigger than the Bloodaxe Crew. Gods, she was bigger than him. Eisa was his fate—was the fate of his people.

Long had the Uppreisna toiled in the shadows—long had they satiated themselves on small-scrap victories. Though he was proud of what he'd accomplished, Rey knew he and the rebels had been nothing more than a small annoyance to the king—gnats buzzing around his head. But with a Volsik alongside them, so much more could be accomplished—they'd be able to quell the infighting in the north and unite under a single banner. And with numbers like that, they could do more than aggravate. They could make a difference.

She could be *everything*.

Rey frowned at that thought. She did not wish for that role. He could see it in her eyes whenever he dared broach the subject. *Time,* he thought. *She needs time.* She'd nearly died in Kopa. She had weathered so much. And Rey could not bear the thought of pushing more on her, not after everything she'd been through.

The door of Harpa's home flew open, and the two women appeared. Even in the dim light of the home, Rey could see frustration etched into their faces. To be fair, it was not an unusual expression to see on Harpa. But Silla—his heart sank at what he saw. Irritation. Anger.

Rey's fist clenched around his rag. He wanted to drag her out of here. Bring her somewhere beautiful and make her smile. But he knew she wanted to get stronger—to master her galdur. Which meant Rey would have to let her fight this battle on her own.

Their eyes met as she stomped the snow from her boots, and Rey couldn't help but recall their sparring session this morning. His skin had heated with each small touch, his heart thundering as her back had brushed against his chest. By the end of their session, he'd been so worked up, he'd needed to douse himself in the stream's frigid waters.

Trouble. This was naught but trouble. He'd been counting the days until he'd freed himself from her pull, and now here he was, sharing a gods damned shield-home with her. Her draw was as strong as ever. Worse, she wasn't afraid of him. Rey needed to distance himself from her. Needed to fortify his defenses.

Silla flopped onto the bench set before the hearthfire, staring into the flames. Harpa busied herself preparing the kettle and cauldron. Soon, the scent of róa bark and cooked food filled the small cabin. After a bowl of mutton stew, Rey set back to his scrubbing and tried not to listen to his grandmother. It was not long before he understood the problem.

"We will work first on clearing your mind. Do not think of the heart of your magic. Do not think of your galdur. Focus on stilling your mind. On pushing all thought from it."

Silla's lips pressed into a line as she nodded curtly. Closing her eyes, she shook out her body, but Rey saw the tension lingering in the tendons of her neck, in the way she clenched then unclenched her hands.

After fifteen minutes of bearing witness to this torture, Rey slipped out the door. It would not be pretty, and he suspected his presence would only worsen the situation. Harpa was stern and relentless, yet her methods were effective. Rey had grown to be one of the most powerful Galdra in the kingdom—his control impeccable, his strength built up over years upon years of practice.

Harpa's voice could be heard outdoors, barking commands to Silla.

"Clear your mind."

"Relax."

"Focus."

Over and over, she repeated them, making Rey's insides twist. He channeled his irritation into chopping wood.

Vig's worries floated to the forefront of Rey's mind. Livestock vanished, wool and a strange smell the only remnants. And Váli, lost somewhere in the wilds.

The small detail of the decaying scent brought to mind the skógungar and wolfspiders that had attacked them along the Road of Bones. He'd forgotten all about them in the aftermath of Kopa. But now Rey found himself pondering the unnatural smell of them and those eyes, red like burning coals. Could something be amiss in Kalasgarde as well? Was it all connected?

Rey had been quick to dismiss Vig's fears, but with each swing of the axe, the gnawing feeling only grew. Hours this went on as the sun sank ever lower from its pinnacle in the sky. Rey split log after log until his back screamed and at least a year's worth of firewood was chopped.

By the time he'd stacked the last log in Harpa's decrepit shed, his mind was made up. The knowing feeling inside him told Rey it warranted a look. And so he would ask Vig to take him to the pasture where the sheep had vanished. In the very best case, assessing the site would quell his worries. And at worst? Well. Rey could not consider that yet.

Dusting his hands, he assessed the clearing. The sun was low, casting long shadows. It was time to return to the shield-home.

On the ride down the mountain, Silla was silent, her misery so potent that it seemed to bleed into the air. A dozen times, Rey opened his mouth to speak but could not find the words. She could not clear her mind, that much was evident. This, he knew, was the trouble with older students. While Rey couldn't help her with this, he could provide a diversion.

"Do you want to spar?" Rey cast a look over his shoulder. Her head had perked up, a glimmer back in her eyes. He found his lips twitching. "After the evening meal. I'll run you through a new routine. See how badly you can slaughter it."

And if Rey's blood heated at the prospect of another evening spent torturously near to her, he refused to acknowledge it.

CHAPTER 23

Sunnavík

The morning after her meeting with Ana, Saga sat in the great hall, prodding her daymeal with a spoon as she pondered her options. It was quieter than usual in the hall, the king and his retinue having ventured south of the city to tour the Zagadkians through timber camps and iron-rich bogs. There was also the fact that Lady Geira was still abed. Despite the silence, Saga could not decide where to start in her quest to uncover the identity of Signe's liason with the Klaernar.

It had to be someone who had access. Someone who did not fear Ivar Ironheart. This person would have to be bold . . . or perhaps stupid. Punishment for such a thing would undoubtedly be a long, painful death. And should the king discover his wife had commandeered his army for her own purposes, even she would not be beyond the king's wrath.

"Magnus has been pushing your father toward a betrothal to the Karthian prince again, darling," Signe said, disrupting Saga's thoughts.

Yrsa blanched. "What about Leif?"

Leif, Saga remembered, was a Norvalander cousin, one whom Signe had been pushing as a suitor for Yrsa. But Magnus wanted to use the princess to forge connections and to keep an eye on Karthia's inner courts. Like Saga, Yrsa had no say in whom she wed. But unlike Saga, Yrsa would not know her future husband before wedding him. A fierce wave of empathy filled her at the thought.

"Don't fret, my sweet girl," Signe said with a sigh. "I shall find a way to convince your father that Norvaland is the far safer option for his only daughter."

Yrsa looked as though she wished to say something but brought her cup of róa to her lips instead.

"What is it?" asked Signe. "Come, darling, with your father gone, you can speak freely."

Yrsa toyed with the cuff of her dress. "What of Zagadka?"

Signe's bondswomen tittered in agreement, bringing a pink flush to Yrsa's cheeks. But the queen set her spoon down.

"It's only—" Yrsa looked flustered now. "I've been speaking to them and thought perhaps—"

"Darling, no." Signe's voice was calm, but firm. "Have you not heard of their barbaric customs? I say this woman-to-woman, and I trust word will not spread from this table." Signe shot a stern glance at each person seated before turning back to Yrsa. "It is a brutal, backward kingdom, Yrsa, unfit for a gentle soul like yours. The high prince is an old, senile man. And his beastly heir renowned for his fits of anger? No. I could bear not to see you wed to a man like that."

Yrsa looked down at her plate.

"Besides," continued the queen, "they've not allowed a foreigner on their soil in hundreds of years. This treaty shall be a step forward, but I doubt they'd be ready for such a leap."

A tense silence filled the air but was soon broken as little Hávar rushed into the room and settled on his mother's lap. Usually he dined with his nursemaids, but with Ivar and his retinue gone, it seemed he would join them for the daymeal. The youngest of Signe's brood, Hávar was two years old, all plump pink cheeks, bright-blue eyes, and adorable smiles. Saga would never call herself fond of children, but Hávar . . . he was all right.

The queen was patient as her youngest selected a juicy blueberry and pushed it rather roughly into her mouth. Signe's smiles, reserved only for her children, made it easy to forget that she was hunting Saga's sister.

As she picked at her daymeal, Saga decided that the most likely candidate for Signe's liaison was someone of high rank in the

Klaernar—a kaptein or perhaps a kommandor. And as the queen departed the room, Hávar clinging to her shoulder, Saga decided to visit the room of records.

She spouted a story to the Keeper of the Records—that she was compiling records into a book celebrating King Ivar's "militaristic accomplishments," which she'd gift him at the feast of Ursir's Slumber. At the promise of inclusion as coauthor, the Keeper was eager to share the records and had agreed not to let word of her research reach the royals. After scouting a path through the old defensive walls, Saga stashed bundles of documents that she then secreted to her chambers bit by bit.

For the first several hours, she scoured the Klaernar's incomes and expenditures for evidence of bribery, but she quickly got lost in lists of fines. As she moved past Flóki Gundarsson, fined twenty sólas for drunkenly entering the wrong home and urinating in the hearthfire, and on to Ása Ingolfsson, fined five sólas for calling her neighbor a *lazy hóra,* Saga questioned if her efforts would be fruitful.

Moving on to expenditures was a test of her will. Many expenses were, in Saga's opinion, wildly irresponsible. Five hundred sterling silver rings with hollow cavities to house doses of berskium powder. Dozens of goats purchased for sacrifice to the Bear God. Casks upon casks of ale ordered to "build harmony among the soldiers." All this excess while the people of Íseldur went hungry.

Saga's eyes rolled so many times, it surprised her they weren't stuck in her skull.

The scrolls were maddening, and her task was feeling more impossible by the hour. Thousands of transactions had been recorded. The search for a single misplaced expenditure among them was daunting.

By the time she found herself reading the same line of text for the fifth consecutive time, Saga relented to rest. She stashed the documents in her trunk. Blew out the candles. Collapsed in her bed. And was asleep in a matter of seconds.

Saga dreamed of a man straddling her chest, one hand wrapped around her throat. She fought for her life. Tried in vain to push him off her, but he was too heavy. Too strong.

"Punished," he growled, slapping her hard. "You deserve to be punished."

Somehow, she got free. Reached for a statue. Crushed the man's skull.

She woke with cold sweat slicked on her brow. Heart thundering, she tried for deep, calming breaths. "Not real," she told herself, trying to push the panic from her body. But it had felt *so real,* that man's grip lingering at her throat . . .

"Killed him," Saga told herself. "You killed him—"

The idea coalesced like clouds around a mountain peak. The expenditures seemed endless, a search for a single feather among a flock of birds. What if, instead of bribery, she searched for Klaernar deaths? More specifically, those who had risen to fill vacant spots.

Her body pleaded for sleep, but Saga threw back the covers and marched to her trunk. She was still poring over the records two hours later, when Sunnvald began His Rise.

CHAPTER 24

Kopa

Jonas strode along the black cobbled streets of Kopa, hands dug deep in the pockets of his cloak. People bustled about with irritating cheer, going about their day as though nothing were amiss. As though their lives had not been smashed to bits. Jonas's gaze trailed above the spires and rooftops, past the tangled towers of Ashfall Fortress, to the fire mountain they called Brími.

It loomed over the city, green and treeless, a dusting of snow at the top of the dome. Jonas knew he could thank Brími for the warm baths he'd come to enjoy, that the heat from underground made Kopa a pleasant place to live during Íseldur's harsh winters. Long had it been dormant, yet there was still a hint of menace from the volcano—the ever-present thought that the past could be made present easily enough.

Do you ever think that perhaps our past is not our future?

Jonas jolted at his brother's remembered words. Chest tightening, he forced himself to breathe. Forced himself to keep walking. Memories like this speared through him a dozen times a day, grief's piercing pain never seeming to dull.

As he rounded the corner, the mead hall came into view. Jonas blew out a long breath, striding toward it. He was running out of halls to visit in this black city—he'd been kicked out of nearly ten now, for brawling. Some might call him an undisciplined warrior, a bringer of trouble. The fact was fighting was the only time Jonas wasn't thinking of everything he'd lost.

Reaching the mead hall's door, Jonas paused.

Rey's *axe eyes* glowered at him from a birch plank nailed to the door. The burn in his stomach ignited at once under the judgment of those eyes. *Betrayer,* they seemed to say. *Deceiver.*

But Jonas's gaze strayed lower, reading the letters scrawled beneath Rey's likeness.

REWARD FOR INFORMATION ABOUT THIS MAN. SEEK KAPTEIN ULFAR, EASTERN GARRISON HALL.

Some unshakable part of Jonas, still Bloodaxe Crew to the core, smiled at that. It seemed the Klaernar'd had no luck in capturing his former brother-in-arms and were now changing tactics.

With the hint of a smile, he pushed into the hall.

Lit by a pair of hearths and a large iron chandelier, the mead hall was busy with a late-afternoon crowd. Jonas was proud of himself for not rolling his eyes at the establishment's choice in decor. As if two full-sized taxidermied bears weren't enough, Ursir was everywhere he looked. Jonas scowled at a tapestry—depicting the Bear God's great battle with the Moonwolf—while ignoring all the tattooed faces looking his way.

Jonas sighed. He should have guessed the mead hall closest to the garrison hall would be a haunt for all the Klaernar in this godsforsaken city.

He spotted a space at the long table and slid onto the bench. A barmaid quickly found him and set down a horn of ale. Jonas took a long draught, gaze unfocused. Seeing Rey's likeness left him feeling unsteady, making Jonas's thoughts drift to better days. As the weeks passed, his grief for Ilías had melded with a new sort of sorrow. Jonas had lost not only his brother but also the people who were as good as kin. He missed the Bloodaxe Crew more than he'd imagined—missed the camaraderie and banter. Missed knowing that someone had his back, no matter what. He considered how restless he'd grown in recent years, how he'd been ready to move on. But now Jonas questioned the rationale of such thoughts. Had it really been so bad, sleeping on the hard earth, traveling about the kingdom?

If this was the alternative, the answer was no.

Jonas felt unmoored, utterly lost. The rage he'd felt in the aftermath of Silla's escape had cooled, grief settling heavily in his chest. And with it, the guilt. Jonas didn't feel an ounce of regret for handing *her* over—she'd deserved it and so much worse. But he'd left his Bloodaxe brothers and sisters without so much as a goodbye. It had been a selfish thing to do, a thing Ilías would have despised. And slowly, his guilt was eating him away.

For all his life, Jonas's goals had been clear, sharp things. But now, he lived in a state of in-between. He hadn't enough funds to buy back his family's lands, yet the thought of seeking another mercenary crew made his insides twist. Fighting alongside others—without Ilías—was more than Jonas could bear right now.

And as he thought of Gunnar, Hekla, and Sigrún in Istré, his spirits sank lower. Would the job proceed without him and Ilías? Without Rey as their leader? He should be fighting alongside them, helping them rid Istré of its deadly problems.

Jonas took another long draught of ale, trying to drown his guilt.

Laughter down the long table caught his attention, and despite Jonas's desire to wallow in his misery, he found his ears straining toward them.

"Aye, we've had leads, plenty of kuntas trying to sell false information." The speaker appeared to be a Klaernar of rank, based on the bear pelt wrapped around his shoulders.

"How can you tell it's false?" asked his comrade.

"We've withheld some details of the pair. When the deceivers don't have the right answers, we know it's false tales they peddle."

"Are you not concerned, Ulfar?" asked his comrade. "The more time that passes, the harder they'll be to find."

"All we know is Svangormr Pass," grumbled the kaptein, his sigil ring catching the light as his fingers drummed on the table. "But it's been too long. Damned warband should've found them. Vanished into the Nordur wilds, it seems."

Kalasgarde, thought Jonas bitterly. Rey had mentioned his tiny hometown in passing during one of the countless nights they'd spent drinking brennsa around the fire. Though Rey had never expressed a desire to return to Kalasgarde, it didn't seem outrageous to think he'd have allies there.

Stop, he admonished himself, his guilt smoldering. It was none of Jonas's business. Yet he couldn't help but think . . . if he listened in on these Klaernar, perhaps he could, somehow, help his Crew leader. Feed Rey information to keep him safe.

No. That meant helping *her.* Anger burned his guilt away, and he drained his horn in a few quick gulps.

"Any news on the hindrium?" asked one of the Klaernar down the table.

"Should be soon," replied Ulfar. "When it's ready, it might change the game, lads."

"Galdra kuntas won't know what hit 'em," said his comrade.

The barmaid was back, handing a fresh horn of ale to Jonas.

"How long has the warband been searching for the Slátrari?" asked one of the Klaernar.

"Must be a week, perhaps two. Don't understand it. We pointed them right there."

Kalasgarde, thought Jonas, his brow twitching.

"Someone must know him."

Ulfar growled. "Aye. *Someone* in this kingdom knows something."

Kalasgarde! Jonas's mind screamed. He threw back his ale, swallowing it with several large gulps.

"Maybe they're waiting for a larger reward."

"Truth is," said the kaptein, his voice lowering, "the Black Cloak would pay a right fortune. He wants 'em. Both of 'em. And his patience wears thin."

Kalasgarde, Kalasgarde, Kalasgarde, chanted his mind, in time with his thundering pulse. Another horn was placed before him. Jonas drained it before the word could break free.

Reward, hissed the voice, dark and deep within him. *Easy coin. Restore your family's lands.*

No. He needed to retain some shred of himself, some dignity and honor.

What honor is there in lying to you all these long years? retorted the voice. *He led you into that battle. Is partly to blame for your brother's death.*

Jonas closed his eyes. Took several deep breaths.

Kalasgarde, chanted the voice.

His eyes flew open. Jonas glanced down the bench. The group was just there. One word. One word uttered, and he'd earn some coin . . . coin to put toward buying back his lands. Could put everything behind him and move on with his life.

But Rey. His brother-in-arms. The one person left in this kingdom who knew and respected Jonas. Turning on Rey would be a new low. One he could never come back from.

He pushed to his feet, ale spilling from his horn. He felt the Klaernar watching him. Waiting for him to betray his former brother-in-arms.

Jonas threw coins on the table.

Stumbled from the hall. Pushed into the black stone streets of Kopa. Bending double, he gasped in deep, desperate breaths.

"Kalasgarde," he whispered.

CHAPTER 25

Sunnavík

Saga's charcoal raced across the parchment, smudging along her mother's jawline and into the curve of her chin. After sneaking past guards patrolling the northern wing, she'd stolen into the secret passageway she'd foolishly revealed to Rurik. Now she waited for the Zagadkian to join her so she could give him his map.

Saga glanced at the doorway, irritated. Rurik was late, and with each passing minute, her nerves grew. In part, it was the anticipation of seeing him for the first time since The Incident, as she'd taken to calling it. Saga had told the man he *smelled good* and had proceeded to hand him all the kindling he needed to burn her to the ground...

She cut the thought off before it could grow roots. Suffice it to say, she was not ready for the mortification of seeing Rurik once more. But the map... she owed him the map, and after days spent touring the timber mills and bogs just south of Sunnavík, he was finally back in Askaborg.

Saga had been so busy poring through the Klaernar's records, the days had flown past. After changing tactics, it hadn't taken long to find the first suspect's name. A year ago, a Reykfjord kommandor had been thrown from his horse, suffering a fatal head wound. A kaptein by the name of Thord had been quickly installed in his place. Saga had diligently recorded the man's name as one to investigate.

In Midfjord, not three months later, Kommandor Bjarki replaced the old kommandor, who'd died in his sleep. A weak heart, the records noted. And then there was Svaldrin's kommandor, who'd held his position for a decade and a half until he'd succumbed to an undisclosed illness. A man named Hilja had replaced him.

Saga now had three names, three kommandors who, at the very least, warranted investigation. She was dying to speak to Ana and had ventured to the falconry tower half a dozen times. But so far, there had been no sign of the white linen. It was good, Saga assured herself. No letters from the queen—or Alfson and Lady Geira—meant Signe had not yet discovered the results of Saga's tampering. It meant Eisa had more time.

As her charcoal danced along the parchment, Saga became a clear, glassy pond on a calm day. Drawing always had this effect, allowing her to escape without the need to set foot outdoors.

Pausing, she examined her work in the guttering torchlight. Svalla Volsik stared up at her, but something was not quite right. Was it her nose—too narrow, or perhaps too pointed? But then it struck Saga—the scar was missing. Pursing her lips, she made a charcoal slash along the base of her mother's neck, then held her drawing board back in appraisal. Yes. Now it felt complete.

Stone ground against stone, the door grating open. And there he was. As he crouched low to fit his large frame through the doorway, the torchlight cast shadows along the rugged lines of Kassandr Rurik's jaw and in the cleft of his chin. And with that, ripples shattered her waters.

"Beautiful," he murmured, igniting a burn low in her stomach.

He's looking at your drawing, featherhead.

Saga pushed to her feet, pulling the map from her pocket and thrusting it at him. Best to get this over with quickly.

Brows hitching up in amusement, Rurik took the parchment. "You were able to send letter?"

Saga managed a crisp nod. "You have your map. Now I must be on my way." But the passageway was narrow, and Rurik didn't seem inclined to budge.

She met the man's gaze. His eyes were irritatingly bright despite the darkness.

"Again, you are striving to rid yourself of me?"

"Was I being so obvious?"

The man had the audacity to *smile*. Light caught on the curve of his upper lip and in the shallow grooves bracketing his mouth.

"And here I was thinking you liked my company in our last meeting," he replied smoothly. "I thought we might even call each other *friends*."

Her hands curled into fists. Did friends refuse to help each other unless they got something in return?

"I can assure you, Lord Rurik, it was the tonic's doing," Saga replied, staring longingly at the door. "Though I *should* thank you for your assistance and for . . . returning me to my chambers." Gods, but she hated being in this man's debt. Saga forced herself to soldier on. "And let me reassure you, I shan't *ever* take such a tonic again."

"Good," said Rurik. "It was making you reckless." The corner of his lip tipped up. "Is lucky I found you. Proved to be quite useful." He waved the map.

"I'm so glad my misfortune was *useful* to you," she snapped, then pressed her lips shut. But mortification wriggled through her at the thought. He knew she'd tampered with the queen's mail. Knew of her ailment. Knew far too many things.

"And last days when I was gone"—the man's voice had taken on a teasing and far too familiar tone—"were you missing my . . . show in sparring grounds?"

"What do you mean?" she asked, but her voice was too high. Too guilty.

"You liked what you saw, yes?"

Embarrassment flooded her, followed quickly by curiosity. How had he seen her through that crowd of bloodthirsty Klaernar? "I saw nothing to impress me."

"Perhaps you are merely ashamed your countryman cannot best me."

She huffed an irritated breath. "If they cannot see through your tricks, they don't deserve to win."

"Tricks?"

"You bait them. Wear them down with your relentless circling.

Drive them to anger, which makes their attacks emotional and reckless."

A large hand went to Rurik's chin, stroking it in thought. "You are seeing much."

"It's a pity," she continued, unable to help herself. "Had they watched more carefully, they'd have noticed how protective you were of your left side. An obvious vulnerability. What is it?"

Rurik's green eyes took on an alarming glint. "You are seeing *too* much. Can be dangerous thing in this world, Saga." Rurik meandered closer in a move that was casually threatening. "A rib"—he patted his left side—"is healing. And now you know this thing about me, you must share something about you."

Saga took a cautious step back. "That's not how it works. I discovered this about you, purely from observation."

"From *watching* me."

Her cheeks flushed hot, but she stood her ground. "You're doing it to me now," she snapped. "Circling me. Driving me to anger. What do you want from me, Rurik? Do you want me to attack?"

He chuckled softly, stepping closer. "I admit, I enjoy making you squirm."

She blinked twice. "Why?"

"Because is"—he paused—"true. Is *real*. Not pretend like you show to others."

"Well, stop it."

She could hear his smile as he said, "Then I would be needing new ways to make you squirm."

Saga closed her eyes. Let his words seep into her blood, hot and languorous and full of ideas that would get her killed. But then anger ignited low in her stomach. *He* could play games like this without fear of repercussions. Because that was precisely how it went—men paid with a rap on the knuckles, while women paid with their lives.

"Do you say whatever slides through your mind?" Saga seethed, her anger growing hotter. "How could they send *you* to broker the treaty? Are you truly the best that Zagadka has to negotiate?"

"Best from the best," he replied wryly.

"Based on what I've heard come out of your mouth, I struggle to believe that."

Rurik chuckled, his gaze falling to the tenderest part of her throat. "You are not knowing the magic of this mouth."

His words sent a sweet, warm rush pulsing through her body. And for the briefest moment, the thought slipped into her mind: What *would* he do with that mouth?

"I must go," she said dazedly. Good gods. Too many nights spent poring over records must have addled her mind. She needed a good night's sleep to restore her sanity.

"Very well," said Rurik, though the reluctance in his voice told her this conversation wasn't over. As he stepped back, Saga released a long breath. "Word must not reach the others of my involvement," said Rurik, all amusement gone. "I will hold your secret for you, and you, too, will hold mine. Do you agree?"

Saga nodded.

"Good," said Rurik, staring at her. After a long moment, he turned to the door, shoving it open with a quick thrust of his shoulder. As he moved to allow space for Saga to shimmy past him, his lips tugged up in amusement. "Was pleasure, Saga, as always."

"I'd say the same," she huffed, "but we'd both know I was lying."

Behind her, Rurik choked in disbelief, and Saga had a moment of trepidation—had she gone too far? But as the sound shifted to laughter, Saga allowed herself a secret smile.

A fleeting thought entered her mind. Perhaps there was some truth to what he'd said about seeing the real her. Because when this man provoked her, Saga was incapable of keeping her anger tucked away. And based on his laughter, he seemed to enjoy the burn.

Quickly, she pushed the thought aside. And then, with her drawing board tucked under her arm, Saga strode on.

CHAPTER 26

Days later, Saga's heart raced as she prepared to meet Queen Signe for róa in Askaborg's solarium. As she stepped through the doors, Saga looked down, examining her gown for a thread out of place. For an hour or more, she'd been braided and poked and yanked until Árlaug had proclaimed her worthy of meeting a queen.

After days of fruitless scouring of records, she'd leaped at the queen's invitation to join her for róa in the solarium. Not only did it mean doing something besides *reading*, but this one-on-one meeting was also the perfect opportunity to use her Sense on the queen.

Saga hadn't failed to notice that the invitation had been penned by Lady Geira. Distantly, she wondered if Geira still believed her ill health to be Ursir's doing or if she suspected Saga. Though Saga supposed it didn't matter—Geira wouldn't say anything if she thought Saga had a page of her salacious Bear God story.

"The table has been set near the fountain, my lady," said the thrall, holding the door open.

Saga nodded. As she stepped into the solarium, the scent of moonflowers and sweet florals hit her with such force that her feet faltered. She closed her eyes, inhaling deeply as she walked toward the fountain. Like the hearth hall, the solarium was hewn from plain granite, though color throbbed throughout, clambering green offset by bursts of pink and white.

Sunlight filtering through the Galdra-made sky windows warmed Saga's cheeks and, combined with the scent, triggered a fierce wave of nostalgia. Memories bloomed in her like a garden—playing spinning games with her small brown-haired sister and hiding in the foliage with her mother, waiting for those winterwing birds to fly from their cage. The indoor gardens had once been Saga's favorite place in all of Askaborg. But like many corners of the castle, she frequented them rarely these days.

As she rounded a corner on the pathway, the fountain came into view. Saga murmured a silent prayer to Marra as she settled into a chair. Today, she'd need all the wisdom she could get to steer conversation toward the Klaernar. How would she do it? The King's Claws were not exactly a common topic discussed with the queen.

Thankfully, Queen Signe soon arrived, glimmering in an ivory gown and golden jewels. Standing to curtsy, Saga drew a deep breath and unraveled her mental shields.

"Saga," said the queen, taking a seat. "You look gorgeous, darling."

... That shade gives her a sickly complexion, wafted Signe's thoughts. Saga wrangled a smile, despite the desire to sag. An hour of torture, and for what?

"As do you, Your Highness," Saga forced herself to say, sinking into her own chair. As her eyes met the queen's, Saga's stomach lurched. A fading purple bruise covered Signe's left cheekbone.

Signe's lips drew down. "If you have a question, Saga, then voice it."

"I apologize, Your Highness. How did you—"

The queen's glacial eyes sharpened. "I was careless and ran into the wall."

But Saga knew better than to believe it. It wasn't the first time Saga had seen such marks on the queen, nor the first time she saw her future. A loveless marriage. A husband who bedded countless others and used violence to get his way.

"Do not worry for me, child," continued the queen in a demure voice. "I should have paid better attention."

... and I know better than to voice my displeasure aloud, thought Signe, waving to the cupbearer. *What is it Skraeda would say? The rabbit comes easily to the clever wolf who waits...*

The serving thrall scurried forward with a kettle and poured steaming róa into a pair of silver cups. Saga added a spoonful of honey to hers, stirring slowly as the spiced scent filled her senses.

"I thank you for meeting me, Saga," said the queen, setting her own spoon aside and meeting her gaze. "Long have I wished for us to speak honestly with each other."

Saga's heart sped up.

"Mother-to-daughter," said Signe. "Woman-to-woman."

Saga clasped her gloved hands tightly on her lap as new alarming thoughts surfaced. Had Signe discovered the wax sealer's theft? Had word of the tampered letters reached the queen? Saga's heart thudded as the attending thrall placed a trencher of steaming oatcakes with butter and strawberry preserves on the table. The urge to flee to her chambers was high, but she fought against it, reciting the solarium's exits.

"It is a delicate matter, darling," continued the queen. "But one that must be addressed." The queen leaned closer. "We must discuss your womanly duties."

Saga exhaled slowly, staring at the queen. "Womanly duties," she repeated.

A coy smile tilted the queen's lips. "What is expected of you upon marriage to Bjorn."

Gods, Saga thought she could be sick, right here, on this table.

The queen frowned. "Now, don't be so dramatic, Saga." She watched Saga over the rim of her cup as she took a sip. "Things we do not understand can sometimes appear frightening."

Saga opened her mouth to tell the queen she knew more than she ought, thanks to those books from the Southern Continent, but decided against it. She bit into an oatcake with vigor, determined to let this go where it must.

"I'm certain you know what makes a man and a woman different, don't you, Saga?"

Saga nearly choked, managing a nod at Signe.

"When a man appreciates a woman, his . . ." Signe paused, looking down at the table. She picked up the silver teaspoon. "His *spoon* can grow in size."

"It can become a tablespoon?" Saga could not help but inquire, lips beginning to quiver with suppressed laughter.

"For some men," said the queen, "it can even become a serving spoon."

Saga choked on her mouthful of oatcake, washing it down with a gulp of róa.

"And when a woman appreciates a man, her"—Signe's gaze fell back to the table, settling on the jar of honey—"her *honeypot* becomes coated in . . ."

"Honey?" suggested Saga. Her entire face tingled as she tried to maintain a neutral expression.

"Yes, darling," said Signe, a smile curving her lips. "And a man will take a woman into his arms and"—the queen dipped the spoon into the honey—"stir her honeypot with his spoon."

Saga closed her eyes, a strangled sound escaping her throat.

"Now, Saga," said Signe. "It is important to know this is not the only way to please a man. You can also . . ." Signe pulled the spoon out of the honey and began lifting it up.

She wouldn't. Saga's eyes began to water. She couldn't.

But the queen placed the spoon into her mouth, pulling the honey from it with her lips. Her eyes met Saga's as she withdrew the spoon and set it back down. "Do you understand, darling?"

Saga's lips were pressed together so tightly, they were probably white. And at last, she could not help the laughter that burst free, echoing through the solarium and frightening a knot of birds from a tree.

"I know, darling," said Signe, a rare smile on her lips. "It is rather strange. But it is a thing men enjoy."

. . . and a rare source of a woman's power, thought Signe, selecting an oatcake.

"It shall hurt the first time you lay with your husband," continued the queen. "But then it is not so bad. You must simply . . . lie there and let him have his way."

Saga felt her brows draw together. Not so bad? What about the pleasure, the romance, the undying need? Though when Saga considered it, she could never imagine such things with Bjorn, anyway.

"Have you questions for me, Saga?" asked the queen, smearing strawberry preserves on her oatcake.

So very many. Saga desperately tried to wrangle her thoughts. "You were frightened?" she heard herself ask.

"Oh, yes," replied the queen, in a surprising display of vulnerability. "I was terrified when I first lay with Ivar. My entire family had just been slaughtered, and I was handed over to a man I did not know. It was very frightening indeed." The queen leaned forward, her ice-blue eyes suddenly burning. Signe's voice lowered. "But I let no one see my fear, Saga.

"Which brings me to the next thing we must speak of. I see you trying, darling. You've joined my ladies and me for many social engagements and have resumed taking your meals in the great hall. But I fear you've a long way to go before you're fit to be queen."

Klaernar, Saga reminded herself, searching for an opportunity to steer the conversation in that direction.

"In this world," continued the queen, "perception is everything. To have power, you must always project it. Which is why, Saga, you must learn to harden your heart, to put on a mask." The queen paused, looking her dead in the eye. "If you're perceived to be a mouse, the snakes will slither in."

Saga's lungs seemed to stop working at that.

. . . The girl needs to grow teeth and armor if she wants to survive, thought Signe, biting into her oatcake. She chewed slowly, then swallowed.

"When you marry Bjorn, you'll represent him. You'll represent this family, and you *must* display strength. Your husband must feel your support as he sets to raid and conquer his kingdom. And if you do your job well, you'll be rewarded with the crown. It's important, Saga, that your husband feels the full support of his wife."

. . . She'll find out soon enough the truths of being a woman in this world, came Signe's thoughts, and unease slithered in Saga's belly.

"As queen, you shall sacrifice your own wishes for the greater good of your kingdom. Be a good wife, provide heirs, and show the kingdom a unified front, whether or not your heart agrees."

Saga found her gaze drifting to the queen's bruised cheek, pondering her words. It was clear the queen had no love for her husband, that she'd sacrificed much to wear the crown. But Saga reminded herself of the queen's insincerity—behind her words, Signe plotted at things she should not.

"Ours is not a life bound by love, but by duty, Saga," said the queen. "I know Bjorn will be pleased with your womanly efforts. He is a good man. Perhaps you will not have love, but you will have friendship at the least."

... and an enemy in your bed at the worst, thought Signe, biting into her oatcake.

"But surely there is a way to have both. Love and duty together?" The words sprang from Saga's tongue before she could swallow them back.

Signe's gaze snapped to her, and Saga forced herself not to recoil.

... Is the girl dim-witted? came Signe's thoughts as she chewed. *After all I've said, does she still not understand? I've always thought her malleable, but if she cannot grasp the games at play ...*

"No," Signe said after swallowing. "There is not." The queen's face was tranquil and smooth, but beneath her beauty, something burned. "You enjoy those fairy stories from the Southern Continent, Saga, but let me tell you this: They are naught but tales. In our world, the princess does not find true love and live happily ever after. And let me remind you, there are a thousand girls who'd die to take your place." Her voice lowered an octave. "Who would *kill* to take your seat."

The temperature in the room seemed to drop.

... The Urkans love to mix with the royal bloodlines, thought Signe, *but what if an accident were to happen? She could be replaced with someone unbroken, someone easier. Perhaps that Anita with the golden eyes ...*

Pulse throbbing, Saga reminded herself to breathe.

"Do you have a better understanding now, Saga?" asked Signe. Saga felt herself nodding. "You are so fortunate, darling. But I've seen the apprehension in your eyes, and I hope our conversation has smoothed the rough edges over. Bjorn needs a supportive wife. One who'll be *devoted* to him. And now that we are both on the same page, I know you'll do well."

Saga was beyond befuddled. Of all the topics she'd anticipated discussing with Signe, the seduction of her thirteen-year-old son was not one of them.

"It's important for us women to speak frankly about such matters." Signe sipped her róa.

"I'd like to . . ." Saga wasn't sure where she was going with this, only that if she had to sit through the spoon-and-honeypot talk and weather veiled threats, she damned well wasn't leaving without the information she needed. "I'd like to learn about a queen's ruling duties."

Surprise flashed in Signe's eyes as she patted a linen against her lips. "Oh?"

"I've always had a mind for books," Saga prattled on. "I thought I could prepare myself. Perhaps I should . . . study the tributary systems, or Klaernar hierarchy, or—"

"Darling," interrupted Signe. "Let me assure you, neither of those matters will fall into *your* hands." She set her linen down, a secret smile crossing her face.

. . . unless, filtered Signe's thoughts, *you grow a backbone and steal them for yourself.* The secret smile fell, Signe's gaze growing distant. *We ought to have heard from that warband by now. The knowing feeling in my stomach tells me we should send the Black Cloak himself after Eisa—*

Saga's spoon fell from her hand, clattering on her plate. Shaking herself, she retrieved it and stirred her róa frantically. But the thoughts rattled inside her skull. *The Black Cloak.* She'd heard the name before—had *seen* it in Lady Geira's scribed letter. *It would be wise to send the Black Cloak after Clever Tongue.*

It had to be him. Exhilaration filled her. She wasn't sure how she'd missed it before. The queen's liaison to the Klaernar went by the name of the Black Cloak.

"Are you well, Saga?" asked the queen, her ice-blue eyes shining in concern.

. . . She looks as though she's seen a draugur . . .

Saga was nodding frantically. "Yes, my queen," she asserted. "I'm fine. Just a . . . tremor in my hand."

. . . Alfson insists no sign of galdur has ever manifested in Saga, the queen thought, folding her hands on her lap and watching Saga carefully. *But what if his test missed something . . .*

A shiver rolled down Saga's spine as her memory careened back to her meeting with Alfson—his thoughts of testing her for galdur in her adolescence. But Saga's galdur had not manifested until she was sixteen, soon after her menses. She'd been told sixteen was rather late for her woman's tide to flow. Was the same true with her galdur? Regardless, the small smile Signe sent her told Saga she needed to be careful, lest her Sense be exposed.

"You and I are a lot alike, darling," said the queen. "I know what it is to wonder." The queen's voice held the softness usually reserved for her children. "I know what it is to survive while all others have perished."

Signe had been a princess of Norvaland, had witnessed the slaughter of her entire family when Harald the Hard had taken the isle. The parallels between them were too great to ignore, and Saga felt a foreign feeling—pity for Signe. What must the queen have endured when the Urkans invaded her country all those years ago?

. . . Síssel, Gymir, Arvíd, Falki, and Eylín. Sweet Eylín, who should be where I am now, thought the queen, chewing her oatcake in silence.

Saga fought to keep her face neutral, but the five names pierced her heart through. Five children, slaughtered because of their bloodline.

"I'm so sorry, Your Highness."

"Don't be," said Signe, her voice cool and smooth as fresh-fallen snow. "It's been many years now. Of course, it feels impossibly sad in the moment, but time heals all wounds. Ursir has plans for us all, and unfortunately for my siblings, their fate was to perish young."

. . . Had they lived, I never would have been queen, thought Signe, sipping her róa. *Third in line and a girl at that . . .*

"I made the decision to embrace my fate, not to fight it," said Signe aloud. "To love my husband. To take the crown and power granted to me." The queen studied her carefully. "Fighting the current only depletes you of energy, Saga. You must go with the rushing waters."

... and look for opportunities to take what you truly want ...

"Are you certain you're all right, darling?" asked the queen.

"Yes. N-no, Your Highness. I have . . . I've been battling a headache all day," stammered Saga. Exhausted, she reached for her mental shields, weaving them back into place. "You're right. Thinking of the past, fighting the present, it is all quite draining. I thank you for your wisdom. It has been most helpful."

Signe's lips tipped downward. "Yes, darling. Go and rest. And when you wake, think of the future, of what is at stake. And I shall see you at the evening meal. Oh!" Signe reached across the table, her hand encircling Saga's wrist. "Yrsa's birthday feast."

Saga forced herself to look at the queen.

"You and Bjorn should make an entrance at Yrsa's feast, Saga. It will be a wonderful way for you to show your affection for him publicly."

"Yes, Your Highness," said Saga through gritted teeth as the queen released her wrist. "My apologies, but I must lie down. I am feeling a touch dizzy now."

"Yes, of course, Saga. Off with you."

Saga turned and strode from the solarium, the palace thrall stationed at the door hardly able to yank it open in time as she flew past him.

Her feet carried her through the hallways. Despite what she'd told Signe, she did not, in fact, wish to lie down. Instead, Saga was filled with building energy that drove her at a furious pace toward the door to the falconry tower.

And when she reached it, there flew the white linen.

CHAPTER 27

Kalasgarde

The sun had melted the snow from the forest pasture, yet the shredded wool clinging to rocks and brambles gave the space a decidedly wintry look. Bracing himself against a frigid breeze, Rey couldn't keep his mind from drifting to Silla. He hoped her second day with Harpa went better than her first. With a shake of his head, he forced himself to refocus.

"The same," Rey muttered, the gnawing in his stomach only growing. The scent of decay was not altogether unique, but immediately brought to mind the skógungar and wolfspiders they'd clashed with on the Road of Bones. Several weeks it had been since Vig's sheep had gone missing, yet that smell lingered as though it had stained the ground, the air, the trees.

"Hmm?" asked Vig from beside him.

Rey surveyed the space. Typical for Nordur lands, the forest pastures provided protection from the brutal northern elements while allowing livestock to graze lands difficult to cultivate. Tall pine trees were interspersed with wild grasses and shrubs in the pasture, which was at least an hour's ride from Vig's steading.

"How many sheep?" Rey asked.

"Two dozen. They were brought here early summer to fatten until our roundup in a month's time."

Inwardly, Rey cringed. Two dozen sheep would be a tremendous blow to Vig's family, who relied on their milk, meat, and wool to survive the harsh northern winter. And if the chill in the air told Rey anything, it was that they were in for another long winter.

His gaze slid back to the pasture. It climbed to a steep cliffside, fenced for the sheep's protection. White fluff was stuck on rocks and brambles and low-hanging tree branches. But there was no blood. No bodies. Like Váli, the sheep had vanished without a trace.

A curious sensation brushed down his spine—the feeling of being watched. Rey spun in a slow circle, staring into the shadowy forest surrounding the pasture, finding nothing but varying shades of gray.

"The fence is intact," murmured Vig, breaking him from his reverie. "We've examined the entirety. No loose rails, and the gate was secure. Nothing to suggest the sheep squeezed under."

"And your hound?" asked Rey, shaking off the unsettling sensation and striding to the fenced cliffside. A streak of dark blue cut through thick forests below, and he traced the river to the glacial terraces on the adjacent mountain.

"Hounds," answered Vig glumly. "Two of our best. No sign of either, and they're trained to protect the flock."

"No blood," murmured Rey, scratching his beard. "No bodies. Outlaws? Could they have been stolen?"

Vig shook his head. "Should it be outlaws, were the flock brought through the pass—"

"Someone would note two dozen sheep," finished Rey. He wove through the forest until he reached the opposite fence line. Still, that feeling of being watched clung to him. He stared hard into the bushes, looking for any sign of life, but again came up empty. Next, he searched for hoofprints or wool tufts beyond the fence, any scratchings in the posts and rails that might suggest grimwolves. But the forest floor was pristine, the fence weathered but intact.

He glanced at the skies, then to the woods at the base of the pasture. "Does it seem strangely quiet to you, Twig Arms?"

"Strong Arms," snapped Vig. "Now that you mention it . . . there are no birds here."

Rey crossed his arms, scowling.

"Care to fill me in on your thoughts, Galtung?" asked Vig irritably.

"I am wondering," said Rey, "if the birds know something we do not."

Vig's brows drew together, and he cast a nervous look over his shoulder. "The smell? Perhaps it repels them?"

"It could mark a creature's territory," Rey mused. But something caught his attention before he could elaborate. He took off at a quick pace, striding to the highest edge of the fence line.

"Will you tell me what you're thinking, Galtung, or must I learn to read your various scowls?"

But Rey did not answer. His sole focus was on the top corner of the meadow. Heather bushes and shorter wild grasses were interspersed with the pine trees, all except for this one place. As Rey neared, his heart quickened. The plants here were flattened, forming a large, circular shape that was at least six paces across.

Rey's arm shot out, stopping Vig from stepping into the depression. "What?" bristled Vig.

"Something bedded down here," said Rey, crouching. "Long enough to flatten the grass for several weeks afterward." He plucked a piece of grass and brought it to his nose.

Vig picked a blade of grass, sniffed it, and gagged. "Malla's tits, Galtung," he muttered, wiping his mouth with the back of his hand. "Your guts must be forged from steel."

"It's almost as though it needed to rest after gorging on a large feast," said Rey absently. "Or perhaps it was too large to escape the pasture."

"'It'?" asked Vig, surveying the woods nervously. "As in, a *creature*?"

"Perhaps a winged beast too heavy to fly or something that could not leap the fence," Rey said.

"You don't—" Vig cleared his throat. "You don't suppose it could still be here, do you?"

Rey's stomach tightened as he glanced over his shoulder. "They say some creatures like to return to the scene and relive the glory of their kill."

Vig blinked.

Pushing to his feet, Rey stared into the forest beyond the fence.

His fingers slid along the hilt of his longsword, but his gaze snagged on something nearby. "There," he said, striding around the circular impression. "This. What is this?"

"It appears to be a rock, Galtung," said Vig drily.

At first look, one could easily mistake it for a boulder. But Rey knew better. "That, Vig, is shite."

"What is it, then?" asked Vig, obtusely.

"Shite," Rey repeated, toeing it with his boot. "Dung. Feces. Meadow bread. Call it what you want. The beast lay there"—he pointed at the circular patch. "Then produced that"—he pointed at the excrement. "And only then was it able to leave."

Vig's brown eyes narrowed. "It's too small. And where are the sheep bones?"

"You'd be amazed at the digestive abilities of some creatures, Vig," said Rey. "They can use many parts of the animal that we humans cannot. Surely you can use your imagination."

"Bones," repeated Vig, swallowing hard. "You mean to tell me there are creatures that can digest *bones*?" His skin leached of color at Rey's nod. "Hábrók's bollocks. What—how—"

"The answers," said Rey, "will be in the excrement." The hairs on the back of his neck lifted, and Rey glanced again into the forest beyond the pasture. "I do not like the feel of this place, Vig. Let us carry it down and examine it in the shield-home's yard."

Vig spluttered. "The shite? You want to carry the shite—"

"There will be clues buried in it," said Rey, righting himself. He sent Vig a stern look. "Answers to what befell your sheep. And, perhaps, Váli."

At the mention of the missing boy, Vig quickly mastered his emotions. "Very well. Let us get on with it."

Rey'd thankfully had the foresight to drag a sledge up the mountainside. While he'd hoped to have bones or a carcass to examine, it appeared they had dung instead.

"I'll have to burn these clothes," grumbled Vig as they loaded the feces onto the sledge. "And scrub myself with ash and lye."

Rey was well used to dealing with unfortunate smells, and as he glanced over his shoulder once more, he was glad to put distance between himself and this pasture.

"I've been thinking," said Vig as they made their way toward their horses, the sledge sliding across the grass behind them.

"A rare—"

"Yes, Galtung, a rare thing. But the . . . shite. It's too small. If this was done by a winged creature that became too heavy to fly, or even something that might leap over the fence, surely expelling that did not much help it lighten?"

"Hmm," said Rey slowly. "I agree with you, Twig Arms."

"I suppose there's a first time for everything."

Rey ignored him. "The lack of blood and corpses suggests the sheep were devoured whole. 'Tis curious indeed. Perhaps we will glean more answers when we—"

"I, for one, am *not* digging through shite, Galtung."

Rey glowered at him. "You asked for my help. Do you expect me to do everything?"

"Only the parts that involve shite," said Vig smartly.

"The same as always, Vig," said Rey, disapprovingly. "Content to sit by while others dirty their hands."

"And you're the same sour man who turned his back on his kin!"

"Kin," repeated Rey, frost spreading through him. "My kin are dead, Vig."

"Harpa," spat Vig. "You have Harpa."

Rey laughed, a caustic sound. "Harpa cares only for her weavings."

"And Runny?" exclaimed Vig. "What of the twins?" *What of me*, he did not need to say. "No. You cast them aside easily enough in favor of chasing glory."

"Chasing glory," repeated Rey, numbly.

Vig raked his hands through his hair, irritated. "What else would you call it? You left this place, while I . . ." As Vig's voice trailed off, Rey understood.

"This hasn't a thing to do with my leaving," he said slowly. "You are bitter about your own situation."

Vig huffed but did not reply.

"You always were a man of words, not deeds," continued Rey. Vig had prodded his wound, and Rey was eager to hurt him in turn. "In truth, you are content to cower in the north, while good men and women die for our cause."

"Cower?" sputtered Vig. "I have *duties,* Galtung! You would never understand. *I* am the man of the house. I have kin who depend on me, my mother and sister. My brothers—"

Rey's mind clamped down in a futile effort at self-preservation. But memories flooded forth—a stone placed on a burial mound. An owl blinking down at him. Harpa, weaving at her loom, as though nothing had happened. Vig, holding Snorri on his lap. How was it fair that Vig had three brothers *and* a sister, while Rey had nothing. No one.

But it seemed Vig was not done. "I'd rather be happy in the north than live a life of misery in the south."

"What does that mean?" demanded Rey, anger flaring.

"It means you've chosen a cold, bleak life and begrudge that I have not."

Rey trudged on. "Don't concern yourself with my life."

Vig scoffed. "Fine, Galtung, keep your empty, miserable life. Deny yourself the thing you want—"

Rey whirled on him. "Speak plainly, Vig. I haven't time for games."

"I see the way you look at her," Vig pushed. "You can deny it if you want. Or you can have her if only you—"

"Enough!" Rey bellowed so loud the air seemed to shake. Anger rushed through his body, boiling his blood.

Tense silence hung between them as they made their way to the edge of the pasture. Rey wanted to drive his fist into Vig's jaw. Wanted to curse him. Wanted to ride down the mountain on Horse and never set eyes on his former friend again.

But as they reached the forested fence line where the horses grazed, Rey's eyes snagged on the trunk of a tree on the edge of the clearing. Immediately, his anger turned to confusion, then fear.

Carved into the bark was a symbol—a straight line, with two downward slanting arms.

"The protection rune?" asked Vig, breaking the silence.

"No," said Rey. "It is upside down, which means . . ." He cleared his throat. "That is the death rune."

CHAPTER 28

Sunnavík

Saga found herself in Asla Tower early, pacing the floor as she awaited Ana's arrival. She was grateful for the moonlight spilling through the window, as she'd left her torch at the bottom of the stairs so as not to be seen through the tower windows.

Pulse thrumming, she rifled through her satchel to ensure her supplies were all there—fresh parchment, a quill, an inkwell, and, of course, the sealer stamp. After days of waiting, tonight was the night of action, and Saga could barely contain herself. All day she'd found herself wondering what the letter Ana had intercepted might contain—directives for the north? Perhaps an update on Eisa?

The door's iron hinges groaned, making Saga jump in her skin.

"It's only me, Your Majesty," said Ana, sliding through the doorway, a pair of scrolls held in hand.

"Two?" asked Saga eagerly.

Ana nodded, hurrying over. "One addressed to Reykfjord, the other to Svaldrin."

"Svaldrin?" Always, it was Svaldrin. It was becoming increasingly apparent something was afoot in that city.

The pair settled on a patch of floor bathed in moonlight, Saga carefully slicing open the first scroll. As she read in stilted silence, her spirits sank with each word. Svaldrin's letter was a summons to a seamstress requesting her services for the production of a bridal gown. Ana glanced at her, setting the letter wordlessly aside.

Saga busied herself with the second letter, pretending she didn't know who the bride would be. But as she read it, what little hope Saga had grasped slipped through her fingers. The second letter was an invitation for a jarl's family in Reykfjord to attend Princess Yrsa's birthday feast.

Silence filled the room as the pair stared at the letters.

"Well," Ana sighed, "there will be more letters. Sooner or later, we'll find something worthwhile." Saga felt the woman watching her, felt the questions piling up. But Saga did not know Ana well enough to reveal what she was looking for. Eisa's existence was best kept secret, and an absence of news was good.

She gave herself a mental shake, pulling a square of parchment from her bodice. "What do you know of the Black Cloak?"

Ana's brows drew together as she pondered the question. "'Tis a name I do not know."

"I believe it's the name for Signe's liaison," said Saga, handing the list to Ana. "Three kommandors have perished under questionable circumstances, and these men have replaced them. Perhaps one of them is the Black Cloak."

Ana's eyes widened as she unfolded the parchment. "Brilliant, Your Majesty!" Ana read the names, a line forming between her brows. "Thord, we've investigated. Midfjord's kommandor, as well. But Hilja, this is new."

Saga tried to keep her disappointment at bay.

Ana pursed her lips in thought. "It is a start, to be sure. I shall bring this to my foreman."

"Perhaps," said Saga cautiously, "if I knew more details about your . . . concerns, it could help me narrow my search."

Ana's apprehension could be felt in the air, and Saga readied herself to lower her mental barriers. But Ana surprised her by answering her question.

"Galdra have gone missing." Saga met Ana's determined gaze. "Taken for the pillar yet never executed. They vanish from the Klaernar's custody as though they were never there."

"And you believe Queen Signe is involved in this?" At Ana's nod, Saga's mind raced. Missing Galdra. The queen. Svaldrin. Eisa and her Galdra companion. It must all fit together . . . somehow.

"We believe the queen is plotting against her husband."

Saga pondered the statement in silence. It matched what Saga had gleaned from the queen's inner thoughts . . . her ambition to take for herself . . . an enemy in her bed . . .

"Ivar strikes her," murmured Saga.

Ana scowled at that. "In truth, we'd not mind her scheming one bit were it not for our missing kin."

"Kin?"

"Oh, bother this!" exclaimed Ana, pushing to her feet and pacing the confines of the tower room. She turned, leveling Saga with a look of pure fire. "Again, the high chieftains want to protect you, but I'm tired of their rules . . . tired of stepping around the truth. You're a *Volsik*. You ought to be treated like a queen, not a child."

Saga blinked, but Ana was not done. "The group I work with is called the Uppreisna. In the old language, it means 'the Uprising.' We are those who wish for a change in this kingdom."

Saga stared at her. "What do you mean?"

Ana's eyes shone. "I mean . . . there are many in Íseldur who oppose the Usurper. Those whose families he's persecuted without cause. Whose land and titles he's stripped and who he's forced into hiding. We seek justice and a better future for this kingdom."

"Usurper," Saga repeated, stunned at Ana's daring to voice such things.

Ana turned, gaze settling back on Saga. "We've reason to believe the queen is using the Klaernar to steal Galdra for her own purposes. We believe she is building a weapon to seize control of the kingdom."

"A weapon?"

"Or perhaps she's building an army," said Ana. "Truly, we know little of her plans. But it is clear the queen plays at something. Alfson is involved, several Klaernar kommandors—"

"Svaldrin," Saga burst out.

"Your Majesty?"

"Something is afoot in Svaldrin. Patients and testing of some sort. A maester by the name of Lekka. They are . . . dosing them with herbs." She closed her eyes, trying to recall the details. "Alpine catspaw had the most success. And . . . their best *stock* of something was stolen by a person named Skraeda."

"Skraeda," growled Ana. "A traitor." She grew thoughtful. "I do not know what kind of herb would weaponize the Galdra. But I shall send word to the Uppreisna at once. They'll send out our best Shadow Hounds. If our kin are held in Svaldrin, they'll find them."

"Shadow Hounds?"

Ana's lips curved up. "I forget, Your Majesty, you know so little of the Galdra. A Shadow Hound is a type of Galdra able to weave light in various ways. Most often, it helps them blend with the shadows, giving them the gift of stealth."

What Saga wouldn't give for that. "Are there Galdra who can . . ." Saga hesitated, her mind at war. Keeping parts of herself hidden was how she had survived. Yet after years of wondering, Ana was here, filled with tantalizing answers. And after what the woman had just shared, Saga felt bold enough to share her own damning secret.

"Are there Galdra who can read thoughts?" Saga forced out. Her skin felt too hot, too tight, as she waited for Ana's reply.

"Readers," said Ana softly. "Galdra whose gift allows them to read threads of thought. Extremely rare."

Reader. Saga's brows drew together. After all these years, she had the true name for her Sense . . .

"Readers," continued Ana, "belong to the class known as the Mind Galdra. These Galdra are highly intuitive—meaning their gift flows passively, without need for their source, or for Cohesion. After the Cohesion Rite, however, they can exert their will upon the threads."

Saga's gaze snapped to Ana's. "That all sounded like another language."

Ana paused in thought. "Before Cohesion, a Reader can *read* the thoughts. But after Cohesion, a Reader can"—she hesitated—"*write* the thoughts."

"Cohesion?"

"'Tis a Rite that Galdra go through to come into their full power."

Saga swallowed. "And after this Rite, a Reader could *write* thoughts . . . what does this mean?"

Ana's smile turned excited. "It is said a Reader can exert their touch to threads of thought. That they might influence them."

"*Influence* thoughts," repeated Saga. This revelation made her feel like a minnow in a very large pond. There was so much she did not know...

Lost in thought, Saga busied herself with the scrolls. Gathering a sheet of outer parchment, she copied the addresses in Lady Geira's handwriting.

"My foreman has sent word to the Uppreisna's high chieftains," said Ana eagerly. "It's time to stir them from their comfortable halls in the north. We must attempt another rescue."

Saga blinked.

"You should not live among these vile murderers." There was an edge to Ana's voice. "Nor should you be among those who betrayed and deceived the Volsiks."

Saga's chest clenched, emotion threatening to claw forth. She shoved it back, focusing on dripping melted wax over the letter's seam. It pooled, and she counted ten heartbeats before pressing the sealer stamp into the wax.

"I cannot be rescued," Saga finally murmured.

"Surely you can—"

"You watched from the tower while I attempted to cross the courtyard, Ana," snapped Saga. "You saw what happened. My... affliction prevents me from stepping outdoors."

"Then you shall not step outdoors," was Ana's stubborn reply.

Saga was silent, trying unsuccessfully to stamp out the glowing ember of hope. *Dangerous,* she thought. *Heartache.*

"There are herbs," continued Ana, "that, when placed into your drink, will make you fall into a deep slumber."

"And... what? You'd *carry* me from Askaborg?" Saga's hands trembled at the terrifying thought of leaving Askaborg—the only home she'd ever known, with its secret passages known to her alone. The thought of waking in a strange place, surrounded by people she didn't know, made her feel positively ill. How would she know where the exits were, the shadowy places where she might hide?

"There are many ways to bring things in and out of the castle,"

Ana replied. "Parcels are constantly arriving and departing. Perhaps a large trunk . . . a sack of grain . . . a warrior's armor with a face shield. The southern branch of the Uppreisna is based out of Midfjord—a large enough city for us to blend in, yet close enough to Sunnavík to travel to and from swiftly. 'Twould be but a few days' travel to reach it . . ." Ana's voice trailed off as she took in whatever expression was on Saga's face. "We have time to consider it, Your Majesty."

Despite the fear her words drew, Ana's enthusiasm was catching. Saga couldn't keep herself from dreaming. What if she were to leave, to plant her roots in soil less toxic? Would she be able to bloom again? Saga took a tremulous breath, preparing to voice the thing she'd never allowed herself to hope for. It had always felt impossible. Too much to even consider.

"I want to leave," she said, her hand reaching up to clasp a winterwing earring. "But my cage feels safer."

Much to her chagrin, Saga's entire body was now quivering. Ana's hand slid into Saga's gloved palm, squeezing gently. Such tenderness was foreign to Saga. So long she'd lived in this cold place. So long she'd kept her thorny protections in place.

"Think on it," said Ana. "Give yourself time to adjust to the idea. In the meantime, we have other diversions."

"Svaldrin," murmured Saga, breathing deeply.

"Svaldrin," confirmed Ana, picking up the freshly sealed scrolls. She hesitated. "It is possible the Black Cloak's information is too closely guarded to be found in public records." Ana turned her back to Saga. "Bolder action may be required. Keep an eye out for anything that might be kept under lock and key. Cupboards. Drawers. Cabinets."

"How would I ever gain access to these?" Saga asked, despair creeping through her.

"That, I do not know," said Ana, brushing her skirts. "But I'm certain you'll find a way."

Saga nodded. One way or another, she'd figure it out.

"Until our next meeting, Your Majesty," said Ana, sending a weary smile her way.

And with that, she departed Asla Tower, leaving Saga in contemplative silence.

CHAPTER 29

As she descended Asla Tower with her satchel clutched in hand, thoughts chased themselves around in Saga's skull. Missing Galdra. The Black Cloak. An escape plan. But first, locked cabinets. Immediately, the cabinet below Maester Alfson's worktable came to mind. Be it instinct or something else, when Saga had touched the lock, she'd known with such certainty that she *needed* to get into that cabinet. But how would she obtain a key? And besides that, how would she even get into the room with said locked cabinet?

It was too much to think of all at once. She needed a cup of mead. A warm bath. Needed to ease the tension coiling around her spine. *One step in front of the other,* came from the back of her mind. Saga frowned, wondering where such a chipper thought had materialized from.

Reaching the bottom of the spiral staircase, Saga collected her torch from an iron loop on the wall and paused. Asla Tower was located in the remote northern wing, and they were in the dark hours of the night, but she let her Sense stretch out to alert her of nearby patrols.

Silence.

With a deep breath, Saga stepped into the corridor, leaving her mental shields down. Immediately, the hairs on the back of her neck rose. She paused, glancing over her shoulder, but was met with utter darkness.

Rounding the corner, Saga held her torch aloft as she found the tapestry with the mad-eyed berserker. Pulling it aside, she fumbled for the latchstone and shoved her shoulder into the door until it gave way.

"Is strange how this door is missing from your detailed map."

Saga yelped, torch tumbling to the floor. Heart galloping in her chest, she whirled. The torch remained lit, illuminating the bottom half of Kassandr Rurik's face. Saga stared at his cleft chin, covered with the untidy beginnings of a beard. Her gaze trailed up to his mouth, twisted into a look of pure displeasure.

"What are you doing here, Rurik?" she bristled, trying to gather her senses. Gods, but this man was proving meddlesome. And why could she not hear his thoughts? Saga peered at him, concentrating. Her barriers were down, yet she could not hear a thing.

Rurik stepped closer, his piercing green eyes coming into view. Usually the man had a cunning look to him, yet there had always been a playful edge to it. Now all traces of amusement had vanished. And in this light, with shadows pooling beneath his eyes and nose, he had a dangerous look about him.

"I could ask what *you* are doing here, Saga, in deep of night. But I think you again would deceive me."

Saga swallowed, eyes dropping to the map clutched in Rurik's hand. This was one tunnel she'd deliberately left off the map. Though she knew Rurik had seen Ana's note when he'd left it for Saga—*Asla Tower, tomorrow, 20th chime*—that had been days ago. How had he known she'd be here *tonight*?

Saga's gloved hands curled into fists. "Were you *following* me, Rurik?"

Rurik lifted a shoulder in a maddening shrug. "Your face is pulsing."

Fire ignited in her chest and licked up her spine. "You're like a gnat!"

He seemed to puzzle over the word for a moment until a smirk slid into place. "You want for me to bite you? I am not opposed."

Saga let out a shaky breath as her mind's eye showed her the image: his teeth sliding along her skin, dangerous, yet teasing.

Rurik's low chuckle broke her from her reverie. "I see you are not against this, Winterwing. Shall we try it?"

"Someone ought to put a muzzle on you," she muttered, trying to ignore the fact that he'd just called her Winterwing. "Must I remind you, we're *done,* Rurik?" Saga bit out. "You have your map, and I have my . . ." Her voice trailed off as the man stepped nearer. He was tall, impossibly broad, and in that moment, she was overtly aware they were all alone.

"We are not done," Rurik growled, waving the crumpled parchment in the air. "Give to me the complete map." His hair was mussed, day-old scruff was on his jaw, and Saga realized for the first time that Rurik's usual casual refinement was gone. The man was just a little undone.

A prickle ran down her back and settled low in her belly.

"How many tunnels you have left off?" demanded Rurik. Her spine hit the wall as she stared up at him. Backlit by the torch, his silhouette seemed impossibly large. And yet she was not afraid so much as . . . curious.

"What's wrong?" she asked.

"What is wrong is missing tunnels!"

"No," she murmured, watching him. "There is something else."

"There is not," he snapped, green eyes flaring.

Saga frowned, waiting expectantly.

"Winterwing," he said, voice softening a touch. "Always, you are seeing too much."

Saga pressed her lips together, hoping her silence would spur him on.

"I am disappointed to discover your deception."

"It was only fair," she retorted, pushing back against the twinge of guilt. "You made a bargain with me while I was befuddled by that tonic! I'd never have agreed to this had I been clearheaded."

"Why?" he demanded, his anger stirring the air.

Saga stared up at his shadowed face, too flustered for anything but the truth. "Th-the tunnels are my only ally. The only place where I am truly safe in this castle." To her horror, she felt emotion burning up her throat. "You wouldn't understand."

"You are right, I do not."

Shocked at his admission, Saga swallowed.

"But," said Rurik, irritation plain in his voice, "we had agreement, and I have little time left."

Surprised, Saga tried to recall when, precisely, the Zagadkians were leaving Íseldur. Was it this week already? Part of her burned with guilt at having deceived Rurik, but the part of her that needed an exit—that needed somewhere safe—fought with vigor.

"Locks," whispered Saga, the idea settling in the forefront of her mind. Rurik had clearly been sneaking into places he was not meant to be. "Do you know how to pick a lock?"

Rurik watched her with preternatural stillness. "Yes."

"Teach me."

"This does not have smart sound about it," grumbled Rurik. "Queen's letters is one matter, but this . . . what are you doing, Saga?" He ran a large hand through his hair, drawing her attention. Saga fought the urge to reach out and touch it.

She forced her gaze back to his shadowed face. "Tell me what you're searching for, and I'll reveal my secrets."

His low chuckle in the darkness was somehow *more* than a mere sound . . . it was like a living thing, whispering along her skin. "Very well, Winterwing," he rasped. "You keep your secrets, and I keep my own. But how do I trust you will not again deceive me? As I say, in Zagadka, this brings to you great punishment."

"We are not in Zagadka, Rurik."

"Kass," he said in a low growl she felt all the way to her toes.

"We are not in Zagadka, *Kass*," she said tartly. Saga blew out a long breath. "I will add two new tunnels to your map right now as a show of goodwill." She gestured for the parchment crumpled in his fist. Rurik handed it to her, and Saga slid past him to the torch lying on the ground. After sinking down beside it and flattening the map out, she pulled her quill and inkwell out of her satchel.

Rurik hovered above her, studying every flick of her wrist. His presence made it difficult to think, and Saga had to rally all of her focus to place the tunnels correctly on the map. Within a few minutes, Saga had the one behind the berserker tapestry drawn, as well as the passageway hidden in the kitchen's dry storage.

"Kitchens," Rurik scoffed from behind her. "I should have guessed this, *Árlaug*."

Pushing to her feet, Saga looked him in the eye. With the torch on the ground between them, his rough edges seemed only intensified, causing a tremor of exhilaration to rush through her.

"After you teach me to pick a lock," she said, pulse fluttering, "I will complete the map." Saga put a gloved hand on Rurik's forearm, trying to convey trust. "I swear it to you, Kass."

A muscle in his jaw flexed, his eyes intense as he stared at her hand. "Last time, we shook hands for it," he said. "How can I trust in you now? Unless . . ."

"Unless what?"

"I could believe, perhaps, if you partake in Zagadkian tradition." He paused, his lips curving up in a mischievous smile. "A kiss."

Saga's heart must have stopped dead in her chest. "Kiss?" she spluttered. "What has this to do with trust?"

He looked down at her through unfairly thick lashes. "Is . . . how do you call it . . . superstition."

Saga made a sound—half laugh, half wheeze. "Don't tell me you believe such things?"

"Of course. In Zagadka, we take such things *very* seriously."

Saga was not sure how true this statement was. But to her great surprise, she found she didn't much care. Her heart was pounding with the same thrill she'd had while opening the scrolls with Ana. Anticipation. The delight of doing something she ought not to. Each small act of rebellion seemed to power her further. These were choices *she'd* made, and Saga found herself craving more.

"Very well," she said cautiously.

A sound came from deep in Rurik's chest, his green eyes flashing with surprise. It seemed he hadn't expected her acceptance.

"Good," said Rurik, stepping around the torch. Even in the dim light, she could feel the intensity of his gaze roaming her face and settling on her lips.

Saga drew in a shaky breath. It wasn't as though she hadn't considered how those lips would feel against hers, how it might feel to be wrapped in his arms. But the man was so large, and Saga's instincts had her stepping back, away from the torch and into the safety of the shadows. Once. Twice. Her back hit the wall.

"Your heart is beating very fast," said Rurik, his voice a low whisper. He was nothing but an enormous silhouette, blocking out all light.

Darkness—its comfort wrapping around her like a blanket. Safe. Hidden. Exits all around.

"Do not be frightened."

Saga's breath caught as his fingertips landed on her waist and skimmed around to the small of her back. Palm splayed wide, his hold became firm. Rurik's boot edged against her own as his other hand grazed along her jaw.

Eyes falling shut, Saga submitted to the darkness. There were only the rhythmic beats of her heart, the herbal scent of him surrounding her. Only the feel of him, so large and unyielding, yet his hold so tender. He cradled her as though she was something precious—something cherished.

"*Krasavitsa*,*" he said, tilting her jaw up with gentle pressure. "*Dolgo ya zhdal*.†"

Rurik lowered his face to hers, his breath heating her skin. And then their lips brushed against each other. Saga was hot and cold all at once. And for one infinitesimal second, she was lost to this world.

But as soon as it had started, it was over. Rurik drew back, his hands falling away. Saga felt the loss of his touch like an ache.

As her eyes flew open, irritation lashed through her. "That's *it*?"

She could feel his smile in the darkness. "You were expecting more?"

Saga had somehow been reduced to a creature of need. Grabbing him by his jacket, she yanked him back to her, pushing onto the tips of her toes to slide her lips against his. Saga hadn't a clue what she was doing. All she knew was that if this was to be her first kiss, she wanted it to be something worth remembering.

---

*Beautiful.
†I've been waiting for a long time.

"Your fire," he breathed as their lips broke apart and came back together. "It drives me mad."

"No more talking," Saga said, hands skimming along his jaw to hold him to her.

Rurik made a sound of satisfaction from somewhere deep in his throat, sending a thrill spiraling through her, burrowing deep in her belly. Hands sliding around her waist and up her back, Rurik crushed her to him. He was so large, so sturdy, so utterly warm, and Saga molded into him.

All of her sharp parts, the defenses she'd erected over years in this place, were slowly melting away. Her body was growing soft and supple, and Saga realized distantly she was letting go. Not fearing for her safety. Not searching for an exit. Was this what it felt like to just live in the moment? To *feel* with no fear?

"I should be in my room." She gasped in glee as his lips moved to her neck, his stubble driving her mad as it scraped along her sensitive skin.

"Do you wish for me to stop?"

"Don't you dare." Saga's head tilted back, thunking against the wall.

Rurik laughed into her skin, the vibrations making her body throb with need. "Good," he rumbled. "I am not nearly finished."

His lips moved back to hers, teasing them apart, tongue sliding into her mouth. Everything was molten and so loose, so free—her insides were liquid heat, her knees buckling, but Rurik held her pinned in place.

Saga moaned into his mouth, causing Rurik's kisses to grow more urgent, hands roaming over her like he could not get close enough. And Saga arched into his touch with an urgent, needy sound.

The minutes blended together, light dimming as the torch burned lower. There were only the shadows, only *them*, their hot mingling breaths and exploring hands. Rurik's palm cupped her backside, yanking her closer. His rough handling of her made hunger knot tightly in her stomach. And she had the fleeting thought that this man wasn't afraid she would break.

She curved her body against him, feeling the hard ridge pressing into the center of her being. Here, they were at one with the darkness. Here, they were protected. Here, she could be reckless. Could throw everything away for a night of carnal passion. But somewhere, deep within Saga, remained a shred of sense.

She pulled back. "Wait," she panted, her mind spinning. Rurik pressed his forehead to hers, and they remained like this for several silent moments, catching their breaths.

"In case you were wondering," he said at long last, "in Zagadka, would be considered acceptable kiss to confirm deal."

Saga couldn't help it—she laughed. And before long, Rurik was laughing with her. A confusion of want and logic warred within her as she righted herself and met his gaze.

This was easy. *He* was easy.

And as much as she wanted to linger with him, she knew the hour grew late. "I must return to my chambers," she said at last.

"I am this way," nodded Rurik, indicating the opposite direction. He retrieved her torch from the ground and helped her into the passageway behind the berserker tapestry. And after a weighted look, Kassandr Rurik closed the door behind Saga.

Alone again, in her place of safety, Saga allowed herself to smile.

She'd had a moment of freedom. And in that moment, she'd chosen, of all people, *him*.

CHAPTER 30

Kalasgarde

Rey was grateful for the unseasonably cool morning as he pulled apart excrement with a dull blade. He knew all too well how such an activity went beneath the full brunt of a summer sun. But between the lack of heat and the fact that the dung was several weeks old, so far there was very little odor involved.

"Why do I gather this is not your first time doing this, Galtung?" grumbled Vig from beside him.

"It's not," Rey found himself saying. "Be glad it is old and dry."

They'd parted on bad terms the day prior, and Rey had fully expected Vig to abandon him to this unsavory task. But as Vig had ridden through the wards this morning, Rey'd felt both relief and a note of respect. Now a fragile sense of peace hung in the air between the two men, the kind easily shattered with a single ill-placed word.

Whether he wanted to be or not, Rey was distracted, his mind circling back to the words Vig had spoken in anger.

I see the way you look at her. You can deny it if you want. Or you can have her.

Gods, were his thoughts so clearly written for others to see? Rey hoped not, because this morning, as he'd looked at her across the long table, he'd imagined flinging the dishes away and peeling her tunic and breeches off. Of spreading her out and mapping her body with his tongue . . .

He blinked the thought away. She was not meant for a man like him, a man bathed in shadows and blood. Rey had known this long before he knew her true name. But learning Silla was Eisa Volsik had only solidified it. Eisa needed a partner with political power, someone with a noble house and standing. And Rey had more honor than Jonas. He would do what was best for *her*, not take for his own selfish reasons.

Rey forced his attention to the task at hand. Vig crumbled a chunk between his gloved hands, pulling more matted wool and a few bone shards from it and setting them with the rest.

"Between the wool and hooves and bone fragments, it's clear to me this *thing* ate the flock," said Vig. "Must we continue?"

"Yes," Rey asserted, prying a denser layer from the "loaf," as Silla had insisted on calling it.

Vig sighed for at least the tenth time that hour. "'Yes'? Haven't you anything else to say?"

Rey glared at the shite. "I'll tell you when I find it." Truly, it could be any small clue that could break open an investigation. A stone, a seedpod, a shell unique to a specific area. They were looking for . . . *something* in the excrement. His knife rammed into a hard object. As he pried apart the dung, Rey assumed it was another hoof or bone shard. But as he loosened the debris, it quickly became clear this was different from the rest.

"This," said Rey, holding the item between thumb and forefinger. "This is what we're looking for."

Vig squinted at the thing. A handspan long, it curved and tapered to a jagged point. "A . . . fang?" he guessed. "But what could this belong to? It's enormous. Nothing like that roams these parts."

Rey turned the fang this way and that, examining each side. "The fang is hollow," he murmured, thoughts shifting to a job the Bloodaxe Crew had taken in the south of Íseldur. Holt and its infestation . . .

"For the love of the gods!" exclaimed Vig. "I beg you to finish your thought. Fangs, Galtung, focus!"

Rey cast his sharpest *axe eyes* at Vig. "Hollow like a serpent's, you eelhead. Venom flows through the inner part and into their prey."

"Serpent? We've no serpents in the northern wilds." Vig made to rub his brow, then thought better of it.

Rey placed the fang on the table, next to the assortment of bone fragments and wool. "Snakes do not survive in these parts," he said. "Which means the serpent must have been consumed by this creature somewhere south."

Vig looked irritated, and Rey didn't blame him. They'd confirmed the dung belonged to the sheep's killer, but this fang raised only more questions. "So this *thing*," said Vig, "ate a giant serpent in the south, then came to the north and ate an entire flock of sheep. Then the *thing* had a nice little rest before shitting it all out? This is . . . madness."

Rey pried another layer of excrement from the loaf. The fang's discovery had spurred his enthusiasm.

"I cannot believe this," muttered Vig, watching him. "I thought you would bring answers, not raise more questions."

Rey merely ignored him. And after a moment of muttering under his breath, Vig settled down. They'd been sifting through shite for the better part of an hour when Vig finally broke the silence.

"I spoke in anger yesterday, and for that, I should apologize."

Rey turned to his former friend in surprise. Vig watched him uneasily, making Rey grind his jaw. Gods. Must they do this?

"As did I," he forced out.

Vig's gaze slid to the tarp above them then back to Rey. "Runný says the same, you know." Rey waited expectantly. "She thinks it cowardly to sequester ourselves in the north. She wants to take up arms with the Uppreisna, but I've forbidden her to do so."

"I cannot imagine Runný would allow you to forbid her anything."

Vig chuckled. "No. I don't imagine my word will hold her for long." He frowned. "I worry about her. I worry for our kin. There has been so much suffering, and I wish only for peace. Perhaps it is craven of me—"

"It is not craven," Rey asserted. "It is bold to see the life you wish to live and take it." Discomfort slithered through him. Burning fucking stars, he hated speaking of sentiments. But Vig had once been like a brother to him and had answered Rey's summons for help. At the very least, he deserved respect.

"Perhaps there is some truth to what you said as well," said Rey. "Perhaps I do live a bleak life. Perhaps I punish myself for living when he did not."

Vig's sigh was long and heavy. "You are not to blame—"

"I do not wish to speak of it," Rey said sharply. "Let us put our disagreement behind us." He paused, examining the face he'd known so well in his youth. "And let me tell you this one last thing. My leaving had nothing to do with you, Vig, and everything to do with myself."

Rey thought of Vig, surrounded by his kin; he thought of the emptiness that had spread through him when he realized he was all that was left of the Galtung bloodline. Leaving Kalasgarde had been the only thing Rey could do to keep darkness from swallowing him whole—vengeance the only thing to assuage his grief.

"I should have visited or written or . . . something," he muttered.

Vig moved to put his gloved hand on Rey's shoulder. Realizing it was covered in excrement, he thankfully stopped. "You are here now, Galtung," said Vig. "It is all that matters."

Rey felt unburdened at that, a weight he had not been aware of lifting from his shoulders.

"Now," said Vig. "This loaf of shite won't pull itself apart." And with that, they dug back in.

But it wasn't a moment later that Runný burst through the wards. As she tightened the reins, her horse pranced to the side, agitation clear in beast and human alike.

"What is it?" demanded Rey, unease scraping along the back of his neck.

"Ástrid," she said, her face twisting into grief. "Our neighbor. She was mustering their flock, but only the sheep hound returned. She's vanished with a dozen sheep."

Nausea twisted in Rey's gut, his mind at war. He knew he should keep his face hidden about these parts. Should keep a low profile. But how could he stand idly by as people went missing?

"Take me to the paddock," he said.

To say Silla was in a foul mood when Vig arrived to retrieve her from Harpa's was an understatement. Another afternoon spent within the toxic confines of her mind. Another afternoon failing at this task. It was clear even Harpa was tiring of this routine.

"Why do you wish to master your galdur?" the old woman asked after hours of practice.

Silla met Harpa's stern gaze. Forced herself to hold it. "Saga," she replied. "I must grow as strong as Rey so I can save her. And then . . . something good might come from all the bloodshed."

"You cannot move forward if you are stuck in the past," was Harpa's reply. "There are times for fighting, and there are times for surrender. I see the fight in you. Perhaps it is all you've known. But you will not move forward unless you give yourself over. Let go. Surrender."

"Surrender," Silla repeated numbly, trying to understand. But there was only the frustration twisting in her stomach, the fear of the voices that would greet her the moment she tried to find the quiet corner of her mind. Wearily, Silla said, "Very well."

And so, perhaps she'd been dreaming of Rey's surly face riding through the wards for the last hour of her training. And perhaps, when instead it had been Vig, she felt a pang of disappointment. But as Vig informed Silla that another Kalasgardian had vanished, she felt like a fool. People were being taken—were possibly being killed—and she was wallowing in self-pity.

As Vig recounted the hours he and Rey had spent out searching for the missing woman with the rest of Kalasgarde, she forced her spine to straighten. And by the time they arrived at the shield-home and rode through Runný's wards, Silla had pushed her misery deep down inside her. She could not stop thinking of Váli and Ástrid. What had happened to them?

Eager to return to his steading and patrol the fence line, Vig excused himself and departed. With a sigh, Silla dismounted and searched the yard for Rey. She wanted to help, wanted to join in the search. Her feet faltered halfway across the yard.

Rey rounded the corner, naught but a blanket wrapped around his hips. Water droplets glistened in his curls, her eyes tracking one as it slid down his neck. Silla had once called the man a walking mountain, and now she understood she hadn't been wrong. He was broad from his shoulders to his hips, his body carved by years of exertion on the battlefield. Her gaze followed the water droplet as it continued down his chest, but her eyes snagged on the creature etched into his skin.

"A dragon?"

Rey's head jerked up, eyes meeting hers. His grip on the blanket tightened as he came to a halt, and Silla's gaze quickly found her feet. "You're back," said Rey. "How did you fare today?"

Silla found she could not muster a smile, nor could she resist another glance at his tattoo. Membranous wings spread across the planes of Rey's chest, sharp talons poised to lash out. The dragon's mouth yawned wide, spewing midnight-blue flames up Rey's throat and over his shoulder, while its barbed tail snaked down his left arm. The detail was incredible, from the diamond-shaped scales to the spiny protrusions along the dragon's back.

"Another day spent weathering Rykka's insults," she said with forced brightness, whirling away from him.

Silence suggested Rey was choosing his words. "Are you hungry?" he asked at last. "Gyda sent the evening meal for us."

Keeping her back to him, Silla shook her head. "Vig told me about the woman. I want to join the search."

"No," answered Rey, his voice immovable. "You know we must keep our presence hidden. We cannot risk your face being seen."

Frustration gathered in Silla's gut. "And you?" she demanded, her frustration roaring back. "What about your identity?"

"I can take care of myself."

She couldn't clear her mind. Couldn't join in the search for the missing people. Was there anything she *could* do?

"The locals know these parts," continued Rey, as though reading her thoughts. "The mountains are harsh and dangerous, especially after nightfall."

"I suppose you're trying to tell me I'd only be in the way," Silla said bitterly.

Rey let out a long exhale. "If you need to move, then we shall spar. Fetch the practice swords while I dress."

Silla heard the shield-home's door close and tried not to imagine that blanket falling away. She gave herself a mental shake. "Gather your wits," she chided, leading Brown Horse to the stables.

After removing the saddle and retrieving the practice swords, she returned to the yard to find Rey waiting for her. He'd changed into a tunic of charcoal gray, exposing a tendril of tattooed smoke at his nape. Rey lifted a questioning brow and she passed him a sword.

Silla settled into the defensive stance he'd shown her the day before. Rey's dark eyes locked onto hers, his grip on his wooden sword firm. As he lunged at her, her sword lashed out, their wooden blades clunking together.

"Good," murmured Rey, circling her.

Silla whirled, her heart rate kicking up. This time, she attacked, rushing at his left side. He parried her blow with a casual flick of his wrist, sending her sword flying. Gods, they had run through this move in the morning and she'd fared far better. It felt as though her failure with her galdur was bleeding into this, too. Yet Rey said nothing about her sloppiness.

Blowing out an irritated breath, Silla retrieved her sword and charged at him once more. A sidestep had her stumbling over a rock and landing on hands and knees. Still, Rey said nothing.

"Stop it," she growled, pushing to her feet. "Stop being nice to me."

"Will it help you pull your head out of your arse?"

She glared, and Rey's lips twitched up in silent challenge. This was what she needed. For things to go back to how they were on the Road of Bones, before everything got so gods damned complicated.

Silla rushed at him, ducking under his sword, but not low enough.

The wooden blade collided with her shoulder, and she lurched away with a curse. Righting herself, Silla sent Rey a withering glare.

"You'll have to be faster than that, Sunshine," he chided, but it only made a grim smile spread on her face. Her frustration now had an outlet. She pivoted and attacked, raining blow after blow upon Rey.

"You've got spirit tonight," he commented, switching his sword to his left hand and blocking her attacks effortlessly. "Unfortunately, it's come at the expense of your wits." With sudden movement, he caught her with the broad side of his sword, sending her sprawling.

Silla shot to her feet and brushed hair from her face. The man's eyes gleamed with amusement.

"Do you think this funny?" she demanded.

"Not particularly," Rey drawled. "Get your head in line and knock me on my arse."

Gods, but she wanted to send the man flying and wipe the amusement from his face.

"I meant knock me on my arse with your *sword*, Sunshine, not with your eyes." His lips twitched.

Clenching her teeth, Silla swung upward with her wooden blade. Rey blocked it, twisting his wrist and flicking her sword free. He moved far faster than she could react, and before she knew it, she was spun around, the solid strength of him behind her. As his arm locked around her throat, practice blade poised at her cheek, a blast of heat rushed through her.

Rey lowered his head right next to her ear, and despite herself, Silla's eyes fell shut. "Stop telling me what you're going to do," he said in a low voice.

Her eyes flew open at that, elbow driving into his ribs, foot slamming down on his boot. Silla swung loose, grabbing her sword in a swift motion. Pushing the hair out of her eyes, she glared at him.

"I'm not telling you a thing!" she seethed.

"Oh, but you are," said Rey. His gaze meandered from her boots to the top of her head, and all of Silla's blood seemed to flow downward. "Always watch your opponent for cues. If you look closely enough, they'll tell you their plan." He nodded at her. "Your left thigh. You tense the muscle before driving forward. It's your tell." That irritating almost-smile curved his lips.

"You're awfully pleased with yourself," she said tartly. "For besting a beginner."

Rey cocked a brow. "Today's most important lesson: Never let emotion rule you in battle."

"I'm not!" she exclaimed.

His brows rose, and she lost all control. With a cry of rage, she charged at him. Rey's foot hooked out, and the rest was a blur. Before Silla knew what had happened, she was flat on her back, Rey looming above her. She blinked up at the smug look on his face, and anger gathered in her stomach. Her foot kicked out with speed that seemed to catch him off guard. Rey's feet were swept out from beneath him, and, with a shout of surprise, he crashed to the ground.

Silla launched herself on him, pinning his shoulders to the ground and smiling victoriously at the look of disbelief in his eyes. "What was it you told me, Axe Eyes?" she gloated. "Ah yes. *You must learn to react swiftly and without mercy.*"

A small smile curved his lips, and despite herself, Silla's gaze was drawn to them. "You like it when I tell you what to do, Sunshine?" His voice rumbled through her, and she felt it in all the places they touched.

"Well guess what?" With a ruthless burst of speed, he flipped her onto her back, pinning her to the ground with his hips. "I like telling you what to do."

A rough breath gusted out of her as she tried to comprehend what had just happened. With his elbows braced on either side of her head, his face was inches from hers. How easy it would be to reach out and slide her fingers into the coarse bristles of his beard. To pull his lips to hers and channel her frustration in an entirely different way.

But Silla had vowed Rey would not be another distraction from her troubles. And he was right—her emotions had gotten the best of her tonight.

"Are you done?" Rey asked, his voice cold and merciless.

Silla drew in a deep breath. "I'm done," she whispered.

Rey's throat bobbed, and for a moment, she thought he had something more to say. But he rolled off her, raking both hands through his hair. Pushing to his feet, he loomed above her. "I'll heat the evening meal."

And with that, he stalked into the shield-home, leaving Silla lying in the grass, trying to calm her racing heart.

CHAPTER 31

Sunnavík

S aga's fingers tapped against the stone wall as she waited in the hidden passageway for Rurik to teach her how to pick a lock. The hairs on the back of her neck stood on end as she heard the heavy footfalls of patrol guards strolling past the tunnel's entryway. But soon they'd retreated, leaving Saga listening to the creak of timber beams and the scuttling of small, unseen creatures.

After the day she'd had, Saga was eager to meet Rurik. Not only had she been forced to listen to a skaldic rendition of the Urkans storming Askaborg, but Signe had taken the opportunity to present her with a bridal veil.

"I wore this," the queen had said, "when I wed Ivar, uniting the Urkan and Norvalander lines. And so it seems fitting that you shall wear it when you wed Bjorn, weaving Íseldur and Urka together for good."

With the eyes of Sunnavík's nobility upon her, Saga had accepted the veil with all the grace she could muster. The wedding loomed like an impending storm, blowing ever nearer. But Saga forced her mind to the task at hand. If she wanted to get into Alfson's locked cabinet, she'd need to learn how to pick a lock.

And of course Rurik was late, leading Saga to question her good sense for the thousandth time. The mystery of what the man sought in Askaborg's tunnels nagged at her. Was it a weapon? Jewels? A book, perhaps?

For the dozenth time she questioned involving the man in her schemes. But they'd struck a bargain, and there was no going back. At the very thought of how they'd sealed this deal, heat unfurled in the pit of Saga's stomach. Last night the man had invaded her dreams, and today, her thoughts, and Saga decided it was a very good thing he would soon depart Íseldur.

The door shoved open, slamming into the wall with a loud bang. Saga cried out, hand flying to her chest.

"Dreaming on your feet?" asked Rurik, filling the doorway with his large silhouette.

She scowled. "Dreaming of pushing you off a tower."

"Ah, but then you would be needing to walk outside, would you not, Saga?"

Her teeth ground together as she searched for a reply, but before she could find one, a second figure appeared. Yuri Rovgolod stepped into the passageway, a look of pure displeasure etched into his face.

"Rov," she said, hand flying to her chest. "What are you doing here?" Saga's stomach twisted at the realization—yet another person now knew of the passageway, and, she suspected, the purpose of this meeting. This was . . . not ideal. She sent Rurik a panicked look.

At least the man had the good sense to look irritated. "He discovered my late return last night." He sighed, running a hand through his wavy hair. "This man is too good at pulling truths from me."

"I pulled nothing from you, *nochnoy vor*.* The truth was written all over your face."

Saga felt her own face flush. Not good. This was not good at all.

Rov turned his dazzling smile on Saga. "Is pleasure to see you, my lady." His smile dimmed slightly as he glanced at Rurik. "I am . . . how do you say it . . . *chaperone*."

"He is not trusting me," grumbled Rurik.

"Is reason for that. I know you well, Rurik. And so I am here as . . . nursemaid. To force impetuous man to behave and not start a war."

Rurik muttered something in Zagadkian, causing Rov to release

---

*Night thief.

an exasperated sigh. "He has sworn an oath to me," said Rurik, turning to Saga. "I promise you, Lady Saga. He will not speak of this to anyone."

The knot in Saga's gut eased just a touch. "Ravine Tower," she said, eager to move on. "It's locked. In the western wing. This way."

Rurik sidled up beside her and placed her gloved hand on his forearm, as though strolling like this down an abandoned corridor was completely natural.

"*Ty ispytyvayesh' moyu volyu*,*" muttered Rov from behind them.

"Which sights will you show to me today?" Rurik asked genially, ignoring his countryman.

"On your left, there is stone," said Saga. "On your right, more crumbling stone."

"It is far to Ravine Tower?"

"Five, perhaps ten minutes." Saga tried to ignore the feel of his large, warm body beside her—tried to shake the memory of that body pressing her into a wall.

"Let us play a game while we are walking," said Rurik, a smile in his voice.

"A game?"

"Game of smacking some sense into your head," muttered Rov.

Rurik ignored him. "Is game of discoveries. I will tell you a thing I have discovered, then you do the same."

Saga pressed her lips together in thought.

"As fine upstanding gentleman—"

Rov and Saga snorted at the same time. She glanced over her shoulder and they exchanged looks of agreement.

"I am choosing to ignore that, my lady," Rurik said jovially. "And you, my boot polisher." He glared over his shoulder at Rov. "As I am saying, I will go first so that you might learn. I have discovered I do not care for famous Íseldurian oat pies."

"Oat*cakes*," Saga corrected before she could stop herself. "How could you say this? Our oatcakes are *renowned*!"

---

*You are testing my will.

Rov made a dismissive sound. "Is 'oat-stone' other name for oatcake?"

Saga huffed indignantly.

"Hard like rock and having no taste," said Rurik. "Someday, you will taste the *blini* of Zagadka. Then you will know."

More incoherent mutterings came from behind them.

"Ignore him," said Rurik. "Is past his bedtime."

Saga smothered a smile. "I thought Zagadka's lands were closed to foreigners."

A muscle in Rurik's jaw feathered. "Is true. For now."

Saga raised a brow.

He sighed. "Like oatcake, the older generation in Zagadka is also like stone—unmoving in their beliefs."

Rov grunted his agreement.

"Zagadkian elders are fools," continued Rurik. "They think secrecy keeps peace and safety in the realm. They are comfortable and lazy . . . no. Is wrong word." He paused in thought.

"Complacent," offered Rov.

"*Complacent,*" repeated Rurik. "Younger generation is eager for change—to modernize, to gain allies and learn from them."

"Is that why you've come to Íseldur?" asked Saga. "I know you're searching for something. What is it?"

Rov barked a rapid flurry from behind them, but Rurik merely chuckled. "I must be guarding my mouth around you, Saga." He leveled that green gaze at her, causing prickles to dance across her skin. "You will try to charm my disobedient tongue."

Mention of his tongue made a flush creep up her neck. "Is your turn, Winterwing."

"Troublesome man," muttered Rov.

Rurik sent a sharp glare over his shoulder. "I believe chaperone is meant to be silent." At Rov's low growl, Saga couldn't help but snicker.

"I've discovered that even when life seems like a straight road, there is always the chance of unexpected twists." Being in this passageway with two Zagadkian dignitaries in the arse end of the night was certainly something Saga could never have predicted.

She felt Rurik's keen gaze on her skin, as though he noted each minute movement. "You are not alone in this."

"Oh?" asked Saga. "I suppose you thought Íseldur would be filled with bear-worshipping warriors and meek women? Are we not what you expected?"

"Not at all."

She knew he spoke of the *kingdom*, but a shiver ran down her spine all the same. They reached the end of the passageway, climbed a set of stairs, and crept into the western wing through a concealed doorway. After another minute, they stood before an iron-hinged door.

"The Ravine Tower," she whispered. After releasing her arm, Rurik tugged on the handle, but it did not budge. Saga watched in mild amusement as he pressed his ear to the wood. The man worked quickly, drawing two sharp instruments from his pocket and inserting them into the keyhole. With a few deft twists of his fingers, he had the door open.

"And now," said Rurik, pulling her through the door. Reluctantly, he held it for Rov. "I will show you how to do it."

Rov settled on the ground with a grumble, his back leaned against the wall. "I give him five minutes," Rurik said with a sly smile, "before old man is fast asleep."

Saga shook her head. "Are you ever serious?"

"There are some things I will never joke about." His look grew intense, eyes gleaming in the torchlight, before Rurik turned to the door. "Now we will begin."

And as Kassandr Rurik showed her how to pick a lock, Saga decided that there were indeed many twists in her seemingly straight road.

"Rotate bolt," repeated Rurik.

"I am!" hissed Saga, throwing the lockpicks on the floor in a rage. Rov snorted, his head lolling to the side as he settled back into sleep. An hour now, she'd been at this, an hour without success. And all Rurik had to say was *rotate bolt,* over and over, as if saying it for the thousandth time would suddenly work.

"*Tvoy gnev prekrasen,**" he murmured, bending to gather the lockpicks.

"*Tvoy gnev prekrasen!*" snapped Saga, hopeful it was the most heinous of insults she'd flung back at him.

He chuckled, straightening. "You do not want to be saying that to me, Winterwing." Rurik paused. "You are saying this quite well. Are you certain you do not know Zagadkian?"

She blew out an irritated breath. "I have an aptitude for languages," she said. "But apparently not for locks."

"Is easy."

She opened her mouth to retort, but the words dried up on her tongue as the warmth of his body spread along her back, the strength of his arms sliding along hers. Gently, Rurik placed the lockpicks into her hands, his large palms settling on the backs of her gloves.

His voice was close to her ear, low and soft. "Slide it through keyhole, finding notch in the bolt." Rurik's hand pressed down over hers, and Saga was so distracted by the unyielding pressure of his chest against her back that she nearly forgot to pay attention. But she felt it then as the lockpick sank into a depression in the bolt.

"Now," whispered Rurik, "we push just here"—the pressure of his hand increased—"and rotate like so." His hand twisted hers, the bolt rotating with a scratch, then falling with a thud.

A breath gusted out of her. "You make it seem easy."

"With practice, is easy." He stepped back, and she missed his warmth already. Swallowing, Saga tried to force coherent thoughts into her mind. She glanced at Rov, leaned against the wall with his head tilted at an ungodly angle, drool gleaming at the corner of his mouth. As Rurik had predicted, the man hadn't lasted five minutes. And Saga was beginning to feel fatigue creep up on her as well.

"My hands have begun to ache," she said softly. Turning, she looked up at Rurik. "I suppose I should not expect miracles."

---

*Your anger is beautiful.

He looked down at her expectantly, and Saga's hand found the completed map in her pocket. Some part of her didn't want to hand it over—once he had it, what need had he for her? But she had things to accomplish, and this man had proven far too distracting. Her resolve hardening, Saga thrust the map at him.

His throat bobbed as he took it. "My thanks." But he didn't move, and when Saga looked up at him, Rurik had that same look on his face—as though he fought against himself. A heavy exhale escaped him. "Saga." His voice had shifted. There was weight to her name. Meaning she could not untangle.

"You are uncommon. No, is wrong word. You are *rare*. Not what I expected." He stepped nearer, so close she could feel the heat radiating off his body. She found herself incredibly attuned to his size. His nearness. His masculine scent.

"*Khotel by ya posmotret', kak ty letish' svobodno.*"*

Saga stared up at him. Her mind was gauzy, her limbs tingling. She felt his gaze on her, so heavy it seared her skin.

"What does that mean?" she whispered.

"That I am wishing you well," he said softly.

Rov snorted, shattering the silence. The Zagadkian jerked upright, looking around. "What?" he demanded, gaze landing on Rurik. "I am awake. I did not sleep."

Rurik's lips tipped up, Saga's quickly following. With a reluctant sigh, Rurik turned to his comrade. "No, old man? I suppose was just resting of eyes?"

Rov pushed to his feet, bleary eyes blinking rapidly. "You are done? Yes? Good." And with that, their session was over.

As they walked in sleepy silence through the passageway, Saga couldn't help but dwell on Rurik's words. Somehow, it had felt a lot like goodbye. It was for the best. Yet for some reason, Saga couldn't shake off her disappointment.

---

*I would like to see you fly freely.

CHAPTER 32

Kalasgarde

For Silla, the days limped past like a wounded animal, each more painful than the last. She and Rey settled into a routine of sorts. Mornings started with the daymeal followed by ill-fated attempts at feeding Brown Horse. Sparring lessons came next, and then they rode to Harpa's. During daylight hours, Rey was off with Vig, scouring the woods for any sign of Ástrid and Váli, while Silla spent hours in the unpleasant confines of her mind. By the end of the day, she was bone-weary, ready to drive all memories of her lessons away with a second sparring session.

Practicing swordplay with Rey was the best part of her day. Here, she was in control. She felt herself growing stronger—could see herself getting faster. Rey had taught her both offensive and defensive routines, and while she was far from his skill level, the movements were becoming ingrained in her memory.

But so much time spent near Rey seemed to have befuddled her mind. Twice this week, Silla had dreamed of her fingertips tracing the curve of a dragon's wing, chased closely by her lips and tongue. She'd woken misted in sweat, her body tight with unfulfilled desire. During the day, she caught herself watching Rey as he went about the mundane. The way his eyes fell shut as he took his first bite of porridge. The flex of his shoulders as he hefted the saddle up. The twitch of his lips as he stroked Horse's cheek.

Close quarters. It was merely the product of sharing the shield-home with Rey. She could not allow herself to get caught up in such things.

Silla's days were spent sitting for hours upon torturous hours, working on what Harpa called *surrendering*. She was failing. Silla knew it; Harpa knew it. She could not master her mind. Each time she closed her eyes, each time she allowed herself to retreat into herself, *they* were there.

Ilías Svik. Matthias Nordvig. Skeggagrim.

They waited for her. Reveled in her misery. Taunted her with the perfect combination of words to unravel her. She shoved them into cages, slammed the doors shut. Swallowed the keys and tried to refocus her mind. But the task was futile, and time was slipping away.

Time, she'd wasted *so much time,* and she had nothing to show for it.

———◇◇◇◇———

Silla swung the axe, striking the log's edge and sending it skittering to the ground. With a growl of frustration, she wiped sweat from her brow. Her back ached, and a blister was forming on her thumb. But still, it was better than sitting in that cabin, listening to Harpa chant "surrender" over and over.

Frustration twisted her insides at the mere thought of that cabin. Obviously weary of Silla's failures, of Rykka's reminders that "this is why you don't take older students," Harpa had relented and tried something new.

"You will chop wood," Harpa had said. "And when you can swing the axe no more, you will rest in the steam bath."

"But Rey has chopped enough firewood to last you a year—"

Harpa's amber eyes had flared. "You will not succeed with your galdur until you surrender. Do as I say and do not question my methods."

Now she stood in the yard, breath clouding in the cool northern air. Movement from the forest had Silla gripping the axe tighter. Everything these days seemed to raise the hairs on the back of her neck, had her looking over her shoulder in search of man-eating creatures. According to Vig, this creature had the whole of Kalasgarde on edge. Despite countless searches, there had been no sign of Váli nor Ástrid. And with each passing day, Rey's agitation only grew.

"It strikes on a seven-day pattern," she'd heard him tell Vig. "First, your sheep. Next Váli, then Ástrid. Do not let your guard down. Have Runný freshen the wards daily."

Silla readied herself to rush into Harpa's cabin, but as she gazed into the woods, she saw a clear flash of blue darting toward her.

"Ice spirit," she murmured, taking in the white-blue form of a tiny woman. The sunlight caught her diaphanous wings, crystalline and gleaming with frost.

Days now, Silla had tried to catch sight of the ice spirit in the woods near the stables, seeing nothing but blue wisps as it darted within the foliage. But now the spirit revealed herself fully to Silla. It felt special, somehow.

"Beautiful," she whispered, smiling dumbly. The ice spirit twirled, hair and skirts flowing outward, as though she were preening for Silla. "Rykka says I'm not to trust you." She paused. "Then again, Rykka named me after a squirrel, so perhaps I needn't listen to her."

The ice spirit ceased her dance and opened her mouth, revealing long, pointed teeth. A horrid hissing sound escaped the creature, sending goosebumps down Silla's spine.

"Oh," murmured Silla, brows raising. "You're rather ferocious."

The ice spirit zipped back and forth while continuing to hiss. Intrigued, Silla watched. Was it trying to communicate with her? Could this spirit not simply speak to her, as Rykka could? "You seem agitated," she said. The spirit looped in an excited motion with a series of softer hisses. "Yes?"

The sun vanished behind a cloud, and Silla's gaze fell on her axe. "I must complete my task. But it's lovely to meet you." Yanking the axe from the stump, Silla hefted it overhead.

But the ice spirit would not be dissuaded, darting into Silla's vision with startling speed. Reeling back, Silla watched the winged woman make an agitated loop.

"Is this your territory?" guessed Silla.

The ice spirit hissed. Flashing a brilliant blue, she zipped away, then back.

"What is it?" Silla asked in mild irritation.

Baring her teeth, the ice spirit burst into a small blizzard that vanished into the air. But with a quick swirl, she re-formed, flitting back and forth in the periphery of Silla's vision.

With a shake of her head, Silla turned back to her task. She placed a log on the chopping stump and tipped it on end.

The ice spirit zipped in front of her, a blur of ice blue and shimmering white.

"What?" snapped Silla. The ice spirit darted to a patch of exposed rock in the ground, gesturing at a frosted symbol she seemed to have drawn. It was the protection rune, though upside down.

"I thank you for your protection, kind spirit," said Silla, as calmly as she could manage.

The ice spirit looked as though she were about to hiss once more but zipped into the bushes as Harpa's door banged open. After trudging across the yard, Harpa examined Silla with an unreadable expression. Then, she dragged her by the elbow to a small hut near the shed, smoke puffing from a hole in the roof.

"Strip," ordered Harpa, watching Silla expectantly.

Silla's mouth fell open, protests gathering on her tongue.

"Stop questioning," barked Harpa, and Silla's mouth slammed shut. "Surrender yourself. You will strip down to your underclothes and warm in the steam bath."

"Steam bath," repeated Silla, shimmying out of her overdress.

As she stepped into the steam bath in naught but a shift, Silla sighed with contentment. Steam poured from an oven of burning stones and hung thick in the air, clinging to Silla's cool skin. As she eased onto the bench, Harpa spooned water over the stones, standing in the doorway.

"Clear your mind," she said, then closed Silla into utter darkness.

Silla blinked. In here, there was only darkness and the sizzling stones. Her body ached, exhausted from her wood-chopping efforts, but as the heat slowly penetrated her, she began to relax.

She closed her eyes. Tried to focus on the backs of her eyelids.

This is a waste of time, said her father.

Irritated, Silla shook out her shoulders. She focused on the beat of her heart, on the slow slide of sweat along her temple.

I gave my life for you, and yet you squander it.

Silla found that cage, shoved the voice behind it. Locked it in then boarded it up.

Come and find me, sister, said Saga. *I need you.*

"I'm trying," whispered Silla. "But first I must—"

There is no time!

Reluctantly, Silla corralled Saga's voice into the cage. If Harpa's aim was to tire her mind into submission, then it was a failure. She was letting down those who'd given their lives for her—who'd sacrificed for her safety. Her throat stung as tears scratched forth.

Cold tension purred in her veins, and Silla's eyes flew open. White light glowed from her forearms, catching undulating clouds of steam in the air. Silla vaguely recalled Harpa telling her that both heat and tension could make priming and expression easier. Something about energy barriers.

"Express," she muttered, imagining light flaring in the steam bath. "Express!" Jaw clenched, she tried to wrangle it like a wild horse, tried to push, shove, enslave the thing to her will. Nothing happened.

Surrender, she heard Harpa say in her mind. *Lean into it. You must surrender.*

Tears welled, then spilled down her cheeks. Why couldn't she do this? Why did she continue to fail, time after time?

Silla burst into the yard, steam and white light spilling from her. Her eyes met Harpa's. "I cannot do it!"

Harpa was unmoved. "This is why you continue to fail. You must believe. You must stop fighting." She paused. "And then you must surrender."

Surrender.

Silla wanted to pull the hair from her head, wanted to throw and break and smash. Already, she'd surrendered her dreams. Her happiness. The life she'd known. Was it not enough?

Bitterness filled her. No. It was not enough. Because the gods hungered for her misery. And it seemed they would not be satisfied until she was utterly broken.

CHAPTER 33

Sunnavík

Long had Saga thought herself a woman of horrid luck. But the day a leak sprang in the roof of Ursir's House, she wondered if the winds of change had finally blown her way. With prayers canceled, a private Letting in the confines of Saga's chambers had been a great improvement on one before a crowd. After a cup of yarrow tea to replenish her strength, Saga had taken a stroll to the western wing of Askaborg, thrilled at what she discovered.

The white linen flew.

The rest of the day had moved at a snail's pace. Anticipation of meeting with Ana once more had Saga vibrating with excitement. Would this letter prove more revealing than the last? How did Eisa fare in the north? Had anyone offered information about her accomplice?

Apprehension knotted her stomach as she ran a comb through her hair. She hadn't any information to bring Ana this time, though it was not for lack of trying. Each spare minute was spent practicing her lockpicking skill. It had taken her a day to master a door lock. One more to conquer her trunk's padlock. She was feeling ready. And the way things were going, she found herself increasingly optimistic.

The comb stilled as she stared at her reflection in the polished metal mirror.

Things had been going *too well.*

"Gods, Saga," she chided herself. Why couldn't she just accept good fortune for what it was? Why couldn't she just hope for the best? But she couldn't. Hope was like a carnivorous plant, lovely and bright to lure you in. That was when the gods sprang their trap.

Pulling on her gloves, she glanced at the door. Soon, Árlaug would arrive to ready Saga for tonight's feast. She breathed deeply, pressing a palm to her stomach. Her first feast in several months. In contrast with the fifty or so who joined them for prayers, tonight, hundreds of Sunnavík nobles would gather to honor the Zagadkians and the new grain treaty. It would be loud and raucous, and Saga's attendance after a long absence would most definitely be noted. She could look forward to a night of usurping Ivar's bears as prime entertainment.

"They don't matter," she told herself, trying to quell her rising nausea. She'd get through the feast, meet Ana in the tower, and hope that there would be something useful in the letter.

Stop fighting, came a voice, bitterness prickling through Saga. *Surrender. I've surrendered my whole life. What more does she want from me?*

The hairs on the back of her neck lifted as Saga wheeled around. Alone. What was—

"Good evening, my lady," said Árlaug, bustling into the room. "Let's get you ready for the feast."

Saga sank onto the chair set before her dressing table, probing inwardly and confirming that her mental barriers were intact. Cautiously, Saga lowered them.

. . . The girl's hair is dry as a hag's broom. Perhaps a treatment of bear grease would bring some shine . . .

Saga's nose wrinkled. Árlaug's thoughts were both louder and lower in tone than the voice she'd heard. Was she losing her mind?

Giving herself a mental shake, Saga set her barriers back in place and forced her thoughts to the present. Árlaug braided silver twine through a side section of Saga's hair, wrapping the ends tightly. Next, she helped her step into her dress, a finely woven black gown with shining knotted embellishments running down the front. "Lovely," said Árlaug, admiring her hard work.

And as Saga examined herself in the polished metal, she decided she was, in fact, dressed finely for a woman planning to end her evening with a bit of forgery.

The noise of several hundred guests mingled with drumbeats and the soft notes of a lyre. Seated beside Prince Bjorn in the great hall, Saga pointedly ignored the other end of the high table. She had absolutely *not* noticed Kassandr Rurik seated beside Princess Yrsa, their heads bowed together in low conversation. But as Rurik's irritating voice carried across the room, soon followed by the princess's soft laughter, Saga bit into her flatbread with a little extra vigor.

Rows upon rows of feasting tables were filled, jarls and wealthy Sunnavík merchants drinking mead and ale in ceremonial horns. They watched her already, scarcely bothering to smother their voices. Saga fought the urge to jump onto the high table and turn around in a full circle so that they might look their fill.

Here she is, Ivar's pet.

Saga scowled at a raven-haired woman who stared unabashedly. The woman's eyes widened as she whirled away, head bowing to whisper in a friend's ear. With irritation, Saga glanced down the high table, gaze landing on Lady Geira in a high-collared dress, presumably to conceal any lingering lesions.

Saga shook herself, forcing her attention back to her betrothed.

Tonight, Bjorn's blond hair was woven into a warrior's braid, though without a beard, his youth was only pronounced. With rings far too large for him adorning his fingers, and a crimson tunic that emphasized his narrow shoulders, it seemed that Bjorn was trying to emulate his father's style, with awkward results.

"And then, we tested the new Karthian steel, and it cut through a hare as though it were butter," Bjorn was telling her, swirling ale in his goblet.

"That's . . . wonderful," Saga managed. She waved over the cup-bearer to refill her own goblet, reflecting that there was not enough mead in the kingdom to make this evening pleasurable.

"'Tis promising indeed. Is only a fraction heavier than Íseldurian metal and—" As his voice cut off abruptly, Saga followed Bjorn's gaze, settling on a figure whose presence made her blood chill.

Jarl Skotha was here.

Once, Skotha had been a trusted member of King Kjartan's retinue. But when the Urkans had landed and it was clear who'd be victorious, Skotha turned his back on the king to whom he was oathsworn. Over the years, whispers had reached Saga's ears, rumors that it was Skotha who'd revealed Saga and Eisa's hiding place to the Urkans.

And Jarl Skotha had risen to prominence among Ivar's new regime. But his lands were south of here, and she thankfully hadn't seen him in some time.

"The bread is dry," complained Signe, diverting Saga's attention. "Can nothing in this castle go right?"

Seated on Bjorn's other side, the queen had been quiet thus far. Easing forward as subtly as she could, Saga examined Signe. A delicate clawed crown of polished steel sat atop her head, and her white-gold hair was immaculate. But what was most beautiful of all to Saga was the irritation etched into the queen's face.

Had Signe and the Wolf Feeders finally realized the warband had wasted weeks traipsing in the wrong direction? Or had something gone amiss with Signe's dealings in Svaldrin?

"Is it the thievery you speak of, Mother?" inquired Bjorn.

"Thievery?" asked Signe.

"In the garrison hall's undercroft. The place was sacked—barrels of ale tipped over, weaponry strewn about."

Rurik, thought Saga at once, *you delinquent.* Who else could it be, brashly ransacking the castle, but him? His departure was imminent. The man must be growing desperate to find whatever it was he sought. What could it be? Without thinking, she glanced down the table to the Zagadkian lord. A smile spread wide across his face as he entertained the princess and several of the queen's bondswomen. Saga's brows drew together as her gaze fell on Yrsa. The princess gazed at Rurik with unabashed wonder.

"How awful," said the queen, drawing Saga's attention back to this end of the table.

"Father is rather furious."

"I imagine he is," murmured Signe. "I've heard so little of what has transpired with the Zagadkians. Won't you share a bit with me, my Little Bear?"

Bjorn's cheeks reddened. "Mother," he hissed. "I've told you before not to call me that in company. And I am not to speak of our dealings. To *anyone*."

Signe's face filled with hurt. "Surely you can speak of it to your mother, darling."

Bjorn only folded his arms over his chest.

"Signe, don't bother the boy," boomed Ivar as he seated himself in the high-backed chair beside Signe's. "He's doing a man's work now. Nothing for the women to brood over."

Oh, this was getting better and better. From the corner of her eye, Saga watched the queen's face sweep a furious shade of red. How had she gone her whole life without noticing that Signe was a ball of quietly contained rage?

"Of course, darling," Signe said in that demure, queenly voice of hers. Unfortunately for Saga, the queen's gaze quickly fell upon her. "Saga darling, you look so pretty when you put in a little effort. Doesn't she, Bjorn?"

"Yes," said Bjorn, a red flush creeping up his neck. "Your"—he stumbled over his words—"... *eyes* ... look as blue as a"—he paused in thought, then his expression brightened—"as a Norvalander hound's," Bjorn concluded. "And your hair as yellow as a fire serpent's scales."

Saga blinked, unsure how to take that. "My thanks?"

King Ivar's chair scraped across the stone floor as he pushed to his feet. He was garbed in a wine-red tunic and bearskin cloak, and the twin braids of his beard were set with golden rings. The crowd quieted, finding their seats.

"Thank you all for coming," thundered Ivar, raising his cup. The crowd raised their drinking vessels in unison. "We've much to celebrate tonight. We've reached a treaty with our Zagadkian brothers." Ivar tilted his cup toward Rurik and his Druzhina. "They've delivered fine-quality grain with the promise of shiploads more!" A murmur swept through the crowd, some nobles nodding, others stricken with relief. "Tonight we pay tribute to our Zagadkian guests and induct them as honorary Brothers of the Hearth." The crowd bellowed in approval.

The doors to the great hall burst open. The High Gothi entered, trailed by acolytes with the altar stone and an assortment of leashed animals—a swan, a sheep, a hog, and, to Saga's great dismay, a man.

Her temples throbbed.

"To the Zagadkian Druzhina, we honor you with a tradition passed down through the Urkan lines. A sacrifice to grant you safe passage back to your country."

Rurik stood, eyes blazing. "We are thanking you for this gesture, Your Majesty. Is unnecessary."

A collective gasp filled the room, the crowd holding absolutely still.

Saga froze. The impulsive fool. As horrid a ritual as it was, to refuse this sacrifice was a blatant insult to the king. She watched Ivar's dark eyes cool and sharpen. But Rurik's own gaze was undeterred as he stared back at the king. All those weeks to broker a deal between their kingdoms, and the brash man might shred it in this one move.

"We are thanking you, Your Majesty," Rovgolod burst out, shooting Kassandr a look that could slice through steel. Rov succeeded at last in pulling Kassandr down into his seat. "Please forgive my colleague. You see, is difference in customs. We are pleased to accept this gift of yours. Is large honor."

The king nodded at Rov, then threw a look of unconcealed dislike Rurik's way. And with a wave of King Ivar's hand, the bloodshed began.

The animals were slaughtered with ruthless efficiency, blood collected and poured over the altar stone. Saga could not keep her eyes from Rurik as he watched unflinchingly.

The man was waved forward last of all. Gray-haired, he was all bony, sharp angles. And yet there was a quiet dignity to him as he stepped willingly to the altar. Saga tried to take solace that this man had come of his own accord, that perhaps he considered this a great honor. But it did not erase the barbaric nature of it.

The High Gothi tilted the man's head up to bare his neck as two acolytes held him firmly in place. Forcing her gaze to the table, Saga tried to recall the good things in this world. Sketching; her winter-wing earrings; the silk pillow with red tassels . . .

The blade *shucked* across the man's throat. Saga's eyelids fluttered, her body growing light. She could hear the soft gushing of the man's lifeblood as they collected it in cup after cup and washed it over the altar stone. When at last Saga allowed herself to look, the High Gothi, the altar stone, and the acolytes were gone; the sacrifices were being dragged over to Ivar's pet bears.

Over. It was over.

The king was standing, though his voice sounded distant from the ringing in Saga's ears. "We honor our Zagadkian brothers with a feast of boars. It is one of Ursir's most revered creatures, and I would ensure nothing but the best for our new friends." There was no mistaking the sharp note on the last word—a warning of how tenuous this friendship truly was. "Tomorrow, you will leave, but the bonds of brotherhood will persist."

Ivar let the crowd utter their agreement. From the corner, a bone popped as the bears began their own feast.

"To my Íseldurian fellows. Our Yrsa turns eighteen soon, and we hope to see you all at her birthday feast. My lovely wife has been busy with preparations—wine and food made with spices from the Southern Continent. There will be a tournament, skald tales, and mead fermented specially for the occasion!

"Enjoy the food and drink!" Ivar lifted his silver cup to the center of the room, drained it in two large gulps, then slammed it onto the table with a resounding thud. The rest of the crowd followed suit, the room echoing with bangs as horns and cups slammed down. Saga pursed her lips, then forced herself to do the same.

Conversation hummed to life as serving thralls poured into the hall. Sadly for Saga, the turnaround from bloodshed to revelry was something she'd grown accustomed to, and her stomach soon growled at the scents wafting from trenchers placed on the table—rabbit dressed with juniper, thick slices of boar topped with rich gravy and roasted vegetables. Saga's silver cup was refilled, and she snatched it, draining it quickly. Her stomach was acid, though the mead provided a pleasant, pillowy haze.

"It's good to see you again, Lady Saga," came a cool, deep voice. Startled from her thoughts, Saga's gaze met large, dark eyes. Her teeth clenched together. Jarl Skotha. He looked just as he had as a trusted member of her father's retinue, though deeper lines now grooved his brown skin, the black of his hair and beard peppered with gray.

Saga swallowed her bitterness back. "Good evening, Jarl Skotha."

"I'm pleased to see you in good health, my lady," said Skotha smoothly, studying her face.

Just the royal pet trotting out for inspection, Saga thought, jamming a buttered parsnip onto her spoon.

"Lady Saga shall soon take the name Ivarsson," said Signe, grabbing Bjorn's hand and giving it a squeeze.

"Is that so?" asked Skotha.

Bjorn nodded, pulling his hand back and adjusting his over-large rings. "We shall wed before winter's fall."

Saga's hands gripped each other beneath the table linen.

"That is wonderful news," said Jarl Skotha. His voice was level, but something passed behind his eyes.

"And I hear congratulations are in order to your family as well, Skotha," said Signe demurely. "I'm told your daughter's husband has risen through the Klaernar's ranks with impressive speed."

Jarl Skotha's lips spread into a proud smile. "Yes, Your Highness. We are quite pleased. I'm told Kommandor Hilja is the youngest of his rank Svaldrin has ever seen."

Saga's brows drew together, a vague memory stirring. She prodded deeper into her mind, trying to recall the details. Svaldrin's kommandor had been on her list. A respected kommandor who'd recently suffered an undisclosed illness. He'd perished rather quickly and had been replaced by a young man.

A young man by the name of Hilja.

Saga's gaze snapped to Skotha, and she examined him afresh. He hadn't hesitated to turn his back on her father, and it did not seem a stretch to think he might turn his back on King Ivar. But if there was a link between Skotha and the queen, neither of their expressions betrayed such a thing.

Jarl Skotha's attention landed on King Ivar. "My king," he said. "I would ask for your ear. My hounds have found a lead on the thief."

"Oh?" The king looked up with great interest, pushing to his feet without hesitation. "Fetch Magnus. Bjorn, with me."

As the king and Bjorn disappeared through a doorway and Skotha went to fetch Magnus, Saga glanced at Rurik. Completely unconcerned, he'd reverted to his far-too-jovial self, spoon waving in the air as he regaled two of Signe's bondswomen with a tale.

Saga waved over her cupbearer to refill her goblet.

It was going to be a long night.

CHAPTER 34

Shortly before the eleventh chime, Saga picked her way along the narrow corridor in the northern wing's old defensive walls. Torch held in one hand, a satchel with her supplies in the other, she stepped over a pile of crumbled stone and ducked under a dangling cobweb.

Celebrations continued in the great hall, with skald tales and drumbeats and plenty of ale, making it all too easy for Saga to slip out unnoticed. Now, taking the stairs to Asla Tower two at a time, she wondered what information the letters might hold and whether she and Ana would be able to *do* something this time.

Having stowed her torch at the bottom of the tower, Saga climbed in darkness. As Saga pushed into the tower room, moonlight revealed Ana at once. With her knees drawn up, head tipped back against the wall, the woman's face was etched with exhaustion.

"Good evening, Your Majesty," said Ana, climbing to her feet and dipping into a curtsy.

"Ana, please . . ." Saga sighed, then held out a linen-wrapped lump. "I thought you might want a sweet roll."

"My thanks!" said Ana, taking the linen eagerly. "With feast preparations, there's been little left for the help."

Saga frowned as they settled to the floor, unease prickling her stomach. She knew there was a grain shortage—knew starvation was a very real threat to the lower class—but she'd been so insulated from it in Askaborg, and now she felt like a muttonhead. She should have brought the woman a whole trencher of breads.

"We've had word from Svaldrin," said Ana, after swallowing the last bite. "The Shadow Hounds tracked Maester Lekka to an old fort at the edge of town, but I fear they were too late."

"Late?"

"The place was abandoned—rows of beds left behind in one room and something akin to a kitchen in the other. But it was filled with curious instruments—crucibles and small cauldrons, phials whole and shattered. And they say the place had a horrid smell—sulfuric, like rotten eggs."

Saga's brows drew together. "What does it mean?"

"We haven't a clue, Your Majesty," sighed Ana wearily. "Our Weaver searches for answers, and our people have remained in Svaldrin to search for clues to Maester Lekka's whereabouts."

"This fort . . . it must be the location they discussed in the letter," said Saga. "*She made off with our most vigorous stock,* Lekka had written. What does this mean, *stock*?"

Ana shook her head. "Stock . . . goods . . . wares . . . livestock . . ."

"Some sort of herbal remedy, perhaps?"

They exchanged a silent look. "Was there any evidence linking the missing Galdra to those beds?"

Ana chewed her lip. "It was clear someone had recently occupied the beds based on the blood and urine stains, but there was nothing to reveal their identities. And I regret there is more." Ana's jaw hardened. "The Shadow Hounds dug up the yard behind the fort. Corpses were discovered."

Saga's stomach twisted. She reached for Ana's hand and gave it a gentle squeeze.

"Near two dozen bodies, crammed into a single pit. Just . . . piled atop one another. No dignity. No ceremony. No provisions for the afterlife." Ana's gaze grew distant. "They were several weeks old, at the least. And based on the bloodstains, it appears whoever had lain in the beds was taken when Lekka fled."

"Taken," repeated Saga numbly.

"I tell you this against the Uppreisna's wishes," said Ana bitterly. "Because you deserve to know. But also because you alone are in a position to find answers. We believe the Black Cloak orchestrates the removal of Galdra from Klaernar custody and delivery to Maester Lekka. But now that Lekka has fled Svaldrin, we must determine where he's gone. And we still do not know the identity of the Black Cloak."

"Skotha," suggested Saga, fire igniting in her stomach. "His daughter's husband is Kommandor Hilja of Svaldrin. I'm told he's their youngest kommandor ever."

She watched Ana, waiting for a look of conviction... for any sort of reaction. But Ana merely stared at her hands.

"Skotha betrayed my father," continued Saga vehemently. "I'm certain he wouldn't hesitate to betray King Ivar if the price were right."

Ana shook her head slowly.

"What is it?" asked Saga.

With a sigh, Ana looked up. "It is not Skotha."

Saga opened her mouth to demand how Ana knew this, but the woman had pulled out a pair of scrolls and two small boxes.

"Packages?" Saga asked, a thrill rushing through her.

"It seems our Maester Alfson means to send goods to the north and west," said Ana, a touch of enthusiasm back in her voice. "His adherent dropped these off this morning."

"Truly?" Saga examined the first pair. "It's addressed to Kaptein Ulfar in Kopa," she read eagerly. Heart pounding, she sliced through the wax seal and unrolled the parchment. Based on the cramped letters, Maester Alfson had penned it.

Heat hindrium alloy until liquid. Dip quills until tips are coated and allow to set. Dose once per day. Subjects last seen in Svangormr Pass.

Saga turned the parchment over, but there was nothing more to be found. "Hindrium?"

"'Tis a galdur-neutralizing metal," said Ana slowly. "Most often used in manacles and prison cells. But—" She paused. "—If they've found a way to liquefy it . . ." Her voice trailed off, but Saga understood. A liquid form of the metal might be used on blades and arrows, neutralizing their targets from afar.

Saga swallowed, the words on the parchment blurring together. With the mention of Svangormr Pass, it was clear Alfson intended for the hindrium to be used on Eisa and her companion.

"The other letter," said Ana, passing the scroll to Saga. "The package is larger, yet lighter."

"'Tis addressed to Rökksgarde," said Saga. "Where is *that?*"

Ana shrugged.

"'Alpine catspaw,'" read Saga. "'Dry for two weeks, then grind to a fine powder.'" She stared at the letter, willing new words to appear. But no matter how many times she blinked, it was still maddeningly sparse.

"We must change the addresses," said Ana eagerly. "Send the catspaw to the north and the hindrium to the east."

Saga nodded and pulled her supplies out. This would be simple enough; she'd merely change the addresses on the outer scrolls without need to touch the inner message. Saga worked letter-by-letter to replicate Alfson's cramped style, then resealed with the queen's wasp sigil. A small smile spread across her lips.

Leaning against the stone wall, Saga eyed Ana. "Might I ask you something personal, Ana?" she asked cautiously. "Why do you do this? Why do you risk yourself like this?"

Ana drew her knees against her chest, wrapping her arms around them. "I dream that no one else's sister should suffer the same fate as mine."

An ache grew in Saga's chest. "Your sister was—"

"Put to the pillar," said Ana. She lifted her head, opening her mouth as though she wished to say more. But whatever the thought was, Ana decided against voicing it.

"I'm so sorry, Ana."

Ana shook her head. "It was long ago. I scarcely remember her. But I've never forgotten her."

"I understand that sentiment well," said Saga.

A look crossed Ana's face, lasting for less than a heartbeat. But it was enough. Because in that moment, Ana had revealed something crucial to Saga.

"You were about to contradict me."

Ana rolled her lips together, as though to keep herself from speaking.

"You *know*," whispered Saga, realization settling into place.

The mask Ana had wrangled into place fell free. "I know something. Do you know . . . something?"

Saga's mind was frantically trying to piece things together. But before she could cobble together words, Ana spoke.

"Your sister is alive." Ana's eyes brimmed with tears. "I should have told you, but I—"

"How?" Saga interjected. "How do you know this?"

"I know because . . ." Ana's gaze met Saga's for one heartbreaking second. "Because my sister was put to the pillar in Eisa's place."

Saga felt like she'd be sick.

"It was for the Volsiks," continued Ana. "For Íseldur. A Protector of the Realm must *always* sit on the throne. And so a sacrifice had to be made." A haunted, vacant look had crossed Ana's face. "I was but five, and little Bryndís was nearly three."

"It was wrong of them," muttered Saga, revulsion coursing through her. "They murdered a *child*—"

"It was my parents' choice," said Ana, anger sharpening her words. "*They* chose that fate for Bryndís."

Nausea twisted Saga's gut. "The body," she whispered, unable to finish. The Urkans had made a spectacle of it—had brought all of Sunnavík into Askaborg's pits to witness the deaths of her family. What terror little Bryndís must have suffered. And they had left the corpses on display for a full year in Askaborg's pits; they'd been subjected to all manner of disrespect, which Saga tried desperately not to think of.

Saga awkwardly wrapped her arm around Ana's shoulder. "I'm sorry," she said, unable to find the right words. There *were* no right words. But her mere presence seemed to soothe Ana.

"*I'm* sorry," sniffed Ana, wiping tears from her cheeks. "I've forgotten myself, Your Majesty—"

"Just Saga," said Saga, brows drawing together. "No more Your Majesty between us. We are friends, Ana."

More tears spilled down Ana's cheeks, and Saga smoothed her hair. "Who else knows, Ana?" she asked. "Do the Uppreisna know of Eisa?"

Ana shook her head slowly. "Back then, there *was* no Uppreisna. It was a secretive affair. Only my parents and some of your father's retinue knew. We were ordered not to tell anyone. There were leaks and traitors; it was uncertain who could be trusted. Most who knew were killed when the Urkans breached the walls. My mother survived, though her mind never recovered. She took her own life when I was twelve. And now it is only I who carries the secret. I've kept it close to my heart all these years, so my sister's sacrifice would not be in vain. It seemed safest for Eisa this way."

"She's in the north," said Saga. "But Signe hunts her, and I . . . I will do what it takes to keep her safe."

Saga's jaw clenched, emotion clawing up her throat. *Don't cry,* she told herself. *Do not cry.* Thank the gods above, the moment soon passed, and in place of emotion was hardened resolve. Hearing of Ana's sister only made her eager to do more. "What do we do now, Ana? What is next?"

"We keep pushing," said Ana. "Have you uncovered anything new?"

Saga shook her head. "I've tried, but—"

"Keep trying," encouraged Ana. "Keep digging. If we know the Black Cloak's true name, we can send our best assassins after him. Make him disappear. And if we discover where Lekka has taken the Galdra, we can form a plan to rescue our kin."

Saga nodded.

"You've done well, Saga," said Ana slowly. "But if we want to uncover these answers, you may need to be more daring." She paused. "Once we've brought down Lekka and the Black Cloak, we will take you from the castle. Settle you in Midfjord."

Saga felt bone-weary. Tonight's feast and learning of Ana's sister were reminders of what her future held. If she remained in Askaborg, she would become one of *them*. Would be complicit in spilling the blood of innocents. The thought took the slightest edge from her panic at the prospect of leaving the castle.

"Midfjord?"

Ana nodded. "Near the southern border of the Western Woods. It's a hub for the southern Galdra. A place where you'll be safe. In time, we could bring you to Kopa."

Saga swallowed down her nausea. Ana was offering her a chance for freedom. A chance to choose for herself. A chance to see her sister one day. It wasn't a choice, really. It was the only path forward.

"I shall get the information, Ana. I swear it to you right now. I won't rest until we have it."

Ana nodded, eyes sparkling. "Good." She pushed to her feet, gathering the scrolls and parcels and placing them into a satchel. "I'll send these tonight. Check for the white linen."

Ana made to turn but paused. "Thank you, Saga," she said. "Thank you for everything."

Emotion burned in Saga's throat as she thought of little Bryndís, who'd died so Eisa could live. She would not allow Signe to steal Bryndís's sacrifice. Would do anything to keep her from capturing Eisa.

With a shy wave, Ana slipped through the door of Asla Tower, leaving Saga alone.

Sitting in the moonlight, Saga tried to wrangle her thoughts into some semblance of a plan. Alfson's study would be her next task. She'd practiced her lockpicking. Knew precisely where that cabinet lay. Tomorrow, she'd map out her path to his study, would count the steps and observe the Klaernar's patrol patterns so she could make it there in the dead of night.

But tonight, there was only fatigue. Tonight, there would be sleep. After the day she'd had, the prospect of her bed was tantalizing. Stifling a yawn, Saga decided enough time had passed for her to safely retreat to her chambers.

But then, she heard it—a faint groan of hinges from the bottom of the stairs.

Someone had entered the tower—was slowly climbing the stairs. Saga's gaze darted desperately around the tower room in search of a place to hide, but the room was unfurnished, open and exposed.

Trapped, she was trapped, no exits to be found. She was cornered, just like that day long ago . . .

The door pushed open.

And Kassandr Rurik stepped inside.

A ragged breath escaped her as panic quickly morphed into anger. "What are you doing here, Rurik?" she demanded.

"I came to show you something," he said. He leaned his long body against the stone wall with irritating nonchalance.

Gods, the man had scared her witless, and for what? Surging forward, she pushed against his chest, but he was unyielding. "Then show me tomorrow. Don't sneak up here and frighten me, you arse!"

Rurik *tsk*ed, an infuriating brow cocked up in amusement. "I did not want to wait." Two large hands wrapped around her shoulders, turning her. "Look," he said.

But it was impossible to focus when he was behind her. Saga's eyelashes fluttered as Rurik's large body crowded her toward the window. "Look," he repeated.

"What is it?" she croaked. The window looked out over the castle grounds and Sunnavík beyond. It was a clear night, the sister moons glowing brightly—Malla a bold crescent, while Marra was soft and round.

"A full moon?" she guessed.

"There," he whispered, his breath tickling her ear.

Everything felt hazy and dangerously hot, but Saga forced herself to search the shoreline. Just down the hill, at Sunnavík's harbor, she spotted it—a pulsating orange glow.

"A fire?" Saga squinted, leaning closer. "At the harbor." She gasped. "Is it *your* ship?"

Rurik chuckled, the sound rumbling straight to her toes. He released her shoulders, and Saga blinked. It was then that a curious scent met her nostrils.

Smoke. Kassandr Rurik smelled faintly of smoke.

Saga whirled, staring up at him. "You."

He watched her with a strange, unreadable look.

"You burned your boat!" she burst out. "Why—what—weren't you due to leave in the morning?"

"Yes. Is very sad indeed. Rovgolod yells much and pulls out hair."

"You . . . you're mad!"

"I am preferring . . . *creative*."

Saga's brows drew together. "Why did you show me this?"

Rurik's gaze traveled around her face, his expression unreadable. "We are having secrets, both of us," he said softly. "I like this thing."

Saga blinked, reality swiftly spilling through her mind. This close, and lit by bright Marra, Saga could see more of him than she ever had before—a shallow scar on his cheek, the way one eyebrow arched just a touch higher than the other.

She gripped his elbows to steady herself.

Rurik brushed a tendril of loosened hair back from her face, the tips of his fingers whispering along her skin. "Earring today," he said softly, touching the dangling bird. Rurik leaned in, his breath heating her cheek. He was so near, so very close, so deliciously large.

"I am staying," he whispered, "until I am satisfied with unfinished matters."

Satisfied. The word seemed to throb through her body.

But the warm haze of her mind was shattered by the clang of bells. Saga rushed to the window. Hounds fanned out across the castle grounds below, Klaernar following closely behind. Two broad-shouldered men ambled out last, surveying the progress. Malla's light spilled down upon the figures, revealing the unmistakable profile of Magnus Hansson. Her gaze flitted to the second—broad like Magnus, with a darker complexion and light streaks in his black hair. She gasped as the man turned. Jarl Skotha.

And wrapped around Skotha's shoulders was a black wolfskin cloak.

Saga's hand curled into a fist. "Black Cloak," she seethed.

"You must be getting back to your chambers," said Rurik sharply. "I will watch. If any get near to you, I will frighten them away."

Saga didn't have to be told twice. She gathered her satchel. Rushed down the stairs. And Saga did not stop until she was secured—alone—behind her chamber doors.

CHAPTER 35

Kalasgarde

The morning was cold and gray, a match to Silla's moods. Casting a look over her shoulder, she surveyed the woods for any sign of the beast prowling the area. But there was only Rey, standing in the shield-home's doorway, watching her tread across the yard. His grim prediction—that the monster would strike on a seven-day cycle—had him anticipating violence today.

"Five minutes," said Rey from the doorway, fastening the buckle of his lébrynja armor.

Entering the stables, Silla had the barest flicker of hope. Would today be the day Brown Horse finally took the treat? But the horse swished her tail and turned away, and it took all of Silla's will not to cry. She'd sworn she wouldn't give up, but her resolve was crumbling.

Everything was crumbling.

Rallying cry, she tried, but her mind was empty.

Hearthfire thoughts, she tried, but couldn't muster anything warming.

"Silla?" came Rey's rough voice from the yard.

Him, she thought. *He's my hearthfire thought.* Silla gave her head a shake. No. Sparring was her hearthfire thought.

Silla took a deep breath, then strode out of the stables to join him in practice. She would put one foot in front of the other, until she could no longer walk.

"Focus on the beating of your heart," said Harpa, several hours later. "Feel the blood flowing through your veins. Sense the heart of your galdur, calm and resting."

Though she'd tried it all before, Silla forced herself to try again. She wrangled her focus onto the shapes swirling on the backs of her eyelids. Circles churned until they were singular, and no, this was not a circle at all but a face with two ice-blue eyes glaring at her.

Your fault. It should have been you.

Silla was beyond impatience. Beyond irritation. Where once she'd been filled with warmth and the knowing feeling that all would work out, now she was cold and empty. Everything had been stripped from her when he'd died, and she was only just realizing—

Your optimism is shallow and false.

Rey had said that. He'd seen right through her. Had seen her as a naïve girl. And oh, how he'd been right. And what had she replied? *You do not have to let the awful things define you.* How utterly foolish she'd been.

A bitter laugh fell from her lips.

"Surrender," said Harpa, for the thousandth time that hour. "Surrender to your past. Do not give power to things you cannot change."

"Words are easy," said Silla.

Harpa's sigh was long and weary. It was clear even she was tired of this routine. "'Tis true," said Harpa, much to Silla's surprise. "Even the bravest of warriors still struggle with such things."

Silla's eyes found her mentor's, and she saw it there—an untended wound, something with jagged parts that Harpa hid from the world.

Hypocrite! she wanted to scream. How easy for Harpa to tell her to surrender when she herself could not follow her own advice. The emptiness inside her filled with something ugly. Silla wanted to hurt Harpa, wanted to break things, wanted to wound others as she herself had been wounded.

Hands curling into fists, Silla opened her mouth. But before she could speak, the door to Harpa's cabin flew open. They whirled to find a pair of warriors bursting inside, the largest cradling a woman. It was clear the two men were related, both pale-skinned with blue eyes. But the taller of the two had a bushy black beard with a solitary streak of white, while the other's shaved skull sported swirling blue tattoos. This man's eyes found Silla's and hardened. For a moment, the room stood still, the steady drip of blood tap, tap, tapping onto the floor.

"Hef? Ketill?" Harpa rushed toward them. "What has happened?"

"It's Freydis," the bearded man growled. "Something attacked her. Ate a dozen sheep before turning on her. Hounds startled the thing. Chased it off before worse could be done, Hábrók praise them."

A hand flew to Silla's mouth. Rey had been right. The creature had struck again.

"Silla, bed," barked Harpa, and Silla understood immediately. She leaped to her feet and dashed to the bed in the corner of the hut, sweeping off a book and distaff and pulling back the furs.

Harpa's eyes were hard as stone. "Lay her down, Hef."

The taller warrior eased the injured woman onto the bed, and she writhed, a shrill sound escaping her lips. A strange smell filled the cabin—the metallic tang of blood mixed with an earthy, moldering rot. Blood, so much blood matted the front of the woman's wool dress.

"Hush, Freydis," said Hef, smoothing a hand along the woman's forehead. "You're at Harpa's now. She'll set you to rights."

Room swaying before Silla's eyes, she braced a steadying hand on the wall. It was too similar, so much like the death wounds her father had suffered. She could hear the sardonic laughter of the warrior who'd held her on the road near Skarstad, the black hawk's cry from high above . . .

The sharp rip of fabric drew Silla back to reality. Harpa had sliced through the woman's dress and was slowly peeling the fabric back. It was such a grisly sight, the air caught in Silla's lungs.

There appeared to be two even-sized wounds in Freydis's abdomen. Silla stared harder. Something was blocking one wound, impossible to see through all the blood. Gods. There was so much blood. Silla had only the most basic of healing knowledge, but the knowing feeling inside her told her that removing the thing from Freydis's flesh would cause death to claim her quicker.

Harpa's eyes lifted to Hef's, a silent look passing between them. Silla understood without need for words. This was a death wound.

"Water," snapped Harpa. "Ketill, stop loitering in the doorway and fill a bucket from the stream around back. Silla, fetch the mushrooms third shelf down, fourth jar from the right."

The bald warrior hastened out the door while Silla rushed to find the mushrooms. As she moved, she felt dazed, as though her feet were not planted on solid ground. Suddenly, her woes from earlier felt so small.

She scanned the jars on Harpa's shelves, her eyes snagging on one at the very top corner. Recognition landed like a full-body slap. Silla steadied herself on the worktable as her vision tunneled.

Gnarled green leaves crammed into a jar.

Silla breathed in, then out. The leaves looked like home, like comfort, like poison and lies. *Ten years,* they whispered. *We were so good together. Why did you stop?*

Fingernails dug into her palms as Silla's body trembled with restraint. Her skin felt too tight, her heart racing with need.

One leaf to feel better. A second to forget.

"Silla!" barked Harpa.

"I see them," Silla lied. She moved as though in a trance, with slow, unsteady movements. Silla pulled a chair to the shelf, glancing over her shoulder. Harpa and both warriors were bent over Freydis's broken body, their backs to her. Silla reached up. Took the jar of skjöld leaves. Stepped down and slipped it into her provisions sack.

Guilt slid through Silla's veins, but by now it was an old companion.

With a long breath, she found the jar of withered mushrooms and brought them to Harpa. She recognized them by scent—the same ones she'd been offered during her Cohesion Rite to bring her into the folds of her mind.

And Silla understood. Harpa's goal was to ease Freydis's suffering. To give her peace in death.

Heart pounding, Silla followed Harpa's clipped directions and prepared a tea from the mushrooms. After several long minutes, she approached the bed, a cup of the steeped liquid clutched in hand. Hef's eyes shone, his face taut with grief, while Ketill cast Silla a sidelong glance as she approached. Harpa had covered Freydis's stomach with a blanket—had wiped the grime from her face. Candles were lit around the bed, and Harpa's head was bent low as she muttered something indecipherable. The injured woman's back bowed off the bed, and she released a sound of agony.

"We will give you a moment to say your goodbyes," said Harpa, taking the cup from Silla and setting it on the floor beside the bed. "Call to me when you're ready."

Harpa strode across the room, snatching Silla's cloak and provisions sack. Heart hammering in her skull, her knees, her fingertips, Silla trailed her outdoors.

"We are done for today," said Harpa. "You will rest your body and your mind. Think very hard about what it is you want."

Silla held her breath. Did Harpa know what she'd taken? Had she seen her? But as Harpa handed her bag and cloak over, Silla allowed herself a long exhale.

"Don't return until you're ready to stop running." Harpa paused, watching Silla in that knowing way of hers. Cheeks reddening, Silla stared at her feet like a child scolded.

She felt too much in that moment—sorrow for Freydis; anger at Harpa's bluntness; shame for her own failings. And the ever-present burn of guilt. She craved the numbness—a reprieve from it all. Silla pushed away from the wall.

And as she rode through the shimmering edge of the wards, Hef's voice rang out in the clearing.

"It is time, Harpa."

CHAPTER 36

A flurry of soft peeps met Rey's ears from the crate he balanced on the front of the saddle. The waning sun shone sharply on their backs as they rode down the trail. After a day spent patrolling Kalasgarde and its surrounding farmsteads, Rey was weary. To his knowledge, the creature had not struck after all, which left him wondering. Was the seven-day cycle merely coincidence?

During a last patrol of Vig's farmstead, Vig had mentioned a new hatching of chicks, and the idea had struck Rey. For days he'd racked his mind for a way to put a smile on Silla's face. The corners of his lips twitched as he thought of her surprise when he passed her a handful of baby chicks.

"You must return them to me soon, else Runný will tear me a new arse," warned Vig as he and Rey rode along the trail. "She's gotten rather fond of this brood. Their mother wanted nothing to do with them, so they won't miss her one bit. Just feed them, and they'll love you. Chickens are simple like that."

Vig paused, and Rey could feel his apprehension. "I'll muster the neighbors to patrol the walls tonight, but I'm needed on the steading tomorrow. You'll manage without me?"

Rey nodded, trying to piece together a plan. Without knowing what the creature was, he couldn't build a trap, but he could try to lure it, perhaps with a sheep's carcass.

They crossed the threshold of the shield-home's wards to find Silla slashing a wooden sword through the air. Had she ridden back from Harpa's *alone* with the beast lurking about these parts? Anger gathered in his gut, but it quickly gave way to worry.

Rey had always been attuned to this woman—long had he watched her from the corner of his eye, marking each smile, each flinch, each small expression. So perhaps it was no surprise that he saw it immediately.

Something was wrong.

"Go home, Vig," said Rey.

"Thank you for your help, Vig," replied Vig in a mocking voice. "Thank you for your excellent navigation skills, Vig. Thank you for lending us your chickens, Vig."

Rey fought the urge to roll his eyes. "Thank Gyda for us," he said, just to irritate the man. "For sending the evening meal over."

"Arse," Vig muttered with a scoff, but Rey heard the telltale signs of his mount turning then riding back down the trail.

Dismounting, he watched Silla as he led Horse to the stables. Her hair was loose and hiding her face as she moved through her practice with uncharacteristic carelessness. As she swung the practice sword with upward momentum, her foot caught on a stone, and she stumbled forward with a curse.

Rey had seen a hundred small mistakes in that singular move, but he knew better than to point them out. After pulling Horse's saddle off and freshening her water, he decided to leave the chicks in the stables until he could speak to Silla.

Cautiously, he approached. "In need of a sparring partner?"

She pushed tangled coils from her face, giving him a clear view of her red-rimmed eyes.

"What is it?" he snapped, more harshly than he'd intended. Rey couldn't help it—the evidence of her tears made him want to sink an axe into someone's skull.

"You should visit your grandmother," Silla said, not meeting his gaze.

"What happened?" he asked.

"A woman died."

"Who?" Rey demanded, trying to calm his thudding heart.

"Freydis," replied Silla.

"Hef's wife," muttered Rey, dragging his hands through his hair. "How. What happened?"

"Your creature, I assume," said Silla.

Rey blew out a long breath. Vig had heard that Hef and Freydis were out of town. They'd been to Hef's farmstead and found it vacant; he'd assumed the rumor to be true. Too late—they'd been too late to stop the thing, and now it would be another seven days before he had a chance . . .

"You must go to Harpa's."

"The creature won't attack for another seven days," Rey said, watching her.

Silla shuddered. "It . . . left something in her."

"Something?" Rey fought the instinct to charge off to Harpa's, to discover what was left behind in the woman's body. But there was something in Silla's voice that gave him pause.

"I do not know what it was. I was sent away." Her voice trembled.

Rey strode forward and pulled her to him. Seeing her like this made a chasm of hurt open in his chest. If he could, Rey would take the pain from her and endure it himself. He'd failed to intercept the creature, and he'd failed to help Silla through her struggles over the past days and weeks. Right now, he felt like he couldn't do anything right.

"You must go to Harpa's," she said, her voice muffled against him.

"No," he said, more forcefully than he meant to. But the decision rooted itself deep in his chest. The knowing feeling told him he was needed here tonight. With her. "The creature has struck. I now have seven days to see Harpa." His hand went to her hair, stroking it gently. "Was it an ugly sight?"

"She died and I . . . I . . ." She buried her face in his chest. Rey smoothed his hands over her curls, stumbling for the right words. Inwardly, he cursed himself.

"Why am I here, Rey?"

His hands stilled. It was not what he'd expected her to say. "For safety. To learn from Harpa."

"I cannot do it," she whispered, so softly he barely heard it.

"You've killed one of the most notorious kommandors in the kingdom. You killed a seasoned assassin, one who bested even me." Pride swelled in his chest, and Rey hoped he'd at last found the right words. "You can do anything you set your mind to."

But she pushed him with surprising force. Dragging her hair from her face, she sent him a look of pure fire that had Rey frowning. Not, apparently, the right thing to say at all.

Silence stretched out for several moments, until she said, "Spar with me."

With a nod, Rey fetched his practice sword, and they worked through the motions. She was sluggish and unfocused, but Rey understood that today was less about precision and more about doing *something*. And so, for an hour, he blocked her sloppy attacks and let her gain ground, which he wouldn't ordinarily allow.

As she lunged at him with an entirely predictable slash, he let her land a blow and knock the practice sword from his hand.

"I do not want your pity," she seethed, wiping her sweat-dampened brow.

Rey scowled. "I do not—"

"Stop letting me win."

"Very well." He retrieved his sword, watching her warily. Silla looked like a caged animal, pacing with restless energy.

Setting his jaw, he widened his stance, Silla mirroring his movements. And then Rey let two decades of practice take hold—the flat of his blade slapping her sword hand, a thrust forward to capture her slender wrist in his hand. He wrenched her around until her back was pressed to his chest.

Her scent hit his bloodstream, dizzying his thoughts. Rey tried to still his body's response to the expanse of her touching him—tried not to note the heave of her chest as her mind caught up.

Lowering his head to the shell of her ear, Rey whispered, "You need to rest, Silla."

"Stop telling me to *rest*!" Rey's brows drew together at her outburst. She struggled against him, and he released her. Whirling, she faced him. "I do not need rest. I need to get her."

Rey's mind raced to fill the gaps in her words. "Saga."

Silla retrieved her sword and faced him with those burning eyes. "Again."

"No," he growled. She turned away with an irritated huff. "Silla."

She took an attack position, preparing to run through the sequence once more.

"How long have you been at this, Silla?"

She shrugged.

His eyes narrowed. "How long have you been at this?"

Silence.

"When is the last time you ate?"

She did not respond.

Rey's low growl shook the air. "Come into the shield-house and rest. Eat something. Afterward, if you wish to continue, you can come back out."

"You go. I will stay."

Rey gritted his teeth. "You'll run yourself ragged."

"Sounds like a pleasant improvement," she muttered.

Rey grabbed her shoulder before she could turn away. This was more than Freydis's death. More than a failure to express her galdur. "What happened?"

She wouldn't meet his eye.

He gave her a gentle shake. "What. Happened."

"Nothing."

She tugged against his grip, but he lashed out with a second hand, his hold ironclad. "If you won't take care of yourself, then I'll be forced to do it for you." And with that, he hooked an arm around her waist, threw her over his shoulder, and strode toward the shield-home. Silla cried out, pounding on his back, kicking at his front, but she was no match for his size or strength.

After kicking the door open, he dumped Silla onto the bench near the hearth, pinning her arms firmly in place as she fought like an angry cat. "Must I fetch the ropes, or will you stay?"

To Rey's relief, she stilled at that.

"Now," said Rey, "I don't know what happened, but I do know something troubles you. Loath though I am to"—his lip curled—"*speak* of such things, I think it would benefit you."

She said nothing, so he continued. "As I am not a Reader of minds, if you will not tell me what haunts you, I will hazard a guess that your practice did not go well. You struggle to clear your mind, and I think I know why." His stomach burned. Gods above, but he did not wish to broach this topic, but it had to be said. Rey took a deep breath and forced the words out. "I think you're haunted by what Jonas did. It was a vile, horrid thing. A craven thing. Yes, he acted in grief, but—"

"I don't care about him!" she burst out.

Rey blinked. "You . . . you don't?"

"No!"

"Why not?" It was a question he had no business asking, yet Rey could not help himself.

Her teeth sank into her soft lower lip. "He . . . I . . ." Silla's head tilted back, and she let out a long sigh. "It is complicated."

Releasing her arms, Rey crouched at her level to study her face. He wanted to know . . . *needed* to know. "I have nothing but time."

Her eyes met his, and she puffed a breath of surprise. "You don't want to hear such things—"

"You can say anything to me," Rey found himself saying, "if it makes you feel better." Immediately, he felt a pang of regret—he'd laid himself too bare, and he longed to snatch the words back. But after a searching look, words rushed out of her.

"I thought perhaps I cared for him. But now . . . now I understand I was lonely and sad, and he made me feel good for a time." Silla closed her eyes and inhaled shakily. "He was like the skjöld leaves. A thing to drown my sorrows. A tonic for my grief. A distraction that went very, very wrong."

Though her words held nothing but torment, something in Rey's chest woke up and sang. It was wrong for him to be so pleased, and yet he could not suppress it . . .

Rey forced his gaze to harden. His hand slid around hers, squeezing gently. Her fingers were ice-cold. How long had she been out there? "Distraction or not," he said, "what he did to you was loathsome. You did not deserve—"

"It was *exactly* what I deserved."

"What?"

"Ilías," she said, her voice breaking. And then, understanding grew within him. "Ilías is dead because of *me*. Tell me you wouldn't have done the same had it been your brother."

Rey forced in a deep, steady breath, trying to corral his thoughts. When he spoke at last, his voice was low. "No, I would not, Silla." Her gaze snapped to his, eyes wide and shining. "Now listen, as I will tell you this but once. Ilías's death is not yours to own."

Her brows furrowed, and Rey wanted to reach out and smooth the line that had formed between them. "I loved Ilías like a brother, but he died because he lacked control in that battle. Had he waited for Jonas, for Hekla or Gunnar to cover his flank, he'd most certainly have walked away from it. His death is *not yours to own*."

"He would not have been in battle were it not for me."

"How greedy of you to take his death wholly," said Rey. "Do not I bear some of the blame for leading him into this battle? And what of Ilías himself? Yes, this was the fight that ended Ilías's life, but if not this one, it could easily have been another. He rushed into the fray without waiting for one of us to guard his flank. Do you know how many times I tried to help him master this impulse? How many battles he survived by sheer luck? I warned him time and time again to work on his control. And at last, his fortune ran out."

She was silent for a long while, and so Rey continued. "Understand this, Silla: Each battlefield we step onto, we do so knowing it might be our last. It is the risk a warrior takes. And do not forget, we sat around the fire and voted on entering that battle. Ilías accepted the risk—we all did. Unburden yourself from his death. I know Ilías would not wish for you to carry it. He would want you to forgive yourself and to move on with your life."

Minutes passed as they sat like this in silence—Rey crouched before Silla, holding her hand in his. In this moment, she could have asked him for anything, and he'd have done it. Anything to make her smile, to make the light come back to her eyes.

"I have something for you," he said, remembering the chicks.

Setting her hand down, he trudged outside to fetch the crate. But when he returned to the shield-home, Silla was gone, the curtain slid shut.

Rey sank onto the bench. Pried the crate lid open. Pulled a little yellow fluff ball into his hand and stroked the tiny creature's head. The corners of his lips hitched up as he looked at the thing. The chick looked back.

"I suppose," said Rey, "you'll have to settle for me tonight."

The chick peeped.

Rey's gaze traveled to the curtain, and he released a long sigh. At the very least, sleep would serve her better than training in the cold.

CHAPTER 37

The birds chittered and the sun shone with cheer as Silla crossed the yard, yet inside, there was only gloom. The jar was heavy in her pocket, bumping her hip with each step forward. But she didn't need to feel it to sense its presence. Ever since Silla had descended from Harpa's, she'd been hyperaware of the jar.

The cravings slithered through her, the whispers relentless. It was too much on top of all else, and Silla feared it was a foundational stone pulled—at any instant, she could crumble down.

She'd thrown herself into practice for distraction until Rey had put an end to that. Distantly, she'd appreciated his attempts to assuage her guilt, but his words were no match for its all-consuming burn. She'd stolen the leaves while a woman lay dying, and with that, Silla had lost all sense of who she was. It had been a vile thing to do, so despicable she did not recognize herself.

Who was she?

Loathsome and guilt-ridden and so very tired.

Her hand found the jar, curving around the smooth surface.

A sign. Silla yanked her hand away. She needed a sign. Something—*anything*—that would tell her to keep trying. Last night, she'd nearly slipped. Had been staring at the gnarled leaves lined up on her bed. But then a crate had slid under the curtain, a flurry of soft peeps meeting her ears.

Rey had brought her chicks.

It had been the sign she'd needed. Hold strong for one night. Hope that with a good rest would come some clarity of mind. And as Silla had gazed through the slats in the crate at the tiny creatures within, she'd fallen asleep.

And now it was morning, and the clarity she'd sought was nowhere to be found. Brown Horse. If her mount accepted an oatcake, it could be the sign she needed. Silla's guilt burned hotter as she recalled Rey's expression when she'd told him she would not be going to Harpa's today.

"Why not?" he'd demanded, scooping a baby chick away from the table's edge. The chicks tottered around the tabletop like little drunken fluff balls, gorging themselves on a pile of grain in the middle. Ordinarily, she'd have found the scene delightful. But today was different.

"You should ask her yourself," Silla had said, tugging the curtain shut and retreating within.

He'd made as much of a racket as possible as he'd banged through the shield-home, putting the chickens back in the crate. It sounded as though one had escaped as he crashed around the room. And as the door had shut behind him, she'd pulled the jar from her bag. Clutched it against her chest. Pulled off the lid and breathed in the scent.

Just one. She'd stop at one.

Some slim measure of logic remained in place, hanging by a bare thread. Because Silla knew it would never stop at one. Taking a leaf would open a box that was nearly impossible to shut. She tried to recall the pounding of her skull, the cold sweat slicking her brow, the fever dreams that felt terrifyingly real.

"A sign," she said aloud, stepping into the stables. This was it. If Brown Horse took the treat, she wouldn't take the leaves. But if she didn't . . .

She'd weathered so much. Surely she deserved one. Only one.

Silla fetched the oat treat from her pocket and held her palm beneath Brown Horse's nose. She found herself holding her breath, the last vestige of hope wriggling deep in her chest as this weighted moment stretched on. Brown Horse's tail swished. Her ears flattened. And then she stepped backward with a loud warning snort.

Knees buckling, Silla sank to the cold, hard ground of the stable. A sob choked out of her. She was so lost.

You know how to find your way back to the light.

The thought was a knife slicing through her anguish. With utter calm, Silla reached into the pocket of her cloak. Pulled out the jar. It was small, nondescript. And yet it held her salvation, the cure to her torment.

"Poison," she whispered, but her words were so feeble.

Antidote, it whispered back.

"Trouble," she countered.

Peace, it purred.

Silla twisted the jar back and forth. Back and forth. How easy it would be to pull the lid from the jar, to pluck a leaf and tuck it into her cheek. Her guilt would vanish in an instant, warmth bathing her from within. It would be a homecoming—a reunion with a long-lost friend.

Everything seemed to fade around her. There were only the leaves and their constant, unrelenting draw. With each passing second, Silla's will crumbled just a little more. Why was she resisting? Hadn't Harpa said she must surrender?

It was not the same. But how did she surrender? How did she free herself so she could move forward?

Her father would have been able to explain it to her. But he was gone, and she was alone, missing him so fiercely that it physically hurt. Silla shoved thoughts of him aside, then paused.

That was what she always did—pushed the hurt aside. Locked it in a cage.

Of course she pushed the hurt aside; it was human—instinctive. *Surrender,* echoed Harpa's voice in her mind.

The knowing feeling in Silla's stomach warned her against it. In fact, every part of her fought it. How could something that felt so wrong be good for her?

Silla toyed with this corner of her mind, assessing the bones of her hurt. So long had she sought refuge from the raw, aching wound her father had left behind. It was a hopelessly tangled mess of emotions—she missed him and loved him so much, yet Silla couldn't shake the bitterness of his betrayal or the guilt of his death.

It's your fault, he whispered in her mind. The words burned as they always did. But this time, Silla ignored the instincts screaming for her to cage it away. Instead, she gave it free will to say what it would. *Your fault,* it repeated.

"It's your fault, too," she replied sharply, surprising herself.

I died to protect you, he whispered. *And now you squander it.*

"I didn't ask you to die for me," said Silla, the words rising from deep within her. "And I didn't want you to." Silla's confidence grew. "You *left* me," she accused. "You left me alone and vulnerable."

Silla thought of that night in the Twisted Pinewoods, the feeling of abandonment she'd silenced with an extra skjöld leaf. Realization jostled her. That was the start, the beginning of her desperate flee, not only from the Klaernar but from her past. And she hadn't stopped running since.

"You told me *nothing,*" Silla snapped. "Your lies caused undue hardship for me. They endangered my life."

I wanted to spare you from the pain.

"You did nothing but make it worse."

Like the skjöld leaves. Like Jonas. They'd done nothing but form a temporary dam against her grief. And when they were removed, it had only made the flow so much stronger.

Was it the same with her father? Perhaps he'd begun lying in an attempt to protect her when she was young, but with time, the pressure had only grown. To tell her the truth, to admit what he'd done, would have caused anger and strife between them, when already they'd faced so much.

A strange sort of compassion settled in Silla's stomach. Her father had been put in an impossible situation—to shield Princess Eisa from detection. He was not a father by choice, but a warrior, potentially not suited for the task he'd been given. After King Kjartan's death, Matthias could have abandoned Silla and made an easy life for himself, but he had not. Instead, he'd loved her; had dedicated his life to her protection; had sacrificed his own safety, his own well-being. And perhaps, in his mind, shielding her from the truth was merely an extension of this protection.

Tears sprang to her eyes. "Father," she whispered. "I do not agree with what you did, but perhaps I understand." She paused, knowing what she must do, though still she fought against her instincts. It was like walking against the currents of a rushing river, and yet she trudged on. "I forgive you," she whispered. "And I forgive myself."

Silla did not quite believe the words. Did not feel them in the marrow of her bones. But speaking them, even in the barest whisper, felt monumental. The first step toward something.

Surrender, Harpa had said, and Silla opened the cage in the corner of her mind, surrendering herself to the tide of anguish. The pain was acute, invading each corner of her body. She weathered it like a battering storm, braced against the lashing torment.

Time ceased to exist. There was only feeling—only raw, basic emotions—and Silla let herself feel it all. She wallowed in her pain and anger. Reveled in her love and grief. On and on and on it went, and just when she thought it would never end, the current began to ebb.

Silla found herself shivering on the cold stable floor. She was tender, wrung out, wholly exhausted. As she pulled in a shaky breath, Silla's gaze fell upon the jar of skjöld leaves clasped tightly in her hand. She released it with a start. The jar tumbled to the ground, leaves spilling across the hard-packed floor.

Her pulse thudded as she stared at them.

"What—"

Silla's eyes snapped up, finding Rey's large frame filling the stable entry. She hadn't heard him approach, and now it was too late—he'd seen the leaves. He *knew*.

Shame stung her skin, her rib cage expanding and contracting with each deep breath she took. Silla braced herself for anger but was surprised when a gentle voice met her ears. "Where did you get those?"

"Harpa's."

He cursed under his breath. "Did you . . ." His voice trailed off.

She shook her head, kicking the jar away. How easy it would have been to take one . . . how quickly her life could have been altered . . .

Rey crouched low to the ground, scooping the leaves back into the jar. Then, to her surprise, he sank down beside her.

The moment she'd spoken words of forgiveness, Silla had known what she would do. But Rey's reassuring presence grounded her, solidifying the choice. It was still quite possibly the most difficult thing she'd done in her life.

"Can you get those away from me?" she asked in a quiet voice. Both relief and regret battled in a confusing bid for dominance. "Bring them back to Harpa or . . ." A pungent smell filled her nose. She turned to see a wisp of smoke drifting from Rey's closed hands. He brushed his hands together, ash crumbling to the stable ground.

Gone. They were gone.

She hadn't given in. This time.

A sob broke in the back of her throat.

"Shh," said Rey. She felt him move closer, a heavy arm rolling around her shoulders and pulling her to him. "It's all right, Silla. You didn't take them."

A breath shuddered from her. "I'm one bad decision away from ruining everything." The tremble in her hands intensified. "I nearly ruined everything!"

Her entire body was now quivering. An arm snaked around her waist, and she felt herself lifted and pulled across his lap. He was warm and solid, something she could hold on to, and she sank into him, the steady thump of his heart reassuring against her cheek.

"You didn't, though."

She hadn't taken them. She *hadn't taken them.*

Silla had resisted the pull of the leaves. Had stopped running from her grief. Had faced it head-on. Had forgiven her father and had taken the first step toward forgiving herself. And that was something altogether new.

She felt subtly different. As though everything had shattered, and new, tiny bonds were being forged. Perhaps, over time, these bonds might just grow to be stronger than before they'd broken.

Rey's hand slid into her hair, making tender strokes along her scalp. "You didn't take them. That you're still trying says everything about how strong you are."

A sob grew within her, clawing to get loose in her throat, and her hand moved absently to his chest, clutching the buckle of his lébrynja jacket. "I'm tired of being strong. I'm just tired."

Rey's hand moved from her hair down her back, running gently up and down her spine. "You don't have to be strong all the time. Let me be strong for you."

It was the permission she needed to give herself over, to allow herself to crumble from within and let her emotions fill the emptiness inside her. Once the tears started, she couldn't stop them. Rey's arms tightened, his fingers pressing into her hip and around her shoulder as he held her firmly to him.

She wasn't sure how long they sat like this, but eventually, the tears ceased to flow. Perhaps her emotions had worn themselves out, or perhaps she'd run out of tears. Rey's fingers brushed across her cheeks, swiping her tears away. After a moment's hesitation, he pressed a kiss to her hair with aching tenderness.

"Come into the shield-house," Rey said quietly, pulling her to her feet. "Let us warm by the fire. Perhaps have a midday meal. Then you can rest. Or hold a chick. I'll admit they are . . . tolerable."

The corners of her lips twitched, but at that moment, something soft and warm nuzzled her cheek. Silla gasped, blinking. Surely she'd imagined it, but . . . there! A gentle tug on her hair, hot breath on her neck.

Slowly, Silla turned. Brown Horse stared back, several curly locks of hair held between her lips. Silla fought back tears of disbelief. "Are you hungry?" she asked softly, afraid to break the spell.

"It's not exactly an act of respect," grumbled Rey. But he fetched the oatcake and pressed it into Silla's hand. "Here."

Silla lifted her palm. Flattened it. Held herself unflinchingly still.

And then it happened.

Brown Horse released Silla's hair and dipped her head. Her nose slid along Silla's palm, then the treat was plucked from her hand.

The tears streaked freely down her cheeks, her chest expanding with warmth.

Brown Horse.

Brown Horse had willingly come to her. Had allowed Silla to feed her.

If this was not a sign from the gods, Silla didn't know what was.

Unbidden, Matthias's words came to Silla—a thing he'd said following her mother's execution. They'd fled from the village, leaving behind their friends, their home, their chickens.

Remember, Moonflower, it is always darkest just before dawn.

Tears spilled down Silla's cheeks, and she whispered to Brown Horse, "I have a proper name for you, girl. It is a name for hope and new beginnings. A reminder that it is always darkest before first light."

Rey watched her silently.

"I will call you Dawn."

CHAPTER 38

Kopa

Hunched over a horn of ale, Jonas tried his best to feign disinterest in the pair seated beside him. As evening progressed, the mead hall had grown more and more busy, Klaernar warriors filtering in as the night watch took over. It was perfect, truly. With burly warriors milling about and growing increasingly intoxicated, it forced the men to raise their voices in order to hear one another over the crowd.

Over the past weeks, the sight of claw-tattooed faces and snarling bear shoulder plates had become a regular occurrence. Jonas told himself he kept coming back to this mead hall because he'd been kicked out of all the others in Kopa. But it wasn't altogether true.

It was like a scab he couldn't help but pick at. What had started as a mild case of curiosity had quickly spiraled. Jonas found himself watching Kaptein Ulfar from across the room. Then from just down the bench. And now from directly beside him. Gradually, he'd picked up small details on the Klaernar's investigation into the Slátrari. From the man who'd tried to claim Rey was hiding among the Sleeping Dragons, to the one who'd claimed he was tilling fields near Midfjord, none of the information the Klaernar had received was remotely accurate.

At first, Jonas had felt relief. Relief that his brother-in-arms was lying low. If he knew Rey, the man was concocting a plan, keeping two steps ahead of his enemies. But as the days moved on and the Klaernar grew irritated, new thoughts settled in place.

No one had come forward with *true* information. It was becoming increasingly evident just how well Rey had kept his identity hidden.

Jonas couldn't help but wonder if the Bloodaxe Crew had been merely a cover for Rey while he went about killing people. Why had he never confided in the Crew . . . in *Jonas*? Five years, they'd fought side by side—had saved each other from death countless times. But now that Jonas knew the truth, the past took on new meaning.

All the deeds he'd done with the Bloodaxe Crew felt . . . empty. Naught but a ruse to buy Reynir Bjarg's cover. He was Galdra. Probably belonged to one of those Galdra rebel groups fighting against the king. The thought tasted bitter, but the more he considered it, the more it made sense.

His memory flitted back to that meeting with Magnus Hansson in Reykfjord all those weeks ago. They'd discussed the gods damned Slátrari, with Rey seated beside him. He'd probably gone back to his chambers and had a good laugh about it.

Nausea twisted in Jonas's stomach. It was only one of many meetings he and Rey'd had with Magnus Hansson. Jonas went back over them all. Had Rey been more talkative than usual? Had he pressed Magnus for details on strange things? Jonas could not remember. But the very thought made him feel soiled. Used.

"Makes no sense!" muttered Kaptein Ulfar, handing the letter to a black-bearded warrior, who, Jonas had learned, was called Hagbard.

Hagbard, it seemed, was not so keen a reader. "All-peen catspaw," he labored.

"Ursir's bloody liver," said Ulfar, snatching the letter back. "Alpine catspaw, you kunta. Dry for two weeks, then grind to a fine powder." He looked up at Hagbard. "What does it *mean*?"

Hagbard blinked, clearly just as enlightened as Ulfar. "If it's orders, it's orders," the man said with a shrug.

"Are we to take it in our róa? Smear it on our skin? There's no directions." Scowling, Ulfar drank deeply from his horn of ale. "For all

I know, it could be a poison . . . perhaps a sleep aid to help with their capture."

"Can't capture someone you cannot find," Hagbard said glumly.

The look Ulfar sent him could shatter glass. "They'll be found." He lowered his voice and Jonas leaned closer. "We've a new lead." When Hagbard stared blankly, Ulfar continued. "Haeth."

"Haeth?" repeated Hagbard, dumbly.

"Shhh, you muttonhead!" hissed Ulfar. "Yes. *There*. We've had it from a reputable source, one who's known the man since childhood. He could answer all our questions about the Slátrari, though he does not know the girl. Apparently, they grew up together in Haeth. Says the man went mad a few years back. Burned a few homes before fleeing town."

"No surprise," muttered Hagbard.

Jonas closed his eyes. Clenched his jaw tight. Whoever had provided this information was woefully incorrect. Haeth was in the farthest southern corner of Nordur lands—about as far from Kalasgarde as one could get. Jonas saw this tip immediately for what it was. Deliberate misdirection.

Of course Rey would have mysterious allies to cover his arse. More questions built in his mind, the answers to which Jonas knew he wouldn't like.

Inside, he was at war. Rey had been like a brother to him, but all this time, he'd lied right to Jonas's face. Not small, inconsequential lies. Huge lies. Life-endangering lies. All while demanding the absolute truth from the Bloodaxe Crew.

Rey and his gods damned *honor*.

What was honor to a man who was such a hypocrite—who lied so freely? Where was Rey's honor when he'd led Ilías into a battle without proper forethought?

Fuck honor.

And fuck Rey.

He turned to Kaptein Ulfar. Put his hand on the man's shoulder. Ulfar turned, meeting Jonas's eye.

"Kalasgarde," he said. "The man you seek is in Kalasgarde."

PART 2

DAWN

DAHN

1. The first appearance of daylight in the morning.

2. The beginning of something new.

CHAPTER 39

Kalasgarde

For once, Silla did not dream of death. Instead, she was running through a garden, chasing butterflies with her sister. Her heart was so full, she thought it might burst; her smile so wide, it hurt her cheeks. In this dream, she was free; she was safe and loved. And when she woke, she felt more refreshed than she had in weeks.

Her melancholy hadn't suddenly vanished, but a strange sort of acceptance had settled in her. For weeks, she'd loathed this part of her, had berated and battered it. But all this had done was drive her deeper into the gloom. Only now did Silla realize that what this version of herself needed was compassion. Patience. Forgiveness.

Pulling the furs and blankets back, she climbed out of bed. As autumn neared, the sun rose later each morning, the air growing more crisp. After dressing in legwraps and a loose red tunic, Silla drew the curtain aside. Blinked in surprise.

"Runný?"

Runný reclined on the bench, a yellow chick curled in her palm. Her lips tilted up in a guilty smile. "I missed them," she said, stroking the chick's head.

Silla hesitated. She'd been distant with Runný. Had not been terribly friendly. But putting up those walls had been just as draining as caging away her grief. And in that moment, Silla decided things would change. Sinking onto the bench beside Runný, she pulled a second chick from the crate. "Thank you for letting us borrow them."

"That one is Bandit," said Runný, nodding at the fluff ball in Silla's hand. "He steals from the cat's dish."

"Bandit." Silla scratched the chick's head fondly. "And yours?"

"Craven," replied Runný. "Prefers to let the others fight his battles. But is the fondest of cuddles."

Silla's gaze swept the otherwise unoccupied cabin, falling upon the hard, narrow bench where Rey had been sleeping. His furs and blankets were neatly folded.

"Where has Rey gone?"

Runný shrugged. "I do not know. Only that he asked me to stay with you."

"Oh," Silla started, cheeks burning. "I . . . that's . . . my thanks."

Runný waved off her embarrassment. "That one is Hábrók," she said, pointing to the crate. "The most violent of the bunch."

Silla couldn't help but smile at the tiny tuft of yellow glaring up from within the crate. Tucking her feet up beneath her, Silla relaxed. She and Runný stayed like this, chatting for some time. Runný told her about the steading, indulging Silla's questions about all the animals they kept. She told her of the goat named Helga and the tyrant goose who'd declared war on Vig. She told her of the long winters in Kalasgarde, of being cooped up in a small home with four wild brothers. Of her dreams of going south someday. To Silla's great relief, Runný asked little of her.

Eventually, Silla's stomach growled loudly, and she handed Bandit over. After washing her hands, she busied herself cooking the daymeal. The past weeks had been so trying, Silla hadn't been able to cook. Now, putting herself through the familiar motions of peeling apples, toasting grains, and stirring the bubbling porridge was like stepping into a pair of well-worn shoes.

Just as she was spooning the daymeal into a pair of bowls, the door scraped open, and a rush of cool mountain air carried into the cabin. Rey shut the door behind him. Their eyes met across the hearthfire, and a thousand thoughts crowded Silla's mind.

But Runný was here, and thanking him felt like a thing to be done when they were alone.

"You cooked," said Rey.

Silla nodded, fetching a third bowl and spooning it full as he hung his wolf pelt on a peg. They gathered at the table, chicks pecking around their feet as they ate. Rey went back for seconds and then thirds. Silla smothered a smile as he scraped the bottom of the cauldron with a wooden spoon and licked it clean.

When he caught her watching him, he quirked a brow. "I missed your cooking," he said with a shrug. The words landed like a hug, wrapping around her middle with delicious warmth.

After the daymeal, Runný departed. Alone with Rey, Silla felt a little uncertain. The day before, he'd seen the ugliest parts of her. But he hadn't balked—hadn't run away. And as he beckoned her outdoors for their morning sparring routine, she began to relax.

"Take me down, Sunshine," he said, a gleam in his eye. And with that, her nerves had an outlet. If Silla had worried yesterday might change things between them, Rey's dry commentary immediately put her at ease: "You'll have to do better than that" and "Why are you breathing so hard?" and "You're slower than the tides today."

To Silla's great pleasure, Rey didn't allow her to win a single time.

"You've got a crowd," he said, as she wiped sweat from her brow. Half a dozen shining blue ice spirits peeked at her from behind the foliage, zipping deeper into the woods when they spotted her looking.

She decided the beautiful, winged spirits were an optimistic sign from the gods. "They must like my offerings," Silla said in delight. Indeed, the offerings of sheep's milk and butter she'd left on a stump near the stables were gone.

As Rey stowed the practice weapons away, Silla made her way to the stables. Approaching Horse first, Silla pulled an oat treat from her pocket. Horse, predictably, nuzzled hers at once. Slowly, she approached Dawn, watching the horse's nostrils flare as she scented the treat.

"Now, Dawn, I know we've had a rough path, but yesterday was something special. A fresh start. I can do this alone, girl, but I'd rather do it with you. So I'm going to hold this treat out, and I promise not to look. It's there if you want it."

Silla pulled the treat from her pocket. Flattened her palm and turned her head away. *Surrender,* she urged herself, vowing to love her stubborn horse just as she was, even if she didn't take the—

A breath steamed her palm. Silla's eyes widened, but she did not turn her head. A soft nose nuzzled against her. And then the treat was gone.

An explosion of light and warmth and happiness filled Silla as she hazarded a glance at Dawn. The horse's ears flicked in agitation. "Good girl," Silla whispered, backing away slowly.

As she exited the stables, Silla paused. Squeezed her eyes shut. And wriggled with utter delight. When she opened her eyes, they landed on a tall, dark figure leaning casually against the shield-home's door. Rey's lips quirked into an almost-smile.

And Silla smiled right back.

If Harpa was surprised to see Silla cross the wards on her property, she showed no trace of it. Her arms were folded over her chest, and the swath of white in her black curls shone like snow on a mountaintop.

Dismounting, Silla felt uncertain. Like Rey, Harpa had seen the less savory parts of her. After a moment's consideration of how to approach it, direct felt best. "I'm sorry—" Silla started.

But Harpa cut her off with a wave of her hand. "Do not be sorry. Be open. Be willing."

Silla swallowed. "I'm ready."

A slow smile curved Harpa's lips. "Finally. Come, we have much to do."

And as Silla followed her mentor into the cabin, she felt the strangest thing—possibility.

Days passed without outward success. Mornings were spent working on her mindfulness in Harpa's cabin, afternoons chopping wood in the yard. More ice spirits found her each day, jostling and hissing at one another while she swung the axe. She greeted them and told them about her day while they looped and whirled and wrote those curious runes on rocks and fence posts.

Her lengthy rest in the steam bath's languid heat was the highlight of Silla's day. The whispers persisted, as always, but instead of caging them away, Silla endured them. It was counterintuitive, this kind of surrendering. Rather than seeking peace and shelter, it felt a lot like exposing herself to dangerous elements. And yet the only way out of the storm was through it.

On the sixth day since her breakdown, Silla knew what was to come. She did not fight it when Harpa nodded at the woodpile. Did not curse inwardly or question the rationale of her mentor. She was stoic and determined. Her path was set, and all that was to be done was to follow it.

There was such peace in acceptance.

Silla collected the axe and made her way to the chopping stump. She chattered mindlessly at the twenty or so ice spirits zipping back and forth at the edge of her vision and swung the axe over and over, until her shoulders ached and sweat dotted her brow.

As she worked, Silla considered her progress this week. So much of her suffering had come from fighting against herself. She had fought her guilt and grief, had smothered the things she'd lived through, had clung to her dreams long after they'd been shredded. For so long, Silla had thought surrendering meant giving up. But to her utter surprise, surrendering had only brought freedom.

Silla considered this. Would it be the same with *her*—Eisa Volsik?

The familiar coil of nausea tightened her stomach.

You'll lose your freedom. The name is shackles. More death. More misery.

Silla acknowledged these fears and let them seep into her. There were so many unknowns with Eisa. So many dangers. But what did fighting against her true name accomplish? What would it feel like to surrender to Eisa Volsik? To let go of what could never be and dream of what could?

The nausea did not let up, and so Silla fell into old patterns—pushing the fear down. Burying it. She forgave herself for doing so.

It was only for now. And Silla swore to herself that day by day, she would dig up this fear and surrender just a bit more of herself.

Miracles rarely happened overnight.

At last, the unexpected happened—Silla ran out of logs to split. Wiping her brow, she made her way to the cabin. She stepped inside, and at first it was so silent and still, Silla thought Harpa had left on some errand. But the soft knock of stones had her eyes darting to the farthest back corner. Harpa stood at her enormous warp-weighted loom, fingers moving with rapid, dextrous speed. Beneath it, the weight stones tapped together in an oddly soothing rhythm.

The air held a peculiar quality—a low thrum that pressed lightly against her skin. She opened her mouth to speak but paused as she caught sight of Harpa's eyes—an eerie milk white. Turning quietly, Silla slipped back out and made her way toward the steam bath.

She stripped down to her undertunic and spooned water over the stones; a satisfying sizzle filled the air. Silla reclined on the bench. The heat loosened her tense muscles and eased the cold from her blood. Warm and languid, wrung out from her emotions and hours spent chopping wood, Silla focused on the beating of her heart.

Soon her forearms began to glow, the cool buzz of galdur in her veins. Silla closed her eyes, relinquishing herself to the whispers, letting them have their say before releasing them. She felt herself sinking deep down, filled with utter awareness. Her blood pumped through her veins in a sure, steady rhythm. Her lungs pulled hot, steamy air in then out. And her galdur whispered coolly through her, that familiar tension building.

Then she sensed it—the lessening of tension. Like a tiny crack in a cup, her galdur leaked out. She opened her eyes.

Stared in disbelief.

Tiny motes of light drifted up from her forearms, rising through the steam bath and melting before her eyes. A thrill of victory zipped through her. After weeks of trying, she'd finally done it! But the moment she let herself celebrate, the crack sealed over, the specks of light vanishing. And then the tension began building anew.

Silla probed inwardly. Now that she knew how it felt, it took only a few minutes to find the fractured place again. To Silla, it felt like a crevasse—cold and deep, with a surface that could be thawed or frosted over at will. Like a muscle, controlling this thing would take continued effort. But eventually, perhaps, it would be as intuitive as breathing.

With a smile, Silla tugged on her clothes and rushed to the cabin. Harpa was slumped in a chair, a damp linen draped over her eyes. At Silla's entry, she pulled the cloth off and looked at her expectantly.

"I did it," said Silla, biting down on her smile. "I expressed."

Harpa nodded wearily. "I knew you would do it."

And as the faintest hint of a smile curved Harpa's lips, Silla felt as though she could fly.

CHAPTER 40

Some might call Rey tenacious, others stubborn as a rock goat. But when he set his mind to something, he always saw it through. And six days ago, as he'd examined the tooth Harpa had pulled from Freydis's abdomen, he'd known they were another step closer to solving the vexing mystery of what, precisely, was hunting Kalasgarde's citizens.

The fang was a perfect match to the one they'd excised from the excrement.

"What does it mean?" Vig had asked impatiently.

Rey had remained silent for a ponderous moment, examining the hollow groove through the fang's center. "It didn't eat a serpent. It *is* a serpent."

"You expect me to believe that?" Vig scoffed.

"It makes no sense," Rey replied. "No sense at all that such a creature could survive in the northern wilds. But the facts are what they are: Serpents are known to swallow their own teeth *and* digest the bones of their prey. They eat at timed intervals and can grow to cumbersome sizes after a large feeding. It fits, Vig."

"Hábrók's flaming bollocks!" sputtered Vig. "Two dozen sheep, Galtung! What kind of serpent eats *two dozen* sheep?"

"That," said Rey, "I do not know." He wasn't sure he *wanted* to know. His thoughts drifted to the skógungar that had attacked Jonas along the Road of Bones. Another creature acting outside its nature. It, too, had carried the scent of rot, which had lingered on Freydis's corpse and in Vig's paddock. He thought of Istré, with the pulsing mist and curious Klaernar deaths. What the fuck was happening in this kingdom?

"At least it hasn't any teeth now," Vig said.

Rey had scowled. "I very much doubt that. Serpent teeth grow quickly."

"Again, we find answers, but they only create new questions," Vig had said. "Very well, Galtung, I shall put word out . . . and prepare myself to be laughed out of the Split Skull."

And that was precisely what occurred. Vig spread news in Kalasgarde's mead hall and sent word to neighboring towns. All they received was heartfelt laughter. Rey couldn't blame them. A giant serpent hunting the wilds of Nordur was about as believable as Ivar Ironheart suddenly embracing the Galdra.

Rey was unmoved by their reaction. "We will build a trap," he said, which led to days spent engineering it. The contraption he settled on was long and narrow, with dual snares that caused a panel to slide down, trapping the creature in place. Rey and Vig built the trap in a narrow valley backing Vig's farm and would bait it with a fresh sheep carcass. Armed with grit and a plan, Rey was eager for the day the serpent would slither out of its nest.

This time, he'd be ready.

"Take the bed, Galtung," Silla implored. "There's room enough for both of us." Perhaps it was Vig and Runny's influence, but she'd taken to calling him by his last name in the past few days. And Rey had decided he liked it.

He tried not to look but was pulled into her dark gaze. The candle she held cast flickering light on her cheeks—rosy from a day spent training with Harpa. Rey couldn't help but feel a burst of pride.

"I expressed!" Silla had exclaimed when he'd arrived to fetch her from Harpa's. She'd rushed at him, flinging her arms around him. "I did it!"

And Rey had celebrated it as though it had been his own victory. She'd fought so hard for this moment.

After her breakdown in the stables, everything had changed. Grief and guilt persisted in her eyes, but there was a lightness to Silla that had not been there before. She dedicated herself all day long to his grandmother's Galdra training, then poured herself into sparring with him. Unfortunately, Rey's body seemed to take her nearness to mean something altogether different, and he had taken to bathing in the glacial waters of the stream behind the stables afterward.

And Vig's teasing had turned relentless. "Gods, I can't take any more of these long, pining looks," he'd exclaimed one day, exasperated.

"There's no pining, Twig Arms."

"You actually believe that, don't you?" Vig had replied, shaking his head. "Just tell her you want her to stroke your axe."

"Shut your mouth, Vig, or I'll do it for you."

But Vig was only getting started. "Tell her you want to raid her shores."

Rey's glower deepened.

"That you wish to plunder her womanly cavern with your manly serpent."

At that, Rey tackled his friend, forcing his mouth shut. "Stop stirring the pot, Twig Arms."

"Strong Arms," Vig had said, words smothered by Rey's fist.

But Vig's teasing had only raised Rey's hackles. He needed to keep a distance between them, for himself and for her. He was better than Jonas. More masterful of his own desires.

"We shared a tent," Silla now reminded him. "Just get in the damned bed!"

"I don't share," was Rey's low reply. Distance was good. Distance was *necessary*.

With a huff she retreated to her bed with the candle, flinging the curtain shut. He watched her silhouette as she set the candle down. Peeled off her tunic. Rey's skin heated, and he could not look away. His eyes traced the contours of that silhouette—the slope of her neck and curve of her breast. She'd picked up a comb and was working it through the ends of her curls.

How simple it would be to walk to the curtain. Pull it aside. Take the comb from her hand and push her back onto the furs . . .

Rey's body was as tense as before a battle and aching with need. Gritting his teeth, he fetched his soap and a linen to dry off with.

"I'm bathing!" he barked and strode out into the night. *Another cold bath for him.*

Rey was the cleanest he'd ever been.

He was deep in slumber—a rare feat on the bench that currently waged war with his spine—when someone pounded on the door. Logic pierced through sleep's veil, and he was on his feet in an instant, answering the door in only his breeches.

"Vig?" he mumbled, rubbing his face.

"Another boy," was Vig's brisk reply. "Ketill's just told me. Up near Archer's Point."

Rey blinked. "But it's only been six days."

"Perhaps our serpent can't count."

Rey reached for his tunic. Was just pulling it over his head when Silla stumbled out from behind the curtain. Her hair was wild, and she was dressed in naught but a tunic.

With a growl, Rey placed himself between her and the door, blocking her from Vig's view.

"Who is it?" she asked, dark eyes glazed with the remnants of sleep.

"Only me, Silla," called Vig from behind him, and Rey wanted to drive his fist into his friend's skull. Vig rolled his eyes. "I'll saddle your horse, Galtung." The man wisely retreated into the yard.

Rey turned to Silla, unable to keep his eyes from wandering down to her bare toes and back up again. "A boy's gone missing. I must—" He broke off with a sigh. He'd *promised* he wouldn't leave her alone at night. "I'll stay," he said, resigned. "I won't leave you."

But she surprised him, as she so often did. "Go," said Silla, giving him a small, encouraging push toward the door. "There's a boy out there who needs you. Go, Galtung. I shall be fine."

Rey studied her face, searching for any trace of fear or apprehension, but all he found was determination.

She pushed him again, gently. "I'll be fine. I have the chicks now. And you must do this."

Relief rushed through him. She understood his need to see this through. Was willing to face her own fears so readily. And thank the gods above, she didn't insist on coming with him this time. She had the wards. No one knew she was here. And they would only be gone for an hour . . . perhaps two.

As Rey fastened the last buckle on his armor, Silla charged at him, wrapping her arms around him in a tight hug. He cupped the back of her head, holding her to his chest. It took every bit of his restraint not to bury his nose in her hair.

"Be safe," she whispered.

He drew back. Looked down at her. It was strange to see the concern in her eyes—to have someone worry after him. It felt like warmth. Like a reason to come home.

His insides writhed in discomfort.

"I will," was all he said. And with that, he exited the shield-home.

As the door slid shut, Silla curled up on the bench, pulling a fur over her bare legs. It smelled like *him,* and she couldn't help but worry for his safety. But there was a missing boy . . . people who depended on Rey and Vig to chase down that gods-forsaken creature.

"They will return," Silla whispered to the chicks as she pulled them from the crate. They settled in her lap, huddled in a fluffy pile. Hábrók alone remained alert, keeping watch over his brothers and sisters.

The shield-home was quiet, yet Silla knew better than to settle back in bed. Sleep would not find her so long as Rey and Vig were out there.

The man has pond sludge for brains, came a strange voice. *Burning his own boat. What was he thinking?* Silla's spine straightened as she glanced around the cabin to confirm she was alone.

"Hello?" she whispered, concentrating with all her might. But all she heard was the snap of embers in the hearth, the distant whinny of a horse. Silla tried to relax her clenched muscles—tried to sink back into the bench. What had that been? Was her mind playing tricks on her?

"It was nothing," she said aloud, Hábrók peeping in reply. "We must get you a hammer like your namesake." She stroked little Hábrók's fluffy head.

But a horse called out once more, closer this time.

Silla's heart pounded a little harder. "You're being ridiculous," she chided herself.

A log collapsed into the hearthfire, making her jump. The chicks peeped in protest, but she scooped them up, the fur tumbling to the floor. As she deposited them safely in the crate, little Hábrók looked up at her, chirping shrilly.

"Hush, now," cooed Silla. "'Tis only for a moment."

Silla secured the lid in place and turned.

Stumbled backward.

Stared into the eyes of five men. Tall. Bearded. Ropes in hand. And dozens of blades sheathed at their hips.

"This is her?" asked a man with ragged blond hair.

A bald man in the bunch held something in hand—a slab of birch bark, Silla realized in horror. More time, she'd thought they had more time before their images reached Kalasgarde. Gripping the back of the bench to steady herself, Silla took in the familiar blue tattoos scrawled on the pale flesh of the man's shaved head.

"You," she said. "Y-you were at Harpa's. With Hef and Freydis." She pulled the name from the depths of her mind. "Ketill."

Ketill scowled at her, holding up the etching. "Told you it's her. And that was Galtung leaving just now."

A black-haired man with very few teeth danced a jig while the blond man smacked Ketill on the back. "Well, I'll be shitting pinecones. It's *her*. Hiding in Kalasgarde. We'll be rich, boys!"

Ketill's just told me, Vig had said. *Up near Archer's Point.*

But it's only been six days, Rey had replied.

"There's no missing boy," she guessed. "You lured them away." Goosebumps rushed up her bare legs.

Ketill didn't bother to answer. He took a heavy step forward. She took one back. The hearthfire was between them. A bench. But the room was so small, and there was only one exit, and there were five warriors blocking it . . .

The blond man pulled a rag from his pocket, a sickly-sweet scent filling the air. Slowly, he rounded the other side of the fire. "Come now, girl. Have a sniff of this and then a good nap, and it'll all be done when you wake."

Silla's hand found the patch of hair cut by Kommandor Valf. "Won't go back," she muttered.

Her gaze settled on a handaxe propped against the hearth. At some point, Rey would realize the missing boy was a ruse and would come back to the shield-home. If she could delay them, perhaps she had a chance. Because Silla knew that even with all her practice, even with good odds, she could not best *five* men.

On the other side of the hearth, the blond-haired man closed in on her. "If it's money you want, then let us talk."

"It has already been decided," grunted Ketill. "We will take you to Kopa and collect a reward."

Won't go back, she thought desperately. And as Silla glanced the blond warrior's way, she saw his tell—the flare of his nostrils. She lunged for the handaxe. Turned on her foot. Slashed it downward.

Blood splattered her face, hot and sticky, but she was already turning, swinging at Ketill. The blade met flesh, then bone. The man bellowed and drove his fist into her jaw.

Her world became nothing but white-hot pain, but she whirled, screaming. The handaxe was knocked from her grip. She was jostled, wrists yanked behind her back. As she blinked, her vision came back, revealing Ketill pulling the axe from his shoulder.

"Oh-ho," he sneered. "Got a feral one, have we?" His gaze fell to the figure lying prone on the floor—the blond man, a gash opened wide in his neck. Ketill's eyes snapped to Silla's, an angry flush creeping up his neck. "You killed my friend," he growled. Ketill nodded at the men holding her. "Release her."

"Need her alive, Ketill," warned one of his companions, hand wrapped tightly around her shoulder. "Just give her the valerian and—"

"She killed Bredi!" snarled Ketill. "Release her!"

With a heavy breath, the man behind her let her go. "No death wounds," he warned.

Silla's chest heaved, confusion muddling her thoughts. Ketill offered her the bloodied handaxe, pulling his own from the loop on his belt. And then she understood. He wanted a fight. Her gaze flicked to the door, then back to Ketill.

She had to draw this out. Give Rey time to return.

Silla took the axe. The warriors eased away, leaving her and Ketill in the space between the bench and the shield-home's wall. The hearthfire cast harsh shadows on Ketill's face, but his eyes burned bright with rage. And in that moment, Silla could only think of that cell in Kopa, the kommandor with his tapestries woven from human hair. She wouldn't. Go. Back.

She rushed at him, axe slicing through the air. Ketill ducked easily, sweeping her feet out from under her. Silla landed hard on her back, her skull missing the bench's edge by scant inches. The warrior's jeers were distant, but she sensed what would come next. Towering over her, Ketill hefted his weapon. She rolled just in time—the axe hacked into the floor inches from her head, splintering wood in all directions.

"*Alive,* bog-brain," said one of the warriors.

"Get up," sneered Ketill, and Silla did not hesitate. Scrambling to her feet, she shoved into his injured shoulder. Startled, Ketill grunted in pain, giving her the opening she needed to drive her axe into his boot.

Ketill howled, stumbling into the bench. Silla pulled the axe free, ignoring the shouting warriors while she assessed Ketill. It seemed she'd wounded more than his foot.

Ketill charged at her with the intensity of a riled bull, and Silla's swing was just a heartbeat too late. Ketill ducked, the full weight of him ramming into her stomach. She was airborne, slamming into the wall and sliding to the ground.

Her chest seized, unable to draw breath. As she tried to force air in, a dark form blotted out the light from the fire—Ketill, glaring at her with utter hatred.

"Get up," he growled.

At last, she was able to draw air into her lungs. Gasping, Silla grabbed her axe and clambered to her feet. Pushing the hair back from her face, she took a defensive stance. Bared legs and feet, bloodied tunic, hair wild, and eyes set. Fury churned in her veins.

"Won't go back," she said through gritted teeth, waiting. Watching.

A quick breath in, and she knew he'd be coming. Ketill swung, and she blocked him, but the force of his blow rattled down her arms. Another swing. Another block. Her teeth clanked together.

He was too strong. She was barely holding on. Cold tension slid through her veins, and Silla knew her fear had primed her.

Ketill's gaze darted to her forearms—glowing where her sleeves had slid up. He sneered. "We're using galdur now, are we?" Dropping his axe, Ketill vanished into thin air.

Shadow Hound.

Silla wasn't calm. She wasn't relaxed. But in the midst of battle, she found herself remarkably clearheaded. There was no space for anything but the here. The now. In a heartbeat, she found the fractured lines of the crevasse inside her. Forced it open. Light sparked from her forearms, hissing in the shield-home's warm air.

It tasted like winter. Felt like destiny.

Ketill's invisible form crashed into her, bringing them both to the floor. Silla's fear channeled straight into her galdur. With a burst of white light, Ketill screamed above her, and he flicked back into view. She shoved him off her and watched in disbelief as he writhed on the floor.

The surrounding warriors roared, and then it was chaos—Ketill thrashing about; the warriors seizing her arms, wrenching them behind her back; the chicks peeping frantically from their overturned crate.

The cabin door crashed open, a large figure filling the frame, and Silla knew a moment of pure fear. It was Rey as she'd never seen him—a lethal combination of Axe Eyes's brutal intensity and the

Slátrari's burning wrath. And in that moment, she knew this man was unmatched. The most deadly of warriors and Galdra alike.

Rey's eyes were an inferno of rage. Smoke spilled from his palms, curling around his arms and flaring with bursts of embers.

The warriors released Silla, stumbling away, but it was too late.

"Six days," said Rey, his voice low and lethal. "It was only six days. You've all just made a grave mistake."

"Wait," pleaded the warrior nearest to Silla, hands raised placatingly.

"How brave you were, five against one," mused Rey, stepping deeper into the shield-home. Wisps of smoke split in the air, churning like wrathful thunderclouds. "Now look at you, begging. Have you no honor?"

The man fell to his knees, shielding his face from the heat of Rey's galdur. "It was Ketill! He promised us sólas. 'Twas *his* plan!"

"Ahh, but you chose to follow him," said Rey bitterly. "Own your choice." Embers detonated within the seething smoke, making the warriors flinch.

"Mercy!" begged the man.

Rey laughed, a dark, jagged sound. "I'll grant you the mercy of choosing your death. Will you die like a coward on your knees or on your own two feet with honor?"

The man swallowed. Pushed to shaky feet. Retrieved his axe and ran at Rey.

Silla knew she should look away but could not. She watched as the smoke surged at the man with the rage of hungry wildfire. It tunneled down his throat, smothering his screams, and swarmed along his skin, leaving blisters in its wake. The other warriors rushed Rey and met the same fate. She watched as their eyes bulged. As their flesh sizzled. As they screamed and clawed, then fell to the floor and contorted wildly.

Rey stepped over the nearest warrior's writhing form, making straight for Silla. Her heart pounded, muscles trembling, and as he crouched, she threw herself at him.

"Thank you," she sobbed into his shoulder. "Thank you. Thank you."

Rey's cloak was off, wrapped around her shoulders. Gripping her chin, he tilted her head left to right, examining her face. Rey closed his eyes. Took a deep breath. And when he reopened his eyes, they burned with anger.

He swallowed, glancing around. Ketill wailed from the room's corner, face still hidden in his hands. But Rey's gaze landed on the blond man, neck split wide by Silla's handaxe. His lips tilted up at the corners. "Your work?"

Silla nodded. "I tried . . . to keep them . . . to buy time . . ."

"You did well." His eyes met hers. "No one is getting through that door without my say."

Rey prowled over to Ketill and crouched before him. Ketill must have sensed his presence, for he dropped his hands, revealing his face. Silla gasped. Where her light had landed, angry red craters had formed on his flesh.

"You," muttered Rey, staring at the man.

"Galtung," pleaded Ketill. "I did not know—"

"You did, Ketill," replied Rey, his voice cold and brutal. "You lured me away. Tried to harm her. And now you'll die in agony."

No more death, Silla wanted to scream. No more people dying because of her.

Rey had turned to her. Must have read her expression. "Your mercy will be your downfall." Straightening, he walked to Silla. In a single, agile motion, he scooped her up, then stepped over bodies and out the shield-home's door. Vig's horse rushed through the wards, and he leaped off in a hurry.

"Fuck, Galtung, I lost you—" He broke off as he spotted Silla. "Silla! Are you . . . is she . . ."

Words were beyond Silla's grasp, and she was thankful Rey answered. "The shield-home has been breached. We need somewhere to—"

"Go," said Vig. "Go to the steading. Take my room and have Runný set new wards in place."

A cry from within the shield-home had Silla burrowing into Rey's chest.

"Ketill," Rey was saying. "I do not know the others. He . . . we . . ."

Rey growled. "There are things you should know, but they must wait for now." He slid Silla into Horse's saddle and climbed up behind her.

Vig moved to the doorway, cursing loudly at the carnage within the shield-home. "Gods damn it, Ketill!" Vig gritted out. He turned to Rey with a thunderous expression. "He came to *me,* knowing I'd go straight to you, Galtung. He must have followed. Watched me ride through the wards."

"The shield-home," said Rey gruffly. "I must know if we've been compromised. I'll need to question him."

A heavy silence followed.

"Aye," said Vig, reluctantly. "I'll bind this walking sheep shite and begin cleaning up while you get her settled."

Silla swallowed, resting her head against Rey's chest. Reality was sinking in. Kalasgarde was not safe—of *course* it was not safe.

"Rey," she whispered, as they rode into the darkness. Questions had begun to gather. The birchbark etchings had made their way north. What did this mean? Would they have to leave Kalasgarde?

"Shh, my warrior," he said with remarkable softness. "Do not think of it now. Rest. I've got you."

He had her.

Thank the gods he had her.

CHAPTER 41

"My wolfsbone dagger." A low voice pervaded her dreams. "My obsidian-hilted dagger. My hevrít. My whetstone..."

Silla's eyes fluttered open to torchlight dancing across the rafters of an unfamiliar room. Her heart took off at a gallop as memories surged back. Trapped. Not safe. Where were the exits?

"Peeling the flesh from Jonas's face..." Rey's voice.

Whipping toward him, Silla's pulse eased. She recognized the shield slung on the wall as Vig's, and recalled it was his room in which she had slept. A wall-mounted torch illuminated Rey's form, crammed into a chair far too small for him.

"You're awake," he said, watching her curiously.

Her eyes met his. "What are you doing?"

The man's lips twitched. "Thinking hearthfire thoughts."

Rey was here. Safe. She was safe. Taking a calming breath, Silla tucked her hand under her cheek. "Am I to understand all your hearthfire thoughts involve blades?"

He blinked slowly, his gaze meandering down to her lips. "Horse was included." Rey leaned forward and whispered loudly, "The chicks as well."

Silla choked on her laugh. Gods above. Was he drunk? "What else?"

Rey lifted his flask to his lips. Tilted his head back. Frowned when nothing came out. "Empty," he muttered, dropping it to the floor. "Sweet rolls," he said, his dark gaze homed in on her.

"Sweet rolls?"

He nodded. "And . . . sunshine."

His gaze was on her lips once more, and Silla felt suddenly very warm. "Sunshine," she repeated.

"Chases away the storms."

Flustered, Silla pushed into a sitting position, wincing at the vicious throb of her temples, her back, her ribs . . . everything hurt. But Gyda had examined her before she'd settled into bed, deeming her only bruised. And then, leaving Silla under Gyda and Runný's watchful eyes, Rey had returned to the shield-home to deal with Ketill.

"I gather you're drunk," she said carefully.

Rey shrugged, a flippant, careless gesture so unlike him. Even through the drink, his eyes held a haunted look. "Had to question Ketill," Rey mumbled, head knocking against the wall as he stared at the roof. Anders, back on the Road of Bones, flashed in Silla's memory. Fingers sliced off. Bones broken. The look in Rey's eyes as he'd slit the man's throat . . .

"You killed him."

"Had to know if he'd spread word—"

"But *killing* him—"

His gaze speared right through her. "No loose ends, Silla. Never."

"Loose ends . . ."

"I left one in Kopa. 'Tis how they knew my likeness. I let one live."

Silla's brows drew together, discomfort tightening her stomach.

"They already want me for murder. What is the harm in one more?" But there was something in his words, a certain . . . self-deprecation she didn't like one bit. "Chicks are unharmed," Rey said. "Runný fetched them."

"Good," said Silla, mind drifting back to the shield-home. Those men, thirsting for her blood. Ketill, his face seared by her galdur. She winced.

"Bodies are with Kálf."

"Kálf?"

"He's . . . chieftain around here."

Silla was growing uncertain. "And . . . the shield-home? Do you think it safe?"

A muscle in Rey's jaw flexed. "Ought to have been safe all along. How Ketill discovered—"

"Harpa," Silla cut in. "Ketill was in Hef's company when he brought Freydis to her home. He must have recognized my face."

Rey scowled. "Ketill. Did you know I grew up alongside him? He always lacked honor, but never did I think . . ." He scrubbed a hand down his face. The man looked exhausted. "He's forced us out. What is it you want to do, Silla? If you wish to leave, then so we shall."

We shall, he'd said. Silla wasn't certain when they'd become "we," but the very thought made her heart feel too big for her chest. "I wish to stay." She was more certain of this than anything in her life. "At last, I am making progress with Harpa." Silla turned her wrist over, examining her forearms anew.

"You expressed," said Rey. "Right into his face. Wish I could have seen it."

"I owe you my life, yet again." She hesitated, then shifted, making space for him on the bed. "You look exhausted, Galtung. Come here."

Rey pushed to his feet, then stumbled to the bed, flopping onto his stomach with all the grace of a walrus. Silla snickered, crawling onto his lower back. As she leaned forward, kneading the rigid muscles of his shoulders, she tried not to think of all the parts of her that touched him.

"You've not slept," she guessed.

Rey shrugged, turning his head to the side.

"Rest," said Silla. "I have you."

"I said that." A soft, raspy chuckle, and Silla caught the corner of a smile. Her heart flipped over.

"You're smiling."

"Your doing," was his only reply. But his smile fell. "You truly wish to stay? What if . . ." His voice drifted off.

Her hands slid between his shoulder blades, kneading gently, and Rey let out a groan she felt through her entire body. "What I know, Galtung, is that nowhere in this kingdom is truly safe for me. I can keep running, or I can take matters into my own hands. I *must* learn my galdur. Here, we have Harpa. Here, we have friendship. Allies we can depend on. I wish to stay."

"Brave girl. The bravest I know—"

Warmth flowed through her at his praise. Finding a group of tense muscles flanking his neck, she worked her fingers in soothing circles. Rey's eyes fluttered shut with another low groan.

"You wanted to hold my hand," he said sleepily.

"I what?"

"The day you earned your scar. Two-year-old Eisa wanted to hold my hand while walking on Sunnvald's fountain."

"You must have been appalled."

"Disgusted," Rey agreed. "But then you fell . . ." He exhaled. "And I felt such a fool, so prideful that I let harm befall you. When you cried, I carried you into the castle and found the healer. And while they stitched you up"—he paused, gathering himself—"I did not let go of your hand."

Silla's lips parted.

"And you," said Rey fondly, "have always lacked common sense."

She snorted, her hands slipping away. Reluctantly, she climbed off him, moving to the end of the bed and working the buckles loose from his boots. After tugging each one off, she placed them neatly on the floor. She then climbed into the bed beside him, pulling the furs and blankets over them both.

Rey wriggled clumsily onto his back. "I thought blood and vengeance would make it better, but it's only grown worse."

Silla turned onto her side, examining his face. Soft black lashes fanned out along his cheeks, but his brow was lined with tension. "What better, Rey?" she asked softly. "What blood?"

"The darkness. Their deaths. All of it." He lifted his hands to examine them. "There's so much blood on my hands."

Her insides surged with a protective instinct. Carefully, Silla took one of his hands and laid it on his chest. "These are good hands," she whispered, lacing her fingers through his. "The best hands."

If he heard her, Rey made no motion. His breaths grew slow and even, his brow relaxing at last. Silla stared at him until the torch burned out and darkness engulfed them completely.

The last thought Silla had before falling into slumber was that even after eighteen winters, she still very much wanted to hold this man's hand.

Rey dreamed of Kristjan. They raced through a field on horseback, Kristjan's head thrown back with wild laughter. Pine and crushed moss and crisp mountain air filled his senses, and Rey felt a curious sensation. Freedom. Happiness. Utter contentment. Everything was perfect for one infinitesimal second. And then it slipped through his fingers.

His eyes fluttered open to an altogether different scent. Sweet, perhaps floral. *Her.*

In sleep, she'd turned toward him, as though seeking comfort in his touch. Her arms were tucked against her chest, her cheek resting against his collarbone. He buried his nose in her hair. Drew in a deep breath. Settled his hand on her hip, holding her to him.

Another moment of perfection before morning stole it away.

CHAPTER 42

Sunnavík

The night Kassandr Rurik burned his boat, all of Saga's plans went awry. According to Bjorn, the scent Skotha's hounds had picked up proved the arsonist and the person who'd sacked the garrison hall's undercroft were one and the same. In the incident's aftermath, Klaernar flooded into the castle at the king's behest, crawling through the corridors, day and night.

It was impossible for Saga to leave her chambers without coming face-to-face with a guard. Needless to say, all plans to break into Alfson's study were immediately halted. Saga would admit she felt a twinge of worry for Rurik. She wanted to warn him, but with all the extra eyes in Askaborg, she couldn't risk it.

And much to her chagrin, Saga couldn't shake the man's words from her mind.

I am staying until I am satisfied with unfinished matters, he'd said, generating only more questions. What did the Urkans have that Rurik and his people needed? A weapon? A book? She couldn't fathom what it might be.

The Zagadkians, forced to linger, had a grim air about them. From what she'd pried from Bjorn, the boat's frame had been salvaged, and they needed merely to plank and reseal. If Rurik had meant to buy himself time, then he'd succeeded. And based on what she'd heard from Signe's ladies, the Zagadkians' delayed departure saddened none of them. Yrsa, in particular, was delighted to have them attend her birthday feast.

Saga went through her days as she was expected to—attending meals with the royal family; enduring wedding talk with Signe and her ladies; embroidery and Lettings and measurements for the gown she'd wear to Yrsa's birthday feast. She didn't dare stroll to the falconry tower to check for a white linen and was certain Ana knew well enough—now was no time for bold acts against Signe. They needed to be patient. Lie low. Wait until the search for the arsonist died down.

Saga kept herself busy with lockpicking practice and searching the Klaernar's records for any connection between Skotha and the Black Cloak. But after rolling up the last scroll, she concluded that if there was evidence, it was not in these records. Glumly, Saga had returned them to the room of records.

By the end of the week, Saga was restless and irritated. She was desperate to resume her plans. She could pick a lock in under a minute. Had counted the steps to Alfson's study. Had mapped out alcoves and shadowed corners she might hide in. She was ready.

And after a long week, it happened. A quarrel in the market over the last loaf of bread soon turned into a brawl. The King's Claws were dispatched, but the crowd turned on them. By nightfall, the city was rioting.

And as the Klaernar rushed out from Askaborg to quell the violence, Saga knew it was time.

Creeping down the darkened corridor, Saga pulled a black hood over her tightly braided hair. Her body thrummed with anticipation, with the excitement of *finally* doing something to help Eisa.

One hand clutched her satchel with supplies—an ink pot, spare parchment, and quills—while the other closed around the twin brooch pins in her pocket. A month ago, the simple act of leaving her room had disarmed Saga. Would she ever have guessed she'd be prowling the halls in the dark hours of the night, plotting to break into Maester Alfson's study?

A brittle cough set her hair on end. Saga slid back against the wall, pressing deeper into the shadows, as a pair of Klaernar strolled past. After several long moments, their retreating footfalls could no longer be heard, and Saga dashed down the hallway before she could second-guess herself.

It wasn't long before the narrow hallway yawned open into the expansive blackness of the grand stairwell. Saga descended quickly, not stopping even as a loose stair groaned. Lightning-quick, Saga folded into a shadowy corridor, waiting for Klaernar to investigate the sound. She counted to ten, then back down again.

No one came.

Soon, she was darting down the corridor to Maester Alfson's study. And then she was staring at the door. With a deep breath, Saga stepped forward, reminding herself of all who depended on her. Ana, Eisa, the missing Galdra.

And so with trembling hands, Saga inserted the brooch pins into the keyhole and set to work. With only a week's practice under her belt, she was far from an expert. But now she knew the feel of the brooch pins sinking into the hole—knew the force she'd need to twist. She hadn't expected her trembling hands and racing heart to complicate the process.

"Bog serpents," she cursed at her fifth failed attempt to find the hole in the bolt.

". . . fifty dead, all told . . ."

Saga froze, goosebumps rushing up her arms. Footfalls sounded down the corridor, drawing nearer with each heartbeat. Panic seized her. It was too late to retreat—they'd catch sight of her for certain. Her only escape was through this door.

Redoubling her efforts, Saga pushed harder as the voices grew louder.

". . . such a fuss over bread . . ."

She felt the pin slide in, and her heart leaped.

". . . heard it was right ugly. Clawing like animals, crushing one another underfoot . . ."

Saga twisted the pin forcefully and felt the bolt grate against wood as it slid from the lock. Relief swept through her, but there was no time to celebrate. Silent as a cat, she slunk through the door and closed it quietly behind her.

"... thought it would calm once the Zagadkian grain arrived..."

The muffled voices moved past the door, right where Saga had stood moments before. And then it was silent. After sliding the bolt back into the locked position, Saga tried to shake the tension from her muscles. She'd made it through the door. Now she had all night to dig through the cabinet.

The curtains were cracked, a column of moonlight spilling across the floor and illuminating the maester's worktable. Saga crept over to it and sank to her knees before the cabinet. As her fingers made contact with the lock, a strange, dark sensation whispered across her skin. With a shiver, Saga got to work, picking the lock in under a minute.

There were two shelves. On the top was an assortment of scrolls; on the bottom, a stack of parchment bound by twine. Longing uncurled deep in her stomach, a need to devour this information.

Shaking it off, she reached for a scroll. After loosening the waxy outer parchment, Saga gently flattened it on the floor. She drank up the words scratched in ink. *Extracting the Míkrób*, it read. *Ensure Dragon's Belch slumbers. Collect life-forms in clean wool from inside the hollow and seal in a glass jar. Store near a fire pot and feed frequently with broth. Míkrób must be kept as warm as possible...*

Saga's gaze fell upon a curious illustration. Holding the candle closer, she examined the drawing. Though crude, it appeared to depict water gushing into the air from the midst of a flat plain of stones. The Dragon's Belch. Saga had never seen it, but this drawing matched the descriptions of a place where sulfuric water burst from the ground at distinct intervals.

With a frown, she reached for the next scroll. This one had a strange drawing of dishes and curving tubes and instructions to isolate the Míkrób from other tiny creatures through repeated separation into phials containing different broth recipes.

It was the third scroll that made her blood frost over. *Introducing Míkrób to a host*, it read. *Ingested under a black moon, host must be kept near the fire and well covered. A full moon cycle is sufficient for Míkrób to feast on the galdur and produce enough spawn to introduce to the next host. This is verified by a strong sulfuric smell.*

Saga's heart began to pound. This . . . this was what they were doing with the missing Galdra. Using these . . . creatures to eat their galdur. But as she turned the scroll over, horror and revulsion filled her. *Reaping,* it read. *Carve legs, arms, buttocks.* A diagram of a human indicated these regions. Nausea roiled in her gut, but she kept reading. *Flesh must be consumed raw. Secondary host must fast for a full day before and after consumption.* A note was added in Alfson's cramped lettering: *Block wound healing to speed spawn growth.* Beside this was written: *alpine catspaw.*

She wanted to stop, but there was more, and she needed to know . . . needed to tell Ana. *Secondary host may reject Míkrób within the first three moons. If they survive, secondary host will be able to reproduce primary host's galdur.*

Saga's hand shook as she reached for the last scroll. Unrolled it. In Alfson's lettering was written *For Rökksgarde,* beneath which was a to-do list of sorts. Saga's eyes scanned the list, picking out items at random. *100 ells of flax linen . . . 1 pound losna leaves, harvested by the largest full moon . . . Rhodium, sterkium, iron, steel for dungeon— 100 pounds each . . .*

Saga put the scroll down. Pressed a hand to her stomach. She thought she might vomit. Because the picture beginning to shine through was utterly despicable. Harvesting galdur from unwilling Galdra. Consuming their flesh so this secondary host might gain magic. It was vile to even think of. But the abandoned kitchens, those beds, the missing Galdra, the buried corpses behind that fort in Svaldrin . . . it all fit into a sickening tale.

Rökksgarde . . . it sounded like Rökksgarde was where they moved this horrid galdur-harvesting practice after Svaldrin. Saga took a steadying breath. She ought to copy these scrolls. But as her gaze fell on the bottom shelf of the cabinet—on the stack of parchment, bound with twine—the hairs on her neck stood on end.

A strange sense of recognition settled in her, a sense of something more ancient than the castle itself. She found herself reaching out, power brushing along her fingers as they swept over the top page. Tucking her index finger under the twine, Saga lifted the bundle and placed it gently on the floor in front of her.

A breath of air caressed her cheek, sending Saga's heart skittering. But it vanished so quickly, she wondered if she'd imagined it.

Saga examined the stack. Binding tracks peppered the long edge of each parchment, suggesting that, at one point, these pages had been bound in a book. The cover and title pages were missing, and as she flipped through the manuscript, Saga found many portions water-damaged and illegible—page numbers skipped in sizable bunches as if entire sections of the book were absent.

At last, she came to a page with portions of legible text. Eagerly, Saga devoured all the words she could read.

> *. . . from the deepest roots of the woods, made from Sunnvald's own heart, light will not destroy it, only a thing made of the same darkness . . .*

She flipped the page, eager to read more, but found only an illustration that made her blood run cold. Creatures she knew, and yet did not. There were strange, mutated grimwolves with maws stretched too wide; ravens with enlarged talons and shredded wings; fanged bears with elongated limbs.

She continued to search through the book, paging past curious charred sections, as though someone had tried, and failed, to set it alight. Saga's fingers paused as she reached a page titled *KRAUGEIR*. Frowning, she stared at the name. She'd told Rurik about Kraugeir all those weeks ago—the dragon of legends who'd once woken to burn the world. As she gazed upon it, Saga felt a strange stirring in her chest, like the faintest ruffling of wings and long, dark limbs stretching out.

Cold prickles climbed across her neck. It was wrong, this book, yet so very familiar. So very seductive. She must have this book, must drink up all of its knowledge, must—

Someone coughed from beyond the door.

The sensation retracted in an instant, leaving an aching hollowness in its wake. A strange longing filled her. Saga blinked, forcing logic into her mind. There was something wrong with this manuscript—

she needed to get away from it. With shaky hands, Saga stacked the parchment and tied the twine in place.

The bolt rattled.

Lightning-quick, Saga shoved the scrolls back into the cabinet, sliding the padlock back in place.

A key slid into the lock.

Panicked, Saga yanked her satchel from the ground and threw herself into the shadowy back corner of the office. Her heart raced, breathing shallowing.

Metal grated against wood as the bolt slid to the side.

Oh gods, oh gods! In a heartbeat, someone would step into the room, and she'd be caught. She was trapped . . . no exits . . .

Saga pressed herself farther against the wall, wishing it could swallow her up. A stone dug sharply into the small of her back, but suddenly, it retracted. The entire portion of wall swung inward.

A door. Alfson had a hidden door in his study.

After scrambling through the doorway, Saga found herself in a dark alcove. There was no time to think, no time to do anything but shove herself against the door. It rasped shut, enveloping Saga in inky blackness and damp, musty air.

Safe. She sagged against the wall, her pulse calming. She was safe in the darkness.

Beyond the door, there was movement within the study. Whoever it was, their thoughts were muffled by the stone, but Saga guessed it had to be Maester Alfson. Would he know someone had been in his study? Did he know of this doorway?

Her brow furrowed. *She* had not known of this doorway. And as someone who hoarded Askaborg's secrets the way Signe did ivory gowns, it was unsettling to discover there were things she did not know.

Turning, Saga felt her way around the space, thankful she was not afraid of the dark. Was it merely a closet? But as she toed around the dark landing, she found the edge of a stair. Cautiously, she descended the first step, and began what she soon discovered was a long climb downward.

Disoriented, she relied on her sense of touch as she fumbled through the blackness. After a curving set of stairs and a long corridor, she rounded a corner, and her heart swelled at the faint bloom of light. As she neared, she could make out a torch mounted on crumbling stone walls at the juncture of three doors. Reaching this juncture, Saga paused, her ears primed and Sense stretching out. Nothing but silence.

She steeled herself, her hand wrapping around the iron ring of the door to her right and pushing it open.

Saga stared down yet another corridor, this one lit by wall-mounted torches. She blinked as her eyes adjusted to the light. There was a heavy feeling to the air, an unpleasantness she could not name. Gripping her satchel tightly, Saga forced herself to walk.

The guttering torchlight illuminated a prison cell on her right, a rust-red stain in the middle of the stone floor. She passed more cells, all empty, but heavy with the scent of iron and urine.

With each step farther down the hall, the ominous feeling grew. She reached the doorway at the end of the hall. Hand poised on the ring, she felt a premonitory shiver run down her spine.

With a deep breath, Saga pushed it open and stepped inside.

CHAPTER 43

Saga was not certain what to expect beyond the door, but it certainly wasn't what she found. The room was long, with rough stone walls, curving into a low, arched roof. Soft, dancing light came from a large fireplace set at the far end of the room, illuminating neat rows of beds pushed against the walls.

Saga's heartbeat accelerated at once.

Beds. Could these be the missing Galdra? The ones taken from Svaldrin?

Closing the door silently, Saga eased deeper into the room. She pulled an unlit torch from the wall and crept to the fireplace, dipping it into the flames until the pitch-soaked cloth caught. Her heart beat with sharp, rapid strikes as Saga crept to the nearest of the beds. There were so many furs piled on it, it was impossible to tell if it was occupied.

Saga peeled back the furs, a cold sense of foreboding growing low in her stomach. Instantly, the sulfuric scent of rotten eggs met her nose. Smothering a gag in the sleeve of her dress, Saga blinked back tears. Gods, but that was foul. As the seconds passed, the smell dissipated, and Saga held the torch aloft to examine the bed.

The bed was empty. With a sturdy iron frame and a ragged straw mattress, it seemed a typical bed to Saga. That was, until she saw the manacles secured to the headboard. Her gaze flew down the row of beds. Were any of these beds occupied?

Her eyes settled on a lock of mousy brown hair peeking out from the furs one bed over. "Hello?" whispered Saga, approaching.

As she pulled back the blankets, that same pungent smell swarmed her face, momentarily blinding her. But as the tears cleared, a woman's slumbering face came into view. Saga leaned closer, holding her torch aloft to examine her face. The woman's complexion was sickly, sweat matting her hair. But most curious of all was the webwork of dark blue veins climbing up her neck.

Saga's gaze drifted down to the corner of a bandage on the woman's left shoulder. Nudging the furs lower, Saga took in the linen bandages wrapped around the woman's upper arms. The woman groaned, then fell silent, leaving Saga's heart drumming in her ears.

Everything seemed to slow. Saga reached out and pinched the linen between her thumb and forefinger. Tugged ever so gently. The bandage fell away, loosing a fresh sulfuric wave.

She knew what she would find but was not prepared for the sight. The wound was perfectly rectangular, cutting from shoulder to elbow—a perfect match to the diagram on Alfson's scrolls. Horror and revulsion churned in Saga's stomach. This woman, this poor woman, was in the midst of her Reaping, her Míkrób-filled flesh carved from her to feed to others.

The woman's eyes flew open.

Saga had no time to assure her she meant no harm. The woman's face twisted into a mixture of terror and rage as she lunged, teeth snapping like a feral dog. The manacles caught with a rattling clamor, making Saga cry out as she stumbled back. Her legs hit the bed behind her, and she dropped her satchel and torch, snuffing out the light.

"Wait," she hissed. "I'm here to help—" But it was too late.

"No!" the woman screamed, lunging at her once more, the manacles clanging. The corners of the woman's mouth frothed, madness in her eyes. "You won't have it! You cannot!"

Saga's gaze flicked to the door and back to the woman, her hands held up in a placating gesture. But the woman was too far gone, wild with rage and thrashing against her restraints.

"Let me help you," Saga pleaded, hands finding the brooch pins in her pocket. Could she pick the manacle locks? But the woman did not hear her, and soon, a man's voice joined in, then another. Gods, but this was bad. She could *not* be discovered in this room.

Escape—she needed to escape! She looked around in terror for the exits. But there were no other doors in this room, only the one through which she'd entered, and Saga was frozen in place, so distraught she did not see the large, dark shape charging at her from her periphery. One hand slammed over her mouth, another wrapping around her waist. She was dimly aware of the torch and satchel kicked under the bed—of the blankets shoved over the shouting woman. Screaming against the rough, dry palm, Saga fought her captor, pulling the brooch pins from her pocket and sinking them deep into his hand. Unfortunately, it did nothing but draw a string of rough, incomprehensible words.

"Calm, Winterwing," came Kassandr Rurik's accented voice. "They are coming."

She froze.

He stopped at the unoccupied bed opposite to the screaming woman, pulling the furs back. Hand falling on the small of her back, he gave Saga a gentle push. Understanding, Saga threw herself onto the bed, tossing an elbow over her nose to stifle the foul smell. To her utter horror, Rurik climbed on the bed with her, flipping the furs over both of them.

"Again, you are seeing things you should not," whispered Rurik.

"What are *you* doing here?" she hissed.

"Finding another thing that was not on your map," was his infuriating reply.

"Shut up!" yelled out an angry male voice from beyond the furs, a door slamming shut. "Shut your mouths, you foul beasts!"

Muffled footfalls approached. Saga's heart beat fast and uneven. The excitement of doing a thing she should not had morphed into remorse and pure terror. She gripped the arm Rurik had slung over her.

"Ursir's hairy scrotum!" came the man's voice. "Should've known it would be *you*. How did you pull your bandage loose?" Silence stretched out. "You must be kept warm, 'tis not my orders, now. Cannot allow the cold to touch you."

Saga's body trembled.

"Easy," whispered Rurik. "Calm, *malen'kaya ptichka*."* She forced in a steady breath of the foul-smelling air, tried to relax against the solid form behind her.

"You have one job, Gorm," came a voice from the far end of the room. Even muffled by the furs, Saga knew it at once. Maester Alfson. "And you've failed at that. Have I not told you their silence is imperative? How precarious our situation is until we can move them to Rökksgarde?"

"Forgive me, Maester," came Gorm's voice. "Something's rattled them! Started squealing like pigs at the slaughter. Draugur, it was, I'm certain of it. This one's bandage pulled free."

"Draugur," repeated the maester, much nearer now. "You fool, the dead would not trouble themselves here." After a few moments of wordless movement, the maester spoke. "Luckily, I've just returned from harvesting more losna. An extra dose will set them right."

"But—Maester, but their teeth is snapping!"

The maester muttered a string of irritated curses. "This batch has weeks left in their Reaping, Gorm. I won't have them wasted to your incompetence. Do it like this." After a moment, the woman's screams grew muffled, then dulled completely.

"Administer the losna to beds three, five, seven, and twelve," said Maester Alfson, "or you'll be volunteered for consumption, Gorm."

"Y-yes, Maester," stumbled Gorm. "Where are you going?"

"I have a strange feeling about this. I'm fetching Skotha's hounds."

Cold trickled down Saga's spine, pooling in her stomach. She should be in her bed, slumbering soundly, not hiding in this place of horrors. As the maester's footfalls faded and Gorm busied himself quieting the screaming patients, her fear did not subside.

"What do we do?" she whispered to Rurik. "We must leave before the hounds arrive."

He was quiet for a long moment. "No," he said, to her surprise. "The hounds will not trouble us."

"How do you know that?"

---

*Little bird.

"This smell is hiding much."

She bit her lip, unconvinced. "Can you not just knock Gorm on the back of the head?"

A low chuckle rumbled through Saga's back. "Such violence you crave, Winterwing. Is only one way out of this place, and I fear they will come before we can escape. Let the hounds come and discover nothing. Will satisfy the maester to know no one is here. And then we are free to leave."

"I don't know—"

"Do you trust me?" he asked.

Saga considered for a minute. "Against my better judgment."

"I will show you," he said, shifting on the mattress.

"I want this place scented," the maester was saying from beyond the furs.

"'Twill be a challenge, Maester," came a gruff voice in reply. "What is that smell?"

"It is none of your concern," was the maester's terse reply. "Scent the place!"

Saga's heart thundered in her chest, nausea churning violently in her stomach. What if they were discovered? The rattle of a chain grew closer, closer, closer, the dog huffing softly from beyond the furs. She squeezed her eyes shut, waiting for the fur to lift, waiting to come face-to-face with a snarling hound—

As though reading her thoughts, Rurik's hand made the softest of taps on her hip, slow and rhythmic and decidedly calming. She focused on the sensation with all of her mind.

Tap. Tap. Tap.

A low growl filled the air. It seemed to come from everywhere at once—in front, below, behind. The breath lodged in Saga's throat, and she was sure that this was it; in moments they'd be discovered. But the dog beyond the furs whined.

Tap. Tap. Tap.

Up seemed down and left seemed right, everything twisting and turning in the dark dread beneath the furs. Saga was distantly aware of a clank and rattle, growing gradually softer, but she could not trust her senses, not with the dizzying swirl of her mind.

Tap. Tap. Tap.

"Nothing, Maester," called out a man. "I'm sorry to tell you, but there's nothing to trace, not in this stench."

"Go," ordered Alfson. "Get out."

After the sounds of the man and hound had vanished entirely, Gorm said cautiously, "They're dosed, Maester. What should I—"

"With me, Gorm," came the maester's even voice. "We must speed our plans for relocation. In my study, *now*."

The men retreated from the room, and Rurik rolled on top of her, bracing himself on his elbows. Saga's heart spun and twisted as he lifted the edge of the fur and peered out.

"They are gone," he said, throwing the covers back and looking down at her. "You should not be in this place."

Saga pushed Rurik off her with a huff. "Nor should you." She swung her feet off the bed, assessing the room. The screaming woman lay utterly still.

"We must help them," she whispered.

"Is no place of rest. Is place of death," muttered Rurik.

Glancing at the door, she stepped toward the woman. "They've been taken against their will. We must help them—"

Rurik cursed in Zagadkian, his hand wrapping around her shoulder and stopping her. "You cannot, Saga. You must go back to your chambers and pretend you never saw such things."

"But these people—"

"They cannot be helped!" he snapped. "They are altered in ways that cannot be undone."

She was silent, recalling the feral look in the woman's eyes, the froth at her mouth. "Have you no mercy?" she asked. "We cannot let them suffer. Let them have a good death, at the very least."

"Winterwing," Rurik said softly. "I should never have shown you how to pick the locks. Is a curse on me for letting you find such troubles." She felt herself being turned around, rough fingers sliding beneath her chin and tilting it up. "Promise to me, Saga, you won't come back here. It will bring danger to you."

Clamping down on her back molars, she did not reply. With a

soft growl, Rurik wrapped his hand around her upper arm. "Your fire is strong, Winterwing, but caution is needed to keep the flame burning." After a silent moment, he dragged her to the door and pressed his ear against it. "Is clear through this way now."

"How do you—"

"I have excellent hearing."

Saga swallowed. Pushing the door open, Rurik tugged her into the hallway lined with cells. "I am taking you to your chambers, Saga, and then I will be watching. You will not go back to that room."

"*Excuse* me?"

They paused at the juncture of three doors, Rurik turning to look down at her. "You are brave, Winterwing, but your soft heart will get you killed. Your plans are written on your face."

"I must help them," she said, stomach twisting.

"I am sorry," he said, with surprising sincerity. "But those in foul room are lost already. You gain nothing by rushing into danger. If you wish to help them, you must be smart and quiet." Rurik pulled her straight through the juncture of doors, rather than left toward Alfson's study. Cautiously, they climbed a set of torchlit stairs.

"You are right," whispered Saga as they paused at a landing. "I must think more rationally." She scowled. "As do *you*. Bjorn told me the hounds have linked the arsonist to the person who sacked the garrison hall—"

"I thank you for your concern, Lady Saga, but hounds do not concern me."

Her scowl deepened. "How can you be so unbothered?"

The man's flippant shrug made her teeth clench. She forced in a calming breath and whispered, "Did you find what you've been seeking?"

Rurik pulled a pin from his pocket and picked the lock with a few deft twists of his hand. "No."

"I'm sorry." Saga bit her lip as he pressed his ear to the door, then pushed it open. "If you tell me what it is—"

"I cannot."

"I see," said Saga, rebuked.

"Would betray my kin to speak of it," he added, a strained note in his voice. "Is a thing taken that must be returned."

"Have you searched the old armory?" asked Saga. "I drew it on your map."

He nodded. "It would not be there, but I looked all the same. Nothing. Have looked in all your places. Has vanished, it seems." As he ushered her into the safety of her chambers, Rurik said softly, "I will watch your chambers, Saga. No more troublesome ideas."

And with that, the door clicked shut.

Numbly, Saga stripped off her clothing and went to the washstand. After dipping a cloth into the basin, she tried to scrub the rotten scent from her skin. But she could not scrub that woman's face from her mind.

She was being harvested—sliced into time and time again, until Alfson had taken all she had to give. Saga pulled on her nightdress and slipped between the covers.

Her stomach was in knots, her mind spinning in circles. Rurik watched her door; he would prevent her from leaving tonight. But he could not stay forever. Sooner or later, he'd have duties to attend to.

And so, as sleep gradually crept in, Saga made plans. That room was all the evidence she needed to damn Signe. At the first opportunity, she'd go straight to King Ivar and expose the queen's lies.

CHAPTER 44

Kopa

"Describe the tattoos once more," commanded Kaptein Ulfar. Jonas gripped the arms of his chair, trying to quell his rising temper. Days, they'd been at this. A dozen times, he'd tried to explain. But these fool Klaernar were content to lounge in the comforts of the kaptein's private quarters, dining on a constant flow of ale and food.

It seemed the kaptein had inherited the decor from his predecessor, the infamous Kommandor Valf. In the days he'd spent in this room, Jonas had grown used to the obsidian busts lining the shelves, but something about the strange tapestries above the hearth unsettled him.

"Dragon," Jonas forced out. "Across his chest. Tail down one arm. Smoke along the other."

Ulfar stroked his long gray beard, his sigil ring glinting in the torchlight. Rumor had it the Klaernar kept a dose of berskium powder inside their rings for times they'd need a quick boost of strength. "And you claim you did not know he—"

"Was burning people alive along the Road of Bones?" A brittle laugh escaped him. "No."

The kaptein grabbed a jug from the table and poured himself a fresh cup of ale. "It is true you know details we've not made public. But others have as well—"

"They were deliberately misdirecting you," Jonas shot back.

Hagbard shuffled into the room, glaring at Jonas with clear dislike. "Another falcon from Sunnavík," he said, handing a scroll to Ulfar. "She's . . . oof!" The kaptein's elbow landed hard in Hagbard's stomach, and ale sloshed from his cup. "*He's* demanding new information."

Jonas rolled his neck, trying for patience. "I know it's the queen," he said blandly. "And if she thinks she can command this search all the way from Sunnavík, then either she's being pandered to, or she's a fool."

Kaptein Ulfar's gaze snapped to Jonas. "Do not speak such—"

"She's *not* a fool." Jonas regarded Ulfar with cool calculation. "What have you told her? You've got it under control?" As the kaptein paled, Jonas knew he'd made a mark. He leaned in. Went for the jugular. "How much longer will she tolerate your failures?"

Ulfar and Hagbard shared a tense look.

"This entire search is a mess," Jonas continued. "You're collecting information on Axe Eyes while warriors comb through the arse end of Nordur and the queen tries to control it all from the south." He shook his head.

Incompetent fools, he wanted to lash out. "I know them," Jonas said instead. "Know how they think. Know how they fight. They're clever, Ulfar, and if you think this mess of a hunt will prove successful, then you're poised for yet more failure."

"Enough!" Ulfar's fist slammed onto the table, sending an apple wobbling. "What do you propose, Svik?"

Hagbard protested, but Jonas cut him off. "First, you need to stop pandering to the queen. Tell her you must control the search from the north. That you'll send her daily updates." Gods above, but their ineptitude was exhausting. "Sending a warband after the pair will not be enough, Ulfar. You'll need to be cunning. You need a plan." Jonas reclined in his chair, resting an ankle on his knee.

"Perhaps *you* should go," sneered Hagbard. "See what you're made of."

Jonas's gaze landed on the brute. Hardened. "I said *cunning*, you shite beetle. I'm not foolhardy enough to face Axe Eyes alone. I've fought beside him for years; I know how he wields a blade. And now that I know he's had galdur all this time . . ." Rage burned inside him, red-hot and ceaseless. Jonas leaned into the anger. Let it fuel him. "You'll need to match his wits with your own."

Ulfar stood and began pacing the room, muttering under his breath. Jonas waited for the man to come to the inevitable conclusion. Ulfar paused. Turned. Asked again, "What do you propose, Svik?"

"You'll need both numbers and the element of surprise," said Jonas, slowly. "Corner him. Play to his weakness." His lip curled. "You can bring him to his knees without even drawing a blade."

Rey was a protector—but this was information Jonas kept to himself for the time being. The memory of Rey pulling Ilías and him from Sunnavík's streets flashed through Jonas's mind. He'd saved them. Had said he admired Jonas's loyalty. The memory twisted as he saw it in new light. Rey, finding two young men desperate enough to trust him. To buy into his lies. After all, they were too busy being grateful to look closely at Reynir Bjarg.

"You think such basic tactics will earn your reward?" glowered Kaptein Ulfar.

Jonas leaned forward, bracing his elbows on his knees. "I require half the payment up front. After I have the sólas, I'll hand you everything you need to best him."

"Up front!" guffawed Hagbard. "What do you think this is?"

"I think," said Jonas, scowling at the warrior, "I've been burned by the Klaernar once before. I brought the girl to Kommandor Valf. Had her imprisoned in your keep. *I* held up my end of the bargain, and yet I was not paid. Because of your predecessor's incompetence."

Ulfar's glare was sharp as daggers. "Your knowledge of the man's tattoos and the girl's scar is not proof you know their minds. We'll need a . . . demonstration before we can trust your word."

"Send a missive to your warriors. Send them to Kalasgarde to observe only." Jonas's jaw worked as he tried and failed to voice the next words. This felt too personal. Too . . . much. But his mind's eye helpfully showed him Ilías rushing into battle. The blades protruding from his back. His little brother's final moments, as Jonas spoke of the elm tree.

Jonas's hand wrapped around the pendant strung around his

neck and squeezed. "Rey had a younger brother," he forced out. "Kristjan was his name. I assume he's buried in Kalasgarde." He closed his eyes. Tried to unclench his jaw. Tried to block the swelling tide of self-loathing. "I imagine he'll visit the burial mound at some point."

Ulfar nodded, studying him far too closely.

Jonas swallowed. Gazed into the hearthfire. "Have them watch the burial grounds for Rey." Remorse tasted bitter, but there was no time for that. He'd committed himself to this path, and there was no turning back. "Once you have confirmation they're in Kalasgarde, then you'll provide half my fee. And then I'll tell you how to best Axe Eyes in combat."

Ulfar watched him. "How do we know you're not like the rest of the reward hunters?"

"Because," said Jonas, "for them, it's just sólas." He leveled the kaptein with a hard look. "For me, it's personal."

CHAPTER 45

Kalasgarde

Rey had decided the birds hated him. Why else would they be gathered just outside the window, screeching like berserkers? They'd infiltrated his dreams. Had dragged him violently from sleep. He reached for his dagger, ready to send it sailing through the window. But rather than the unyielding surface of that gods damned bench, his hand met unfamiliar softness.

He sat up. Rubbed his throbbing temples. Decided that the birds might in fact be screaming goats because this was Vig's room. And that was Vig's voice, filtering through the window . . .

"Good, Helga, just a little closer. Yes. Now sing!"

The screeching restarted, driving into Rey's skull like a thousand knives.

"Vig!" he bellowed, flinging the furs aside. Snickering beyond the window confirmed his suspicions.

"Let him sleep," came Silla's voice, making Rey's stomach tighten. And a curious memory filled his mind's eye—Silla, curled into his chest, soft breaths puffing against his skin. He'd thrown an arm over her hip, hauling her closer. Had slept with his nose buried in her curls.

With a grumble, he dangled an arm over the side of his bed, his hand meeting the smooth curve of a waterskin. Grabbing it, he sat up and choked the water back. What had he been thinking the night before, drinking more brennsa than Kraki on Longest Day?

He *hadn't* been thinking.

The need to obliterate his feelings had blinded him. Discovering an axe-wielding, blood-splattered Silla, clad in only her tunic, was bad enough. But to discover it was Ketill—that a Galdra he'd grown up with had so readily betrayed him—was altogether different.

After getting Silla settled into Vig's room, he'd looked her in the eye. Had told her what he truly did not wish to. "We must tell Vig the truth of who you are. Runný and Gyda as well."

He'd watched her swallow—watched her gaze grow distant. "You can tell them," she whispered. "You can tell them who I am."

It was enough that she'd allowed him to share this, yet Rey found himself frustrated. How long would she need to grow comfortable with Eisa? He could only hold off the Uppreisna for so long, and after tonight, avoiding the local chieftain would certainly grow more difficult. No one would believe a craven like Ketill would go toe-to-toe with Reynir Galtung. How would Rey explain the bodies?

Time. She only needed time.

Rey had relayed her identity to Vig and Runný with cold calm. Had ordered them to share it with Gyda alone. Had threatened to thrash them if they treated her any differently. And then Rey had needed to find the cold place inside him before facing what came next.

He'd returned to the shield-home to find the bodies laid out in the yard. Rey had stared at these men, trying to place them, but neither he nor Vig knew them. And with that, he'd turned his sights on Ketill.

Known for his ruthless efficiency, Rey knew precisely how to draw answers. But this was different—this man had intended *her* harm. So perhaps his cuts had not been as precise. Perhaps he'd not been quite as in control as Axe Eyes would have been.

Sobbing, Ketill had explained that he'd been in Eystri selling sheepskins for Hef and Freydis. That he'd come across a birch plank with Rey's likeness and had recognized him at once. He'd enlisted the group over ale at the mead hall and had brought them north to Kalasgarde with the purpose of capturing Rey. They'd planned to slip seeds into Rey's ale when he showed his face at the mead hall, but each night, he'd failed to arrive. And when Ketill saw Silla at Harpa's home, his plans had changed.

To Rey's great relief, Ketill vowed no one else in Kalasgarde knew of the reward—swore that he did not know the girl's true name. But Rey had to be certain.

No loose ends.

He'd erred in Kopa and would not do so again.

When he'd finished and Ketill lay lifeless in his own blood, piss, and vomit, Rey had been surprised to find his hands trembling. His stomach had twisted. And to his great horror, he'd rushed to the bushes and retched.

Another life taken. More blood on his hands.

Draining his flask was all he could do to keep the trembling at bay. After washing himself, Rey had run straight through his stores of brennsa, then stumbled into Silla's room at Vig's steading and watched her sleep. *Safe,* he'd reassured himself. *Safe.*

But then she'd woken and had seen straight through his façade. Of course she had. She'd seen through Axe Eyes from the start. When she'd lured him onto the bed and massaged the knots from his spine, Rey's long-frozen heart had dripped with meltwater.

But now he ached with remorse—with that feeling of sharing too much.

You wanted to hold my hand. Rey raked a hand down his face. Had he truly told her that part of the story? He felt flayed open and exposed, wishing he could snatch those words—and many others—back. Thank the gods Silla was not in the bed. He could not face her yet.

And Rey was *never* drinking brennsa again.

As pain speared through his head, he drained his waterskin. From the brightness of the room, he could tell it was at least midmorning. Vig's and Silla's voices carried from outdoors. He cursed. It was the seventh day—the serpent was due to feed *today.*

Rey climbed from the bed, eager to throw himself into work. Pulling on a fresh tunic and lébrynja armor, his fingers smoothed the Galdra-made scales down. He stepped into the common room, then paused. Unlike the shield-home, Gyda's longhouse had the look of a place well lived in. Herbs were strung from the rafters, tapestries and shelves lined the walls, and an enormous cauldron bubbled over the central hearth. Seated on a bench before the fire was Gyda herself.

"Ahh, you've risen," she said. In her right hand she held a distaff wrapped with raw wool. A spindle beneath it twisted the fibers into yarn. Her eyes twinkled with mischief. "You've gotten your rest, haven't you, Rey?"

He nodded curtly.

"I've brought sweet rolls from town," she said, nodding at the table.

"My thanks, Gyda," grumbled Rey. He snatched a sweet roll from the table and tore it in half.

"She's in the yard, sparring with Vig."

Rey's jaw hardened. "Has Vig told you?"

"About the attack?" asked Gyda. "I'm afraid so. Thank the gods above you returned in time." She paused, giving the spindle a hard whirl. "Ketill was a fool of a kunta."

Rey's brows rose.

"'Tis true and you know it," Gyda said with a shrug.

"He was," admitted Rey, biting into the soft, flaky roll.

"Vig told me the rest," said Gyda casually, tugging the raw wool down along the distaff. "That she's Eisa Volsik. And now, it all makes sense." Gyda met his gaze. "She's a survivor, that one."

"Braver than any I know," Rey admitted. "Though she's had some trouble . . . adjusting to the name."

Gyda nodded. "She's . . . quite fond of you, Rey."

He scowled into the fire, unsure of how to respond.

"'Tis plain to see you share the sentiment."

Rey exhaled in irritation. He'd forgotten how perceptive Gyda was. "She's been hurt. Betrayed."

Gyda's lips curved into a knowing smile. "And with each passing week, she heals just a little more. As I said, a survivor, that one. Perhaps more resilient than you think." Her eyes met his, pure mischief shining from within. "I see you're sharing a bed now."

"It is not like that," Rey said sharply. But he paused, mid-chew, the memory of her body pressed against his so vivid, his skin heated. "She's not meant for a man like me, Gyda."

"What does *that* mean?"

He swallowed the last of the sweet roll, sending his best *axe eyes* at her. "I've done too many terrible things. I'm no good for a woman like her."

Clearly unconvinced, Gyda set the spindle turning with a brisk flick of the wrist.

"I'm a *killer*, Gyda."

"But your heart—"

"Is made of ice. I am not capable of softness. I excel in cruelty and violence."

She merely shook her head.

"I am what I am." Rey scowled. "And that is unsuitable for her. Best you understand it." Snatching another sweet roll, he stormed into the yard.

His feet faltered.

Vig's broad form was wrapped around Silla. With one hand on her hip, the other skimming along her collarbone, Vig's mouth was right beside her ear, saying something in a low voice. Silla nodded in reply.

Curls pulled back from her face showcased the pink apples of her cheeks, the graceful curve of her neck. And her eyes, gods, those eyes could make a man forget his own name. Dark yet always sparkling, set between long, sweeping eyelashes.

Was the light playing tricks, or was she always this gods damned beautiful?

But that palm on her collarbone made a hot, poisonous feeling slide through Rey's veins. He wanted to snatch Vig away from her—wanted to drive his fist into his friend's jaw.

The goat screeched, breaking the moment.

Silla smiled, those eyes daring to brighten as they landed on Rey. His knees felt weak, his heart pounding too hard.

"Good morning, Rey," she said, and he could have sworn the pink of her cheeks swept down her neck. Was she thinking of the night before? The tenderness they'd shared? No. She *was not* flushing. But his cock unfortunately noticed, throbbing eagerly and flooding his blood with a single, cycling word.

Her. Her. Her.

"Fuck," Rey muttered, grateful that his lébrynja armor covered his stupid, single-minded appendage.

"Vig is teaching me about Blade Breaker intuition," she said spryly. "Did you know it is much like Ashbringer intuition but expressed *inside you*?"

Gaze snapping to Vig, he found his friend's eyebrow quirked, lips curved up in a knowing smile. Rey tried to school his face into an impassive look, but he knew it was too late.

"Fuck, *fuck*," Rey muttered with an inward groan.

Vig's fingers trailed along Silla's collarbone, watching Rey as he mouthed, *Liar*. Gods, but Rey had never wanted to punch someone so badly in his life.

"*Burning*, Vig calls it," continued Silla, oblivious. "He burns his galdur into energy and energy into strength. It happens so swiftly he hardly needs to think of it."

"I know how it works." Rey glowered.

Silla's teeth sank into her soft lower lip.

Hábrók's hairy arse. He forced his gaze to Helga the goat, gnawing on the longhouse's siding, then to the dung heap across the yard. Anything but her . . . lips . . .

But she was still talking. "Curiously, burning galdur does not feel the same for Vig as it does for me," Silla said absently.

"What do you mean?" said Rey, again too sharply.

She scowled adorably at him, and a bit more meltwater dripped from his cold dead heart. Shaking Vig loose, she put a hand on her hip. "You needn't punish the rest of us for your poor choices, Reynir."

Rey let out a long, suffering exhale.

"If you want answers, you'll need to ask nicely," continued Silla. Vig snickered behind her, earning himself a glare.

She was baiting his temper. Had she no sense of self-preservation? Not when it came to Rey. She'd never been afraid of him. He remembered her face when she'd stormed up to him and spoken the words that had first stirred his blood.

You cannot frighten me away.

With an irritated breath, Rey tried again. "How does your Breaker skill feel different?" he asked in his softest, most placating voice.

"Better," said Silla in amusement. "Next week, we'll work on the word *please.*"

Please, he heard her begging in his mind. *Please, Rey. Please!*

Rey shook out his shoulders. "Do not play games with me, woman," he growled. "I am not in the mood."

"Did you just growl, Galtung?" said Vig with a chuckle.

"He does that," said Silla blandly. "Don't worry. I'm unaffected."

Vig's eyes were alight with glee as he watched the exchange, and Rey took another threatening step forward. Helga the goat screeched.

"All right, Axe Eyes. Lay down your weapons." Silla sighed. "When I pushed you across the field, it felt like a . . . vibration in my hands. Like a thousand popping bubbles. But for Vig, his Breaker skill feels like a bright heat, radiating from his chest."

Rey's brows drew together. That *was* curious. "Did you access your Breaker skill last night?"

She shook her head. "I haven't since Kopa." Since her fight with Skraeda, then. Rey recalled the way she'd pushed him—with such strength he'd flown. How could she have done that without Breaker skill? But surely if she had a second source, she'd have some awareness of it . . .

"I suppose it will come in time. You must continue your training."

"We'll work together," said Vig with a mischievous smile that Rey wanted to wipe right off his face. The man was taunting Rey. Daring him to act.

"You shouldn't be out here," he said in a low voice. "The serpent is due to strike today. And you"—he leveled his gaze at Vig—"you and I have traps to set."

"Vig has already baited the trap," answered Silla. Rey's brows rose in surprise. "Runný has added an extra layer of wards, and Vig is far too valiant to allow harm to befall me in his own yard."

"Valiant," repeated Vig with a broad grin. "I think I like that. Valiant Vig of the mountains, protector of goats and curly-haired women."

"Valiant Vig whose mouth was so smart, it was sewn shut," muttered Rey.

Silla made a face. "Thank you, dear Rey, for your concern, but I cannot stay indoors. Not when I've work to do."

Rey saw the stubborn look in her eyes—could tell there was no convincing her. Whirling on his foot, he strode to the stables to saddle Horse and begin his patrols. Rey hoped Vig had some brennsa stashed away in his saddlesack. What he needed right now was a good nip of fire whiskey.

So much for sobriety.

CHAPTER 46

Sunnavík

Saga rubbed her gloved palms together as she stood outside King Ivar's study. Cursing her erratically beating heart, she forced in a deep, calming breath.

It was only Ivar. But the thought did nothing to calm her. Only the man who'd murdered her parents. Only the man who'd given her like an object to his son. Saga despised that when Ivar looked at her, he saw victory, and as a rule, she spent as little time with him as possible.

But this was bigger than Saga's discomfort. Those Galdra, strapped to beds in the chamber beneath Alfson's study, had haunted her all night. Each time her eyes had fallen shut, she'd seen the woman's snarling face and the bone-deep wounds cut into her arm. Alfson was carving her up. Feeding her flesh to others. And Saga had left her there.

Those in foul room are lost already, Rurik had said.

Perhaps they were lost, but if Saga could stop this from happening to others, she would do what she must. During her long, restless night, Saga had vowed she would gather her courage and go to King Ivar. The king who had outlawed the Galdra's very existence would be furious to discover his wife toying with galdur right under his nose. In these strange circumstances, Ivar was an ally to Saga. And so the moment Saga was certain Rurik had abandoned his post watching over her room, she made her way to King Ivar's study.

Just tell him of the scrolls and manuscript in Alfson's study, she recited, pressing a hand to her queasy stomach. *The passageway to that horrid room.*

With a deep breath, she rapped on the door. After a long moment, it opened, a thrall peering down at her. "Have you an appointment?"

"No."

The man frowned. "You can be seen tomorrow—"

"It's urgent. I must see the king."

The thrall smiled stiffly. "I'm afraid the king has been called away from Sunnavík."

"Step aside, Kul," came a familiar deep voice—one that sent a shiver through her. And then his large frame filled the doorway. "Lady Saga."

Saga swallowed, trying to calm her galloping heart. He was the last man she wished to see. The one she'd successfully avoided for years.

"Magnus," she managed.

Clad in a tunic of fine black wool, the king's chief hirdman was both tall and imposing. Saga met those cold brown eyes with forced neutrality. Inside, she stumbled, trembled, curled into a ball, and rocked back and forth.

Were it Ivar, Saga would let down her mental barriers. Allow her Sense to pull his thoughts to her. But the last place in the kingdom she wished to be was inside this man's mind.

"I must speak to King Ivar," she said. "Do you know when he'll return?"

Beneath his heavy beard, she saw his lips curl. "I'm afraid he's gone for several days, Pet."

Her hands curled into fists as a vicious wave of nausea rose within her. But she thought of the screaming woman, thought of how many others might have been manacled to a bed before her. She had to speak for them. Had to put an end to Signe's plotting. And Magnus was the king's right hand. If anyone shared Ivar's hatred for galdur, surely it was he.

Saga drew in a deep breath. Forced herself to look Magnus in the eye. "Perhaps you could help me, Magnus."

He stared at her long and hard, then widened the door, allowing her space to pass.

You can do this, she told herself, breaths quickening as she entered the room. Saga's gaze darted around, noting each exit. Glass-paned windows that could be opened; the thralls' hidden exit next to the fireplace; the door through which she'd just entered. Her pulse eased just a touch as she drew another long breath into her lungs.

Magnus gestured to a chair set before a heavy ashwood desk. "Sit." He shot a pointed look at his thrall. "Róa, Kul."

The door fell closed behind the thrall, and Saga was alone with the Heart Eater. *Ally,* she told herself. *In this, he is an ally.*

"I'm surprised to find you seeking the king's counsel," said Magnus. "Why did you not request an audience with the queen?"

"It is . . . complicated," Saga said, trying to rub the goosebumps from her arms.

"You're agitated, Pet. Something is bothering you."

"Alf—" Saga's voice broke off, and she tried to gather her courage.

"Alfson," Magnus urged. "What has the man done now?"

Surprise jolting through her, Saga studied his face. Magnus seemed irritated, though not with her. "Between you and me, Pet, Maester Alfson is on thin ice. He's been shirking his duties. Has grown unreliable." He leaned forward on the desk, his voice lowering. "The king and I have been looking for a reason to strip him of his maester's robes."

Saga chewed on her lip, her mind a tangle of confusion. Magnus was the king's right hand, she reminded herself. Currently, he was the only man in the castle with the power to stop Signe. Gods, but if only her heart would calm down.

"If you know something," said Magnus slowly, "that could help our . . . cause, I'm certain the king would be quite appreciative."

"Maester Alfson schemes at something devious."

Magnus's face twitched. "Devious."

There was no going back from it, so Saga soldiered forward. "He has a room beneath his study, with Galdra chained to beds. He is cutting the flesh from their arms and feeding it to . . . others." Magnus was silent, waiting for her to continue. "He uses something called Míkrób to steal their galdur for his own use."

Kul bustled into the room with a pot of róa and silver cups upon a tray. Saga forced deep, calming breaths as Kul poured steaming liquid into two cups.

"Leave us," said Magnus coldly, and the thrall scurried out.

Magnus reached for his cup, blowing steam while staring out the window. Saga held her breath. The fire's crackle was the only reprieve from the agonizing silence stretching between them.

"Alfson is harvesting galdur," she said desperately. "There are scrolls and a manuscript. The king should know—"

"Stop," said Magnus, setting down his cup of róa. He leveled her with a stare that shredded through her. "You dare spew such *lies* to me?" Magnus's nostrils flared. "The king and his family have been more than patient with you. Far more forgiving than I would be, I might add." He sent her a knowing look.

No, she thought, her gloved hands clasping tightly together.

"We all know you've been unwell these years, Pet. 'Tis a shame how you've hidden away when you're such a thing to look at." His oily gaze slid over her. "You're having delusions—dreaming on your feet. 'Tis the only reasonable explanation."

Taking a sip of róa, Magnus gazed thoughtfully out the window. "I might have a reputation for brutality, but it's not for lacking a heart." He chuckled darkly. "I shall grant you a favor."

A tremor started low in her body, radiating outward.

"I shall keep this conversation between us." He leaned on the desk, a chilling smirk spreading. "A *secret*, Pet. Should word of these accusations spread, I'm certain it would be unpleasant for you."

Saga stared at him numbly, gripping her chair's arms.

... If Signe would only allow me, I'd set the girl straight ...

Saga inhaled. Her mental walls must have frayed through in her agitation. Gods above, she could not survive the mind of this depraved, vile man.

... I would take my time with her. I would mark every inch of her skin ...

Saga felt her icy exterior beginning to crack as her rising panic hindered attempts to weave her barriers. She pushed to her feet, gulping in a breath. "You are most generous, Magnus. If you'll excuse me, I feel a touch unwell. I shall go lie down."

... I suppose we don't need the hounds to scent the satchel now ...

Saga stumbled as she rushed out the door.

Satchel.

Satchel?

Satchel.

Pieces slid into place, one after the other, until a horrible picture formed before her eyes. Rurik had kicked her satchel and the torch beneath the bed before they'd hidden. And in their rush to leave, she'd forgotten all about them. Clearly, they had been discovered.

And Magnus knew about them.

"No," whispered Saga. "No. No. No. No. No."

Realization slithered through her veins. Saga had been so distracted by the idea that Jarl Skotha could be the Black Cloak, she hadn't seen things clearly. Who had access to both the queen and the Klaernar? Who traveled freely through the kingdom? Who hungered for power? For violence.

Magnus Hansson was the Black Cloak.

And she'd just told him everything she knew.

CHAPTER 47

Kalasgarde

In the aftermath of Ketill's attack, Silla spent three nights at Gyda's farmstead while Rey and Vig tried to trap a serpent. But it seemed the creature, who'd been remarkably punctual, had suddenly grown shy. For days, Runný and their neighbors kept vigil around their cluster of farms, never so much as venturing to the privy without a hound as company. Meanwhile, Vig and Rey kept watch over the trap. But day seven from the last serpent attack passed, then eight and nine, with no sign of it.

Rey was left scratching his head, while Vig asked around at the mead hall. But all Vig had to say upon his return was, "Kálf grows restless. I cannot hold him off for much longer, Galtung."

Between the serpent and the aftermath of Ketill's attack, things in Kalasgarde were growing more complicated. Silla tried to ignore it—tried to keep her head down and her mind focused on mastering her galdur. But staying with Gyda and her brood of loud boys, she felt rather out of sorts.

Three days after Ketill's attack, Rey finally deemed it safe enough to return to the shield-home. As they'd sat by the hearthfire, Silla had felt him watching her as she stared at the place where she'd parried Ketill's axe blows. But rather than fear, Silla only felt her resolve hardening. Kalasgarde was where she was meant to be. She was progressing with her galdur. Was growing stronger. She hadn't bested Ketill, but she'd held him off. And that in itself was progress.

In the wake of the attack, Rey had grown more vigilant, his shoulders more tense. He swept the yard for threats each morning. And to her great relief, he'd relented to sharing the bed.

"For safety," he'd grunted, sliding a dagger under his pillow. "Keep your cold toes on your side," he'd warned, making her bite down on a smile.

Positioning himself between Silla and the rest of the shield-home, Rey had placed his back toward her. But in the morning, she'd woken with his chest curled against her back, his nose buried in her hair. A sleepy smile had crossed her face as she'd hugged his arm to her chest and tumbled back into slumber.

The man who'd once avoided her like the plague now seemed unable to keep from touching her—a tendril of hair he tucked behind her ear, a hand on the small of her back as he led her to the stables. And in the evening, when he sprawled on the bench and caught her staring at the Silla-sized pocket, he merely rolled his eyes and beckoned her over.

She knew he watched her. Could read the hunger in his eyes in those rare, unguarded moments. And Silla would be lying if she said it didn't feel good.

But she couldn't shake the memory of Jonas's betrayal. And despite what she'd told Rey—that Jonas was merely a diversion—Silla was forced to acknowledge that Jonas's actions had wounded her, nonetheless.

Silla spent long days at Harpa's, working on expression. She'd learned that with gentle enough release, the motes of light could be drawn together, cohesing into a wobbling orb. Curiously, this seemed to stabilize them, making the light last from minutes up to an hour.

"Bonding," was Harpa's explanation. "Imagine tiny tethers between each speck of light, globbed together. It is you who controls the shape of these bonds. Give them structure and order—weave them into an organized webwork—and you'll find they are yet more secure."

It was difficult to imagine, but Silla tried her best. The weaving comparison did not exactly help—cloth work was hardly her forte. And Silla found herself fighting with the light and trying to force it into order, only to have it rebel.

Yet the light was progress, and she refused to let impatience get the best of her.

It was five nights after Ketill's attack when Silla had the dream. She scurried down a cobwebbed corridor, the cold, dark presence growing ever stronger. The cravings awakened, sliding through her veins, pulling her forward. She entered the room. The Dark One's shadow was stark on the stone wall. He laughed, and the sound vibrated through her chest, like strings on a harp plucked.

Too late, the Dark One whispered. *You're too late.*

Silla whirled. And there he was—Rey, manacled to a bed, arms and legs sliced down to sinew and bone. *Too late,* she agreed, tears streaming down her face. She'd been too late to save him. She'd been . . .

She woke with a start, heart pounding in a deafening beat. *A dream,* she thought, rolling to face Rey. She needed to see him. Needed reassurance. But the bed was empty.

Unease crept down her spine. Each morning, she'd woken with him by her side. To find him missing in the wake of that dream was unsettling. Climbing from the bed, she wiped cold sweat from her brow.

After dressing, she pulled the curtain back. Her brows drew together. Where Rey should be, sat Runný instead. A few weeks past, this had been a regular occurrence. But now, paired with the dream, Silla's unease only grew. "Well met, Runný," she murmured. "Where is Rey?"

Runný merely shrugged, the silver rings adorning her black braids clinking together. "Out."

Silla strode to the window and pulled the animal hide covering back. A light dusting of snow covered the ground, footprints leading out through the wards and beyond.

"What is it?" asked Runný.

"Dark dreams, and now . . ." Silla raked her hair back, trying to shake the feeling that the dream had been a message from the gods. "I do not like that Rey is gone."

Runný watched her silently. "He's gone to visit his brother."

Silla's gaze met Runný's and held it. "Kristjan?"

Runný nodded. "The burial grounds in Kalasgarde."

Motion from the yard diverted Silla's attention. A large black bird had landed on the pristine carpet of snow. Slowly, it lifted its head and stared at Silla with dark, knowing eyes. Her heart leaped into her throat. Curved yellow beak. A swath of white on its tail feathers.

"Black hawk," she whispered. The herald of death. The last time Silla had seen it was the day her father had died. And in that moment, the knowing place deep inside her told Silla she needed to get to Rey. Her cloak was on in a heartbeat, her boots and weapons belt next.

"I'm under orders to keep you here," said Runný, standing. "It's not safe."

"Something's wrong," said Silla, strengthening her spine. "I feel it in my bones." She held Runný's gaze, trying to convey her urgency. "Do you believe in the signs from the gods? Because now, in the yard, sits a black hawk. Perhaps it is nothing, but with Rey, I cannot take the chance."

To Silla's great relief, Runný merely nodded. "Let's go," she said, grabbing her cloak and pushing through the door. The pair followed Rey's footsteps along the road and toward Kalasgarde. In a matter of minutes, they were rushing through the stockade walls, weaving between homes and shops, coming to a stop before the burial grounds. A wide-open space, bordered by woods and dotted with thick clusters of trees, the burial grounds contained orderly, snow-covered mounds, oriented in the path of the sun. And there he was, a dark form folded over his knees near a group of trees.

"He's safe," Silla exhaled. The battle thrill coursing through her began to ebb at the sight of him. Perhaps she should warn him of the strange dream . . . of the black hawk. Silla glanced around the burial mounds, eyeing the forest edging the back border. She'd just give him the warning, then return to the shield-home. "Runný," Silla whispered. "Can you wait here?"

The dark-haired Galdra let out an exasperated sigh, but as her gaze landed on Rey it softened. "Very well."

"Thank you!" whispered Silla, hugging a startled Runný before following Rey's footsteps into the burial grounds. Nearing the copse of trees, she studied him for any sign of trouble.

"Why have you come?" grumbled Rey without looking.

"I had . . . a dark dream," she said, feeling foolish. Yet seeing him well and whole relieved some of her unease. "I had to know you were safe." Silla cleared her throat, glancing around. To her knowledge, the serpent had never breached Kalasgarde's stockade walls, but she didn't like the feel in the air. "Perhaps you should not linger too long—"

"Sit," said Rey, making room on the cloak he sat upon. "We'll leave in but a moment." Reluctantly, Silla drew nearer and eased down beside him. Warmth tingled wherever they touched—thighs, hips, shoulders—slowly easing the tension in her body. Silla gazed at the burial mound, noting the three stone clusters swept clear of snow.

"We had nothing to bury but needed a place to visit our parents." Silla did not need to ask who the other was in the *we*—Kristjan, the brother Rey had lost to skjöld leaves. The brother he never spoke of. Her heart pounded as she waited for him to say more.

"I scarcely remember my parents now," he said. "Each year, the memories fray a little more. Sometimes"—his voice cracked—"days go by, and I don't think of them once."

His elbows rested on his drawn knees, and she looped her arm under his with a gentle squeeze. Several moments of silence passed before he continued. "I've not returned to Kalasgarde since I—" He cleared his throat. "For five years. I've left their burial mound unvisited for five years. What kind of son am I?"

"You're here now," Silla whispered.

"It is your doing."

Silla's pulse pounded. "Me?"

"I've watched you face your grief day after day. And I thought that if you could do it, at the very least, I could try."

Warmth unfurled in Silla's chest, and she couldn't help but smile.

"I missed your smiles," he whispered. "I'm glad to see them back."

Embarrassed, Silla pressed her nose into his shoulder, breathing him in. "You," she said softly, "helped me more than you know. Having you at my back gave me the strength I needed."

He looked incredulous. "I did nothing. Words are not . . . I am better with actions."

"Your words *and* actions helped," she said, turning her head so her cheek rested on his shoulder. "Will you tell me about them?" She felt shy asking, fearful he'd retreat.

"I recall little," he said, staring at the burial stones. "But there are flashes of things. My mother could be as stern as Harpa, but my father was as playful as a wolf cub. He'd wrestle us for hours—taught us how to hold a sword and how to tell if a man is lying. He taught us how to cheat at dice and how to slip the parts of our meal we did not care for to the hounds without catching Mother's eye."

Rey let out a long breath. "On the surface, it might not seem that my parents were suited, but I think they brought balance to each other. He drew out a carefree side of her, while she helped him achieve things he could not on his own. Together, they were stronger than apart."

Silla squeezed him gently. "And your brother?" she prompted, greedy for more.

But Rey's guarded expression told her not to press. "I'm sorry," she retreated. "I . . . if you ever wish to speak of him, I am here to listen."

He was silent, and Silla's mind raced for a way to open him back up—to bring him back to where they'd been moments before. "Your work for the Uppreisna," she tried. "It is for them. For your parents."

The muscles beneath her fingers eased just a touch as he released a long exhale. "Yes."

She was silent for a moment of quiet contemplation. "You're a caregiver," she said, understanding at last. "You care for others, dead or alive. You do *everything* for others. The Bloodaxe Crew. Your family. Me." Silla paused, looking up at him. The sun glowed brighter behind Snowspear, catching in his eyes—threads of gold woven with the deepest of browns. "Who looks after *you*, Rey?"

He held her gaze for a long, weighted moment. "I do."

"I could do it," she said, the words quiet and loud all at once. "If you'd let me."

"I don't need anyone to look after me." He glowered.

She laughed—she couldn't help it. "Obstinate man."

"Repulsively cheerful woman." He pinched her ribs, and she squirmed.

"I'd warm your bed with heating stones." She gasped, wriggling away as he pinched her again. "Massage the ache from your shoulders. I'd knock you on your arse each night to keep your pride in check."

Rey huffed, gaze settled on hers. His lips twitched, and then it happened.

He smiled.

It was like molten sunlight pouring through her veins. She smiled back, reaching up, skimming fingers along the soft contours of his lips. "Your smiles," she whispered. "I find myself willing to do anything to see them." Her finger settled in the divot of his bottom lip, pushing down. "And I find myself wondering . . ." She pushed onto her knees, bringing their faces level.

Edging closer, she watched Rey's pupils grow impossibly wide. Something deep inside her fluttered. Impulsively, Silla leaned forward, sliding her lips against his.

As far as kisses went, it wasn't her best work. She pressed her lips to his just a little too hard. Lost her balance as the world seemed to tilt. Putting a steadying hand to the ground, she drew back, her face as hot as a thousand suns.

"I didn't want to die without doing that," she blurted, easing away. Panic gripped her. What had she done? She'd just kissed him—Reynir Galtung. Oh, gods.

But his hand slid around her shoulder before sliding up her neck to cup her face.

"Then do it right," he muttered. And his lips were on hers.

Silla was torn between a curious mixture of surprise and relief. Surprise that Reynir Galtung was cupping her face so reverently, kissing her with all the tenderness in the world. Relief that at last, this was happening. A warm rush of tingles flowed through her body, and time seemed to stand still for a single perfect moment.

But the moment shattered.

A cry echoed across the burial grounds, and their mouths wrenched apart.

"Runný?" gasped Silla, head whipping around. But before she could see anything, she was slammed to the ground and rolled once, twice. Cold seeped into her back, Rey's powerful body covering her own. For a moment, Silla thought she was dreaming.

But Rey's low voice cleared her mind in an instant. "When I get up, move as fast as you can to the trees, and don't come out."

CHAPTER 48

Heart thundering, Rey hauled Silla to her feet and pushed her toward the woods. At first he'd thought the serpent was attacking, but now he knew better.

"Archers," he hissed, tracking movement in his periphery. The light streaming over Snowspear was near blinding, shadows in the burial grounds growing deep. "Take cover in the trees!"

"But I want to fight!" she protested, reaching for her sword.

Another arrow whisked past his ear. "Not this time." Rey left no room for compromise in his words. "It is too dangerous. Get into the trees and *do not* come out until I signal."

After casting him a scathing look, Silla rushed to the trees, and just in time—another arrow thrummed by, missing her by inches and embedding in a trunk. This arrow, Rey noted, was far smaller than a longbow's, with curious red fletching.

Drawing his sword, Rey ducked low and rushed to the largest of the burial mounds, swerving side to side to confuse the archers. He was two steps away from the stones when warriors emerged from behind the barrow. Gritting his teeth, he quickly assessed. Eight of them, clad in boiled-leather armor, greataxes clutched in both hands. His gaze fell upon their sigil and he cursed.

Wolf Feeders.

Rey dropped, rolling behind the barrow while simultaneously yanking his galdur with all the force he could muster. By the time he sprang up on his knees, the veins in his hands were oil black, the prickling heat of his galdur building higher with each heartbeat.

He had only seconds for this to work—the archers would have to wait as he took on the warriors rushing around the mound. Flicking his palm open, he drew from the halda tattooed on his chest, expressing his smoke in a churning rush of darkness.

With an exhale, he split his power into eight wisps of smoke, channeling every fiery ounce of anger into his galdur. His smoke swarmed at the nearest warrior's face.

The familiar anguished screams and spit of burning flesh filled the air, the warrior before him falling to the ground just as the churning smoke met the next one. An arrow whizzed by Rey's ear, diverting his attention for the barest of moments. His galdur faltered, but he refocused quickly. Three warriors fell, but the rest were closing in on him.

"Shit," he muttered, trying to maintain his focus. But they were too near, and his galdur was better used from a distance.

"'Tis a nice trick," grunted a warrior from behind him. "But it is no match for cold steel."

"Unfortunately for you, I have both," growled Rey, drawing his sword.

Rey whirled just in time to duck beneath the swinging greataxe. The warrior was a match to Rey's own size, his red beard glinting in Sunnvald's glorious Rise. Bringing his blade up to parry a bone-rattling blow, Rey was forced to relent his galdur. The hair on the back of his neck lifted, and he dove not a heartbeat too soon as another warrior swung from behind.

"Give up and you'll keep all your parts," spat the man. "Or keep on, and you'll leave in pieces."

Rolling to his feet, Rey widened his stance, the warriors advancing on him. "Give up and I won't use you as firewood." He wouldn't allow them to know that he couldn't maintain swordplay and his galdur simultaneously.

Rey had learned long ago to steel himself against emotions in battle. *The hothead is more apt to lose his head,* as Kraki liked to say. And so Rey found that cold place within and became the ruthless warrior he needed to be. Lunging at the red-bearded warrior with a burst of aggression, Rey caught him off guard. The man parried, sending Rey's blade flying to the ground, but it was no matter. Rey grabbed him by the collar and pressed a sizzling palm to his face, his grip unrelenting as the man's flesh turned as red as his beard.

A blade sang through the air, and Rey released the man's collar, ducking low just in time. The warrior's greataxe collided with the red-bearded man's shoulder, leather splitting as the blade sank right through.

Yanking the greataxe free, Rey swung it overhead, burying it deep in an advancing opponent's neck. The last warrior, having lost his weapon, tackled him to the ground. It was not a pretty fight. There were no handsome swings of the blade or fancy footwork. This was a struggle—a fight to the death. The warrior had enormous fists that returned Rey's own blows in equal measure. As his opponent's fist crashed into his nose, Rey pressed his still-hot hands onto the man's face, finding the soft curves of his eyeballs.

The warrior screamed, bucking like a wild animal and sending Rey flying. But it was enough. The man's sight had been compromised. Breathing hard and trying to regain his senses, Rey scrambled to his feet. Unsheathing his dagger, he dispatched the writhing warrior. But pain speared suddenly from the back of his neck. Shock was chased quickly by fear, then relief. Had it been a longbow's arrow, he'd be dead.

Distantly aware of yet more approaching warriors, Rey yanked the arrow out and examined the strange, pointed tip. This was no arrow—it was a skarpling's quill. Most alarmingly, with each passing breath, the heart of his magic grew increasingly quiet until at last he could sense it no more. Rey clutched at his chest, at the hollow place where his source should lie. This was different from being drained. Rather than being empty, it was simply not *there*.

What had they done to him?

Rey fought his panic as more warriors swarmed at him from all corners of the burial grounds. He tried to assess, tried to find that cold, unfeeling place, but Rey was unsettled by the absence of his galdur. Battle cries surrounded him, and he retrieved his sword, bracing himself for impact . . . an impact that never came.

He watched in disbelief as one charging warrior veered unexpectedly to the side, crashing into his comrades and landing hard. A wound opened in the man's throat, blood arcing through the air and staining the snow crimson.

"Runný," he exhaled. "Thank the gods." Just then, Vig hurtled from his periphery, his bare arms swinging a greataxe through the air and hacking through the man from shoulder to hip. Before he'd tumbled to the ground, Vig was already cutting down another Wolf Feeder.

"Seems you cannot stay out of trouble," yelled Vig, a broad smile on his blood-flecked face as he struck down another Wolf Feeder.

"My life was quite in order until *she* showed up," muttered Rey, slashing into the neck of a warrior charging at Vig from behind. "Trouble stalks her like a jilted lover."

"'Twas too quiet around these parts anyway," Vig replied, ducking an incoming blade while chopping the man down at the knees. "Needed a good fight to liven things up."

"Don't let them prick you," yelled Rey. "Their arrows quell galdur."

The world became a blur of blades as Rey fought side by side with the Shadow Hound and Blade Breaker. Red sprayed across the snow as he edged toward the trees where Silla took cover. It seemed each warrior he felled was instantly replaced by another.

"She's in the woods," came a man's voice, chased by Silla's scream. Rey's stomach clenched. Too many times had he failed her—today would not be another. With a ragged cry, he forced his way toward the woods.

"Get her!" someone yelled. "Someone get her!"

"Archers!" someone else bellowed.

"No," Rey grunted, shoving his shoulder into a man's gut and sending him stumbling backward. He could not fail, not again—

Pain exploded from the back of his skull, consuming his entire world.

Life throbbed back to Rey with every excruciating pound of his heart. He blinked, prone on his back, as snow melted through his armor. Cold steel pressed into his throat, and the three warriors glaring down at him came into focus.

His vision warped, the men above him shifting. One turned, calling out over his shoulder. "We've got your man, love. Put that away and we won't hurt him."

Put what away? Rey wanted to ask, but his tongue felt too large for his mouth.

A male roar filled the air, growing higher and higher until it reached a shrill pitch. It was not the sound of victory, but one of agony.

"Release him," snarled Silla, "and I'll let you live."

Rey expected laughter, perhaps a patronizing grin. Instead, the warrior flinched.

"Shoot her!" he bellowed.

Everything happened so quickly he could not make sense of it—footfalls and grunts, a warrior's terrified cry. Something heavy fell onto his chest, punching the air from Rey's lungs. And he found himself staring into the blank eyes of a man's severed head.

Looking up, Rey blinked. Limned by the rising sun, a goddess with iced hair and crystalline eyelashes stood over him, a sword of shimmering frostfire clutched in hand.

Silla's eyes widened, the sword dissolving into the air like shining stardust. "Oh, gods," she breathed, covering her mouth. "I've cut his head off." Turning, she retched into the snow, instantly breaking the spell Rey'd found himself under.

Rey pushed the severed head from his chest and crawled to his feet. His skull screamed in protest, but he tried to shake the grogginess away. Bracing himself on his knees, he took in the corpses on either side of him, so engulfed in frost they seemed at one with the snow. Another pair lay toward the copse of woods where Silla had hidden. Irritation prickled through him. The bodies wove a clear picture—she'd left her place of hiding to confront them on her own.

The telltale signs of the Wolf Feeders retreating brought him back to focus. Vig had appeared at his side, Runný naught but a pair of boot prints on his other. "No one leaves here alive," Rey rasped, retrieving his sword. "No loose ends."

Vig nodded, and together the trio stormed into the woods bordering the burial grounds, sniffing the archers out and making quick work of them. Vig was a horrific sight, slashing through body after body, while stealth was Runný's ally as she snuck up on the fleeing archers, slitting their throats before they knew she was there. And Rey, well, anger had honed his blade to the sharpest of points. They'd spilled blood in this, of all places, and for that, he made them pay. By the time the last of the Wolf Feeders fell, the snow glinted red, raven cries filling the burial grounds as they feasted.

Rey trudged over to Silla, tight with anger. He wanted to shake her, wanted to scream at her. Wanted to glory in this new revelation of her power. But most of all, he wanted to gather her up and finish what they'd started moments before the warband had attacked. His skull still rattled, and he could not find the words; and so he merely watched as her gaze found Vig and Runný.

"A sword!" exclaimed Vig, clapping Silla's shoulder. "You wove your galdur into a *sword*! How did it happen?"

A tentative smile curved her lips as Silla stared down at her pale forearms. "It happened so *fast*," she murmured. "I cannot say precisely how."

Runný nodded. "It is a common thing, the first time your galdur takes its natural shape. Often it comes in times of duress."

"You must go to Harpa," said Vig eagerly. "Reshape this thing while the feel is fresh in your memory."

As they chattered on about Silla's galdur, a growing unease spread through Rey. He could not sense the heart of his magic. It was unnatural, like a part of himself missing. Swallowing his nerves, he strode to an archer's corpse and plucked one of the curious skarpling quills to bring to Harpa. They must identify the substance on the tip. Determine if there was a way to counter it . . .

"I found the shield-home empty," Vig was saying, prodding what would soon be an impressive black eye, "and followed your footsteps."

"Well, thank the gods Valiant Vig arrived when he did," said Silla. "Not to mention Ruthless Runný. The pair of you are merciless."

They limped their way back to the shield-home in silence. Runný kept invisible, traveling ahead of them to scout for danger. Thankfully, she did not find anything. And as the sun crept higher, their footsteps vanished with the melting snow.

At the shield-home, Silla stoked the fire and boiled water to dress wounds. Rey collapsed onto the bench, Vig beside him. "I'll talk to Kálf," said Vig in a low voice. "But he'll need an explanation for the corpses at the burial grounds." Vig's gaze darted to Silla for a heartbeat. "You must tell them. Today has proven extra eyes and blades will be needed to keep the pair of you protected."

Rey grunted in understanding. The meeting he'd put off for so long was now breathing down his neck. With a long exhale, he considered his options. He did not want to force Silla to do anything she was uncomfortable with. But keeping her identity hidden was getting trickier with each passing day.

From the corner of his eye, he watched her clean a gash in Runný's arm. She hummed as she worked, and Rey's irritation began to grow. She'd left the shield-home. Had put herself in harm's way. They could have overpowered her. Could have injured her . . . captured her. *Killed* her.

Yet still she hummed, approaching to spread salve on Vig's swelling cheek. After some time, Vig and Runný departed with a quick farewell, leaving Rey and Silla alone in the shield-home. An ember snapped in the hearth as Silla moved about the room. Any moment now, she'd admit her mistake. Would apologize for breaking his orders. But she didn't. In fact, she ignored Rey entirely.

A thousand angry thoughts crowded his mind, but all that came out was, "When I say stay in the shield-home, I mean *stay in the gods damned shield-home.*" He glared into the hearthfire. "And when I say stay in the trees, I mean *stay in the gods damned trees.*"

He heard her turn, felt her sharp gaze on his back. "I believe you meant to thank me, Galtung."

Rey stood, turning to find her with hands on hips.

"'My thanks, Silla,'" she continued, "'for saving my life. *Again.*' 'Tis not so hard to say."

Rey's glower deepened. "Gods above, woman! Have you no sense of self-preservation?"

"More than you, it seems." She huffed. "I told you I would look after you, and I meant it. I won't watch your throat be cut open simply because you're too proud to ask for help."

"Proud—" Rey spluttered, moving toward her. "Pride has nothing to do with it! You cannot risk your life like that. It's *worth* something!"

Silla stepped closer. She was small yet so fierce. He wanted to hold her, wanted to shake her, wanted to kiss her and strangle her all at once.

When she spoke, her voice was low and dangerous. "You'd best not suggest your life is *not* worth the risk, Galtung. I would do it all over again."

He stood a head taller than her, but it was clear she was not intimidated in the least. Glaring at him, Silla put a finger in the middle of his chest and pushed.

"Let it sink into your thick skull: Your life is worth the risk."

All other thoughts spilled from his mind as her words echoed in his head. So long, he'd been alone in this cold, hard world, keeping everyone at a distance. But the warmth of her outrage reminded him of what it was to have someone. To feel cared for. His ribs felt too small, his skin too tight.

As her expression turned to hurt, his chest squeezed. "What happened to the man who let a vampire deer attack me?"

"That was before—"

"*No,*" she snapped. "I thought better of you. You always had such confidence in me, even when I did not. This is exactly what I fear . . . why I don't want to be *her.*" Silla's brows drew together, uncertainty written all over her face.

Rey struggled for the words. "You *are* capable. Stronger than any I know. When I saw you . . . and I thought you could be lost . . ."

He couldn't finish the sentence. Couldn't tell her that in that moment, Eisa Volsik had been the farthest thing from his mind. It was *Silla* he'd feared for.

Her hurt melted away as understanding settled in. Those dark eyes fell to his mouth, the air seeming to crackle between them. All he could think of was how soft her lips had felt.

The tip of his boot edged against hers. This close, he could count each freckle scattered across her nose, trace the crescent scar at the corner of her eye. Her gaze met his, and it felt as though she'd reached right through his chest and squeezed his heart. And then his hands were sliding along her jaw, and he had to kiss her.

Warmth exploded through him as their lips met. Soft, she was so soft and tender, so responsive to his touch. Her hands wrapped around his, holding them in place, and as his lips moved against hers, all thoughts melted from his skull. Why had he fought against this? Why had he thought this was a bad idea?

Silla's face flashed in his mind's eye, bruised and terrified as she fled through Kopa's woods. Jonas. She'd been hurt by Jonas. Rational thought surged back, along with all the reasons he shouldn't be kissing her. She was Eisa-gods-damned-Volsik, and Rey had *vowed* to do right by her.

He broke the kiss, running a hand down his face as he tried to gather his wits. But all the blood in his head seemed to have rushed south to his cock. Desire thrashed through him, and gods, he needed to kiss her again.

"What is it? You don't want me?" There was a note of uncertainty in her voice, a note that snapped clean through his restraint.

His hands were on her waist, pulling her hips flush against him. Silla gasped, looking up at him with eyes dark as midnight, and he knew she felt just how wrong she was.

"I want you every minute of the day." He rolled his hips against her. The friction was maddening, and not nearly enough. "If you knew the sordid thoughts I've had, Silla, you'd run the other way."

Rey's nose was in her hair, drawing deep pulls of her scent. She smelled like a gods damned meadow. Felt like everything he could never let himself have.

She tilted her face up to his. "Then what is it?"

"I have no business wanting you."

But his mouth was on hers once again, a low groan escaping him. Kissing her was more than mere need. It was a compulsion against which he was helpless. Closer, he needed to be closer. Needed to hold her and touch her and learn the shape of her everywhere. But he pulled his mouth from hers, running his nose along her temple.

"I'm not a good man."

"I disagree."

Outwardly, Rey scowled, but inwardly, it was as though a hook had caught in his belly, pulling and twisting his insides up.

"You need someone of standing. Someone who can guide you—"

"You," she replied, her fingers sliding into his beard and drawing his lips to hers. "I want you."

His heart sang loudly, cock straining against his breeches, and Rey knew he was in trouble. His grip on her waist tightened, fingers digging into her skin, as he fought desperately for control.

"I'm not *nice*, Silla."

"And I can't be so easily frightened away, Galtung."

With a growl of frustration, his lips found hers in a demanding kiss. *I'm not soft,* he told her with his lips and tongue, *and I'm not gentle.* But rather than retreating, she gripped his elbows, arching closer. And as a soft sound came from the back of her throat, lust surged through him.

Rey groaned, wrenching back. Her lips were swollen, begging for more, and it took everything he had not to devour her.

"I'm violent," he tried. He was holding on by his fingertips. Soon he'd wash away, and there would be no turning back. "I'm a killer."

"You have reasons."

"Gods damn it, Silla! You should run the other way." But he was walking her backward with slow, deliberate steps. "You never did have the good sense to be frightened of me."

His palm skimmed along the curve of her backside.

"You're precious, and you deserve to be treated as such."

The hand slid up her spine, settling at the base of her neck.

"That's . . . sweet, Rey."

Their slow retreat across the room had halted as they'd reached the bed, and the realization made Rey's teeth clench tightly.

"You deserve sweet, Silla. You deserve kind. You deserve to be worshipped and respected and treated right."

"Show me," she whispered. "And I will show you—the man who is so busy caring for others, he forgets about himself. Let me show you what it means to be cared for."

Her eyes met his in silent challenge. "You're running out of excuses, Galtung. Tell me why else I shouldn't want you."

Rey opened his mouth, but no sound came out.

"Good," she said. She fell back onto the bed, pulling him with her.

CHAPTER 49

As Rey's lips moved against hers, Silla's body seemed to sigh, bowing up toward his. *This,* her heart beat out. *Him.* As he kissed her, she was infused with such happiness, it seemed to spill out everywhere.

Bracing himself above her, Rey deepened the kiss, and she clutched at his forearms like she might otherwise fall. It didn't matter how they'd started. Didn't matter that they should be all wrong for each other. Kissing him was like the first spring day after a long, brutal winter. Like finding one last sweet roll hidden in the bottom of the basket. It was like all the hearthfire thoughts she'd ever had combined.

There had been a moment when she'd thought she'd read him all wrong. That tendril of fear, borne of Jonas's betrayal, had wriggled and grown. But as his tongue dipped into her mouth, as the hand at her hip fisted her tunic, all worries were burned up with the rest of her. Gods, but she wanted this man. Wanted to discover the taste and feel of him.

Rey dragged his nose down the length of her neck. "Do you know how long I've wanted to do this?" he whispered into her skin.

She made an incoherent sound, trying to pull his mouth to hers, but Rey resisted.

"Weeks," he muttered, trailing his mouth along the edge of her jaw. "Months."

His touch was maddening and not nearly enough.

"Silla," he pleaded. "You feel . . ." Whatever he was going to say was drowned out as he kissed her again. The world sharpened where they touched—their slanted lips, the heat of his chest melting into hers, the drag of his hand along her hip, her waist, higher, higher.

Rey's hands were everywhere—under her bottom and around her back, crushing her to his solid body as though he could not get close enough. And she was unraveling, strand by strand, beneath his touch, growing soft and boneless.

It was too much, and yet not enough.

"Rey," she whispered.

A husky groan from the back of his throat turned her insides liquid and scalding hot. Her hands raked down his back, seeking the edge of his armored coat. She needed to touch him, needed to run the pads of her fingers along his smooth skin. Discovering a tunic beneath, Silla growled.

"Did you just growl?" Rey teased.

"Off," she begged, yanking at his tunic.

"Ask me nicely," said Rey in a low, dark voice.

Silla scowled. "*Please.*"

Rey made a low sound of satisfaction, and she felt it in all the tender places of her body.

He climbed off the bed. Staring at her with dark eyes, he toed off his boots, each thud sending shivers down Silla's spine. As his hands began working the buckles of his lébrynja armor, Silla propped herself up on her elbows to get a better view. Slowly, he pulled off the bloodstained armor, stripping down to his breeches and undertunic.

Gods, but this was . . . doing things to her.

Is this finally happening? Silla thought as he stalked toward the bed.

"Only if you want it," he answered, uncertainty flickering in his eyes.

Silla blinked. Had she said it aloud? "Gods, yes," she said, grabbing his collar and yanking him down eagerly. Rey covered her body with his, bracing himself on his elbows. He hovered above her, so near their breaths mingled in the darkness.

"Truly?" he asked.

She nodded. And then the words flowed from her, unfiltered and embarrassingly honest. "Since the first time you smiled, I think. I couldn't stop thinking about it. Those dimples. Gods, when you smile . . ." She exhaled shakily. "I cannot stand it. I want to be crushed under your weight. Want to feel your bare skin on mine. Want to watch your face as you fall apart—"

Stop! warned the protective part of her, and Silla sealed her lips shut before more words could spill out.

"Gods, woman," came Rey's low voice. "You'll be the death of me, won't you?"

And with that, all embarrassment fled her. She opened her eyes. Met his fiery gaze. *Him,* her heart pounded, again and again. He lowered his hips against hers and . . . oh. She felt *all* of him.

And then his lips were on hers, and Silla was pulled under by the current of lust.

Rey had been reduced to pure visceral want. He needed her more than air. More than vengeance. He'd fought so long, so hard against the pull of her, but it had always been futile. *She* was inevitable.

Drawing back, he ran a finger along the waist of her breeches. "Take these off."

Silla responded with such enthusiasm, lust and amusement battled within him—it seemed the obstinate woman didn't mind being told what to do after all. But Rey should have known Silla would surprise him. After pulling off her breeches, she reached for her undertunic, yanking it off and tossing it aside. She settled back in the furs, utterly bare.

Rey couldn't breathe for a moment as he took in the goddess before him. Wild dark tendrils spilled around her face, her bare skin pale against the brown furs.

"Your turn," she said softly.

But Rey could only stare dumbfounded at the expanse of bare skin. "So beautiful. So lovely." It was all he could say. She truly was exquisite, inside and out. He reached to touch her, but her hand encircled his wrist, sending sparks shooting up the length of his arm.

"You," she insisted, as though that single word was all she could muster. Deft fingers slid under the hem of his own tunic, and Rey's heart thundered so loudly he was certain she must hear it. But the thought of her skin sliding against his made him wild and reckless, and before he knew what he was doing, Rey's tunic was off.

"This dragon," she murmured, staring at his chest. Her fingers skimmed across the tattooed creature's curving body, along a membranous wing. "I want to map it out."

"Later," he muttered, his palm sliding roughly against her jaw. Rey kissed her deeper, harder than before, losing himself in the sweet taste of her mouth, in curves and dips as he explored her bare flesh.

"Do you know how badly I want you?" Rey's voice was rough as sand, his body hard as granite as he sank against the softest part of her.

"I might want you more," she gasped, rolling against him and sending shivers of pleasure up his spine.

Gods, Rey's restraint was nowhere to be found. He thrust against her, imagining how the hot, slippery clasp of her body would feel. How deep she would take him. He moved against her with a soft groan, pure satisfaction filling him as she trembled with need.

Words were spilling out of him completely unfiltered. *So lovely,* and *so brave,* and *I've wanted you for so long.* He was carving himself up, handing pieces right over. *Take it all,* he wanted to say. Nothing mattered except her. Here. Now.

"More," she moaned, and Rey found himself rolled onto his back, Silla clambering on top with amusing determination. Her hair fell around them in a cascade of curls, and she hauled it over her shoulder.

"Easy, my eager girl," Rey said with a soft chuckle.

"Your laugh," she whispered. Gods, she was beautiful, smiling down at him, with that wild hair and bare skin. "You're smiling." Her fingers slid along his lips, and he realized he was, indeed, smiling. "I want them all, Rey. Your smiles. Your laughs."

"Come and take them," he said, hauling her against him and kissing her. Rey's fingers skimmed down her stomach, then slid through her intimate flesh and dipped inside. A thrill ran through him at the wetness he discovered. Proof that she wanted him, too.

Rey sat up, bringing her with him and settling her on his lap. One hand slid down her spine, the other pushing two fingers inside her, all while she rolled against him. The friction was maddening, intoxicating.

"Gods, woman," he rasped as he pumped his fingers. Straining against his breeches, Rey bucked up, rubbing himself against her sensitive skin. He was beyond restraint. Beyond reason. "I've no control where you're concerned."

"I don't want you in control," she said breathlessly. "I want you reckless." A moan slid from her as her inner muscles clamped tighter and tighter.

Her thighs clenched against him. Silla's fingers dug into his back, and she released a soft cry. Burying her face in his shoulder, she tried to smother her sounds. And as her body began to quake with her ecstasy, Silla's teeth sank into his skin. The pain was sharp and distracting as Rey pinned her to him and bucked up against her, again, again, again, relentless in his desire to break her apart as she'd broken him.

Closing his eyes, Rey clenched his teeth as she sagged against him. He tried to distract himself from the fact that he was painfully hard by focusing on the thundering of her heart.

At last, she drew back, a sated smile curving her lips. But his errant cock twitched against her, and Silla's smile vanished.

"You needn't—" But he hissed as her hand slipped beneath his breeches, wrapping around him. She paused, her brows drawing together.

"What are you hiding down here?" she asked, scooting back on his thighs. Her eyes met his. "They feed you something special in the north?" And with that, she pushed his breeches down to free him.

"Silla," he warned. "You do not—"

"Oh, but I *do*," she insisted. "Gods, Rey, you're—" One small, hot hand encircled him, and it was too much. Gods, he'd imagined this a thousand times, but the touch of her was more than he could have dreamed. Her other hand joined the first, working him up and down with torturous slowness. "Rey, I don't know if you'll—if I can—if we'll—"

"I didn't take you for a coward," he grunted, shoving into the tight clutch of her hands, trying to urge her on. Silla scoffed, and he caught the competitive gleam in her eye. And in that moment, he could see how it would be with her. The teasing. The games they'd play.

It wasn't long before he found his own pleasure, showers of sparks racing across his vision and down his spine as he thrust into her hands. He groaned into her hair, clutching her close as heat burst from him. He could smell and feel her everywhere, and it was almost too much sensation for him to bear.

Resting his head on her shoulder, he labored for breath. But Silla pushed him onto his back. Cleaned them up with her tunic. Curled her body around his with a soft sigh.

"That was . . ." She let out a shaky exhale.

Rey tipped her chin up and pressed a soft kiss to her lips. A disorienting blast of warmth radiated through his body, leaving him feeling off balance. She felt like she belonged there, curled up against him.

The thought was enough to make panic surge through him. *Kristjan,* he tried to remind himself, but even the memory of that loss did little to rebuild his defenses.

"Why a dragon?" she asked, tracing a tattooed wing spur.

"A dream I once had," he replied, thankful for the diversion from his muddled thoughts. "It is my halda."

"Halda?" Silla asked, looking up at him. "Why do I know that word?"

Rey found himself rambling. "Harpa, most likely. The tale goes that Sunnvald's ash fell upon the stones, creating halda deposits. Some say they have their own source of galdur, but as they are stone, they lack the mind to control it. When ground into a fine powder and tattooed upon one's skin, they serve as a . . . reserve of sorts. A place to store galdur outside one's own source. It is handy when you need a great supply."

"In battle," Silla mused, her nails scraping along a wing spur. Her fingertips found the bite mark on his shoulder, and she pressed a soft kiss to it. "I'm sorry. I've marked you."

Should he tell her he would wear it like a badge? *Hers,* it seemed to say. "Thank you," he said instead.

She blinked.

"Thank you, Silla, for saving my life. *Again.*"

Silla burst into laughter. "That was painful, wasn't it?"

He frowned affectionately. "Horrible. But you summoned a sword of light and turned yourself into an ice goddess to protect me. I suppose I ought to thank you."

Her fingers slid into his beard, stroking gently. "I'd do it a thousand times over, Galtung."

He pressed a soft kiss to her temple, then jerked back with a frown. Rey had been so distracted, he'd forgotten the absence of his galdur. Now, as he probed inwardly, a hot, restless feeling filled him. It was unnatural, an empty space where the heart of his magic should lie. It felt as though a part of him had been wrenched free.

"What is it?" asked Silla.

His lips parted, but he forced them shut. Yanking on his breeches, he searched for his tunic. "We must get to Harpa's," he said brusquely.

And before she could answer, he was out the door.

CHAPTER 50

Kopa

"What do you mean, 'lost contact'?" Kaptein Ulfar growled. Jonas shifted in his chair. The Klaernar standing before them was young, with a wispy blond beard that barely concealed his chin.

Immediately, the lad reminded Jonas of Ilías, making his chest clench with grief. Gods, but he missed his brother. Missed the Bloodaxe Crew. Found himself wondering how things had gone this way. But here Jonas was, partnering with the Klaernar to fulfill the oath he'd sworn on Ilías's burial mound.

Clearing his throat, the younger Klaernar shifted nervously. "It is only that . . . it is to say . . ."

"Spit it out, boy," said the kaptein in a low and dangerous voice.

"All our falcons have returned to us unanswered. We've lost contact with the Wolf Feeders."

A flush crept across Ulfar's cheeks. "Out," he told the boy.

As the door closed, the kaptein turned to Jonas. "Kalasgarde," he spat. "We sent them to Kalasgarde, Svik." The kaptein pushed to his feet, hands braced on the scarred table. "Do you think me a fool?"

Jonas kept his gaze impassive—he was no stranger to ill-tempered warriors. Still, he understood this situation would require careful navigation.

"You're working with them," said Hagbard from the farthest corner of the room. The man's meaty arms were crossed over his chest, his claw-tattooed cheek pulled into a scowl. "You sent the Wolf Feeders to Kalasgarde, right into a trap."

"I'm not working with them," muttered Jonas, turning over this latest development in his mind. He knew the Wolf Feeders by reputation—they were not so undisciplined as to ignore orders. "What were your directions, precisely?"

"That's enough information shared with the likes of him, Kaptein!" exclaimed Hagbard, pushing from the wall and striding toward the table.

Jonas stood, glaring daggers at the black-haired warrior. His anger was growing, a hot restless feeling sliding through him. He needed an outlet—needed to brawl. And oh, how he'd love to rearrange this lout's face. "I said," growled Jonas, "I am not working with them."

"But—"

"If I *had* sent the Wolf Feeders into a trap, why would I wait here for you to discover it, you eelhead?"

Hagbard's brows drew together as he pondered the question.

Jonas turned his attention back to Ulfar. "What were your instructions?"

Ulfar scowled. "They were told to wait at the burial grounds until the Slátrari appeared. To follow him back to his hideaway and send word at once."

Jonas stood. Began pacing the room. What had happened in Kalasgarde? He paused. Turned to Ulfar. "Did you instruct them not to attack until they heard from us?"

Ulfar and Hagbard exchanged a look.

Jonas clenched his fists, trying to comprehend the imbeciles before him. "You were to confirm their location, pay my reward, and *then* I was to tell you how to defeat them. Did I not tell you he's no ordinary warrior? Did I not tell you we'd have to be *clever* to disarm him?"

Ulfar did not reply.

"The Wolf Feeders have not made contact," Jonas said, trying to grasp this situation. "How many warriors is that?"

Ulfar stared at him hard.

"Do you want to tell the queen, or shall I?"

"Twenty-four," muttered Ulfar, looking away.

"Twenty-four," repeated Jonas in disbelief. "Twenty-four seasoned warriors felled by a single man." A small part of him was proud, but he quickly stomped it down. He scowled at the map pinned to the wall, tracing the mountains surrounding Kalasgarde. "No. Rey is a capable warrior, but twenty-four—"

"He roasted twenty-one at the gates of Kopa," Hagbard said.

Jonas stroked his beard, considering this new side of Axe Eyes—a side he'd never known. "Rey had the element of surprise in Kopa," said Jonas. "But the Wolf Feeders knew him to be Galdra; they had the advantage in Kalasgarde. You sent them the phials of that—" Jonas tried to recall the name of the parcel that had recently arrived from Sunnavík after some sort of mix-up.

"Liquid hindrium," supplied Hagbard.

"The liquid *hindrium*," spat Jonas. "This was the Wolf Feeders' battle to lose."

"They were under orders to take them only if both targets were sighted," said Ulfar, sulking.

So she was there with him. Jonas's stomach twisted at the realization that Rey had shared something so personal with her. Meanwhile, Jonas was realizing he scarcely knew Rey at all. But he knew well enough how good she was at getting a person to open up.

I did not wish to lie to you, rang her voice in his ears. All while drawing out his hopes and dreams—his greatest shame. And then she'd smashed everything to bits.

The smolder in his stomach burned hotter, higher.

"So," he forced out, "*she* was with him. A battle ensued. The Wolf Feeders must have been vanquished, else they'd have checked in by now."

Ulfar nodded in agreement. "It seems that way." He sighed. "What do you propose?"

"What do I propose? I *proposed* the Wolf Feeders wait. Assess. Determine numbers, strength, formations." He was echoing Rey leading the Bloodaxe Crew into battle, and the realization made his stomach lurch. But Jonas kept talking. "Now I don't know. You'll need a way to gain the upper hand. Retake the element of surprise."

Ulfar and Hagbard watched him expectantly.

Jonas blew out a long breath. He'd been happy to direct the Wolf Feeders from afar. To feed them Rey's weaknesses and helpful information. But as he looked at the kaptein and his half-witted second-in-command, he was beginning to understand.

If Jonas wanted to get the job done, he might just have to do it himself.

A knock on the door.

"In!" barked Ulfar.

The young Klaernar warrior sidled back into the room and handed Ulfar a scroll. "This just came from Kunafjord." Ulfar slashed the wasp sigil open with his dagger. Flattened the scroll on the table. A wolfish smile spread across the kaptein's face as he read.

"Out," said Ulfar, and the young Klaernar left.

"What is it?" asked Hagbard as the door thunked shut. "What's it say?"

He handed the scroll to Hagbard. "It says we have our element of surprise." The kaptein's eyes met Jonas's. "The queen's Chosen will arrive in two days' time."

CHAPTER 51

Kalasgarde

Silla stood in Harpa's yard, bitter traces of replenishing tea lingering on her tongue. She glanced over her shoulder in search of Rey and found him leaning against Harpa's cabin, his umpteenth cup of replenishing tea clutched in hand. Based on the troubled look on his face, the heart of his magic had yet to return.

Silla tried to push her worry for Rey from her mind, but she couldn't help but remember the way he'd looked before rushing from the bed—their eyes had met, and he'd opened his mouth as though he wished to say something. *Tell me,* she'd wanted to beg. *Talk to me!*

"We must get to Harpa's," he'd said instead, yanking on his clothes before heading outdoors.

She didn't want to admit that his sudden coldness made her uncertain. Already, her feelings for Rey felt altogether different from what she'd had with Jonas. Now she was left wondering what this was between them.

Silla tried to bury her doubt, focusing instead on the beautiful sword of white light. She could still feel its imprint in her palm—could recall the power she felt wielding it. There had been a rightness to that blade, her galdur taking its fated form.

After countless cups of replenishing tea and a trip to the steam bath, she came to a realization. It seemed certain motes of light had affinity for one another, that they need only be guided together to make these connections snap into place. It was an intuitive thing, impossible to explain to another. While Harpa thought of it as *weaving*, to Silla it was more like . . . *herding*. And once she started thinking of herself as a shepherd of sorts, everything slid into place.

When at last she looked down at the sword of white light, she was filled with exhilaration. It was cold against her steaming palm, the familiar taste of winter on the back of her tongue.

"Malla-blessed," Harpa breathed, a note of wonder in her voice. "In all my years, I have not seen such a thing."

Silla's eyes found Rey leaning against Harpa's doorframe. His lips formed an almost-smile, but his gaze was distant, as though his mind was not in this realm. Coldness grew in the pit of her stomach.

"Relinquish your sword," instructed Harpa, forcing Silla's attention back to her task. "Practice summoning it again."

And so the next hours were spent doing just that. As she practiced, Silla wondered if a sword was such a great thing. Other Ashbringers could express blasts of fire, taking out multiple warriors at a time. But the more she considered it, the more potential Silla saw in the weapon. An unbreakable blade, sharper than any metal in the kingdom. A sword she need not carry but could summon at the ready. Light as air, it was easy for a woman of her stature to swing.

"You have an affinity for this thing," murmured Harpa, returning to the yard as the sun sank behind Snowspear. "It is the natural structure for your galdur."

Indeed, it felt natural, allowing her to move with far more ease than she had with the practice swords. Once summoned, it felt steady, pulling continually from her source to stay alight.

As Silla mounted Dawn at the end of the day, she was bursting with excitement. After weeks of hard work, she'd finally summoned this sword! But one glance at Rey had her tensing.

"Any trace of your galdur?"

A slow nod.

"Thank the gods," said Silla.

Rey nudged Horse forward, and Silla urged Dawn to do the same. "Sparring tonight?" she asked, desperate to break this strange silence between them. "The routine you showed me yesterday?"

But Rey did not reply. She wasn't certain he'd even heard her.

And as Dawn trekked down the hill, the uncertainty Silla had pressed aside all day took full control.

An hour later, Silla's wooden sword slashed through the cool evening air. The sun had long since set, Malla and Marra now beginning their Rise. Rey had reported his source was growing stronger with each passing hour. It should bring her relief, yet the coldness in Silla's core was absolute.

This morning there'd been the exhilaration of surviving the Wolf Feeders. It had been all warm feelings and strong convictions. She'd been so certain, it had felt so *right*. But all day, there had been empty spaces, silences, gaps for doubt to creep in. She found herself dissecting each small expression on Rey's face. What was he thinking? Why didn't he confide in her?

Her mind swirled with irrational thoughts. In the aftermath of Jonas, Silla had lost all faith in her own judgment. Did Rey only want some fun in the furs? Didn't he understand that when she said she'd care for him, she meant in all ways? They should have spoken more plainly about it. Now Rey was pulling back, and Silla's worry only grew.

She flipped her thick braid over her shoulder in irritation and tried to get out of her head. Widening her feet, she readied to launch into an attack routine.

"In need of a partner?" asked Rey from the shield-home's doorway.

"What?" Her gaze caught on his, and she felt it *everywhere*.

Rey stepped toward her. "In need of a partner?" he repeated.

Nodding apprehensively, Silla tried to corral her fears and shove them away. Rey ambled closer, one hand held behind his back. There was a look in his eyes—one she could not untangle. Again, she did not understand what was going on in the man's head, and everything in her tightened.

"What is it?" she asked sharply.

"I . . . have something for you," he said, pulling his hand out from behind him, revealing a garment.

She took it, frowning as she smoothed her fingers over gleaming black scales. "Lébrynja armor," Silla murmured, her eyes meeting his.

"For you," said Rey, the corners of his lips twitching up. "Put it on so I can see how you'll look in the next battle."

A reluctant smile spread across her cheeks. A gift for her, and so much more—it was an apology for forcing her to hide in the bushes at the burial grounds, a promise to trust in her skills going forward. "My thanks. Where did you get it?" She dropped her practice sword and pulled the armored jacket over her tunic. It fit like a glove, hugging every curve of her body.

"I had it commissioned from the Tailor," he said. "It was delivered to Vig—'tis why he came to the shield-home this morning." Heat flared in his eyes as his gaze skimmed from her toes to the top of her head. "It suits you well."

His focus dropped to her mouth, but Silla busied herself by retrieving her sword. If she'd expected Rey to go easy on her in the wake of the morning's events, Silla was very wrong. He blocked each blow, pushing back with strength. Her blood pumped harder with each swipe of her sword, her worries from earlier swept aside. She rushed at him again, and his wooden blade whipped out, knocking against her own. A smile curved her lips as she dodged his next blow.

After several long minutes, Rey broke the silence. "Are you ready to speak of it?" he asked, and Silla stumbled back.

"What?" she asked, regaining her balance.

"Whatever it is that troubles you."

"Nothing."

"Liar."

She wiped the sweat from her brow, staring over his shoulder. "'Tis merely the Wolf Feeders," she managed. But Rey's expression told her he didn't believe her in the slightest.

His sword swung low, and she danced back with not a heartbeat to spare. Rey moved into one of their routines, his movements so swift, she could only duck his blows. "You can keep lying," he said, driving her back, "or you could tell me the truth." Silla's spine hit the wall of the shield-house. There was nowhere to go.

She swallowed, trying to decide what to say. But Rey beat her to it.

"You want to know my truth?" he asked, that deep voice soft and rough all at once. "Today I was unsettled." He ran his tongue along his teeth. "I couldn't feel my galdur. I thought I might have lost it forever." A look of discomfort crossed his face. "And I did what I always do. I kept everyone out and weathered it alone."

His gaze landed on her, pinning her in place. "I'm not used to letting people in," he admitted. "And I'm not used to voicing my . . . sentiments." His lip curled up in obvious distaste.

The tension in Silla's stomach eased just a touch.

"I should have considered you might take my behavior to mean something else." His hand found her waist, then skimmed along her back. "Let me make this clear to you, Silla. There is nothing uncertain in how I want you."

She could not look away from the intensity of his gaze.

"It's the most maddeningly certain I've ever felt. I want you all the time. I want you *everywhere*. It's become a real problem."

Her stomach rolled and flipped, heart pounding in her chest.

Rey put one hand on the wall, leaning down toward her. Even in the dimming light, his eyes were scalding hot. "I wanted you on Longest Day when you came out in that dress," he said, voice ragged. "I wanted you when you pushed me across the field on the way to Kraki's. I wanted you when you killed the vampire deer, when you blackmailed me, even when you tried to steal my gods damned horse. I've wanted you since the night you stormed up to me and told me I couldn't frighten you away. That was it for me, Sunshine."

Where tension had once weighted them, her limbs now felt light as air. Silla stumbled over her words, but her mind didn't seem to be working.

Rey leaned closer, his breath mingling with hers. "And now that I've had you, it's only worsened. I cannot stop thinking about this morning. How glad I am you were brave enough for the both of us. The disbelief that you might possibly want me as I want you." Vulnerability flashed on his face, but it was quickly chased away by a look of pure hunger. "Are we clear now?"

Breathlessly, she nodded.

"Good." His hand skimmed up her spine, coming to rest on her nape. "Because in my mind's eye, I've had you naked and spread out before me on every surface of the shield-home. Have done the most wicked things to you."

Silla stared into his gold-flecked eyes. Swallowed her worry.

"Show me," she heard herself whisper.

And before her mind could follow, Rey had hefted her into his arms and was kicking the shield-home's door open.

CHAPTER 52

Rey thanked the gods as he carried her into the shield-home. His day had been disorienting. The empty space where his source should lie had been a void in his chest. And though Rey often bragged that nerves were a wasted emotion, he could not help the worry that had gripped him. What if his source didn't return? Who was he without his galdur? Without his work for the Uppreisna?

At the first faint glimmer of the heart of his magic, he'd exhaled a long breath. Had shaken the tension from his bones. Unsettled didn't even begin to describe his mood. Losing his galdur had shaken him to his core.

It had taken him far too long to realize what he'd done. She'd trusted him with her body. Had been brave enough to open herself up to him. And he, the eelhead that he was, had run from the bed. Had shut her out all day.

He felt her surprise as he paused by the long table. Transferring her to one arm, he swept the dishes onto the floor with the other. Wooden plates bounced, clay cups shattered, cutlery and candlesticks clanged.

"What—"

"I want you here," he muttered, setting her down and finding the hem of her tunic. "Right on this table."

"You can have me anywhere," she breathed, lifting her arms so he could yank her lébrynja, then her tunic, over her head.

His hands found her braid and pulled until her back arched. "I want you *everywhere*," he whispered into her skin, dragging his nose along the underside of her breast. "I want you all the time."

Silla moaned, and he felt the sound straight down to his cock.

"When we're done sparring, I must douse myself in the stream's icy waters." Releasing her hair, Rey kissed her roughly. "When you lean over to stir the porridge, I have to count the beams in the wall." He rocked his hips against her. "And when your hair falls into your face"—he dragged his mouth down her neck—"it takes every ounce of my will not to bury my hands in it."

She gasped as he kissed a path downward, avoiding her breast. She was soft as silk, warm as sunshine. Silla made an indignant sound, hands sliding into his hair, as she tried to pull him to her.

"Are you trying to tell me something, Sunshine?" he asked, his tongue tracing along her smooth stomach, chased by the bristle of his beard. She squirmed, so naturally, he repeated the motion. "Here?"

He kissed a path upward to her sternum. "Here?" he asked. She strained up, trying to pull his mouth to her breast. But Rey resisted. "You like to rush, don't you? I like to go slowly."

He pressed a kiss to the underside of her breast. "To savor."

He dragged his nose up her sternum. "I want to learn you. What you like. And I won't be rushed, Silla."

He saw the moment she understood—this was a new version of their game, of their push and pull. If she thought she'd be able to control it, his touch told her otherwise. He teased her with another pass of his mouth, then hovered over her breast, just where he knew she wanted him. At last, he relented. Rey pulled the soft bud into his mouth, drawing a low moan from Silla.

Gods, he ached for her. Wanted to bury himself deep inside her. But Silla had rushed things before, and he wanted to be certain she was ready. And there were plenty of other ways to amuse themselves. Rey's attentions slowly moved downward, along the sensitive skin of her ribs, the curve of her hip, the waistband of her breeches.

"Take these off," he said in his sternest Axe Eyes voice. He watched a shiver roll through her as she rushed to comply. His eyes slid slowly over every dip of her body, trying to decide where he'd start. She was beautiful, so absolutely lovely. Their gazes met. Held.

"Lie back. Hold on to the table."

He dropped to his knees. But Silla remained braced on her elbows, brows drawing together. "What are you—"

Rey's head lifted, pure fire racing through him. "I want to taste you."

"Taste me," she repeated, dumbfounded. And then her brows drew together in realization.

A shaky breath escaped him, fingers digging into her thighs. "Do you mean you've never . . ."

Slowly, Silla shook her head.

Rey didn't care if he was her first, and yet this pleased him. "Let me taste you, Silla. Let me worship you. Let me show you all the ways you deserve to be treated."

"All right," she managed, her voice shaking. And the trust in those two words made Rey's insides melt into a puddle of pure heat. Lying back, she braced her feet against the table's edge. But Rey's fingers tightened on her thighs.

"Don't be shy," he said in a low voice, yanking her to the edge and hooking her feet over his shoulders.

Chest heaving, he felt Silla watching as his head lowered. His fingertips glided along the sleek skin of her inner thighs, chased with teasing kisses. And then Rey's fingers slid through her.

"So soft," he murmured into her skin. "You're so lovely, everywhere."

His fingers dipped inside her body, stroking gently, soon followed by the wet heat of his mouth. Silla's body jolted upward, and she sat up, staring dazedly at him.

"Lie back," ordered Rey, adjusting his breeches. She fell backward with a moan, and Rey's own pleasure grew as his mouth moved slowly against her. With his tongue and fingers, he learned her—finding the spots that made her insensible, and those that made her clench down. She was close, he could tell, tightly wound up. Her feet flexed, searching for traction, but Rey drew back, peppering kisses along her thighs.

Silla grasped his head, trying to guide him back to where she needed him. His eyes met hers. "I told you, Silla. I won't be rushed."

With a frustrated cry, she curved her hands into fists, but Rey only smiled. He wanted to tease her, to drive her to the edge of madness. Bending down, he pulled her into his mouth with a gentle suck.

"Oh, gods!" she cried out, arching off the table. It sent a jolt straight through his body. Rey tightened his grip, holding her in place. His fingers slid back in, teasing, coaxing, while his tongue swirled, and soon he felt her climbing back up, reaching, reaching, reaching . . .

Again, he relented when she neared that very pinnacle. Again, she cried out in frustration. Her head swung back and forth, incoherent sounds spilling from her lips. But Rey only laughed.

"Please!" she begged. Her body writhed as though she was not in control. And she wasn't, in the least. She was utterly at his mercy.

This time, when his tongue found her, she received the full weight of his attention. He found a rhythm and was relentless in his touch. Her heels dug into his back, knuckles white from her grip on the table's edge, but Rey held her firmly to him.

At last, she reached the peak, breath seizing as her back bowed. Silla cried out as her body clenched down again, again, again. It seemed to go on endlessly until at last she lay limp on the table.

"That was . . ." Her inability to find words was the highest praise. Silla raked her hands over her hair, as though trying to drag her mind back to her body.

Rey pushed onto his feet, his large body covering hers as he leaned over her. "You're exquisite," he said, pressing his lips to hers. "Those sounds you make . . . I want to hear them every night, Silla."

Her hand trailed across his chest, resting over his hammering heart. Their eyes met and held. Then her expression shifted to mischief.

Silla's mind was dazed and tangled, her heart beating out of her chest. Rey's ministrations had left her weak, and as she slid off the table, her knees buckled beneath her. But his hand was there to steady her, helping her stumble to the bed. As they reached it, Silla twisted them so Rey landed on his back.

"Silla..." His eyes were glazed with desire, and she wanted—no, *needed*—to see him completely undone.

"I want to make you feel good." Her eyes met his as she climbed onto the bed, settling on his thighs. Slowly, her hand delved under his breeches, pulling him out. "I want to taste you as well."

The gold flecks in his eyes brightened as though a fire raged behind the brown. Rey trembled with restraint, closing his eyes as she stroked him. "Silla," he rasped, his hand finding her jaw. "You needn't—"

"I need," was all she could say, fingers finding the bead of liquid at the tip and swirling it.

"Fuck," cursed Rey, bucking into her hold.

"Language, Reynir," teased Silla, a thrill running through her. He'd driven her to madness, and now he'd pay penance. Dipping her head, she took him into her mouth, twirling her tongue. He groaned, throwing an arm over his face.

"Now," said Silla, drawing back. "Let's see if we can learn a few things about you." She licked her way up the length of him, studying his every reaction. By the time she'd drawn him back into her mouth, Silla was pleased to see a sheen of sweat across his brow.

"How does it feel, Reynir?" she asked. "Being teased?"

Rey just grunted, his gaze growing hard. Her hands slid back up his hips and settled on his stomach, where they moved in soft circles. But where Rey was the model of control, Silla had always been unapologetically eager, and this game was beginning to torment her. Unable to sustain this ruse any longer, she held his gaze as she drew him into her mouth, taking him as deep as she could.

"Fuck," muttered Rey, squeezing his eyes shut. His pulse pounded furiously, chest heaving, and a small smile curved her lips.

"I've been imagining you like this," she admitted, giving him a teasing lick. "Axe Eyes, at my mercy." She took him deep once more, adding a hand to work in tandem.

She pulled off him, smiling at his groan. "What do you like, Rey? Show me."

His eyes met hers. "Don't be gentle," he rasped.

A strangled sound came from her. She tried to gather herself, but she felt dizzy, disconnected from her body. Instead, she pulled him back into her mouth, meeting the thrust of his hips. She'd done this before, but had never felt so lost, so utterly aroused at another person's pleasure.

Each groan she drew from him made her own desire spiral only higher. Each involuntary buck of his hips made her wild with need. He cursed roughly, his hands resting on her hair, yet never pushing down. They cradled her, stroked her scalp, let her know just how much she pleased him.

"Close," muttered Rey.

She drew him deeper, growing heady with the sensation of driving him wild. Rey's hips shot up in short, involuntary thrusts, guttural sounds coming from the back of his throat. And as she swallowed, Silla watched him. Gone were the masks, the tough, sharp man she knew well. Here was Rey, undone. Dismantled. At his very purest self.

He lay on his back, panting. And as she settled into the crook of his arm, Silla once again placed her palm on his chest, his heart striking against it with rapid beats.

"Gods, woman," Rey heaved. He rolled onto his side, resting his head on his bent arm.

He was sated and soft and impossibly warm, and as she stared at him, Silla couldn't help but smile. "I told you I'd take care of you."

Rey's lips curved into a smile, that dimple creasing his cheek. He shook his head, watching her.

"I'm glad your galdur is back."

He drew a deep breath. Let it flow out. "As am I." His gaze locked onto hers. "I'm sorry," he said.

She blinked.

"I will work on not being stubborn as a mule."

"And I," said Silla, "will try not to let fear rule me." She rolled onto her back, gathering her bravery. "I thought I was past it. Past *him*. I did not feel for him what I—" *feel for you,* she could not add. "But he hurt me all the same. And I cannot let that man take any more from me."

Rey leaned over her, covering her lips with his. As he rolled back, Silla mindlessly expressed her light. The orb formed, wobbling above them.

"Look how far you've come," said Rey, expressing a ribbon of smoke. Silently, Silla watched as light and dark swirled together, marveling at how his darkness made her light shine so much brighter. At how her light cast the deepest shadows from the darkness.

"How do you give it a light touch?" she asked. "If I wished to bathe you in starlight, but not . . . remove body parts."

"Practice," was Rey's reply. He extended a hand, reaching for the orb. But as the light made contact with his finger, he hissed and retracted it.

Silla released her galdur, taking his hand in hers and drawing his finger to her mouth. Eyes meeting his, she sucked gently, melting the frost. Instantly, Rey's eyes heated. His smoke melted away as he rolled onto her, and she felt his body reawakening.

"Again?" she asked, her own desire stirring deep in her belly.

"I told you," he grumbled, dragging his nose along hers. "I *always* want you. It's a problem."

Silla slid her lips against his, then whispered, "Let us find a solution, shall we?"

CHAPTER 53

Rey picked at the knots in her curls with gentle tugs of the comb. Seated atop the furs and clad in only his breeches, he'd nestled Silla between his thighs as he teased out the tangles. Sunlight crept beneath the animal hide window coverings, catching motes of dust in the air. The room was scarcely large enough to fit the bed on which they sat, the timber beams overhead showing signs of decay. By anyone else's standards, the shield-home would be a grim place to lay one's head. And yet Rey could not think of anywhere he'd rather be.

As Silla loosed a wide yawn, Rey's lips curved up. He'd woken her with soft, sleepy kisses, smiling at her sounds of protest—at the way she'd curled into his chest and tried to fall back asleep. Silla was one who rose at first light with an irritatingly cheery air, but today, she was truly exhausted. Her grumpy demeanor, paired with the disheveled state of her hair, had filled him with satisfaction.

He'd quickly changed her mood with soft strokes of his hands, pulling the blankets back and crawling down her body. And as he'd energized her with his fingers and tongue, Rey decided it wasn't so bad, sharing a bed with Silla and her cold toes. He'd submitted himself to her idea of retaliation but when his hand had gotten stuck in her tangled curls, Rey had felt a mild twinge of guilt.

"And after Geirborg?" he now asked, picking at a stubborn knot.

Silla hissed in protest, and he eased back. "We settled in Holt," she answered, irritation in her voice. "You simply *had* to unbind my hair, didn't you, Galtung?"

Rey thought of those tendrils sliding against his fingertips as he'd unwound her braid the night before. "Yes."

She was silent a moment. "I was an underbaker, which meant most of my time was spent bent over the quern-stone, grinding the grain for hours at a time."

Rey frowned at the thought. "That would've been backbreaking work."

Silla nodded, then flinched as the motion tugged on her hair. "I still bear scars from the blisters. Right here." Silla held up her hand, showing the red mark on the side of her thumb. Capturing her elbow, Rey directed her hand to his lips and placed a kiss on the scar. Then he returned his focus to the tangles.

"And you, Galtung?" Silla urged gently. "Jarl Hakon and the Uppreisna's high chieftains sent you south to apprentice with Kraki. What happened next?" Rey could hear the hesitation in her voice—as though she were afraid he'd rebuke her.

His stomach tensed instinctively and Rey wondered if he'd ever get used to sharing such details with another. "Much as Kraki told you, I suppose," he grumbled. "I'd trained with a greataxe, but he would not take me on unless I learned how to wield a longsword."

"I imagine Vig would turn foot and return to the north at that."

Rey chuckled. "I imagine so." His brows furrowed as he recalled those days. The pride he'd felt at being the Uppreisna's youngest covert warrior. The youthful optimism that he'd bring change to the kingdom. Back then, he had yet to feel the frustration that came from years of toiling with little to show for it.

"I practiced with the longsword at first and last light every day for years. Sigrún, Jonas, and Ilías joined us a few years later in Sunnavík. Hekla that spring in Midfjord. Gunnar two years later in Kunafjord. And slowly, we became the Bloodaxe Crew you knew." He was telling only half of it, skipping the part where his world shattered.

"Ha," he muttered as the comb broke through the knot. He began dividing her hair into small sections. For so long, this hair had been just under his nose, driving him mad. Now he wanted to touch it—to care for it. "You might have noticed," he murmured, "in the north, the style is to wear several small braids, cuffed with silver rings." His fingers deftly wove the tendrils together.

"I had noticed," said Silla, with a deep, satisfied sigh. "Though I'll admit, you surprise me. To think the fearsome Axe Eyes has any interest in hair."

Only this hair, he could not say aloud. He pressed his nose into it and inhaled, noting the shiver that ran through her body. Rey forced his focus back to the task, twining a handful of small braids and securing them with leather strips. He decided he'd get her silver cuffs the next chance he had.

"You want the good news or the bad news, Galtung?" boomed a loud male voice, the shield-home's door banging open. Silla gasped in fright, Rey reaching for his dagger. But the moment he recognized the voice as Vig's, he relaxed, running a soothing hand down Silla's spine.

"Still abed?" bellowed Vig from beyond the curtain. "Lazy hearthfire fool."

But he said it with affection, drawing a small smile from Rey. "A minute, Twig Arms!" he barked. "I'll talk to him," he whispered in Silla's ear. "Rest and take your time."

She nodded, another yawn breaking free, and Rey slipped from the bed, pulling on his undertunic. A moment later, he was through the curtain, sliding it back to shield Silla from view.

Vig's smile was wide and knowing, and Rey realized he, too, was smiling. He forced his expression into a scowl. "What is it, Vig?"

Vig slid onto the bench and rested an elbow on the long table.

"Let us talk outdoors," Rey said quickly. After what they'd done on that table, there wasn't a chance he could hold a serious conversation while seated at it. After pulling on stockings and boots, he strode into the yard.

"Galtung?" asked Vig, grinning like a wolverine as he sauntered toward him. "Anything you need to tell me?"

"No." But Rey cursed inwardly as he smothered a yawn with his hand.

Vig chuckled. "Mmm. I suppose you were up all night, *gazing at the stars.*"

Rey ignored his friend.

A knowing look spread across Vig's face as he folded his bare arms over his chest. "Thank the gods, Galtung, I was getting sick of all the longing looks—"

"Enough, Twig Arms."

Gleaming white teeth shone from within Vig's black beard. "So touchy, Galtung. And here I'd thought a good romp in the furs would loosen that stick up your arse."

Rey merely scowled.

"Good news first, then," said Vig with a shrug. "The serpent struck again, but our victim escaped unharmed. And we have a sighting."

Immediately, Rey's mood lifted. The serpent . . . gods, in the wake of the Wolf Feeders' ambush, he hadn't thought of it once. He tried to count the days since the serpent's last attack but quickly lost count. Far more than seven days, whatever the number was.

"Bjalla Gray Locks," continued Vig, "takes his ale at the Split Skull. We'll talk to him today."

"Good," grunted Rey.

Vig scratched his beard, his gaze growing wary. "The bad news is that Kálf is no longer *asking* to see you. He's *demanded* your presence at the Uppreisna meeting tonight. Has threatened to have you dragged before him if you don't answer for Ketill and the Wolf Feeders."

Rey let out a long exhale. In truth, he'd been bracing for this. Had he been alone, he'd have gone to see Kalasgarde's local Uppreisna chieftain immediately upon arrival. But he'd been trying to buy Silla time, trying to give her the space she needed to grow into Eisa . . .

Now it seemed time was in short supply.

"Very well," muttered Rey. How could he explain the invasion of their peaceful town by a violent warband? Would they buy that the Wolf Feeders were here to hunt the Slátrari? But Ketill had lured Rey away. Had tried to take *her.* And surely those birch planks would be making their way through the north. It was entirely possible they'd reached Kalasgarde.

After arranging to meet at the Split Skull later, Vig departed, and Rey strode into the shield-home. Silla was bent over the cauldron, the nutty scent of toasted grains filling his senses. Clad in a red tunic and black breeches, Silla straightened and turned.

"What . . ." she asked sleepily.

"I need you to come to a meeting with me," he said in a rush.

"What happened to *rest and take your time?*" she grumbled.

"Come here," he muttered, grabbing her arm and pulling her to him. Hands sliding under her jaw, he cupped her face and brushed his lips against hers. It took every ounce of his will not to drag her back to that bed, but he forced himself to draw back.

He looked into her eyes. "I need you to come to a meeting with me."

Her brows dipped low. "Are you trying to kiss me into agreeing?"

A laugh rumbled low in his chest. "Did it work?"

But a look of concern had crept into her face. "What is this meeting?"

Rey licked his lips, searching for the right combination of words. "It is run by Kalasgarde's local Uppreisna chieftain." Now there was no mistaking the panic in her eyes. "A gathering of local Galdra. I need to explain why there are two dozen bodies in the burial grounds, Silla."

"It *is* a place for the dead," she murmured, pulling free from his grip and avoiding his gaze.

"I can go alone, but I don't want to lie. Not to the Uppreisna. There's only so long . . ." Rey didn't want to pressure her, but he didn't understand. "Can you explain it to me?" he tried as gently as he could. "Why you have no interest in her?"

Silla whirled away, but not before he caught the redness creeping up her throat.

Frustration gathered in his gut. "Why are you still afraid?" he asked, more harshly than he'd intended.

Silla turned to him, aghast. "What?"

"Eisa," said Rey, stubbornly shouldering forward. "You've faced so much. Have come so far. But still, you always steer the conversation away from her. Don't think I haven't noticed you've never asked about your birth parents."

Silla would not meet his eyes, but he could read her body language well enough—tense and ready to flee. It seemed she was still not ready for this.

"I let you reveal my identity to your friends," she muttered. "Is that not enough?"

"Yesterday's attack proves we cannot do this ourselves. They'll come for us again. We need men. More eyes, more blades. Come to the Uppreisna meeting tonight and reveal your identity. They'll understand the urgency of our situation. They can *help*. Offer better protection."

"No," she said forcefully. "I cannot. Not yet . . ."

"These are *Galdra,* Silla," said Rey. "Good, honorable Galdra. You needn't fear them. They would never turn on their own—"

"Like Ketill?" she spat.

Rey rubbed his forehead, trying to choose his words.

But Silla had turned on her foot. "I need more time."

And with that, she rushed to the sleeping quarters and slung the curtain shut.

Sitting on the bed with the curtain separating her from the rest of the shield-home, Silla wished she'd stormed into the yard. With only a shred of linen separating them, she could hear as Rey moved around the space, adding wood to the fire and pouring water into the cauldron.

Silla forced in deep breaths, trying to tame the panic thrashing through her veins. She did not know how she could simultaneously want to punch Reynir Galtung in his beautiful, cruel mouth while also wanting to climb into his lap and press her lips to his.

Why are you still afraid?

What an arse. Anger flared through her. Rey had always been assertive—had always pushed her. But there had also always been a measure of restraint. Today, he'd broached the subject of Eisa with the subtlety of a broadsword.

How could she explain it wasn't simply a change of names? That becoming Eisa meant rewriting her entire past. It meant mourning the loss of dreams she'd had for so long and coming to terms with what her future now held—duty, responsibility, and expectations she could never live up to.

Each day, she tried to surrender to Eisa. Each day, it grew a little easier. Yet still she had a long way to go before she could summit this mountain.

Time. She needed more time.

But the daggers she'd pointed at Rey soon turned inward. Why *did* Eisa frighten her so much? Why could she still not do this? As a sob broke free, Silla held her head in her hands. She needed to calm her racing thoughts. To get back to a place of stability.

Perhaps Harpa's mind-clearing techniques would be good for more than controlling her galdur. Sitting on the edge of the bed, Silla closed her eyes and found the quiet corner of her mind. It was dark and calm and utterly still.

You'll never be ready to be Eisa, Matthias soon whispered. Silla greeted his words. Let them settle into her. And released them.

Perhaps I won't, floated the thought. Perhaps she would never be ready to be Eisa. Perhaps she would always mourn Silla's dreams of a quiet life with chickens. This thought, too, she acknowledged and freed.

You're not strong enough to be Eisa, whispered Matthias. *Too soft. Too scared.* They stung, these thoughts, but she did not push them away. She let herself feel them, let them do what they would before letting them go.

Magnus is the Black Cloak, came a new voice—a woman's voice. *How could I not have seen it? How do I get word to Ana with them watching me?*

Silla's breath caught. The woman's voice . . . it was so familiar. *Who was that?* thought Silla. From beyond the curtain, Rey coughed, but Silla kept her thoughts focused inward.

This fresh delusion is splendid, came the woman's sarcastic voice.

Silla's hand flew to her chest. *Silla Margrét, you are going mad.*

If you're mad, then that bodes poorly for me, said the voice. *I'm already quite out of my mind. And now I've taken to speaking to myself. I wonder if Alfson has a tonic for this?*

Who is this? thought Silla, bewildered.

Oh, fine, said the voice. *I can play along. 'Tis I, Saga Volsik. How absolutely splendid to meet you, Silla.*

Silla's hands clenched around the furs she sat upon. *Is this a twisted joke? W-who is this? Has someone put you up to this?*

Wonderful, thought the would-be-Saga. *My delusional voice is now yelling at me.*

Who? demanded Silla. *Who is this?*

Silla felt a foreign trickle of irritation. *Look,* thought the would-be-Saga. *It's not the best time for me to be hearing voices. I'm in a bit of a predicament. I need my mind to myself, if you please.*

It's not the best time for me either, thought Silla, her current woes forcing their way forth and flooding her mind. *How can I go to an Uppreisna meeting and tell them who I am? If I tell them, they'll expect things of me. Things I cannot ever give them...*

Would-be-Saga seemed to hesitate. *Uppreisna? What is this? A joke?* Another pause. *Are you a friend of Ana's? One of the Mind Galdra?*

Galdra? thought Silla, her thoughts spiraling quickly. *Do you think... is this... a Galdra trick? Are you... infiltrating my mind?*

A pause from would-be-Saga's end, then, *I don't know. In truth I know little of my Sense. But Ana would know. If only Signe's mice weren't watching me...*

An incredulous feeling crept through Silla. She heard the crackle of the shield-home's hearthfire, felt the tickle of furs beneath her fingers. Yet foreign sensations also filled her—the damp scent of old stone in her nose, the whisper of fine-spun linen against her skin.

Could it really be? Silla thought, shifting on the bed. *But no. This is madness. But Signe, and she knows of the Uppreisna. And I know nothing of Mind Galdra. What if this really is Saga?*

Your thoughts are rattling my skull, thought the would-be-Saga. *You* think like a squirrel on its fifth cup of mead. I've just checked outside my chambers, and no one is there. I do not understand...

Tell me something, Mind-Saga, thought Silla. *Something only the real Saga would know. Tell me about your sister's scar.*

A flash of confusion, and then, *Eisa cut her eye on Sunnvald's fountain...*

Gods' sacred ashes, thought Silla, confusion and wonder and incredulity battling within her. *Is it really you, Saga?*

Hesitation and doubt filtered from the other side.

It is you! erupted Silla's thoughts. *I know it. Gods, Saga, I don't know how this has happened, and I don't think you'll believe me, but it's me, Eisa, though I prefer to be called Silla. Tómas stole me from the castle. He couldn't get to you in time. But now he's dead, and I've fled to the north. Oh, gods, maybe I shouldn't have thought that.* Silla clasped her hands tighter.

How do you know such things? demanded Saga. *If this is a joke, it's not the least bit funny. Tell me why you contacted me.*

Silla's nostrils flared in irritation. *I did not contact you; you contacted me. I was only trying to clear my mind, and I heard your voice. You thought about Magnus the Black Cloak and someone named Ana—*

Plague and boils, thought Saga.

Silla blinked, then smiled. *Did you just think about the plague and... boils?*

How in the gods' names do you know about the Black Cloak? was Saga's reply.

You told me!

Delusions, replied Saga. *The queen must have slipped something into my food. She's onto me. Knows I've been interfering with her letters.*

Wait, thought Silla. *You've... what?*

I sent the Wolf Feeders to the east, but I'm certain it's only a matter of time until they discover it was forged.

Tears pricked Silla's eyes. *That is... incredible. Though I daresay, you needn't worry about the Wolf Feeders anymore.*

What happened? asked Saga, a phantom pang of worry knotting Silla's stomach.

We killed them.

A trickle of relief came from Saga's end. *Thank the gods. Though of course I can't trust this. If the queen has drugged me, what will she do next?*

Are you safe? asked Silla, hands balling into fists. *Have they harmed you? Please, Saga, tell me you're safe.*

Define safe, thought Saga, with a distinct note of unease.

What has happened, Saga? she thought. *I sense worry.*

I fear I've made a mistake, thought Saga. *I've stumbled into something. And by now the queen surely knows . . . there will be consequences to be sure.*

Silla's heart squeezed. *I'm sorry. I wish I could be there with you.*

A bitter feeling flowed from Saga's end. *I wish you were real, Mind-Eisa. I miss you every day. I wish I could see you. Hug you. Feel like I have someone in this world . . .*

You do have someone in this world, Saga, insisted Silla. *You have me.*

Saga did not reply.

I am practicing, continued Silla. *Getting better each day. And when I have mastered my Galdra skills, I will come and get you myself. We will walk away from the castle, arm in arm.*

I want to believe you, thought Saga. *But I learned long ago that hope is a wasted emotion.*

Silla's eyes brimmed over, tears tracking down her cheeks. A sense of tenderness reached through the bond, as if sunshine had warmed her through.

You used to climb into my bed when you had a bad dream, thought Saga. *I would stroke your hair and sing you that silly song about Kisa the cat. We got into trouble, you and me, stealing sweet rolls and hiding under the table to eat them—sneaking out of lessons to chase butterflies in the gardens.*

I . . . I don't remember you, Saga, Silla thought with a heavy heart. *But I've carried you with me all the same. I dreamed of you. Of that night.*

That night, sighed Saga.

Tell me of our parents, begged Silla. Moments ago, the thought of asking had made her queasy, but with Saga, she felt like the little sister, begging for one more story. She drew her legs up onto the bed and sat cross-legged.

There was a long stretch of silence. *Father was stern, but you could get him to do anything you wished.*

Truly?

Saga laughed, and the warmth wrapped around Silla like a hug. *Yes. You'd mastered the look... a tilt of your head, your eyes extremely large. One look, and Father could never say no to you. It made Mother rather cross.*

And Mother? Silla prodded.

Father called her his light. They loved each other very much. She smiled often and made up incredible bedtime stories. Saga paused, and the warmth faded as though a dark cloud passed over the sun. *I scarcely remember them.*

Silence stretched between them.

It's not right, thought Silla at long last. *What they did to our family. What they've done to Íseldur.*

Saga was silent.

I will find a way to free you, Saga. One day, we'll look each other in the eye—will wrap our arms around each other and never let go.

I'd love that, Mind-Eisa, thought Saga. *Though like you, I'm certain it's naught but a dream. Already I feel you fading.*

Silla felt it, too—Saga's presence grew more distant with each passing second. *Stay,* begged Silla, desperate to keep her. *One more minute. Please!*

Saga replied, but it was muffled, impossible to understand. And at last, she was truly gone, leaving Silla with a hollow, aching pit in her chest. For a moment, she'd had her. Impossible though it seemed, she believed it with every bone in her body: That sarcastic, sad voice had belonged to Saga.

Her brows drew together as she pondered her sister. Alone, drowning in that poisonous castle. Silla's fear and apprehension suddenly felt so insignificant compared with whatever Saga faced.

Saga *needed* her.

From beyond the curtain, the fire crackled, the wooden spoon scraped along the cauldron's bottom—normal, everyday sounds. And yet inside Silla, *everything* had changed.

She closed her eyes and tried to picture her family. All she could imagine was a young Saga, a phantom girl in a torn nightdress. She couldn't remember her birth parents. Couldn't even see them in her mind's eye.

Silla's hands curled into fists.

The Urkans had robbed her of her family. Had murdered her parents. They'd held her sister captive and had come for Silla time and time again. Her mind skipped to Metta, locked in a prison cell in Kopa. To Silla's adoptive mother, Ina, strung up on a pillar. To all the innocent people who were killed for no good reason. Every Íseldurian who was forced to cast a stone.

Someone needed to do something. Someone needed to make this stop. Someone needed to make them pay.

Her thoughts crystallized, cold and sharp.

She wrenched the curtain aside so hard it tore, and Rey whirled in surprise. As he stood near the hearthfire, his dark brows rose. She marched toward him, wrenched the wooden spoon from his hand, and stirred the porridge violently.

The warmth of the fire amplified the white-hot rage simmering in her blood.

"Are you well?" asked Rey warily.

"No," she said.

She took a deep breath. Rested the spoon against the cauldron's edge. Turned to face Rey.

"I'm not ready to be Eisa," she said sharply, "but I might never be. So I suppose I'll simply try." Silla crossed her arms over her chest and sent him a challenging look. "I'll go to your meeting, Galtung. I'll explain everything."

Rey exhaled slowly, pulling her against him. He smelled of porridge and smoke—he felt like safety. And in that moment, Silla knew she didn't have to feel ready. She could jump off that cliff, just as she'd done with the skjöld leaves. Once again, she was frightened. And once again, Reynir Galtung was by her side.

Silla blinked back tears as realization settled into place. She wasn't alone anymore. Rey was there, and he had her back.

"One foot in front of the other," she whispered into his chest.

CHAPTER 54

Sunnavík

In the wake of her disastrous meeting with Magnus Hansson, Saga returned to her chambers only to discover more bad news. In her absence, a small square of parchment had been slipped under her door. Unfolding it, Saga read eagerly.

Winterwing,

Room is gone. Everything taken. Do not go seeking more danger. Burn after reading.

Yours,
Kass

She crumpled the parchment in her fist, then threw it into the fire in a rage. Pacing her room, Saga tried to gather her thoughts. The room of horrors had now been cleared out, which likely meant the scrolls and manuscript in Alfson's office would have been moved as well. What evidence did she have linking Alfson and Signe to the missing Galdra? Having burned all the correspondence she'd intercepted with Ana, Saga had nothing but her word.

That night, she was unable to sleep. Her satchel had been discovered in that horrid room. And after her meeting with Magnus, they knew to whom it belonged. By now, Signe would have been informed. Perhaps, she'd link Saga to the Wolf Feeders' troubles.

Ana. Surely Ana would know what to do. Perhaps she could speak to her Uppreisna group. Perhaps they could move up their plans to smuggle Saga from the castle. But Saga could not sneak to the falconry tower without painting a target on Ana. By now, Signe surely had her mice watching. Saga would have to be clever. Find another way to reach Ana.

But no matter how she spun it, Saga knew there would be consequences. At least Queen Signe could not have her killed—not without raising Ivar's suspicions. Besides, murder seemed too *obvious* for the queen.

One foot in front of the other. It is all you can do.

The words came from somewhere deep inside her, the kind of irritating positivity that made her want to gag. *Mind-Eisa, is that you?* Saga sent out. Gods, she was truly losing her mind. But the memory of the conversation filled her with inexplicable warmth. Saga was a Reader . . . one of the Mind Galdra. Was it truly so hard to believe it could have been the real Eisa?

Perhaps Mind-Eisa was sleeping, or her mind was not in tune, because Saga was met with silence. She frowned. There truly was nothing to be done but to face the consequences of her actions. With a sigh, she submitted to preparations for the daymeal, stepping into a dress of black Zagadkian silk and letting Árlaug braid her hair.

Saga was the last to arrive, and all eyes in the great hall fell on her as she entered—all eyes except the king's, that was, seeing as he was absent. Saga had vowed to keep her cool, to play the pliant version of herself. The queen didn't need to know that Saga had been growing and changing these last few weeks—that there was no going back to the girl she'd once been. And if Signe thought Saga would simply allow her to perform such gruesome experiments on the good people of Íseldur, then she was in for a surprise.

But for now, compliance. She molded her face into a placid expression, making her way to the head table. Magnus sat beside Queen Signe, and it took all of her efforts not to scowl at the pair. If Saga had ever wondered what Magnus gained from this arrangement, as she took in the ease with which he sat on Ivar's throne, she understood well enough. Power. Wasn't it always about power? Men who had it, strove to keep it. Men who did not, schemed to steal it.

Saga settled into the chair beside Prince Bjorn, ignoring his curious look. Food was laid out, and she busied herself filling her plate with berries and griddle bread and spoons of skyr, trying to pretend everything was as it should be.

"I see you've finally graced us with your presence, Saga," said Queen Signe, bringing a silver cup to her lips. "Why did you miss last night's evening meal?"

Because I thought I might retch on the table, Saga thought. She met Signe's gaze. "I felt unwell."

The queen pursed her lips, her ice-blue eyes darting to the warrior's table. "Thorir, come here." The enormous, red-bearded warrior stood. "Saga, darling, Thorir has agreed to help you arrive at your engagements *on time.*"

The large man grunted in acknowledgment. He was tall as a bear, with thickly corded biceps and hands that could crush her bones without a second thought. A prickle of unease ran down her spine.

"How kind of you, Thorir," Saga said, forcing a bland tone. She must give no reaction. So Thorir would act as an overgrown child minder. In terms of punishments, this wasn't as bad as Saga had expected.

Glancing down the table, Saga's eyes met Rurik's sharp gaze as he brought a silver cup to his lips. She could tell he was doing that thing—seeing more of her than she wished. Saga had the strange urge to ask him to meet her in a hidden passageway—to confide in him. But the look in his eyes told her Rurik knew Saga had already found more trouble. Hopefully, he wouldn't try something foolish like chivalry.

"Saga, darling," continued Signe, spreading butter onto her griddle bread, "since you missed the evening meal, you've missed today's excitement. 'Tis execution day. And today, we shall hold them in Askaborg's pits."

It required every ounce of Saga's energy to keep her face impassive, but her hands began to tremble at the mention of the pits. "Fantastic news, Your Highness."

Signe studied Saga with distaste she didn't bother to veil. "It's been many years since you've attended an execution, has it not, Saga?"

"Yes."

"What a treat for you." Signe punctuated her statement with a bite of her bread. "Thorir will ensure you arrive early, won't you, Thorir?"

As Thorir grunted, Saga forced her gaze to her plate. *The pits!* her insides screamed. The pits where her parents . . . where Ana's little sister . . . Saga could not finish the thought. Her heart churned violently, and her gaze darted around the room, focusing on the exits.

As the tension squeezing Saga's chest slowly eased, murmured conversation started up around her. Beside her, she felt Bjorn sending sidelong glances her way. But whatever was on his mind, he seemed to decide against voicing it. Instead, he turned to the Zagadkians.

"How fare the repairs on your ship, Lord Rurik?"

"They are going well," said Rurik, gaze flitting to Saga's for the barest of moments. *What have you done now?* his eyes seemed to say. "We shall be sailing after Printsessa's birthday feast."

"I am glad to hear it," replied Bjorn. "With any luck, we'll have the arsonist captured before that time, so you can witness justice with your own eyes."

Saga took a sip from her too-hot róa, then dropped her cup to the table with a distracting clunk as she fanned at her burned tongue.

"You are well, Lady Saga?" asked Rurik, with the barest traces of a warning. *Gather your wits, fool of a girl,* she imagined in his gaze.

"Burned my mouth," she rasped, her tongue singed so badly, she knew she'd feel it for days.

He leveled her with a heavy look. "You must be more careful. Is not fun to burn oneself."

She choked on her laugh. "It's too late for that, Lord Rurik."

Too late indeed, she thought bitterly, tearing into her griddle bread.

CHAPTER 55

Kalasgarde

"Over there," the barkeep told Rey, nodding to a man in the dark corner of the Split Skull.

Kalasgarde's mead hall hadn't changed in the five years since Rey had last visited. Same scarred long tables. Same crumbling hearths. Same bust of Ivar Ironheart, chipped and cracked from years of target practice. He paid no heed to the heads swinging his way, his gaze focused solely on the old man clutching his horn of ale as though it were the elixir of life.

Rey had a moment of doubt. Could this man truly provide a reliable description of the serpent?

He'd been reluctant to leave Silla alone with Harpa in the wake of the Wolf Feeders' attack, but they needed to hear what Bjalla Gray Locks had seen. Vig had assured him Runný and a trusted friend watched the narrow valley—the lone route in and out of Kalasgarde. If any suspicious warriors were to enter, they'd soon find an avalanche crashing down upon them. With that in mind, Rey had begrudgingly relented to leaving Silla at Harpa's for an hour while he and Vig rode into Kalasgarde and questioned the man who'd seen the serpent.

"Old Man Bjalla's been spouting tales of late," said the barkeep, pouring ale from a jug, "but he can't tell a door from a wall." Handing the filled horn to Vig, the man glanced at Bjalla. "Been telling all who would listen he's seen Svangormr about these parts." The man chuckled, shaking his head.

"My thanks," muttered Rey, turning back to Bjalla.

"The hungry serpent. That'll help our cause." Vig's words dripped with sarcasm.

Rey did not respond as they made their way to Bjalla Gray Locks. As the name would suggest, the old man had a shaggy head of gray hair, and he watched them with steely eyes as they approached.

"Gray Locks," said Rey with a nod. "I'm Axe Eyes, and this is Twig Arms—"

"Strong Arms!" Vig protested.

Rey ignored him. "We've heard you saw a disturbing sight. Might we share a cup with you and hear it for ourselves?"

The man drank deeply. "Here to ridicule me, are you?"

"No," said Rey. "We wish only to hear what you saw."

Bjalla did not reply, watching them with suspicion.

"There've been attacks in the area, Bjalla," said Rey carefully. "Vig and I are investigating. One woman killed, another missing along with a young boy."

Bjalla let out a heavy breath. "'Twas Svangormr, I swear it to you. Long as ten stallions strung together, with scales of glistening blue and long, white fangs. But its eyes"—the man's gaze grew distant—"they were red as blood."

"Where did you see it?" asked Rey.

The man had a haunted look. "Was on me way home from the mead hall when I saw it just beyond the stockade walls. First, I thought I was too deep in my cups. But it turned and locked eyes on me, and I knew . . . knew it was real, that I was as sober as a newborn babe."

"What happened next?" prompted Vig.

"Startled away," Bjalla muttered, turning his attention to his ale.

Vig and Rey shared a knowing look. "Freydis was killed," Rey tried. "Váli and Ástrid have vanished without a trace. We wish to give their families some peace. Prevent anyone else from being harmed."

Bjalla seemed to chew on these words, but he did not reply.

"No one has seen the creature except you, Bjalla. We must know precisely what you saw. No detail is too small. It is a matter of life or death."

"Axe Eyes and I are northerners through and through," Vig chimed in. Rey watched his friend, a warm wave of gratitude filling him. He was glad Vig was here, glad they were doing this together. "We are friends to *all* Íseldurians," continued Vig. "You can trust us with details that might otherwise draw troubles to your doorstep."

Bjalla eyed them both, taking another long drink of ale. Wiping his mouth on the back of his hand, he leaned in. "Not certain I believe it myself." With a shake of his head, Bjalla muttered in a low voice, "Ice spirits."

"Ice spirits?" repeated Rey numbly.

Bjalla continued, waving his hand in a mad gesture. "Whole cluster of 'em swarmed in on it. The beast stopped in its tracks, snarled 'n' yapped at 'em. But they was persistent little hissers, and he soon turned tail. Moved without grace, as though it were encumbered by its great size. But when it slid into the river, it swam away right quick."

Bjalla's voice grew faint beneath the rush of blood in Rey's ears. The bench swayed beneath him as he grappled with his thoughts. The ice spirits had been visiting Silla in increasing numbers—a dozen or more had played in the bushes while they sparred that morning. Why would they seek her? Did it have something to do with the serpent? A pit opened up in Rey's stomach.

"Thank you, Bjalla." Rey pushed abruptly to his feet, ignoring Vig's perplexed look. He'd heard all he needed to. Right now, there were more urgent matters. "We need to get back to Harpa's."

CHAPTER 56

The air was so cold it burned Silla's cheeks, each breath like tiny knives in her lungs. Yet still she plodded, step after step, along the pathway to the glacial terraces, thankful for the trees that sheltered her from the brutal wind.

"Today you will fetch meltwater from Jökull's lake," Harpa had told Silla, handing her a bucket.

"Why?" asked Silla, before she could stop herself.

Harpa's glare was so like her grandson's *axe eyes,* Silla wanted to laugh. "You agreed not to question my methods, did you not? I believe this will help tease out your Blade Breaker skill, and so you will do it."

Silla had chewed on her lip. "But the giant serpent . . ."

"Do you not trust me?" Harpa had folded her arms over her chest, a challenge in her gaze.

"I do," said Silla slowly. Harpa might not be the best at explaining the *why,* but Silla had to admit, her methods were effective.

"Go now," said her mentor, nodding at the door.

And with a sigh, Silla had surrendered. Accepting the bucket, she'd wordlessly stepped through the wards and begun her trek up to the glacial terraces.

As she climbed, Silla glanced over her shoulder frequently but thankfully found no sign of the serpent. The lush pine forest of the lower mountains soon dwindled to short scraggly fir trees amid thick drifts of snow. And soon, even those sparse trees fell away and there was nothing but snowfields, so windblown in places that black rock had been exposed. The wind started up in earnest, and Silla pulled her scarf higher.

Jökull loomed before her, giant stacks of blue-tinged ice as far as the eye could see. From a distance, they had such graceful shapes, all nestled into the curve of Jökull's mountain. But up close, the rugged shapes were apparent, jagged peaks with rough cracks, the ice battered and shaped over centuries. As she neared, the cold seemed to fade. Silla felt small, humbled when faced with a thing of such magnitude.

Beneath the lowest terrace, the ice arched around a dark opening, a heavy lip of snow jutting out over an entry. A cave, it seemed, but hadn't Harpa mentioned a lake? Silla surveyed the barren landscape stretching between her and the ice cave, gaze falling on a windswept patch of ice. Clearly the lake was frozen solid. Had she misheard Harpa's instructions?

Silla made her way to the entry of Jökull's caves, where the trickle of water met her ears. With a deep, bracing breath, she ducked under the snow shelf and entered the cavern. And gazed about in complete wonder.

The tunnel was a more brilliant blue than the most beautiful cloudless sky. Light diffused from a rippling glacial roof, and Silla found she could not look away. Her gaze traced the build and crest of each undulating wave. There was a rhythm to this place, like the flow of an ocean trapped for eternity.

With a shake of her head, Silla set to her task. A small stream flowed along the black rocks on the cavern's floor. Part of her itched to explore the cave, but she reminded herself that she was here for one reason alone. Dropping to her knees, Silla dipped her bucket into the stream.

Movement caught her eye, and she glanced up, spotting an ice spirit. Her frosty blue wings were a near-perfect color match to the cavern's roof, and as the spirit flew in an anxious loop, a trail of tiny crystalline shards drifted in her wake.

"Well met, friend," said Silla. "I did not expect to meet you here."

A pair of ice spirits joined the first, hissing and pointing deeper into the cavern.

Silla frowned, setting the bucket down. "Is this your home?"

Another half a dozen ice spirits dashed from the cavern's depths, jostling against one another for Silla's attention.

"It's lovely," she said, apprehensively. There was a certain aggression to the spirits she hadn't seen before. "Is something wrong?"

The ice spirits dashed down the corridor and back again. It seemed to be a *yes*. They watched Silla expectantly.

"You want me to follow?" Another happy response from the spirits. In the back of Silla's mind, doubt lingered. "It does not seem smart."

But a low, distant wail met her ears, raising each hair on the back of her neck. Silla grew preternaturally still, wondering if she'd imagined the sound. It had seemed human. A child, perhaps.

"Help!" called a voice, shock prickling down Silla's spine.

Discarding her bucket, Silla pushed to her feet. "Show me," she said, determination settling in place. Was it Ástrid or Váli? Silla rushed after the ice spirits through Jökull's caves.

The cries grew louder, the ice spirits more restless, the deeper they went. And as Silla hurried after the spirits, a dark tendril stirred within her.

"Help!" cried the voice, louder, more frantic. The distinct smell of rot met her nose, and Silla had the vague thought that it would be wise to turn back. But the dark tendril unfurled and stretched out, a seductive caress soothing any fears.

As she rounded a bend, Silla entered a cavernous space and met with a chilling sight. To her left were strange bulbous rock formations, some of which were cracked. Directly ahead, tufts of wool, bones, and torn sheep carcasses littered the space. And the smell—she knew that smell. It was just like the forest walker Jonas had slain on the Road of Bones—the smell of dead, moldered things. Most curious of all were the strange, twisted lengths of material, thin like parchment, yet scaled like . . .

Gasping, Silla stumbled back. *Nest,* her mind provided. This was the serpent's lair. And that parchment-like matter was a snakeskin. Hardly daring to breathe, she looked for any sign of movement. Nothing. Silla looked harder at the shed snakeskin. It was far too short to belong to the serpent Vig and Rey had described. And as she looked at the nest with fresh eyes, a picture formed.

The curious cluster of rocks to her left were not rocks at all. Some of the domed tops had been cracked open, revealing hollow, empty cavities within. Eggs. Gods above, they were eggs. The sheep carcasses must have been left for the hatchlings, and as she examined the state of the corpses, Silla guessed they'd been torn into bite-sized pieces.

And suddenly, it made sense why Rey and Vig had found no sign of the great serpent for several weeks. The mother had been holed up in her nest, laying her eggs—some of which had already hatched.

Silla had to get out of here. Had to tell Rey . . .

"Help," came a child's voice from the far end of the cavern. The ice spirits had gathered near it, swarming over something.

"Váli?" whispered Silla, hugging the wall to edge around the nest. "Ástrid?"

"Here!" said the voice. "Help me."

Heart pounding, Silla stepped over another snakeskin, avoiding the gaping rib cage of a sheep carcass. The back of the cavern came into view, and Silla stifled her scream. A pile of broken skeletal remains lay in the corner.

"Váli?" whispered Silla, shock and nausea battling within her, "Ástrid?" But then she saw the symbols frosted all around the corpses. The upside-down protection rune was drawn over and over, dozens, perhaps a hundred times. Beside the bones, steam rose from a wedge-shaped opening in the floor of the cave. The ice spirits flew in agitated loops, hissing and gesturing to the pit. This, apparently, was what they wished to show her.

Come closer, my darling, whispered a voice. It was a voice she'd heard before—a voice coming from nowhere and everywhere all at once. It was the thing she'd heard and felt in her vision during her Cohesion Rite.

The Dark One.

His presence seeped freely from the crack in the deepest part of Jökull's ice cave, a rumble from deep below rattling Silla's bones.

"I should not be here," she whispered, fighting against the seductive need to approach the abyss, to give herself over to the dark tendrils sliding through her. She glanced back at the pile of bones.

Her gaze caught on a bronze cloak pin shaped into the form of a leaf. If she could retrieve that pin, she would have proof that she knew where Váli and Ástrid's final resting place lay.

She stepped forward, nausea churning in her gut as she fought the intense desire to lean over the chasm—to let the dark force emanating from it consume her. But Silla was no stranger to withstanding powerful longings; for that, perhaps she should be grateful to the skjöld leaves. Clenching her teeth, she shoved back at the presence.

An ice spirit zipped to her, so near that Silla could see each tiny, frosted lash framing her wide blue eyes, and could make out the delicate iced veins on her wings.

"This is where the monster came from?" asked Silla, unfastening Váli's cloak pin and sliding it into her pocket. The ice spirit nodded. "I will find help. I'll bring others who will know what to do." The ice spirit zipped in a gleeful loop.

Another low rumble shook the ground, sending goosebumps racing up her arms. *Closer,* came the voice. *Come to me, Malla-blessed.*

Silla fought the drugging compulsion, forcing herself to step backward. "No."

Daughter of Svalla, said the thing. *Let me look upon you.*

Hearing her mother's name startled Silla, but as the ground beneath her feet rumbled, her senses rushed back. Stumbling backward, she cried, "No!"

A pulse of the thing's anger filled her, but she shoved it back. *I'll have you soon enough. Surrender now and save yourself the pain.*

At Silla's silence, there was another pulse of anger. *A poor choice,* said the thing. An odd splintering sound began from behind her. Slowly, she turned. Beside the cave's exit, fractures spread across one of the eggs. A fragment chipped away, landing on the dark cavern floor.

And from within the small opening, a long forked tongue flickered out.

"Oh, gods," whispered Silla, backing away.

And then she ran.

CHAPTER 57

Pure panic filled Silla as she fled through the ice caves, stumbling over rocks and slipping on icy patches.

"Help!" Váli's screams chased after her. "Come back!" But then they shifted into the Dark One's voice. *Save yourself the suffering and give yourself over!*

Laughter echoed in her skull, but Silla knew better than to surrender to this voice. And then the hissing began.

"Oh, gods," Silla whispered, digging deep for whatever energy she could spare. She had to get out of here. The ground rumbled, and Silla dared a glance over her shoulder, promptly wishing she hadn't.

Half a dozen serpents had hatched, all ice-blue scales and glowing red eyes. Each was as long as two full-grown warriors, with glinting fangs. Yet their movements were clumsy, undulating wide and jostling against one another. As a pair of serpents collided and one struck the wall, the entire cavern rumbled.

Oh gods, oh gods, oh gods! Silla tried to push her despair back, but the serpents were gaining on her. Light burst from her palms, flaring through the seams in her wolfskin gloves. Silla stripped them off and cast them aside. She was primed, the cold tension begging for release.

Teeth snapped behind her, an angry hiss soon following. The distant light of the cavern's exit met her eyes, fueling Silla with hope. Near, she was so near . . .

Pain speared from her ankle as a pair of fangs sank through her boot. With a cry, Silla whirled, finding that crevasse and pulling it open. The creature reared back at the flare of light, giving Silla time to herd the bonds into place.

It was bare moments before she held the sword of cold light. The serpents recoiled, watching Silla with red eyes, glowing as though lit from within. Their scales were ice blue, though their underbellies were closer to white.

"Find something else to eat!" Silla growled, swinging her blade through the air. It bounced harmlessly off the nearest creature's scales. Silla hadn't the chance to feel disbelief because the snakes were lashing out . . .

A swarm of crystalline blue forms surged at the creatures from below. The snakes recoiled, crashing into one another as the ice spirits mobbed them, driving them back.

Silla noted the ice spirits attacked from below, focusing on the hatchling's undersides. An idea coalesced, and then she was swinging upward, her blade sinking through the nearest creature's stomach like butter.

She whirled and ran. As she dashed through the caves, Silla's coordination quickly deteriorated. She stumbled over rocks and slid on patches of ice. The ground rumbled behind her, and she guessed the hatchlings had broken past the ice spirits.

They could not escape. She needed to block the exit. The roof of the cavern thinned, and soon, her vision exploded with disorienting light as she burst outdoors. Her mind felt as though it were stuffed with wool, but Silla turned on the cave entrance, hacking at the overhanging shelf with her sword.

Again and again, she brought her sword down on the snow-covered opening, hoping, praying that it would be enough. A clump of ice fell, sending another crashing, then another. The ground rumbled, and Silla stepped back. Snow cascaded down, landing with a solid thump and sending powder pluming into the air.

The rumbling stopped, a muffled hiss coming from beyond the snow. Silla let out a long breath. The exit to the cave was sealed—for now.

She needed to get out of here—needed to bring help to destroy the creatures for good.

Turning, Silla rushed away from Jökull's caves.

As she stumbled down Jökull, Silla became aware that the snake's bite was no mere flesh wound. It started with a low throb in her leg, but with each passing step, it grew and spread, until feverish heat burned through her body.

A life for a life, whispered that malevolent voice, seeping like venom into her mind.

Silla grabbed on to a scrubby tree as her feet slid out from beneath her along the snow-covered path. Sweat dotted her brow, the ground swaying beneath her.

Use the knife.

Pushing to her feet, Silla edged down the trail. It seemed to take all her energy to keep her focus on the ground, to keep from tripping over tree roots and rocks. Thankfully, the snow soon receded, the trees growing taller.

A good girl you are, my darling Svalla.

Her vision swirled, the voices growing louder. Images flashed in her mind—a fountain; a rosebush; a blood-soaked dagger.

Gods, but there must have been venom on the serpent's teeth.

I miss her so much.

Her vision warped, and Silla felt herself stumbling aimlessly among the pine trees. She fought to maintain her grip on her mind, but it was slipping through her fingers. Reality blurred, swirled, twisted around her. And then Silla tipped into the realm of her mind.

Silla saw a girl, blue eyes just like Saga's, but dark curls just like her own. And then she was one with the girl, skipping through a stone-paved courtyard, a doll tucked under her arm. She smiled as sunshine heated her cheeks, and Silla could smell spring—sweet floral blossoms and freshly turned earth and bright grassy things.

She was going to the fountain. How glorious it was to see the last of winter's snows melted. Soon there would be flowers and midday meals in the garden and trips to the shore. And it also meant Cook would set fresh berries out with every meal, and that was her favorite—crowberries with a drizzle of honey.

But today, she would go to the fountain and give three wishes to Sunnvald. The first, of course, would be for a baby brother or sister. The second would be that Grandpapa would feel happy again. She missed his smiles and the stories he used to tell before Grandmama got sick and went to the stars above. The third wish she had not yet chosen. A hundred days of sunshine? Or perhaps she should wish for something more, as her papa would say, "noble." The absolute best harvest season ever? The most bountiful fishing hauls for everyone?

Silla pursed her lips, skipping past the bush she'd helped Mama plant. A rosebush, Mama had said, from the Southern Continent. Apparently, it would soon be filled with luscious pink blooms, but she wasn't sure she liked this one. It had thorns all over it, and they bit. What kind of pretty flower had sharp parts?

When she rounded the corner, Sunnvald's fountain came into view, carrying the soft tinkling sounds of water. She pulled the offering from her dress pocket, loosening the ties of the small hemp sack and tipping it upside down. Metal shavings fell to the fountain, hitting the water with sharp strikes, then sinking slowly to the bottom.

Sunnvald likes shows of fire and might, her father had told her. *When making an offering, lay mead, meat, or a well-crafted weapon on the altar.* Well, mead would not fit in a pocket, and meat was too messy. And Silla did not have a weapon, save for the small wooden sword for sparring with Papa. But being clever as she was, she'd snuck into the blacksmith's forge and collected metal scrapings from the floor.

She kissed her knuckles and closed her eyes. "Oh, Bright One," she whispered, but something crunched behind her. Eyes flying open, Silla whirled. An old man stood, flanked by a dozen guards. "Grandpapa!" she gasped, filled with shame. Caught escaping from her nursemaid for the third time this moon cycle. Surely she'd weather a blistering reproof. She brought a finger to her mouth and gnawed on the nail.

"Come here, my dear," came the king's watery voice as he sat on a stone bench. She blinked, taking in the dark circles under his eyes, the deep wrinkles in his forehead. He'd always been old, but he'd never looked sickly until the queen had died.

But now, as Silla looked at him, there was a glimmer in his eye, a hint of the man who'd told her of the great battle of fire and ice. With a cautious smile, she stepped forward, taking a seat on the bench beside him. Chewing on her fingernail, she waited anxiously.

"Fallgerd," said the king, waving at his chief guard. "Allow me a moment with my granddaughter."

Fallgerd was the biggest man she'd ever seen and was a little bit scary. But Mama had told her he was really a kind and gentle man, that it was only Fallgerd's job to look frightening. Now Fallgerd had a funny look in his eyes, and Silla thought perhaps he didn't want to leave.

"Yes, Your Majesty," he said, beckoning the guards to follow him out of the courtyard.

Sitting on her hands, she swung her legs, wondering what Grandpapa would say. A confession was building inside her, and she pressed her lips together to hold it in.

"A good girl you are, my darling Svalla," said the king, much to her surprise. He sounded sad, but that was not unusual. "But I miss her so much." The king let out a long breath, and his whole body seemed to sag. "I'm sorry."

Silla looked at him, confused. "What do you mean?"

"A life for a life," said the king. A blade flashed in his hand.

There was a sharp pain in her neck, and everything went warm and cold at once. Fallgerd was suddenly there, knocking Grandpapa to the ground, and there was an awful clamor as the rest of his guards surged around.

Silla's eyes went wide, her mouth falling open as she took it all in. A white-hilted knife had fallen to the flagstones, and she stared at it hard. There was something evil about that knife, a vile, horrid presence pouring off it and into the air. The tip was red, and a warm trickle dripped down her neck, wetting her dress.

A life for a life, someone whispered in her ear.

"What?" she tried to say, but the sounds wouldn't form. The warmth on her neck was spreading down her tummy, and when she reached up, her small hand was slicked with blood.

Fallgerd was there, and he looked furious. She recoiled, but his voice was soothing.

"Hush now, Princess," he said in a soft voice, putting his hand on her neck. Little lights floated in her vision, like *flíta* dancing all around. "A healer is on the way, and they'll fix you up. But I need to keep my hand on your neck, and I need you to stay calm. Can you do that, Svalla?"

She was nodding, staring up at Fallgerd and trying to understand. There were voices all around, fearful and frightening, but Fallgerd was there, and she focused on his face, on his voice. The edges of her vision blackened, like night closing in on all sides.

"The king is dead," someone cried out.

And then the darkness was absolute.

CHAPTER 58

Sunnavík

Saga was growing desperate to talk to Ana but did not know how to do so. Sneaking to the falconry tower had grown more challenging in the past weeks. But with Thorir now trailing her every step, it felt downright impossible.

But Saga had to get word to Ana. Not only did she need to inform the Uppreisna of the Black Cloak's identity, but that Signe knew Saga had been meddling in her affairs, and Saga was eager to plot her escape from Askaborg. For so long, escape hadn't been a possibility. With her condition, Saga could not set foot outdoors. But the seed Ana had planted—and the realization that there were others willing to help in this endeavor—had bloomed in her mind.

After a day spent thinking of reasons to avoid the executions, Saga knew she had no choice. She would have to attend to appease Signe, would have to watch others killed on the same pillars as her family. Gathering every ounce of grit and determination she possessed, Saga promised herself she would not crumble.

Thorir ensured Saga's timely arrival at the pits. With a sprawling roof held up by dozens of granite pillars, the pits had once functioned as a gathering place in the cold winter season. Stands circled the central, dirt-packed arena, flat stone benching climbing dozens of rows high.

For seventeen years, she'd avoided this place.

Under her father's rule, the *pits* had been the *ring*, a friendly place of gathering for celebrations. Saga could recall viewing everything from fighting contests to horse shows to performers from the Southern Continent who bent their bodies in impossible ways. It had been a place where even the poorest of Íseldurians could experience a few hours of joy.

The Urkans had done what they did best—ruined this place.

Now it smelled of violence, with three V-shaped pillars pounded into the earthen floor. This was where Volsik supporters had been taken—where they'd been tortured in disturbing displays with mandatory public attendance.

At age five, Saga had thankfully been excluded from such events, but it hadn't shielded her from the whispers sweeping through the palace. She'd heard of the good people slathered in raw meat and sent into the pits with Ivar's pet bears and hounds. Had heard of those who'd been starved for a month, then pushed into the pits to face Ivar's armed retinue. There were tales of some spread wide on the pillars, hundreds of cuts administered over days, weeks, until they begged for the mercy of death.

While the nobles sat on the dais and surrounding stands, Sunnavík's peasants remained in the arena. And as Saga stepped onto the packed-earth floor of the pits, they turned to watch her. She forced herself forward. *No reaction,* she reminded herself, searching for the cold place deep inside.

"Forward," grumbled Thorir, his hand pressed firmly between her shoulder blades. The gathered crowd quieted as it parted, eyes falling upon her as she made her way through.

As she walked past the pillars, it felt as though her heart was trying to hack its way free from her ribs. Forcing herself forward, Saga kept her expression neutral. Not trapped. Public exits all around. She tried to regulate her breathing, but each breath came short and ragged.

Though it was only a short walk across the arena floor, it felt like an eternity. Her head spun with the openness of this space, and her palms were slick with sweat. But at last, they reached the dais. Centrally located and slightly raised, the dais had, to Saga's misfortune, the best view of the pillars. She climbed the stairs. Crossed the platform. Settled into the chair beside her betrothed. Exhaled at last.

Signe soon entered the pits, a pair of broad warriors parting the crowds as her bondswomen held the train of her ivory gown. More and more people spilled into the pits, gleaming stones of black obsidian clutched in hand.

Reciting the exits, Saga tried to ignore the building anticipation. The shuffle of boots and soft greetings to her left disrupted her thoughts, and as she turned to investigate, Saga's gaze locked onto eyes of a depthless green.

Rurik sent her a look, and she understood at once—the fool was here on her account. Declining a seat, he crossed his arms over his chest, leaning against the stone wall that sectioned the dais off from the stands. Rov joined him a moment later, looking entirely unimpressed.

A cheer rose from the crowd, and Saga turned to find the Klaernar dragging three figures toward the pillars. The condemned, muzzled in iron bridles, were fastened to the V-shaped pillars with arms spread wide.

She would be a rock, hardened against the world. Would see but not feel. Saga's gaze landed vacantly on the condemned. She would not look away, would not flinch, would not—

No.

Saga couldn't breathe. Couldn't think. Couldn't do anything but stare at the woman in the middle. Those unmistakable brown eyes, which had been so filled with determination when last she'd seen them, were now framed by an iron bridle.

No. Not her.

But no matter how many times she tried to clear her vision, no matter how many prayers she uttered, nothing changed. It was Ana.

Ana, who had given her a taste of hope.

Ana, who had risked everything to save anyone else's sister from the pillars.

Ana, whom Saga hadn't dared contact in over a week.

The blood drained from her face. How? They'd been so careful.

How had Ana been discovered? The roar of the crowd grew muffled, as though she'd been plunged under water. She forced in a breath, her evening meal churning in her stomach. Saga tried to think, tried to come up with a plan—to no avail. Every option led to death.

She could not save Ana.

Realization seeped into Saga, chilling her blood. Thorir was not her punishment, nor was attending this execution.

Ana was her punishment.

How foolish Saga had been to think that *she* was the one who'd pay for her rebellion. Saga should have known Signe had sharper knives and knew how to use them. She forced her lips shut—attempted to wipe the panic from her face. Her eyes locked with Ana's, wide and fearful.

The High Gothi had entered and was reciting the charges of witchcraft, but his words did not reach Saga's ears. She kept her gaze on Ana, determined to be a calming anchor in a sea of horror. It was the only thing she could do. A last act of kindness.

Something tugged at her, instinct perhaps, and without thinking, Saga dropped her mental barriers and allowed her Sense to awaken. A jarring wall of noise crashed upon her, the thoughts of the angry crowd intense and unrelenting, swarming in from all sides. It was disorienting, so loud, their violent thoughts rattling through her.

Kill the scum.

Let us get on with this.

They must pay in blood.

Saga tried not to let these unsettling thoughts grab ahold of her, instead focusing on Ana, stretching toward her through the chaos.

I would do it all over again. I regret nothing. It was the right thing to do.

It was Ana. Saga grasped the thread, pulling it to her.

Ana, she thought. *Ana, I'm sorry. It's my fault.*

But Ana made no sign she'd heard. The Gothi sliced into her vein, collecting the slow crimson drizzle in a cup. *I get to see my sister. Finally, I'm going home to her.*

Saga's hand flew to her mouth.

"You may now cast your judgment," came the Gothi's voice, and the crowd surged forward.

Saga held on with all of her might to the thread of Ana's consciousness, clutching it through the violent efflux of thoughts. Something snapped, the thread falling loose, and Saga balled it up, holding it to the warmth of her heart.

Stones were cast, and Saga was distantly aware of the cheers of the crowd, thudding rocks, the crunch of bone and cartilage.

A stone hit the softest part of Ana's stomach, and pain ruptured from Saga's middle. She wheezed as disbelief hurtled through her—Ana's face did not so much as flinch. Pain speared through Saga as a large stone crunched sickeningly into Ana's shoulder.

Saga gritted her teeth. Ana's eyes were vacant, her face calm and peaceful. A jagged stone slammed against the side of her face, and Saga's vision exploded, pain slicing through her skull and consuming every part of her being. Ana's thread was fading, like footprints swept clean by an ocean wave. But Saga held on, determined not to let go.

Gripping the arms of her chair, Saga held Ana's empty gaze as pain ripped through her, rocks crashing into her chest, her pelvis, her face, her shoulder. Her body was on fire, an explosion of heat and pain, obliterating the crowd, the noise, the dais, the pillars. It was just Saga and Ana, alone in the pits, the last wisps of Ana's thread fading until, at last, it was gone.

The pain vanished in a sudden flash, her vision rushing back. Ana's head lolled to the side, but the crowd's thirst for blood had not been sated. With the last of her energy, Saga wove her barriers back in place and slumped against her chair. The execution continued for an excruciating eternity, until the last stone had been cast, and the three women hung bloodied and limp.

It was over. They'd feel no more pain. And Ana would soon be among the stars with her sister.

Saga closed her eyes to keep her tears at bay. She would *not* cry. Would not grant the queen such a victory. But as the sounds of the crowd dwindled, Saga felt a prickling sensation on the side of her face. Her eyes opened and snapped to the right, locking with Signe's.

The queen's lips curved up.

Pure hatred dripped down Saga's spine, pooling in her stomach.

"Saga?" asked Bjorn, wrenching her gaze away from Signe. "Your nose is bleeding." Bjorn handed her a square of linen. With a trembling hand, she dabbed at her bloody nose.

"Are you well?" he asked. "You look sickly."

"I'm fine," she snapped, closing her eyes as she held the linen to her nose. She swallowed her remorse, wishing she'd been softer with him. She breathed in deeply. Let it out slowly. Tried to calm her rising panic.

Movement beside her. The royals were leaving. Saga stood, gripping the chair for balance. Gods, she needed to lie down. As she moved toward the exit, her eyes landed on Rurik. A line had formed between his drawn brows as he stared at her with an unreadable expression. But then he pushed off the wall and followed Rov down the stairs and out of the pits.

Saga trailed numbly behind Bjorn, his movements stilted as though he was affronted. She was too weary to consider it. How she made her way back to her chambers on her own two feet, Saga could not recall. She collapsed onto her bed and fell into a dreamless sleep.

Until Thorir pounded on her door the next morning, ordering her to get dressed for the daymeal.

CHAPTER 59

Kalasgarde

Rey ran his thumb along the freshly sharpened blade of Harpa's axe. It was honed to a deadly point, as were Harpa's kitchen knives, daggers, and every other blade he could get his hands on. Yet no matter how many passes of steel across the whetstone he made, Rey could not ease the tightness in his chest.

The sun was sinking lower toward Snowspear, the slanted light casting Harpa's yard into stark shadows. No sound. No voices.

She must still sleep.

Gritting his teeth, he strode to the cabin. Enough was enough.

His mood had been foul since he'd rushed from the mead hall to his grandmother's home and discovered she'd sent Silla up Jökull. Rey had stared at Harpa with incredulity. He knew well enough which methods his grandmother used with her students—after all, it was Harpa who'd taught Rey the benefits of giving his apprentices a taste of danger. And if Rey had allowed a vampire deer or two to attack greener members of the Bloodaxe Crew, that was well enough.

But this was Eisa-gods-damned-Volsik, and there was a giant-gods-damned-serpent hunting these parts. He couldn't understand what head injury his grandmother must have suffered for her to think this wise.

When he'd discovered Silla stumbling through the woods near to Harpa's property, his foul mood had turned to pure, incinerating anger. Her brow had been slick with sweat, incoherent words spilling from her lips. And as he'd searched for a wound, he'd found naught but a puncture through the back of her boot. Curiously, it was too small to have belonged to the fang he and Vig had found in the excrement.

After he raced her to Harpa's home and stripped her boot off, his brows drew together. It was shallow, yet the woman was shaking, mumbling the same thing over and over.

"The king is dead."

Did she mean Ivar? But it made no sense. Rey stared up the mountain, Jökull's ice shields glinting through the trees. He wanted to charge up there and find what had done this to her. Yet he was confused... beyond confused. Had she encountered the giant serpent described by Bjalla, surely she'd not have lived to tell the tale.

He pushed through the door to find Silla still slumbering. Harpa stepped out from the shadows, and Rey's teeth clenched so hard they almost cracked.

"She sleeps, Reynir. Let her rest."

"We haven't time to let her rest," he growled. "I must know what she saw up there. Must know if it was the serpent."

Harpa squeezed her woven belt, an unreadable expression on her face. "It will take time," she said softly. "It has the feel of chaos magic, causing disorder within her aura. But it has no permanent hold on her and should work through in a few hours."

"I do not know what you were thinking," he muttered.

His grandmother was silent for a moment. "I saw curious threads. Disruptions in the weavings, coming from Jökull," Harpa admitted. "I thought perhaps it was a vampire deer and that it could be helpful in drawing out her Breaker skill."

Rey's temples throbbed. "Eisa Volsik, Harpa."

"Perhaps it was risky," confessed his grandmother. Shocked at her uncharacteristic admission of guilt, he peered into Harpa's eyes. Gods, but they were so similar to Kristjan's—a soft shade of amber, like honey when sunlight hit at the right angle. He forced his gaze away.

"You're angry with me," Harpa observed, and somehow, he knew she was no longer speaking of Silla.

Rey turned to the hearth, watching Rykka dance in the flames. Embers burst within her smoky wings as she looped and twirled.

"It is understandable," said Harpa. "I am angry with myself."

Rey's brows drew together, and he turned.

Her overdress swallowed her small form, and Rey examined the gaunt lines of her neck, the grooves in her brow. Always, Harpa had seemed a fortress of strength—untouchable and indestructible. But now his formidable grandmother looked *old*. "Say what you must, Reynir. I fear I deserve it."

Anger burned low in his stomach, and he drew his hand into a fist. "You were selfish. You cared only for yourself."

Harpa winced, but it brought him no satisfaction.

"You should have checked on Kristjan. Should have seen..." He drew in a long breath. Blew it out sharply. "You should have sent for me."

Harpa nodded. "I should have." His grandmother closed her eyes for a moment. When she opened them, they shone with emotion. "When you're a child, you think adults know it all. But then you grow old, and you realize the truth. We're all bumbling fools."

Rey blinked.

"I wish I had done it differently." Harpa's gaze drifted to her bed, where Silla's dark curls splayed across a pillow. "Motherhood never felt like my calling, and when my children were all grown, I'll admit I was relieved. I took a place in Askaborg, training young Galdra and using my Weaver skill to better my kingdom. It felt as though I'd found the thing I was fated to do."

Harpa drew a deep breath. "But then the war happened. King Kjartan sent many of the Weavers to the farthest reaches of the kingdom so we might preserve the stories of our ancestors, should Íseldur fall. A wise man, the king was, though I did not see it as such. While my peers fought on the front lines, I was relegated to hiding in the north. It did not seem an honorable thing to do. I fought against charging south every day. By the time you and Kristjan were thrust into my care, I was . . . bitter. Resentful. I was not a good mother to you, and I knew it."

Surprise rushed through him, and for the first time in his life, Rey felt the smallest glimmer of understanding.

"I miss your brother," she admitted. "I miss him every day, Reynir. I sit in the yard and feed the birds and imagine Kristjan beside me, naming each one."

Emotion clawed up Rey's throat, but he forced it back. "The birdhouses," he rasped.

"I had them built for Kristjan," said Harpa, observing him. "So he might have a reason to visit his old grandmother. So he might know how sorry I am."

Rey tried to rub the burn in his chest away.

"I cannot go back in time and be there for Kristjan. But I can be there for you." Harpa swallowed. "I want you to be happy, Reynir. You deserve to be happy." Her gaze fell to the bed. "She is good for you."

Rey shifted in discomfort.

"I see changes in you since you've arrived. You smile more—"

"I cannot do this," muttered Rey, raking a hand down his face. "I cannot—" He found he could not finish.

But his grandmother seemed to understand. "She will be fine. She needs only to work the venom from her system. Give her another hour. If she has not woken, we'll rouse her, and you'll get your answers."

Rey could only grunt. His stomach was wrenching, twisting, tying itself in knots. "I have something to show you, Reynir," said Harpa, breaking him from his thoughts. She beckoned him to the back corner of the room where her loom leaned against the wall. On it hung a partially woven tapestry, all grays and blacks.

"What is it?"

"Dark threads," murmured Harpa, frowning. "The darkness I first sensed in Jökull has grown greater today. It is gathering elsewhere in this kingdom as well. I do not yet know the meaning."

He examined the weaving, trying to guess what it would reveal. A dark curve formed the left side of the tapestry, and he leaned closer to inspect it. "Is that a leaf?" he asked.

"Perhaps," was Harpa's reply. Her gaze grew distant. "I must keep weaving. We must discover which secrets it has to reveal."

A cough from across the room had Rey whirling. And there, in the bed, sat Silla, rubbing her eyes. He rushed to her side. "You're all right," he told her—told himself. And for the first time in hours, Rey felt as though he could breathe.

But her eyes met his, wide with fear.

"Jökull's cave. We must go back!"

CHAPTER 60

Malla and Marra had begun their Rise, spilling moonlight across the cobbled streets of Kalasgarde as Silla followed Rey to the mead hall. It was so still, so silent, it felt as though the entire village were holding its breath.

And Silla held her own along with it. She was about to meet the Uppreisna—others like herself. Would share her truth and tell them about the caves and what she'd seen in them. Her heart pounded viciously in her chest, in her temples. The venom had thankfully worked through her, though a touch of light-headedness remained.

The aftermath of her awakening had been a whirlwind. She'd relayed everything to Harpa and Rey—about the cave at Jökull's base, the serpent hatchlings, the chasm, and that strange, malevolent voice.

"The dark threads . . . this chaos magic," muttered Harpa, testing the pulse in Silla's wrist. "It feels far more sinister than I first sensed. Do not go back alone."

"The Uppreisna meeting is tonight," Rey had said. "We could rally the Galdra to our cause—"

"I will tell them what I saw," said Silla, pulling the furs back and climbing from bed. She pulled Váli's cloak pin from her pocket and passed it to Rey. "I will show them this."

"The chasm," murmured Harpa, glancing at her weaving. "The chaos magic . . . the ice spirits . . . the dark threads. It must be connected. The chasm may be the source of the serpent."

"We will close it," Rey concluded.

"I will come with you," Silla had asserted. "You need someone who's seen the creatures. Who knows the feel of their venom and where the chasm lies."

She'd watched Rey battle his protective urges and had feared that he would tell her no again. But he'd swallowed his apprehension and nodded.

First, the mead hall. Silla was going to do this. Her body tingled with anticipation, but her stomach knotted with apprehension. *Not her,* pounded her head. *Not ready.* But she thought of Saga in that castle; she thought of Váli's and Ástrid's corpses in the back of that cavern.

Ready or not, it was time to be Eisa.

"The Split Skull?" she asked, making a face at the sign. "The name hardly inspires thirst."

Rey pounded on the door. "I suppose you'd call it something revoltingly joyful. Hearthfire's Shelter." He paused. "Knowing you, I'm certain it would have an animal included. The Frothy Fox—"

"The Cheery Chicken!"

"No warrior in his right mind would be seen in such an establishment," muttered Rey. He glanced at her sidelong. "You'll do fine. Try not to talk too much."

Silla's sharp reply was interrupted as the door to the mead hall opened a crack, revealing a pair of blue eyes.

"Galtung," came a deep male voice. "It's been an age."

"It has indeed," said Rey. "Well met, Erik. I've brought a guest for whom I can vouch."

Wood dragged against stone as the door widened, revealing a broad-shouldered blond man. Silla's eyes slid to the hevrít gripped tightly in his fist, and she chewed on her cheek.

"This is Silla," said Rey. "Silla, Erik."

Erik did not return her smile. "She's not from here."

"No."

"And you've not been about these parts for, what . . . eight years?"

"Five." Rey glowered.

"It is strange you should return after so many years with an unknown, right when suspicious things are afoot," said Erik, eyeing Silla once more. "I do not like the feel of it. But it is for Kálf to decide." Thankfully, Erik stepped aside, allowing them to enter the Split Skull.

Silla followed Rey into the mead hall, all eyes swinging their way.

"Two men watch the front—Erik at the door, and another in the shadows of the street," explained Rey, nodding in greeting to a scowling woman. "Should problems arise, there is a back door and a cellar beneath the bar with exit tunnels."

At Silla's look of concern, Rey added, "There has never been trouble in Kalasgarde." But she heard the words left unsaid—there *had* been trouble in other places. Because this gathering was forbidden. Not only did the people in this room live a life in hiding, but they actively schemed against King Ivar. Suddenly, Erik's suspicion felt entirely valid.

Rows of feasting tables were arranged end-to-end, the scent of ale mingling with woodsmoke and urine. Above, iron chandeliers cast shivering light upon the hardened warriors—two dozen, Silla guessed. She waved at Vig and Runný, but Rey led her past them and to the front of the room.

A large warrior sat in the middle of the long table, his glinting brown scalp a stark contrast to the thick black beard covering his jaw. He watched Silla with stern, unnerving eyes, as though he analyzed each small detail. This, she supposed, must be Kálf. Her eyes slid to the man's left, landing on a pale-skinned warrior with a lone streak of white in his black beard. She recognized him at once—Hef, who'd carried Freydis to Harpa's house. Hef, whose cousin Ketill had attacked her with an axe.

"Kálf," said Rey briskly, pulling Silla forward. "This is Silla. I vouch for her."

Warriors lined the bench on either side of Kálf and Hef, all watching her with marked suspicion.

"Well met," she managed.

Kálf sent a hard look at Rey. "Why has it taken you so long to present yourself, Galtung? Word is you've been here for *weeks*."

"I meant no disrespect," said Rey, carefully. "My identity was revealed, and I was forced into hiding."

"Interesting," said Hef sourly, "that the letter Vig procured for us makes no mention of yourself." He drew out a piece of parchment, reading the words slowly. "'Accommodation for one Galdra, Ashbringer.'"

Silla's palms began to sweat as she looked from Kálf to Hef. This felt less like a meeting and more like an inquisition.

"Many curious happenings since your arrival, Galtung," said Kálf. "And now you stand before us, lying—"

Rey shifted uneasily. "I have not spoken a single untruth—"

"Half-truths are as good as lies, Galtung," spat Kálf. "Explain yourself. And start with Ketill."

Rey cleared his throat. "He attacked Silla, and I was forced to stop him."

Kálf's heavy gaze landed on Silla, brows drawn together. "And why would he do such a thing? I know Ketill was not the sharpest of axes, but even he would have had a reason."

Silla's heart pounded. Now was the time for her to reveal her identity. But the words were stuck in her throat.

"Silla has seen the serpents," said Rey, an obvious attempt to change the subject. "Has discovered a cave beneath Jökull where hatchlings are nested. We come to you asking for help to destroy them before they wreak havoc in the north."

Kálf took a long drink of ale, then wiped the froth from his mustache. "More than one, is it now? Have you struck your head, Galtung? You sound just like Gray Locks."

"Rey speaks the truth." Silla fumbled in her pocket, pulling out Váli's cloak pin. "I found this in a cave beneath Jökull before being chased by ice serpents twice my size."

Kálf assessed Silla with a cold, hard look, his gaze then falling back to Rey. "You expect us to believe this *girl* faced down these . . . serpents?"

Silla crossed her arms over her chest indignantly. "I've seen twenty winters, which does, in fact, make me a grown woman."

"Do not make the mistake of underestimating her, Kálf," said Rey in a low voice.

Kálf's eyes narrowed as he examined Silla. "Where have you come from?"

Now. She needed to reveal her identity now. But her insides rebelled. *Not her, not her!* they screamed. "Skarstad," was all Silla could manage.

"What brings you to these parts?"

"Safety. A refuge from the Klaernar."

Kálf's thick fingers tapped on the scarred surface of the table. "Found yourself in trouble with the King's Claws, did you? What, did you escape from the pillar?"

"Something like that." The image of Kommandor Valf's crushed skull flashed in her mind's eye, causing nausea to churn in her stomach.

"And you fled from Skarstad to Kalasgarde all on your own?" Kálf's eyes were filled with mocking amusement.

"I had help," she said, irritated.

"She trains with Harpa," Rey cut in.

Kálf seemed surprised by this revelation. "I thought Harpa no longer took on apprentices."

"Silla is special. Harpa was intrigued."

A blond warrior put his pale elbow on the table. "What's your intuition, sweetheart?"

"Ashbringer," Rey answered sharply. "And I assure you, Rannver, she's not sweet in the least."

The men at the long table chuckled at that. All except for Kálf. "We'll require proof that you are, in fact, one of us."

At a nudge from Rey's elbow, Silla swallowed. "It can be a shy thing," she said, trying for levity. But the warriors before her did not look amused. With a sigh, Silla reached for her source, drawing it into her veins with a soft exhale.

Murmurs arose as her forearms grew cold and undulated with stark white light. "I am learning," said Silla, her breath frosting the air. "Priming has come naturally, but expression . . ." She closed her eyes, trying to relax into herself. But they were watching her, and she should have revealed her name already, and how would they rally these warriors to their cause . . .

When she opened her eyes, she found a weak version of the orb, which quickly shattered into shards of crystalline frost.

"I'll admit, I've never seen Ashbringer skill like that," said Kálf. "But I can hardly believe you managed to face down any sort of creature with *that*."

Silla drew her galdur back into her heart, shaking the cold from her hands. "As I said, it is a timid thing. It seems my skill will require more time to hone."

Kálf watched her impassively. "How is it you've seen twenty winters and are only just mastering your galdur? About ten winters too late, I would think."

"Harpa sent Silla up Jökull as an exercise in training," said Rey. "She discovered the cave and came across the creature's offspring. They match the description provided by Bjalla Gray Locks—"

"You believe the rantings of a madman?" scoffed a woman warrior. Her dark eyes and brown skin tone were a dead match to Kálf's, but her round cheeks and the short, neat styling of her hair set her apart. Sister, Silla guessed, or niece.

"Yes, Mýr," replied Rey coolly. "I do. We ask for half a dozen warriors to help us hunt the hatchlings."

His request was met with utter silence.

"You still haven't told us why you've dragged your sorry arse back here, Galtung." Hef glowered. "Nor why my cousin lies cold in the ground."

"Klaernar," grumbled Rey after a long pause. "I was forced to reveal myself, and there are etchings posted with my likeness on them. Your cousin"—he glared at Hef—"tried to make some easy coin."

Hef scowled, but Kálf was not impressed. "Vig said you were lured from the shield-home," Kálf said. "Which means, again, you speak in half-truths, Galtung. Ketill was after *her*, wasn't he?"

Say it, Silla urged herself. *I'm Eisa Volsik*. But her insides had frozen like a frightened deer.

"And the corpses discovered in the burial ground a few days past. Wolf Feeders, it seems. They were here for *her*, too, weren't they, Galtung?" asked Mýr.

Rey gritted his teeth but did not answer.

"You fool of a man," growled Kálf. "What have you done, Galtung? Why have you brought such attention to our corner of the kingdom?"

Gods, but they pecked at this man like ravens at a corpse. And he would stand there, enduring it.

"Enough!" she exclaimed. "You are right. Ketill was after me. The Wolf Feeders as well."

All eyes slid her way. Silla's heart was drumming wildly, her palms slick with sweat. *Not her*, her insides screamed. But she forced her thoughts to those serpents—to Váli and Ástrid. She had to stop this from happening to another. Rey's boot edged against hers, and she felt him building her up, as he'd always done. It was time to surrender.

It was time to own her truth.

She closed her eyes. Drew in a long breath.

"I am Eisa Volsik."

Her words were loud and quiet all at once. But before she could let the doubts creep in, Silla began to tell her story.

She started with Skarstad. With Matthias—Tómas to these folk. She told them of Reykfjord, of climbing into Rey's wagon, of Skraeda's mad pursuit. By the time she relayed the events of Skutur, of discovering her true name, the hall had fallen utterly silent. Silla continued, telling them of Kopa and Istré, of how she and Rey had fled to Kalasgarde.

"So you see," she finished, "we had no other choice."

She could see disbelief and wariness in the eyes of some and wonder in others. And she understood completely—Eisa Volsik was long thought dead. It was as well known as the sky being blue.

"I did not believe it myself, when first I was told." Silla laughed coarsely. "I have yet to accept it truly, I suppose. But there are too many things I cannot explain. My father's deception and ability with a sword. My scar—" She tapped the crescent-shaped mark beside her eye. "And the fact that all my life, I've dreamed of my sister, Saga."

Silla could tell many remained unconvinced. "I've spoken my truth, and that is all I can do. If you don't believe me, there's nothing more I can say to convince you. But does it truly matter? I could be a flying cat, and it would not change the fact that your northern refuge is no longer the safe haven you wish it to be."

Kálf sent her a sharp look, but she continued. "Good people have died because of those creatures, and no one has done a thing, save for Rey. He's trekked all over that gods damned mountain searching for clues—has been elbow-deep in excrement and built a ridiculous contraption to trap the thing."

"And Vig!" called Vig, from the back of the mead hall.

"And Vig the Valiant," she added with affection, before scowling at the warriors surrounding Kálf. "Believe my story or do not. Hold your poisonous grudge against Rey if you must. But if any wish to do something to protect Kalasgarde, then I'll be at that table there, waiting to tell you what I know." And with that, she turned on her foot, pulling Rey along with her. He slid an arm around her shoulder, dragging her close.

"You did well," he whispered into her hair.

As they slid onto the bench beside Vig and across from Runný, Silla felt their amusement.

"It takes a lot to silence Kálf," said Runný with a wry smile. "That was impressive."

"Too much?" Silla asked, glancing down the mead hall. "Was I too unkind?" The warriors had clustered together, several casting suspicious looks her way.

"Unkind?" choked out Vig. "Your *unkind* has all the fierceness of Helga the goat." At Silla's glare, he continued. "I suppose only time will tell. Sad though it is, the Galdra can sometimes be a bit like sheep—it is frightening to break from the flock. But if one strays, others might follow."

"You mustn't think badly of them," Runný added. "Fear can make even the largest warrior feel small."

Silla sighed. "At the very least, I've done all I can to sway them—" She broke off as a large form slid onto the bench beside Runný. Silla stared into the warrior's ice-blue eyes.

"Hef," she croaked. His cousin lay cold in the ground because of her. Did he seek vengeance? Wish her life as payment for Ketill's?

Hef folded his arms on the table, leaning closer. His eyes were like cold steel. "My cousin was a sniveling kunta who has dishonored our family. I owe you an apology."

"I . . ." Silla blinked in shock. "Might I express my condolences for Freydis?"

Hef's eyes shone in the dim light of the mead hall. "I'd rather you tell me what you saw in that cave, Your Highness."

CHAPTER 61

To Rey's great relief, after Hef joined their table, it was not long before others came as well. Kálf had been the first to slide onto the bench after Hef, talking little and listening intently. And after that, a flood of others had followed. Rey did not care if the men and women who joined them were driven by curiosity or by an honest desire to help. The more people who joined, the better their chances up Jökull.

Within half an hour, a plan had formed. Silla described how she had collapsed the cave entry with an avalanche of ice and snow, but it was unclear if it would hold. This task could not wait until first light. The warriors would collect their armor and meet at Jökull's trailhead in one hour's time. The cave entrance would need to be dug out, the hatchlings and mother serpent dispatched.

Ástrid's and Váli's bodies would be retrieved. And then Ashbringers would bring down the cavern roof over the chasm while Breakers held open a passage from which they could escape.

Energy rushed through Rey as the plan came together. After weeks of feeling powerless, of fruitlessly searching for the creature, progress was being made. He only hoped the Bloodaxe Crew fared as well with the mysterious, pulsing mist in Istré.

At last they rose from the benches, warriors trudging off to fetch battle provisions. Rey lingered, waiting for Silla. Kálf sidled up to him. "Despite the attention you've brought to our quiet corner of the kingdom, I *am* glad to see you back, Galtung," the older man admitted.

"It seems I'm glad to be back as well," said Rey with a shake of his head. He'd never have believed he'd feel this way about Kalasgarde.

Rey's eyes found Silla across the hall, pushing a coil of hair from her forehead. Her cheeks were flushed, and a smile was on her face. She had not stepped timidly into Eisa's shoes, but had leaped with astonishing bravery. Rey couldn't help but feel proud.

"Tales of your doings in the south reach our ears, courtesy of the high chieftains," Kálf was saying as they made their way toward the door. "The explosion at Reykfjord's berskium mines—that was you?"

Rey's lips twitched. "Aye."

He chuckled. "I'll wager those Klaernar were spitting mad when their berskium caches were ruined. And Kommandor Valf in Kopa? That had to be your doing."

Rey nodded at Silla. "I'm afraid I cannot take credit for that."

Kálf's mouth opened and closed, much like a fish. "I do not believe it," he spluttered. "How—it is not possible—"

"As I have said," said Rey, "she's more than she seems."

"Her tale is . . . much to take in," continued Kálf, allowing a pair of warriors to pass. "But I'll admit, I cannot understand why a person would make such a thing up."

"Sometimes the truth is wilder than the most imaginative tale," said Rey.

"Ready to slay some serpents, Galtung?" asked Vig jovially as he and Silla joined them.

"More than you know," Rey replied, eyes landing on Silla. "We'll see you at the trailhead, Vig." Ignoring his friend's scoff of annoyance, he steered Silla out the door and into the frigid nighttime air.

As they stepped out from the Split Skull and into Kalasgarde's streets, Silla's head tilted up with a gasp. The black night skies were painted with brushstrokes of luminescent green.

"Up here, they call it the dawn of the north," Rey said, unable to look away from the wonder in her eyes. And in that moment he knew he had to show her the lake.

Grabbing her hand, he pulled her forward, and they walked in silence to the gates of Kalasgarde. Rey paused. "We've some time to spare before we must meet the others," he said, turning away from the route back to the shield-home. "And I've something to show you." She trailed him along the path as they began to climb a small foothill. White lichen, clinging to slender pine trunks, had unfurled beneath the moonlight, the northern lights casting a slight green tinge upon the luminescent gills.

"You did well tonight," he said.

"I am glad it is done," she admitted. "It earned us the help we needed. And . . ." She paused. "And it feels good to be a part of something."

It wasn't long before they crested the hill. Rey removed his wolf-skin cloak and spread it on the ground at the edge of the trees. As he and Silla sank down on the cloak, her mouth fell open.

They sat on the edge of a precipice that cut sharply down to Kalasgarde Lake. All around them were impossibly tall snowcapped mountains; lunar-blooming plants dotted the landscape. The star-filled sky undulated with green light, reflected in the lake's glassy surface.

But as Silla watched the river of green cresting in the skies, it was she Rey could not stop watching.

"Some say it is Sunnvald's show for the kin He misses dearly," he said, forcing his gaze to the lake and trying to see it through her eyes. But when he looked out, Rey was transported to a different time. Instead of Silla beside him, it was Kristjan, the pair of them grouching about Harpa. Rey would make a wry comment about their grandmother, and Kristjan's head would fall back in laughter, his entire body shaking. That was how his little brother had been. He never laughed halfway.

"You came here with your brother?" Silla asked, reading whatever was written in his face.

As he swallowed back his emotion, all he could manage was a curt nod. Rey was filled with sudden regret. Why had he brought her here, of all places? Of course he'd react this way, and she'd want to know more.

"Will you tell me about him?" she asked. Rey could hear the caution in her voice, and beneath it, her gnawing need to know more.

Years of defensive instincts kicked in all at once, clamping down on all memories, all thoughts of Kristjan. Rey wordlessly forced his gaze to his boots. Sharing about his parents was one thing, but his brother was another. The wound left in Kristjan's wake had been untended too long. He'd learned to live with the dull pain of it. To speak of him now would be like slicing it open—would be subjecting himself to the sharp agony all over again.

"I'm sorry," Silla mumbled.

Rey heard the disappointment in her voice, saw the hypocrisy in his own actions. Hadn't he just pushed her to stand before the Uppreisna? To share her true name with them?

A sound from above had Rey leaping to his feet. The barn owl had settled on a branch, and gods but its presence was as good as a knife, slicing without Rey's consent. "Go away!" He waved his arms at the owl, trying to frighten it, but the bird only stared at him with unnerving black eyes.

"Please," he begged, hands wrapping around the tree's scaled trunk as though he could shake the owl free. But the owl was unmoved by his request, and as Rey felt Silla's concerned gaze on his back, panic began to flood his veins.

"Kristjan rescued an owl once," Rey heard himself saying. Desperately, he searched for the cold, unfeeling place inside himself, but couldn't seem to find it. "He made Harpa set its wing. Trapped mice in the fields to feed it. Nursed the owl back to health. The day he set the owl free might have been the happiest I'd ever seen him.

"After burying him, I came here to get mindlessly drunk. But then I looked up and saw the owl, and it felt as though *he* was there with me."

As he stole a glance at the owl, Rey felt it all—the bright, sharp guilt of failing his brother, the sorrow of burying his little brother, the blackness that had dogged his steps for a full year afterward. Throwing himself into his Uppreisna work had been the only way Rey could claw himself out of it. He'd taken every assignment no matter how dangerous. Had built his walls, high and impenetrable, to keep this from happening again.

How could he have forgotten? Rey had barely survived it.

"Would you believe an owl guided me through the Twisted Pinewoods?" Silla's voice was fast and excited, but Rey felt as though he were underwater, mere fragments of her words meeting his ears: "The Owl's Hollow Inn," and "sign from the gods," and "brought us together."

Her words barely penetrated him. Rey stared up at the owl, trying to breathe through his remembered pain. It was worse than any battle wound he'd suffered. Worse than anything he could imagine. And in that moment, Rey understood the owl's presence.

"A reminder," he muttered. He rested his forehead on the tree trunk, a singular thought circling in his mind: *I cannot survive this twice.*

"What is it, Rey?" asked Silla, that gods damned concern in her voice. "You can tell me."

Rey pushed away from the tree and began pacing. His breaths were too quick, his thoughts spiraling out of control.

Cannot! his insides screamed. *Cannot survive it.*

"If you only shared a little," she tried again. "I know this is about Kristjan. Talk to me, Rey. Tell me about him. It could help. I know losing him shook you to your core—"

"I cannot give you what you want."

Her eyes were wide, black pools, and Rey forced his gaze away.

"What does that mean?"

"I don't know!"

His words were loud and sharp, and as she recoiled, he despised himself. He felt her watching him. Felt her dismantling the meaning in his words. Felt the moment she realized they were no longer speaking of Kristjan but of something altogether different. Rey turned and met her eyes. Registered the fire.

"You said there was nothing uncertain in how you want me," she challenged, pushing to her feet.

"Wanting you is not enough."

Silla stared at him hard. "And what does *that* mean?"

Rey's self-loathing reached new heights. How did he explain that the people he loved were never long for this world? That he could not survive this twice? Rey had never been one for words. And in this moment, he felt like a cornered animal, desperate and lashing out.

"I've let this go too far. I should have put a stop to it sooner."

He braced himself for tears. Readied himself for her to crumble to pieces. But Silla only folded her arms over her chest.

"No," she said, gaze unflinching. "I see what you're doing, and I do not accept it. You are trying to frighten me away, Reynir Galtung, and I'm sorry to say, I won't let you." And with that, she turned on her heel. Retreated down the foothill.

Rey stared after her, dumbstruck.

A minute stretched out, his hot, restless panic burning away and leaving numbness in its wake. His mind was at war, uncertain if he wanted to let her walk away or chase after her. But as the gods damned owl stared down at Rey, Silla's words sank into his mind.

You are trying to frighten me away, Reynir Galtung, and I'm sorry to say, I won't let you.

She'd seen through his ugly words, straight to his very core. He felt exposed. Vulnerable. Gods, but he should have known, with her, there was nowhere for him to hide.

And the anger he'd seen on her face was a revelation, sparking warmth in his numb chest and bringing him back to life. This woman challenged him at every turn and might well drive him to madness. But now, Rey understood: She would fight for him. Fight for *them*.

Disoriented, he trudged after her.

CHAPTER 62

Sunnavík

Ana's charcoal eyes smiled at Saga from the parchment secured to her drawing board. She sighed, setting it down on the bench and strolling to the window. Dawn was still hours away, the blackness absolute. But as she stared, Saga's heart squeezed in her chest.

A flare of light. A star streaking across the sky, then glimmering into darkness.

"Ana," Saga whispered, sorrow and nausea battling for dominance.

Then, as it often had in the execution's aftermath, Saga's last glimpse of Ana invaded her mind's eye—head lolling to the side; part of her skull crushed; blood trailing from her Letting and countless other wounds.

Saga's stomach twisted violently, and she rushed to the bathing chamber, reaching the chamber pot just in time. Over and over she retched, until acid stung her throat and there was nothing left but bile. Saga rose, hands trembling as she picked up the jug of water on the wash station and poured herself a cup.

She leaned into the listless, fuzzy sensation from lack of food and sleep. It was better not to think too clearly, better to keep her mind from picking apart Signe's expression after Ana's execution. In this place, Saga could convince herself that making herself pliant and small would keep her from harm.

But Eisa.

But Eisa. It was a pesky rock in her slipper; it was a solitary hair on her oatcake. The name ruined it all. She could not give in. Could not let Signe harm her sister.

But Saga did not know how to fight the queen alone. Ana had been her anchor, her link to the Uppreisna. And now that she was gone, Saga was alone and exposed. And why? Because that cursed Zagadkian man had kicked her satchel under the bed. It was childish to blame him, but she needed somewhere to channel her anger.

She sighed. After rinsing her mouth, Saga made her way back into her chambers, and nearly jumped out of her skin.

"Rurik?" she gasped. For a moment, Saga thought her sleeplessness had overcome her. She'd just thought of him, and now here he was—all broad shoulders and square jaw and those emerald-green eyes.

"You are—" Rurik paused. "—spouting?"

And with that, Saga knew he must be real. A confusing mix of irritation and embarrassment rose within her. Putting her hands on her hips, Saga sent him a hard look. "You shouldn't be here."

"I disagree," he said, studying her carefully. Weariness lined his face, yet his eyes shone with strange eagerness. "I needed to check on you."

Saga's gaze flicked to the balcony door—slightly ajar. "Did you . . . Rurik, did you *climb* the balcony?"

He shrugged.

"That's fifteen feet of smooth pillar. How did you—it is not possible—"

"Red troll man is outside your door. Impossible to come through doorway." The intensity of his gaze sent a rush of heat to her stomach. "Tell me, Winterwing. Are you safe? Are you well?"

"Well," repeated Saga, swaying on her feet. *No!* she wanted to scream. She would never be well again.

"Your friend," continued Rurik, holding up her drawing board. Saga frowned. She hadn't quite captured Ana's true likeness. It was the smile—just a little too forced and decidedly somber. Saga took in a ragged breath, fighting with all her will not to crumble. She refused to cry. But her throat tightened, and her eyes stung. She would never see Ana's real smile—would never have the chance to capture it.

Saga snatched the parchment from the drawing board, crumpling it and tossing it into the fireplace. It curled, then flaked into ash, joining dozens of its predecessors.

"I am sorry," said Rurik, standing just behind her. Saga stared listlessly into the flames. "You did her a kind thing, did you not?"

She turned slowly. "I don't know what you mean," she said. But her stupid, insufferable voice betrayed her.

"You were taking her pain," Rurik continued.

Saga forced her gaze over his shoulder, swallowing a lump in her throat. Her mind's eye showed her Ana's crushed skull, then shifted to the woman manacled to the bed, flesh carved from her arm. Which fate would be hers should her Sense be exposed?

Rurik's hands wrapped around hers, squeezing gently. "You can trust me, Saga. We keep secrets for each other, do we not?"

"Not this one," she whispered.

He watched her carefully—too carefully. "Do they know you are a . . . what are you calling this?"

"Galdra," she breathed.

"Galdra? Do they know this, Saga?"

Her eyes met his, but she could hold his gaze for only a heartbeat before looking away. "They might now."

Rurik's hands slid around the small of her back, pulling her to him. He was so warm and solid, a reminder of resilience when she felt herself washing away. Dazed, she leaned in. Let him stroke her hair. Listened to his soft murmurs, soothing, though she did not understand them.

"*Chto ty sdelala, malen'kaya ptichka,**" he said. "You are in danger." Saga did not reply, but his arms tightened. "You will come with me when I leave."

Wrenching herself free, she started pacing. "I cannot, Rurik. I cannot leave this place."

---

*What did you do, little bird.

"I will help you," he asserted. "Rovgolod has seeds for ocean sickness. You will take them and sleep, and I will steal you out."

But Eisa, she wanted to scream. If Saga left, who would protect Eisa? Who would stop Signe? The room swirled, Ana's bloodied corpse sagging on the pillar. Saga whirled away from Rurik, closing her eyes.

She would. Not. Cry.

"Look at me, Winterwing." Gentle fingers gripped her chin, tilting her face upward. Saga stared up at Rurik. This unyielding man was used to getting what he wanted, and he wanted to steal her away. It was a tantalizing offer. And yet . . .

"I cannot leave," Saga whispered. "It is more than my ailment. I must keep her safe."

"Who?"

"My sister."

"Yrsa?" asked Rurik.

Saga looked away.

"Not Yrsa." Rurik was silent for a moment. "Which means it must be other one. Esa."

"Eisa." Saga swallowed. She felt disconnected from her body, from this entire conversation. Had she truly just told him that?

"Eisa," Rurik repeated. "She is not dead, then." He did not wait for an answer. "And you are helping her by . . . what? Reading queen's letters? Sneaking through tunnels and hearing things you should not?" Rurik clicked his tongue, muttering something in Zagadkian. "You cannot help her if you are dead, Saga."

Her heart slammed against her ribs. Because, of course, he was right.

"You are in danger if you stay," said Rurik in a low voice. "And so you will leave."

"But the treaty, Rurik—"

He let out a dark chuckle, gazing at her with predatory green eyes. "Here is another secret, Saga." He leaned closer. "I do not care about treaty."

Saga's brows furrowed. "What?"

Rurik shrugged, a maddeningly casual gesture. "I'm afraid I cannot say more."

Saga watched him suspiciously. The man was an irritating enigma. She could not allow herself to forget—Rurik knew Saga's most damning secrets, while still she knew little of his.

"I will help your sister if you wish it," Rurik said casually. "Tell me, Winterwing. What must be done?"

"I don't trust you," she hissed.

A slow smile slid across his face. "You are not in position to choose. Is myself or Urkans."

Gods, but she hated that he was right. Ana was gone. Signe knew of Saga's scheming. Any minute now, her world could crash in on her. And Rurik was right—Saga would be no help to Eisa or her kingdom if she were killed or locked away.

"I will give you drug for sleeping to sneak you out of castle. Give you nice room on boat. Many soft furs and books for reading."

"Doors?" she asked, her heart pounding.

"One door to lower deck. Not to outdoors."

"Windows?"

"One window, so you might look at ocean if you are wishing. Or cover if you are not."

"People?"

"Rov and Druzhina. Good, trusting men. Crew stays on deck—they are having shelter above."

Saga ran her hands through her hair absently. "What if they see me? What if I panic?"

"I can sit in your room if you wish," he said. "Can help you with tapping. And if you wish it, you may take seeds." A mischievous smile curved his lips. "And Rov tells me *medovukha* was saved in fire, thank the Autumn Crone. Lady Saga, you can *pit** if you are liking."

Against her better judgment, a smile twisted Saga's lips. "What is that?"

---

*Drink (alcohol).

Rurik chuckled. "Get drunk, *ptichka*.* You can get pickled on *medovukha* for whole trip. I won't tell anyone."

"Another secret?" she asked wryly. Despite his teasing, Saga couldn't help but feel strangely honored by the way he anticipated her needs, and the way he never judged her. And she wouldn't deny that her skin heated at the thought of sharing a ship with this man... a room, perhaps...

"My sister," she said, trying to shake some sense into herself.

"When we get to Zagadka, we will speak to high prince. Make plans for your sister."

Saga chewed the inside of her cheek, her stomach twisting. It was not merely the prospect of leaving the castle or venturing to the unknown space of the boat that had her anxious. It was Zagadka.

"I thank you for your offer, Rurik," Saga said at last. "But I cannot leave my people or my sister in their time of need. I would like you to take me instead to Midfjord."

Rurik's jaw hardened. "Zagadka."

"No."

Irritation settled in his face. "Midfjord is not on way. Urkans might catch us."

Saga crossed her arms. "It *must* be Midfjord."

"Zagadka!" he hissed.

"No!"

Desperation settled into Saga's bones. Her place was in Íseldur. Her kingdom. But how could she convince this irritatingly stubborn man? "You are not here for the treaty," Saga said. "You are searching for something, but you have not found it. Not in the armory. Not in the hidden passages. Perhaps it is not in Askaborg at all." She thought of the name *Rökksgarde*, which had come up time and time again.

As Rurik's thick dark brows dipped down, she knew she was onto something.

"I uncovered something in Alfson's study before stumbling

---

*Birdie.

across that horrid room of beds. If what you seek is not in Askaborg, perhaps it was taken somewhere else."

"Where?" he demanded, his voice a near growl.

"Take me to Midfjord," said Saga. "And I shall tell you."

"Tell me now, Winterwing," he pressed. "Lives are at risk—"

"As they are if I do not get to Midfjord."

The air between them crackled with intensity, and Saga second-guessed herself. He approached, and she retreated until her back hit the wall.

"In Zagadka, no one dares to tell me no," drawled Rurik.

"Must be why you're so arrogant," retorted Saga. Gods, this man was impossible, infuriating. And yet his wild green eyes flashed with delight.

"They are knowing what happens when I feel disrespect."

Saga's eyes narrowed. He was so close she could feel the heat rolling off his body. He lifted a hand, ran it slowly down the column of her throat. Warmth pooled low in her stomach. "Shall I show you?" he asked.

"Stop trying to provoke me," she muttered.

"But I like your fire, Saga." Rurik laughed, low and deep. "Is a thing you show only to me. Another of our secrets." He leaned so close, his breath misted across her cheek. His gaze slid down, landing on the fluttering pulse at the base of her neck. "You are frightened. Your heart is fast like hummingbird's wings."

Saga took a shaky breath, trying to drag some sense back into her skull. "I'm not frightened, I'm irritated."

He turned preternaturally still, his eyes like green flames that would blind her if she stared too long. "Tell me of this place. I must know if your information is worth such a bargain."

Saga swallowed, trying to keep up. "A fortress of some sort, I believe. I discovered a list. Items to be shipped, including herbs, metals for a dungeon, and—"

"Dungeon?" Rurik cut in.

She nodded.

His large hand wrapped around her shoulder in a firm grip. "You must tell me."

"Midfjord," she whispered, holding her breath. This had to work. It was all she had.

He muttered in Zagadkian under his breath, then met her eyes. "What is in Midfjord? How you are knowing it is safe?"

"Ana," Saga whispered.

Understanding settled in Rurik's eyes. A curt nod was his only acknowledgment.

"You agree then?" Saga pushed. "Midfjord?"

Letting out a long, low breath, Rurik gazed at the fireplace. "Is not on way. Rov will do much yelling." Finally, his eyes met hers. "Very well, Saga. I will take you to Midfjord. And you will tell me on boat about this place."

Saga nodded, relief flooding her. The boat. Then she would tell him of Rökksgarde. And then . . . Midfjord. Gods, but this was truly going to happen . . .

A slow smile curved his lips. "Good," he said. His hand slid down her arm, slow and deliciously warm. "We leave morning after Printsessa's feast. At the daymeal, drink large cup of your—" He paused. "—róa. Will crush seeds and put in there."

"How?"

Rurik cupped her jaw, his thumb sliding up her chin. "Do not worry about that, Winterwing. Do not worry of anything. Soon you will be away from this place. You will be safe."

Open skies. New places. His *safe* sounded an awful lot like danger.

His thumb skimmed her lower lip, and her eyelids fluttered. "*Glaza boyatsya, a ruki delayut*. Is Zagadkian saying that means 'The eyes are afraid, but the hands are doing.' You understand, Saga?"

Numbly, she nodded. Fear was a thing to be felt, not obeyed.

Rurik smiled, all flashing teeth and predatory eyes. "Good. You are fighter. Long have I seen this. But Urkans, they are cunning. We must be careful and clever."

Saga nodded again. This conversation had exhausted her. But there was a plan. A new purpose. "The morning after Yrsa's birthday feast," she repeated.

"Good," said Rurik, guiding Saga to her bed. "Now rest *malen'kaya ptichka.* Soon, you will be out of this place." He smoothed the blanket over her.

And then he slid through her balcony door, leaving Saga in the quietude of her chambers. She stared up at her crimson canopy, letting his reassurances sink into her.

One way or another, she was getting out of this place.

CHAPTER 63

Kalasgarde

Silla joined more than a dozen fur-clad men and women climbing up Jökull to collapse the ice caves. The northern lights had gradually faded, leaving a blanket of stars illuminating the sky. Silla gazed up at them as she climbed, wondering if her birth parents were up there watching over her. If they'd be proud of her, stepping into Eisa's shoes.

The last time she'd hiked up this mountain had been a solitary event for Silla. But in the dead of night and surrounded by Galdra, it felt entirely different.

Of course, it could also be the anger in her chest whenever the owl flashed in her mind's eye. Couldn't Reynir Galtung get it through his thick skull? The owl was a sign—be it from the gods or from the spirit of his brother—that they were meant to be together.

I've let this go too far, he'd said coldly instead. Silla had seen through his words in an instant. Rey saw only the reminder of his brother; he was frightened and tried to push her away. Perhaps she ought to have been softer. But his willingness to give up on them so easily made her burn with anger.

For the time being, Silla shoved her emotions aside, focusing on her actions. Destroy the hatchlings and mother serpent. Retrieve the bodies of Ástrid and Váli. Collapse the ice cave over that chasm.

And so she trekked up the mountain behind a burly Blade Breaker named Nefi, who, from the smell of things, had not washed his furs in quite some time. The moons were high in the skies, foliage glowing all around them—the strange, tentacled plants unfurling from nooks in trees and between rocks, huddles of moonflowers glowing brightly. It should have been magical, but Silla was numb.

Hearthfire thoughts, she thought as she walked. *Harpa's steam bath. The ice spirits. His almost-smile.*

Within an hour, the flat, frozen lake spread wide before them. When last she'd seen it, the lake was covered in snow, but the howling winds had blown it clear. Now the stars reflected on a sprawl of black ice.

Her gaze darted across the lake, landing on the cave's entry. Silla let out a relieved breath as she saw the crumbled snow and ice sealing the entrance—the small collapse she'd caused had held. As they crossed the lake, Silla looked down. Swept free from snow, the lake proved larger than she'd expected. It was impossible to tell the depth; beneath her feet was only the reflection of stars. A loud groan came from below. Stopping dead in her tracks, Silla stared hard but found only the black gleam of ice.

"'Tis merely the ice shifting," said Mýr, clapping her on the shoulder. "Do not worry, Eisa, this ice is as thick as Rannver's skull."

Rannver grumbled his annoyance from behind her. Exhaling, Silla hurried to join the rest of the Galdra gathered at the ice cave's entrance.

"How did such a cavern appear?" asked Hef, unstrapping a shovel from his back. "Do you think the mother serpent could have carved it?"

"Perhaps," said Rey, beckoning them all closer to run through the plan. "We dig out the cave. Take out each hatchling as they emerge."

"What if the mother shows up?" asked Nefi.

Rey leveled him with a stern gaze. "The mother is not in the cave, else the blockage would be gone. But if she shows herself, we work together. Aim for the eyes and underbellies." His gaze shifted to Silla, and it looked as though he wished to say something more. The man seemed uncomfortable. Miserable perhaps. Throat working on a hard swallow, Rey looked away. "Once the entrance is cleared, we move through the cave as a group."

Hef and the other warrior began digging out the cave's entrance while a pair of Ashbringers pushed their fire on a targeted location. Silla knew they'd planned to widen only a small area—to allow a single hatchling out at a time—but it quickly became apparent that the icy wreckage was unstable. Each time they tried to create a single, narrow hole, the top section of the debris crumbled away. Before long, an unintended hole had formed at the top of the snowpack, a forked tongue darting through the gap. One warrior fell back with a yelp, while Hef's shovel slashed into the snowpack. It struck the serpent's nose with a clang, causing Hef to curse and shake out his arm.

"Underbelly," Vig reminded him.

The tongue had vanished into the blackened cave, but with the hole now widened, they could hear the rest of them hissing in unison. How many serpents were trapped in the cave?

Behind them, the ice groaned, loud and so long it set the hairs on the back of Silla's neck on end. Beside her, smoke peeled up from Rey's palms, while Kálf formed a whip of crackling flame. Heart pounding, Silla primed, closing her eyes while she expressed and herded her light into place. Within moments, she was holding a sword of shimmering frostfire.

Murmurs rippled through the Galdra as they took in her sword, but they quickly refocused on the cave's entry. Anticipation rattled the air as the group listened to the serpents begin to slam against the wall of snow.

A bang from the lake behind made Silla's heart leap into her throat. Snow crashed down from a nearby tree. And then the debris blocking the cave's entry exploded as the serpent hatchlings smashed through.

Any hope of quick, orderly executions was immediately lost. The hatchlings swarmed out of the cave, Galdra stumbling back in shock as the sheer number became apparent. When Silla had sealed the cave, there had been perhaps six hatchlings in pursuit. Now there were easily ten times that number.

The world descended into chaos. The heat of Rey's galdur radiated from her left, smoke tunneling down serpent throats and wrapping around their bodies. An ice-scaled beast lunged at her, and Silla's sword swept up in reply. It sank through its underjaw and into its skull, the glowing red eyes extinguishing as the creature fell.

The Galdra battled all around her, the serpents' moldering stench mingling with charred flesh. But there were too many serpents, and it was impossible to contain them. One then two slithered past the group, escaping into the trees beyond.

"Do not let them break free!" bellowed Rey, rushing at a hatchling sneaking between Hef and Mýr. A trio of hatchlings took advantage of the gap, advancing with those unnerving red eyes trained on Silla. One lunged, and Silla's sword whipped out, embedding deep in the snake's underbelly. As she pulled her sword free, the other two slithered past her, making their way toward the woods.

"No!" she cried out, rushing after them as they neared the lake's edge. She would not let them escape. Would not let them harm another child. Anger and battle thrill powering her, Silla threw herself at the nearest hatchling just as it whirled. Her sword sliced deep into its underbelly. But tears of frustration burned in her eyes as she watched the third serpent's tail vanish into the dark woods.

"Silla!" boomed Rey. "Shore up!"

She began to trot back to the group but was soon greeted by a cloud of writhing blue: The ice spirits, freed from the cavern, were in a frenzy, jostling and crashing into one another as they pointed to the lake's surface. Brows furrowing, Silla looked down.

It lasted for barely a heartbeat before it vanished. But that moment was enough for Silla to make out movement beneath the ice—and the unmistakable red glow of an eye. Goosebumps rushed up her arms. Something was *under* the ice, and it seemed to be very large.

Silla ran.

The ice beneath her buckled upward with sudden impact, making her stumble. Thunderous sound filled the air, the ice spirits darting feverishly about. Eyes wide, Rey charged toward her, and Silla picked up her pace.

She didn't make it far.

The next impact broke through the ice, a thing of nightmares breaching the surface a few paces ahead of Silla. Its long, serpentine body was covered in icy scales, spear-sharp fangs visible as it opened its mouth and screamed. The noise was demonic, not of this world.

The mother serpent. It had to be.

Time slowed. Her feet stopped moving, yet her momentum and the smooth surface of the ice carried her hopelessly toward the monster, toward the widening hole in the ice. The ice spirits pelted the creature, drawing another shriek, but they could not divert it from its prey. Faster than lightning, the beast swung toward her, its mouth agape as it waited for her to slide within striking distance.

Instinct took hold of her, and Silla swung her sword at the creature's underbelly. The beast reared back before her blade could make contact, then plunged below the ice. Silla was vaguely aware of Rey shouting as he stormed toward her, but the ice beneath her disappeared.

And then she was in the water.

A thousand knives plunged into Silla's skin; the pain was so intense, it robbed her of the ability to think. It might have been the span of a heartbeat, or five, or perhaps thirty before shock flooded her, numbing the pain. Silla kicked toward the surface, her muscles stiff and slow.

Something brushed against her calf.

Her sword had miraculously held steady in her palm. Curiously, the blade did not freeze the water; it sent a strange vibration as it cast shimmering light into the darkness. For the first time, she saw the full scope of the serpent. It was enormous—at least thirty paces long, rippling the waters as it undulated in place. And those eyes—glowing red like embers—were homed in on her.

As Silla stared at certain death, her awareness sharpened, and she could feel it *all*—the frantic churn of her heart; the burn of her lungs; and a strange dark thread writhing somewhere deep within her.

The serpent lashed forward. Silla managed a clumsy swing, the water's friction proving a new hurdle. Despite her awkward motion, the beast recoiled, and she kicked furiously. Breaking the surface,

Silla sucked in great mouthfuls of air and searched for escape. She needed to get onto the ice. And then she needed to run.

"Silla!" Rey was lying on the jagged edge of the hole, an arm stretched out. "Swim!"

Silla kicked frantically, hope blooming brighter as the distance closed.

Ten paces.

Nine.

Eight.

She was going to make it.

Seven.

Six.

Before she could think to scream, Silla was wrenched backward by her tunic, dragged under the surface. The deafening roar of water against her ears drowned all else out; her terror climbed higher as the serpent pulled her deeper, deeper, deeper.

It released her.

It was blacker than midnight on the Shortest Day. By some miracle, her sword held steady through the confusion and terror of her descent, though its light was dull and flickering. She spun until she caught sight of the creature coiling nearby, watching her with its eerie red eyes.

It was playing with her.

Silla shivered, though she was beyond cold at this point—she was so cold, she actually felt hot. The darkness was smothering, pressing in on all sides.

Escape, came a voice from within. *Exits. Not trapped.* With one eye on the serpent, Silla fluttered her feet, pushing toward the dim gloam of blue above. Her muscles slowed, her lungs ached, but she just kept moving her feet.

Her senses sharpened, instinct warning her of the creature's approach. It was as though Silla watched herself from above. She turned, sword low. Swung upward through the turbid waters. Sank the sword deep into the soft underside of the serpent's jaw. The serpent's agonized shriek vibrated through the lake, water billowing as it drew back. Twitching and shuddering, the beast slithered deeper until the light of her sword could no longer illuminate it.

Silla didn't have long. Lights danced in her vision; her lungs were going to burst. She pushed, and kicked, and fought her way up through the icy waters.

Her head bumped into a hard surface, hands groping along it.

Ice.

She was at the surface but trapped under the ice.

That was the moment Silla realized—she was going to die.

CHAPTER 64

"Silla!" Rey bellowed, fighting against Vig's grip as he tried to reach the chasm's edge.

"Think, Galtung," growled Vig, his hold only tightening. "You cannot help her if you're dead."

Rey's heart was in his throat, nausea twisting his stomach. Get to her. He had to get to her. Never mind that most of the hatchlings had now slithered free, that Nefi had taken a bite wound and lay unconscious as the venom worked through him. Mýr, Rannver, and Kálf had formed a protective circle around the unconscious warrior, ready to cut down any hatchling that got close enough.

"You jump into that water, and you'll die," reminded Vig. "Be clever, Galtung. Do not let emotion—"

"Silla!" Rey shouted, driving his elbow into Vig's gut and wrenching free. He threw himself onto his stomach, easing toward the edge of the hole in the lake. Dozens of ice spirits flitted about frantically, only fueling his panic. How long had it been since the beast had pulled her under?

Each heartbeat felt like an eternity. Rey's throat was closing up. He struggled to breathe. Where was she? He surveyed the scene, looking for her curls, for her dark, vibrant eyes. But Silla was nowhere to be seen. Where once the waters had frothed with the mother serpent's rapid movements, now they lay still.

Rey forced in several deep breaths. His gaze raked across the lake, trying to formulate a plan. If something happened to her . . . A sob built in his throat, and Rey swallowed it back. She was a fighter—she would never give up.

And neither would he.

The spirits had flocked to a patch of ice not far off, looping and hissing excitedly. He saw it then—a dull throb of light beneath them. He pushed to his feet, legs moving before he could think. And then Rey was yanking on his galdur and shoving it at the ice where white light flickered, then vanished.

"Silla!" he yelled. And then Kálf was beside him, and Rannver, both Ashbringers working to melt the ice. Vig rushed forward, greataxe in hand, Erik soon joining him.

The frozen surface of the lake sizzled as their collective fire burrowed into the ice. Vig and Erik chipped gently with their axes, deepening the hole as the ice spirits hissed, urging them on. Slowly, a depression formed, deepening until a glimmer of water appeared.

It wasn't fast enough. Warm prickles rushed the length of his tattoo as he drew from his halda. A hole in the ice formed, half a handspan, then a full hand. Then two. Then five.

She floated face down, hair fanned out around her.

No. Sliding on his stomach, Rey yanked her from the water, then tugged her limp body onto his and cradled her to his chest. She felt small. So vulnerable.

The surrounding commotion grew muffled as blood rushed in Rey's ears. This was all wrong. Her cheeks were a pale corpse gray. They should be pink. Should be curving up at the apples when her smile stretched wide. And it hit him all at once, with a blow that left him spinning. He could lose her.

"Sunshine," he pleaded, fingers fumbling around the base of her neck. The fear he felt was staggering. She might die with Rey's words ringing in her ears. *I've let this go too far.*

He felt it then—a faint throb beneath his fingers. "She has a pulse," he said, and a murmur of relief spread through the Galdra. Swiftly, Rey rolled Silla onto her back, a pair of ice spirits darting away before she could crush them. Her lips were blue against her pale, unnatural complexion, her chest unmoving. She wasn't breathing.

Like all Galdra, Rey believed in the old gods, though he'd never been much for prayers. But in this moment, as he stared down at her slack body, he begged . . . *pleaded* with them. *Please . . . please spare her life.*

Rey pressed down on her chest.

Please allow me the chance to make things right.

Another compression.

If you give me another chance, I won't squander it.

Another compression.

I will do better. Be braver.

Silla coughed, water spluttering from her mouth. Rey let out a ragged cry, pressing his forehead to hers. She breathed. She was *breathing*. But if he didn't warm her, the cold would steal the life from her.

"My fighter," he whispered, pulling her into his arms and standing unsteadily. Half a dozen hands reached out to support him. "You're all right, you're *all right*." He wasn't sure if he was trying to reassure Silla or himself but decided it didn't matter. All that mattered was getting her warm. And with an hour's hike separating them from the shield-home, he had to do it here. Rey ran to the shelter of the forest, where the snow was shallow and the winds less biting.

"Cloaks!" he bellowed, pulling gently from his source and wrapping a smoky blanket around Silla. Her body bumped against his chest with each frenzied stride.

Vig laid a fur cloak on a bare patch of ground, and Rey laid Silla down upon it, yanking off her boots and reaching for her belt. He had to get her out of her wet clothes.

Vig lingered beside him, setting more cloaks down. "What do you need, Galtung?" he asked.

"Fire," muttered Rey. "And space."

Rannver rushed forward, expressing a flame and fixing it to the ground nearby. And then Rey heard Vig's gruff voice ushering the others away.

Rey pulled off her battle belt and tugged her tunic over her head. Her blue lips opened and closed, and a jumble of slurred words spilled from Silla.

"Shh," he said. "Don't speak. Save your energy, my brave girl. I won't let anything happen to you. I can't lose—" Rey's voice cracked, unable to finish. Emotion churned inside him so forcefully, he shook.

Shielding her from view, Rey shucked the wet fabric from her and draped the heavy, dry cloaks over her bare skin. With shaking hands, Rey dragged off his lébrynja armor, his tunic, his breeches, then slid beneath the cloaks and pressed his bare skin to hers.

She was colder than ice.

His fear was overwhelming, and he found himself rambling, unfiltered, desperate words tumbling loose. "Come back to me, Silla," he said. "I cannot do this without you." She was softness he hadn't known he needed, light casting away the deepest of his shadows. "Forgive me," he begged. "Please, Sunshine, come back to me."

She cried out, and Rey gripped her tighter, pressing his face to her sodden hair. "I'm a fool and a coward. Please let me fix this."

Rey clung to her, heating them both with his smoky galdur, praying to all the gods that she would come through this. The moons traveled toward the horizon, the skies lightening by slight degrees. Rey was vaguely aware of Vig leading the Galdra into the cavern, of the ground shaking some time later from the depths of the mountain. But his sole focus was held on Silla. And by some miracle, the trembles faded to shivers, and her ice-cold skin grew tepid.

"Rey," Silla croaked. Her hair was matted, her skin deathly white, but she was the most beautiful thing he'd ever seen. Rey's chest flooded with pure, raw emotion, and he leaned over her, pressing his forehead to hers.

"Thank the gods," he said, his voice raw and scraped.

She trembled against him. "S-saved me."

"You saved yourself. I only melted the ice."

Silla watched him with dark, shimmering eyes. And through her clattering teeth, she managed a small smile.

Rey felt shaky. Wrung out. As though he himself had faced death and survived. "You scared me senseless," he whispered. "I can't . . . I don't . . ." He raked a hand through his hair, staring down at Silla. The smallest hint of color was returning to her cheeks, but her eyes held absolute exhaustion.

Still, against all odds, she was alive. All the cold seemed to have drained from his body. How could he feel anything but warmth at this moment? The gods had answered his call.

Silla tried to sit up, but Rey put a gentle hand on her collarbone. "Easy now," he whispered. "The others are just there, and I must let them know you're all right. Rest. Let me take care of you."

Thank the gods, the willful, lovely woman listened.

After dressing, Rey called Runný to watch over Silla. The ice spirits fussed around Silla, keeping their distance from the flames as Runný added kindling.

Rey trudged to the cave's entrance, where Ástrid and Váli's corpses had been laid out. Sorrow filled his chest as he stared at the broken remains. His eyes met Vig's.

"It is done." Vig exhaled. "We collapsed the cavern over the chasm."

Rey nodded, relieved that at least one part of this mission had gone to plan. "And the eggs?"

Vig rubbed his forehead, weariness etched into his face. "Tallied eighty-seven hatched eggs." Vig nodded at the frozen lake where the serpent bodies had been laid out. "Twenty-two hatchling corpses."

Shock jolted through Rey. "Sixty-five hatchlings escaped." Gods above, it was a nightmare. Sixty-five giant serpent hatchlings running rampant in the northern wilds.

"Why in the gods' flaming bollocks was the mother serpent in the *lake*?" Vig demanded, diverting Rey's attention from the unfolding calamity.

"Bjalla Gray Locks," muttered Rey. "He said the serpent was . . . clumsy on land. That it entered the river and swam away." Their gazes met, understanding hardening into place.

"The rivers," said Vig. "They prefer the water." He rubbed his forehead. "We'll send word across the north. The beasts prefer to travel by waterway and might be lured with sheep carcasses."

Rey exhaled, clasping Vig's arm. "Be safe, Twig Arms," he said.

Vig nodded, gaze falling on Silla. "Take care of her."

Rey swallowed the burn of emotion, thankful that Vig turned quickly to the Galdra. He barked out orders to fashion sledges to carry the corpses as well as Nefi's unconscious form. It wasn't long before they were charging down the mountain, eager to spread word of the hatchlings across the north.

Rey's attention was focused solely on Silla. After dressing her in his overtunic and Mýr's legwraps, Rey enfolded her in fur cloaks and lifted her into his arms.

She tried to protest. "This is for *me*," Rey told her. Thankfully, with her pride protected, Silla relented.

Once they hit the trail down Jökull, they made quick work of it. Less than an hour later, he was climbing into Horse's saddle behind Silla. His body curved protectively around her.

He forced himself to exhale. She was safe. She would recover.

And Rey had the chance to make things right.

CHAPTER 65

Kopa

The sound of clashing steel was like music to Jonas's ears. His breath misted the cold air, feet planted wide on the blackened earth behind Kopa's eastern garrison hall. Ducking the slashing sword, he kicked out at Hagbard, felling the large Klaernar warrior like a tree.

Jeers and the thump of shields rattled through the yard, exhilaration pumping through Jonas's blood as he offered the man a hand up. Gods, but he missed this. The battle thrill; moving his body; the strategy in besting his opponent. On the sparring grounds, Jonas was back in his element.

Had this been what he'd chased, brawling in Kopa's mead halls? The thought was confounding. Trading his blades for quiet nights in his family's reclaimed longhouse had been his goal for so long. He'd convinced himself his life with the Bloodaxe Crew was a temporary thing.

What if our past is not our future? Ilías had asked. But these were the words of a younger brother. One who'd never looked into the eyes of his dying grandfather and sworn on a talisman to uphold the Svik family values.

Jonas's hand found the talisman hanging from his neck and clasped it tightly.

Family, respect, duty.

It didn't matter what Jonas wanted. He'd sworn to his grandfather he'd uphold these values. He'd sworn vengeance on Ilías's grave.

And with half the Klaernar's payment buried in a nearby cache, Jonas was halfway to reaching his goal. Once Silla and Rey were locked in the Klaernar's dungeons, he would collect the other half of his reward. Would have enough to buy back his family's lands. He could put this all behind him and move on with his life.

Now there was only the task at hand.

"The man you know as the Slátrari," said Jonas, turning to the contingent of Klaernar, "is a master in combat."

These warriors had just arrived from Kunafjord after taking a ship from the south of Íseldur. *The queen's Chosen,* Kaptein Ulfar had called them. *Elite.* These were no green boys. They were battle-hardened men. And now, they were under *his* command.

"He does not rely on one specific tactic when fighting," continued Jonas. "He uses his whole body. A slew of different weapons. He is cunning and brutal, and that was before I knew he was the gods damned Slátrari. Now we must also account for this . . . fire magic of his."

The warriors grumbled. "Is this meant to enliven us?"

Jonas's gaze snapped to the man's claw-tattooed face. "No," he replied. "It is meant to dispel any illusions you might have. He is one man, yes, but he fights like ten combined."

"Sounds as though you admire him!" challenged one of the Chosen from the back of the group.

Jonas scowled at the man. "I did, once," he admitted.

The men began complaining among themselves. "Why should we trust you when you've fought shoulder-to-shoulder with the man?" one called out. "What's to say you won't change your mind?"

"He took an arrow to the left thigh, and it still pains him when it's cold. He has five daggers sheathed in his belt and one in his boot. He can handle a sword as easily with his left hand as his right." Jonas watched the group, hoping they got his message. "He's a protector. Makes poor decisions when others are in danger."

Ilías had paid the price for Rey's hotheaded decision to protect Silla on the Road of Bones. Jonas's stomach burned, but he ignored it. There was only forward. Only vengeance. "He uses the terrain to his benefit."

"Nothing we can do about that," muttered one of the Klaernar warriors.

"Oh, but there is," said Jonas, surveying the man. "If we control the terrain, we control the battle."

"What do you propose?" asked another.

"I'm not certain yet," admitted Jonas. The men protested. "Not *yet*," repeated Jonas, irritation stirring. "If you're eager for battle, then by all means rush to Kalasgarde and meet the same fate as the Wolf Feeders." The men quieted at that. "This will *not* be rushed. It will be carefully planned and executed. I know how he thinks, how he fights, how he takes his gods damned róa. He does not know I'm working with you. That gives us an edge . . . the element of surprise."

Jonas watched the group carefully. "For now, we train. We plan. We wait. Sooner or later, he'll make a mistake. And when he does, we'll be ready."

CHAPTER 66

Kalasgarde

Silla had thought the naps she'd taken on the Bloodaxe Crew's wagon were the most splendid of her life. But the nap she had in the aftermath of the mother serpent's attack topped them all. After returning to the shield-home, she'd instantly tumbled into bed. And now, Silla woke wondering if it had all been a dream.

But the man seated beside the bed quickly told her otherwise.

Silla looked down to where his large hand enveloped her own. She stared at their twined fingers—his warm brown, hers pale as moonlight—zagging against one another like the weavings of a tapestry.

"You're holding my hand." His eyes flew to hers, relief melting through his face. "How long did I sleep?" Silla glanced around the shield-home for clues, but with animal hides covering the windows, it was difficult to tell the time of day.

"Through the morning and all day," Rey replied, scrubbing a hand over his face. "Dusk is upon us." He studied her as though searching for any sign of illness.

"Have you been sitting here all this time?" she asked cautiously.

"I wanted to be the first thing you saw when you woke."

Silla blinked at him, trying to read his weary expression. "The chasm?" she asked.

"Closed by Vig and the others."

"And the hatchlings?"

Rey closed his eyes, a muscle in his jaw feathering. "Many escaped. Vig's been working tirelessly, sending missives all through the north. They're already building more traps—" He shook his head. "Right now, it is not our concern. The serpents are in capable hands."

Silla stared at him, trying to read his expression. Jaw tight, free hand gripping the chair's arm. The look in his eyes—it was dark and inscrutable. And at that moment, his words under the northern lights came back to her.

I've let this go too far.

She'd had the strangest dream—Rey apologizing, begging for a second chance. But now that she was fully awake, she knew it was only that—a dream. With each passing breath, the warmth in Silla's chest morphed into irritation. He looked just as confused as he had under the northern lights.

Rey scrubbed a hand through his beard, looking utterly unsettled, and Silla braced herself for what he'd say.

"Kristjan was . . . life," said Rey.

Shock rippled through her, but she held herself quiet.

"He was happiness. Like you, really. He saw the best in people." Rey stared at the wall behind her, but he was *talking,* and she blinked furiously to clear her blurring eyes. "Kristjan was a light in my life. The person who reminded me to live. He dragged me fishing, took me to the mead hall, made me play countless games of dice with him. He kept me from the dark places my mind can sometimes go."

Rey dragged a hand along his jaw. "It occurs to me only now that perhaps it was not only for my benefit. Perhaps Kristjan needed *me* to keep him from the darkness as well. And in that, I failed spectacularly."

Silla squeezed his hand, wishing she could say something to take his pain away. But she knew the words didn't exist.

Rey continued. "I thought our parents' deaths would not affect him the way they did me, since he was so young, but I was wrong. Skjöld leaves were known about these parts to uplift the mood. I'm certain he took them to lighten his heart, but he . . . saw them. Our parents. I'm told he had visions, would speak to them. And then nothing could stop him from taking more."

Her chest constricted, an ache filling her. "You cannot blame yourself, Rey—"

"I should have come home," he interrupted. "I am his brother, his only living kin, save for Harpa. I should have watched after him—should have seen the signs and been able to help him. Instead, I was off with Kraki, fighting and drinking and trying to make a name for myself."

"You trusted Harpa to watch over him," she guessed.

"Yes," he said through gritted teeth.

She smoothed her hand up his forearm, trying to loosen the knotted muscles.

"And when I buried Kristjan, I vowed I would never set foot in this place ever again."

It all made sense—Rey's departure, the animosity between him and Harpa. Surely he could not think Kristjan's death his own fault?

"Have you ever spoken to her of it?" she asked with apprehension.

"Yesterday," he said roughly. "I understand better than I did before. Yet . . . I do not know if I can find forgiveness."

Silla's brows drew together as she pondered his words. "I do not understand the workings of Harpa's mind. What I do know is that the people we love wield the sharpest blades of all." Her gaze grew unfocused. "My father lied to me for years. He fed me those poisonous leaves. It was a shameful thing not to tell me the truth." She took a deep breath, then let it out slowly. "I do not like what he did, but I forgive him for it. And it has been such a weight lifted from my shoulders."

Rey was silent but listening.

"I do not know if Harpa deserves forgiveness. But I know *you* deserve it, Rey. Anger is such a burden to carry. There is peace to be found in surrendering it." She took a deep breath. "His death is not yours to own."

His hand tensed against hers. "He would not have taken them had I been here."

Silla's thumb slid along the back of Rey's hand. "How greedy of you to take his death wholly."

Rey released a sharp breath. "You use my own words against me."

"They were wise words, spoken by a wise man," she said softly. "I will not let you carry Kristjan's death on your shoulders. I did not know him, but I know he loved you, and he would not wish for you to carry it. Kristjan would want you to be happy."

Silla counted her breaths as she waited for Rey's response. He hesitated. But then his strong, sturdy hand squeezed hers gently.

Torchlight caught on Rey's textured curls, on his curving cheekbone. His jaw flexed. "I want you," he said in a bare whisper. "More than air. More than anything in this gods damned world, Silla."

She blinked back tears.

He took a deep breath. "You make me happy, Sunshine—so damned happy it terrifies me. But the thought of losing you terrifies me even more. I want this. I want you . . . *us*." Rey paused. "And if you never want to be Eisa, it won't change how I feel. If you wish to rest, I will shield you from harm. If you want to fight, I will draw my sword beside you. If you want a hundred chickens, I will build you a hen-fortress."

The tears were now gathering. She hadn't known she needed to hear this. But now that he'd said it, a great weight lifted from her shoulders.

"But you've seen what I'm like—a temperamental man who is set in his ways." Shame was written all over his face. "If you no longer trust me with your heart, I'll respect your wishes."

He stared at her, and at last she realized what she saw. Gone was Axe Eyes, stern and tough and completely untouchable. This was Reynir Galtung, open and willing and hopeful.

"I'm scared," admitted Silla, her angry bravado from earlier melting away. She let him see everything she felt—how scared she was of being hurt. Of being used and discarded. "Perhaps," she whispered, then faltered. *Bravery, Silla,* she urged herself.

"Perhaps we can be frightened together."

Rey seemed not to breathe for a moment, caught somewhere between fear and disbelief. Silla wanted to kiss the worry from his brow, wanted to rub the tension from his shoulders. Pulling on his hand, Silla drew him onto the bed. As she made space for him, he rolled onto his side, staring deep into her eyes.

"I am not . . . words are not . . ." Rey shook his head, then said in a rush, "I will say the wrong thing often. I'm not a sensitive man. I'll trample you without meaning to," he admitted. "But know that I will fight for you, Silla. For you, I will work to be softer, to be a better man."

"No," she blurted, the blood draining from her face. *I thought you could make me into a good man,* Jonas had once told her. "I like you as you are. And I," she said, "am also sorry. For pushing too hard about your brother."

"Incredible woman." Rey studied her carefully. "I've watched you grow and change, and I know there are mountains yet for you to climb. But I want to be by your side when you conquer them. And I will relish watching others underestimate you."

"Relish?" she asked in amusement.

"I know better than to doubt you, my brave girl," said Rey. "You never were afraid of me, were you?"

"I feared you," she whispered. "But only until I understood the kind of man you are. An honorable man. A protector."

His knuckles stroked along her cheek, lips quirking into an almost-smile. "How do you feel?" he asked.

"I feel"—Silla bit down on her lip—"cold."

A furrow between his brows. Concern in his eyes. Rey leaned closer, placing the back of his hand to her forehead.

Silla looked up at him through her lashes, hand encircling his wrist and gently pulling it downward. His expression heated as she placed his hand over her breast.

"Will you warm me up, Galtung?"

CHAPTER 67

Silla held her breath as understanding settled into Rey's face.
"You nearly died," he protested.
"A weekly occurrence."
"Are you certain?" he asked, with heartbreaking concern.
Slowly, she nodded. "More certain than anything."
Rey's jaw hardened, his voice dropping an octave lower. "Where?" The change in his voice sent a shiver of awareness through her. "*Where* are you cold?"
"Under the blankets."
"That won't do," he said. Standing, he moved to the foot of the bed. With torturous slowness, he pulled the furs down inch by inch to reveal her tunic-clad form. When he reached her bare legs, Rey drew in a sharp breath. Silla wriggled under the intimate weight of his look.
A warm, dry palm cradled her heel, lifting it up for his inspection. Her tunic inched higher on her thighs, but Rey's dark eyes were trained on her foot.
"Here?" He dragged a knuckle along her arch.
Goosebumps rushed straight up her spine, and Silla shifted once more. Slowly, she shook her head.
"Hmm," said Rey, a sound so erotic it throbbed through her body. Slowly, his palm slid up her calf and stroked her inner knee. Silla gasped. "Ahh," he said. "Here?"
The back of her knee seemed to have a pulse, sending a symphony of vibrations straight through her body. Good gods, the man had turned her into a puddle just by touching her knee. Silla opened

her mouth to protest, but Rey had settled on his knees at the base of the bed, dragging his nose along the sensitive skin behind her knee. As she felt the wet heat of his mouth, a low sound came from the back of his throat.

"Rey," she whimpered, her head lolling against the pillow. It was almost too much, almost unbearable . . .

But his hand now slid up her thigh, lightning sparking through her. As the bristles of Rey's beard scraped along the sensitive skin of her inner thigh, her body jolted, but he eased the roughness with the slide of his tongue. "Here?" he asked, rubbing his nose back and forth, back and forth.

"Mmph," she replied, squirming.

"Words, Sunshine," said Rey, lifting his head. "Use them."

She glared at his smug expression, then gave in. "Higher."

With maddening slowness, Rey pulled her tunic upward, baring her to him. "Beautiful," he murmured, sliding an index finger through her. "*This* is where you're cold." He placed the finger in his mouth, then drew it out slowly. "It shall require my fullest attention."

And with that, he settled onto the mattress, hooking her thighs over his shoulders and locking them tight. He hovered for a moment, then licked a searing path through her center. Back bowing off the mattress, Silla moaned. But Rey's grip only tightened, holding her in place.

"You'll be the death of *me*!" she exclaimed, as he drew the small bud into his mouth and sucked. As his tongue flicked against her, Silla's muscles clamped down. Empty, she was empty, she needed . . .

As though he'd read her mind, Rey slid a finger inside her. They both groaned. He found a rhythm at once, a second finger soon joining the first.

"Need . . ." Her head flopped to the side as pleasure built and contracted through her body. Mindlessly, her fingers slid into his hair, tugging his curls as he worked with single-minded determination. Her pleasure reached a sudden unexpected peak, crashing over her like a rogue wave. Silla cried out, arching up, but the man held her in place with unrelenting strength. On and on the pressure swelled and broke through her until her vision darkened and she lay limp in the furs.

Rey kissed his way up her stomach, pausing to work her tunic all the way off, then laving her breasts with affection until lust stirred deep in her stomach. *Again?* she thought. But with this man, she imagined there would be no such thing as enough.

And Rey could already read her body. His kisses moved lower, back to the apex of her thighs.

"Wait," she said, fingers sliding into his curls and pulling him up.

"I need you mindless, Silla," he said, dark eyes molten with heat. "I need you trembling. I need to hear you begging."

"You," was all she could manage, pulling at him. Gods, the man had reduced her to single words. She tried again. "Inside me!"

"Not yet, Silla," he growled, resisting her pull. "Not until you give me one more."

With a cry of frustration, she fell back into the furs, submitting to the torturous movement of his tongue. She was sensitive at first, writhing under his maddening touch, but a low ember of need flared gradually hotter, brighter, until wildfire was coursing through her veins.

She wasn't even sure what she was saying. *Yes,* and *more,* and *you you you*.

The wildfire exploded through her body, burning her up to nothing but feeling. Pleasure raged through her, her body clasping down on his fingers, those glorious, talented fingers stroking the place that had detonated it all, and now prolonged it.

At last, she lay utterly lax, darkness gathering on the edges of her vision. He settled beside her, and she rolled to face him.

"What are you doing to me?" she panted.

"Everything I've wanted to for so long," he replied. Her vision shimmered back, revealing his intense, dark eyes.

"What else? Tell me what else."

"I want to fuck you," he said, the words so raw and brutal, she felt them in her toes. "I want to take my time with you. Make you scream, and curse and forget your own name." He leaned closer, whispering in her ear. "I want to make you forget anyone who came before me."

Silla whimpered, staring at him. "That. *Please.*" Her hand slid down his body, running over the hardness straining against his breeches. "I want *you.* I ache for you . . ."

Before she understood what was happening, Silla was on her back looking up at Rey. His elbows on either side of her head, he caged her in with his large body, nose so close it nearly touched hers. "You want me, Sunshine? You're sure about that?"

Dumbstruck, she nodded.

A sharp exhale vibrated along her skin. "Silla." His lips came to hers. "I've been yours for a long time."

She reached for him, but Rey was already yanking his tunic over his head and working his belt loose. He tugged down his breeches, and Silla swallowed, feeling a moment of apprehension. Because Reynir Galtung was large *everywhere.*

"Are you certain?" he asked, eyes dark.

She nodded, watching the knot at his throat bob with a hard swallow. And as she looked at him, warmth pulsed through her with every beat of her heart. There was weight to this moment, and as they stared at each other, understanding passed between them. This was more than their bodies coming together. This was a promise. *Frightened together.* Because together, they were stronger.

"Contraceptive herbs?" Silla whispered.

"Vig." Rey cleared his throat, casting an irritated look to the rafters. "He brought them as a joke."

"Good," she said, dragging his gaze back to hers.

They stared for another wordless moment, and then his lips met hers. The exquisite weight of him sank onto her, and Silla shifted to accommodate him. Hands sliding everywhere, she felt the solid strength of this man, and marveled at the way he held her—as though she was his entire world. The warmth in her chest expanded until it felt as though there was not enough space to hold what she felt.

"So beautiful," he whispered into her hair. "Your hair, and your lips and your heart." And he was all around her, cradling her, holding her, devouring her. And yet it wasn't enough.

Reaching down, she took him in hand, guiding him to where she needed him.

"Silla," Rey gritted out, burying his face in her neck, holding himself at her entrance.

She had a moment of trepidation, but then he was nudging into her with slow, gentle pressure. Her breath caught in her throat, body instinctively clamping down. It was far from her first time, but with him, it felt as though it was.

"Breathe," he whispered, drawing back and cupping her jaw.

His thumb stroked gently along her cheekbone, lips sliding against hers. Slowly, gradually, she relaxed, letting her body stretch around him, and he pushed a little deeper.

A low whimper escaped her.

"You can take it, Sunshine."

"You've always had such unfounded confidence in me," she breathed.

"Not unfounded," he muttered, coaxing her to accept another inch. "Gods," he groaned, eyelids fluttering. "I could die like this and be happy."

"Don't you dare," she warned, fingers digging into his biceps.

Rey was so patient as he waited for Silla's body to accept him, yet from the pulse throbbing in his neck, she knew he was not as calm as he outwardly appeared. At last he'd eased fully inside her.

"You see?" he asked. "Not unfounded."

Full, she'd never been so full before, yet when he began to move, it felt incredible. He didn't tear his eyes from hers, and she felt him studying her, watching for any sign of discomfort.

She pushed up on her elbows, and together, they looked down at where their bodies met. Rey cursed softly under his breath, his pace growing uneven for a few thrusts. But he soon found a rhythm, slow and languorous, as though he wanted to prolong it as much as possible. And with each measured stroke of him, she melted a little more, softened a little more, surrendered a little more. Silla wrapped her legs around his hips, welcoming him deeper, and he reached a place that made her vision tilt. Nails biting into his arms, she threw her head back, squeezing her eyes shut.

"Look at me," came Rey's low voice.

Her eyes flew open. Locked onto his. And she couldn't look away—he looked at her like she was the answer to every question, like he was the most fortunate man in the world. The man made her feel like a goddess.

Pleasure was building, low and deep-rooted, growing taller and greater with every heartbeat. Rey reached down, adjusting her hips and pressing his thumb firmly against her.

"Oh, gods!" she cried out. Stars shimmered in her vision, everything building, tightening, around him. Close, she was so close . . .

"Sunshine," he murmured. Looking down at her with burning intensity, Rey quickened his tempo in a series of short, quick thrusts that had her gasping and wrenching at the blankets. But he was relentless, and he kept pumping, kept watching her.

The warmth in her chest—the warmth for *him*—reached a breaking point. It exploded, shimmering to each corner of her body.

And through it all, Silla didn't once look away.

Watching her expression while she fell apart around him nearly sent Rey over the edge. Gritting his teeth, he dug for every last ounce of his willpower, holding himself still as she shuddered around him. It felt like an eternity until her body grew limp, and he eased himself out of her. Burying his face in her hair, he inhaled deeply.

"Rey, you . . ."

"Give me a minute," he growled, trying to master himself. He breathed in slowly, then released it through his teeth.

"But you didn't . . ."

He lifted his head, taking her in. Hair disheveled, eyes glazed with pleasure.

"I'm not done," he said roughly. "I warned you, Silla. I plan to take my time."

"Three!" she exclaimed. "Three is plenty! Three is wonderful!"

A slow smile curved his lips. "We can do better."

He watched as her eyes darkened—as her gaze slid down his body. "Better, you say?"

Rey reached for her hips, desperate for the feel of her, but Silla surprised him by pushing him onto his back and climbing on top. "Perhaps," she said, a smile teasing her lips, "like this?"

In smooth motion, he lifted her, settling her over his aching cock. Bracing her hands on his chest, she slowly slid down his shaft. They groaned in unison.

He stared up at her, so beautiful and soft, emotion swelling deep in his chest. This woman—who was soft and so lovely yet would defend his life with the fierceness of a grimwolf—had pulled his defenses down, piece by piece. He should feel exposed and vulnerable, yet to Rey's surprise, surrendering to her had brought nothing but relief.

Silla began slow, sinuous rhythms, her dark curly hair spilling over her shoulders.

"So lovely," Rey murmured, pulling a stray tendril taut, then letting it spring up.

"You're lovely, too," she whispered, pushing harder on his chest, lifting her hips higher and taking him even deeper. "So selfless. So willing to sacrifice for others. I shall show you each day just how lovely I think you are."

Her words were sunshine, pure and bright and shining into each dark crevice in his chest. Rey's hand slid along her spine, up the back of her neck, grabbing a handful of hair and pulling her down. The friction of her breasts against his chest was maddening, her moans even more so. Rey's other hand gripped her hip, holding her still as he pumped into her.

"You feel what you do to me?" he whispered, tugging her hair to crane her neck upward. He needed to look deep into her eyes as his hips surged up. "This is yours. For you, Sunshine."

Her only reply was a whimper. Based on the fluttering of her intimate muscles, he knew she would soon find pleasure once more.

"You see?" His fingers dug into her hip, holding her down as his thrusts grew frantic. "You thought you couldn't have another."

Heat was sizzling through him, gathering at the base of his spine, and Rey knew he wouldn't be able to hold off this time. Slowly, he pulled her hair backward, forcing her spine to arch like a bowstring as he continued to thrust. She was utterly at his mercy, her trust absolute, and he didn't take this lightly. He cherished her trust. Vowed to protect it with all of his heart. Moaning, she pushed her hips back to meet him.

"But I know better."

His carnal words set her off. The arch of her back deepened, her walls squeezed him so tight his vision flared white. And then he was over the edge with her. His thrusts grew erratic, his body seared with heat and longing and emotion and pure, utter pleasure, coiling tight before exploding outward. And then he was groaning, clutching at her, spilling inside her.

He felt disconnected from his body. Distantly, he felt her collapse onto him, the two of them heaving for breath in a tangle of sweat-slicked limbs and thundering hearts.

Rey felt as though he'd been shattered and reassembled. Different, but better. Because now she was there, tucked into his heart.

Minutes passed before either could speak. Silla folded her arms on his chest, propping her chin up. Watched him with a lazy smile.

"Well," she said. "I'm quite warmed through now."

Rey chuckled. Brushed a stray tendril of her hair back and smiled. Because with this woman by his side, he might never feel cold again.

CHAPTER 68

"Hands to the skies or I'll widen your smile," snarled Vig, pressing his blade to Silla's neck.

Swinging herself free from Vig's grip, Silla couldn't help but think of the woman who had ingrained these movements into her. A pang of sadness filled her, and Silla hoped with all her heart Hekla fared well in Istré—that someday soon they'd be reunited.

With a sigh, Silla forced her focus back to the present and probed inwardly. There was no trace of the curious fizzing sensation, nor of the incredible strength she'd had while pushing Rey across the field.

"Shy, your Blade Breaker skill is," muttered Vig, withdrawing his blade.

Silla shook out her limbs, glancing toward Harpa's home. Ice spirits flitted between the offering plates, shouldering one another and baring their teeth, while the wooden wind chimes clunked together. But there was still no sign of Harpa. According to Rey, she was weaving—had been, it seemed, since Silla's encounter with the serpent.

"She searches for answers to the events on Jökull," he'd said, as though that explained anything at all. Silla knew Harpa pulled threads from the weavings of the world, but she did not understand the process one bit. She only knew the tapestries Harpa wove contained the stories of the past, present, and future.

She turned back to Vig and Runný with a sigh. Silla had to admit, they were amusing to train with, but thus far, the results were rather lackluster.

Vig surveyed the woods, and Silla knew he searched for any sign of the serpent hatchlings. He'd been busy since the attack, sending word of the serpents across Nordur and south. Rey's trap had caught three hatchlings, leading to the construction of a dozen more, which were set near local waterways. A total of eight hatchlings had been caught and killed, raising hopes that it was only a matter of time before the rest were as well. But there were still more than four dozen serpents out there somewhere.

As for the mother serpent, she had not yet breached the ice lake's surface. But no one believed for a moment she'd succumbed to her wound. One theory was that the mother had accessed Jökull's lake through underground tunnels. If this were true, it would explain how she'd gotten into the lake without breaking the ice. But it would also mean the mother could potentially slither free without notice.

Runný hopped down from the fence post she'd been perched upon and sauntered toward Silla and Vig. "Perhaps she hasn't burned her Blade Breaker strength yet because you, dear brother, are about as frightening as a seal pup."

"Baby seals are a *delight*," declared Silla.

Vig waggled his black eyebrows. "Are you calling me delightful?"

Silla shrugged.

"Careful, Silla, or you'll get me killed. Axe Eyes over there is sharpening his blades."

They glanced at the stump. Legs spread wide, Rey made a slow, threatening sweep of the whetstone along the edge of his blade while glaring at Vig.

"He's *always* sharpening his blades," she said, trying to disguise her flush with a casual wave of her hand.

"Not enough, it seems," said Vig, examining Rey. "Which blade did he use to trim his beard?"

"What do you mean?" asked Silla, her voice going high.

Vig scoffed. "He's . . . uneven. Looks as though he hacked at it with a longsword."

"It's perfectly even," Silla said defensively. "It was my first time! I need more practice—"

"Galtung let you tend his beard?" Vig bent double, his laughter bouncing off the nearby stable. As he straightened, he wiped tears from his eyes. "And Horse? I suppose you're responsible for the moonflowers braided into her mane?"

"Horse *loves* her braids."

"Hmm. And Galtung?"

"They're . . . growing on him." Silla folded her arms over her chest. "With Harpa busy, I've had nothing but time, Vig."

"Focus!" exclaimed Runný, dragging them back to their original conversation. "The point is, Silla, you don't truly believe Vig will do you harm. And thus, your Blade Breaker skill remains shy. Perhaps you need to feel *true* fear."

Vig scowled at his sister. "What is your grand suggestion, Runný?"

Runný cocked an eyebrow, then vanished from sight.

"Runný," warned Silla, searching for any sign of the Shadow Hound. The compacted snow made it impossible to track footprints. But the crunch of ice had Silla swinging around.

"Ow!" Vig doubled over, rubbing his ribs.

"Runný, don't you dare—" A grazing touch against the back of Silla's neck had her whirling. "Stop this—" A stone kicked across the ground came to a stop on the side of Silla's boot. Her breath quickened, and she backed away. One step, two steps . . .

"Boo," whispered Runný at the moment Silla's back bumped into her.

Silla's heart stopped dead for a second. "You wretched—" She broke off at the telltale cold sizzle of her primed galdur. Silla expressed, herding her light into place until she looked upon the sword in all its glory—a slender, tapered blade of cold fire, the hilt clasped in her right hand.

A pair of ice spirits flitted over, then hovered above Silla's shoulder and watched with interest.

"Well, it's not what I'd intended," murmured Runný, once again visible. Her dark eyes were focused on the blade. "But it *is* a beautiful weapon."

"What can it cut?" asked Vig, sidling up beside Silla.

"Everything I've tried so far," replied Silla, her breath frosting in the air with tiny, shimmering crystals. The ice spirits zipped into the crystals, dancing and frosting the air further.

"Human heads, if I do recall," muttered Vig, backing away cautiously.

Runný rolled the chopping stump across the yard and set it on end. "Shall we play a game?"

Over the course of the next hour, Silla sliced through anything deemed worthless on Harpa's property—logs, discarded nails and horseshoes, an iron axe that was half rusted away. The ice spirits clustered, watching intently and zipping in excited loops. Silla cut through a series of stones, each larger than the last, until finally she cut through a boulder half her size.

"Well," said Runný, hands on her hips as she examined the smooth, frosted surface of the split boulder. "I suppose it's quite sharp."

With a ragged breath, Silla let the sword shatter into glittering frost. She glanced at the cabin from under frozen eyelashes, but it was quiet and still.

"Galtung tells me the pair of you shall return to Kopa when your training is done," said Runný.

Silla nodded, biting her lip. "I'm told Jarl Hakon has the means to help me rescue my sister."

Vig put his hands on his hips. "Has he told you of Hakon?"

"He told me Hakon is a Volsik supporter, but to survive under Urkan rule, he's had to do regretful things."

Vig and Runný shared a knowing look.

"Galtung knows him best," said Vig slowly. "His father and Jarl Hakon were good friends before the war. I know he spent many summers in Kopa with Jarl Hakon and his son Eyvind. Though"—he cast a wary look toward Rey—"there are whispers of corruption."

"You must surround yourself with people you trust," said Runný. She hauled her black braids over a shoulder, twisting their silver cuffs nervously. "I was considering . . ." She glanced at her brother, then quickly back at Silla. "It is merely an idea. Perhaps a foolish one at that." Runný rolled onto her toes, then back down. "I thought of accompanying you and Galtung to Kopa."

The color seemed to drain from Vig's face, but to Silla's surprise, he remained silent.

"You'll need protection on the road," continued Runný. "Allies in Kopa. And I hope"—Runný cleared her throat—"I hope you know you can trust me."

This was the part where a good leader would have wise words, or perhaps oaths to be sworn. But Silla threw her arms around a startled Runný and hugged her tightly.

"You'll need to get used to me, Runný," Silla said brightly, pulling back. "I do love to hug. Of course we'd love that."

"Yes, well . . . good." Runný's eyes met her brother's. "Vig?"

His eyes were shining as he beamed at her. "Yes."

"Yes?"

"Yes. You should go." Vig sent a wistful look at the skies. "Too long have I begrudged others for the choices they've made. I will work on . . . not doing this."

Runný's lips pressed together, but her smile shone through. "I am pleased to hear it, brother."

Vig cleared his throat. "Yes, well . . . *I* must stay in the north. Someone must lead the hunt for the hatchlings and ensure that the chasm remains closed."

"I worry for you," Runný said with a swallow.

Vig sent her a wry smile. "Don't worry for me. I am far more fierce than a seal pup, as you well know." And with that, he wrapped a bare, burly arm around Runný's neck and pulled her into a headlock.

"Arse!" she exclaimed, driving an elbow into his ribs.

Silla watched the siblings spar for a moment, a pang of jealousy filling her. What would it have been like to grow up with a sister? She would never know. The Urkans had robbed her of the chance.

Biting down on her back teeth, Silla turned and approached the cabin. The frost on her hair and lashes had melted, and she brushed the moisture away. Rey watched her, setting his blade aside. "You're getting better at weaving the sword," he said with a quirk of his full lips. At the memory of what those lips had done this morning, Silla fought the urge to crawl into his lap and wrap herself around him.

"I can read your wicked thoughts, woman," Rey said in a low voice, his lips tipping into an almost-smile. He was doing this more and more, each time drawing a full, shining grin from Silla.

Rey's large hand wrapped around her own, pulling her between his spread legs. The way he was seated, she could look straight into his eyes without craning her neck. Rey smoothed a silver-cuffed braid from her face, then cupped her jaw. "And to think I ever thought you sweet," he murmured, drawing her in for a soft, and entirely too brief, kiss.

"And I thought you murderous," she whispered, chasing his lips as he pulled back and recapturing them with her own.

He made a sound of amusement. "I *am* murderous," he managed, drawing back for a bare second before his arms tightened around her back, pressing her firmly to him.

"Runný will join us on our return to Kopa," said Silla, glancing over her shoulder. The siblings were still sparring, Runný leaping onto Vig's back and wrapping her arm around his neck.

"Good," said Rey. "Runný is a good ally to have by our side. There are others who've expressed similar sentiments." His gaze softened to something like pride. "Your presence has already brought a sense of change to these parts."

Silla let out an uncomfortable breath. "I've done nothing but act as serpent bait."

Rey stood, pulling her into him. Sighing, Silla wrapped her arms around his middle, resting her chin on his chest and gazing up at him.

"You know what I used to call you behind your back?" she asked sweetly.

He quirked a brow.

"A walking boulder." Silla snickered.

"Do you wish to know what I called you?" he asked with a glint in his eye.

Silla nodded.

"A pain in my arse."

She dissolved into laughter, squeezing him only tighter. "I bet you did."

CHAPTER 69

The door to Harpa's cabin rasped against the frame as it shut behind Silla. It was cold inside. The fire had burned low, casting dim light onto the bundles of herbs and jars strewn about the room. Like the fire, Rykka slept, her charcoal arms hugging a coal as though it were a pillow. Silla had expected silence but was met with the eerie sound of weight stones thunking together as Harpa wove at her loom.

A life for a life, slid through her mind, and Silla tried to shake it off.

Rey had warned her not to disturb Harpa, but there were too many things Silla needed to ask her. At the forefront of her mind were the visions she'd had of King Hrolf. In the aftermath of the serpent's attack, she and Rey had rushed to rally the Galdra. But now Silla wondered if there was a connection between the visions and the serpents.

She also wanted to ask about the mind-to-mind connection she had with Saga. What kind of Galdra could communicate like this? If she could trust in this voice, could this be the breakthrough needed to free Saga from Askaborg? Days already, Silla had spent waiting, while Harpa worked at her loom. Enough was enough.

A candle lit in the far back corner illuminated Harpa's outline. The dancing light caught an array of coils sprung loose from her braid. As Silla glanced at Harpa, a tendril of worry slid through her. Her shoulders looked thin against her dress, and her shawl was in a rumpled heap behind her. How long had Harpa been at this?

"Harpa?" she whispered, but her mentor continued through her motions.

A life for a life.

Silla shook her head, trying to jostle the unnerving words from her mind. The air was even cooler in this corner, sending a shiver down Silla's spine. Suddenly, the flame shuddered violently. A strange, ominous feeling pulled at her, familiar, yet not. A dream she'd forgotten, a memory she could not recall . . .

Placing a hand on Harpa's thin shoulders, Silla stepped in front of her mentor and gasped. Harpa's eyes were opened wide, but not milky white as she'd seen them before. Instead, they were utterly black.

"Harpa?" asked Silla, louder this time. She gave her shoulder a gentle shake. But Harpa would not be roused from this trance.

Silla turned to the loom and gasped.

Harpa had made considerable progress, and now four figures could clearly be discerned, all woven in threads of midnight black. A serpent. A dragon. A tree. A queen.

A life for a life.

The words curled through her mind and slid through her veins. As Silla stared, the tapestry pulled at her. Nearer, she must get nearer. And with each passing heartbeat, the urge to reach out and slide her fingers along those threads pumped through her body with more vigor, until it rivaled her most vicious cravings for the skjöld leaves.

Silla felt her mind grow slack. Her hand lifting. She touched the tapestry.

And the world went black.

Stone walls. Dank air. And an ancient, familiar feel clinging to the air. She'd been here before.

The room was still crumbling, the alcoves still dark. But instinct told Silla this differed from the before. Instead of the old, solemn king, a woman paced frantically before her.

Clad in lébrynja armor emblazoned with a Spiral Stave, the woman had dark hair woven into dozens of small braids merging into a single, thick one at her crown. As Silla took her in, she realized the woman was in degrees of disarray—blood splattered along her neck and chin, the forearm of her armor slashed open to reveal a bandage.

Silla moved closer. Due to the dim lighting and the charcoal war paint smeared across the woman's face, it was difficult to make out her features.

"Cannot," muttered the woman, pausing to chew on a fingernail. It was a surprisingly childlike gesture, one that stirred recognition. Silla's gaze flew to the woman's eyes, examining them through the dark paint. Blue. Tilted upward.

"Mama?" Silla whispered, love and grief warring within her. As expected, Svalla Volsik was unaware of her daughter's presence. But Silla rushed forward all the same, throwing her arms around the woman. They slipped through her body as though she were made of air.

"Mama!" Silla sobbed, trying in vain to touch the woman.

"Must keep them safe," said Svalla, completing another lap of the room.

Silla urged herself to stay calm. But this was her mother, the woman who'd birthed her. Until this moment, Silla hadn't realized how badly she wanted to know the look of her mother—to map each corner of her face and discover each thing that looked like her.

In Silla's last vision, Svalla had been a young child. But now she was a grown woman. A queen. Silla's gaze dropped to the base of Svalla's neck; a red scar stretched across it. She'd survived the unimaginable—an attempt on her life by her own grandfather. What was Svalla doing in this of all rooms?

"Cannot," Svalla said through gritted teeth. She paused, turning to the shelves carved into the wall. "But what else is there?"

Silla's brows drew together, apprehension knotting her gut. Svalla stepped to the wall, selecting the white-hilted dagger from a shelf and holding the tip to her palm.

"No," whispered Silla, watching numbly.

Svalla let out a shaky breath. Slashed the blade through her hand. Drew symbols in blood on the wall.

"Dark One, I call to you," said Svalla in a resigned voice.

A cold, dark feeling spread outward from the pit of Silla's stomach. Her mother was . . . no. This could not be. This was all wrong.

The candles guttered, the temperature in the room plunging. This time, Silla knew what to expect—an inky shadow blotting up the wall, blurry lines coalescing into the eerie shape of a man crowned with spikes.

"Little Svalla," said the voice, disembodied and chilling, "you're all grown up."

Svalla straightened her spine, facing the shadowy form on the wall. "Do you still thirst for my soul?"

The shadow crackled, then settled, its hunger filling the air. "What is it you want, Svalla?" it asked.

"Protection," she replied, voice wavering. "For them."

"Ahh," said the shadow, tilting its head to the side. "For them."

"My daughters are innocent," said Svalla. "They cannot—" She broke off in a sob. "They cannot die. The Urkans have taken Sunnavík and will soon breach the castle walls. Askaborg will fall. Please, my daughters—they must be protected."

Bone-chilling laughter rattled Silla's skull. "You know the way, Svalla. There is a cost."

"A life for a life," said Svalla dully.

"You agree then?"

Svalla bit her lip, eyes shining with unshed tears. She nodded.

"Say the words, Svalla."

Silla's mother took a deep breath. "Yes. A life for a life."

The candles flared with writhing black flames, power surging through the room and spiraling through Silla's body. She could feel change occurring—bonds broken and reforged, the natural threadwork of the world snapped through and rearranged into something new. And something inside Silla thrummed like the strings of an instrument plucked. The surging power ebbed, candles flashing orange once more.

"It is done," said the voice from everywhere and nowhere all at once.

Svalla exhaled, lifting the white-hilted dagger with trembling hands. "Now?" she asked, the tip of the blade hovering over the pulsing point in her throat. "Here? With this dagger?"

The shadow laughed, a broken and jagged sound. "Oh, Svalla. Let this be a lesson in bargaining. Specificity is of the utmost importance."

"What?" sputtered Svalla.

"I don't want your life, Svalla," said the thing. "You'll be dead soon enough on your own."

Svalla's blue eyes widened.

And then Silla tipped forward into a void of nothingness.

"Wake up!"

Pain lashed across her cheek. Silla blinked, then blinked again. Flickering candlelight. The smells of woodsmoke and herbs. Two forms struggling over her.

"Release me, Reynir!" That was Harpa's voice.

"You will *not* strike her again." Rey.

She stared up as his form gradually came into focus. Candlelight played across his cheekbone, and the edge of his lips were pulled down.

"What . . . happened . . ." Silla tried to sit up, but everything swayed.

"Easy now." Rey's warm palm slid to the small of her back, helping her up.

"Tell me precisely what happened, girl," snapped Harpa. "You disturbed my weavings, then had a . . . a fit."

"Trilla is seeking attention once more," muttered Rykka, a twist of smoke rising from her black hair as she flitted over Harpa's shoulder. "Already she's brought those ice demons to your yard, and now this."

"The voice," whispered Silla. "It would not stop. The voice . . ."

"What voice?" asked Rey.

"The voice. It beckoned me. It pulled me to the tapestry, and when I touched it . . ." Silla's eyes flew to Harpa's. "A life for a life."

Harpa's eyes went wide. "What did you say?"

"A life for a life," repeated Silla. "Thrice now I've heard this in strange visions. The first during my Cohesion Rite."

Harpa's gaze grew distant. "I could not find you that day. I thought nothing of it, but . . ." Harpa scowled at Silla. "Where did you go? What did you see?"

"Hrolf," said Silla. "I saw King Hrolf. Who is the Dark One?"

Harpa recoiled, pressing a hand to her forehead. Slowly, she turned to the tapestry. "Serpent, dragon, tree, queen."

"Does anyone care to explain?" grumbled Rey.

"Myrkur," gasped Rykka. "Myrkur is the Dark One." An ember snapped from within the smoke spirit, and she zipped to the hearthfire, then hid beneath a blackened log.

"The god of chaos?" asked Rey, skeptically.

"I must hear everything," said Harpa sharply. "Start from the beginning."

And so Silla did, beginning with the Cohesion Rite, when she'd watched King Hrolf summon the Dark One, and proceeding with his attempt to murder his own granddaughter. Reluctantly, she ended with her own mother's bargain gone awry.

"A life for a life," murmured Harpa. "Those were King Hrolf's last words, though none understood the meaning."

Harpa watched Silla with keen amber eyes. "In all my time spent with her, Queen Svalla never spoke of it. The attempt on her life was kept silent," she said, a note of bitterness in her voice. "It was decided best to preserve the public's support of the Volsiks. But it was well known that Princess Svalla suffered from night terrors well into adulthood. The servants spoke of her screams. Of the words she cried out in sleep. *A life for a life.*"

Silla's stomach knotted as she thought of her mother pacing in that room. What fear Svalla must have felt facing down the Dark One. But she'd done it for Eisa. For Saga. So that her daughters might live.

"What does it mean?" asked Rey, frustrated.

"It means," said Harpa slowly, "Myrkur has been threading darkness into the Volsik line for generations, and we were none the wiser."

"Who?" asked Silla, dumbstruck. "If He didn't want my mother's life, who then did He want?"

Harpa observed her. "That, I do not know. Perhaps you. Perhaps your sister." She turned to the tapestry. "But I fear—" She paused for a moment. "The serpent, we understand. But the rest . . ."

"Could the tree reside in the Western Woods?" asked Rey, and Silla knew he thought of the Bloodaxe Crew in Istré battling unknown foes in those woods. Fear tightened her stomach as she thought of Sigrún, Hekla, and Gunnar.

Harpa pushed to her feet and paced the cabin. "Serpent and dragon are Myrkur's children. But the tree and the queen. These I do not know."

Rey massaged his temples.

Harpa turned to them, her face lined with worry. "The long winters," she said. "Myrkur's creatures entering through cracks in the world. And the Volsiks—the protectors of Íseldur—captive and forced into hiding. A Volsik must always sit on the throne. To bring balance. To counter Myrkur's chaos."

A premonitory chill ran down Silla's spine.

"It begins with frost and ends with fire," said Harpa, taking a deep breath. "Rökkur is coming. The twilight of our world."

CHAPTER 70

Sunnavík

After countless weeks of preparation, Princess Yrsa's birthday feast was upon them at last. Tugging at her gloves, Saga made her way through the corridors, bracing herself for the night to come. First came the drumbeats; next, the scent of roasted boar. And when the archway leading to the hearth hall came into view, hundreds of voices met her ears. Saga's feet faltered, her heart hurtling inside her chest.

Yrsa's birthday feast was the biggest celebration in Askaborg until Ursir's Slumber. Much to her chagrin, Saga knew everything down to the last exquisite detail. The royal skald had been industriously preparing tales to recite, and a special mead made with heather honey was fermenting just for this occasion. Drums were fastened with fresh cowhide, the boars fattened, and an abundance of fruit and wine shipped in from the Southern Continent. Hundreds of nobles from all over Íseldur would gather to celebrate the nation's princess's coming of age.

Saga drew a calming breath, reminding herself she just needed to get through the night. There was the daymeal tomorrow. The drugged róa. And when Saga woke, she'd be safely stowed away on Rurik's ship.

The thought was utterly terrifying. Five years it had been since she'd left the castle. Her insides kicked and fought at the very idea. But there was no other choice. Askaborg, her refuge, her ally, was no longer safe for Saga.

The eyes are afraid, but the hands are doing, came Rurik's rough, accented voice in her mind. The words eased the tension in her stomach—helped her draw in a deep breath. But so many things could go wrong, and Saga could not stop the questions from shoving into her mind. What if someone saw them? What if they couldn't sneak the seeds into Saga's drink? What if the weather turned rogue and the ship crashed ashore?

"Forward," grumbled Thorir, placing his hand on the bare skin of her nape. Flinching, Saga hastened to escape the press of his palm.

Each of Thorir's heavy steps seemed a reminder from Signe. *Comply, darling, or you'll be crushed.*

"Tell me, Thorir, has Signe asked you to select each morsel of food for my plate tonight?" she asked bitterly. Already, Signe had chosen Saga's attire, down to the slippers she wore and the style of her hair.

He grunted. "You can eat what you like. But Her Highness says you're to sit by your betrothed and show him affection."

Saga couldn't help but cringe. And so the farce of marriage began. All the more reason for her to leave as soon as possible.

"You're to *smile* and make conversation." He paused, then continued. "And there are men at each doorway who'll deny your exit. So I'm afraid, Lady Saga, you'll stay in the hall as long as the queen wishes."

Saga's insides twisted. *Deny your exit.* It was enough to make her heart race and her palms grow sweaty. "My, Thorir," she snapped. "That is quite the list the queen has entrusted you with. I hope you don't strain a muscle trying to remember it all."

"Might I?" the big man asked.

A sly smile curved Saga's lips. He made it too easy. "Oh, yes, Thorir. Over-contemplation can give one a frightening headache." She lowered her voice. "A hearty drink of ale should help."

He hummed, lost in thought.

The swell of voices grew louder as they reached the hall's doorway. Saga took a deep breath, smoothed her stiff skirts, and adjusted the fox fur clasped around her shoulders.

"On," grunted Thorir, nudging her forward.

The hearth hall was barely recognizable. Feasting tables had been arranged end to end, bathed in a buttery glow of torchlight, and fires roared in the enormous twin hearths.

Though the feast fare had not yet been served, the tables were laid with overflowing bowls of fruit, pine boughs, and beeswax candles set in the finest silver holders. An ursine grunt drew Saga's attention to the fighting ring, where Ivar's pet bears tore into a fresh carcass. Gilded collars encircled their necks, lengthy chains securing them to the floor while allowing them enough space to charge any onlookers who got too near. A crowd had gathered around, young warriors jostling and daring one another to step forward.

Thorir's hand on her nape seemed to burn as he directed Saga through the crushing crowd toward the high table. Thankfully, the crowd parted readily for them. Saga supposed that was one benefit of having a half troll as a minder.

She eyed a crew of warriors, their chests bare and painted with Urkan symbols. A pair sat in the front, enormous drums between their spread thighs, and pounded a rhythmic beat with mallets. Others in the back sang, moving as though in a trance.

"Saga, darling," cooed a familiar voice from behind her.

Saga paused, apprehension knotting her gut, but she forced a smile on her face. Just one night, and she'd be free of Signe. With a steadying breath, Saga turned to face the queen.

"Your Highness," she murmured, dipping into a curtsy. Signe wore an ivory gown that made her complexion and white-blond hair all the more pale. But her ice-blue eyes were as harsh as the crown of claws sitting upon her head.

Signe's lips pursed as her eyes swept down Saga's body. "You're wearing appropriate attire."

"You have excellent taste," Saga said stiffly.

Signe sipped from her goblet, a crimson drip clinging to the corner of her mouth. "Enjoy the feast, darling," said Signe. "I'm told it will be a night to remember."

And with that ominous statement, the queen wandered off.

Saga quickly found the deepest corner of the hall, a cup of mead in hand. Scowling, she watched the festivities. Thorir had joined Magnus for a sizable horn of ale, and as the Heart Eater's smug gaze met her own, Saga looked away.

Gods, but she wanted to leave this space. One more night. She only needed to make it through tonight. Irritated, she sipped her mead.

"Is not wise to *pit* tonight." The deep voice reverberated through her body, settling deep in her stomach.

"It would make it far more tolerable," replied Saga, turning to find Rurik tugging at his sleeves. Sipping her mead, she allowed her eyes to slide along Rurik's body. His tailored Zagadkian jacket stretched across the expanse of his shoulders, the fine-spun tunic beneath doing little to hide the muscular cut of his body.

Saga edged nearer to the courtyard's doorway, which was propped open to allow fresh air to flow in. And as Rurik strode wolfishly toward her, she was grateful indeed for the flow of cool air.

Bracing a forearm on the wall, Rurik leaned toward her, placing his mouth near her ear. "All things are set for tomorrow," he whispered. A shiver vibrated through her. "But you must be careful, Saga. Careful and clever."

"Perhaps it is not wise for you to be seen with me," said Saga, glancing over his shoulder.

"Perhaps I cannot help myself." His green eyes seemed too bright, his smile too sharp, and Saga wondered if he, too, was nervous about the next day.

Her eyes narrowed. "Perhaps it is *you* who requires supervision."

"Is no *perhaps* about this, Saga." He chuckled, then drank deeply from his horn of ale. "The problem is, Winterwing"—he leaned closer—"I want what I want. And always I get it." He stared at her for a moment, nostrils flaring. Eyes falling shut, Rurik rolled his neck in agitation.

"Are you feeling well?" she asked in a low voice. "You seem . . . restless."

The intensity of his gaze made Saga squirm. But after a long moment, he blinked, and his eyes softened. "I miss my country," Rurik said, unexpectedly. "I am eager to plant my feet on Zagadkian soil."

Swallowing, Saga nodded.

"Lord Rurik," came a female voice, and Saga's eyes flitted to Yrsa, standing behind Rurik.

As always, Yrsa was perfection. She was clad in a vibrant red gown, and glittering candlelight caught the golden embroidery along the bodice. Glacial pearls—woven into her braids and dripping from her ears—accented her gown.

Rurik turned, bowing to the princess. An acidic pang pierced Saga's stomach as Yrsa's eyes raked over him in appreciation.

"You are looking beautiful as a sunrise," he said jovially. "May your mead never spill, your stockings never tear, and your bathhouse never be haunted by evil spirits."

Yrsa's gaze locked onto Saga's, and they both burst into laughter. "Evil bathhouse spirits?" Saga asked, shaking her head.

Rurik nodded gravely. "Is considered worst form of bad fortune in Zagadka."

"I should think so," murmured Yrsa, cheeks pink. "I thank you for the sentiment, Lord Rurik. I was hoping to have a word with you." Her eyes darted back to Saga's for a moment. "*Alone.*"

"Of course," he replied.

Saga dipped her brow in deference to Yrsa. "Enjoy the feast, Lord Rurik," she murmured, making her way to the high table.

CHAPTER 71

The feast was a revolting show of excess, nobles and royalty gorging themselves while pretending the rest of the kingdom did not starve. After a lengthy five courses, countless boisterous toasts in honor of Princess Yrsa, one failed proposal met with laughter, and the skald's tedious recital, Ivar's bear minders finally stepped forward. After they unchained the bears, the king's beloved pets were led out of the hearth hall.

And then the brawling began.

The youngest warriors went first, grappling and wrestling across the stone floor until the loser fell unconscious or relented and rang the iron bell. Sólas exchanged hands, fresh horns of ale were passed around, and the crowd grew louder. Prince Bjorn stepped into the ring, the crowd giving a dutifully raucous cheer as he faced a trembling boy his own age. It was no surprise when the lanky prince was crowned the victor, yet the crowd cheered as though name alone had not earned this victory.

At last, it was time for the main event. At this point, the long tables had been abandoned as onlookers crowded around the fighting circle. Anticipation rattled the room.

Saga watched dutifully, fighting her craving for another calming cup of mead. Rurik was right: She needed to be careful and clever. With a deep breath, she joined the crowd at the ring. Her gaze caught Rurik's across the pit, his green eyes gleaming as he shifted in agitation.

King Ivar raised a hand, and the clamor of voices hushed. "And now, a tradition long held by our ancestors," he boomed. "The princess has selected a champion to fight for her tonight."

Whispers floated up from the crowd, but Saga's stomach tensed.

The king continued. "As most of you know, it is considered both an honor and a trial to be named the princess's champion."

Saga's eyes flicked to Rurik, but he did not meet her gaze. A slow, tingling chill spread through her limbs.

"This warrior must battle through the most elite among us in order to claim victory. No mercy shall be granted. But if the champion succeeds, they will do what few have. Not only will they bestow great glory upon Princess Yrsa, but they will be honored in the best way we Urkans know how." Ivar turned to his daughter, eyes gleaming. "What say you, Princess Yrsa? Have you selected a champion?"

Bile rose up Saga's throat as realization dawned. *No . . .*

"Yes, Father." Yrsa smiled serenely. "I've selected Lord Kassandr Rurik from the Kingdom of Zagadka as my champion."

The king's eyes hardened at that, whispers of disapproval whipping through the crowd.

Rurik, you muttonhead, was all Saga could think. *How is this either careful or clever?*

"It's a dishonor to all the capable warriors in this room," muttered the man beside Saga. "A foreigner fighting for *our* princess?"

Beside Rurik, Rovgolod gesticulated wildly, the rest of the Druzhina scowling in disapproval. But even from across the fighting ring, Saga sensed the strange restless energy coursing through Rurik as he unfastened his surcoat.

"Are you certain of your choice, Yrsa?" asked King Ivar with a frown. "This is most unusual."

But the princess, like Rurik, seemed set on her choice. "I am certain." Color bloomed on Yrsa's cheeks as she watched Rurik peel off his coat.

Saga felt sick. These contests were notoriously violent—in fact, Saga had never once witnessed a champion claim glory. Instead, they were rendered bedridden for weeks with broken bones and head wounds, if they survived at all. And from the indignation quickly gathering in the crowd, and the knowing look shared between King Ivar and Magnus Heart Eater, Saga's nausea worsened. They would never allow him to win.

All it would take was a misplaced blade, a sleight of hand, and Rurik would be dispatched. The thought of harm befalling him was enough to make the blood rush in her ears. But as it dawned on Saga that Rurik's downfall would leave her stranded, the very room tilted on its axis.

"The champion is to face five rounds!" called out the king. "Single combat within the boundaries of the circle. No armor, no weapons brought in by combatants. The battle continues until the bell is rung or one can no longer fight."

Rurik grabbed the hem of his undertunic and yanked it over his head, then tossed it carelessly at Rov. Torchlight in the hall caught the powerful surface of his broad chest, hard muscle toughened from years spent in rings just like this. Saga tried to remind herself that this was what he did. But another part of her argued at his brash, impulsive nature. What if he'd agreed to something more than he could handle? What if he didn't walk out of that pit?

Leaping into the fighting circle, bare-chested and barefoot, Rurik prowled back and forth like a caged animal. Saga's heartbeat reached a frantic pace.

"The first opponent," bellowed King Ivar, "is Sida Spearhand!"

The crowd cheered, parting for a pale, raven-haired woman stripped down to her fighting leathers. After securing her long, ropy braids at her crown, Sida shook Rurik's extended hand. The opponents backed to their respective corners of the fighting ring. Sólas passed hands. Ale was refreshed. The king raised his goblet, and the crowd hushed.

"Skál," said Ivar.

And with that, it began.

Rurik and Sida circled the ring, two fierce predators studying each other. Though he had the advantage of height and brute strength, Sida's movements flowed like liquid. The crowd soon grew agitated, shouting their displeasure.

"Enough playing about!" bellowed the man beside Saga.

With serpentine speed, Sida drove forward, attacking with a flurry of rapid kicks and punches. Rurik ducked low to evade a striking fist but took a heavy blow to the ribs. Sida took advantage of his momentary startle, launching a powerful kick aimed at his head.

Rurik bobbed backward in the nick of time, righting himself by some miracle. And with that, equilibrium was reestablished. The warriors began circling once more, and the crowd groaned.

"Get him, Sida!" roared a warrior nearby.

Saga studied Sida. The woman's movements were powerful yet agile, and clearly, she had no fear of attacking first. And as Rurik and Sida made yet another circle around the pit, Saga understood.

Sida wasn't meant to win this battle. She was meant to wear Rurik down.

Soon, both warriors were covered in a sheen of sweat as a cycle played out. Sida lashed out. Rurik retreated. And the dance began anew. It seemed Rurik was trying the same tactic she'd witnessed at the garrison hall—angering Sida into attacking. But Sida was too smooth—too even-tempered to fall for such tricks. What Rurik needed was to break the sequence. Break her concentration. Lure her into a trap and go for the match-ending blow.

Before Saga could decide what to do with this knowledge, a gasp tore from her throat. Sida's foot had struck out, Rurik's response a heartbeat too slow. The kick landed with a sickening thud to the ribs and sent him flying back. Sida charged with new intensity, and an upward jab snapped Rurik's head back. Stumbling, Rurik cradled his ribs, spitting blood.

Saga's hand flew to her mouth. His ribs, the ones he'd told her were healing.

The crowd went wild, tasting a hint of victory.

"Some champion he is," snarled a man to Saga's left. "Sida'll take him out in the first round."

Heart thundering, Saga thought of Ana, of how she'd taken her pain. Could she do this for Rurik to give him an edge? But she'd never been able to find the thread of Rurik's thoughts, which meant there was nothing for her to latch onto. It seemed he'd have to win this match on his own.

Saga grew light-headed as Sida advanced, then launched a fierce kick at Rurik.

The match-ending blow.

And it was, only Rurik was not on the receiving end. Throwing himself down, Rurik rolled under Sida's leaping body. His leg swept up. Caught Sida's shins. She crashed toward the floor, an arm thrown out.

The wet crack of bone filled the air as Sida's arm broke her fall, her skull colliding with the floor soon after.

The hall fell silent.

Saga held her breath, counted the heartbeats. But Sida did not stand.

"The victor is Rurik," yelled the king, and the crowd jeered.

Rurik straightened as though his ribs did not pain him in the least. Their eyes met, and Saga stared in disbelief. Had he—did he just—

And in that moment, Saga realized she'd underestimated Kassandr Rurik. Those first successful blows landed by Sida had been nothing but a ruse for Rurik to study her moves. And after enough time had passed, he'd brought her back to that very same sequence and used it against her.

It seemed the lout was smarter than he looked.

Saga felt herself smiling. Shook her head slowly. And decided a nerve-calming cup of mead was most definitely in order.

Rurik quickly proved himself to be a man of many tricks. His moves changed with each opponent, felling one within seconds of starting the match, and another after three-quarters of an hour. He used the crowd to his advantage, deliberately provoking his opponents to anger and using chaos to disorient them.

But Rurik was only a man, and as the matches continued, his energy flagged. He took more hits—to his jaw, his ribs, his knee—

leaving him gritting his teeth. Yet he persisted. The crowd grew more agitated with each passing brawl, their thirst for his blood only growing.

"Victory to Rurik," barked the king after the fourth match, irritation etched in his face. The crowd spat curses, howling with impatience. More sólas were passed around, warriors begging to be let into the ring.

Rov wiped sweat from Rurik's brow, talking in rapid Zagadkian.

"Fifth round," bellowed King Ivar, "will be fought by Thorir the Giant."

The crowd whipped into a drunken frenzy, parting as Thorir ambled forward. Saga swallowed heavily. Of course it would be Thorir—undefeated in this very ring. She took in the warrior—arms thick as tree trunks, shoulders as broad as a grizzly bear's. He was larger and far stronger than Rurik. Saga had seen the man fight in this ring before, had seen his lethal punch crush more than a few skulls. Thorir could take a blow like none other. And while the man might be dim-witted in conversation, he was anything but in battle. This ring was his domain.

Another wave of nausea hit Saga as she watched Rurik shake out his shoulders. The Zagadkian's eyes had a mad sort of gleam to them. Thorir stepped into the ring, a linen undertunic stretched around his broad barrel chest.

The crowd quieted, every eye in the hall fixed on the two men in the ring.

"At last they are sending the red troll man," said Rurik, flashing a sharp smile.

Thorir growled.

The king raised his goblet. "Skál!" he bellowed.

And with that, combat began. Thorir did not waste time before charging at Rurik. But the Zagadkian deftly twisted away. Again, Thorir launched at him, and again, Rurik evaded.

"Fight, you coward," snarled Thorir, swinging hard.

But Rurik rolled beneath Thorir's lethal fist, springing nimbly into a crouch.

"Little frightened girl," taunted Thorir. "Fight like a man."

"Perhaps I wish to fight like a girl," said Rurik jovially, beginning to circle once more. "Is not the insult you are thinking."

The crowd jeered, shouting for blood, while Saga's gloved hands held each other in a vise-like grip. She couldn't watch, and yet she couldn't look away.

"Come here," growled Thorir.

"You come *here*," was Rurik's maddening reply.

"Coward!"

"Careful, troll man," said Rurik merrily. "It seems you are growing angry."

Thorir stormed at Rurik with the force of a raging bull, sending the crowd into a frenzy and Saga's heart into a free fall. Thorir swung. In a move so swift she nearly missed it, Rurik rolled beneath Thorir's fist, bounding to his feet behind the large man and launching onto his back.

Rurik's hands closed around Thorir's thick neck, his thighs clasped around the larger man's middle. Thorir swung madly around, an odd whistle escaping from his increasingly reddening face. But Rurik's throttling grip was relentless, and he held tight through Thorir's thrashing movements.

The crowd howled with rage, but hope kindled in Saga's chest. Perhaps he could do it . . . Rurik could end this now and walk away unharmed, and tomorrow would proceed as planned.

She should have known it wouldn't be so easy.

Thorir fell back, slamming Rurik into the ground with the full force of his weight. The sickening slap of Rurik's bare back against the stone floor made Saga's lungs seize. The two warriors lay—Thorir the Giant, gasping desperately atop Kassandr Rurik, who blinked dazedly. But then Thorir twisted over, driving a fist downward.

Rurik rolled, missing the lethal blow by scarce inches.

As his fist connected with the stone floor, Thorir bellowed in pain. But then Rurik was up behind him, pulling and twisting Thorir's tunic. With a swift yank, the Zagadkian had Thorir's arms wrenched behind him, restrained in the twisted fabric of his tunic.

"You see, large man, strength is not all that matters. What I lack in height, I make up for in wit." And then Rurik delivered a stinging slap across Thorir's face. "Is why I take honor in . . . how do you say . . . fighting like girl."

Gods, but the crowd hated that. Their outrage was only matched by Thorir's own. Face redder than his own hair, he let out a deafening cry. And then, the sharp rip of fabric filled the air as Thorir tore free from his tunic.

Rurik backed away, spitting blood as he reassessed. But Saga saw what he tried to hide—a tightness in his jaw, a furrow as he inhaled. He had not risen from the floor uninjured.

Backed by the crowd's energy, Thorir advanced with new intensity. Rurik dodged one blow, then another. But the third hit him on the left side of his ribs and sent him reeling back. He recovered quickly, a fist striking out and connecting with Thorir's jaw with a loud crack.

It was then that Saga saw a flash of silver from the corner of her eye.

"Blade!" she shrieked above the roaring crowd.

Rurik twisted with preternatural speed, one hand lashing out. The room grew very still as they took in the sight.

The hilt of a dagger was clasped in Kassandr Rurik's hand, the blade an inch from his face.

Saga blinked, then blinked again. Had he truly just snatched the blade from thin air? It was impossible . . .

"Ah, ah," chided Rurik, casting the blade aside. It landed on the floor of the fighting ring with a loud clang. "No weapons."

"'Twas not me," said Thorir, eyes darting to the dagger, then back to Rurik.

"You know what this means, troll man?" A wicked grin spread across Rurik's face. "It means they think you cannot best me. They know you need favors."

The crowd booed at that, and Saga glanced about for any new sign of a dagger.

Rurik spread his arms wide. "Come now, Thorir. *I* will grant you favor. Give you one-second head start."

Thorir's lip curled, his meaty hands balling into fists. "I don't need a favor to finish you off, kunta. I'll gladly knock the teeth from your pretty face. See how smart your tongue is when you can't find it among all the pieces of your shattered skull."

The crowd howled at that, their hope rallying as the two men began circling once more. But in a surprisingly quick motion, Thorir scooped up the dagger as he passed it.

Rurik's eyes narrowed. "This is the honor you speak of, big troll man?"

"A benefit of fighting here for many long years," snarled Thorir, "is *I* understand the rules. No blade can be brought into the ring by a combatant. But this"—he brandished the blade—"was not brought by either of us."

Saga's heart flew to her throat. Already the blade was slashing through the air as Thorir launched himself at Rurik. All honor and discipline flew out the window. The two warriors grappled, Rurik holding the blade off with sheer will. But his left side was weakened, blood trickling from the corner of his mouth, and Thorir would always win when it came to pure strength.

Rurik pounded at Thorir's forearm, trying to loosen the blade. But the bigger man surprised him with an overhand attack, the blade slashing through Rurik's right shoulder.

With a shout of pain, Rurik threw his head forward, his forehead striking Thorir's nose with a wet smack, then flipped over his opponent in an inhuman leap. Before Saga could consider the impossibility of such a feat, Rurik landed behind Thorir and delivered a swift kick to the back of his knees. With a shove from Rurik, Thorir landed with a bone-shaking thud.

The crowd quieted as the enormous man lay motionless. A pair of warriors rushed in and rolled him onto his back. Protruding from his stomach was the hilt of the dagger, Thorir's hand still wrapped around it.

A hush fell over the room.

Thorir's blue eyes were wide in his ruddy face, blood trickling around the hilt of the dagger. Rurik snatched the bell and placed it in the large man's hand. And then, the unthinkable happened.

Thorir the Giant rang the bell.

"Healer!" Ivar's gruff voice cut through the silence. He stepped into the ring, then knelt before Thorir and handed him a cup of ale. "You fought well, Giant. And you will live to fight well again. Let the healer take out the blade."

As King Ivar righted himself, his stern gaze met Rurik's. He was silent a long moment, chewing on words he did not wish to speak. "And you, Champion," he said with a decided note of bitterness, "you, too, have fought well." His voice rose as he turned to the crowd. "It has been many long years since a champion has been crowned in this circle. Let us raise a cup to the warriors who fought valiantly on this night."

Cups and horns and goblets were raised around the room.

Ivar turned back to Rurik. "And let us raise a cup to our new champion, Lord Kassandr Rurik, from the Kingdom of Zagadka!"

The crowd muttered in displeasure, parting in the back corner as a pair of warriors pushed through.

"And tonight, Lord Rurik," continued the king, "we have a special ceremony. One in honor of the princess's coming of age. Tonight, you will partake in an honor experienced by but a handful of my highest esteemed."

Saga's brows drew together as she examined the small chest carried between the two warriors. They descended the steps into the fighting ring and flipped the lid open.

King Ivar reached in. Pulled the item out for all to see.

Saga recoiled, her heart surging into her throat. Gasping for breath, she staggered out of the crowd. The room was spinning; the walls were closing in on her.

Out! her mind screamed. *Escape. Exits. Must get out!*

Her hands met a stone wall. Groped along it. Her gaze bounced from exit to exit, Thorir's words echoing in her mind.

There are men at each doorway who'll deny your exit.

Breathe, she could not breathe. But then she saw it—the doorway leading to the outdoor courtyard. By some miracle, it was unmanned. She moved along the wall, trying to block out all sound. But as Saga staggered through the doorway and into the cool night air, the king's voice chased her.

"Tonight, Lord Rurik, you will have the honor of drinking from King Kjartan's skull."

CHAPTER 72

The rich smolder of the hall extinguished to a dark, moonless night. Raindrops spattered Saga's bare collarbones, and her slippered feet stumbled along the flagstones. All of it felt strangely distant. Another girl in another time, fleeing from the monstrous people who'd killed her father and now drank from his skull.

The skies spun above, the fog of her breath twisting upward and catching in the castle's light.

Laughter and cheers filtered through the door, sliding like knives into her skin. His skull. They were drinking from her *father's skull*, like some sort of game. As though sitting on his throne and dismantling his country stone by stone was not enough, they needed to degrade him further through this abhorrent ritual.

A burn crept up her throat, but she could not give in. Could not cry.

Away! her mind screamed. *Escape.* She needed to get as far away as possible from that room, those people, this castle, this life.

Distantly, she remembered she would be leaving tomorrow. She needed only to make it through the daymeal. But the sight of her father's skull had pushed her beyond reasoning. She could not think, could not wrangle her turbulent mind. The light dimmed... or was smothered by darkness as her feet carried her deeper, farther from those people. Saga found herself in a land of dark, twisted shadows and cool, crisp rain.

Rain.

The realization brought reality crashing down upon her. Rain. She was outdoors.

Punished, came the voice. *You deserve to be punished.*

"No," whispered Saga, whirling. The cold was sharp and piercing, her surroundings so dark. But the fist of panic squeezed around her ribs, and her heart was careening out of control.

You should have been strung on a pillar next to them.

"Please," she wheezed, trying to draw breath, trying desperately to shove that voice, that day from her mind. Saga spun, trying to get her bearings, but in the darkness, it all looked the same.

Lost, jeered her mind. *Trapped. No escape.*

Saga gasped for breath, phantom ravens crying out in her skull. *Punished,* they seemed to say, with each ragged caw torn from their beaks. She stuffed her fingers into her ears, trying to smother it, trying to stop it . . .

Do you know how many men I lost to your vile father? he whispered, the ghost of his fingers skimming down her face.

"No," Saga whimpered, placing a hand out to steady herself, but there was nothing to hold. She stumbled to the ground, gagging on the scent of hay and horse and the blacksmith's forge . . .

Saga curled into a ball, her fingers clasped over her ears. "Please," she begged.

"Please," she'd begged that day as the tall, black-clad forms had closed in on her in the stables. "Let me pass."

But they'd blocked her path, coarse male laughter sending a violent shiver through her. Trapped. No exit. Surrounded. The leader stepped forward, a ruthless man Saga had deftly avoided at all costs. But there was no avoiding him now, not backed into the blacksmith's corner of the stables . . .

He was tall and broad, with a ragged beard braided in the Urkan style, and his dark eyes grazed from the tips of her toes to the top of her head. Magnus Heart Eater had smiled as he crowded his much larger frame against Saga's. But as her back had hit the timber walls of the stables, true panic had filled her.

She'd flinched as Magnus's calloused fingers dragged along her cheek. "Do you know how many men I lost to your vile father?" His hand had tightened into a bruising grip around her jaw, wrenching it up. "Look at me when I speak to you!" he shouted. "Halfdan lost three brothers. Frode, his own twin." He spat, and she recoiled as it landed on her cheek.

Magnus had brought his face down to hers, so close she could feel his hot breath on her skin—could smell the ale he'd been drinking. "You should be dead," he whispered. "You deserve to be dead, like your family. You should have been strung on a pillar next to them."

She'd felt the telltale prickle of tears and squeezed her eyes shut to ward them off. Saga hadn't cried since the day they'd butchered her family, and she'd vowed never to cry again. But Magnus's grip had tightened. "Look at me, you worthless pet!" Saga forced her eyes open, staring at his cold gaze. "Pet," Magnus repeated, an ugly smile spreading wide. "You are a pet. But it seems you've forgotten. Prancing around the castle. Riding with the princess. Wearing the finery of nobles. You look at us all as though you think you're better—"

"I don't—"

"Quiet!" he barked, so loud it vibrated through her bones. "You will listen until I've spoken my piece! You've forgotten your place."

The men behind him grunted in agreement.

"We cannot ruin your virtue without raising the king's ire," grunted Magnus. "But there are other ways to remind you, Volsik. You're property. Owned. Nothing but a worthless pet."

Magnus had turned and nodded at the men over his shoulder. Wordlessly, they closed in on her. Saga opened her mouth to scream, but a hand was clamped over it.

The rest was a blur. She was dragged toward the forge fire, her stomach pressed flat over a worktable. The scent of hot iron met her nose. And then Magnus approached, the brand used to mark horses held in his hand. Saga was reduced to a screaming, bucking, fighting thing, overwhelmed by pure terror.

But it was all for naught. Her palms were shoved to the table, the red-hot brand pressed into the back of her hand. Pain screamed through her, unlike anything she'd ever felt. It became her world, this blistering-hot agony. Sparks showered through her vision, the scent of burnt flesh filling her senses. And then they repeated it on the other hand.

The pain never ended, not even after the men left her collapsed over the blacksmith's table. It burned, and devoured and consumed the frail barriers she'd managed to construct over the past twelve years. Saga was left empty, boneless and trembling.

And then she'd done the most unforgivable thing of all.

Saga had cried.

Liquid heat slid down her cheeks, mingling with the sharp cold of the rain. Saga reached up only to recall she wore gloves. She tugged them off, and the smooth tips of her fingers skimmed along her cheeks, feeling the tears she hadn't allowed to fall for five long years.

But now, she found herself as defenseless as that day. Broken and shaking and shrouded in darkness. The tears came with a vengeance, and Saga relented. She *let* herself cry—for what they'd done to her that day and for the slow withdrawal from life that had followed. Magnus might have branded her a pet, but Saga had been the one to cage herself away.

She cried for the girl she'd been before that day—for the thin flame of hope she'd sheltered inside herself. Back then, there had been happiness. There had been hope that she could make a life for herself amid the wreckage of her past.

Instead, she'd only joined that wreckage. A broken, bitter thing, locking herself in the dark until she could wither away.

When at last her eyes ran dry, Saga was completely wrung out.

She lifted her head from her knees, surprised to find her panic had subsided for the time being. Blinking in the darkness, she tried to regain her bearings. Saga could make out the rugged outline of hedges before her, the tinkle of water just behind her.

And suddenly, Saga knew where she was. Slowly, she pushed to her feet. Turned on the pathway. Her gown was sodden, goosebumps prickling her skin. But as her gaze fell upon Sunnvald's fountain, she felt nothing but warmth. Faint light from the upper floors of Askaborg caught the water bursting from Sunnvald's palms, giving it a magical glow.

"Hello," she murmured to the god of her ancestors—to this light she'd unknowingly stumbled upon in the darkness. Tucked away in the royal gardens, this was the statue that Signe had tried in vain to have removed. Little did she know it was Galdra-made and unbreakable. Each stonemason who'd examined it—each warrior who'd tried to take it down with brute force—had eventually relented.

Tilting her head back, Saga closed her eyes and breathed in this moment. Cool rain landed on her face, sliding along her skin. It was the first time in five years she'd felt rain on her skin.

And it felt like freedom.

Holding her gloveless hands up to the skies, Saga smiled as the rain tickled her skin and collected in tiny pools in her palms.

Her heart rate accelerated, and she longed to retreat to the castle's safety, but she rooted herself in place. Just a little longer. A few more moments of freedom, and then she'd relent.

Movement in her periphery caught her gaze, and she turned, her eyes meeting Rurik's. "Beautiful," he murmured, seeming surprised to find he'd said it aloud.

But the sight of that skull filled her mind's eye, and Saga whirled away. *Retreat,* her insides begged. *Get to your chambers.*

"I did not drink from it," he said, edging into her vision. "You must know I would never do this." He raked a hand through his hair, sending water droplets flying. Rurik had pulled on his tunic, the rain making it cling and highlighting every muscle. "You are outside," he said wondrously.

You must find safety, came the intrusive thought. Saga flinched, trying to refocus. "Are you hurt?" she asked, searching Rurik's face.

"Only this." He tugged at the neck of his tunic, revealing a bandage wrapped around his shoulder. "And my ribs hate me rather much."

A relieved breath rushed out of her. "I tried to be careful," Saga whispered, hugging herself. "But I could not stay, not when they—"

Flee! screamed her mind, preventing her from finishing the sentence. *Get to safety!* A dull ring sounded in her ears, her heart racing. The telltale signs of her panic were returning. Outside, she was *outside,* and this thing she carried could not be vanquished in one night. Her breaths grew fast and shallow as the ring grew louder.

"Breathe," soothed Rurik, approaching slowly. "Is only us, Winterwing. Close your eyes if you must."

But the tightness constricted, like a serpent squeezing the air from her lungs. One hand curved around her shoulder, the other sliding around her waist to her lower back. And then she was pulled against Rurik's powerful body, his hand running up the bumps of her spine as he whispered Zagadkian into her hair. The rapid thump of his heart was so easy to focus on, the heat of his body easing the damp chill.

In a minute, she could breathe, but Saga did not let him go. Instead, she slid her arms around his waist, pressing herself tighter to him. Beneath her, his muscles clenched. "Why did you fight for Yrsa?" she asked dazedly. "Why did you not refuse?"

A sound from his throat rumbled through her sternum and settled in the deepest part of her stomach. "My mouth agreed before my mind was thinking," he replied. "Is problem of mine. I have told you before."

"Impulsive," she murmured, turning her face into the wet wool of his tunic. Saga brushed her nose back and forth against the soft fabric, breathing the scent of him in—blood-tinged sweat and that fresh, herbal thing unique to him. A tremor ran through him, and Saga felt him grip her fur stole as if trying to steady himself. "A brash man."

"Sometimes, they are calling me worse," he admitted. "Sometimes they call me a *chudovishche*.'" His body was so rigid, his muscles straining beneath her touch.

Inside to safety, begged her mind. But Saga wasn't ready for this to end. Tonight she'd found her freedom, and it was both empowering and drugging. She wanted more. Wanted to choose something for herself.

"I'm discovering lately I have a brash streak of my own," Saga whispered, massaging the tense, corded muscles of his back. Relaxing against her, Rurik seemed almost to purr. "There are things I've

---

*Beast.

been told I cannot have, but I want them all the same." She lifted her face up to meet his gaze, studying each rain droplet clinging to his eyelashes.

"Saga," said Rurik, and it seemed a cross between a plea and a warning.

Saga pressed onto the tips of her toes and brushed her lips against his. The touch sent a jolt through her, circling in an endless current. As he kissed her back, a sound came from deep inside him—a pleased noise that made Saga's blood pump hotter. Rurik's arms tightened, pulling her closer, but there was a feel of restrained tension in his body, as though he was holding himself back.

"Long have I craved more of your touch," he said, drawing back. His green eyes had a wild look to them, the hand fisting her wool dress trembling. But Rurik's words sank into her skin, heating her until she melted against him. "*That one*, my heart told to me. *I want that one.*"

Saga's lips parted as she stared at him.

"You are so rare." Rurik's nose dragged along her temple as he breathed her in. "With fierce fire." His teeth scraped gently along her jaw. "And sharp wit." His tongue laved the sensitive skin of her neck. "And so . . . exquisite." He lifted his head, and she saw the hunger in his eyes. "Like you, I know how it feels to be wrongly understood."

Saga's brows furrowed as she pondered his words, but any questions dissolved into pure, shimmering heat as Rurik's lips crashed into hers. This was no slow, restrained thing. This was hunger and need, unbridled passion.

One large hand cupped the nape of her neck, holding her firmly in place as his teeth and tongue clashed with hers. Any thoughts of fleeing the gardens were shattered by his touch. All memories of the feast were demolished by his taste. The kiss was so mind-numbingly hot, Saga imagined the cool rain was now steaming off her skin. His hold grew bruising, the five points of his fingers digging into her skin.

Perhaps some women would be frightened by this man's intensity, but Saga only leaned into him—this man who had become the only solid thing in her life. This man who had reminded her what it meant to be spontaneous—that to reap rewards, one must take risks.

And this felt like the biggest risk of all.

But she could not think of the future, not when he held her as though she was the cause and the cure to his madness. Despite the roughness of his touch, she could sense Rurik's barely leashed restraint, and she wondered what would happen if it snapped through. Saga's hands grew bold, sliding down his neck, along the bunching muscles of his shoulders, then back up his chest. Her hand came to rest over his heart, thundering as though it were trying to break free. The realization that Rurik was as undone as she made her wild with need.

"Saga." Rurik's voice sounded scratched as he pulled away from her lips. He dragged his mouth along the column of her throat, breathing her in. "*Kak ya mogu otpustit' tebya?**"

"What does that mean?" Her lips parted in surprise as she tilted her neck, gasping as his lips trailed rough kisses downward, his close-shorn beard scratching along the sensitive skin of her neck.

"It means you are beautiful."

"*You're* beautiful," she breathed, the scrape of his teeth and the slide of his tongue along her neck stealing all thought from her mind. Hands skimming back into his hair, she held him there, wanting this moment to extend forever.

"*Mozhet ya ne otpushchu tebya,*†" he said in a low growl that reverberated through her entire body.

"And that?" Her chest rose and fell with each rapid breath.

"It means I wish to do wicked things to you."

His hand gripped her waist, and his mouth dipped to hers. This kiss was desperate—urgent, anguished. Rurik kissed her as if he were starving—as if he knew this was the last taste he'd get.

She already mourned its ending—this kiss that had transformed

---

*How can I let you go?
†Maybe I won't let you go.

her soul. How could she go back to a time before she knew what it felt like to be kissed like this—like she was the sun and moons and all the stars in his sky?

But gradually the voice clawed its way back. *You fool!* it screamed, setting her heart hurtling. *You're outdoors. In danger. You must find safety.*

Saga drew back, trying to shake the voice free. Just a little longer...

Come with me, Saga wanted to scream. *Come with me to Midfjord.* But she couldn't drag him into her troubles more than she had already. Couldn't have any more blood on her hands.

Rurik looked like a wild creature, his hair wet and mussed, eyes wolfish and far too bright. He looked like he wanted to consume her—like he was holding himself back by the very finest thread. A warm rush spread through her, and for a moment, Saga wanted nothing but for the thread to snap through. But as Rurik blinked, the ferocity eased, as did the muscles beneath her fingertips.

And then he was looking at her mischievously. "Is wonder enough you have been outdoors so long. Let us return to castle, Winterwing."

The air between them was heavy with unspoken words, but neither wanted to break the spell.

"Yes," said Saga at last. "I must return to the castle." A pang of alarm tightened her chest. Her sodden gown clung to her body, her braids drenched with rain. "I cannot return to the feast."

"I know a door," Rurik said, his voice touched with amusement. "Is secret."

"Oh?"

"A woman more beautiful than forest fairy showed it to me. I was so enchanted, I set fire to my own boat to stay longer by her side."

Saga shook her head slowly. "Brash man."

"Hands were doing without permission," he replied, reaching for her.

As his hand closed around the back of hers, he hesitated. His palm slid against her skin once more, eyes flickering down.

Saga's heart stumbled, and she tried to yank her hand back, but his grasp was ironclad. His eyes locked onto hers, dark brows furrowed as he lifted her hand, holding it up to the light trickling from the palace.

"What..."

Her heart beat like a war drum, and she squeezed her eyes shut. *Danger!* her body screamed. Saga forced in deep breaths as Rurik tilted her hand, sliding his thumb against her disfigured skin.

"What is this, Saga?"

Saga's lips parted, but no sound came out. Her chest was squeezing, tighter, tighter. Forcing her eyes shut, she tried not to think of what he'd find on the backs of her hands.

A bear, its mouth opened in a silent scream. Etched in angry red lines for the rest of eternity.

"They marked you?" His words were a low growl, reverberating down her body and lodging in her stomach. "They *burned* you?" Rurik's rage was palpable, radiating off him into the night sky and sending goosebumps rushing up her arms. "Who... *who* has done this to you?"

She shook her head, lights dancing in her vision. Panic was climbing through her, infecting her body like the plague.

Rurik shook himself, and when he spoke, his voice was softer. "Breathe," he said. "It is me, Winterwing. It is only us." Again, he gathered her to him, then stroked her hair until her body calmed. But when at last she opened her eyes, she was met with a glare that could shatter glass.

"You must tell me who did this," said Rurik. "It was Ivar?"

"No."

"Who?"

She shook her head.

"The name," he gritted.

"I cannot."

"Infuriating woman," he growled. His eyes seemed inhumanly green, the air vibrating all around him. "If you do not give me the name, I will go back into the hall and question every person with my dagger."

Waves of shivers rolled through her, and Rurik blinked, seeming to regain some control of himself. "Forgive me, Winterwing. I did not mean to frighten you. Come. Let us return to castle." Taking her hand in his, Rurik turned.

She wet her lips. "Magnus."

He stilled. Was silent a long moment. Slowly, Rurik turned back. "Why?"

Saga took a deep breath. And then she forced the words out. At first, they took enormous effort, but the more she spoke, the easier it became. And though she'd never intended to, Saga found herself telling him *everything*. "'Now when you look at your hands, Saga,'" she finished, "'you'll remember that you're property. Nothing but a worthless pet.'"

Rurik's eyes shut, his body tense as a bowstring. He was silent for a moment, and when he opened his eyes again, they were filled with regret.

"I called you this when we met. I called you *little pet of Ivar*." He cursed under his breath, reaching for her hands. As he brought her scarred flesh to his mouth, his lips brushed reverently across first one, then the other. "Forgive me."

"You didn't know," she managed, swallowing the hot burn of tears. "Few do."

"What was his punishment?" asked Rurik tightly. "What was done to Magnus for his crime?"

Saga cast her eyes to the ground. "Nothing. The king has never spoken of it. Signe advised me to wear gloves to hide my shame. And that was the end of it."

He pulled her to his chest, wrapping himself around her. Saga closed her eyes, listening to the angry thump of his heart.

"You are no pet. Do not forget this."

"I know," she said mildly. "I told you so when I met you."

He choked out a laugh. "So you did."

Saga sighed into his hold, wishing they could stay like this for all eternity. But the burn of panic was growing hotter within. *Safety!* her body screamed. *Flee!* Yet still, she could not let go. Just one more moment like this, one more before facing reality . . .

If her eyes weren't open, Saga would have missed it. A flash of red at the corner of the hedges. The rain had stopped, and the air was clear and still. And for a full second, Saga stared into Yrsa's widened eyes.

Yrsa turned and fled, and Saga pulled herself from Rurik.

"We must go."

CHAPTER 73

Kopa

Jonas strolled among the sparring Klaernar, hands gripped behind his back. The late-afternoon sun was bright, catching shining minerals in the blackened earth and along the stone walls of the garrison hall grounds. All around him were Klaernar warriors clad in black chain mail, with screaming-bear shoulder plates in shining silver. Each warrior had the bear claw tattooed across his cheek, a sigil ring worn on his second finger. And after weeks of training these men, Jonas knew they were lethal on the battlefield.

Motion at the gates caught his eye—Kaptein Ulfar striding through with a pair of Klaernar leading a horse-drawn wagon. Exhaling, Jonas made his way to the kaptein and greeted him with a firm handshake.

"They're all there?" asked Jonas, pulling the wagon's cover back and inspecting its contents.

"All there," said Ulfar, opening a crate. "Three hundred skarpling quills."

Jonas picked up a quill, holding it to the sunlight. "They're all tipped with the . . . hindrium?"

"Aye. I'm told it locks up their galdur instantly."

A grim smile spread across Jonas's lips. "Good," he murmured. He placed the quill back into the crate and replaced the lid.

"And this," said Ulfar, gesturing to a smaller crate, "is the berskium powder to refill the sigil rings after dosing in battle." He scowled. "After the destruction of Íseldur's mine, we've had to import the berskium at a great cost, so be sure to only use what you need."

Jonas nodded, his gaze roaming over the supply wagon. He tried to ignore the twist of his stomach—the wagon was nearly identical to the one used by the Bloodaxe Crew. Crates of provisions. Iron tent poles. Weapons. Jonas's eyes landed on the pile of furs, and his stomach wrenched violently. He could practically imagine her there, dark hair spread out on wolfskin, lashes lowered on pale cheeks as she napped.

Jonas exhaled shakily. Lately, fierce pangs of nostalgia were interspersed with his grief. He found himself yearning for days gone by, when the Bloodaxe Crew sat around the fire playing dice until Ilías went a little too far and Gunnar tackled him to the ground. True, there had been long days in the saddle, but with the wind in his hair and the endless beauty of Íseldur all around him. A wave of sentimentality hit Jonas so hard, he clutched the wagon's side.

"You've focused much on this... Axe Eyes," noted Ulfar. "Should we not also think of his woman accomplice?"

"She's no warrior," Jonas spat. "Her only true weapon is her poisonous tongue. She weaves lies and deception like a spider does its web."

Ulfar watched him warily. "Ah. She entrapped you, did she?"

A hot flush crept up Jonas's neck.

"I do not care what motivates you, Svik, so long as you bring them in," muttered the kaptein. "The queen will not tolerate another failure."

"We've studied his battle tactics," said Jonas. "Have spoken to the warrior who escaped the Slátrari. We know how he fights, know how he wields his galdur. We *know* him, Ulfar. Sooner or later, he'll have to crawl out of his hole. And when he does, we'll be ready."

"I hope you know what you're doing, Svik," said Ulfar, stroking his beard.

"Kaptein Ulfar," came a breathless voice. Jonas and Ulfar whirled to see a young Klaernar jogging toward them, waving a wad of parchment. "This just arrived from the north."

He handed the parchment to Ulfar, who flattened it on his thigh and scanned the contents. "It sounds like another sundrunk northman," muttered Ulfar, handing it to Jonas.

"No," said Jonas, reading the page. The knowing feeling in his stomach grew more and more certain with each word he read. "It is no madman." He met Kaptein Ulfar's wary eyes. "It's *him*."

Ulfar's brows drew together, doubt written all over his face.

But Jonas was more confident than he'd ever been. At last, the gods bestowed some good fortune upon him.

"This," said Jonas, "is our edge."

CHAPTER 74

Sunnavík

Saga's fingers dipped into the ash of her dead fire, swirling along the stones of the hearth. Normally, drawing was her solace, a place to retreat when things were hard. But now it did nothing to ease the knots in her stomach.

The night before had been a disaster. Moments after Saga had shucked off her sodden gown and climbed into her tub, Signe had stormed into the room, a flurry of white-gold hair and ivory skirts. "You were instructed *not* to leave the feast." There had been an edge to Signe's voice, and she'd closed her eyes, smoothing her hands along the ethereal white of her gown to collect herself. When at last Signe had opened her eyes, they'd cooled and sharpened.

"Saga, darling. If you act like a child, expect to be treated like a child."

And with that, Signe had departed, leaving Saga alone in the tub. She sank beneath the water. Screamed a torrent of bubbles.

Saga had soon heard a noise from beyond the door. After pulling herself from the tub, she'd dried herself off and hastily pulled on the long, white nightdress Árlaug had laid out for her.

"What are you doing?" she'd exclaimed, bursting into the bedchamber. A dozen or more guards had gathered her things and were carrying them from the room. Clothes were pulled from the wardrobe, drawers emptied, jewelry and drawing tools and furs all carted away. Eyes slid in her direction, along her bare feet and collarbones, but the men did not pause in their task.

"Those are my belongings!" Saga tried to block a pair of guards from carrying off her dressing table.

"Step aside, Lady Saga," Thorir's weasel-faced replacement had glowered, "or I'll use force to assist you."

Clad in only a nightdress and surrounded by men twice her size, Saga had no choice but to relent. It wasn't long before they'd taken it all: her bench, her drawing supplies, her furs and blankets—even the rug. All that remained was her bed with a single threadbare blanket.

The room was large without her belongings, so empty and cold. For so long, this room had been her sanctuary within Askaborg. But now it had been violated, and Saga realized it had only been another illusion. There was no safe place for her within these walls.

Tomorrow. Tomorrow she would leave. But the chasm in her chest had expanded. Yrsa had seen her and Rurik embrace in the gardens. Had she told Queen Signe? King Ivar? Saga did the only thing she could think of—she pushed this thought aside, clinging to a thin shred of hope that Yrsa had kept it to herself.

It had been a long, cold night. When Árlaug had discovered her, curled under the single banket, she'd gasped.

"My lady, what happened?"

Saga opened her mouth to answer, but feared she might cry. Thankfully, her lady's maid had understood enough.

"Oh, child. I was barred entry to your room. Told not to return until the morrow." Árlaug tutted. "Not to worry, Lady Saga, we will set you to rights before the daymeal." She'd retreated to the bathing chamber, then returned with something in hand. "At the very least, we have a comb."

After diligently working the tangles from Saga's hair and weaving it into a side braid, Árlaug had disappeared beyond the door, exchanging some sharp words with Thorir's replacement. And after a while, a rumpled garment had been delivered—a gown of plain blue wool, which Árlaug had helped her don.

And now Saga sat at her hearth, drawing with the ashes of her dead fire. Uncertainty gripped her. Today would grant her freedom or imprisonment. Reward or harsh punishment. But one thing felt certain—regardless of what happened, by twilight, Saga's life would be changed.

The ominous thought was disrupted as Árlaug poked her head in, informing Saga that she was now late for the daymeal.

With a sigh, Saga stood and made her way to the door.

"My lady," called Árlaug, eyes landing on her bare hands, "your gloves."

Saga paused with her hand on the iron door ring, looking down at the raised red marks. Showing her marred skin to Rurik had been strangely empowering. It had made her emotions feel justified.

"I shall no longer hide my hands," she said with quiet anger.

And then she pushed into the corridor, her new guard clambering behind her. The walk to the great hall went far too quickly. Reaching the doors, Saga refused to hesitate. She stepped into the room and made her way through it.

Saga quickly noticed that the secondary feasting table was empty. No jarls, no skalds, no High Gothi dined with them today—and no Zagadkians.

Her chest squeezed, but Saga focused with all her might on breathing through it. She nearly tripped as she realized the high table was reconfigured—chairs arranged on both sides, with no vacant seat beside Prince Bjorn. Slivers of cold lodged in her spine as Saga spotted the only empty seat in the room.

Next to Magnus.

With a steadying breath, Saga moved to the empty seat and sank down beside the king's chief hirdman. She stared at her plate, taking stock of who was present from the edge of her vision—Ivar, Signe, Magnus, Yrsa, and Bjorn. Too many people for her Sense to be of use.

"You look terrible, Saga," murmured Signe from across the table. "You must not have slept soundly last night."

Saga was too busy wrangling her spiraling fear to answer. She had to remain calm.

"Saga," snapped King Ivar, his face reddening. "Your queen has addressed you. Show her some honor."

Saga lifted her hands and folded them together across her plate.

She heard a sharp intake of breath but didn't look to see the source. "No, Your Highness," she said, looking at Signe. "I did not sleep well."

Signe's lips turned down as she stared at Saga's bare hands, but her recovery was swift. "A shame, darling. But the greater shame is what Yrsa saw in the garden last night."

Saga's hands clenched tightly. Signe's cruelty was so often a subtle thing, but Saga knew in this instant she'd best brace herself for brutality.

"Saga, why don't you tell us what happened?" asked Signe, her voice light. "I should like to hear your explanation. One must hear all sides of a story before leaping to conclusions." Signe's gaze flicked to her husband; for once, they were a united front.

The king's face was stern, his eyes solemn. "Explain."

They wanted to shame her. Wanted her to writhe like a bug as they pulled off her wings. And there was nothing Saga could do but play along. Go with the currents.

"I should like to speak to the prince in private first," said Saga, her eyes darting to Bjorn's. But her betrothed's cheeks were flushed, and he would not meet her gaze. Clearly, he knew. They *all* knew.

Saga felt the barest moment of regret for kissing Rurik—twice—but found it quickly chased away by a rush of indignant anger. She did not regret it. Those were *her* choices, and in a life where she had so very few, she refused to regret them.

"You will explain to us all, Saga," said Signe, her voice disarmingly calm. "We are your family. We deserve to hear the truth."

Not my family, she wanted to scream. But Saga knew there was only one choice for her here—to play along. "I felt flushed, so I left the hall." Her voice sounded distant to her own ears. "Lord Rurik joined me in the garden."

Signe's chin rested lightly on her knuckles. "And then . . ."

The eyes are afraid, but the hands are doing.

"We kissed." The words seemed to echo in the vast, empty room. Saga hazarded a glance at her betrothed, shame coiling inside her as still he did not meet her gaze. "My apologies, Bjorn. I meant you no dishonor."

"Saga, you've disappointed me," came Ivar's deep voice. "You've brought shame upon our family."

That word, again, kindling anger deep in her stomach. But the king had not finished. His fist bashed the table, rattling the silverware. "The Zagadkians have deceived us. Have made fools of us. 'Twas shame enough that he would not drink from the skull, but this... *this* cannot stand."

Saga's anger quickly curdled to fear. She opened her mouth to protest, but the violence in the king's eyes made her falter.

"That arrogant man thinks he can come into my home and put his hands on *my* ward? On my heir's betrothed?" The possessive gleam in the king's eye told her in an instant that his outrage was not for Saga but for his own pride.

A new realization was dawning on her—one that filled her with panic. Saga's selfish choice last night had far broader ramifications than she'd realized. She'd jeopardized the treaty with the Zagadkians. This risked not only the safety of Rurik and his companions but also the well-being of her people. The good people of Íseldur *needed* that grain.

She had to fix this. "I kissed him. It was *me*. He is innocent."

"You've been used, Saga," spat Ivar, deep lines of tension in his forehead. "The man was trying to antagonize me." He muttered something under his breath. "Already, he opposed our sacrifice at their farewell feast. Then he had the gall to enter the tournament, only to dishonor us by declining the victor's rights. He spits on our tradition. Thinks himself above our rules."

"No," protested Saga. "It was not like that—"

"Poor darling," Signe interrupted primly. "You've been used and abandoned. They've fled like cowards under darkness of night."

White dots danced in Saga's vision. It couldn't be true. But her eyes darted to the empty secondary table, reality crystallizing, cold and bleak. There would be no seeds in her róa. There would be no escape for her today.

Saga had been left behind.

She could not crumble—she would not let Signe win. As she forced breath into her lungs, Saga's gaze slid to Yrsa, but her foster sister blinked furiously at her own plate.

"The Zagadkians will soon know the taste of Urkan wrath." Ivar's voice was rising. "It was wise of them to flee."

"We must seek retribution," said Magnus darkly.

"Swiftly," growled Ivar.

"But the grain," Bjorn interjected. "What of our people?"

"What of our *honor*, son?" boomed Ivar. "It is a lesson to be learned. Trust not a man's words but his actions. We thought the Zagadkians our allies, but their behavior has proven otherwise. Who's to say they'd even deliver the grain we were promised?"

Bjorn opened his mouth, then closed it.

The king's gaze hardened. "When faced with a wolf, you show your teeth or your belly. Are you a sheep, son, or are you a predator?"

"Predator," said Bjorn, though he looked troubled.

"Saga," said Ivar in a cold, hard voice. "You've proven to be a sheep. Weak. Easily misled. And you've fallen prey to the trickery of wolves. You're unworthy of marrying my son. Unworthy of becoming queen."

Saga held her breath.

"I hereby call off your betrothal to Bjorn."

Saga's heart felt as if it had grown wings—as if it might fly circles around the ceiling. She was quite proud of herself for smothering her reaction. But Bjorn was not so impassive. The sadness in his face was like a blade between her ribs.

He couldn't possibly have wished to marry her, could he? But Saga had no time to ponder it. As her eyes settled on Signe, her blood chilled. It seemed there was more.

"Instead, you'll marry Magnus," said the king.

The room tilted on its axis, her heart careening in her chest. Saga gripped the edge of the table, trying so hard to maintain her passivity. But as Magnus pried her hand from the table and clasped it in his, she felt herself shattering into pieces. Not him. Anyone but him. Magnus's thumb swiped over the marks he'd placed on her skin with a low grunt of approval.

"A better match for you, darling," continued Signe, her face as calm as if she were discussing the weather. "You need a firm hand to keep you in line. And Magnus is the perfect man for the job, aren't you, Magnus?"

"I think this will be an agreeable arrangement," he said coolly, stroking her hand once more.

"It's time you settled, Magnus," said King Ivar with a knowing smile. "Time you had a family."

Dazedly, Saga wondered if she'd be violently ill on the table. She wrenched her hand free from Magnus and pressed it to her rapidly throbbing temples.

"We shall expedite the wedding," Signe was saying, though the words were muffled as if she were underwater. "No need to draw things out. We can arrange a lovely ceremony on short notice. How does a week from now sound to you, Magnus?"

"Perfect." His hand fell heavy on Saga's thigh, and she flinched at the contact.

They spoke of her as if she weren't even there. Like she had no say. And she didn't.

She pulled Magnus's hand from her leg, and he chuckled, making her entire body tense. The sound was a promise—of torment, of violence, of games she'd lose, over and over.

You deserve to be punished.

The hum of conversation picked up around her, but white noise filled Saga's ears. Her breaths sawed in and out. She did not want to give Signe the satisfaction of seeing her undone, but Saga was no longer in control.

The man who'd branded her body and called her property would soon be her husband.

The daymeal was served, and Saga drank four cups of róa. But she knew there would be no sleeping draught in the drink. There would be no escape. They'd fled in the night. Left her behind. Tears tried to scrape forth, but she kept them trapped through sheer will. She had vowed there would be no tears. She had this one thing left.

The daymeal stretched to torturous lengths, but by some miracle, Saga survived. At last, the royal family stood, and she followed on numb legs. How she made it back to her chambers, she could not say.

Her guard settled into his chair outside her chamber doors. Standing in her empty room, Saga took stock of her situation—she'd lost her freedom, her possessions, her hope of escape. And soon, she'd be handed over to a monster.

What Magnus had done to her hands was only the start. A fresh wave of nausea churned through her as she considered what else he might do.

Saga stared with unseeing eyes at the heavy oak doors of her balcony. She pushed on the iron ring and stepped into the crisp morning air. The stone balustrades warped before her as her body reacted to being outdoors, tightness wrapping around her middle, squeezing until she couldn't breathe. Everything was wrong, so wrong. Up was down, right was wrong. She stepped forward again, again, again.

Punished, echoed through her skull as her heart pumped violently.

"Yes," wheezed Saga through the tension in her chest. Birds were screaming, the iron forge sizzling in her ears. Her hand wrapped around cold, rough stone. The balustrade. She reached it and looked below to the stone courtyard.

Her body moved, her mind unthinking. Gripping the stone wall, Saga pulled herself up to stand on the rail. The ground below tilted back and forth, like the deck of a ship, and Saga steadied herself with a hand to the wall.

A call from below—Klaernar on the stone walkway, looking up.

She stared down, her skirts whipping in the wind.

Third floor of the palace. How long would it take to fall? The span of two heartbeats, perhaps three? Her vision clouded, and she closed her eyes.

No tears.

Saga thought of her family, tried to picture her mother and her father in her mind, but like the perfection she chased in her sketches, the images were never quite right. The coil of her mother's hair was off, the arch of her father's brow wrong. Her parents blurred until they were no longer an image but only a feeling. Warmth. Safety. Love. Things she hadn't felt in far too long.

Saga was scared but sure. In a moment, she'd be free. She'd stretch her wings and fly from her cage. No one could hurt her where she was going. No one would ever hurt her again.

She smiled, a strange sense of peace settling into place.

As she closed her eyes, a vision flashed before her: a small girl running, a net clutched in her hand, brown hair rippling in the sunlight. The vision twisted. The girl reached for her, eyes wide with fright as Saga was wrenched from her arms.

Don't leave me! Saga had screamed. But they'd left her. Everyone always did.

I'm sorry, Eisa, she thought. *This is the only way to find peace. I love you and will see you again among the stars.*

CHAPTER 75

Kalasgarde

Silla's white blade sizzled through the air as she launched into the striking sequence Rey had been working her through. She ducked low while swiping up, but her back foot slid on a patch of ice. As her hand shot out to balance herself, her blade sliced through a clump of wild grass poking through the snow.

"Focus," said Harpa, perched on a chair.

Silla had been working through the motions for hours already. Her hair was frosted white, her eyelashes crystallized and glinting. A dozen or so ice spirits played among the birds who'd gathered at Harpa's feet, chirping for bread.

Rökkur echoed in her mind, and she stumbled again. Righting herself, Silla released a frustrated breath.

"What happened?" asked Harpa.

"I'm distracted."

"You must learn to block out the noise," said Harpa. "The first battle is always within yourself."

Silla's eyes slid to Rey, who was perched on his favorite stump. Like her, he seemed lost in thought—stuck on Harpa's revelation from the day before.

Rökkur, she'd said. *The twilight of our world.*

Silla and Rey had exchanged an uneasy look at the statement. It was one thing to believe that the gods held sway over minor happenings among mortals—the signs Silla so often looked for, or the weather, perhaps. But to believe that Myrkur, god of chaos and darkness, was waking to bring an end to life as they knew it . . . was a leap.

"None know the full story of Rökkur," Harpa had explained. "Once, there was a tapestry. I saw it in Sunnavík as a young girl. Even then, it was ancient and badly frayed. I fear I do not know what became of the tapestry when the Urkans invaded.

"What I know of Rökkur is that it has happened before. It is said it began with frost and ended in fire. The yarn begins with three long winters bringing famine to the land. And it ends when the Sleeping Dragons wake, cleansing the realm with fire and choking the sun with ash and smoke. From the wreckage, a new era shall begin. But what passes between frost and fire is not known."

"It is but a tale," Rey had interjected.

"It is as real as the gods," Harpa had replied. "As real as the sun and the galdur flowing through your veins."

Silla was wary—it was too large a leap of faith. Yet when she thought of that shadowy presence, of the voice in the ice caves, she didn't know what she believed.

"And the chasm?" prompted Rey.

"A crack in the world," Harpa had replied. "I've been weaving threads from all over Íseldur these past days and see a pattern. Dark creatures not seen in centuries crawling from the crevasses in the north and the deep-rooted woods of the west, through the swamps in the south and the water spires in the east. Through those cracks, Myrkur's spawn have emerged, feasting on the flesh of humans and Sunnvald's other creations."

"The mother serpent—"

"Daughter of Myrkur," Harpa said softly. "Slipping into our world to bring chaos and strife. I am uncertain if the serpent's purpose was to kill Eisa, or if it was an unfortunate coincidence. But it is said only the Volsik bloodline can stop Myrkur's chaos. This must be why He's been meddling with your ancestors. And it seems He's trying to gain access to your mind. We must shore up your protections. Keep Him out."

"Why a Volsik?" Silla had asked in desperation.

Harpa's eyes had grown distant. "I fear it is one of the lost threads. It is said the Volsiks carry an additional blessing from Sunnvald. A gift with which to defeat Myrkur. But the details are not known."

"Istré," Rey had said absently. "The Western Woods. If what you're saying is correct, the Bloodaxe Crew are neck-deep in things they haven't a clue about."

"You believe this?" Silla had asked incredulously.

"I don't know," he'd replied. "But I'll admit, it explains many things. Why the ice spirits sought you, of all people. If the ice spirits believe you are the key to defeating Myrkur—that you have this blessing from Sunnvald—it fits that they'd take you to the source of His spawn to defeat them."

Back in the present, Silla tripped again, falling to hands and knees with a rough laugh.

"What is so amusing?" asked Harpa, tossing another piece of bread. The birds squawked and the ice spirits hissed, all lunging for the bread. An ice spirit soon emerged from the heap, victorious, and was chased across the yard by several more.

Silla rubbed her forehead. "Only that you believe the fate of this kingdom is in my hands, and I cannot even master walking without tripping over stones." More laughter bubbled up.

"You are improving," said Harpa evenly. "Each day you grow stronger. I see your determination. I see your strength. But I also see stubbornness. Unwillingness to believe." Harpa paused. "Until you accept the gifts the gods have given you, you will continue to struggle."

Tears of defeat gathered in Silla's eyes.

"Perhaps a break is in order," said Rey, stepping between Silla and his grandmother.

Harpa pushed to her feet and began toward her home. "I shall brew a replenishing tea."

As the door to the cabin slid shut, Rey's arms slipped around Silla's waist, pulling her flush to him. "All right?" he asked.

She forced a smile to her lips. "It's a lot."

"It's merely a god fixed on destroying the world."

Laughter burst from her, drawing a near smile from Rey. "I wonder if this weaving foretold such a blundering Volsik?"

"You see blundering. I see progress. There is beauty to behold in the in-between."

Silla was touched by his words. "I would never have guessed the infamous Axe Eyes was such a wordsmith."

His eyes were warm and shining. "I've many hidden talents."

"Is that so?" She smiled coyly. "What kind of talents?"

"I can fall asleep anywhere," he replied without missing a beat. "Sitting, standing, on a horse . . ."

"How in the gods' names can you possibly sleep *standing*?"

He leaned in closer, his warm breath fanning along her cheek. "It involved a lot of brennsa and strong friends to keep me propped up."

Silla's fingers slid into his beard, part affection, part searching out any uneven strands she might have missed this morning. "I want to hear them all. Each misdeed. Each adventure."

"No, you don't," he huffed. "Some stories are not meant to see the light of day."

I'm sorry, Eisa.

Gasping, Silla reeled back. Sorrow pulsed through her, so potent she fell to her knees.

"Silla?" asked Rey, but Silla pushed his voice from her mind. Diving deep within herself, she found the dark, quiet place.

This is the only way to find peace. I love you and will see you again among the stars.

CHAPTER 76

Sunnavík

The scream tore into Saga's mind and echoed off her skull, so startlingly clear her eyes flew open. Blinking, she took in the stone walkway below her balcony, the royal forest and northern defensive walls stretching out beyond it. She gripped the wall, trying to understand the taste of fear in her mouth, the scent of hay and mountain air in her nose.

Saga! shouted Mind-Eisa.

Had they slipped something into her róa after all?

Don't do this, begged Mind-Eisa. *Whatever has happened, don't do this.*

Saga's stomach swooped low, disbelief clouding her mind. But more Klaernar had gathered below, watching Saga as though she were sport. Were they taking bets? Wagering on whether Ivar's little pet would take her own life?

I can't live like this, thought Saga, despair climbing through her. She stared past Askaborg's defensive walls. How could freedom be so near, yet so completely unattainable?

I do not know what you've endured, but I know it's not right, thought Mind-Eisa. *I swear it to you, Saga, I will come for you. Fight a little longer.*

A sob was trapped in her chest, pushing and burning, but she would not let it free. *I cannot,* she thought. *He cannot hurt me again.*

A blast of love wrapped around her like a warm hug. *They shall pay, Saga,* came Mind-Eisa's thoughts, determination edged with anger. *They'll pay in blood. Do not grant them victory by jumping.*

To feel such anger on her behalf was startling. Living among these people had twisted Saga's thoughts—had muddled her self-worth. *I'm frightened,* Saga admitted. The very idea of being near Magnus made her pulse race. *'Tis better to die one large death than a thousand small ones at his hand.*

Someone has hurt you, thought Mind-Eisa, righteous indignation flooding through Saga. *It is not fair what you've weathered alone. But know this, Saga: It's always darkest before first light. Keep stepping forward, one step at a time.*

A sob broke, and Saga leaned against the wall. *I'm so weary, Mind-Eisa. I do not know how much more I can endure.*

I, too, have been all alone, Mind-Eisa thought. A prison cell flashed in Saga's mind's eye. Strange tapestries. A vile-looking Klaernar looming above her. *You were there for me, Saga, in my darkest hour. I believed all was lost, but I . . . saw you. Your face. And you reminded me there was something to live for. I promised you one day we'd meet. Help me keep this promise.*

Something to live for. Saga tried to twist her thoughts back to this. But as her eyes caught on her scarred hands, the fist of panic squeezed tighter around her, and she gasped for breath. The castle's northern walls swelled and crested like moving waves, but a foreign blast of love and warmth left Saga disoriented.

Stop, begged Mind-Eisa, and Saga felt her sister's madness, her desperation. *Whatever has happened, Saga, we will get through it.*

Yearning uncurled in Saga's stomach. *I miss you,* she thought. *I miss them.*

Then help me keep this promise, thought Mind-Eisa. *I swear to you, Saga, we will see one another again.*

An ember of warmth flickered deep in Saga's chest. She stared over the castle grounds, to the harbor beyond. Somewhere out there, in the wilds of this kingdom, was Eisa—alive, and breathing, and fighting for Saga. Surely she could do the same, at least for another day.

Very well, thought Saga, *I will help you keep this promise for one more day.* With a deep breath, she eased herself down from the railing and groped her way back into her chambers. As she slid down the wall and collapsed over bent knees, Eisa's relief and love wrapped around her. *I've made such a mess.*

One foot in front of the other, Saga, thought Eisa. *Your path is shadowed, and you cannot see clearly. With each step, it will become clearer.*

Saga hugged her knees tightly, trying to calm her racing heart. *You are wise for a figment of my imagination.*

I've never been called wise before, thought Eisa with amusement. *I think I prefer it to "repulsively cheerful."*

What if he harms me? Saga could not help but think.

Eisa was silent for a time. *I do not know the answer, or the right words. But a friend once told me she considered the hard times in life kindling. She used them to build her fire higher and hotter. And when the time was right, she unleashed her inferno upon her enemy.*

Inferno, thought Saga. *I do like the sound of that.*

You'd like this friend, thought Eisa fondly. *One day, you'll meet her.*

One day, thought Saga wistfully. Her head thunked gently against the stone wall, and she stared at the rafters. Though it was only morning, already she was bone-weary.

Promise me, Saga! Eisa's presence was sliding through her grasp, growing fainter. *Promise me one day we'll be reunited.*

I promise, thought Saga.

The thread of their connection was severed through, and Saga was alone once more. Eisa's warmth lingered on her skin. She had felt so real. And in that moment, mad or not, Saga decided to believe that it had been real. In the bleakness, she focused on one singular emotion.

Love.

Right now, shrouded in darkness, Eisa was her star, her guiding light, and Saga focused on this light with all of her being.

Fight for yourself, she repeated over and over, until the words burrowed into her bones and flowed through her veins. *Rallying cry,* she thought. *You've been bold and daring this month. You've spied on the queen and stolen into Alfson's study. Have greeted your past and stepped outdoors. And you've kissed a man—twice. You've not come this far to fail, Saga.*

And with that, the decision was made. Saga pulled herself up and strode across her chambers, reaching for the bell pull. Árlaug appeared a few minutes later, lips curved into a tentative smile.

"Yes, my lady?"

Saga gathered what remained of her courage. Straightened her spine. "I need you to arrange a meeting with the queen."

CHAPTER 77

Kalasgarde

The morning they left Nordur, Rey found himself standing in Harpa's snowy yard, considering her home. As though the gods were bidding them farewell, Nordur was in full splendor. It was a cool, crisp day, the frosted air shimmering in bright morning sunlight.

At the far edge of Harpa's property, a cluster of ice spirits twirled and danced, chasing a squirrel up a tree and frosting the gnarled trunk. Silla had already said her farewells to the tiny blue creatures after asking them to keep watch over Jökull. She'd asked them to report to Vig, though Rey supposed only time would tell if they'd understood.

Between Silla and Rey's combined efforts, Harpa had five winters' worth of firewood chopped and stacked in her woodshed. Rey had cleaned and polished the interior of her home to the best of his abilities. Had re-thatched the roof near the smoke hole and winter-proofed the home's walls with fresh pine resin. At the very least, Harpa was winter-ready.

"But Eisa is not ready," whined Rykka. After ensuring that the ice spirits were busy at the yard's edge, Rykka had made a rare trip outdoors. Her smoky form now undulated above Harpa's shoulder, casting steam into the cool air.

"Rykka is right." His grandmother's amber eyes were fixed on Silla. "We need to fortify your mind's defenses. Keep the Dark One out."

"Saga needs me," was Silla's only reply.

When Silla had described the mind-to-mind communication with her sister, Rey had been filled with wonder and disbelief—he'd never heard of such a thing. And yet there were always anomalies among the Galdra. Any doubt he might have felt was assuaged by Silla's steely determination.

"We must go to Kopa *now*," she'd insisted.

If you want to fight, I will draw my sword beside you, Rey had told her, and now he would prove his word.

The rest of the day had been a blur, spent chasing down the warriors who would accompany them and sending word to Jarl Hakon. Kopa had long been their plan. Jarl Hakon's resources and connections were essential in arranging for Saga's rescue. But with the trip now imminently upon them, he was filled with apprehension.

Rey did not like making decisions based on emotion—that was how mistakes were made. But Silla would not be swayed. Saga was her last living blood relative. And as Rey watched his grandmother, he understood that duty in his own way. No matter how fraught his relationship with Harpa, if she was in trouble, he'd always come calling.

And so Rey had resigned himself to the preparations. At last count, they had a group of nine warriors, including Erik, Mýr, and Runný. And to Rey's great surprise, Kálf had volunteered, installing Vig as temporary chieftain in his absence.

"Your Blade Breaker skill remains elusive," said Harpa, her displeasure palpable. "A few more weeks—"

"And Saga could be dead," replied Silla flatly.

Rey's mind drifted ahead to Kopa. They would take refuge in Ashfall Fortress, away from the Klaernar's prying eyes. Would set plans in motion to free Saga from Sunnavík. If Jarl Hakon and the Uppreisna refused . . . if it meant gathering warriors of his own and storming the walls of Askaborg, Rey would do it.

He was starting to realize that Silla could ask him to jump off a cliff, and he'd ask which one.

"Reynir," cooed Rykka, "surely you don't support this."

"I support her decision," he replied.

Rykka pouted, her charcoal wings flaring.

"Her training," began Harpa.

"I will continue her training," he answered. "Unless you wish to join us?"

Harpa's laugh was harsh. "My place is here with my loom. You know that, Reynir." But the lines of her face softened, and she studied him for a moment. "I will be searching through the threads. Communicating with the other Weavers. If I discover anything, I will send word."

He nodded. "We will keep you informed of our whereabouts. Gyda and Vig will check on you. Don't hesitate to ask them for anything should you need it."

Harpa's gaze settled back on Silla. "I fear this is Myrkur's doing. That He lures you into a trap before your training is complete." Silla remained silent. "If you must go, remember this: You will never master your galdur until you believe—in yourself, in the gods, in your power. You have come far, but still you fight it. Remember, Eisa, that to win, you must sometimes surrender."

Something passed behind Silla's eyes, and Rey reached for her hand, sliding his fingers through hers with a comforting squeeze.

Harpa's eyes settled on their joined hands. "Very well," sighed his grandmother, meeting his gaze. "Stay safe, Reynir. And you, Eisa."

Silla's hand remained steady at the use of her true name. "And you, Harpa," she said, stepping forward and surrounding Harpa in a warm embrace. Rey battled a smile at the discomfort on his grandmother's face. "Thank you. For *everything*," said Silla, pulling back with shining eyes. "Truly, I leave here a better person. You've changed me, and I will carry a piece of you wherever I go—"

"Very good, very good," interjected Harpa. "Now you'd best get on the road."

Startled at Harpa's quick ushering, Silla broke into a grin. "You'll miss us!"

"I'll enjoy hearing my own thoughts."

"I'll miss your optimistic wisdom," cheered Silla.

Harpa shook her head, but the hint of a smile peeked through.

"And you, Rykka," said Silla, turning to the smoke spirit. "I would hug you if it wasn't a risk to my life. Be well." She lowered her voice. "The ice spirits are a rather welcoming bunch, you know."

Rykka cast a horrified look over her shoulder at the frolicking ice spirits. "Not on your life," she retorted. But then she wrung her charcoal hands, a look of anguish filling her girl-like face. "Be safe, Reynir. And you, Trilla."

Harpa and Rykka retreated into the cabin, and Rey found Silla wiping tears from her eyes. Gods, but she truly was crying—for Harpa and a surly smoke spirit.

"Come here," he said, trying to hide his amusement. Pulling her close to him, he rubbed soothing circles on her back.

"I'll miss them," she sniffled into his chest.

"I doubt that," he muttered, but that only seemed to make her sniffle harder.

"You'll miss them, too!"

He snorted. "Save some tears, now. Vig is next."

Silla wailed, pressing her face tighter into his chest.

Gyda, Vig, and Snorri waited for them at the shield-home. Runný glowered at her feet, a cap of bright red perched atop her head. Rey's lips quirked. One of Gyda's creations, he guessed.

Rey went to his saddlesack and pulled out a small, sheathed sword. Lowering onto his knees, he presented it to Snorri. "Don't let your brother plant lies in your head, Snorri," he said. "A true warrior is adept with *all* weapons."

Eyes wide, Snorri accepted the weapon. "This is for *me*?"

"Mind you don't run with it!" Silla cautioned.

"Aye, you *run* with it," Rey said, trying not to roll his eyes. "What, should a warrior amble into battle at his leisure?"

"He's *twelve*," she retorted.

"Ignore her, Snorri," continued Rey. "Practice each day. And next time I see you, we'll spar."

Straightening, he ruffled Snorri's hair. The boy was already unsheathing the blade, testing the edge against his thumb.

Gyda stepped forward, wrapping Rey in a warm, motherly embrace. "I'm glad to see you came to your senses, lad," she whispered in his ear. "She's a good woman. Mind you treat her right."

To his horror, emotion felt thick in his throat. Gods, perhaps Silla's affliction was catching. "I will . . . try."

Gyda pulled back, her smile warm and knowing. "Don't let it be another five years before I see your face again, or I'll be forced to ride south and find you. I'll storm right into your grand Uppreisna meetings and pull you out by the ear."

Rey snorted at the image. "It won't be five years. I swear it." He paused. "And thank you. For everything."

As he turned to Vig, Rey felt the tightness in his throat spread to his chest. "Be safe," he told his friend. "Follow the plan. Update me on the mother and hatchlings as often as you can." *And on yourself,* he silently added.

"'Course," Vig grunted, an unreadable look in his eye. "You be safe as well."

Rey's response was a curt nod.

"Oh, stop, you two," Silla sniffled, eyes shining as she looked between them. "Ashes, but you'll make me cry."

Warmth filled Rey at the sight of Silla emotional at leaving Kalasgarde when she'd been so reluctant to come. Her transformation here had been remarkable. As, he'd admit, had been his own. Where once he'd felt despair, now he felt . . . renewed. Filled with new purpose.

"Do not worry for Rey," Silla said in a watery voice. "I shall protect him."

"Ah, but I don't doubt it," teased Vig, his eyes softening. "Fierce thing that you are."

"We did not have the chance for a Nordurian ice bath," said Silla, wiping away a tear.

"I believe you did your own ice bath," Vig said with a hearty laugh. "I'd wager that's enough to last a lifetime."

Silla launched herself at Vig, wrapping him in a fierce hug. "I'll miss you, Vig," she blubbered, burying her face in his chest.

Vig patted her back, sharing a lighthearted look with Rey. "I'll miss you, too, Silla of the south. Keep searching out that shy Blade Breaker skill of yours. And watch after Runný, won't you?"

"Of course." Silla sniffed into his chest, unwilling to let go.

Rey pried Silla's fingers loose from Vig and shuffled around the back of the shield-home to allow Runný some privacy in her farewells to her family. After several minutes of crying into his chest, Silla drew back, looking at Rey with red-rimmed eyes.

"You must think me a fool."

"It's an admirable thing," said Rey, wiping her tears away, "to forge such connection with others. Never feel ashamed of that."

Her hands slid up to his collar, pulling his mouth down to hers. "You always know just what to say," she whispered against his lips, then kissed him slowly.

"That's quite the opposite of what I've been told," he said, lips moving along the wet streaks on her cheeks. The salt of her tears burst on his tongue, and he wanted to kiss them all away.

But movement within the forest had him drawing back and reaching for his sword. Rey stared into the bushes, his chest clenching tight.

"What is . . ." Silla's voice trailed off as she followed his gaze.

Together, they stared into the coal-black eyes of the barn owl, peering at them from a low-hanging pine branch. It made no sense for the creature to be awake during daylight hours. Made no sense for it to feel as though the owl was bidding them farewell. But Rey was learning that some things in this world could not be explained by logic alone.

In the days following Silla's battle with the mother serpent, she'd repeated the story she'd attempted to tell him under the auroras. Had explained about the owl finding her in the Twisted Pinewoods and bringing her comfort. Had told him that because of this owl, she'd chosen the Owl's Hollow Inn in Reykfjord. Silla was certain the owl was Kristjan, watching over them and doing the bidding of the gods. And as he stared at the great bird, Rey let himself believe, if only for a moment.

"Thank you." Rey's voice shook with emotion. "For bringing us together."

Silla's hand found his, squeezing it tight.

"Perhaps you might pay Harpa a visit," Rey said. "I know she'd appreciate it."

The barn owl blinked, ruffling its feathers. And with a powerful push off the branch, it took flight, vanishing over the treetops and out of sight.

Gyda's fading voice reached Rey's ears, as did Vig's proclamation that the greataxe was, and forever would be, what a "true warrior" wielded. Soon, the voices were gone. Drawing back, Rey looked down at Silla, wondering how a heart could feel empty and full all at once.

He sighed. "We'd best be getting on the road."

CHAPTER 78

Sunnavík

Saga stood before the door to the queen's drawing room, trying to smooth the wrinkles from her lone blue dress. She'd been nauseous since yesterday's daymeal. An image flashed in her mind's eye—skirts whipping around her ankles, the Klaernar watching eagerly.

Saga forced her thoughts to the present with a deep, calming breath. *One step,* she told herself, knocking on the ornate door. There was only forward.

As a thrall led her through Signe's drawing room, Saga tried to settle her queasy stomach.

Since the wretched daymeal that had altered the course of Saga's life, a dozen plans had been built up and burned down. Ana and her link to the Uppreisna were gone. Rurik and his plans to steal her from the palace were gone. Which left Saga at Signe's whims. This was no longer about grand plans. No longer about a daring rebellion. Saga's world had narrowed to the very dire need to stay alive. Today was about trying to salvage something from the wreckage of her life.

It would be best to appeal to the queen's motherly side, she'd decided. Signe had, after all, proclaimed herself to be "like a mother" to Saga.

"Come in, darling," carried Signe's cool voice.

Saga lowered her mental barriers to free her Sense and forced herself forward. The queen was seated in one of two fur-draped armchairs arranged by the largest of the hearths. Before her was a small table of polished marble, set with two silver goblets. Sinking into the empty chair, Saga folded her hands in her lap and gazed cautiously at Signe.

... Desperation does not become our poor Saga, wafted Signe's thoughts.

"Wine, darling?" the queen asked aloud. She wore an ivory gown trimmed with hundreds of glacial pearls, her white-gold hair twined into a crown of braids upon her head. "Imported from the Southern Continent," Signe continued.

... and a gift from the Zagadkian party, thought Signe, waving the cupbearer over to fill the two goblets.

"My thanks, Your Highness," Saga murmured, eyeing the burgundy liquid. It was the lone spot of color in this whole room, aside from Saga's wrinkled blue dress.

Signe took a sip. "Oh, my," she murmured, her smile spreading.

... I see there is something redeemable about these Zagadkians after all, thought the queen, her gaze landing heavily on Saga. "What can I help you with, darling?"

Setting her goblet down, she looked Signe straight-on. "Your Highness, I've come to discuss my engagement."

... and now I shall savor the sweetness of this moment...

Saga's stomach twisted, but she forced herself to remain still.

With a long sigh, Signe watched her impassively. "Mmm. An abrupt change in plans, I know, darling. But I think we can both agree, Magnus is a far better match for you."

... She deserves worse for shaming my Little Bear...

"You see, Your Highness," began Saga. "I don't feel it is a particularly good match."

Signe hummed, taking another sip of her wine. "An older husband is not such a bad thing, you know. A man like Magnus can teach you a thing or two, darling."

... about pain and about power. About playing within the rules. Magnus excels at such things...

Saga pressed a hand to her stomach to steady the wave of revulsion that crashed through her. "I don't... that's not..."

"You know, Saga, we are so very alike," interrupted Signe. "And I am nothing if not a champion of women."

... I have plans for this kingdom. To make it better—to grant power back to those who are weakest...

Startled, Saga stared at the queen, trying to glean meaning from her thoughts.

Signe's lips tilted up at the corners. "We could have been allies, you and me. It's a shame you didn't heed my warnings, Saga. Things could have turned out differently for you."

... but I cannot allow anyone to impede my plans. It's unfortunate she's proven to be such a deceitful little thing...

Saga pushed on, despite the cold pit growing in her stomach. "You have the power, Your Highness. Please. You've been like a mother to me."

"Hmm," said Signe, watching her carefully. "You know, darling, I'm reminded of a story." The queen waved over the cupbearer, who refreshed her wine in an instant. "'Tis a Norvalander tale my father once told me. A children's fable about two little mice."

Saga took a small sip of wine, feigning interest.

"It begins with a kind brown mouse, happy in her little hole in the wall. One day, the brown mouse spies a white mouse fleeing from a cat. 'Here!' cries the little brown mouse, making space in her hole. The white mouse dashes into the hole in the very nick of time, narrowly missing a swipe of the cat's paw."

Signe brought her cup to her lips and took a delicate sip. "The brown mouse offered nothing but hospitality to the white mouse, sharing her evening meal and allowing the white mouse to stay until she recovered from her fright. But the white mouse was not such a kindly creature. She stayed longer than she was welcome. Ate more than her share. And was careless in the little hole. One day, the brown mouse returned to discover her home crumbling to bits. With great sadness, the brown mouse was forced to leave and search for a new one."

Saga stared at the queen's lips—wine had stained them berry red, stark against Signe's pale skin. "It took quite some time, but the brown mouse eventually found a new hole. It wasn't a few days later she spotted that same white mouse running from the cat. And this time, the brown mouse did not offer her home as a safe refuge."

Signe's ice-blue eyes bored into Saga's. "Why do you think I was reminded of this story, darling?"

A slow shiver rolled down Saga's spine. "I suppose you liken me to the white mouse." She chewed the inside of her cheek. "Does that make you the brown mouse, then?"

Signe's laugh was like tinkling glass. "No, darling. I am the cat. I devour curious little creatures." The queen set her goblet down, staring at Saga with intensity.

And here it was. This game of pretenses finally put to an end.

"We both know this hasn't a thing to do with Rurik," hissed Saga.

Signe let out a delicate huff. "Darling, you've made the most elementary of mistakes." The queen leveled Saga with a long, hard look. "You let the passions of your heart take control. And in doing so, you lost the only thing protecting you. Virtue is so very coveted by the Urkans."

"I-it was only a kiss," Saga stammered.

... Beauty is a weapon, thought Signe, *one that Zagadkian man wielded quite expertly ...*

"It is enough," said the queen, "to bring shame upon my Bjorn."

... and enough, thought Signe, *to rid us of this meddlesome little creature ...*

Saga's desperation reached a boiling point. Clearly, appealing to the queen's sympathies would get her nowhere. She took a deep breath, then let the words flow. "I know you've been toying with galdur, right under the king's nose. I know you've been stealing Galdra and harvesting their magic by the most vile means."

... At last, her backbone shows, thought Signe. But the queen's face was maddeningly calm, silent as though urging Saga to continue.

"I know you had Ana executed to send me a message." Saga's hand curled into a fist as she thought of the woman strung up on the pillar. "I will *never* forgive you."

"Darling, do you think I need your forgiveness?" Signe watched her impassively. "I don't need you at all."

... This wedding cannot come soon enough, thought Signe.

"I'll tell the king," blurted Saga, anger rising in her. "I know about Alfson and Lekka. I know about Rökksgarde."

Signe sighed. "You won't tell Ivar. There is no proof of anything. And why would he believe *you,* Saga? You, who have just proven yourself dishonest? Your word had little value to start. But now it is worthless."

The telltale sting of tears burned through her skull, but Saga forced them back. Signe would *never* have her tears.

"It is a shame, darling, that it has come to this," said Signe. "I have been in your shoes, and I tried to help you because of it. A pity you did not heed my warnings. You could have had power—you could have been *queen.* Instead, you will face the consequences of your own actions."

Saga leaped to her feet, the goblet toppling. A crimson stain spread across the white marble table, dripping onto the floor.

"I cannot recall much of my birth mother," she said, the words coming from deep within. "You're the only mother I've ever truly known. And one day, I shall repay all the kindness you've shown me."

And with that, Saga left the room.

CHAPTER 79

North of Svangormr Pass

Silla stared at the braids spilling down Runný's back as they rode silently along the trail. The mountains looming before them were thick with freshly fallen snow, the cold more penetrative than in Kalasgarde's guarded valley. A river rushed beside them, the top not yet frozen over. As she'd done a dozen other times this hour, Silla probed inwardly, searching for any hint of Saga's presence.

Nothing.

Sighing, she fixed her attention on Dawn. The horse's emerging winter coat gave her a shaggy, unkempt look, but Silla had braided her black mane to match her own hair. When last they'd passed through this valley—on their way to Kalasgarde—Dawn's neck had drooped, a lead tied to Horse necessary to prompt her forward. Now there was pride in each step. Dawn had relented to Silla's brushing and braiding, and she now ate from Silla's palm while maintaining eye contact. She'd even bestowed several affectionate nudges upon Silla.

"You've come a long way, girl," said Silla, rubbing Dawn's neck in appreciation. And so, Silla supposed, had she.

They rode on for hours, through valleys and up foothills, Silla searching constantly for any hint of Saga's well-being. By the time they reached the first true mountain pass, Silla's insides were twisted into at least a dozen knots.

"How do you feel?" asked Rey, sidling Horse up beside Dawn, who nickered in greeting.

"My thighs ache," Silla said absently, then burst into laughter. "Though *not* in the good way."

Rey's hard look conveyed a dozen different plans he had in store for her. "We'll work on the good sort of ache tonight." He paused. "Svangormr Pass is the most treacherous stretch from here to Kopa. We cannot pause until we are through it, but we shall stop for the night in the valley beyond."

Swallowing, Silla nodded. She was eager to warm her toes by the fire, a cup of róa clutched in hand. The trail sloped up sharply, towering pines dwindling to scrawny firs spearing through the deepening snow.

By the time the terrain evened out, Dawn's coat was dampened with sweat. "Good girl," Silla whispered, stroking her withers. "Extra oat treats for you tonight."

The wind howled as long, ridged mountains climbed up on either side of the path. Silla recalled Vig's explanation of the mountain pass. They did indeed resemble a pair of curving serpents, slumbering beneath blankets of snow. Silla couldn't help but shudder. If she never saw another serpent in her life, it would be too soon.

Though trees dotted the mountainside, distinct gaps existed on the steep slopes where avalanches had plowed through. The wind tunneled between the mountains with increasing rage, lashing against Silla's cheeks. Hooves crunched on snow at a smooth pace. In light of the fresh-fallen snow, Rey had instructed their group to remain silent through this stretch, which lent a decidedly eerie feel to the place.

Yet an unsettling feeling grew in Silla's stomach. Her eyes searched for danger, but she saw only more trees, more snow, and the endless curving line of the mountain range.

As they rounded the bend, she heard it—a sound so faint, Silla thought it the wind. Rey held up a fist, and their line came to a halt. Without the crunch of hooves on snow, the sound was more defined, sending a chill straight down Silla's spine.

Hardly daring to breathe, she leaned in the saddle to see past Rey. White and evergreen were disrupted by a mass of ice blue. Silla blinked against the frigid wind, trying to discern what exactly it was, and why, exactly, it was moving. She nearly choked on the realization.

The hatchlings.

Dozens of serpents swarming atop one another in a mob of ice-blue scales.

"We must turn back," murmured Mýr from behind her.

"No," interjected Hef, his voice fortified with steel. "This is our chance to end them."

"Our task is to protect Eisa," interjected Kálf, a surprising note of concern in his voice. "It would be folly to leap into battle."

"They are too many," said Runný. "That must be all the remaining hatchlings—four dozen at least, and in unfavorable terrain. There is no cover, no advantage to be found."

Silla swallowed the lump in her throat as a pair of ember-bright eyes turned to regard them. A forked tongue slipped between gleaming fangs, crimson dripping from each. The hatchling undulated from the mass, tipping off the top of the pile and tumbling to the snow.

"It's not built for land," whispered Hef. "See the paddle on its tail? These creatures are meant for the water. Here, they are cumbersome. I'm telling you, this is our advantage!"

Slowly, Rey unhooked his shield from Horse's saddle. "Unless we can take that one out without the horde's notice, we may not have a choice."

"On it," muttered Mýr from behind them, followed by the *shick* of a bow being slid from its straps. A soft twang signaled Mýr's arrow whisking through the air. It sank into the hatchling's glowing red eye, causing the creature to hiss as it writhed, then still.

"I don't like the feel of this," whispered Kálf, and Silla had to agree. Alerted by the noise, another hatchling tumbled up from the horde. A second, third, fourth . . . Silla stopped counting.

"Dismount!" ordered Rey. "The corpses will trap the horses, and we have a better angle from below. Breakers up front, Ashbringers in back. Silla beside me." Swiftly, the group dismounted, sending the horses down the trail. "Against this rock face," Rey ordered, darting toward a bare, sheer cliff face of dark basalt. "We'll make a small shield wall formation against it. Have a clear view of incoming serpents."

They made a semicircle against the rock wall—Blade Breakers again in the front protecting the Ashbringers. Runný, predictably, was nowhere to be seen.

"Shields up," ordered Rey. "Aim for the eyes, underbellies, as silent as you can."

Rey's eyes locked with Silla's, his steely mask dropping for a bare moment to reveal fear and worry.

"Together," she assured him.

"Together," Rey repeated, smoke peeling up from his palms as he expressed. "Stay beside me."

The serpents fell upon them like wolves on a dying creature, and the world dissolved into chaos. There were only those blood-red eyes, their lashing strikes, the spear-sharp fangs stabbing between shields. Fireballs exploded from Rannver and Nefi, Kálf's whip charring serpents left and right. Hef, Erik, and Mýr shielded the Ashbringers with their Blade Breaker strength. Serpents were torn in two, black blood spraying the snow as they were hurled through the air. And as the underbelly of a serpent split open mid-strike, Silla knew Runný fought beside them.

Rey's smoke burrowed down throats and coiled around serpentine bodies, while Silla's white sword slashed out time and time again. But as beast after beast swarmed atop one another, Rey soon relinquished his galdur for his sword, heating it with his palm until it glowed red-hot. After weeks of sparring together, Rey understood Silla's movements before she did herself; he kept away from her sword with ease. They worked in tandem, Silla's bright sword disorienting them while Rey finished them with a sizzling strike to the underbelly. And where Silla's gaps in defensive awareness existed, Rey seemed to fill them, hacking off fangs and shielding her from attack.

More hatchlings fell upon them, a frantic mass of forked tongues and slashing fangs. Silla cleaved off a fang, shoving the creature back as it screeched in confusion, then plunged her sword deep into its eye. The eerie red glow extinguished to black as the serpent fell still. Her hair was now frosted, lashes glinting.

A shrill male screech filled the air, and she whirled. An enormous figure blotted out the sky. And Rannver . . . he was lifted from the ground, a large fang protruding from his chest.

"No!" screamed Mýr, diving for Rannver. But the mother serpent yanked him back from the group's safety, holding a writhing Rannver out for her children. A hatchling struck at him, sinking fangs into his thigh, then wrenching them free. Blood spurted in vivid streaks of crimson. A third beast snatched at Rannver's middle, but the mother jerked back. Rannver was torn in two, half a dozen serpents swarming upon one another at the scent of his blood.

"Bastards!" howled Erik.

"Shore up!" barked Rey. "We break and we die!"

Their semicircle tightened with one less among them. Serpent corpses were piled all around, forming a protective wall of sorts. But Silla's stomach knotted as another idea settled into place.

"Trapped," Silla warned. "She can pick us off!"

"Burn through them," Rey ordered Kálf and Nefi.

As the Ashbringers got to work, the stench of burnt flesh overwhelmed her senses, but Silla remained focused on the mother serpent lunging down from above. She slashed her sword upward, the mother recoiling just in time. And then she was striking again, and Silla's sword sliced through the air, connecting with hard scales. The impact reverberated through her, yet it was enough to make the mother jerk back.

"Kálf," bellowed Rey, jostled from behind as Erik stumbled into him, "we're running out of time."

"Almost . . . there . . ." was Kálf's labored reply.

The mother struck down, and Rey yanked Silla back, the pair tumbling to the ground and out of striking distance. But it seemed the great serpent had found prey all the same. A glinting fang plunged into Nefi's back and hauled him upward. Dumbstruck, Silla stared into Nefi's terror-widened eyes.

"No!" she screamed, leaping to her feet and grabbing Nefi's foot.

The mother serpent wrenched back, and Nefi's boot slipped through Silla's fingers. Horror and revulsion clenched in her stomach as the hatchlings rushed below the mother, fighting for their prize. But then she was being dragged through a tunnel of putrid, burnt corpses. As they stumbled into fresh, cool air, Silla sucked it in by the lungful.

Her relief was short-lived. The corner of her vision shadowed. Rey's blade whizzed through the air with preternatural speed, blocking the mother serpent's renewed attack.

"Stay behind me!" he bellowed as the enormous serpent reared up. From this angle, Silla could see a black line running under the mother serpent's underjaw—the wound her galdur had delivered in Jökull's lake. But revulsion quickly overtook the slim measure of satisfaction as she saw the scrap of black armor dangling from the mother's fang. Nefi.

Anger burned low in her stomach. A hatchling lashed out, and Silla's sword moved with pure instinct, sinking into its underbelly. Whirling, Silla placed her back to Rey's.

"You take the hatchlings," growled Rey. "I'll handle the mother." Smoke stripped up from his hands, building and coiling above into a churning storm. Sweat beaded Silla's brow as heat radiated from the fiery tempest, ash raining down on the snow-covered ground. She widened her stance and braced herself as a trio of hatchlings surged forward.

Behind her, the mother screeched, and Silla felt a rush of air as she slashed out at the smaller serpents. Rey had rooted himself into the ground, yelling with his exertion. Above, the storm of smoke spun tighter until it took on a serpentine shape. Flesh sizzled, the mother shrieking once more.

Another hatchling struck out, and Silla responded without a breath to spare. It was pure chaos. Silla caught sight of Kálf, lashing a fire whip at a serpent bearing down on Erik from behind—Mýr cleaving one beast in half with Blade Breaker strength while two other beasts closed in on her from either side. But as the minutes passed and Rey's grunts grew more irritated, Silla's worry festered.

"What are you doing back there?" Silla demanded. "Roast her,

Galtung!" She glanced over her shoulder. Singed black scales were patched along the mother serpent's body, but it seemed only to have incensed her anger.

"Thank you for that," he growled. "I hadn't considered it."

Silla slashed through a lunging serpent. "What's the problem?

"She's too fast."

"You need to get closer," she said, an idea taking form. "You need a diversion." A hand wrapped around Silla's arm, squeezing gently.

"What do you need?" asked Runný.

"Guard Rey's flank," said Silla in a low voice. She eyed the mother serpent. "You want me, don't you, spawn of Myrkur?" The mother's enormous, forked tongue slid out, those glowing ember eyes homed in on Silla. "Such a tasty Volsik. But you'll have to catch me."

And then Silla ran.

She felt, more than heard, the mother give chase. The ground shook with each clumsy undulation as the mother plowed after her. Silla dodged and ducked and slashed her way through hatchlings. Behind her, Runný cried out and Rey bellowed in rage. Silla cast an anxious glance over her shoulder and stumbled.

His storm of smoke seemed to have evaporated as Rey clung to the serpent's back, legs flailing with each surge of her body. One hand slipped, and he held on to a single pale-blue scale. The mother serpent paused, head whirling in search of the pest on her back.

"Stop!" yelled Silla. The mother whipped around, nostrils flaring. But besides the giant serpent, dozens of smaller red eyes turned to her as well.

"Not tasty," Silla said, backing away. "I lied! I taste like old socks!" She glanced at the mother—Rey had regained his grip and was shimmying up the mother's neck. Just a little farther and he'd be right where he needed to be . . .

Silla turned and ran.

The ground rumbled as the mother took chase, her offspring not far behind. Hissing set the hairs on Silla's neck on end, and she glanced over her shoulder once more. Rey had reached the mother's head, ash and smoke coiling up from his raised palm.

Silla dove out of the way just in time. The mother's fangs sank deep into the ground, thunder echoing off the mountains surrounding them. By some miracle, Rey clung to the serpent's head, and he hooked his leg back over. Silla felt his galdur thicken in the air, saw smoke peeling up from his hands—a torrent unlike any she'd seen before. The smoke was midnight black, blotting out the skies, embers crackling like wildfire within. Silla shielded her face from the heat, snow melting beneath her.

The serpent yanked her fangs loose from the ground, rearing up. But Silla rushed into the mother's path, desperate to keep her distracted.

It was enough. Rey shoved the full force of his power at the mother, a maelstrom of smoke and embers battering relentlessly down on her. Smoke burrowed into the mother's eye sockets and nostrils, pouring into her body and filling the air with the scent of charred flesh. The mother screamed, writhing about, but Axe Eyes held on, pouring every ounce of his galdur into this monstrous foe. She slowed, then swayed, and Rey was suddenly sliding down the serpent's back, rolling onto the snow-covered ground. The mother crashed down, sending a plume of snow into the air.

She did not rise.

Silla rushed to Rey's side, slashing into a hatchling lunging at him from behind. Two more appeared in its place, and together Silla and Rey cut them down. But where one fell, another appeared. Another. Another. Exhaustion was creeping in, Silla's muscles protesting. There seemed to be an endless supply of hatchlings, their numbers never dwindling.

A curious whistling sound had her looking up in time to catch a flaming arrow sailing through the air. It collided with a precarious-looking shelf of ice, sending it tumbling down with a sharp crack. Snow powdered the air, making it difficult to see, but the low rumble shaking the earth told Silla enough.

"Avalanche!" shouted Rey, grabbing Silla's arm and yanking her away. And again, Silla was running for her life, this time from an altogether different foe. The rumbling grew more thunderous with each passing heartbeat, snow shaking loose from trees. On they ran, until their muscles screamed and their lungs burned, the sound reaching an earsplitting crescendo. Breathless, they turned.

Erik emerged from a cloud of powder, then Mýr and Hef, dragging Kálf between them. Runný flickered into view a heartbeat later.

"Thank the gods," wailed Silla.

Together, the group watched the avalanche plow down the mountain, straight into the mass of clumsy hatchlings. Snow burst into the air, powdering their faces and obscuring their vision. As the snow settled, nothing remained of the battle but an enormous bank of snow.

The serpents were buried.

"The gods have spared us!" exclaimed Mýr, tugging Runný into a tight hug.

Tears sprang to Silla's eyes. It truly felt like a miracle. The mother and the hatchlings were gone. Their group had survived. A hand ran up her spine, settling on the back of her neck. And then Silla was pulled against Rey's chest, his lips pressed to hers.

Silla kissed him back, waiting for relief to come. But despite the reassuring pressure of Rey's lips, a niggling feeling grew in the back of her mind. Where had that arrow come from? And why had the serpents been *here,* of all places? What had the mass of hatchlings been swarming over? Crimson blood had dripped from the first hatchling's lips, which meant they'd been feasting on something . . .

"Well, isn't this sweet."

Silla jerked back with a sharp gasp. That voice. It was . . . *no.* Slowly, she turned to face the man who'd once been her safe refuge, her comfort. A person she'd foolishly trusted.

"Hello, Curls."

CHAPTER 80

Sunnavík

"Where is Magnus?" demanded King Ivar, draining his goblet and slamming it down.

It was the day after her meeting with Signe, and Saga now found herself seated beside the king for this travesty of an engagement feast. The feasting tables were filled with Sunnavík's nobles chatting among themselves and sampling the Zagadkian wine the queen had served. As Saga caught herself searching for a pair of emerald eyes, she scowled.

She had known, *known,* that if she and Rurik were discovered kissing in the courtyard, it would be Saga who paid the price. And yet she'd thought better of him. How, after everything they'd shared in the gardens, could he have just left her?

Saga sighed. Self-pity was not a luxury she could afford. She needed to keep her wits sharp and find an ally.

But this room was hardly filled with the type of people Saga could ally herself with. Aside from the Volsik betrayers and Urkans, many were friends of Magnus Heart Eater. Bile climbed up her throat as Saga realized those same soldiers who'd cornered her in the stables were likely in this room, ready to revel as Magnus claimed yet more vengeance.

Punished, echoed his voice in her ears. *Nothing but a worthless pet.*

Desperation filled her as she surveyed the room. Alone. She was alone in this pit of serpents, and she wanted to scream.

Slanderous whispers carried through the hall, and looks of disdain were sent her way. Magnus's name reached her ears. She shuddered. Days from now, she'd be wed to that monster. Would *belong* to him.

But Eisa.

All day, as her thoughts spiraled into darkness, she'd brought herself back to the light with a single thought. She had her sister—had the mind-to-mind connection. And Saga reminded herself to take things one step at a time. First, she'd get through this evening. Then she'd figure out the rest.

A cupbearer swirled up with a silver jug, wordlessly filling Saga's goblet as Ivar shoved his own forward. "Oh, I'm sorry, Your Majesty," she said sweetly, dropping into a curtsy. "It was the last drop. I shall return with fresh wine in a moment."

"Would you like my cup, Your Majesty?" asked Saga, offering her goblet to the king. She was unused to sitting so near to him and found herself missing Bjorn's dull tales and odd observations. But as he was her father figure, tradition dictated Ivar sit to her left at wedding celebrations.

All night, she'd fought with herself—to tell the king of Signe's schemes or not. Spilling to the king without proof seemed more likely to incense him further. But now she held the king's ear. Perhaps there were other opportunities to be found here.

Ivar waved away Saga's offered goblet, surveying the crowd. "The hour grows late, and Magnus is normally punctual."

Saga swirled her cup, scowling at the Zagadkian-gifted wine. As far as she was concerned, the later her betrothed arrived, the better. Sipping deeply, she let the rich flavors wash over her tongue.

"I must apologize, Your Majesty," said Saga, gathering her courage. "I did not intend to shame the family."

Ivar surveyed her with dark eyes, stroking his blond beard with a large, battle-scarred hand. "I suppose it is in your blood to make poor decisions," he said with a sigh.

Saga gritted her teeth with the effort to keep her face impassive. Slowly, she took a long sip of wine. Gods, but she'd need all the liquid courage she could get to weather this evening.

"I suppose you are blameless for being so easily misled," continued the king. "But as you well know, power is a thing that must always be displayed. My son cannot be seen as a predator while sympathizing with prey."

The cupbearer returned and filled the king's goblet. "So you understand why you cannot marry Bjorn. You'd make him look forgiving. Weak."

Saga's heart palpitated wildly in her chest, restlessness gathering in her. "I understand." She collected every lingering scrap of her courage. "But, by that logic, would I not also make Magnus look weak?"

Ivar watched her with hard, assessing eyes. "Unlike Bjorn, Magnus is seasoned and has already made a name for himself. I cannot think of a single person who does not know and fear the Heart Eater." His eyes landed on her hands—gloved, to appease Signe. "And I think we both know Magnus is hardly the forgiving type."

Saga's knee began bouncing beneath the table.

... Ursir's damnation. Where is Magnus? I don't want this spectacle to go on longer than needed. I have that blond serving thrall to see to ...

Saga straightened, casting a sidelong glance at King Ivar. Her mental barricades must have slipped loose. Focusing on her goblet, she reached for her barriers to pull them back into place. But each time she tried to tug them, they slipped through her fingers like silk.

... The girl is getting what she deserves ...
... I heard the Zagadkians couldn't cast off fast enough ...
... I wonder when Prince Bjorn will select a new bride ...

The discordant jumble of thoughts built slowly in volume. Taking short sips of air, Saga tried again to pull up her barriers, only to discover great frayed holes widening with each passing heartbeat. A sudden onslaught of sound caused her body to tense, and her grip tightened around her goblet.

What was happening? Never before had she lost control of her Sense; never had she been unable to pull up her barriers. Her world became chaos, a roar of thoughts and boisterous conversations, the volume growing unbearable. Hands clapping over her ears, Saga slammed her eyes shut. She gasped for breath, trying to ease her racing heart.

"Saga, I did not know." Yrsa's voice.

Saga forced her eyes open. Took in her foster sister. Yrsa stood before her, with wide, earnest eyes.

"Please understand, I did not know."

... I only wanted Lord Rurik to myself. I never meant for this to happen ...

Saga's lips parted, but the deluge of sound made it impossible to think, let alone speak.

"Magnus hurt you, didn't he?" Yrsa's thumb rubbed against the back of Saga's gloved hand. "That's why you looked terrified at the daymeal."

... They call him the Heart Eater. By Ursir's Paw, I would take it back if I could ...

Saga caught movement down the table. As she turned her head, her eyes locked onto a pale face. White-blond hair. Eyes of glacial blue. Signe's lips curved up.

... Saga, darling, wafted the queen's thoughts, as though she were directing them straight to her. *It seems you've been keeping secrets from me.*

CHAPTER 81

Svangormr Pass

The wind was fierce and biting, but as Silla stared at Jonas, she could not feel it. A range of emotions swamped her—grief for what had once been, shame for her role in his brother's death, and a distinct sense of inadequacy. Jonas had discarded her. Tossed her away. Seeing him again brought her back to that cell, cold and scared, shrinking in on herself.

Jonas looked the same as always. Golden hair pulled back at his crown, strands Silla had run her fingers through countless times. Eyes the color of a summer sky, always with that hint of arrogance. She hated that she knew it was merely a mask to conceal his inner wounds—that she knew beneath Jonas's collar would hang his family's talisman, reminding him of all he'd lost and strove to regain.

A chasm opened wide in her chest. She despised him for drugging her and giving her to the Klaernar yet understood his motives all at once. But as Jonas stared back at her with hard, unfeeling eyes, at last the cold of the mountains penetrated her skin.

Silla chilled further as two dozen armed Klaernar stepped up behind Jonas. Black wolf-pelt cloaks swirled in the wind, revealing handaxes and hevríts sheathed in their battle belts, their claw-tattooed faces reigniting her long-learned fear of the King's Claws.

"A trap," murmured Rey, strong at her side. "They lured the serpents here to thin us out . . . to tire us." He nodded down the path, and Silla understood how the serpents had come to be here. Sheep carcasses were heaped over blood-spattered snow, positioned directly beside the icy waters of the river. "They triggered that avalanche to block our retreat."

Silla's mind whirled, desperate to form a plan. Galdur nearly drained, they were outnumbered and had nowhere to retreat.

"Fuck," muttered Erik, appearing to reach the same conclusion.

Jonas's eyes climbed from Silla's boots up to her face. He scoffed. "Nice lébrynja, Curls. You think yourself a warrior now?" His gaze flitted to his former headman. "I see you wasted no time taking my leavings, Rey."

Beside her, Rey unsheathed his sword and widened his stance.

Jonas's lips quirked. "She's something, isn't she? Skin so soft—smells so sweet. Best you find it out from me, Rey—beneath the pretty face, she's the spawn of Myrkur."

"Not another word," warned Rey in a low growl.

"I still hear her voice when I'm alone in my bed at night. *More, Jonas, you feel so good.*"

"Hold your tongue, or I'll cut it out and feed it to you." Rey stepped forward, but Silla put a hand on his arm.

"Do not let him stir you," she hissed, though her cheeks burned fiercely.

"You turned your back on your kin," snarled Rey. "The man I knew was better than that."

"Kin?" scoffed Jonas. "*She* was never kin. Ilías . . . he was kin."

"What about me, Jonas? What about Hekla and Gunnar and Sigrún? We were your family as well. You betray us all and dishonor your brother."

"You do not speak for Ilías." Jonas spat on the ground. "I swore an oath to my brother and intend to fulfill it. She must pay."

Rey shook his head, and Silla could feel his disappointment. "It was a warrior's death, Jonas. An honorable one."

"A *needless* one!" exclaimed Jonas, a vein pulsing in his forehead.

"This will only end with more of your sorrow," warned Rey.

"Enough, Rey," said Jonas. "My quarrel is not with you."

"That's where you're wrong, Jonas," growled Rey. "If your quarrel is with her, then it *is* my fight. Heed my warning as I'll say it only once: You touch her and I'll open your throat with my axe."

"She's got you wrapped around her finger, Rey. That's what she does. She tricks you. She's a *liar*."

"I know she's a liar. She's *my* liar, though."

"Yours." Jonas huffed. "Ah. That's right, *Slátrari*." His lip curled. "Your own lies have caught up with you at last. All those years lying to the Crew. Hiding what you are while preaching honor."

"Understand that I did not do so maliciously. Some lies are necessary to stay alive in this kingdom," said Rey uneasily.

"Deceitful, the pair of you." Jonas shook his head. "You deserve each other." He turned to Silla, those brilliant blue eyes so filled with hate. "Silla. Or do you prefer *Eisa*?" His lip curled. "There is no escape for you. But if you come willingly, we will spare the others."

To Silla's surprise, Kálf stepped forward, leaning heavily on Mýr's shoulder. "You'll need to cut through us first," he snarled.

"I see she's poisoned the rest of you with her lies as well," said Jonas. "This woman brings nothing but destruction. A foolish choice to put yourself in her path."

"It is not Eisa's doing," spat Mýr. "Let us place the blame where it belongs—on the shoulders of that farce of a queen."

Ignoring Mýr, Jonas returned his gaze to Silla. "This is your last warning, Silla. We can do this by word or by blade. Surely you do not wish for more people to die."

Silla watched him, choosing her words carefully. "I do not wish for more death; in that you are right." Few though their group was, Silla felt their support building her up. "But I will always choose to fight for Íseldur, no matter the odds."

Her blood pumped hot through her veins. "I owe it to my kingdom. To my family. I owe it to Matthias Nordvig, Ilías Svik, to Skeggagrim and Nefi and Rannver, all of whom died to keep me safe. But most of all, I owe it to my people, who've long suffered under the Urkan regime."

Silla had planned to say none of it. Hadn't known she felt it until the words spilled from her heart. But now she *felt* it down to her very marrow. Long had it taken her to get to this place, but here she was.

"Here are your options," Silla continued. "Ride back down that trail or become food for the ravens. I can see you think yourself quite clever. But hear me now, Jonas: A hungry wolf is bound to wage a hard battle. And we, the Galdra, are *starving*."

Jonas let out a bark of incredulous laughter. As the sound echoed off the mountains surrounding them, the distant *whumf* of falling snow met their ears. The group collectively held their breaths, releasing them only when silence was restored.

Jonas turned his gaze to Silla. "Gods. You've spent too much time with Rey. Your arrogance is astounding."

Silla shook her head slowly. "I'm sorry you're hurting, Jonas. Sorry for what you've been through. But this"—she gestured at the Klaernar behind him—"this is not the way. It is not right, and you know it in your heart."

"Do not presume to know my heart," he growled.

"I know family means everything to you," she answered. "I know you wish only to honor them. It is not too late. Leave now, Jonas, and I'll let you live."

He scoffed again. "You'll *let me live*. Curls. Your threats are as soft as your cunt."

With a ragged exhale, Rey stepped forward, but Silla grabbed his hand, yanking him back. She expressed her light; the sword formed quickly. But she could sense a hollowness within—her source was lower than ever before. Frost crackled along the blade's length as she took her familiar defensive stance.

The slightest widening of his eyes was the only trace of surprise from Jonas. Just as quickly, it was gone. "It'll be blades then," he said dully.

With a subtle nod, the Klaernar put their ringed knuckles to their noses, inhaling deeply.

"Berskium powder stored in their rings," hissed Kálf. "'Twill give them berserker power and rage."

Indeed, as they watched, the Klaernar shuddered, a wild look filling their eyes. As a red-bearded man on the farthest end locked eyes with Silla, he bared his teeth in an ugly snarl. The Klaernar squadron growled and shifted, some bashing swords against their shields, others biting down on the rims.

"Do not let their bravado frighten you," murmured Rey, his boot edging against hers. Smoke peeled up from his palms, gathering above him. "The berskium powder makes them strong, yes, but it also makes them reckless."

Swallowing, Silla braced herself for the Klaernar's advance. Beside her, Kálf's flames licked to life. But before their small band of Galdra could unleash themselves upon the Klaernar, the two dozen snarling warriors vanished into thin air.

A cruel smile crept across Jonas's face. "The queen's Chosen are eager to test themselves in battle."

CHAPTER 82

"Shadow Hounds!" hissed Erik, widening his stance while Runný flashed out of sight.

"How?" spluttered Silla, tracking the footprints in the snow as their snarling opponents approached. "How can they . . . they're *Klaernar* . . ."

"The queen has a new class of warriors," growled an invisible foe.

"This is against the natural order of things," said Kálf, standing gingerly on his injured leg. "Whatever this is, the queen trifles with things she should not."

"Queen Signe needs weapons in her arsenal," said Jonas. "And you, Silla, are apparently of great value."

"I'm not a weapon for her to use," Silla snapped, gazing at her frostfire. Was this why the queen had tracked her all this time? Because she wanted this sword? Or was it her power as a Volsik . . . her unknown weapon against Myrkur?

Jonas scowled. "She's come to that very conclusion. And as you've proven more evasive than she'd expected, the queen has decided you must be destroyed."

Footsteps closed in on them, growls vibrating the air.

"We work together," hissed Rey from beside her, smoke and embers building around him. But they were thin, so transparent compared with the maelstrom from earlier—it seemed Rey, too, was drained. "Force these kuntas to show themselves, then take them out."

Rey pushed out a thin wall of smoke, which billowed around several charging forms. Lunging at the nearest, Silla hacked through bone and flesh with her sword of light. An animalistic howl tore through the air, the scent of rotten eggs swarming up her nostrils.

"What is that smell?" Mýr choked out.

"It's coming from *them*," Erik muttered.

But the scent triggered a memory . . . words from a woman long dead. The phial Skraeda had held—the one Silla had smashed against the wall. It had the same sulfurous smell as these men.

I am told there are tiny living things in this liquid, Skraeda had told her. *You will ingest them and host them while they feast on your galdur, acquiring it in their bodies. Once they have gorged themselves and created more tiny spawn, I will take them from you, bring them into my own body, and your magic will become my own.*

"Míkrób," she murmured. It had to be.

Silla tried to gather herself, but her sword flickered, then sputtered out entirely.

The Klaernar charged at them, a flurry of snarls and howls as they collided with the Galdra. Beside her, Rey grunted, his left leg collapsing beneath him. His arms were wrenched back, hands forced behind him. Whirling, Silla pulled everything she had, only managing a clumsy orb of light. With a grunt, she flung it, ducking as an invisible Klaernar's blade swung just over her head. As her light collided with him, Rey's attacker yowled in pain. Twitching, Rey grabbed his opponent's iron shirt, plunging a hevrít into his neck.

A tiny arrow zipped beside her ear.

"Galdur-quelling arrows!" she shouted.

Rey's body flew sideways, and he landed with a hard grunt. Before Silla could try for another orb, an invisible foe's fist collided hard with her jaw. She fell onto her back, her skull exploding with white-hot pain as her assailant clambered atop her with a growl. The berserker's frantic movements only fueled her panic higher, and Silla expressed all that she could manage—another clumsy orb. It was weak, so faint, yet as it crashed into the Klaernar above her, it danced along his skin, revealing his wild-eyed form. He grunted and pawed at the light, trying to rid himself of it, but it was in vain.

The Klaernar's eyes widened as he choked, the tip of a dagger protruding from his neck.

Runný's form shimmered for the briefest of seconds before an invisible hand wrenched Silla to her feet. "Thank you," she whispered, taking in the bizarre scene before her—Rey and Kálf wrestling invisible foes, Mýr yanking a skarpling quill from her neck.

Kálf's head snapped back, a quill embedding in his shoulder. His flame whip extinguished, and he shouted in alarm.

Silla cursed under her breath, trying to count. Silla, Rey, and Runný against . . . she could not say how many Klaernar remained.

Rey took a brutal blow that snapped his head back, and blood dribbled from the corner of his mouth. Animalistic sounds shook the air, Rey's left leg collapsing once more. Were they targeting it? A red haze clouded Silla's vision.

"Leave him alone!" she screamed, springing toward them.

Air hissed beside her ear, a longbow's arrow thunking into the snowbank beyond.

Silla whirled to find Jonas, a second arrow nocked and aimed directly at her. Suddenly, he lurched sideways, rolling with an invisible assailant. But taking a swift, brutal punch, Runný's form shimmered back into view. Eyes closed, her head lolled to the side, but she was still breathing.

A Klaernar barreled at her, and Silla dodged the man's lethal blow. From the corner of her eye, she tracked Rey. Wrestling with his invisible opponent, Rey tried to express with his bare hand, while grappling with the man—men?—with his other. With a shout, Rey crashed his head into what must have been the man's face—a wet crack preceded a hot spray of blood. Rey could finally express, smashing his red-hot fist through chain mail and flesh—straight into his assailant's torso.

But then it happened. A quill sank into Rey's neck. The smoke rising from his hand vanished in an instant. Rey bellowed a loud curse, and Silla's stomach lurched. His galdur was snuffed out.

"Move, and I'll end him," growled Jonas, another longbow's arrow nocked and pointed directly at Rey.

Blood thundered in Silla's ears, blocking all else out. They were surrounded... doomed... the barest trickle left in the heart of her magic. The twang of a bow drew a scream from deep within her, but Rey twisted a Klaernar corpse, using him as a shield.

Pain blazed through Silla as the broad side of a sword came down on her wrist. Quicker than she could react, her galdur collapsed, her arms wrenched behind her back. Her assailant twisted her arms upward, tendons popping, pain lashing sharp and hot until Silla screamed.

The scent of leather and iron surrounded her, driving her anger to new heights.

"Curls," drawled Jonas, pulling her arm tightly until it felt as though her bone might snap. "My, you've learned some new tricks. But it seems you've still got the same weakness."

She struggled against him, disgust curling in her gut. "Don't touch me, you kunta."

Jonas grunted, stumbling to the side. His grip on her loosened, and Silla wrenched free, lunging for a hevrít lying nearby. "Axe Eyes," Jonas growled, pulling Rey's obsidian-hilted dagger from his thigh and tossing it aside.

Whirling, Silla advanced on Jonas.

From the edge of her vision, Rey's chin snapped up as he took a punch from an invisible adversary, and she realized he must have left himself open as he'd thrown that dagger. His body crashed sideways as if he'd been tackled. There were too many of them... and he couldn't see them... couldn't use his galdur...

This ended. Here. Now.

She turned on Jonas, hevrít in hand. It was just Silla and Jonas on snowy terrain, and he had the mountain at his back. She rushed at him with speed he did not expect. Stumbling backward, Jonas crashed into a sheer wall of black basalt. A low rumble sounded from far above, but Silla was driving into Jonas, channeling the anger and bitterness into blow after blow after blow. The moves she'd practiced each morning with Rey came to her like second nature. But Jonas was larger, far stronger, and had years of experience on her. And once the advantage of surprise had faded, Silla was quickly outmatched.

Thunder cracked overhead, diverting her attention for the barest of moments. But Jonas did not hesitate—with a swipe of his blade, he sent her hevrít flying, leaving Silla twisting and ducking, stumbling back in a clumsy retreat. Her foot caught on a stone, and she tumbled to the ground.

"And how sweet this vengeance shall taste," snarled Jonas, advancing on her. "Sweeter still knowing that by ending your life, I will wipe the black stain from my family's name and earn back our lands."

The thunder grew louder, but it did not break—this sound was ceaseless and growing with each passing heartbeat.

"This is no way to restore honor to your family's name," Silla bit out. "You bring more shame upon them than your father ever did."

With a scream of rage, Jonas charged at her. But the clamorous sound reached its crescendo, rattling the ground and clattering Silla's teeth.

Jonas paused. Whirled. But it was too late.

A billowing cloud of white devoured the mountain peak, the trees, the very sky above. Hungry and destructive and unstoppable, it consumed them, too. The powder surrounded them, and Silla choked on her scream as snow pelted her face, her body. And then it slammed into her—a wall of frigid, smothering pressure that jostled her as though she were made of straw.

And at last, there was only blackness.

CHAPTER 83

Sunnavík

The noise was endless, a thing with no beginning and no end. Saga could not think, could not move, could only hold on to herself and try to survive. A sob clawed up her throat, and she bent over the feasting table, cradling her head in her hands.

She tried desperately to think—she needed to escape. But no thought could penetrate through the swamping, all-consuming sound. *Exits,* she tried. *The . . . the eastern exit.* But it was on the farthest side of the room, through all those people, with all those thoughts, pushing, shoving, battering her skull.

Trapped. She was trapped. No escape. No exit.

Panic squeezed around her, trapping the air in her chest. Die, she would die here, surrounded by people who'd betrayed and murdered her family . . .

Saga?

The voice was thin among the inundating thoughts, but there was something about it that gave her pause. A strand of gold amid a weaving line of pure black.

Saga, come to me.

The voice rang true and clear like a bell. She recognized it then—Eisa here, somehow, amid this night of nightmares. A light for her to follow. And as she followed the sound, moving deeper into her consciousness, the feasting hall grew more and more distant. It was black all around her, and yet Saga had always yearned for the shadows. Here, it was peaceful. Restful.

Saga breathed in. Exhaled slowly.

She straightened her spine and examined the space. In the absolute blackness, a distant glow grew larger and brighter with every heartbeat. And as it grew, so, too, did a silhouette, the lines slowly growing more defined. A woman, her hair a tangle of wild curls.

"Saga!" exclaimed the woman, lunging at her and wrapping Saga in a tight embrace.

Saga hugged the woman back, a wintery taste of frost and evergreens tickling the back of her tongue. The scent wafting from her curly hair wrapped around Saga even tighter than her embrace. It smelled of the gardens on a summer night when they'd fled from their nursemaid for one last frolic. It smelled of the blankets they'd curled under as Mother told them stories by candlelight. It smelled of sweet rolls and róa and unconditional love.

"It's you," Saga whispered, squeezing Eisa tighter. "It's really you."

Her little sister, whom she'd mourned for seventeen years. Saga had never dared hope for this—had never truly let herself believe. But this was real. *She* was real.

Drawing back, Saga studied Eisa's face in the brightening glow—large brown eyes framed with thick lashes, a smattering of freckles across the bridge of her nose. She traced the crescent-shaped scar at the corner of her sister's eye.

"Eisa," she whispered. "How are you here?"

Eisa's brows furrowed, a line forming between them. "I . . . I do not know. How are *you* here, Saga?"

"I . . . retreated into my mind," said Saga. "My Sense has lost all control. My shields, I cannot weave them back together . . ."

Eisa's worry seemed to deepen. "You've lost control of your galdur?"

Saga pressed her lips together. "Something like that. I cannot block it. The noise is unbearable—"

"Did you drink something?"

"Wine," replied Saga, realization hitting her—Signe's smug look, the way the cupbearer had served Saga before the king. The queen had drugged Saga's wine.

"The catalyst," breathed Eisa, eyes widening. "You've been given a drug that causes your galdur to flow without control. It merely primed me, but your galdur is of the mind. I'm told things work differently for your kind of Galdra."

Eisa turned, gazing at the light behind her. "Gods, Saga. This is your Cohesion Rite." She turned to Saga, excitement etched into her face. "Perhaps the gods have brought me here to anchor you through it."

"I don't understand a word you've just spoken."

"You've never linked your heart and your mind," said Eisa. "Which means you have little control over your galdur. Once you link your heart and your mind, you'll be able to do incredible things."

Hadn't Ana said something similar? Glancing past Eisa, she took in the brilliant, gilded cage. The light was sculpted into sleek bars, arching together at the top of the cage, while curious, pulsating creatures fluttered about within.

Eisa's hand wrapped around Saga's. "Free them," she whispered. "It won't hurt, I promise."

As they stepped nearer, the small creatures imprisoned within the cage came into view. A sob broke in her throat, tears stinging her eyes.

Inside the cage was a flock of winterwing birds.

A part of herself, caged away for all these years, waiting for Saga to free it.

There was something so circular about it, a rightfulness. These birds were the heart of her being, a part of her she never knew she was missing.

"Claim your power, Saga," urged Eisa.

Saga's fingers stretched out, reaching for that delicate, gilded door. Her fingers brushed it, then pulled it open. The birds flapped feathered wings of light, soaring from the cage. Free at last.

Saga gasped. Pure energy rushed into her, flowing through her veins, like a river freed from its dam. Every part of her felt connected; every thought, every memory, every muscle, every beat of her heart was woven in thousands—millions—of tiny linkages, and in that moment, Saga felt it all.

Deeper inside her, something ancient yawned, stirring awake from its long slumber. The wild, euphoric power in her veins calmed gradually, spilling into a pool rippling calmly behind her ribs.

"You're Cohesed, Saga," said Eisa, clasping her hands together. "I can feel you, sister. I feel you so much stronger now . . . and I feel something else. Something curious." Eisa's brows furrowed.

Saga could feel Eisa, too—cold pressure squeezing in from all sides, the need for air. The terror.

"Eisa," murmured Saga, realization dripping down her spine like cold water. "You're not safe."

Eisa frowned. "No, I'm not." Her hand slid along her throat. "I can't breathe," she whispered. "Oh, gods . . . the avalanche!"

Saga saw memories that were not her own—a sword of light hissing in gray skies; a blond man crashing back into a sheer rock face; a wall of snow plowing down from above.

Eisa's eyes flared, and she grabbed Saga's elbows. "I cannot linger. I must return . . ."

Saga clasped her sister, hugged her fiercely. Alone. She'd be alone again, and she could not bear it.

"Remember, Saga." Eisa pulled back. "Remember your promise."

Saga nodded, her throat burning. "I remember," she said. "Go. Be safe."

A black fog circled around Eisa, whisking bits of her away, like sand in the wind, until there was nothing left at all.

An ache permeated Saga, the loss of a thing she'd never truly had. And in that moment, her promise to Eisa became more than words—it held meaning. Saga *would* be reunited with Eisa, no matter the cost.

Determination settled into place. Saga assessed herself, probing the curious pool of power in her chest. Dull sounds filtered from above, and she knew her destiny was there, in that room. With those people.

It's time, she thought, steeling herself.

Slowly, Saga crawled out from the folds of her mind, into the light, the noise, the utter chaos. A wall of sound crashed into her, so intense it knocked the breath from her lungs. Saga blinked, Yrsa's face coming into focus, brown eyes widened with concern. Turning, Saga took in the deep line between Ivar's brows. Conversation had come to a stuttering halt, each eye in the room on her. Yet still, the thoughts blasted into her.

. . . possessed by spirits, she is . . .

. . . I knew the girl was not natural . . .

. . . a Galdra of the mind to be sure. Perhaps she'll prove useful after all . . .

Saga's gaze met Signe's. Pale eyes in her pale face, framed by the palest of blond hair. But her lips, tinted red from wine, curved in victory.

And a thousand small cuts collected over seventeen years became a raw gaping wound. Saga hated Signe more than Ivar. More than Magnus. More than each member of nobility who'd turned on the Volsiks. *They* didn't pretend. But Signe, with her false smiles and demure beauty, was the vilest of them all.

A beast inside Saga unfurled its wings and stretched its maw wide. It was darkness incarnate, alluring. Empowering. With gentle wingbeats, it fanned the flames of her anger.

Each wound Signe had inflicted was kindling for today, for this very moment. It was time for her to burn.

The creature inside her breathed in her anger—her hatred—and exhaled pure, raw power. It looked at Saga and smiled.

There you are, daughter of Svalla. I've waited so long for you.

CHAPTER 84

Svangormr Pass

Silla returned to a jarring coldness. It pushed in on her from all sides, above and below, penetrating her lébrynja armor, seeping into her hair, pressing into the creases of her ears and the space between each finger.

Trapped.

Buried beneath a mountain of snow, to depths she could not guess. By some miracle, there was a pocket of air around her head. But it was finite. Already she could tell each breath was a little less effective. Bright dots edged her vision as she gave an experimental kick of her foot, a wiggle of her fingers.

Nothing.

Lodged in place. Stuck in a snowy tomb.

Swallowing back her growing panic, Silla probed at her galdur, pulling, dragging, yanking it forth. A flicker of light was all she could manage.

Drained.

"Oh, gods," she whimpered, trying and failing to control her breaths. She was trapped, buried, would die in this snowy tomb. She didn't want to die . . . not like this. And she didn't want to leave Rey. Gods, *Rey*.

Silla was so consumed with panic that she failed to notice the peculiar sensation she'd felt the moment Saga had claimed her power. Familiar, yet not of herself. Slowly, it opened one eye and peered at her.

I've waited for you, daughter of Svalla, it crooned in a voice of shadows and echoes.

Silla started. She knew that voice. Could not forget it, in fact.

Panic tightened her throat. It could not be.

It is, said Myrkur with glee. *How long I have waited for the pair of you to come into your full magic. At last I can fulfill Svalla's bargain.*

Anger surged through Silla at the memory. *You tricked her. You preyed on her in a moment of desperation.*

Svalla is master of her own words. A life for a life, she said. *It was settled long ago.*

Her lungs were burning, her throat, her limbs. Buried, she was buried, lost to this world. Something inside her cracked. *Then take me,* Silla wheezed.

Myrkur's irritation prickled through her. *A life yielded is not what I want.*

What do you want?

I want to play, dear Eisa. Give me access to your heart, and I will save you.

No, thought Silla, anger flooding her.

My, purred Myrkur, His claws kneading her spine in a gentle, sinuous rhythm. *Such delicious passion you mortals have. I can free you from this snowy tomb. Let me in, Eisa.*

No!

He'll die, said Myrkur, fueling her panic. *If you don't let Me in, Galtung will die.* Her mind was flooded with images—Rey strapped to a bed, flesh torn from his arms and legs. Skin ashen, he groaned, head bobbing to the side.

Her vision went black, except for the shimmering stars. Tired, she was so tired. Tired of running. Tired of fighting.

You promised her you'd be reunited, said Myrkur, Saga's face flashing in her mind's eye. *Remember your promise,* rang Silla's own voice. She squeezed her eyes shut, tears leaking down her cheeks.

Give in, said Myrkur, *and I'll make it easy.* Intoxicating tendrils unfurled within her. She wanted to give in, to make it all stop. But what did it mean to grant the god of chaos access to her heart?

What will happen? she asked. Her head spun, the end ever closer.

You let me in. We escape the snow. And then, dear girl, we'll make them pay.

A hunger grew inside her. One that had been long tucked away. Vengeance and death—blood of the Klaernar spilled on the snow. Silla would take their heads for the role they'd played in the downfall of this kingdom; for every soul lost on the pillar; for each woman who'd suffered in their prison cells.

We'll make them pay, Eisa. We shall spill their blood.

Everything faded save for the gnawing desire to kill. But some small thread of rational thought remained within Silla. *What do you gain from this?*

Myrkur laughed, a sharp, grating sound along the inside of her skull. *I get to play,* he said. *I get a taste of human emotion.*

And what of a life for a life?

Myrkur purred, slinking around her spine. *Ahh, but I haven't decided whose life I want.*

The words were hazy in Silla's addled mind. Her air had run out, and soon she would die.

You must choose, dear Eisa. To live or to die. To let Signe win or to take victory for yourself. To keep your promise to your sister, or to abandon her, like all others have.

Distantly, Silla knew there was no right choice. *Sometimes we must surrender to win,* she thought grimly. Had she not told Jonas she would always choose to fight for Íseldur? Had she not promised her sister they would see each other again? And though it made her a coward to think it, Silla did not wish to die.

Come in, she whispered. Myrkur smiled, a cold, toothy grin.

And then Silla surrendered the heart of her magic to the god of chaos.

CHAPTER 85

The avalanche had plowed down the mountain, consuming all in its path. And yet it did not have the same breadth as the previous one. For that reason alone, Rey was left standing. But where Silla had stood moments before was now nothing but white—a mound of hard-packed snow and ice. The entire gods damned mountainside had slid free.

Helpless. He was utterly helpless, hands bound behind his back, galdur quelled with those infernal quills. Yet Rey's heart still pumped hope through his veins. His girl was a fighter. He struggled against his restraints, desperate to get to her.

But Rey's binds held fast, and with each passing minute, his hope dissolved. Ice speared through him. It had been too good, too sweet. Things like that never lasted, not in his life.

It was a small consolation that Jonas was buried alongside her.

"Free me!" Rey bellowed, his throat raw and burning, as the dozen surviving Klaernar ambled about the wreckage, sniffing for Silla's and Jonas's scents. He supposed they'd need a body to prove to their queen that Eisa Volsik was dead.

The Klaernar cocked their heads in his direction but soon returned to their hunt. Too much time had passed, Rey knew it deep inside, but he could not give up on her—*would not* give up. He twisted onto his side, drawing his knees to his chest and bringing his bound hands to his front. Examining his restraints, Rey cursed inwardly. This kind of cuff could only be opened by key or by blacksmith.

The ground rumbled, and his gaze flew up the mountain as he

braced for another avalanche. But the slope was still, and the vibrations seemed to come from below—and somewhere nearby.

The snowpack pulsed. A clump of snow bounced down the mound of avalanche debris, shattering into a dozen smaller pieces. Rey's heart thudded in his chest as he held his gaze on the pile. Had it been a trick of his eye? Or had the hard-packed snow truly moved?

Rey had only just convinced himself it was wishful thinking when it happened. The world exploded in darkness. Klaernar roared. Bodies flew from atop the avalanche track, and snow showered down upon Rey.

"What in the gods' sacred ashes was that?" muttered Runný, sitting up. Face swelling, she'd soon be sporting an impressive black eye. Her question was met with silence—Mýr, Kálf, Erik, and Hef lay unconscious nearby.

Silla. Rey was unwilling to voice his hope aloud.

The Klaernar warrior watching their small group drew his sword and batted it against his shield as he stared at the haze of finely powdered snow. But a figure leaped through it, curls flying wildly behind her.

"Silla," Rey gasped, unable to breathe. Gods above, but it had to be a miracle. Another one—the woman had more lives than a cat. A confusing muddle of emotions battled within him. Rey was furious at her for frightening him but relieved she was alive.

"Release me!" he bellowed to Silla, scrambling to his feet. "Let me help!"

But her face was impassive as she ignored him, dispatching the Klaernar with a brutal blow to the neck, severing his head clean from his shoulders. As she whirled on her next assailant, Rey's brows drew together. The weapon clutched in hand was not her sword of frostfire. This blade's flame was oil black.

Not only that, but her moves were preternatural—sinuous, smooth, impossibly quick—and far more advanced than the ones he'd taught her. She fought with incredible skill—with more strength and speed than the berserkers. And as Silla relieved a second man of his head, a cold feeling spread through Rey.

Something was wrong.

She sprinted at a third and fourth snarling Klaernar, taking them both on at once. Rey watched, horrified and fascinated all at once. Silla whirled and ducked, the black blade slashing out like an extension of her body. She moved as though she knew her foes' moves before even they did. Blood arced through the air, painting the snow red. A pair of heads thunked to the snow, bodies collapsing a heartbeat later.

She turned to him.

Rey drew in a sharp breath. The same crescent-shaped scar. The same pert nose and pale complexion. But along the curve of her neck, dark-blue veins stretched like tangling branches reaching for the sun. And her eyes—no light. Only black.

"Silla," he murmured, taking a step back. "You're all right."

"Yes," she said, from everywhere and nowhere all at once. "The best I've ever been."

A chill stretched down his spine. Not her voice. Not his Silla. "Who are you?" he demanded of the creature wearing Silla's skin. "What have you done to her?" Rey took another step back, hands cursedly still bound, though at least at his front. She approached, black blade held at her side. "Come back to me, Sunshine."

"Eisa sends her regards," said the voice. Silla lunged at him but stumbled, Runný's hand wrapped around her ankle. With a growl, she turned, raising her sword for a downward strike aimed at Runný's neck. Rey launched himself at her, tackling her to the ground. Her sword fizzled, dissolving into the air as he pushed his bound hands into her neck. She snarled like a creature of darkness, her skin so cold and so very *other*.

Silla's knee came up, landing hard in his groin. Rey bellowed in pain. An arm slipped free, her fist cracking into his nose, then clawing at his neck. The hindrium quill that must have been lodged in his shoulder fell free, landing on the snow beside her head.

"Silla," he growled, trying to shake off the pain. Rey pushed his body harder on her, trapping her freed arm under his knee. She fought against his hold, kicking and snarling like a wild creature.

But Rey had the benefit of his size, the full weight of him bearing down on her.

"You won't have her," he hissed in Silla's ear. Rey caged her in with his body, his grip on her throat unrelenting. "She is not yours to take." Guilt and anger battled for dominance, but his determination won out—he would fight for her, like she'd fought for him.

"What's got her?" asked Runný. "How do we stop it?"

"I don't know." Rey gasped for breath. His muscles screamed in protest as he held her down, his fear climbing higher as her arm began to slip loose. How could he subdue her without causing her real harm?

His gaze fell on the skarpling quill, resting in the snow beside her head. "Runný, get me a fresh one of those quills and hurry!"

Silla's head lunged forward, crashing into Rey's with such force his teeth knocked together. He blinked to clear his vision, but it was too late. Silla had slipped free and was scrambling to her feet. Rey threw his body at her, but she danced backward, a long taper of black flame forming from thin air.

"Shit," muttered Rey, backing away.

A malevolent smile curved Silla's lips as she advanced on Rey. But her feet suddenly stopped, a look of confusion crossing her face. Her hand lifted to her neck and yanked a skarpling quill free. Slowly, Runný edged out from behind Silla.

"No!" screamed the creature inside Silla's body, the sword of black flame flickering before vanishing entirely.

Rey was a man used to doing dark deeds for the greater good. And so he didn't hesitate. He tackled Silla to the ground. Tightened his hands around the throat he'd lavished with kisses earlier in the day. Her movements grew feeble, black eyes bulging as she fought for breath. Placing his lips next to her ear, he whispered, "I'm sorry, Sunshine. Forgive me." Her hands gave one last flap before her eyes rolled back, and Silla moved no more.

Rey collapsed alongside her, the anguished sob he'd held back finally breaking free.

CHAPTER 86

Sunnavík

Daughter of Svalla, said the voice in Saga's mind, *I've been waiting for you.*

She blinked. The strange thing arched its back and protracted its claws in a delicious stretch. Was this her galdur? A living thing that spoke?

When she'd claimed her power from the shimmering winter-wing cage, it had felt like part of herself. But this . . . this was decidedly different. Decidedly *other.* If only Eisa were here, if only she had someone to ask. But instead, Saga faced a room of people who looked at her with disgust.

Together, said the thing, *we will make them pay. Would you like that, Saga?*

Her anger burned brighter, hotter, so deliciously potent. For so many years, she'd been powerless. Forced to comply.

Let me in, Saga, and together we'll make it end.

In? she thought, confused. Saga could sense this creature within, now pacing to and fro.

We can make them pay, said the thing. Saga's anger flared as she gazed at the feasting tables. An entire room of betrayers and deceivers, staring at her as though she'd done wrong.

"Seize her!" cried Signe, pushing to her feet. Guards rushed in from the corners of the room, causing Saga's heart to beat wildly.

They'll put you in the dungeons, said the voice. *Then to the pillar. They'll make a spectacle of it, just like your parents.*

A sob built in the back of Saga's throat. She thought of her mother and father. Of Ana and her little sister. The guards were upon her, Saga's arms seized and wrenched behind her back.

Let me in, and I will stop them. Let me in and we can avenge your parents and Ana. And poor little Bryndís.

A child's broken body flashed in her mind's eye, anger and revulsion churning within her.

Yes, thought Saga, dazed and enticed. She tasted vengeance on the back of her tongue, but it was not nearly enough.

"Signe!" boomed Ivar. "Explain what is going on."

"She's Galdra," exclaimed Signe. "I placed a drug in her wine, and she's reacted!"

"Mother!" exclaimed Yrsa. "Surely you're mistaken!"

The king stared hard at Saga, as though searching for proof. Fear crossed his face, quickly twisting to rage. "Get her out of here!" he bellowed at the guards, backing away. Saga was dragged away from Ivar, but Yrsa followed along the table's opposite side, arguing with the guards.

We can avenge all the innocents they've slain, said the thing, strumming her veins. *We'll make them hurt.* The creature paused, a grin slowly spreading. *We can make the queen hurt worst of all.*

An ugly feeling spread through Saga. She thought of Signe's story—of the cat and the mice. *I am the cat,* Signe had said. *I devour curious little creatures.*

Saga dug her feet in, bringing the guards to a halt. "I'm not a mouse," growled Saga over her shoulder. Her gaze bounced from the queen's widened blue eyes to Ivar's cold, hard ones. "Nor am I prey."

Let me in now, Saga, purred the voice as the guards yanked her forward.

"I," Saga snarled, "am a predator. And I will no longer be caged away." *Do it,* she told the thing, relinquishing control.

It drew from her essence, draining it to the last drop, then . . .

changed it somehow. Bonds snapped, rearranging, forged anew into something that was no longer *self*, but altogether *other*. Instead of a gently lapping pool behind her sternum, it was a raging torrent of power churning through her veins—a thing that could not be tamed, because it was chaos itself. She was merely a vessel for this power—destruction incarnate.

The guards were knocked aside with a casual flick of her hands, and as Saga rounded on the king and queen, she caught sight of something beneath her gloves. She tugged them off and stared at the dark blue spreading through her veins, like ink through water.

"Seize her!" roared Ivar, though he sounded strangely distant. He backed away, but Yrsa stood transfixed, her widened eyes on Saga's dark-blue veins.

Saga's hair lifted, blond tendrils floating around her head, twisting like the crown she was owed. The crown they'd stolen.

Yours, purred the creature. *They will pay.*

A wave built inside her, high and mighty as a tidal wave. It rolled on, pulling in more power as it built in height and momentum. The tension was excruciating, the energy clawing at her veins. Saga's hands burned like scorched lava stones, dry and so unbearably hot.

And then she exhaled. The beast roared. The wave crested. Heat seared from her hands. And the room was swallowed in darkness.

Engulfed in pure black flame.

The fire burst to the farthest end of the great hall, singeing the walls and shaking the foundation of the palace.

Just as quickly, the flame snuffed out, light trickling into the room from windows and torches in the corridor beyond. The air smelled burnt, like after a lightning storm. Stones tumbled from the ceiling, powdering the room. It was silent, but only for a moment.

Then the screams began.

People rushed through the room; a man sobbed over a woman's limp body, blood gushing from his brow; blistered and broken bodies were strewn throughout the hall.

You did well, said the voice, yawning.

Contentment rushed through her at his approval. She'd done it—had made them pay.

Now that you and your sister are awakened, we'll have fun ... more fun than you can imagine. But now it's time to rest. The beast curled up and laid its head on its paws.

Exhaustion surging through her, Saga sat and laid her own head down on the feasting table. And then more blackness as she drifted into sleep.

CHAPTER 87

Kopa

Silla dreamed of darkness—of smothering snow and a bargain gone awry. She dreamed of a creature caressing her spine, whispering wicked things in her ear—of a sword of black flame and Rey's hands wrapped around her neck. And when she woke, it was only to more blackness.

But as she blinked, the blackness sorted itself into soft, pleated linen, curving downward from a canopy. Silla looked down, disoriented. She was in a bed, the blanket tucked around her woven from the softest, most luxurious textile she'd ever felt.

As she rolled to the side, Silla's head throbbed in protest. The room's walls were hewn from black stone, the floor a mosaic of polished black tiles. Golden braziers burned in each corner, and finely woven tapestries hung from the walls, but none of that mattered to Silla. Because before her was Reynir Galtung's large frame slumped in a chair. He was clad in a blue tunic and black breeches, a sheathed hevrít balanced on his knees. In slumber, his face was softer, almost boyish. Long black lashes swept across his brown skin, his lips parted ever so slightly. But as she took in the awkward angle of his neck, Silla scowled.

"Why are you not in the bed, you muttonhead?"

His head jerked up, and he stared dazedly at her for several heartbeats. Then Rey bolted from the chair, his hevrít drawn before she could blink.

"What are you . . ." Silla pushed herself upright, the hairs on the back of her neck rising. "What is it? What's wrong?"

Rey's eyes searched her face frantically, causing Silla's heart to lurch. "Is he there?" he demanded. "Can you . . . feel him?"

Silla's brows furrowed as she tried to puzzle his words together. "I don't understand."

Rey released a long breath. "Your eyes," he said, a note of incredulity in his voice. "They're normal." He approached the bed but paused a pace back from it. "Are you hurt?" he asked, sliding his blade into its sheath.

Silla assessed her body, discovering nothing out of the ordinary. "I'm only tired," she murmured. "What happened? Why did you draw your blade?"

"You don't remember?" Rey folded his arms over his chest. "Perhaps it's for the best." He regarded her with a troubled expression. "What is the last thing you remember?"

Silla pushed through the fog in her head, trying to recall what, precisely, had happened. The serpents, and then, the Klaernar. And Jonas.

She scowled at that. But then the memory of a mountainside sliding free and crashing down on her pushed itself forth. Silla's hand flew to her mouth. Trapped. No escape. She'd been buried alive. She should be dead. She should have *died.*

"The avalanche," she said. "How did I escape that avalanche?" But those hazy nightmares were growing more vivid by the moment. A bargain with the Dark One. An explosion of snow. Her blade slicing through flesh, over and over and over . . .

Bile rose in her throat. "It was real," she gasped. "Myrkur. My mother's bargain . . ."

"So it *was* the Dark One," muttered Rey. "It was clear something had possession of your body. You were . . . not yourself."

Another face flashed in her mind's eye. Black braids snaking along the snow, dark eyes wide in the woman's pale face. Silla's empty stomach turned over. "Runný," she muttered. "Oh, gods. Is she . . . did I . . ."

"Runný's fine. She pricked you with a skarpling quill. It seems whatever galdur-quelling substance is on them works on Myrkur's magic as well."

"He needed access," Silla said numbly, "to the heart of my magic. He could not take it for Himself—I had to grant it to Him." She closed her eyes. Took a steadying breath. "Do you think He's still there? I do not feel Him."

Rey began pacing on the shining black floor, but he did not answer her question. "I carried you on my horse to Kopa. Jarl Hakon set everything up for us—a pillar execution paired with a guard change on the walls—it was enough for us to slip through Kopa unnoticed and reach Ashfall's gates."

"Ashfall," repeated Silla numbly. The fortress carved into the fire mountain. But then her mind took several steps back. "I slept the entire ride to Kopa? But that's . . ." She tried to count the days but gave up.

"Seven days," said Rey. "We moved with haste."

Silla's mind reeled. Seven days. How could it be? "Oh, gods! Saga! We must—" Silla threw the covers aside, making to leap out of bed, but was stilled by a firm hand on her shoulder. Rey dropped to his knees before her, taking her hand in his and stroking it softly. His eyes met hers, and Silla's heart lurched violently. "What is it?" she demanded, fear and worry tangling inside her.

"We've had word from Sunnavík," Rey said slowly. "There was an explosion."

Her free hand went absently to her mouth. "Was she hurt? Was she—" Silla couldn't finish the thought.

"We don't know," he answered. "The Uppreisna has spies in the castle who feed us information. Princess Yrsa is confirmed among the dead, and the king sustained survivable injuries. But Saga has not been found."

Silla exhaled slowly. But then his words caught up with her. "Not been found. But what does that *mean*?"

Rey stroked her hand, looking up at her. "You've just woken. Do you want me to send for food? Some bread perhaps?"

Silla's brows dropped low. "Tell me, Galtung."

His jaw flexed, but he continued. "She is missing. No trace has been found of her in Askaborg Castle. Ivar"—he scowled—"he accuses Saga of working in concert with the Zagadkians to attempt his assassination."

Silla's lips parted on an incredulous breath. "Do you think it true?" Saga. Her beautiful, resourceful sister.

"I do not know," admitted Rey. "It is said they've scoured the castle high and low, with hounds and men alike. There's no trace of her. Our spies have reported that Saga's engagement to Prince Bjorn was recently broken over some indiscretion of hers. It was her engagement feast to . . . Magnus . . . when the explosion occurred."

Silla sank back on the bed, thoughts whirling. "Did she escape?" she asked in wonder. "When last we spoke mind-to-mind, I guided her through her Cohesion Rite. She'd been slipped the catalyst . . ." Her voice trailed off. "Surely she'd have told me if she planned to assassinate Ivar. And surely, if it was the Uppreisna who had her, your spies would know." But where did that leave Saga? Silla's heart pounded with fear and cautious hope.

"I must contact her, mind-to-mind, and confirm her safety." Closing her eyes, she sought the deep folds of her mind—the place where she'd twice spoken to Saga. But as she probed inwardly, Silla realized she could not feel the heart of her magic.

Silla's eyes flew open, panic sliding through her. "I cannot feel it."

Rey dragged a hand through his hair, his gaze growing distant.

"Reynir?"

He scowled at her, running a tongue along his teeth. "For your own safety, we've been dosing you with those quills."

Anger gathered within her. "You *what?*"

"Some suggested securing you to the bed with hindrium cuffs. I thought this a milder solution."

Silla's mouth fell open, and she slammed it shut. Visions of decapitated Klaernar filled her mind's eye, and she took a steadying breath. "I understand," she muttered. "It was wise of you to do so. But now . . . I cannot access my galdur?"

He shook his head.

"What of Saga? I must try to contact her."

"Sunshine, it's too dangerous," said Rey uneasily. "If you'd seen what I did . . . but surely you recall some of it?" He drew a deep breath. Held her gaze steadily. "It is only for a time—until we understand how to release you from the bargain."

"But what about Saga?" Tears of frustration welled in her eyes. All those weeks of training with the goal of freeing Saga. And now that they were in Kopa, with Jarl Hakon's ear, Saga's whereabouts were unknown. It was maddening . . . infuriating.

Rey's hand slid along her jaw, thumb swiping a tear from her cheek. "We can do nothing but wait for now. Wait for more news from Sunnavík."

Another tear slid down her cheek. "What if harm has befallen her?"

He stared at her, the determination in his eyes feeding her strength. "I think our spies would know it by now. But if it turns out she's been harmed, we shall make them pay in blood."

She stared at him for a beat, then pulled him toward the bed and slid her lips against his. "Promise?" she whispered, drawing back.

"I'll swear an oath—"

And with that, the tension broke; laughter burst from Silla. "You and your oaths."

She studied Rey's face once more, fingertips tracing his healing black eye, tracing a cut above his eyebrow and a bruise on his neck. Dark circles hung under his eyes, his hair and beard untrimmed for some time. Clearly, the man had not been caring for himself.

"Why are you not in the bed?" she demanded.

Rey's dark brows dipped down, sending a tame version of his *axe eyes* her way.

A warm shiver ran down Silla's spine. "Come here, you obstinate man," ordered Silla. "Is this how it will be with us? Shall I use force, or will you come on your own?"

The corners of his lips tugged up cautiously, making her heart sing. As she shifted over, he climbed onto the bed, his large body bowing the feather mattress. Silla found her place, tucked into the crook of his arm, and slid a hand onto his warm chest.

"I feared for you," Rey admitted. "I did not know if you'd be . . . *you* when you woke."

"I'm *me*," Silla said, probing inwardly once more. "I cannot feel Him. Nor my own galdur." She frowned. It was like an essential piece of herself, severed from her body. But she focused instead on Rey, on the steady beat of his heart through the wool of his tunic. Slowly, she felt his muscles easing, as though they'd held taut until this very moment.

She tried to gather her thoughts, but it was like wading through a bog. "What happens now?" she asked, uncertain if she wanted to know the answer.

Rey's eyes fell shut. "We wait," he said. "Sooner or later, Saga's whereabouts will be confirmed. In the meantime, you rest. Recover from Svangormr Pass. We must search out all we can on Myrkur and His bargains. If King Hrolf truly did as you described in that vision, *someone* knows something."

Silla chewed on her lip, lost in thought. "And the Bloodaxe Crew?"

A long exhale. "They've not yet found success in Istré. I fear the job may be more complicated than we ever thought." Rey cleared his throat. "Jarl Hakon wants to meet you. He has . . . things he wishes to discuss."

Silla's gaze met his, conveying her worries. A thumb skimmed along her jaw, smoothing some of her distress away. "Later," he said softly. "All of it can wait until tomorrow."

Silla snuggled closer. Soon she was lost in thought. Troubles in Istré. A meeting with Jarl Hakon. An assassination attempt on Ivar, and Saga now missing. Not to mention this gods damned bargain living in her body.

"Rey?" Silla asked softly.

"Mmm?"

"Everything's about to change, isn't it?"

He drew in a long breath. "Aye," he muttered.

But his hand slid to where hers rested on his chest, and he threaded their fingers together. He was warm and sturdy. Her rock in this crumbling world.

"Together," whispered Silla.

"Together," he replied.

CHAPTER 88

Unknown

Scent returned to Saga first—wool and fresh timber and the salt of the ocean. Next came the warmth, the soft scratch of a blanket, the muss of fur against her cheek. And finally sound—rushing water, the groan of wood, muffled voices from somewhere above.

Eyes fluttering open, Saga's gaze settled on the wooden panels overhead. Her heartbeat quickened. Where was the familiar crimson of her canopy? The scent of wet stone and woodsmoke? Slowly, it sank in.

Not in Askaborg. Warning bells chimed. *Danger. Not safe.* Sitting upright, Saga winced against the vicious throb at her temples.

"You woke," came a deep male voice from across the room.

She scrambled back in an uncoordinated rush until her spine collided with the wall. Her vision spinning, it felt as though knives plunged into her skull. The memories collided all at once—the feast; the drugged wine; Eisa and the cage of undulating light.

The explosion.

A low, animalistic sound wrenched free from her. Saga's chest tightened with the stirrings of an imminent crisis.

"Winterwing," said the voice, a figure approaching.

"Kass," she whispered, her breaths shallowing as her chest constricted tighter, tighter. *Not safe,* chanted her mind. *Where are the exits? Must escape . . .*

"Breathe, Saga," said Rurik, his voice low and soothing. "May I touch you?"

She nodded, her gaze focusing at last on those green eyes as she fought for breath—the eyes she'd sought for days. But they hadn't been there. *He* hadn't been there . . .

But he was here now.

As his large hand slid over her shoulder and his fingers tapped on her back, three words ran through Saga's mind on an endless loop. "Didn't leave me," she gasped. "Didn't leave me."

His taps stalled, then resumed. "Of course I did not leave you." Rurik muttered something in Zagadkian. "You were thinking . . ."

The panic she'd held at bay burst free, inundating Saga. Her throat burned with each choking breath, the room spinning in a dizzying rush. She was gathered against a warm, sturdy body. "Breathe, Saga," he whispered into her hair, barely discernible above the punishing strikes of her heartbeat. "Safe. You are safe now."

Not safe, countered her mind, her body primed to flee. *Danger. Escape. Exits.* Time grew hazy, but his warmth was constant. The tap of his fingers and his nonsensical Zagadkian wove together, creating a new sensation—*safe.*

She was safe.

Because he'd come back for her.

He hadn't left her.

Gradually her breaths eased, and her pulse softened. At last, Saga straightened, looking up at Rurik. Dazed, she brushed her fingertips across his cheek. "You're real." Her voice was reedy and thin. "Everyone leaves. But you didn't."

Darkness gathered in his eyes, a low growl rumbling through his chest. Rurik pulled her against him. "You will not worry about this any longer, Winterwing." His fingertips dug tightly into her hip, but he eased his hold on a slow exhale. "You now are under my protection."

She let herself breathe in the smell of him—juniper and sage, fresh and herbal. Real. This was real. She was safe. But this space, this new place filled with unknowns, made Saga feel vulnerable. "Tell me about the room," she whispered, closing her eyes.

Rurik's heartbeat seemed oddly erratic beneath her ear, and for a moment, Saga wondered if something was wrong. But when he spoke, his voice was calm. "Is nicest room on ship. One bed, one door, one window with lovely view of nothing."

"And the people? Will they see me?"

"No one is coming in to see you, Winterwing, only myself. But there is Rovgolod on deck with Druzhina and crew. Sadly, he has not yet jumped overboard."

Slowly, she opened her eyes and surveyed her surroundings. As he'd said, it was a small space with a single bed, a small side table and chair wedged against the wall. She was too tired for humor. Too exhausted for anything but honesty. "Thank you," she murmured. "For never making me feel like a burden."

Rurik huffed, the arm wrapped around her tightening. "Is a word I loathe, Saga. *Burden*. I wish never to hear you speak it again."

As his muscles tensed and released beneath her, Saga drew back, studying his face. Smudges beneath his eyes and a pallid complexion spoke of a less collected version of Kassandr Rurik. Much like the night of Yrsa's birthday feast, Rurik's eyes seemed too bright, his demeanor strangely restless.

"Are you well?" she found herself asking. Her fingers slid along the coarse beginnings of a beard, but she drew them back. Soon, she'd be in Midfjord, and he'd be in Zagadka, and their garden kiss would be naught but a memory.

Rurik rolled his neck. "Before long, I will be on Zagadka's soil, and all will be fine."

Did that mean he was not, in fact, fine right now? Questions gathered on Saga's tongue, but she swallowed them back. Instead, she asked, "What happened in Sunnavík? How am I here?"

Rurik ran a hand through his hair, leaving it askew. "Rov forced our leaving, but I—" He paused. "—*convinced* him to hide boat and return. I could not get message to you, Saga. They were laying many traps. And we set traps of our own for night of feasting. But explosion demanded change of plans." Rurik stared down at her with an intensity that sent shivers all through her. "What happened?"

Saga swallowed, her pulse picking up. Safe. She was safe in this unknown space, safe with *him*. She took a deep breath, then told him everything that had transpired since Yrsa's birthday feast—her broken betrothal to Bjorn, how she'd nearly jumped from her balcony, Mind-Eisa, and the explosion at the feast.

As she spoke, Rurik's palm slid up and down her spine, a spasm jostling him at the mention of her betrothal to Magnus and Saga's near jump.

Tentatively, Saga probed inwardly in search of that *thing*, but she could detect no trace of it. She questioned how her darkest, most vile wants had been pulled to the surface—to wreak havoc and destruction. To kill and avenge. If this was her galdur, Saga wanted nothing to do with it.

"I rushed with Rov to hall after explosion shook the castle," Rurik said, dragging Saga from her thoughts. He stood and began pacing the narrow strip of flooring. "We discovered many bodies. Crumbling columns. The roof, broken and falling."

Saga brought a shaky hand to her mouth. She'd done that. She'd killed people—had thirsted for their blood . . .

"We took you from high table. Ivar lay in blood beside you. Printsessa Yrsa . . ." A muscle in his cheek flexed.

Acid burned Saga's stomach. "Is she . . ."

"She could not have lived."

The words were like blades slicing into her sternum. Saga gasped in a breath, fighting off nausea. Yrsa. She'd killed Yrsa. Yrsa, who'd stood before her, asking for forgiveness, demanding the guards release her. Oh gods, *oh gods*, what had she done?

"We did not see the others—Signe. Bjorn," continued Rurik. "Was impossible to see. We took you and left quickly."

"I didn't want for that to happen." *Lies!* her mind screamed. She'd wanted them dead. Had willed this to happen. "I was not in control . . ."

"I understand," Rurik said, taking her hand in his and running a thumb over her scars. His grip on her tightened. "More than you know."

Saga bit her lip, trying to digest his words, but his touch was all she could focus on. As he relaxed his hold and turned her hand over, she was surprised to find no burnt flesh, nor any hint of the flames that had exploded from her. As Rurik pressed one hand into a tight fist, then splayed her fingers wide, Saga hissed through her teeth.

"Is swollen. I will have compress made for you."

Rurik brought her hand to his lips, caressing the screaming bear branded on it. Her gaze caught on his, and she let herself stare. "What if it happens again?"

"Then I will help you through it before control is lost. And if not, I have these." His hand slid from his pocket, revealing a small, stoppered bottle. "Seeds," he said, a mischievous glint in his eyes.

Saga watched him. How could Rurik be so nonchalant about the danger lurking inside her? And what would happen when he left her in Midfjord and sailed to Zagadka? What if it happened again? "How many nights until we reach Midfjord?" she asked tentatively.

Before he could answer, a knock at the door had Saga's hand tightening around Rurik's forearm. "Is only evening meal," murmured Rurik. Embarrassed, Saga eased her grip.

But the mere mention of food made her stomach growl. Rurik's lips tilted up in reply. "I will bring it." After setting her gently aside, he crossed the room, shielding her from view as he exchanged a low murmur with the person beyond the door. When Rurik turned with a tray clutched in hand, his eyes seemed to sparkle.

"Eat, Winterwing," said Rurik, setting the tray down on the table. Saga scooted eagerly to the edge of the bed and inspected the bowl of soup and flatbread. Rurik began pacing the confines of the room again. "When you have your strength, if you are feeling brave, I have something to show you in ship's hull."

Saga looked up. There was something in his eyes—mischief and eagerness and that strange restlessness. "What is it?"

"Is . . . surprise for you." Rurik rolled his neck, chuckling at her answering scowl. "Already you are feeling better. Good. I missed your fire."

Eating in silence, Saga surveyed each corner of the room. She was growing used to this space, her initial panic softening to a vague unease. She considered venturing to the hull. In Askaborg, she'd gotten to a place of comfort moving within the castle's walls. If she locked herself away in this room, she worried she'd fall back into old habits. Perhaps with Rurik beside her, a trip to the hull would be achievable.

"We won't step outdoors?" she asked, setting the spoon down in the empty bowl. Saga's head felt clearer, glimmers of energy returning to her limbs.

He paused in his pacing with a wide smile. "No outdoors. Is short walk down corridor, then climbing on ladder."

Saga watched him quietly, curiosity gnawing at her from within. What could there possibly be to show her in the ship's hull? "Very well," she said, pushing to her feet. The roll of the ship was jarring, but Rurik steadied her with a firm hand before she could stumble.

"You will tell me if you wish to return," he said, pulling her to the door. "And I will bring you back right away."

She nodded, her pulse pounding furiously. But he was so sturdy, so understanding about her condition, and Saga reminded herself over and over that she was safe.

The corridor beyond her room was dark and narrow, disorienting as the ship swayed to and fro. Gripping Rurik's hand, Saga forced her feet forward, one after the other. Reaching the end of the corridor, Rurik knelt down, flipping a hatch in the floorboards up on iron hinges.

His eyes met hers, dancing with trouble. "Come. Is worth it. I promise."

Saga's brows furrowed, but darkness had already swallowed him in the bowels of the ship and she hurried to follow. The moment her feet hit solid ground, goosebumps raced across Saga's skin. Rurik's arm slid around her back, and she blinked at the tremors running through him.

"Are you certain you're—"

"I'm fine," he asserted, pulling her through a doorway. "This way."

Saga's feet froze in place, her vision twinning at what she saw. "What—"

In the middle of the room, a man was strung to a beam, arms spread wide, feet bound. Hair an unkempt brown, twin Urkan braids adorned his beard, and a large bear tattoo stretched across his chest.

"Magnus?" Saga placed a bracing hand on the wall.

His head lifted, cold, dead eyes meeting her own. "Kunta," seethed Magnus. "Traitor."

In two loping strides, Rurik was at Magnus, striking him across the face. "Magnus, Magnus. Have we not already learned this lesson? You must use manners. Is no way to speak to a lady."

Magnus spat blood onto the floor. "She's no lady. She's a loathsome pet. A useless ornament." His eyes were a thousand knives dragging across Saga's flesh. "Should have been executed."

"Your ears are broken, are they, Magnus?" The Heart Eater's head snapped to the side as Rurik struck him again, harder.

Flinching, Saga stepped back, taking slow breaths.

Rurik grabbed Magnus's beard, tugging until their faces were inches apart. "You and Lady Saga are no longer betrothed. Understand?" Magnus glared at him but made no move to respond. "Need I fetch Rov, Magnus? Is magnificent with the blade. Knows where to cut to make your screams loudest."

The older man's eyes narrowed as he stared at Rurik. "Is what I thought. Now tell me you understand—you will never touch her again."

Magnus merely grunted, but that seemed acknowledgment enough for Rurik. As he turned to Saga, a smile stretched wide, but it was too sharp—too fierce. "You like my surprise?"

"What—" she spluttered. "I—you—you're mad! You stopped in the midst of the explosion to steal Magnus?"

Rurik's eyebrows rose, those green eyes flaring brighter. "Ah, my dear Winterwing. Magnus was stolen long before that. Was, how do you say . . . *priority*."

Disbelief flooded her. "I don't want this—"

A shadow crossed Rurik's face as he stepped toward her. "Look at your hands, Saga," he said in a low, dangerous voice. "Remember how much you endured. Here you can pay back what he did. And no one will ever know it." He drew a dagger and held the hilt for Saga to take.

Saga stared at the dagger, vision tunneling as she pondered the idea. But then the voice whispering to her in Askaborg's great hall slid through her mind.

We can make them pay.

"I'm not a monster!" she exclaimed. "I'm not like that." *You are,* came the thought, floating through her mind. She'd wanted Signe dead. Had yearned for her pain. And Yrsa's blood was now on her hands. But Saga shook those thoughts loose, focusing on Rurik.

"We each have a monster in us, Saga," he said darkly. "Is healthy to exercise it." Saga blinked at Rurik, trying to understand.

Magnus chuckled. "A skald's tale in the flesh," he muttered. "The Beast of Zagadka and the little pet princess—"

Rurik leaped at Magnus, driving his fist into the man's jaw. But it was too late to drive the words from Saga's mind.

"Beast," she repeated, staring at Rurik's broad back. The Beast of Zagadka—heir of the high prince. "You're sorely mistaken, Magnus." But she heard the doubt in her own voice—felt the shiver roll down her spine.

"Ask him," challenged Magnus.

Rurik turned slowly, the muscles in his jaw held tight.

"Is it true?" she asked, her voice just above a whisper. A low buzzing began in her ears.

Rurik swallowed. "It was plan to tell you—"

"You're the heir?"

It could not be. And yet it made sense—why the Druzhina always deferred to him, the way he was used to getting what he wanted. The way he'd been so eager to hear Saga's thoughts on the Beast of Zagadka.

High prince has forbidden his heir to come. Is not good man for . . . diplomacy, Rurik had told her. Now Saga sagged against the wall, the room warping before her as she tried to understand.

Magnus's laugh lanced through her skull. "That's not all, Pet. Not even close."

Rurik whirled on Magnus, his anger stirring the air. "You will not call her that."

"What should I call her? Hóra? Traitor?"

Rurik struck Magnus again, but the Heart Eater only laughed. "Ask him how he earned the name, Pet. How he became the Beast of Zagadka—"

"You will stop!" bellowed Rurik, his anger rattling the air, sending goosebumps rushing up Saga's arms. Another punishing blow cracked across Magnus's jaw.

Spitting blood and a tooth, Magnus persisted. "He's a *monster*, Pet. A thing of nightmares. And when he transforms, his anger is a thing of legends. How can he keep you safe when he is the monster—"

The room seemed to undulate, Saga's knees growing weak. *Danger. Not safe.* She'd trusted him. Had let herself feel safe with him. Her stomach twisted, panic stirring. She didn't even know this man.

"Enough!" roared Rurik, punching again.

Saga hugged herself, looking away from the violence. *Not safe not safe not safe.* Saga's panic was clawing to get free, but she couldn't fall apart. Not here. Not now. Her chest was growing tighter . . .

The air thickened, then relaxed, energy rippling through the room. Saga blinked at the guttering torchlight, at the tingle that spread across her bare skin. Hunched over, Rurik's shoulders rose with heavy, shuddering breaths.

Magnus laughed, wet and malevolent. "It's been too long, hasn't it, Rurik? You've been holding it back." His gaze fell on Saga. "Has he told you why he was truly in Íseldur? Not for a treaty, oh, no. He searched for his kinsman. You thought I did not know, Rurik? Your man is long dead, buried in a mass grave in Svaldrin—"

Rurik let out a guttural, animalistic sound. Saga took a step toward him but stumbled back against the wall. Along Rurik's bared forearms, ink-black lines slid downward, crossing the backs of his hands where tattooed claws extended along his knuckles. Saga gaped as the tattoos moved—as if something beneath his skin ached to be set free.

The sharpened tips of the tattooed claws stretched, then burst from his knuckles.

"You see!" exclaimed Magnus. "He lacks control, Pet. Mere taunts have forced his true nature. And now we're at his mercy."

Rurik's shoulders broadened, fabric ripping as fur burst through. A low growl rattled the air, drawing a soft cry from Saga. He whirled on her, and she gasped. Jagged teeth glinted from a snarling maw, his body a mixture of unnatural angles. He was covered in shaggy gray fur, except for sharp protrusions jutting the length of his spine. Thickly muscled hind legs contrasted with long, angular forelegs, which he used for balance as he ambled forward.

It was the barbed tail lashing back and forth that tore the scream from Saga's throat. It couldn't be. But those eyes—those luminescent green eyes—were unmistakably Kassandr Rurik's. Panic wrapped around her chest, squeezing, constricting, tighter, tighter.

"And to think you feared *me,* Pet!" spat Magnus. "Now you can lie in the bed you've made for yourself."

The creature turned. Lunged at Magnus. The Heart Eater's laughter quickly shifted to screams, so shrill they scraped down her spine.

Saga scrambled to the doorway, chased by the wet sounds of flesh ripping from bone and soft, keening moans. Her fingers fumbled on the ladder's rungs, a foot catching on her skirts as she clambered upward, fighting for each burning breath. As she burst through the doorway and into the dark corridor, Saga came face-to-face with Rov and a woman in Druzhina garb.

"He's," she began shakily, but she could not find the words. Rov extended a firm hand and pulled Saga to her feet. "He's . . ."

"I understand, Printsessa," said Rov crisply, easing Saga toward her chamber. Turning his head, he barked in sharp Zagadkian as the woman descended into the hull. The floor beneath Saga shuddered, shouts rising from below. The corridor writhed before her, and she leaned against Rov as they reached her door.

"Is all right, Lady Saga," said Rov, helping her onto the bed, then cursing. She scratched at her throat, at the maddening constriction.

Not safe not safe not safe!

"I am sorry for this, Printsessa," Rovgolod said, his voice smothered as though underwater. And then his large, warm hand covered her mouth, her head tilted back, tiny objects landing on her tongue.

Die. She'd die here, so far from her kingdom.

"You must swallow the seeds," came Rov's rough voice. She clawed at him, scratched at the hand over her mouth, but his grip was unrelenting.

She couldn't breathe, couldn't string her thoughts together. All she knew was she was away from Askaborg, trapped on a ship. *No exits. No escape.*

"The seeds will make you sleep, Saga," said Rov. "Let you escape your terror."

Escape, she thought. *An exit.* Saga went slack.

And swallowed.

CHAPTER 89

Saga's sleep was blissfully absent of dreams. No little brunette girl. No pillars. No screaming bears. It was an abyss—a cocoon encasing Saga away from reality. From the truth.

She woke too soon, sleep clouding her mind as she took in her quarters. But as her eyes settled on the man slumped in the chair beside her bed, a scream wrenched from the deepest part of her chest.

Rurik straightened quickly, green eyes sliding over her, assessing. There was no trace of the beast she'd seen in the ship's hull, nor even the tattoos on his forearms. But Saga scrambled back into the farthest corner of the bed.

"Stop," he growled, the air rattling just as it had down there, before he'd turned into—

Saga closed her eyes. Tried to shove the memory from her mind. But all she could see were those wild green eyes; those long, sharp claws; the way he'd stalked toward her as though he intended to devour her.

"I apologize, Saga," Rurik said softly. And she could hear it in his voice—the remorse. The shame. He lifted his hands in surrender. "I will come no closer."

I was not in control, she'd said when last they'd spoken. And Rurik . . . his reply . . . *I understand. More than you know.*

Her mind was overflowing, everything spilling out. This was too much on top of all else.

"I must get to Midfjord," she murmured to herself. She would count down the hours. "How many nights until our arrival?"

Rurik's lips pulled into a thin line. "Saga . . ."

"How long until Midfjord?" she demanded, her voice sharp.

His jaw flexed. "We passed it many days ago, Saga. Did you not know you slept for seven nights after the explosion?" Saga gripped the bed. Surely she had not heard him right. A week . . . how could that be?

"Our deal has fallen," he continued. "And you will not go to Midfjord."

"W-what?"

"You will come to Zagadka, Winterwing. With me."

Her mind was spinning, twirling, whirling, as though she were in a dream. Saga pinched the skin on the back of her arm again and again, but she could not wake. And so she laughed. What else could she do? It was madness, all of it.

Rurik's brows pinched in worry. "I regret to tell you of danger in Zagadka. But there I can watch you. Can keep you safe."

All she heard was her choices being snatched away, yet again. Captivity, yet again. She wanted to scream. Wanted to break things.

"Had been a full moon cycle since I had shifted," added Rurik. "Was . . . easily baited. On Zagadka, will not happen like that. I have . . . ways to control." He paused. "I apologize for your fright."

"I do not even know you," Saga whispered, hugging herself. "I cannot trust you."

"You have no choice, Saga." His eyes bored into her. "No choice but to believe me when I promise to keep you safe. Is an oath I swear to you now, and I take such things seriously."

"You've broken our agreement!" she spluttered. "Midfjord was the deal—"

"And Magnus told to me where the person we sought is located. Buried in Svaldrin was not answer we wished for, but now we know. I did not receive your information, and so our deal has fallen."

"We sailed past Midfjord *days* ago!"

But Rurik ignored her. "You must know one more thing. A secret Zagadka long has held. A thing we have *killed* to protect." Numb.

She was numb against the revelations that kept coming. "On Zagadka, all have what you are calling galdur. Is different for us. A shifting, as you have seen, into new forms."

Saga stared at him blankly.

"Though my shifting is . . . different from the rest. A beast they have called me, but only my enemies. They spin many slanderous tales." His tongue ran along his lower teeth. "The man we searched for was called Nostislav. Was like a brother, a great man stolen from our lands on a day when Íseldurian sails passed through nearby waters. And now Magnus has confirmed—Nostislav was stolen and killed in the place called Svaldrin. And if Magnus knows these things he should not, it means Zagadka's secret is exposed."

"Experiments," whispered Saga. "They were harvesting magic from Galdra at Svaldrin."

"They attempt this on Zagadkians, too, it seems," said Rurik bitterly. "But our secret is out, and this signals a change for Zagadka. A thing long needed."

Saga stared at him incredulously. The man was mad. How could she not have seen it before? "Rurik, my kingdom needs help. I *must* return to Íseldur. My people are starving, are being persecuted by the Urkans—"

"No."

Anger sparked within her. "No?"

His gaze hardened. "No. You come with me to Zagadka." There were no cracks in his words, no room for compromise.

Bitterness coated her tongue. "Why."

Rurik's chuckle held a note of hostility. "Because, Winterwing. I will not leave you behind."

Saga's hands curled into fists.

"You will come to Zagadka with me. The rest we will figure out."

"There is nothing to figure out!" she spat.

"Come now, both of us know your words are false."

Desperation clawed through her, but she refused to cry.

But it seemed Rurik was not done. "Some will not like you to be in our kingdom. There will be fighting among the factions and danger for you. But I swear it, Saga, I will keep you safe."

"Don't play at being my savior," she seethed. "Not when you're yet another person taking away my freedom! I belong in Íseldur, Rurik. Not with you. Not in Zagadka."

The air shifted with restless tension.

"You need someone to help you with your . . . condition, Saga. How can you walk into new place when you cannot step outdoors?" He raked a hand through his hair. "We go to Zagadka, and when time is right, I will return you to Íseldur."

Anger flared in her, sending fire blazing through her veins. "Get out!" She groped around, her hand finding a waterskin. Without thinking, she threw it at him. Rurik whipped a hand up faster than was humanly possible, ripping it from the air and tossing it to the floor with a snarl.

Her hand fell back between the mattress and the wall, closing around something smooth and round. Pulling it out, she realized it was a looking stone.

"Leave me!" she screamed, hurling it at him.

Rurik snatched the stone out of midair, closing his fist around it until it cracked, then crumbled to dust. He loosed a growl so loud that the entire ship rumbled.

"You've been nothing but a plague on my life!" she yelled. "Everything you've done has made things worse!"

His nostrils flared, and the air crackled once more. Saga pushed deeper into the corner of the room, curling in on herself. "Leave me," she begged. "Please."

She heard his heavy breaths. Felt that strange, rattling tension in the air. "I know drawing eases your nerves. There is drawing board just there and charcoals. And I leave seeds for you on table. Take them and rest. You will need energy. Soon we will arrive in Zagadka."

His footsteps retreated, the door clicking shut.

And then the dead bolt slid into place.

PRONUNCIATION GUIDE

Many of the words and names in this book are derived from Old Norse and/or Icelandic; ð and þ characters have been converted to *t*, and *æ* to *ae* for readability.

Bjáni – byan-ee
Dúlla – doo-la
Eystri – ay-stree
Flíta – flee-ta
Hevrít – hev-reet
Hjarta – h-yar-ta
Hver – kvehr
Hvíta – kvee-ta
Íseldur – ees-eld-oor
Klaernar – klite-nar
Kunta – koon-ta
Lébrynja – lyeh-bryn-ya
Myrkur – mihr-koor
Nordur – nor-door
Reykfjord – rake-fyoord
Róa – roh-a
Signe – sig-nuh
Skjöld – shkuld
Skógungar – shkoon-gar
Slátrari – slow-trar-ee
Stjarna – styat-na
Sudur – soo-door
Urka – oor-ka
Vestir – vest-eer

GLOSSARY

Berskium – a powder mined near Reykfjord and taken by the Klaernar to maintain their large stature and strength
Bjáni – fool (an insult)
Brennsa – fire whiskey
Dúlla – doll (a term of endearment among women)
Eisa Volsik – a former princess of Íseldur who was murdered by King Ivar, her body impaled upon a pillar in the pits of Askaborg Castle
Eystri – the easternmost territory of Íseldur
Flíta – phoenix-like butterflies whose wings light up when they fly; in their old age, they burst into flames, and a caterpillar emerges from the ashes
Galdra – a magic-wielding person, also called Ashen; outlawed by King Ivar
Galdur – magic itself
Gothi – a priest of the Ursinian religion
Hábrók – the god of battle, honor, luck, and weather; one of the old gods of Íseldur
Hevrít – an Íseldurian long-bladed dagger
Hindrium – a specialized metal that inhibits the magical abilities of the Galdra
Hóra – whore
Illmarr – a scaled vampire of the sea; it can be lured by eel blood and felled by rowan arrows
Íseldur – kingdom of Ice and Fire; the island nation where this book takes place
Ivar Ironheart – the new king of Íseldur who seized the crown from King Kjartan Volsik seventeen years ago
Kalasgarde – a town in the north of Íseldur, located in Nordur lands

Karthia – an isle to the south of Íseldur

Kjartan Volsik – the former king of Íseldur, murdered by King Ivar using the blood-eagle method in the pits of Askaborg Castle

Klaernar – King Ivar's specialized soldiers, also known as the King's Claws

Kopa – a large stone city in the northern parts of Eystri territory

Kunta – cunt (an insult)

Lébrynja – specialized, lightweight armor made of tiny leather-like scales and worn by the Bloodaxe Crew

Malla – the goddess of love, war, and death; one of the old gods of Íseldur; also, the name of one of the moons

Marra – the goddess of knowledge, healing, and peace; one of the old gods of Íseldur; also, the name of one of the moons

Medovukha – a Zagadkian alcoholic beverage similar to mead and made from fermented honey

Myrkur – the god of chaos and darkness; one of the old gods of Íseldur

Nordur – the northernmost territory of Íseldur

Norvaland – the isle northeast of Íseldur, it was overthrown by Ivar's father, Harald, who now sits on the throne

Róa – a hot beverage served in Íseldur, made from the bark of the róa-bush

Saga Volsik – a former princess of Íseldur, she was seized by King Ivar and raised as his ward; she's betrothed to his son, Prince Bjorn

Skald – a poet who composes a type of Urkan poetry, often exaggerating the deeds of kings past and present

Skarpling – a small, mouse-sized creature with quills on its back

Skjöld – a dried leaf taken to treat headaches

Skógungar – a forest walker; a peaceful tree-like creature that lives in the Western Woods

Slátrari – "the butcher"; a murderer who burns people from the inside out

Sólas – Íseldurian coin currency

Stjarna – "mother of stars"; Sunnvald's wife and the goddess of weaving, fertility, and guidance; one of the old gods of Íseldur

Sudur – the southernmost territory of Íseldur, it houses the capital city

Sunnavík – the capital city of Íseldur, where Askaborg Castle is found

Sunnvald – the Sun God; the god of fire and might; king of the old gods of Íseldur

Svalla Volsik – the former queen of Íseldur, she was murdered by King Ivar, her body impaled upon a pillar in the pits of Askaborg Castle

Thrall – an enslaved person; in the Kingdom of Íseldur they are most often brought in from Norvaland and marked on their inner wrist

Urka – a large nation to the east of Íseldur where the line of Urkan Kings, including Ivar Ironheart, originated

Ursir – the Bear God worshipped by King Ivar and fellow Urkans; belief in Ursir has been imposed upon Íseldurians

Vampire deer – carnivorous deer that hunt mammals and drain their blood

Vestir – the westernmost territory of Íseldur, it houses the Western Woods

Wolfspider – a large spider covered in shaggy gray fur

Zagadka – the mysterious island nation to the south of Íseldur

ACKNOWLEDGMENTS

This book was so many things: a labor of love, a refuge from the brutal news cycle, and a therapeutic outlet. Bits of myself often make it into my characters, and with Saga, it's her anxiety and self-isolation. I wanted to write a protagonist living with mental health issues—not necessarily trying to conquer them, but merely accepting them as a part of herself and honoring her boundaries. That's why in this novel, Saga makes little to no effort to overcome her agoraphobia.

I will admit, having her (almost) never step foot outdoors was a struggle for the plot. But our girl Saga is resourceful. Smart. And so incredibly brave. Her agoraphobia is part of her, but not all of her. Her cage door is now open. She's looking through the bars. And I can't wait for you to see what happens when she finally flies free.

First and foremost, I want to thank you, the reader, for trusting me with your time. Each person who picks up my book—who becomes lost in Íseldur and in Silla and Saga's adventures—fills me with such gratitude, it's hard to express.

I must also thank my incredible agent, Jessica Watterson, and the rest of the team at Sandra Dijkstra Literary Agency. Thank you to my editors Shauna Summers and Mae Martinez, and the team at Penguin Random House: Brianna Kusilek, Taylor Noel, Megan Whalen, Mark Maguire, Christa Guild, Fritz Metsch, and Saige Francis.

Several books and resources were indispensable in writing this novel. First I must shout out *The Surrender Experiment* by Michael A. Singer. This book helped me reshape my thoughts during the pandemic, focusing on the things I could control, while letting go of those I could not. If you guessed this book was the inspiration for Silla's surrendering storyline, you are correct!

As well as the books I cited in *The Road of Bones*, *Icelandic Magic* by Stephen E. Flowers, *Viking Warfare* by I. P. Stephenson, and *Life in a Medieval Castle* by Joseph and Frances Gies were incredible resources in understanding the mindset and setting for *Kingdom of Claw*. I've tried to keep things authentic to the Viking age, with a few leniencies: the prominence of books and a written/non-runic language, leather armor, glass-paned windows, and Rurik's boat with cabins and a storage hull. And, of course, the magic, monsters, and religions in this world.

Thank you to Chersti Nieveen for insightful discussions that changed the entire shape of this book. Thank you to Rony Bermudez for giving life to these books with your gorgeous cover illustrations. Thank you to my author friends for their support and friendship and for fielding my endless questions: MT Sear, Jess, Nisha, Elayna, Daniela, Penn, Lisette, and Julie.

I must thank my sensitivity readers for ensuring the portrayals of characters outside my lived experience were done respectfully: Ruthie Bowles and Nicole Neuman. Thank you to my beta readers: Ashlyn, Kelli, Ashton, Diana, Becca, Georgie, Julie, Emma, Kaitlyn, Sarah, MT Sear, Ana, Josie, Bree, Louise, Maggie, and Danielle, your feedback has been so helpful in getting the book just right.

Thank you to Tanya, for your help with the Zagadkian (aka: Russian) translations. Thank you to Sophie for your thoughtful comments on Saga's agoraphobia. Thank you to Sarah for putting up with all my endless horse/chicken/goat/animal questions. And a HUGE special thanks to MT Sear for suggesting Lady Geira should write fanfic. By far the best decision I made in this book.

I have to thank my family, including my uber-supportive parents, who insisted on reading the books even though I begged them not to. But most of all, thank you to my "husband" Ben, for your unfounded confidence in me. I don't know how or why you believed I could write a fantasy series, but your support means everything to me. And look: We're doing it!

About the Author

DEMI WINTERS is the author of romantic fantasy books featuring softer female leads, grumpy heroes, and immersive worlds. Lover of all things fairy-tale, fantasy, and romance, Winters lives in British Columbia, Canada, with her husband and two kids. When she's not busy brainstorming fantastical worlds and morally gray love interests, she loves reading and cooking.

demiwinters.com
TikTok: @demiwinterswrites
Instagram: @demiwinterswrites

ABOUT THE TYPE

This book was set in Hoefler Text, a family of fonts designed by Jonathan Hoefler, who was born in 1970. First designed in 1991, Hoefler Text was intended as an advancement on existing desktop computer typography, including as it does an exponentially larger number of glyphs than previous fonts. In form, Hoefler Text looks to the old-style fonts of the seventeenth century, but it is wholly of its time, employing a precision and sophistication only available to the late twentieth century.